Last Post for the Winds of Freedom

David de l'Avern

authorHOUSE®

AuthorHouse™ UK Ltd.
500 Avebury Boulevard
Central Milton Keynes, MK9 2BE
www.authorhouse.co.uk
Phone: 08001974150

First published by AuthorHouse 7/2/2008

ISBN: 978-1-4343-6916-1 (sc)

Printed in the United States of America
Bloomington, Indiana

This book is printed on acid-free paper.

In memory of Chris (Kika)

*He showed us how to die with his gentle spirit
leading the way with a smile and in quiet dignity.*

We will meet again on that other shore…

My Grateful thanks:

To my wife Katy von Kötlitz *(kiss me Kate!), for her patience and for reading the 'pretty rough draft' during the summer of 2002.*

To my children *who often pestered me to read them a story when they were quite young; Cameron, Margaret, Sabine, Susanne*

To Margaret Jennings *for applying her literary mind when I was piecing things together in the early days of 2003.*

To Rear Admiral Peter Dingemanns, CB, DSO, RN; *for reading the manuscript while it was still on the 'slipway' being tidied up, and for his generous advice peppered with insights into naval warfare, appropriate technology timelines, realistic co-lateral damage, etc.*

To Lt Cdr Tristan Lovering, MBE, RN *whose cheeky grin, incisive humour, and sharpness of brain kept our feet on the deck. Whose book on amphibious warfare is an education in itself -happy landings!*

WO1 Peter Woods RN *who kindly read the beta-test version of the manuscript prior to completion. May the winds of good fortune favour your journeying across the great seas.*

Scamp (MIA). *For his mischievous games that included biting my ankles, a fondness for pinching the ham out of my bread rolls and his ever present readiness for taking a snooze on my lap while working at my desk during the two years that it has taken me to get this book into shape. May he do well for himself wherever he may be!*

Were it in my gift I would say to one and all: "Splice the mainbrace!"

....

The sun rises and the sun sets, and hurries back to where it rises...
The wind blows to the south and turns to the north; round and round it
goes, ever returning on its course. All streams flow into the sea,
yet the sea is never full...
There is no remembrance of men of old, and even those who are yet to
come will not be remembered by those who follow...
I have seen all the things that are done under the sun, all of them are...
a chasing after the wind.

Ecclesiastes

Contents

So it begins………... xiii

1. BLACK SMOKE-FIRE IN THE GALLEY 1

2. SNOW STORM IN LONDON 20

3. CLIMBING BACK...39

4. CONVOI EXCEPTIONEL 57

5. SLEIGHT OF HAND 109

6. THE MARK OF A TYRANT 130

7. THE DRAGON'S LAIR 173

8. A CHASE IN THE FENS 215

9. CRUISING THE MED 235

10. THE BLACK PIRATE 245

11. RECKONING 266

12. RUNNING THE LINES! 319

13. LOSING TIME 354

14. DARKNESS CLOSING IN 423

15. DON'T LOOK BACK 438

16. BITTER HARVEST 481

17. GATHERING STORM 489

18. DAYS OF TRIBULATION 527

Glossary of Terms 551

So it begins...

No one was really sure how it all began. How events all came together that started the war. It seemed as though we had escaped the helter-skelter of the cold war era of our grandfathers' day only to fall headlong into another more openly hostile war on all fronts. Where world peace had been undermined by superpower 'foreign policies', the US had emerged, as they had claimed, a force for good - only the gloves were still on. Not much later on they attempted to rampage across the world in search of immense power and dwindling fuel reserves by declaring war on anyone who was "not with them", and by demanding unconditional access to all nations in search of those whom they declared terrorists or just plain anti-American. Thus it was that the rest of the world became the enemy. Then there was the Canadian war a decade or so ago that tore the heart of their dream. The allies fought them off after a naked land grab in the Northern Territories provoked bitter fighting. Pushing the Yanks south all the way back down to the Great Lakes to where they started out, over the border. The Canadians did it again like they did once before, long ago.

All in all, the damage had been done. Back home in Blighty the old folks saw themselves losing everything that centuries of social and political evolution had brought. Our personal freedoms have of course, long gone, no monarch to graciously rule over us like Elizabeth the Great -God rest her soul, we now have a political elite each with their own dachas in the more exclusive parts of the stockbroker belt. Not that they are much interested in us as a nation any more. We live in walled towns and cities like mediaeval dwellers subjugated by their petty lordlings, except they are now Governors with Parliamentary warrants to rule over us as they see fit. The French and Spanish have fished us out of existence and when we try to fend off their 'illegals' in our waters the French just send in a couple of frigates to shoot up our patrol boats. It's their other national sport -we gave them football and they steal our fish stocks. A short while ago one of those French frigates in concert with a German one had a go at one of ours -the Gloucester, and damn near wrecked it, were it not for its escort of skimmers fighting back hard, saving the day. If I were to put my finger on it, I'd say that was when hostilities really began to take shape, with an air raid shortly afterwards by a squadron of French flyers attacking a couple more of our own ships in the Thames estuary.

We had a British president, would you believe, as a constitutional head of state, among others, in a quasi-socialist republic, reaching from Eire all the way east to the Black Sea. There was an attempted coup-d-etat in the last month, carried out by an extremist group spurred on by the President's resignation, and it certainly seems to be going their way with open rioting on the streets and Parliament being sealed off.

It's a war we are sailing into as we round Cape St. Vincent. Come nightfall we'll probably set alarm bells ringing when some Spanish lookout sees us rounding into the Med. We've had no live broadcasts from home for some time, especially, since we sailed with our VIP on board. The government has switched off all channels, and President Muller-Weiss is sending over police battalions from the continent, or so they say. I'm told we're using other free to air systems to get news about what's happening. The skipper's a good guy, he's all for that sort of thing. He's an ex-flyer who actually owns the boat along with the First Lieutenant. You see we're a high-speed transport built to naval specs in case war breaks out, now hauling military stores and personnel as required. It was just after we broke out of Portsmouth harbour when the Admiral came onboard, next thing we know we're running for Portland, a quick turnaround, then out towards the farthest reaches of Biscay running a southerly course. That's another story -sort of 'sneaky-beaky' and all that. It's getting darker outside, I'll soon be on watch, and I am glad to note there's no time for lurks on this ship, but hey, who wants to be a navigator all his life? Not me! Someday I want a command of my own. We may be a mixed bag onboard this vessel, but she's no slouch and packs a punch of her own with some panache. Ah, there goes the action stations alarm, have to go for now.

****

Up to now it had been an ordinary day in the life of Lieutenant JC Cornwell: "JC" to his friends and colleagues. He'd been given the red light and waved off three times now in the gathering gloom of nightfall in the Straits of Gibraltar. Increasing his speed slowly by feel, not glancing at the throttle he slid past the pitching carrier's deck a worried man. With positive lift he raised the wheels once more shooting heavenwards in a roar, leaving hot plasma trailing behind him. Turning the slim aircraft in a gentle turn he began a large circuit around the carrier towards a position far astern of her where he would once again commence an approach homewards to the warm safety of 'tween decks'. "Raptor five one five, we have a situation down here with a fouled safety net. Take about fifteen minutes to clear." JC Held his breath just long enough as he looked at the odds stacked against him. 'Some idiot desk-jockey; senior air commander, dumb-wit, whoever; ordered that the rookies go up for an afternoon's training, and now look what we've got!' He sighed before transmitting. "This is Raptor five one five, roger that. Don't keep me waiting too long I'm running low on fuel."

It was bad enough to have to take a flight of rookies up and have them go through the hoops, but to allow them to face a pitching carrier deck in diminishing daylight while passing through a busy, narrow channel seemed like sheer lunacy. "Roger that, make your turn at fifteen miles and bring her in slow," replied the approach controller. The US carrier and her escorts were entering the Straits of Gibraltar, making a show that the locals could not miss. The grey looming outline of the Rock on her port side with the mountains of Africa on her starboard side looking dark and stern in the distance under the dwindling daylight. A sudden break in the cloud base painting the Rock and the distant mountain tops in pure gold, but like a giant shutter the lamp went out with the clouds closing ranks and all were surrounded by murk once more. "Roger that." He returned and sneaking a look outside of his canopy he could see the lights ashore running from Algeciras off into the distance towards Rota on his starboard side. On his left he saw the carrier's escorts flash past below him with their riding lights twinkling in the darkening shadows. Another quick glance to the right, then a second as something caught his eye.

JC was a Texan with the keen eye of a marksman, especially for anything out of the ordinary. Since the US had broken just about every treaty that they had with everyone of her so-called allies; he mused; it pays to keep on the lookout for any chance encounter with someone bearing a grudge who may fancy a pot-shot at such a huge target. The outline of a long, low grey painted hull bearing down on the relief Mediterranean Fleet, approaching from the north-west at a shallow intercept, slid under his right wing tip. Noting the vessel's naval lines and the warship grey of her hull and superstructure the word transport flicked across his mind as he entered the cloud base and turning his attention to the panel he flew on forgetting about it. About half way down the line before his turn for home the radio came to life once more. "Raptor five one five the deck is clear for landing." Ali McGrath the flight deck ops officer sounded extremely smug on the radio, and JC imagined his hugely smiling face. "This is Raptor five one five, roger that." Shortly after that and checking his range, he continued, "Raptor five one five makin' my turn now," banking the aircraft as he spoke, simultaneously looking sideways to catch a glimpse outside the cockpit. A split second after levelling off on the compass needle and slowly reducing power to the engine, lights began turning red on the panel while beginning his descent by dipping the nose downwards towards the tops of the clouds below him.

Desperately fast and with lightning speed his hands passed over the panels checking, noting, selecting, making alternative switch positions to by-pass perceived problems. In cloud now, he was flying blind, no gyros to steer by, hydraulics -showing amber –fading. He could not see the coil of smoke rising behind him, or smell the acrid odour of burning electronics. The plane began to sag a little towards the left. He corrected it only to find that it now sagged a little to the right. The gentle yawing of the aircraft remaining about the same on the way down through the clouds. "This is Raptor five one five, I have a problem with hydraulics… partial pressure, no gyros… and she's yawing from side to side… slight rise in plasma regulation chamber temperature… doesn't make sense." Lt Gunnar Olavsson on duty in the fish tank picked up the conversation with equal speed. "Approach Control to Raptor five one five, continue your approach." He pushed the panic button next to his seat. "Roger that, Raptor five one five continuing approach." He tried to sound calm; it would never do to show how anxious he had become in the last eight seconds. 'Be cool at all times' was the dictum that they picked up while at the navy's flying academy. As he broke through the cloud he found the carrier as a distant 'lump' on the horizon, dead ahead. Reaching for the landing gear lever he prayed a swift prayer and thought of Nancy and the kids at home in Maryland. 'Dammit boy! Fly the plane!' All thoughts of home expunged as the lever went down. He waited for the dull thud and the expected change in the aircraft's attitude that he would duly correct, but nothing happened. At a thousand feet and six miles to run he was sitting astride an eighteen and a half-ton rocket of an aircraft that did not want to play ball with him. "Tower, this is Raptor five one five, wheels up, I repeat wheels up." Again that insane desire to stay cool when your guts are screaming at you to get the hell out -any way you can!

He was doing a hundred and sixty knots, fighting to keep on the line and no wheels into the bargain. The scuttlebutt had travelled around the carrier faster than a Roadrunner being chased by a coyote with the result that goofers began appearing everywhere on the superstructure to see what was happening. Lt Cdr Paddy Mulvaney, the senior air engineer who was normally a jovial man and known prankster had appeared at the air engineer's station just ahead of Billy Mathieson the squadron C/O when the alarm went off. He took a few seconds to scan the incoming telemetry from Raptor five one five. His face a cold mask of concern. JC suddenly became very afraid when he saw from his position high up in the sky that his home plate was heading straight towards a large passenger liner. It was like slow motion, he could only hear the sounds that were familiar to him in the cans clamped over his ears, yet he saw an even larger dilemma enfolding before him, and he knew that he had nowhere to go. The yawing was becoming more demanding, more pronounced. Mulvaney almost shouted the words across the fish tank to Mathieson, "Billy, he's losing plasma regulation, she's going to blow! He has to eject now or it will be too late!"

A split-second later JC saw the first wisps of smoke twisting around him, confirming in his own mind that he had better punch out. Mercifully, Billy Mathieson came on the radio. "Raptor five one five, this is Mathieson, eject! Eject! Eject!" He was five seconds from home plate when he pulled up left and began to pass down the port side. With the ejection charge removing him unavoidably from his flying coffin there was a white flash as the burning electronics came to the end of their operational capability with an explosive finality of their own. The dying bird reared nose up, yawing to the left, finally pitching down heading for the surface in a death dive. He watched it disappear in a huge fountain of water and then turning his attention to his own situation found that he was abeam the tower as the carrier slid past him. It was a surreal moment, they were all waving at him and cheering like mad –he'd made it, got out alive! It was a natural reaction to Ali McGrath's cheery salute; "What in the world are you doin' over there, boy." Quipped Ali. JC returned the salute as he sank out of sight from those on the flight deck. The cheers died in a strangulated howl when the plasma drive in the aircraft exploded a few feet beneath the waves. The greenish white light lit up the sea for miles around and the pressure wave slammed JC into the side of the carrier with such a force that he broke his arm, severely bruising his ribs into the bargain. Men ducked and dived to get away from the searing plasma field, which for most of them did not rise above the flight deck. His chute caught on the corner of one of the lower sponsons towards the port-quarter where he dangled in the slipstream dazed and confused, just ten feet above the crest of the waves. His last thoughts were of Nancy, far away.

It must have been about five minutes before he became conscious again. He felt the motion of the ship heard the hissing of the waves beneath him and it was a bright light not too far away that was distracting him into wakefulness. The sun had dipped well below the horizon giving the seascape an eerie appearance as night and the weather closed in. A smaller vessel long and with a fairly low superstructure was signalling in his direction. He fleetingly remembered seeing something like it on his way around just before his troubles began. It was the little ship's signal lamp flickering away in its own urgent manner that had caught his eyes waking him to his full predicament. From high above him somebody acknowledged receipt and the flashing lamp stopped. He felt completely at peace, though he knew he should be trying to escape from his dangerous situation. A few minutes later his reverie was broken by shouts from above as sailors scrambled to find their missing airman. He watched the little vessel slip away aft of the group into the darkness, apparently on station somewhere out of sight. Rain began falling, and like a veil covering the face of a lovely woman, it finally removed all knowledge of her presence from the outside world around her. Little did he know, or indeed no one in that mighty fleet were to know that the naval transport was sailing into history, destined to set alight the imagination of the world, and that they would meet again upon the face of the waters.

****

1. BLACK SMOKE-FIRE IN THE GALLEY

The Blake slipped into the fogbank with her sharp bows slicing through the water at high speed. "Pray to God that last salvo took away her radars." Whispered the navigator, echoing the private thoughts of all those in the ops room. The rear guns fired and the ship shook like a consumptive old hag tottering down the Gut. "Ops room, Aft fire party!" Blared the loudspeaker. "Ops room, go ahead." Came the almost silent reply in the wake of the detonations from down aft. "The fire is under control sir we're damping down in the Junior Rates messdeck at 3F1" The Captain looked at the engineer briefly and asked." Give me the status of the compartments below that please Brian. "Ops this is the aft fire party," blared the speaker again, "We cannot gain access to the plummer block compartment. The deck is too hot to walk on right now, we're cooling the deck before going in." The two men nodded as the second announcement answered the unspoken question. "Rear fire party this is Ops can you give an estimate of the time to get down into the lower deck compartments?" There was a click as the microphone button down aft was pressed, followed by a brief pause. In The background could be heard bedlam as men shouted and encouraged each other. All the while the sound of running water could be heard as the jets from the hoses hit their target at close quarters, the water cascading through the aft messdecks. "Ops this is Mr Evans with the aft fire party, give us about twenty minutes, the deck is still glowing and the control room confirms that the bearing temperature on the port plummer block is in the red. I suggest we stop the port screw Sir or we'll lose it for sure." That was bad news! If either of the plummer blocks supporting the ships propeller shafts seized for any reason the vessel would be slower to handle or worse, become dead in the water. "Very well Mr Evans." He agreed, pausing only momentarily before giving the order. "Stop port engine, maintain present heading." The order was repeated over the intercom with the wheelhouse. The Captain looked at his tactical officer and then at his navigator. "Gentlemen, will this fog bank give us time assuming what we have seen indicates the enemy's masts have gone and their radar as well?"

The pilot being a local man spoke up. "This is a usual fog for this time of year sir it should burn off by about mid-day. If that's correct we have about two and a half to three hours of cover. But there's a chance that our topmasts may be visible from time to time sir."

Ten minutes earlier the Blake had been engaged in a fierce exchange of fire with the Bölkow and the Agilité, both of the European standing naval forces. The light destroyer had taken on the two frigates at missile range on receipt of the telemetry from the command ship HMS Bradford 45 miles to the south. The Blake's tactical weapons computer had been updated by the signals and four missiles rammed home a decisively destructive message to the Agilité, with only superficial damage to the upper mid-ships superstructure and stern of the Bölkow who was effectively in the shadow of the Agilité's radar echo. Within seconds the Agilité started to heel over, and turning away from the engagement she disappeared behind clouds of black smoke billowing ominously from her stack and from the breaches in her hull. Two of her Guignol Mk25s had struck the Blake in a soft spot as one of them passed through the aft messdeck harmlessly before breaking out of the port side plating, exploding violently on the waterline. The whipping action throughout the ship caused a spate of minor injuries such as broken arms and wrists, to half a dozen or so cases of concussion. The other missile had been drawn off by a combination of subtle EW signature manipulation and 3" rocket screens. The Blake pressed home the attack with rapid fire from her guns raking the decks of the Agilité as she withdrew, and then the Bölkow as she came into her sights. The last thing they saw before the Bölkow started firing back was her for'ard mast, including two of her radar spinners taking a direct hit and, sagging like drunken tart, it fell into her W/T aerial wires. The Bölkow sent a returning wall of hot steel that peppered the superstructure and the stern of the Blake before she turned and disappeared back into the fog. The friendly but often perilous cloud around Portland was only an effective screen against the curious eyes of the enemy, but not to modern radar or satellite reconnaissance.

Captain Wilding scanned the chart and decided to put the shallows between himself and the Bölkow, after taking evasive action under the cover of the morning fog. "Pilot, make our course 045 degrees for three minutes to put us due east of the shoal here, then bring her almost about to follow the coast on a heading of 245 degrees. That way the Bölkow can't engage us closely with the shoaling sand between the two of us. This will give the Bradford time to come up channel and between us we can catch the

Bölkow in crossfire, and leave us an escape out of the funnel at the other end of the shoals"

As the orders were given over the intercom to the wheelhouse in the depths of the ship the senior officers scanned the various electronic state boards and reported collectively that despite the damage and a serious fire down aft they were in surprising good shape. Injured men were relieved and replacements filled the gaps in the damage control parties. On the upper deck the Oerlikon guns crews were checking their hardware and ditching shell cases over the side while the laser gun crews charged their cannons during the apparent lull in the firing, waiting for the next time. Back in the ops room they felt the deck shuddering beneath their feet, while almost simultaneously hearing the muffled launch of two Stingray missiles. They vanished in the fog and everyone held their breath. Skimming just above the surface they had locked on to their target milliseconds after launch.

Captain Manfred Schuler placed the Agilité between the Bölkow and the British destroyer. "Verdamnt und mist!" He swore under his breath as the Petty Officer called out missile launch. "Two incoming, five seconds to impact!" He shouted into his microphone. "Everyone braced themselves instinctively even as the smell of burning and scorched metal permeated the air around them from the fires outside on the superstructure. The EW system was still working but hampered by failing power supplies and twisted aerial horns. The Agilité managed to launch a rocket screen as both incoming Stingrays shot out of the fog bank heading straight for them. One more missile slammed into the Agilité four and a half seconds later. "Five seconds after we should have heard another explosion; Shiser, Friedmann where is that other missile?" He called across to the radar operator.

"It's just coming out of the clutter Sir, it's going wide!"

"Now we're in trouble," said Schuler openly. The rogue missile headed off in a wide sweeping arc just above the surface passing close to the bows of the Agilité. Climbing gradually to fifty metres as its computer controlled guidance system looked for alternative means to lock-on to a target. "Acquire target missile and fire a single missile-round!" He shouted at his fire control officer." Squinting down at his chart Schuler looked for a way out. "Can we go after them Captain? We know the Blake has taken both our missiles and we could finish her off!" The tactical officer was over confident about their ability and too keen to see the failings in his plan. "No Rudi. Look at the situation and see what's on the chart. Look here at where we are." Schuler grabbed a compass point and tapped the chart.

3

Now see where the Blake is heading over here. Don't you see; he's trying to draw us onto that shoal standing between us; no I'm not going to clean up after that French idiot. He's done enough damage today and killed a lot of people." If it weren't for the sounds of machinery and water running down the superstructure outside they could have heard a pin drop. "Get the radio room and link us to Blake, in the mean time let's take a look at the Agilité and get what we can before she goes to the bottom."

On the Blake the lookouts had shouted a warning of the Bölkow's missile launch. The Warrant Officer included the cautionary detail that the missile had been launched away from the Blake's position. "Where's that second rocket got to Mr Standish!"

"It's going wide Sir, on an arc about fifty degrees relative to the target. Looks like a misfire!"

"Very well Mr Standish, keep your eyes peeled and let me know the second it turns back towards us!"

Aye, Aye Sir!"

"Captain, Sir. Captain Schuler sends his compliments and wants to speak to you!" shouted a radio op. The Captain grabbed the microphone swinging back and forth from the deckhead on a length of 'curly' cable.

"My compliments Captain Wilding," saluted Schuler, "may I suggest a tactical withdrawal by both sides?"

"What's your point Schuler?" returned Wilding tartly.

"I think we both know nobody can win by continuing this action Captain. I do not wish to clean up someone else's dirty laundry, and we both have our hands full I believe."

Wilder thought about that for a couple of seconds. It was obviously an allusion to the Frenchman's idiotic attack on the Bradford off Start Point just before dawn, and the German commander had a point about not wishing to get involved any further than decency allowed.

"Captain Wilding here Schuler. Don't think that you can attack our ships, invade our territorial waters and then call the shots without paying a price for your actions. You take yourself and that damn piece of wreckage -the Agilité- and you clear away from our waters. You have a quarter of an hour to make your intentions clear. After that we will engage you."

The young lieutenant, Shröder, went white with anger "He can't tell us what to do Sir, he..." Schuler raised his hand sharply and shut up his subordinate. "Oh yes he can, and he just did Lieutenant." A white haired lieutenant commander spoke out of the gloom from one of the radar consoles. It's what the Americans call 'kicking ass.' and he is right. By firing on the Bradford earlier today Captain Lafecke not only broke with the protocols of international law, but also invaded the territorial limits of an ally. "The fact that he was the senior Captain doesn't absolve us from any blame and the Britisher is doing his job. He kicked the Frenchman's ass and ours just for being there."

"I am Glad we agree Captain. Until we meet again in better circumstances. Good day." Schuler replaced the microphone into its holster and gave orders to manoeuvre the Bölkow closer to the Agilité. She was burning badly and the list was almost 10 degrees. With her own damage control parties clearing away debris and burning wreckage from her upper decks the Bölkow started taking on the wounded survivors from the Agilité. Spare engine room crew and a fire party went over with the medics to sort out what they could. Meanwhile, the Agilité's Captain lay mortally wounded on his bunk. The command team was either wounded or dead, so it fell to the wiles of a burly Lieutenant the ship's Bosun. A proper seaman by all that knew him; he had whipped the remaining crew into action and brought the ship back under command after the second missile attack had made it clear that no one was left to take any tactical decisions. Seamen got a line across from the Bölkow and were rapidly pulling in a towrope. There was a sudden detonation in the distance to seaward and everyone flinched at the sound. Schuler's tactic had worked. The stray missile had locked on to the Bölkow's own missile sent after it, and at over eight hundred knots the two met in a distant fireball. The Blake's crew heard it too, but since tactical had followed the missile firing it made sense to assume that both had run their courses far out of harm's way.

On the Blake the casualty list included five seamen from the guns crews on the upper decks and two stokers in the steering gear compartment who had been hit by shells passing through the transom, six stewards, the sick bay tiff and the leading patrolman. One shell had ended up inside the Senior Rates lounge destroying the bar and causing some of the beer kegs to rupture spectacularly. One shell had bounced diagonally through the ship, finally spinning into the dumb-waiter shaft from the main galley to the wardroom. Whereupon it exploded behind the hatch in the wardroom showering the sick bay team with hot splinters of steel and mahogany.

Without a medical team of first-aiders each damage control party was going to have to fend for itself.

Chalky White, Pusser Hill and Fred Hines were hammering softwood wedges into the split bulkhead forward of the aft messdeck. They could feel the heat of the deck through their footwear, but were confident in the fact that their mates were keeping them hosed down in a water wall of spray. Chalky hammered home the last wedge and the water finally stopped pouring through. "Take that big split over there Chalky," Yelled Pusser over the din. As the killick he was in charge of the small group and the last thing any of them wanted was to lose their home right now and get fried into the bargain. "Fred you take that end of the pipe and I'll take the middle. The three of them started hammering away at a salt water main that had cracked length wise for about six feet. "Fred, how are you for wedges?" yelled Pusser. He could just make out Fred's form in the cascading water. All of them had running water up their sleeves as they lifted their arms to the pipe, and it ran into their shirts and down their bodies, through their trousers and into their boots and shoes. It was a miserably cold job despite everything else. "Only six left Pusser, how about you two!" Between them they had 24 wedges of assorted shapes and sizes. The round ones wouldn't necessarily be right. Not quite enough for the job at hand. Pusser made his way to the water wall and yelled out up through the torn hatchway to the deck above. "Chief!" The Chief's head and shoulders came into view "Down below!" he yelled back. "We need more wedges, otherwise we can't plug the fire main down here!" The chief nodded and signalled for him to wait. Chief Baxter conferred with someone else out of view and then turned back to look down through the hatch. "There's no more, use anything you can find, bedding, sheets, whatever, and wrap it round the pipe. Just as long as you slow it down, is that clear!" Pusser nodded, "Yes Chief!" The deck heeled beneath them as the Blake turned on a so' westerly course along the inner channel behind the shoals. The wreckage about them groaned and shifted momentarily.

The C-in-C Naval Home Command Admiral 'Screwy' Driver looked at the chart thoughtfully, pondering on the news of the latest 'skirmish' in the English Channel. Has the Bradford made good her damage?" He enquired.

"Yes Sir, the Skimmer squadron that's escorting her managed to chase off the attacking ships and also made good with a fast turn around of repair crews."

"Signal the Bradford to proceed up Channel at full speed to engage the Bölkow and the Agilité'. Brownling should be aware of the tactical situation… Let's hope the Americans stand by their commitment to maintain the TACSAT system, eh." The senior Captains and the various ADCs took the last remark as a serious observation on the strategic weakness of relying on a fickle former ally three thousand miles distant whose own interests may include dropping the TACSAT data link to the UK forces at any time. Chris, David, I want to talk to you in my office. Two of the senior Captains present looked up and then joined the Admiral as he walked from the chart room. Admiral Driver walked over to his desk and pressed a button on his intercom. "Is Captain Brading in the Ops Centre?" He enquired. The detached voice of a woman acknowledged in response. "Sub-Lieutenant Gad here Sir, he's just arrived, do you want me to send him to your office?"

"Ah, Brian, good to see you back. We need the Fleet Air Arm to provide air cover for the Bradford and Blake off Portland, scramble 685 Squadron immediately. They are to engage any hostile vessels or aircraft if fired upon. Oh, and standard weapons delivery –thank God they didn't shut down Yeovilton in 2023 like they said they would! And Brian, work with the RAF Liaison Officer for backup and intelligence, we need your Airbus Mk 5s up there with their sensors running full tilt."

"Yes Sir. Can I take it we provide air cover for the Marlborough and the Lofoten as well?" Came the quick reply.

"Marlborough? Where is she Brian?

"She's the last through deck cruiser on her way to a scrap yard on Tyneside. The Lofoten is acting as escort." The response was slightly smug if not coming with a hint of an impish gleam in the eye. After all how would an Air Arm wallah know about such things – unless he had hurled metal skywards off her flight deck! The Admiral didn't miss the subtlety behind the point and chose to ignore it with just a faint pursing of the lips to indicate his understanding. "Where are they now?" he enquired. "Somewhere off North Foreland Sir with a skeleton crew aboard." An idea had crept into the Admiral's mind. With so many defence cuts the job of disposing of vessels no longer meant towing them to the knacker's yard, but sending them off with enough fuel and sailors to make the final journey. The Lofoten was a Courier Class frigate providing escort and transport for the Marlborough's limited crew on the return journey back to Portsmouth. Looking at the chart spread across his desk he cast his eye at several points coming to rest on the north coast of Kent. "Yes Brian, ask the Liaison Officer to scramble air cover for them into the Medway. Wait." The Admiral pressed another button on his intercom and asked for the duty signals officer and the Flag Supply Officer. Later, with orders fresh in their ears they departed to co-ordinate the change of plans for the scrap yard flotilla.

"Chris, you're the political graduate here give me a view on the escalation scenario. And David, do you have the information you were waiting for from our friends in Washington?"

"Yes sir," replied Captain David Ansty, "it arrived just after three this morning.

"Good, Chris you first please."

Captain Christopher Hayward opened a blue folder, briefly scanning and reordering the sheets of paper he removed from it. "The formal announcement by the British government to withdraw from the EU in the wake of the recent referendum will create several reactions from the European Parliament Sir, who regard the result as disastrous. The weight of political argument here will not stand in the face of aroused public opinion that already regards the British government at home as 'treacherous.' Further rioting in response to the government's failure to begin the process of our 'detachment' from the EU is inevitable, fuelled further by last week's commons' revolt over implementing the increased taxation from Brussels, which the government argue they had already signed up to before the referendum. Continuing unemployment growing in excess of 25 million in conjunction with the age-old habit of Parliamentarians awarding themselves, shall we say, 'fat-cat' salary increases to maintain parity of income with their city counterparts, continues to anger the public. Not just the normal minority extremist elements, but now includes a polarisation of something in the order of 69 to 75 percent of public opinion violently opposed to the government. The financial implications aside, we have to consider the Government to have lost its mandate to rule and it is likely to fall within the month, and an increase in armed hostilities between ourselves and our allies in Europe." The Admiral nodded and thought for a moment. "What's your opinion on the collateral effects of all three – I mean the collapse of civil law and order, the apparent armed aggression from Europe and the fall of the government?"

"We cannot respond to both the requirements of the civil power and the defence of this nation Sir. Three decades of defence cuts and no political will to ensure the security of our trade routes, including our own shores have rendered our fleet incapable of more than a stand-off for six months."

"Any suggestions?"

"Yes sir, we concentrate on consolidating our defence of the realm, and let the politicians sort out the mess they made and make peace with the electorate."

"A tall order." observed the Admiral wryly.

"David, how are we progressing with the Americans?"

"They give all the appearance of maintaining the status quo over the availability of their TACSAT data link Sir."

"Any noticeable change in their language?"

"Not entirely, but I have detected an increase in the number of 'passives' in their last dialogue with the Chief of Staff."

"Hmm. You're the diplomat David, what do you see as possible scenarios for and against their direct involvement?"

"I would have to say it worries me that they have to trade their own interests in Europe. In the balance is their own commitment to the European 'powers' through post NATO accords, and what is now the hackneyed euphemism of our 'special relationship,' and of course, their increasing trade aggression. – Take for example the last GAT15 summit and the environmental summits they have continued to disrupt since before living memory. In one sense all they have to do is wait for the outcome having fanned the flame of disunity. The end result will be a weakening of European trade barriers particularly if we have a bitter, armed internal feud, and that seems likely in any event. They will trade arms and supplies to both sides in their usual 'balance of powers' strategy knowing that long term they will be the only ones to gain from it. Just like Northern Ireland, and many of the former colonies of the European colonial nations. On the other hand, the expectation that the US will 'assist' the UK breaking from the EU could be a possibility if they could find a political answer to the NIMBY syndrome coming from Brussels. This may be facilitated by the Russians, but it can be assumed that the NIMBY ticket is only good for distraction when coming from the Russians."

"What exactly do you mean?" asked the Admiral looking straight at a world map on the wall opposite, depicting Western Europe including the Russian Federation. "Do you mean that they would see the Russians volunteering to help the British in any way or the European 'powers'?

"The Russians need the EU and the US for continued growth. The Pacific Rim can't help them now, since the pandemic has wiped out two thirds of the population. That leaves both Australia and New Zealand in an isolationist position trading only agricultural resources with either Britain or the USA. The Russians not only need technology, but diplomacy with which to continue rebuilding their own political and social 'wastelands.' By that I mean they need both of us to trade with so they can achieve their own 'corner' of bargaining chips. You see it's falling in to place, at present the US has been aggressively exploiting every third world nation for minerals while undermining every other colonial power by funding armed insurrection in their colonies. Russia is in the same category and can only trade in minerals. They have limited technological achievements with which to trade. Therefore, the US must guard their investment in Russia as well. They've been doing it for years. Quite effectively under the noses of the western powers who signed up to the high technology trade embargoes of the US in the latter part of the twentieth century, so they will use diplomatic force of argument to make the Russians stay out of the conflict. The Russians will be seen to be doing something, but they cannot be allowed to get too deeply involved. However, any weakness in the EU through internal conflict will be seen as strengthening the Russians' position. The key to any diplomatic solution is oil Sir. Our new fields in the Falklands and the combined gas and oilfields off the coast between Poole and Dungeness. The Americans are running dry having forced a cheap supply out of Mexico all these years without restraint, and the Russian oilfield in the Caspian, albeit a different type of oil is also badly needed by the Americans, but it represents a strategic disadvantage. We may see the development of the current situation where our South Atlantic oil is used as a bargaining chip in exchange for armaments."

"Thank you David. Just one more question for both of you. Where do we stand with our legacy of goodwill in Europe since the Second World War of a hundred years ago? Perhaps, Chris you could give David a rest.

"Firstly," he began with a knowing smile, "there's the French. Although they have twice had the benefit of British rescue missions in the past they remain as equally indifferent to us because they are hooked into the EU as founding members to the Treaty of Rome. The Germans remain equally committed as founding members and both countries would take a strong disliking to losing control over the EU bank since it represents the basis for their national recovery programs in the wake of the industrial depression. Other than hoping for individuals or small groups of sympathisers I perceive no German attempt to renegotiate individually. Certainly, the Belgian, Dutch, Danes and the Norwegians are sympathetic, and it seems they may also be making their own bids to secede. I base this on the assumption that they too appear to have grown weary of providing an income to their large neighbours at the expense of their own economies. On balance, we could foresee a time where non-intervention by some of our near neighbours is a possibility because of our own past involvement, and because we are probably like minded enough to come to terms using the diplomacy David has just illuminated?"

"Thank you, Chris. David, your perception on this point."

"We see a government losing its grip Sir, and quite unable to deal with diplomacy while it's head is in the vice. European Parliamentary representatives from the UK are already streaming back home before the cut-off date for secession is finalised. I doubt that any of them will be hindered in their attempts to get back. The French and German leaders have recognised by now that the planned appointment of a European Governor General over the British people was crass. While our people see it as a cynical deconstruction of British independence. The government could stand down leaving diplomacy wide open to confusion just as in Belgium and the Netherlands. One good point in favour of a long diplomatic wrangle is the crushing of Belgian opposition to the proposed governor-ship six months ago. It has exposed the intention of the European Presidium to rule more or less an empire while hiding behind the anonymity of the Commission."

"Do you mean Paris and Berlin?"

"Why yes." Our government will of course cling to power for as long as they can. Even using the wartime expedient of a coalition, but they would have to escalate our present circumstances to a war footing to do that. That's disastrous from a political and diplomatic point of view that would wrong-foot Britain in the eyes of its international observers. Besides, our national defence has been diluted so much that we are going to be pushed to force a tactical solution. What is needed is a political tactical withdrawal by way of an interim government that can play the diplomatic tunes that Whitehall is feared for –at its best- while restructuring our political system without European interventionism. The worst that could happen is a sell out that leaves us free of, yet tied in some way to the EU with punitive tribute of some kind. The best that could happen is as I mentioned earlier. Those other States in the EU that are sympathetic to us remain uncritical as such, even joining us in secession. Either way it would remove any psychological and political initiatives to 'hurt' Britain because of the groundswell of anti-European feelings in the other nation states. However, hostilities are already under way, started by the political leaders in mainland Europe. That gives us the political and psychological advantages of being another victim of Brussels' mismanagement. We have only a few weeks, maybe three months to re-jig the civil power back into shape and get a grip on ruling our country before any full scale hostilities do hit us."

"Thank you, can you summarise all that you have said in the past ten minutes?"

The summary concluded that Parliament would be dissolved and a new government would be formed to manage internal affairs. While at the same time putting into place the format of democratic elections required for a new government to go forward with a mandate from the people to achieve political and economic independence from the EU. That it was inevitable armed conflict would continue and escalate until diplomatic, political and economic arguments could hold sway against EU opposition, with the Americans and the Russians agitating in the background for predominance. What was obvious to all three and countless others throughout the nation, was the lack of firepower to back up the bid for secession.

****

The Agilité sank in mid-channel after having received the tow from the Bölkow. The engagement in British home waters was brief and disastrous. A Squadron of Dutch and Belgian Super T fighters screamed in at low level right up to the old 12 mile limit and in a spectacular formation loop pulled up directly above the wounded ships. Moments later a squadron of Zed-6s met them at eight thousand feet after executing a perfectly tight split S formation intercept. As they drew level Commander Bill Shankly looked hard at the wing leader of the opposing force and nodded briefly giving him thumbs up signal. Wing-Commander Triff Zonderman gave the same signal in response and followed it with a wave-off signal with his right hand. "Red 5 break for 12 and hold position!" He paused and spoke to his wingman in person. "Willi, I'll join you in two minutes, Red 5 Leader out."

After a few moments the two flight leaders were by themselves. Instinctively Shankly changed radio channel for privacy. His own squadron circling gracefully a few miles away closer to the shoreline. He knew the EU air force Commander was no immediate threat. Their weaponry had been deactivated 50 miles from the British formation. The British pilot spoke first. "That was a clever idea Triff. Thanks for that, it's made our job easier." Shankly was greatly relieved he was facing a remarkably intelligent and wise old man of aviation and he didn't want to fight an old friend. He and Triff had met many times and they often vied with each other on the ranges. "Ja you're OK Bill, I think we see this out together." Came the voice of his friend in that typical flattened accent of the Dutch voice. "Let's keep it simple Triff. You look after your lot and I'll try to make a convincing cover for the two old ladies down there."

"OK Bill, we put ourselves between you and the French coast for now. I'll try to give you enough time if they come back."

"Agreed, keep in touch Triff. Shankly out." Shankly changed back to the designated frequency and rejoined the flight. The two squadrons patrolled in a series of elegant manoeuvres. Keeping far enough apart, giving the appearance of a stand off on radar.

Matters took a slightly different twist five miles off Margate. Five French 'Rainbow' fighter-bombers swooped low across the channel from airfields north of Paris. Their weapons systems ranging and locking on to the Marlborough and Lofoten. Pierre Larusse their wing commander had no doubt in his mind what they were about. The Grey and rusting hulk of the Marlborough could be seen clearly rising out of the smooth calm seas. Alongside it he could see the tiny, slim shape of the Lofoten rocking idly in a gentle swell. He knew of the reputed capability of the Lofoten's weapons and had his wingman tucked in to him in tight formation, taking advantage of the early morning sun behind them. At 10 miles he was locked on and signalled for joint weapons release, before he and his wingman turned on their starboard wingtips heading north in a climbing turn to twenty thousand feet to engage the 'rebel' British aircraft bearing down on him from East Anglia. High above them at 25 thousand feet the remaining three aircraft dropped their guided bombs towards the two ships. Lofoten's electronic warfare screen was the most agile and sophisticated the world had ever encountered. It dealt a severe blow to the pride of the French airforce by successfully deflecting the first four missiles away from the little convoy. One apparently stopped working and fell into the sea while another went wide off the mark, turned sharply to the left and acquired the

Herne Bay Court Hotel as its target. The bombs proved more difficult to dodge. Two missed their mark but only just, causing the little greyhound to whip from stem to stern as they exploded into the sea close by. The Marlborough just kept on going not feeling a thing. The fifth bomb struck her on the ski lift flight deck smashing the upper part of the hull above the bows into oblivion. With flame and smoke billowing from her front end, the Captain decided to make a break for it, bringing her up to full speed leaving the Lofoten behind. The wind was onshore and to some extent it blew off to port giving a little clarity of vision ahead. The sixth bomb exploded next to the hull under the island taking out a lot of the command and control wiring between the bridge and the ops room. The Lofoten managed two more missile salvos before she was hit a glancing blow by the last bomb. Skittering across the port quarter it penetrated the deck just under the aft superstructure, blazing red hot it emerged out of the starboard side just above the waterline and exploded taking the part of the visible hull with it. On its journey through the hull it severed a fuel line from the helicopter fuel storage tank and started a chain reaction that became unstoppable. With her EW destroying the French missile targeting, firing her own missiles and dodging bombs she disappeared in a burning white hot roiling dome of flame. Metal vaporised along with the guns and their gunners on the upper decks. The rear mast vanished with all her communications aerials and the stubby funnel collapsed like soggy newspaper. With burning fuel spilling into the bilge below and scuppers 'topside,' it was only a matter of time before the inevitable. High above them a dogfight was being thrashed out between the opposing air forces. Missiles and cannon fire wove a deadly pattern in the skies. Two French aircraft went down immediately as missiles banged home. A British Zed-6 spun out of control, it's starboard wing blown away. The pilot ejecting in a spinning rolling fashion a fraction of a second before his fighter blew up. He could see the French parachutes below him and another partial kill twisting like a falling leaf passed him by. He watched the burning wreck of the Lofoten three miles away. Down by the stern, he could make out moving sailors on the decks with hoses and she was still firing missiles and banging away on her guns.

He didn't know it, but the quickest way to offload high explosives from a burning ship was to fire them off into the distance since the automatic weapons systems were faster than human muscle. The tortured steel ribs and alloy hull slowly gave way and a third of the ship disappeared beneath the surface in a lurch. As if in slow motion he noticed the firings had ceased and a tide of blue and white erupted from the ship as the sailors prepared to abandon her. From two thousand feet above the waves he saw the bows thrusting skywards, and then sag a little before twisting sideways to heel over on her way to the sandy bottom. Bodies still emerging from the open hatches he could only imagine the shouting of desperate men and women trying to get out. Then she was gone and all that was left were the small spots of survivors' heads floating in the water. Some swam around to the life rafts that rose to the surface as the Lofoten sank; others disappeared as they were sucked down. Stray cannon fire zipped about him as he hung there in shock. Looking about him to see two more Zed-6s go down. The Lofoten settled on a sandbank where she slowly righted herself leaving her topmasts visible just above the surface.

In total three Zed-6 combat fighters were scratched with one fatality. 'Scotty' Johnson disappeared in a ball of fire when a French missile slammed into his jet exhaust. Sixty sailors out of 185 got out of the Lofoten before she dived. Three 'Rainbows' went down, one limped off across the North Sea escorted by the only untouched enemy fighter as escort, but flamed out somewhere near mid channel and the pilot was forced to ditch. It was 10:45 and it was over. In the pseudo-silence that followed, the British flight-commander marshalled his remaining aircraft and together they made a low pass in formation over the place where the Lofoten went down. Each pilot responded unfeelingly in their hearts to the tight commands of their Wing Commander as they dipped and then roared off to the Marlborough to give her air cover. Their baptism of fire had passed, but for some the ordeal was far from over. For over 120 years the British had not fought in any major European war and it seemed that it was about to change.

The sailors clung desperately to life in the two remaining rafts not damaged by fire or projectile. There was no naval presence in the area for over a hundred miles. No support vessels or maritime unit. All that was left of a once proud naval tradition was a rag-tag collection of small craft loaded with high-tech weapons based in two ports. No Search and Rescue helicopters and no coastguard facilities to lend a hand. All gone as defence cuts and taxation rose to stifle even voluntary organisations into oblivion.

The ancient Skimmer terminal at Ramsgate, now run down, but still providing the only fast surface route to mainland Europe by skimmer craft, often provided a valuable commercial outlet for ex-naval types. Chip Woodingdean late of the European Standing Naval Forces (ESNF) steered his Skimmer 'Privateer' through the water with a half-load of freight on the enclosed deck behind him. He had seen the French aircraft coming in as he changed course en-route to Ostend. Having cleared the maritime control boundary he was listening to his personal radio, a battered old 'music box' jammed into a corner of the cockpit windshield. He could hear his disk jockey girlfriend's voice chattering away in the background as she played popular music. 'Margate AOK' was a partnership venture between them. While he sunk the bulk of his gratuity and savings into the Privateer, he underwrote a small portion of the radio station until it started to take off. Travelling light and fast on a calm sea the Privateer could make Ostend in just over sixty minutes allowing for traffic control and other skimmers. With a guaranteed delivery to the hover track terminal in Ostend any merchant could see their goods delivered into the Capital cities of western Europe in just half a day. He followed the jet aircraft with his eyes. "You take her Fred, keep her steady on 085." With that he left the cockpit to his co-pilot and climbed through the hatchway onto the roof clutching a pair of old-fashioned Electro-B, Mk 3 intensifiers. The targeting option was still functional and he soon caught a close up view of the receding aircraft. Returning to the cockpit he took out his flight plan and checking the way-points took a final bearing on Broadstairs before taking the skimmer up on its wind-effect hull at full speed. They bounced along happily for ten minutes when the radio suddenly played its identity jingle. *"We have a news-flash just coming in. Apparently military aircraft are attacking two navy ships just off the coast of North Kent opposite Reculver. Several members of the public have phoned in describing the incident as a strafing attack on what looks to be an aircraft carrier and a small frigate. We will continue to update this story as we get more news."*

Observing the speed limit in the traffic lanes the Privateer was seven miles off the English coast and ten minutes into the skim when, for a second time, the programme was interrupted. This time the change of note registered in Chip's ear and he looked up reaching for the volume control. *"...Over to the BBC in London for a news flash on the attack on two British ships earlier this morning."* The announcer spoke in the popular negative tones reserved for grave occasions, lengthening the syllables for dramatic effect. *"We have been informed that there has been an unprovoked attack on two of our naval vessels several miles off the Kentish coast. The attack began at approximately ten o' clock this morning with early reports suggesting that one of our vessels is severely damaged. While the other, an aircraft carrier has been badly damaged. There will be a further announcement from Downing Street in the next hour. Until then we return you to your original programmes."*

"What the hell is going on?" asked Fred. "You don't suppose it was those aircraft do you? I mean that's bloody terrible" Chip quickly folded his chart over and scanned the soundings in the area. "There's nothing but fishing boats and a few tugs between Margate and the Isle of Grain. Hell Fred, if that's one of ours that's sunk there's nothing fast enough to get over there to pick up survivors –not even a coastguard cutter!" Chip reached for the radio panel in the centre of the cockpit between the pilots' seats. He changed channel on the number-two radio to the naval and military distress channel and then reached over to turn up the volume on the emergency receiver system. "We should pick up anything on those two channels if anyone is in trouble. Pass that 'notice to mariners' over will you?" He scanned the three sheets of paper looking through the notices. There it is 07:00 this morning Marlborough with Lofoten as escort passing up-channel en-route. It's the Lofoten; they damn well sank the Lofoten. She only finished sea trials last December. That's just four months, and the Marlborough, she's that old rust bucket on her way to the scrap yard up north, somethi…." Radio number two started to sound off, but there was nothing coming through the mush coherently. "Damn the UHF, there's too much land between us and them!" Chip fiddled for a few seconds. "Fred, get up there on the roof and clean the insulator will you. She's on auto pilot so don't worry about things down here." Fred dutifully climbed onto the ladder that led to the cockpit roof with a dirty rag in his hand, wishing he had four gold bars instead of just two. As Fred wiped the salt away from the aerial insulator the static lifted and bellowed in the cabin below. *"...Mayday, mayday, mayday, warship Lofoten, under attack, sinking, position..."*

"They did it! Those bloody Rainbows, they did it! They sank the Lofoten! Fred, turn her round onto a heading of 360 while I plot a course for the Lofoten."

Chip informed maritime control of his intention, giving him clearance to proceed immediately. They could not legally prevent any response to a maritime emergency by international law. In a medium swell the Privateer covered the distance around North Foreland to Reculver in twenty minutes. The long cargo deck was half empty, and it shook abominably, but the containers stayed where they were fastened to eyebolts in the deck. Looking through the canopy with his image intensifiers he saw the thinning smoke first, then the two life rafts bobbing in the water five miles ahead under the cloud. The two crewmen from down aft had been shaken out of their morning coffee and reverie by the news, now stood at the back of the cockpit for almost the entire journey. "Right, Jim you and Murray get those lines ready to drop over the side and standby with those heaving lines to bring in the rafts. Let them get off the rafts first then drag them inboard, we can use them as padding for the injured so don't deflate the main flotation chambers. We may have to go looking for survivors in the water afterwards." The two men disappeared onto the main deck and out onto the open stern beyond with ropes at the ready. The two huge stern doors to the cargo deck wide open behind them.

They picked up the crew of the Lofoten including a few stragglers and the downed English pilot. He told them there were two French pilots somewhere in the water, but could not be sure where. As morning gave way to early afternoon two merchant marine tugs out of Sheerness under Admiralty orders and with a small crew of navy men aboard came into view. Chip radioed brief details and warned them about the two French pilots unaccounted for. Those who were fit transferred to one of the tugs. The casualties and the pilot remained onboard the skimmer. Drawing away from the tug he set the Privateer on a course for Whitstable. There was no hospital ashore for miles except at Ramsgate; the powers that be had arranged for a fleet of ambulances to ferry the casualties to Canterbury General Hospital until further notice. Chip radioed ahead and asked the harbour master to check out the present status of diplomatic clearance to continue on to Ostend. The answer came after twenty minutes that the government had effectively closed all ports and harbours, all airports and airfields to international traffic until further notice. It took a further two hours to offload the casualties and the life rafts onto the quay. Chip and his co-pilot watched in sombre silence as civilians cradled the injured into a mixture of assorted vehicles acting as ambulances. Four hearses drove away carrying the bodies of those who died of their wounds during the rescue. Many of the injured women who were on the Lofoten had simply switched off and it was left to the men who could either walk or stumble around to chivvy them along. Many were crying and it could be seen that the company was polarising into two groups. The injured men who could lend a hand and did so to help their shipmates and the women who just wanted to be left alone helping no one.

The crewmen on the tug were put ashore at Southend and flown out by military transport that evening. The other tug from 'Grain' found the two pilots swimming slowly towards the coast. They gave up willingly after a token resistance and were hustled below in short order.

The whole incident reminded Chip why he'd left the navy in the first place. He saw how the European system had rendered it pitifully ineffective as a maritime force. He had seen the fleet reduced to a gunboat flotilla and like many people had rejected the political spin about 'joint effort' and the European Fast Response Forces. He resigned in disgust that Britain could barely fight her own corner. Her fishing grounds had been raped by the French and Spanish, The North Sea was a desert and all raw materials had the imposition of the European levy in addition to the Environmental levies and so on. While Franco-German mega–industrials bought out native British industries, effectively wiping them out one by one. Now this! The Privateer reversed slowly from the quay and set course back to Ramsgate and home. The music of AOK Margate could not lift the serious mood in the cockpit as the skimmer lifted on to ground-effect hull and sped eastwards along the coast.

On arriving at her berth the harbour master sent a runner down with a message. "The Harbour Master wants to see you as soon as you finished tying up Sir." announced the messenger. Chip and Fred trudged slowly along the quays and around to the stone building where the Harbour Master's office lay. The two crewmen skipped off towards home via the pub taking with them the exciting news of the day's events. Chip had privately thanked them for their 'splendid effort' and informed them of the unofficial news he had heard from the marine radio network. The Belgians were temporarily impounding six skimmers and their British crews at Ostend. Latterly, the Harbour Master officially confirmed all international journeys across the Channel were forbidden, and all crews were to report to the Harbour Master at 09:00 next day. The meeting broke up as rain began to rattle sombrely against the Harbour Master's office windows. A chilly gust of wind greeted the seamen as they crammed out of the doorway towards the docks.

19

2. SNOW STORM IN LONDON

The Prime Minister's voice rose and fell during the blistering cabinet meeting that followed, continuing into early evening. They, –he, –was under pressure, the early evening editions and the electronic news media were already vilifying both the government and the Prime Minister for gross ineptitude in allowing this to happen. 'Surely they had contingency plans for an orderly and diplomatic withdrawal from the European Union? If not then why are they in government at all?' and so on. The Britz Democratic party, a coalition of the right wing and unionists, blazed away in scathing attacks on the Liberal Nationalist government. 'Nothing could be worse!' the papers screamed with historical diatribes listing the failings of the government including the spiralling taxation, interest rates and growing poverty. The Greens joined forces with the 'Action Against Poverty' party and led a similar campaign quoting endless figures in the media. However, figures did not mean action. Nobody was doing anything.

As the afternoon wore on crowds of people gathered in the streets milling around. Small groups wandered towards the city of London to be turned back by armed police. Others emerged from the underground stations only to meet with a blue line of police who jostled them back down the stairways and on to trains out of the city area. At sunset the city lit up with thousands of lights. The rich corporations could afford to spend the money and advertised their wealth every night. The banks and insurance companies, the dealing rooms, traders, and so on.

"The no confidence vote will go ahead this evening railed the Prime Minister." If we lose we have to stand down. We have a weakened mandate from the electorate and the House will not allow us to continue if the vote is carried." There was a pause into which spoke a cabinet member. I'm sorry to say this Prime Minister, but it's you who will have to go." Everyone in the room turned to the new speaker. "You see it's very obvious, you just insisted for too long to become a media personality giving all that spin and believing your own rhetoric." The Prime Minister goggled and a strangled yell came from out of his mouth. "It's all very well standing there gawping like that, but you brought it upon yourself and upon this government." You have become as it were, your own spokesman, and the only way for this party to remain in political power, to assuage the public outcry is for you to resign. Let someone else step in and restore firm government. That's all there is to it."

The Chiefs of Staff met in their underground bunker far below Whale Island. They reviewed the intelligence reports, scrutinised the casualty list, read the reasons why the losses had been more than expected, and finally reviewed pre-set plans to mobilise the nation's defence. The main threat was perceived to be from the German and French airforces still linked together in the ESAF agreement of 2015. However, it was noted that there was a possibility that not all the European based commanders were persuaded about decisions calling for hostile actions against the British.

With only sixty three warships that included just six destroyers, the rest of the compliment being made up by frigates, fast patrol boats, five submarines seventeen skimmers and nine tugs was deemed parlous. The air force fared little better with only twenty four Zed-6es, eight heavy bombers, two airborne command-and-control centres otherwise known as the 'Airbus squadron' as it was called. A squadron of fourteen Dominies doubled up as armed interdiction and patrol aircraft when fitted with weapons and the right sort of radar, and that was it. The Army could muster four regiments of infantry, two squadrons of tanks each having eight tanks. One regiment of artillery with sixteen guns between them, and four squadrons –if you could call them that- of Royal Engineers. The Army Air Corps had been grounded since the last purchase from across the Atlantic twenty years ago had proved too dangerous and unreliable to fly. Their sleek looking 'Black Angel' helicopters had earned the name 'Dumbwit' since the fly-by-light photonic systems had failed to meet expectations. This left just one Royal Marine Commando unit, the RM band, and a scaled down SBS unit in Plymouth consisting of 20 men. There was a regiment of 'Red Berets' of sixty men and two aircraft. The RAF Regiment of 150 officers and men could be fielded if necessary in support of the infantry. Essentially the British forces stood at just below twelve thousand men and women, six regimental mascots, a mobile kitchen, 36 retired senior officers of flag rank or equivalent in their dotage, and next to no uniformed maintenance personnel. All civilian support would cease at the commencement of hostilities which meant that thirty five thousand civilians, more or less, would be unemployed overnight, unless they joined the armed forces.

"You know," said the Chief of Staff, "I have often wondered where all our taxes went in the last fifty years or so." The remark did not fall on deaf ears. The subject had been the butt of frequent satire in the media, and of numerous name and shame television programmes taken from within the growing ghettos around the bigger cities. Without a heavy industry to speak of, few raw materials except oil, and no time to reopen the coal fields closed during the Thatcher era over a hundred years previously; in a fit of political pique. The sobering assessment concluded with the bitter statement that no real response could be made if European forces attacked Britain. Funding had to be provided to support industry, rearmament and the training of new recruits. That high technology weaponry requiring high cost, high frequency maintenance budgets was financially crippling, and that prolonged skirmishing could be perceived as a way of whittling down British defences within two years.

Admiral Driver and the Defence Chief spoke at length in the privacy of a small function room set aside for private discussions, aides, secretaries, and so on. What passed between the in conversation nobody knew for certain, both men left the room looking resolved with a purposeful mien as if a gauntlet was about to be thrown down with an absolute certainty.

That evening, the motion for a vote of no confidence in the government was shelved. Tight bargaining in the wings and corridors of power dispensed with a Prime Minister as if he were just the wrapping around a bar of chocolate. In such a way the new Prime Minister was ushered in, announcing a package of sweeping changes that were for the good of the people and made plain common sense for the nation. Hot on the heels of the announcement came the news that everyone was waiting for. A diplomatic mission to Brussels that would be 'seeking urgent answers to the reasons for such an unwarranted attack on this country, and recompense for the loss of lives and equipment.'

At three o' clock the following morning, after a long and arduous madhouse in the Commons, the new Prime Minister met with the Defence Chiefs in their ancient and semi-abandoned Sanctum Sanctorum in Northwood. Although accompanied by his own Parliamentary Secretary, the Defence Minister, his Deputy and an under-minister involved with procurement issues, the Prime Minister remained closeted with the Chief of Staff for nearly two hours before a more formal meeting with the assembled board of the Chiefs of Staff. "This is not going to be easy." murmured a General to his Air Force Colleague. "He doesn't know the worst yet does he." Came the soft reply.

At 05:30 a white faced, tight-lipped Prime Minister and his small entourage left for Downing Street. The cavalcade of vehicles moving swiftly through the quiet streets of London kept to the restricted lane reserved for official cars. Anyone improperly using the reserved lane was fined a "Prezzah." So named by the irate population after some long forgotten politician who brought them in under the guise of instituting fast bus lanes to ease traffic congestion. The route took them around those areas of town that were deemed as 'difficult' or 'awkward' for members of the ruling class to behold. The Prime Minister spoke into his scramble-phone outlining preparations for his imminent return. He had addressed three topics on his agenda, now he had to find the cash to pay for them. He put the phone down muttering to himself. "What the hell was the world coming to."

The board openly backed up the Chief of Defence. Consistent cutting of funds over thirty years had made Britain incapable of fighting no more than another cod war. In reply to his unbridled criticism of the nation's defences a Rear Admiral had interrupted him in mid-sentence. "You cannot expect to have an effective defence system unless you are willing to pay for it. You criticise yourself Prime Minister. You were the Defence Minister for five years were you not. Yet you persistently pared away funding for new equipment, new recruits and training budgets. Now you come here blaming us for what you have done to us. If this goes on we'll end up like the bloody Russians. They cannot even pay their men's wages, so like them, ours will simply walk out. We are way past the Belize scenario Prime Minister where we could make the choice to go in or appear to fumble it for the sake of a few million pounds! We cannot respond with more than a token resistance! There is nothing we can do unless there is the provision of the funds that we need to mount an effective rearmament programme. Note, I said re-armament, because what we have at present is outdated compared to our 'friends' on the mainland of Europe!" The Prime Minister was livid and it showed. No one was going to talk to him like that and get away with it! He had just started to bite back hard when the Chief spoke up interrupting him. "Prime Minister, what my colleague has said is nothing short of the plain truth. I see no point in continuing in negative argument, apportioning blame when it is external factors that determine what we can or cannot do. If you want us to follow-up on our strategic planning and deliver the goods, as it were, you must be prepared to pay for it. If you don't there is no point in even trying. You have effectively given us a white flag by not paying for adequate defence."

The Secretary of State for Defence inwardly baulked at the strong language these men used. They had closed ranks and knew damn well that they had right on their side. The Prime Minister stared coldly at the entire assembly of men seated around the table. He was not a man to be thwarted and yet he could see both their argument and solidarity. For too long he and others before him had been using defence as a political punch bag on the way to the top of a political career, maintaining the rot in defence spending. "How long can we hold out if we have to face full scale hostilities?" asked the Prime Minister. "A few weeks at best. Say three months." Came the swift reply. "I'm appalled General, absolutely appalled! Is that all?" demanded the PM acrimoniously. "Yes Prime Minister it is," answered the Chief of Staff, "but there is a way around the problem," and as if to forestall an inevitable 'I thought so' interruption from the Prime Minister the General carried on speaking a little more urgently. "If you can stall the European Parliament for a year, even two years, and give us the funding we need by diverting central taxation from Brussels into defence spending. Then we can raise the forces we need by conscription, we can train them, rearm with better, more reliable weapons, and then we could hold them off. In addition, our intelligence is telling us that it won't be all the member states against us." The Prime Minister took time to consider the statement. Here was something. Here at last was a chink of light remembering the aggressive response that the Commission hurled at the Belgians when European Police Battalion units flooded the capital. "What about the Americans?" ventured the PM thrusting forward a broader argument. "Not directly Prime Minister," ventured another voice, "Not since the trade wars of 30 years ago when the EU finally brought down the shutters on cheap foreign imports. Anyway, they are too busy fighting the separatist states backed by the Arab-American Alliance. No, their industries are collapsing and were it not for their internal problems they would probably remain isolationist. On the other hand they might spare some intelligence, but we have nothing left to bargain with."

An armed police patrol stopped them about a mile from Whitehall on the embankment. "Sorry Sir, you can't go any further there's rioting in Parliament Square with a mass of people crammed all along Whitehall. You'll have to find another route." The Prime Minister and his private secretary remained passive in the rear of their limousine. The driver thanked the police and indicated that he was going to do a U-turn. With the rest following he made a diversion bringing them safely to the imposing façade of Millbank Tower where he pulled up in the yard deep inside the quadrangle. The occupants wearily entered the building and took a lift up to the topmost floor. The PM silently brooded over what had been a near total confrontation with the Defence Chiefs as the lift moved slowly upwards. He silently resolved to make sure that would never happen again.

Ten days later the Marlborough slipped out of 'Grain' having been patched up by repair crews flown in from Portsmouth dockyard. It was 10 o' clock at night and the tide had been high for two hours. "Time to go number one!" Ordered her Captain, and without fuss or noise the crew singled up and made ready to slip. Carrying no lights they let slip at 10:10 with a single tug in attendance to escort them through the deep channel until she made open water. At 10:45 she rendezvoused with a similarly darkened-ship escort of two skimmers and a brace of FPBs from Rosyth. Hugging the coast, as far as the shallows would allow the convoy steamed round the Essex coast heading north. By daylight they were just over the horizon and out of sight of land, and hopefully out of sight from hostile eyes. Discreet air patrols provided round the clock cover until they reached the waters of the Firth of Forth.

During the lull that followed in the next three months, all naval and military establishments were put on full alert. Reservists were quietly re-called and the 'old grey hairs' that had retired in the previous seven years were invited to return with an appropriate bounty to go with their acceptance. Five thousand men swelled the ranks of blue in a campaign of gentle persuasion. Another three thousand went back into the army while fifteen hundred were tempted back into the repose of the Air Force. Small beer, but carefully orchestrated to resemble nothing more than a precautionary step for the digestion of the media and the hostile European Commission.

Fly posters on the wall outside the Black Horse in Nuthurst called for the repeal of Article 60026. The infamous edict from Strasbourg that did away with the independence of the British military armed forces and laid the foundation for the removal of the monarchy. Admiral Driver climbed out of his Super Safari and walked across the gravelled car park. Passing through the gate into the beer garden he went in by the back door and ordered a beer at the public bar. Sitting down under the old oak beams he began toasting himself in front of the great roaring fire. Half an hour later he was quietly joined by three gentlemen of similar age. Together they sat by the fireside chatting affably for a while until the locals thinned out. The noisy celebrations of a birthday party coming from the rustic dining room providing sufficient background noise to cover their own conversation. Air Vice-Marshall Crimmond, Major-General Haslet and Commandant Royce of the Royal Marines sat around the open fireplace like a picture painted by an Old Dutch master. "…That's now in hand Admiral," said Royce, "if the harbours are blockaded by chains we have launches standing by fitted with cutters. The men have been hand-picked and know what to do given the circumstances." He looked across at the Air-Vice Marshall who nodded. Together they confirmed a measured response to the latest government blunder. "The RAF regiment," is on standby," confirmed Crimmond, "with heavy lifting equipment to clear away any obstacles laid down on our airfields and airports, should they choose to block our movements. The Major General looked into the fire and after a few moments of silence spoke for all of them. "Of course we will provide discreet command and control where we can and our communications boys have been briefed on the new network under the guise of commissioning our new equipment. On your call we will provide appropriate security at those key sites, but I would urge you once more to speak to the king before we hand in our resignations as one."

The Admiral nodded slowly in agreement and broke the news. "He knows, I was with him this afternoon at the Cowes marina." There was palpable relief among the assembled men. Crimmond shot the Admiral a penetrating look.

"What does he say?" asked the General.

"He was naturally very alarmed and saddened by recent events." Replied Admiral Driver carefully as the latch on the old front door clicked upwards. The General, staring at the fire leaned back in his chair rocking it backward on two legs, while the Commandant picked up his newspaper and blinked at the crossword. "5-Down, seven letters ending with E, anyone got any ideas?" The Air-Vice Marshall took his pipe out of his mouth looked at it, placed a box of matches onto the top of the bowl and sucked noisily. The door opened as a young couple walked in. "5-Down you say," he spluttered convincingly. The Admiral looked at the ceiling and thought for a moment and said, "I think that should be adipose don't you Bryan?" The General nodded. "I think you're right." He lowered his eyes just enough to observe the couple head off across the bar into the restaurant. The newcomers were greeted with squeals of delight and the Admiral continued as if nothing had happened. "…But he does understand that the freedom of movement of the people of this country is their right and has given me to understand that in his book we are doing the right thing. He wants no part in it, otherwise that will be seen as a political move to re-establish the monarchy in defiance of Article 60030." Everyone knew what was at stake, and each one knew that they had reached the top of their career paths where they could go no further. It stuck in their throats that they should ever have been asked to draw up plans to close all harbours, ports, airports and airfields. The first anyone knew about it was when the Prime Minister had broached the subject in an official letter giving the order to make preparations.

A week later the news broke. 'Prison Britain!' howled the tabloids. 'PM closes borders!' announced the Daily Telegraph in a somewhat muted fashion. Probably because of the censorship imposed on it recently as it voiced an increasingly anti-government, anti-European opinion. 'Nowhere to go!' whined other periodicals. The European Socialist, an unofficial organ of the European socialist movement at large, was incensed and vented its anger on the government it had formerly crowed about. 'Britain shuts down! PM to Blame.' and so on. Regular TV channels broke into their schedules to announce the dreary news causing public alarm and a hue and cry. Within the hour the streets of every major city were filling up with angry citizens. People left their work places to join in. In some towns the population erected barricades around official buildings and vilified local politicians, particularly those of the ruling European Socialist Union party or so-called ESU. European MEPs were jostled in public places. Angry crowds assembled in Parliament Square, up Whitehall, spilling into Trafalgar Square. The leader of the Opposition with other opposition party leaders was addressing the mob from a hastily constructed platform put together from scaffolding and planking.

Somebody had blabbed, but who was it? The PM was apoplectic. "Those two-faced scheming bastards!" He spat venomously. "I want to know who it was and have him or them strung up. The lot of 'em if need be!" By the end of the day the crowds had swelled enormously causing deep alarm in both Downing Street and party HQ. The ESU party chairman had been attacked while getting into his car after a congress meeting in the East End. Stones were thrown at the building where the ESU itself resided in London, while burning effigies of the Prime Minister wrapped in the EU flag were strung up from lamp posts outside. Public opinion had had enough. The nation had lost its currency, its sovereignty and its king in the name of progress, and foreigners were now running the country. People who did not live here! Frustrated at everything being taken from them that represented their national identity the public went mad.

Armed police were much bloodied after three solid days and nights of rioting. The civil power finally stood in the face of failure and ordered the military to step in. Not for over a hundred years had the civil power used the military to quell its opponents. The real cost became known within hours. Police Chiefs reported mass on-the-spot resignations as scores of their officers refused to continue defending what they saw as the indefensible will of the government. In a short public address that was televised to the nation the Prime Minister gave his government's reason for wanting to close the borders of the country. "It is for the safety of the people of this nation and to protect them from the current dangers that exist on the continent of Europe. As you know we have suffered from attacks by the ELF and ESNF and we must ensure that our borders and our citizens are safe… and of course we must safeguard our economic position within the community to which we belong…"

No one was listening because very few people cared. The Chiefs of Staff did not know how long it was before someone in the scheme of things would leak the information. Neither did they go out of their way to ensure it wouldn't happen.

In Strasbourg there was a quiet tension in the European Commission building. Ministers were alarmed at the messages they were seeing on their viewers and through diplomatic channels from home. "What has become of Britain?" asked some of the junior members from the east. Not knowing or understanding what they were doing, the ministers gradually signed away the rights and privileges of nationhood throughout the European peninsula. For the poorer nations it meant a start in life. For the older member states, like those who founded the union in the original 'Treaty of Rome,' it was a huge gravy train where they could milk the system of as much cash as they dared. Using a barrage of legislation hamstrung with so many conditions that only a very few could hope to gain any benefit. Those that did benefit were the larger nations who engineered such legislation in the first place. The key lay in the subtle ransom of huge development grants available to member states. Yet even these grants were small by comparison to the amounts salted away by the founders. The principle mechanism for forging alliances lay in the granting or the insinuated threat of withholding grants to the poorer nations. Both ministers and their bureaucrats were sucked into a huge bandwagon of growing corruption. It was something that had always offended the British sense of fair play. Most people working for the commission and the parliamentary representatives were salaried at two and a half times the rate for company executives within a particular band. All of them with few exceptions were milking the expenses system for all it was worth. A commission enquiry into members claiming their pension contributions on expenses was quietly disbanded once the brouhaha died down in the public gaze. The report never saw the light of day.

The Council of Member States passed a resolution to provide immediate support to their British 'colleagues' to quell the rioting and to restore public order. As a gesture of goodwill and with the benefits in mind they issued orders for riot police supported by army units from the ESA (European Standing Army) to be despatched without delay. This being one of the very few orders issued by the European Parliamentary representatives. Laws and edicts were usually put together and enacted by the legion of un-elected civil servants who made up the 'Commission', with scant reference to ministers. The Presidential cavalcade left the Parliament building with the President seated smugly in the back of his Mercedes Benz. He was almost completely secure in the knowledge that the British had just handed him an excuse to send 'reinforcements' –in effect, as one of his aides put it. "...The first foreigners on English soil to give policy to the British for over a thousand years..." President Albrecht Muller-Weiss savoured the moment feeling gratified that his political manoeuvring for the last two years was about to bring down those 'insel affen' and bring them to heel. This was better than the CIA's disastrous meddling in Irish and middle-eastern affairs. This was not going to blow up in his face like it did for the Americans. It was a tightly run gambit, but he was sure that they could be relied upon to feed their lust for success and use the CIA to destabilise Britain even further and so walk into the trap that would allow him to close the net around Europe. His agents had kept him informed and, after all, they were well paid into the bargain. As he understood it, there was no freedom-fighter movement to feed arms, ammunition or money to. The general perspective in Europe was that this was a matter of unity and Federal Authority. The British were still laughably running around asking if they were doing it right while all the time they could not see the inevitability of it all. What war had failed to do, politics was about to achieve quite unspectacularly, and it was understandable that there was going to be a minority of objectors along the way. He smiled to himself as the limousine drew up alongside the small jet aircraft parked on the apron of Strasbourg's small municipal airport. Walking briskly to the cabin door he acknowledged the presence of the local dignitaries, shook the limp hand of the Mayor and then he was off down the runway with his thoughts his own in the privacy of the small cabin. He inwardly laughed at the recent memory of the British senior representative's acute embarrassment. An embarrassment that turned to white-hot anger as he was shouted down by both the French and German representatives along with their supporters. Then there was the hasty withdrawal, the final act of political disagreement by walking out. The European MPs watched him go, some smugly laughing to themselves, a few deriding him as he walked through the chamber towards the nearest exit, others shocked and disturbed by a deepening concern for the outcome. Both for the British and for their own situations back home.

Alarmed by the imposition of what could only be seen by the population as a foreign invasion, the Cabinet put together a plan of appeasement to stall any such move by the European Parliament. The Party hacks back at HQ had no inkling of what was happening at Downing Street. Indeed, they were coping with the damage inflicted by two weeks of rioting and with the ever-increasing resignations of its rank-and-file membership. "It's designed to demonstrate to the European Parliament that we are still in control. It will show them that we mean business and at the same time, give an indication that we prefer to handle our own affairs with the guaranteed autonomy that Chapter 189 allows us." argued the Home Secretary. We cannot maintain civil order unless we bring in the military to assist the police…"

 "Yes." rasped the Secretary of State for Defence. "What about the police – eh? You seem to forget that we've lost nearly two-thirds of the force up and down the country in the last ten days! What d'you expect the military to do – shoot every damn member of the public for voting with their feet?"

"No, no, that's not the intention, but we now have looting on a large scale in all our big cities. Even the urban preservation areas are being targeted. You must understand that with industry at a standstill we only have about five months before our energy reserves run out, and we're already seeing regional power cuts." He dared not breathe a word about the cross-channel power link. If anyone thought that for a second the government on the mainland would 'pull' the power on Britain it would cause uproar in the already heated atmosphere of the Cabinet Room. They all knew it for what it was. Chapter 156 had decreed that electrical power generation be centralised into key production areas. Britain was not one of them per~se. With an enforced reduction in local facilities the smaller member states had subsequently to rely on their larger neighbours for a substantial portion of their electricity. Behind the lie of organisational needs lay the minds of deceit. With dependency came control. But other than the expected level of objections the bill was pushed forward with the familiar words of European unity, co-operation and mutual benefits for member states being the goal of providing energy in a cost-effective and fair manner across the Union. The arguments and counter-arguments raged until early the following morning. Before dawn drained looking Cabinet members left Downing Street in small groups via the tunnels leading to the other side of Whitehall, and to their awaiting vehicles.

The following day saw Army units moving into the towns and cities along the main highways. As a precaution infantry and missile units were placed near the 'Chunnel' while Customs officials were heavily in attendance at the Folkestone railhead and at Manston International Airport. A detachment of Royal Marines kept out of sight in vehicles parked in the Federal Police compound across the road from the main terminal building, while their colleagues openly patrolled the Harbours at Folkestone, Dover and Ramsgate. Naval vessels appeared in the harbours at all ports along the south coast, remaining a discreet distance from the immediate dock areas and out of the way of shipping. All eyes were turned towards the distant coast of mainland Europe with bated breath.

Chip drove his sporty little roadster up Euro-route 2 to Chatham. The E2 was once a busy highway between London and the Channel ports. The concrete road now cracked and pock marked with large craters through lack of proper maintenance. The hydrogen fuel cell produced enough energy to take the little car up to 140 kliks on the flat. He turned off onto the E222 towards the Medway Urban Preservation Area. Here the necklace of overhead lights along the middle of the roadway was all lit up, unlike the string of lights along the E2 that never seemed to be working. Large signs greeted him along the way reminding drivers to have their IDs and UPA passes ready at the gates to the Medway UPA. A UPA patrol helicopter dawdled overhead as he passed the 5km signs, the sound of its engine whispering above the chop-chop-chop of its rotor blades. He looked up at the aircraft as it passed across the carriageway some distance in front of his vehicle and wondered if they – meaning aeronautical engineers- would ever replace the ageing 'notar' principle for something more exciting. As the road climbed the gentle rise in the land he could see the lights of the complex a few miles ahead. His parents had lived in Old Medway for the last fifteen years near to the old naval dockyard. It had become a popular residential complex with a central marina surrounded by bars, fashionable boutiques and Italian restaurants. Passing through the outer gates he was waved through by two UPA security guards dressed in their distinctive brown-yellow uniforms. At the inner gates they brought him to a stop and the gate guards there checked his ID. The car licence plate had already been scanned by roadside security systems, so they knew it was legally on the road. "Can you confirm the name and address of the people whom you are visiting Sir?" Asked one of the gate guards pleasantly enough. "Yes, it's the

Woodingdeans at number three The Sail Loft in the Chatham District." The second guard nodded politely and waved him through. The darkness hid the ten metre high bank encircling the UPA complex that included Strood, the ancient port of Rochester, and the towns of Chatham and Gillingham. On the outside it was partly hidden by a screen of trees and bushes preceded by a sward of neatly clipped grass. One hundred metres beyond the bank stood a fifteen metre double fence. The first inkling that any 'outsider' received that a UPA was more than just a little different.

The UPAs represented the new era of urbanisation without the trappings of industrialisation. They also represented a haven for the smaller communities of the better-paid workers, administrators and white-collar staffers along with independently minded citizens. In the past travel tax, city tolls and environmental levies had crippled industries and communities. While the environmentalists whined on about pollution and the damage to the eco-structure nobody noticed at first that successive governments were exploiting the issues by setting up new layers of taxation. As industrialisation waned it became evident that some if not all of the basic necessities of life would not be around for much longer. Communities became moribund to the extent that the larger cities by-passed the doughnut-effect, going straight into economic collapse early in the 21st century. Recognising the fragmentation of society into distinctive communities with different needs, the Salisbury accord; so called after the Late Lord Salisbury who put forward the idea; UPAs were set up by a Royal Charter given to designated areas on application and ratification of compliance to stringent set of conditions. Towns and cities were the targeted communities. It was easier for them to transition from local town councils with an elected mayoral system to a UPA Administration headed by a Lieutenant Governor. This left a larger majority outside the pale. Farmers, those working in designated industrial enterprise zones (IEZs), the unemployed, and those who still worked in the remaining industrial complexes. In 2016 the last independent mining operation ceased production in the coalfields due to the rising costs associated with the environmental legislation and transportation. The British oilfields in the North Sea were handed over to the European Energy Commission by Chapter 4056/2009, which called for pooling resources in energy catchment areas. All energy was apportioned according to a population-diameter ratio that translated into Britain's subsequent complete dependence upon the mainland of Europe for its energy resources for the first time ever. Similarly, agriculture collapsed, transport systems failed and both those inside the UPAs as well as those left outside them became isolated from each other with ever increasing demands for security at the gates as resources thinned. Inevitably, poverty grew and those who could not pay the UPA local levies were ignominiously ejected from the UPAs after a period of grace of just six months.

Chip headed along through an expanse of open countryside dotted with fields and inquisitive livestock that occasionally lifted their heads to watch him go by. Sometimes the beams of his headlamps caught their eyes producing an eerie red-eye glow. He picked up the riverside ramp upon entering the built up areas of town, drove past the new Van Alten complex where signposts painted in brown with yellow lettering pointed the way to shopping malls, sports and leisure domes and to the different marinas. The advantage of living in a UPA that contained a harbour was immense. Chip's father retired from the navy and had done enough homework to know that any such place would have the ability to maintain its links to foreign trade, principally from the continent. He was the last of a cadre of officers to hold a government commission signed by the Secretary of State for Defence. The new commissions were now being issued by the European Defence Council (EDC), and had been looked down upon ever since the change had taken place. Particularly since Dartmouth training had long gone with the only alternatives being Mürwick or Brest. He followed the route around the river past restaurants and boutiques that lined the riverside walks. All looked clean and tidy with shrubs and trees lining the pavement areas and promenades. Subdued lighting among the greenery adding a certain quality to the casual observer. He slowed for traffic at the entrance to the Kitchener underpass, taking a filter lane halfway along the tunnel he branched left on to the flyover that dumped him at the back of the old dockyard complex. He drove slowly round a wide bend down the hill catching a view of the wide spaces of water twinkling under the lights of the many walkways and pontoons of St. Mary's Marina. His parents lived on the very edge of the Chatham District; in fact it was almost surrounded by the boundary with the neighbouring Gillingham-Strand District that ran along the top of the ridge above the riverside basin complex. He drove over the short bridges and pontoons that connected the far side of the marina to the mainland accompanied by the clanking of the steel plates as the vehicle ran over the metal sections. He heard the occasional raucous cry of a seagull overhead as it wheeled around chasing after food. He was beginning to feel at home. At a T-junction he turned left opposite the Burma Road Inn following the signs to St. Mary's Island. The Sail Loft was a small complex of three modern townhouses decked out with plasti-board lapped planking on the upper half, with solid decking, iron railings and coloured brickwork completing the style. It gave the impression of being an old waterside warehouse that came even with a mock cantilever wooden beam jutting out from the centre of the wall just above a false wood panelled doorway set high under the eaves. He parked his car under a large archway next to a pink SEAT Puccini. 'Ah, good Meg is here.' Chip sighed with satisfaction as he got out of the car and pressed a button on the facing wall next to a door. There was a gentle scraping sound while a large double door automatically slid downwards into place across the entrance to the archway. He swiped his ID card along the security terminal and an inner door opened silently onto dimly lit softly carpeted hallway.

Chip was warmly greeted by his parents and lovingly hugged his darling Meg. From out of his bag he produced flowers for his mother, Belgian chocolates for his sweetheart and small green box for his father. "Here dad, I think you'll like these." He said as he handed over the box. "Got them from Rotterdam a fortnight ago. Better than my old Mk 3s any day." His father carefully unpacked the intensifiers from the box and looked at them proudly. He went over to the window and switching on the binocular system scanned the world beyond. "They've targeting and relative bearing options as well, my word will you look at that, the night vision option is crystal clear." Together they talked and experimented for a while during which time the ladies made themselves scarce in the kitchen. "How's the radio doing Meg?" asked Chip's mother. "Is it going well?" She thought it was awfully exciting for a girl to run a radio station, especially in a little place like Margate. "Yes, it's starting to pick up a bit, especially since that fracas off the coast a few months ago. We were the first to break the news and I think people woke up to the new radio in town." Chip's mum balanced the conversation between taking steaming dishes out of the oven and putting them aside a small pile of plates. "I don't know how you manage it dear, it's all very technical to me. How can you be here and still turn out your evening programmes it puzzles me." Meg giggled as she helped to set out the plates. "Oh, that's so easy, it's all recorded and managed by my broadcast system. It has a computer that measures everything to the smallest fraction of a second. I only have three staff and we work a shift system so that we can be there if anything goes wrong and to handle live news coverage. We do the entire recording ourselves during the days when we're not on shift. It takes about three to four days to put the programmes together and about seven to ten days for them to come back from the Broadcasting Information Office." Meg shrugged casually replacing the strap that had slipped off her bare left shoulder. "How on earth do you cope with those people I really don't know, it must be awful to have someone looking over your shoulder all the time making sure there's nothing about the government or the Commission. I mean how do you put up with it?" Gabriella Woodingdean, 'Gabbie' to her nearest and dearest, peered over the top of her glasses and gazed briefly at Meg who was spooning gravy over meat on a plate. "Well, it's a bit of a nightmare really. We, I mean, I, had to work my way through the Broadcast Information Act before I could get the licence, and then undergo a personal profile to make sure I wasn't a closet anti-European, anti-government activist. They're just making it so hard for people to make a living these days. I paid 18 thousand Ecus just to get a copy of the document from the information office, and then I had to pay twenty five thousand to sit the examination to prove I had read it. As if that was not all, I had to pay 59 thousand just to take their profile analysis. Honestly, if it weren't for Chip I never would have stuck with it. "Gabbie glowered over the chicken joint that she was carving. "It just seems as though they only want us to hear their radio stations and nothing else."

The men folk were still messing with the imaging binoculars when the videophone issued a low-pitched beep. Chip continued to scan the low hills on the other side of the river outside, while his father went over to the phone. He checked the caller data and left the video facility switched to off. Hello "Woodingdean here." He responded neutrally. "Oh hello Mr Woodingdean, this is Strood gate security office, we have a Mr. Nigel Woodingdean arriving from Portsdown. Are you expecting him Sir? It's just that he's forgotten his pass." Lazlo Woodingdean tut-tutted sympathetically at the blank screen. "Yes we are expecting him. He's such a rascal. I think he's left it in his other pair of trousers knowing him. I'll send my authorisation code in just a second." Lazlo pressed a blue button on the console and waited a few seconds. "It's through now Sir, thanks very much. Good evening to you." The gate-guard broke the connection and a colleague waved on through the gates a nippy little saloon carrying the errant Woodingdean junior. Meg came out of the kitchen carrying plates and Chip turned round holding the binoculars to his eyes and pushed the auto-focus button. "Ho, ho, ho!" He leered. "What have we here?" He demanded as the device picked out the curvaceous lines of his amour. "She looked at him and stuck her tongue out at him. "You men are all the same." She responded tartly and turned away towards the kitchen wiggling her hips in mock defiance. As she did so he pressed the phase compensation button and was immediately surprised. It wasn't a true x-ray vision view he received of Meg's rear end, but the result was stunning. He quickly snatched the viewer away from his eyes in disbelief. He'd heard rumours about phase compensation, particularly in night vision mode, but this was awesome. With a sly grin he lifted them back to his eyes and waited until Meg emerged from the kitchen again, this time carrying a dish of potatoes. Meg wore nothing underneath the top she was wearing. He could tell that from the way the front of her blouse became contoured as she moved around, and by the way her breasts moved with a gentle rippling motion against the material, but this was different. There she was as if her blouse was no more than the merest shadow of chiffon. "What are you laughing at?" She queried as she went over to the table. He slowly lowered his gaze as much as he dared and made out as if he was larking around. She mistook his sudden inwards rush of breath as another murky gesture and sauntered back into the kitchen. As casually as he could make it look he turned back to the window and scanned outside again. He was doubly amazed at the amount of hidden detail that now could be seen in this mode of operation. Switching off the phase compensation mode he handed the new binoculars to his father without saying a word. Secretly he hoped that his father would not discover this particular facet of the 'new toy' until he was long gone, hopefully for several months. Just then, the door opened and his older brother walked in with a large stiff paper shopping bag clasped in his left hand.

After dinner they all gathered around a low table in the lounge and chatted about old friends, politics and what was happening in the outside world. Nigel and Chip found themselves sitting at the table permanently set on the wide balcony overlooking the outer basin and their father's yacht lying motionless upon the still black water. Chip looked idly at the stars high up above, content to let his brother continue in conversation for a while until his father arrived back with more drinks. Nigel fell silent for a few moments and then asked a question. "Have you considered re-joining Chip?" Chip was drawn from his quiet reverie and looked around him. First at his brother and then at their sire. "Er, … only when those bloody French cowards attacked the Lofoten and the Marlborough. I would have given my eye-teeth to be back in the air at that moment in time." His father looked out at the dark line of hills across the main channel of the river and said nothing, slowly lifting his glass to his lips to sip a little whiskey. Nigel continued to press his brother gently. "What would make you come back in?" Chip thought about it for a moment or two and responded a non-committed answer." I guess it's down to money, the fact I've got a reasonable chance running my own shipping company and, yes, I'll admit to it, meeting Meg." He stopped and smiled a little furtively perhaps, at the very recent memory of using the binoculars in phase compensation mode. He looked at his brother and saw him looking in his direction somewhat quizzically. "Ah, it has to be a woman," said Nigel with a mild laugh, totally mistaking the sheepish grin of his younger brother. "Is that serious then?" asked Lazlo, his father. Chip pondered the question for a moment before answering. Since leaving the navy he had, up to then, little or no time for the fairer sex. First his basic training, then flying training and finally deployment to qualify as a naval pilot left him a little short of social engagements. "Ye-es, I'd say it was serious. She's totally different to anyone I've ever met before, capable and at the same time very open about things. I think that's because her father's a vet, and they're a very pragmatic sort of people." Lazlo smiled and looked at his younger son with a good deal of sympathy. "The poor boy is smitten I think Nigel."

His brother took a long quaff from his glass of beer and looked out into the late evening darkness beyond the river. "How's the business doing these days now that the travel restrictions are an almost permanent feature in these parts?" Lazlo paused and continued. "It can't be easy for any shipping company at the moment. Even the big boys are feeling the pinch and hammering on the doors of the Parliamentary Assembly demanding action along with a mighty big claim for damages." He was referring to the new name for the British Parliament that had been reduced to nothing more than a State Legislature, along with all the other political chambers of the other member states'. "Well that's the problem right there isn't it," groaned Chip. "I wasn't serving my country any more, but another country across the channel. They're all foreigners telling us what to do and they seem to be intent on converting us to first German rules and then French rules and then turning us into a backwater while stealing our industries and our energy reserves by legislating against us. No that's not worth fighting for, and I couldn't in all honesty serve in someone else's navy, no matter how cleverly they explained it away."

"Where do you stand with your skimmer sitting idly alongside the wall in Margate harbour Chip? Especially for weeks on end with no destination to go to?" Chip's father made the point very succinctly, but it was still a surgical question that cut right to the heart of the matter. "Quite frankly I don't. It's like this. Either I'll pick up an occasional coastal jolly and try to break even or I'll have to become a smuggler – or sell up and try something different." Both his father and his brother could see the growing frustration in his current situation, acknowledging that unless the impasse was broken Chip would lose his business and his skimmer. "How would you like to work for us Chip, say, indirectly at first, and if things changed you could review your position some time in the future." Chip was now suspicious. "What exactly do you mean by that Nigel. Come on, be more specific." Nigel looked carefully over the rim of his glass and finished off his beer.

"It's like this. You can't work your present contracts because of the closure of the ports to British shipping on the other side of the Channel. Right?"

"Right."

"Then We're looking for someone to move stores about, someone who we can trust and be discrete."

"Oh, I get it, cloak and dagger stuff you mean?"

"Er, no. We want someone, with a proper contract to provide shipping for us and we want to be particular about who we choose to do it. But mainly it has be someone who can be a little circumspect about his destinations and other minor details."

"OK, just who do you mean exactly by 'we'?"

I mean the navy of course. Nothing more, nothing less."

"Ah, you mean a contractor working for the navy moving naval stores from one port to another, that sort of thing?" His brother nodded. "Well why didn't you say so in the first place?" Somewhat naively he took the lifeline his brother threw in his direction and accepted the offer of working for the navy. "It's a good decision Chip, I don't think you'll regret it, and it doesn't mean you'll have to move to another port as a base from which to operate. Margate is fine for what we want, but I do ask you not to tell anyone about it for the time being. If you have to, just tell them you're hoping for a government contract to tide you over, something like that. Oh, don't worry about a crew, I know you paid them off last month when they got an offer from the harbour authorities to work as temporary lighter-men between here and the port of London. I'm sure they'll do well. You'll be using our seamen and I think I'll leave it there for now. Except to say that you'll be hearing from C-in-C Naval Home Command Procurement Officer in the next ten days or so."

3.   CLIMBING BACK

The house sat with bated breath during the televised ministerial announcement at the beginning of Prime Minister's question time. "And so I can inform The House, that by mobilising the army to assist the police forces in the process of restoring law and order in those communities affected by the rioting. We no longer face the prospect of Europol involvement in what is, after all, a local matter for us to deal with by ourselves. I spoke to Deputy-President Augsburger earlier today, who has assured me that our own efforts to restore civil order is sufficient to defer the decision to provide enforcement by units of the European Police Battalion based on mainland Europe." The house erupted into a roar with members rising to their feet shouting a barrage of questions at the Prime Minister. The speaker called for order many times and eventually gave up standing in a dignified posture until a lowering in the volume of disagreement and catcalling across the floor allowed him to be heard. The house being suspended for fifteen minutes to allow members a 'cooling off period to regain their composure.'

Small eddies rippling the dark surface in the harbour under the moonlight gave way to the steady swell of open water as the North Sea started its daily process of decanting into the Atlantic Ocean. Chip turned his skimmer to starboard once outside the harbour wall making a course along the south coast towards Beachy Head. The tide was on the turn and sucked at the submerged fins of the high-speed transport pulling her to one side. He turned off the sound coming from the small screen viewer to concentrate on clearing the outer breakwater. "Load of old rubbish if you ask me," ventured Fred waving to the Marine guards patrolling at the end of the mole. Fred engaged the autopilot while Chip activated the auto-throttles and checked the GPS was locked into the satellite cluster 350 kilometres above them in space. Chip waited until the signal lock alarm burbled it's signal acquisition alarm and the figures started rolling on the electronic navigation information system display, or ENIS as it was generally known. With the advent of Europort every commercial vessel within the European marine navigation area had to carry transponders, GPS and collision detection systems in addition to the normal navigation and marine communications systems. All cadged from the world of civil aviation. Private craft had to carry a minimum of a transponder, VHF radio and flat-pack GPS. In the latter case this was a general reference to the plethora of cheap hand-held devices produced by the Hungarian Republic's huge electronic conglomerate ME Systems. The electronic revolution that had saved Hungary during its post-communist era eventually grew big enough to challenge and wipe out its Franco-German predecessors within twenty years of liberation from the Russian occupation. For those who could afford private craft over a certain length and weight, the rules required a full commercial fit as for commercial traffic.

The dark humps of the Seven Sisters and the distant glow from the lighthouse at its base at Beachy Head became the only external reference points for the two-man crew in the skimmer's cockpit. More lights came into view as they traversed the slash in the cliffs at Burling Gap. Beyond that lay the densely populated coastal strip that began to unfold as the downs moved away from the shore into the hinterland out of sight, laying bare the brightly coloured lights of the seaside towns.

****

Sam Ryall, Principal Geologist at San Antonio's Institute of Geological Sciences ran a scan of the pressure readings in the crust under Yellowstone recording number 575/28. Frank Ritchie stood beside her as they peered into the geological computer screen. Frank had just got his PhD at Edinburgh's renowned IGS. He had taken the field evaluation trip as a break from his three year effort to get his 'letters' deciding that the result of his viva-voce could wait, or at least they could send him the news electronically. "Hey will you look at that!" Squealed Sam, tucking a wayward strand of her raven hair behind her right ear. "The temperature has gone up by 150 degrees in the last six days." The ground beneath their tented cubicle moved and the tent flapped as a minor earth tremor shook the surrounding area. It's definitely going to blow one day Frank, but not right now. I mean when this blows it will be the biggest thing since Krakatoa, but they reckon it's got another hundred years or so before that happens, and we're camped right on top of it." Frank nodded almost absently while looking at the data. Sam was a lively twenty four-year old Texas girl whose British parents had moved out to Houston following her father's career in space aeronautics. While her dad and her brothers were either in space or aviation she chose the more practical career of collecting and studying rocks. The shallow social life of Houston jarred with her deep thinking mentality and she sought the escape mechanism of travelling around the world looking at the widely different geology offered abroad.

The huge mound that first appeared as a small rift in the surface soil, way back in the late twentieth century now stood at one hundred and seventy five metres tall and something like ten square kilometres of land had changed shape to accommodate the bulging crust below it. Historically, geologists had discovered evidence of a massive basaltic eruption that pre-dated the end of the last millennium by about sixty thousand years. A trail of erupted materials, mostly basalt had been traced for up to a thousand miles 'downwind' of the original eruption, long before human memory. The trail led straight back to Yellowstone. Another tremor shook the campsite

The National Geological Survey had begun to keep a watching brief in Yellowstone National Park since changes to the most noted landmark 'Old Faithful' were first observed some seventy eighty three years ago. The geyser remained locked in its synchronism with time, more or less, but pressure changes in the earth deep below was causing the geyser to produce higher columns of scalding hot water at much higher temperatures. The conclusion of scientific opinion had been made and it was the subject of many debates in geophysical circles. The senior scientists heading up the small field survey team made up of a couple of post-grads and second years, organised the collection of data from a number of strategic outposts that automatically logged the tedium of figures registering changes in temperature, pressure, gaseous composition and so forth. It was half-past six in the morning and all the team were out checking the systems, replacing power cells and cleaning up the equipment that had lain unattended for the last three months. They followed their careful instructions cleaning the insulators from the microwave aerials that relayed the transmitted data to a receiving station a few miles away in the basement of one of the many visitor centres. Frank's gaze scanned ahead looking lower down the printout as it emerged. His sudden in-drawn breath hissed a warning in Sam's ears. She adjusted her gaze downward at the place where Frank tapped the sheet with his stylus. "Let's get a plot on the screen for the last seven days Sam, I think we need to see that right away." Without breaking his conversation he walked to an encased portable computer and spoke to the command processor input. Computer, run program DP 1090 slash 17."

"I see what you're thinking Frank." Said Sam slowly looking up from the readout at her computer station. "Frank?" She stared at her colleague who had turned ashen, shaking his head slowly from side to side. "Sam." He called in a hoarse whisper. "Get the gas analysis for the last four weeks, quickly. I'll get that plotted out next." She looked at him and blinked in silence. "What is it Frank?" she asked with a mounting sense of urgency. "He lifted a hand slowly into the air and spoke to the computer again. "Computer, run program DPGAS slash 693 and include correlation matrix program FR 0252." The first plot was emerging from the printer station as the computer began processing the last request from Frank. "Frank, Frank! What's that program doing, I've never seen a plot like that?" He stared at the screen with Sam peering over his shoulder. "See, there it is. The rise in pressure is the greatest there and it's still rising, but the rate of change over the last seven days is beyond existing models. No one has ever seen live a basaltic rift like this before." Sam looked at the plot and saw the trend line curving upwards more sharply towards the right. "Yes, that's pretty obvious to see, but what makes you think that's any different from previous activity cycles along this particular rift formation?" Sam was getting a little impatient, as Frank waited in silence for the second program to finish the plot. "There it is Sam, just a little bit more data and I'll show you what this means." Different coloured lines had been appearing across the view screen in the last ten seconds. Some of them had woven undulating trails that occasionally crossed other lines in the plot. Three of the lines rose and fell in huge dome like lines as the plot slowly emerged across the view screen.

Another minor tremor rattled the tables and kitchen area as crockery and utensils left out to dry shook and fell onto the light floor panelling in the mess. "The correlation-matrix is a set of curves derived from a particular algorithm based on known geological fault parameters, Sam. You see here where the blue line rises, that's a pressure dome plot of the rate of change in pressure, against the gas density efflux rates of change within the same period. That orange line with the green are both telling us that the levels are changing far more rapidly than in the last three months. The correlation is telling us that given similar parameters for other eruptions, like for example, Vesuvious or Santorini there's a strong indication that the magma plug is at the point of failing."

"You think this is a good time to pack up and go, Is that what you're telling me Frank?" Sam was now getting really cross. "Look Frank that can't possibly be the case. The perceived wisdom is that with modern field methods showing current data, this thing will blow out in about a hundred to hundred fifty years or so. We'll all be long gone before then." Frank took the sheet out of the printer and laid it on the table. "Sam, the data has been correlated with known eruption parameters from a hundred and sixty nine eruptions, least twenty five of those classified as major disasters both on the local environment with associated global impact." Frank looked at her directly and waved the paper in front of her as an expression of his concern. "Yes, Frank, that's just fine, but Sternbach & Michelson have stated categorically there is an underground system of branching basaltic flows relieving the pressure in local eruptions through minor fissures in the Yellowstone area." Frank nodded, interrupting her citation. "Yes I've read their paper and understand what they are saying, but they did not have access to all of the data on which to make a better assumption."

"Oh that's great Frank, simply great. Here you are a visiting geologist and you disagree with the foremost experts in the field. Not any old field Frank, but this particular mound of earth that both these guys studied for ten years or more." Frank had trodden on hallowed ground. Professor Hiram G Sternbach and Doctor Miranda Michelson were her heroes. The post-pubescent Sam had sat at the feet of her heroine Miranda Michelson, and hung on every word she uttered during several youth workshops and field studies that she ran for youngsters interested in geology. Later she went on to take her Master's degree at Princeton under the tutelege of her idol and received a distinction. "Sam, it's not me that's challenging their paper, it's the data right in front of our eyes."

About a mile and a half away Miles Villager, Damian McReidy and Sylvia Fernandez were finishing off the maintenance on a remote sensing station on the side of a small valley dotted with trees. Sylvia was a curvaceous tease of Hispanic descent that the boys always wanted to be with. Her ample bosom and wide hips gave her that classic hourglass figure accentuated by the low cut toppers and short dresses that she wore. As the boys finished bolting down the covers on the transponder casing she felt the urge to go for a leak for the umpteenth time, getting to the point where she could no longer hold on. Leaving the boys to finish off she crossed the floor of the valley and crouched down behind some bushes about a hundred yards away. Carefully making sure there was no wildlife in the grass in and around her feet, she slipped her clothing over her buttocks in a single movement and squatted over the grass Indian style. As she fumbled for some tissues in her jeans' pocket she became aware of a sudden difference in the air around her.

An ominous silence fell heavily as birds stopped singing. A small flock of lapwings flew off disturbing the eerie calm settling on the little valley. She heard rustling in the bushes and saw small brown shapes as rodents and other small animals pushed their way through the low tangle of branches and leaves. Startled Sylvia stood up half-hitching her clothing up to her knees. There was a sudden loud crack as an explosion of hot gases and steam erupted from the floor of the valley thirty feet away from where she crouched. Screaming out of shear amazement and surprise she tried to run while trying to pull up her clothing around the lower half of her body. She fell headlong into the grass as a large globule of boiling mud and grass shot out heading straight for where she had been standing. Sitting on her bare bottom on the grass she watched in terror as the ground split open in a wide fissure exuding yellow gas that flung more boiling mud into the air around her. Mud was beginning to splatter her in tiny drops that stuck to her shirt scalding her skin beneath it. In a panic she wriggled her way back into her jeans in one swift move. Not daring to stay there any longer she ran the other way holding her trousers up with one hand while fending off branches and bushes with the other. The boys jumped like rabbits startled by a polecat. Just as they saw the eruption of a tall geyser from the floor of the valley nearby they heard Sylvia screaming. McReidy who had been watching Villager tighten up the last nuts on the casing, stood up and looked down the valley. "You finish the casing and I'll go see what's happened to Sylvia." With that he headed off down the slope giving the site of the eruption a wide berth in the process.

"Sylvia! Sylvia!" He called twice. There was no answer. Over on the other side of the little valley, low down he caught a glimpse of Sylvia's pink shirt close to the ground as she ran crouching over, moving away from him and the eruption. Damian ran a parallel course along the other side of the valley noting how the wind was blowing droplets of mud and water along the valley floor. Sylvia screamed again, barking her shins on a root and fell hard against a sapling. Her collarbone took the force of the impact causing her to scream again before coming to a prone position on the grass. Guided by her screaming Damian ran forwards and then took a faster run across the valley floor, taking his bearings from her sobbing he found her on all fours with her jeans falling over the backs of her legs. He was tempted to laugh were it not for another dreadful burst of sound coming from the site of the eruption. The valley floor split wide open along its length spewing rocks pushed upwards under immense pressure. White with fear he grabbed Sylvia by the arm and dragged her to her feet. She screamed again "My shoulder! My shoulder!" she wailed, and then he could see where the light material of her shirt had become stuck to her skin with a growing patch of dark red blood beginning to blossom around her upper torso. He looked at her near state of undress and in gentlemanly fashion gave her time to rearrange herself. Finally offering to do up the zipper and her belt when it became obvious it was impossible for her to do so because of the pain. She flushed a little, but he didn't notice for she was already in a state of high colour caused by her panic. Looking over his shoulder she saw a large wall of molten mud surging towards them. All she could do was point and scream again. Startled, Damian looked back and saw what was coming. He turned and grabbing her by the back of her belt half-lifted, half carried her up the side of the valley as fast as they could go.

Miles Villager threw the tools into the plastic toolbox and ran in the general direction taken by Damian, towards the screams. He felt the ground shudder beneath him as the valley beneath split open and watched in horror as the wall of boiling mud and rocks gushed from the fissure. Further down the valley he saw the other two and started running towards them shouting and yelling a warning. At the last moment he saw Damian grab Sylvia and drag her up the slope out of harm's way. Cut off from the other members of his team he started to panic not knowing what to do. He ran along the side of the valley until he reached a spot opposite the point where the other two disappeared up the slope. Further along he could see where the fissure had caused a partial collapse of the soil layer back into the mouth of the gash in the earth. He darted down to the valley floor mindful of the apparently slow moving wall of boiling mud. He sailed over the danger in a giant leap of athletic proportions and moved swiftly up the opposite slope. He caught a glimpse of the other two moving over the ridge at the top of the valley and continued running. He arrived at the top to see the other two transfixed on a small outcrop below. Below them flowed a super heated stream of lava straight across their escape route. From his higher vantage point he could see the ridge descending slowly into a small dell before the land dipped away towards a nearby rivulet. The stench of rotten eggs effectively gagging him before he could call out to the other two. By a miracle of coincidence Damian looked up at the way they had come and saw Miles waving at them, pointing in the direction along the ridge. He looked in that direction and saw what Miles was driving at. If they could get to that dell and cross it before the lava flow reached it they could all get back safely to base camp. "Come on Sylvia, it's our only way out of here!" A huge roaring hiss broke forth as lava ejected into the air about the height of a two-storey house.

Continuing to drag the sobbing Sylvia between them they ran apace to the dell. The lava flow simultaneously reaching the outer limits of the greenery causing saplings and the bushes to burst into a fierce wall of flame. They crossed the dell in front of the advancing lava, scrambling across the rock-strewn riverbed sliding and tripping their way up to the top of the slope on the other side. Lava bombs started to rain down on the grass nearby causing a myriad of hissing burning fires that burned deep into the soil cutting through the vegetation instantaneously. Miles dropped his toolbox in his rush to get to the top and stopped looking downwards over his shoulder watching it tumble back down to the stream. He was about to run back and fetch it when a lava bomb smacked into the earth beside it with an ominous heavy thud. They all looked up briefly to see a cloud of small bombs, each about the size of a large buzzard, arching over towards them through the sky. Damian looked at Miles and shook his head. The whole of one end of the box had vaporised and the steel tools within it were burning then melting as the lava reduced the contents and the box to slag and then vapour. They continued running over the rough terrain for about half a mile until Sylvia could stand it no longer. She tripped over a tussock of grass and fell to her knees dragging Damian with her. From then on they walked at a pace that she could bear, eventually coming into view of base camp about an hour later.

The other teams had made their way back, some had had narrow escapes with erupting mud, but none so far had seen any lava flows. Sam and the other girls fluttered around the injured Sylvia while Frank and Bruno Sangonella discussed what they should be doing. "I definitely agree that we should strike camp and move back to the visitor centre. With those fissures occurring at these points on the map that puts us somewhere in the middle of them. If they should meet up we would be stranded and somebody would have to come and get us out." Until the trio had arrived Bruno had been unaware of the hidden eruptions two miles away. Both Bruno, Frank and Sam were joint expedition leaders, which gave them an odd number as a quorum that would settle any debate over important decisions, but no one expected a decision like this over situations such as an ill-timed eruption. "OK, guys, listen up. Sam will you get over here for a minute, the rest of you start packing your personal stuff and get ready to move out!" Sam joined the two men with a quizzical look on her face. Bruno was the eldest and most experienced, and the de-facto leader of the group, but she was beginning to feel that her place in the team was being undermined. "What's going on Bruno? What do you mean by telling them to start packing their things?" She demanded with an edge to her voice. "Yes, quite, Sam, have a look at these readings." Bruno handed her a printout and then drew her attention to the map pointing out the general direction of the boiling mudflows around their campsite. "Hey Bruno!" Called Miles, "We've just seen this huge lava flow erupting in the valley below station 165C where we were just working. Man you should have seen it, it was awesome!" The leadership team looked at each other and on the map. "Come over here Miles and show us on the map." Taking in the route of the lava flow and the lie of the land it suddenly became urgent to be long gone.

Sam started to argue the point, she wanted to be seen as a participating member of the leadership, but in her anxiety to be 'noted' she failed to grasp the full weight of their situation. "He's right Sam." Said Frank, "This is the best way to ensure the safety of the members of the team, especially since they are mostly undergrads, we have to withdraw to a safe distance and watch what happens." Sam bit her lip and nodded feeling out of joint. "The lava flow's the thing that's bothering me," said Bruno almost as a matter of fact, as if it was a regular thing in his experience. "We would have an estimated hour or so before the mud flows really threatened to cut us off, but the lava flow is goin' to come rushin' down this river bed here and threaten the bridge across the stream cutting us off." Sam could see now what he meant, and realised that the last piece of information handed out by Miles had much more serious implications.

They struck camp and headed off down the dirt track towards the stream. The pungent aroma of volcanic gases mixed with burning vegetation began to affect them as the small convoy of four vehicles wound round the undulating countryside. Here and there they caught glimpses of steam rising out of the many clefts and gullies where new fissures had formed. There was a new urgency in their desire to be gone from that place and eventually they reached the small wooden bridge. They gasped as the lead vehicle slid to a halt at the bridge. The lava flow had almost reached it and they could feel the intense heat emanating from the gully where the stream had once flowed. A three metre high wall was advancing within a few yards of the track as Bruno in the lead vehicle frantically waved them on. Taking his foot off the brake pedal and gunning the engine he raced across the bridge as fast as he dared drive the laden Trailblazer, swerving round a bend thirty or so metres further on bringing the all terrain vehicle skidding to a halt. He saw the second vehicle come round the bend, then the next, and waited for the last one being driven by a spotty young undergrad who was becoming more scared as the wall of fire rolled ever closer. They were towing a long base trailer carrying all their heavy field equipment. While the other vehicle slowed up and stopped behind his own, Bruno and Frank started running back the way they had come to the bridge. Rounding the bend in the road they could hear the engine of the remaining vehicle revving like mad, closer still they could hear shouting and screaming. Running down the slope to the bridge a terrible sight lay before them. One of the wheels of the trailer had jumped the rail at the side of the wooden planking and was hanging over the side of the bridge. Nick Allsop the undergrad in question was trying to literally drag the trailer; 'by the seat of its pants;' along the side of the bridge come hell or high water. The two girls in the vehicle were screaming and flailing around in blind panic while the lava flow advanced to within ten metres of them. The trailer was edging further over the parapet while they moved slowly forwards. "What the hell happened!" Shouted Frank as they came to an abrupt halt against the front of the carrier. "The car in front just stalled as we were coming across and I had to brake really hard or hit it!" shouted Nick choking on the fumes. Bruno and Frank ran along the other side until they reached the end of the trailer. The heat was intense and they could see thin wisps of smoke rising off the tyres. "We're goin' to bounce it. When we give the word you just put your foot down and pull away slowly, ya hear me!" bellowed Bruno. "OK girls, get out of the vehicle and run across the bridge!" Frank & Bruno started to bounce the trailer as the girls ran off with their arms crooked at the elbows swinging out sideways. The trailer rose and fell getting higher at each bounce. Finally the height seemed to be at the same level as the low wheel trap that doubled as the side of the bridge, and they simultaneously heaved it inwards at the summit of its flight. The wheel caught on the top of the lip and for an agonising few seconds they stalled with the wheel half on, half off the bridge. "Now!" shouted Bruno the back of his throat dry with fear. Nick saw them straining through the rear window and slowly let out the clutch. With the vehicle inching forwards the elevated side of the trailer moved slowly towards the centre of the bridge, landing with a heavy thud onto the scorching planks. Nick drove like a bat out of hell up the other side of the bank. While Frank and Bruno, half ran half-walked off the bridge, dizzy from their efforts in the blistering heat and smoke. The lava connected with the lower supports as they reached the bend in the dirt road. They didn't look back until they had turned the bend and the safety of the waiting vehicles.

President Barclay T. Shaw of the United States wearily finished going through the final details of his impending trip to Europe with his private secretary. In spite of the growing political problems at home over the demands of some of the states in the mid-west for greater autonomy. Sinking production output, higher interest rates, the poor exchange rate of the dollar on the international markets, he knew it was political suicide not to make his trip to Europe his first priority since being elected. Looking momentarily through the bullet proofed glass of the oval office he watched the sunlit view of the lawns and bushes outside and longed to get away. Yet he knew that this important visit, the first by an American President for over thirty years, was crucial.

It was left to the Senate to sort out the gasoline replacement scandal that had rocked the states from New York all the way down to the Florida Keys and across to California. By the time he returned, he mused, a Congressional Board of Enquiry would have been set up, ready to grind its way through mountains of papers and bureaucracy in their inexorable drive to get to the truth. Somebody somewhere had defrauded the Federal authorities of millions of dollars of revenues in the share dealings and licensing agreements over the green gasoline replacement, popularly referred to as 'VGS' as a result of one enterprising oil company's re-branding of the product. Everybody knew what it stood for –vegetable gasoline substitute- and the transition had been rumbling on for ten years or so. The problem came to light when the previous government, Democrat by persuasion, disciplined two of its erring members for being enmeshed in problems brought assiduously to light in lurid detail by the media explosion following the 'discovery' of skulduggery. It knocked a very big hole in the Democratic presidential election campaign much to the delight of the Republicans who swept to power with a convincing majority.

This turn of events left unpalatable problems facing the new administration concerning the failure of the power utilities in the mid-west and western states to broker enough leverage to guarantee supplies over the grid from their better-off counterparts back east. As more and more companies 'switched off' the grid supply system, the population in the vast continental spaces of the US resorted to other means of generating power. The Indian nations had a large stake in the new energy markets, particularly since most of their territories were out in the arid regions where sunlight fell inexorably hot all day long, and they were beginning to be noticed as an influential trading bloc on the smaller exchanges. As always the government found ways to tax the alternatives. The already exasperated population in the city areas changed their voting habits and many, like their country cousins, found clandestine ways to generate their own electricity. Like their British counterparts before them, many recycled their own oils while turning to local sources of home made gasoline substitutes for other machines like lawn mowers and the smaller electrical generators. Not since that fatal explosion of the nuclear power station at Fishers Creek in the Carolinas, eighty years ago. Had there been such a long and bitter feud between the Federal authorities and the people. Safety and heritage had become major issues that politicians could not brush aside with long-technical arguments over the supremacy of nuclear power. Oklahoma, well known for its prodigious agricultural output led the way stockpiling its grain in an effort to broker favourable legislation to meet its needs for more power generation. The 'green states' held back on their food production diverting their surplus output to making bio-fuel and oil substitutes. The government sent in the State Police and then latterly State Troopers as increasing resistance from the people moved up a couple of notches. Californians watched as their key industries shrank, not before adapting alternative energy methods to supplement the dwindling supplies. High technology began to founder as intermediate technology was seen as the saviour of the day for the remote towns and cities of the western communities.

No one is quite sure how it started, but some enterprising types in the Nevada-Californian desert region had worked out that by growing and harvesting certain kinds of green crops, boiling the leaves in a homespun concoction and by distilling the fumes in their elicit stills they could make fuel. It was possible to make a virtually free, albeit pretty raw, source of energy that worked pretty much the same as the VGS-gasoline substitute. Some college kids got hold of it and found ways to refine it, and by then the rumours became a reality for big business. With a speed to match those rumours, unlicensed fuel sources sprang up all over the place, and thus began a legend that would fuel the creation of a new set of folklore heroes throughout the less densely populated regions of the United States.

The Brits had adapted their cars to burn cooking oil as a diesel fuel substitute before the turn of the twenty-first century. It's beauty lay in complete simplicity. The fact that the fuel could be harvested from used cooking oil led inevitably to the birth of a new sub-culture of motor enthusiasts setting up small workshops providing fuel system adapter kits and cooking oil purifiers. Used cooking oil was collected, mostly from restaurants, fish and chip bars and in fact from any organisation that had a catering facility. For their part, those establishments were absolutely delighted to be relieved of their tax burden, because it afforded them a reduction in their environmental levies at disposal. The engine gurus 'cleaned' the cooking oil using a centrifugal filtration system, and in a matter of minutes the laundered product became available for immediate use. Later, when the fuel problem finally started hurting the average American who, just as enterprising, took a similar route developing grain based fuels and similar green oil substitutes. These were being grown specifically as the new cash crop with a potential value of astronomical proportions once it was realised they were not for eating, but for powering electrical generators and vehicles with the profits going into the pockets of the once rustic enterprising farming communities. Simultaneously, the old hydrogen fuel-cell technology was becoming too expensive to maintain from dwindling resources and had begun free falling from favour. With the resurgence in homespun fuels, clever conical gearbox systems, adaptive drive train, and magnetic fuel injectors the average punter could achieve a rewarding 37 percent increase in engine efficiency.

As the sales of VGS declined, almost completely within a year in some states, fuel cell recycling levies increased until it was no longer affordable or sensible for anyone to continue using either. The blinkered federal authorities realised too late that they had a problem. Much had been invested in VGS, by the huge oil corporations and by many 'in the know'; bankers, financial institutions and politicians had joined the bandwagon as investors, now only to watch in dismay as profits slumped. Like the bootleggers of olden times, everyone connected with the production, and distribution of DTF, which was the popular cult name given to it, became the target of much FBI activity designed to stop them. Not with much luck either. The majority of the population was in on the 'deal' and beyond the boundaries of the far-flung VGS gas stations the world ran on DTF cocking-a-snook at the Feds. The legendary tales of 'Smokey and the Bandit' -a one time bootlegger who ran liquor across the British lines in huge trucks during the war of independence grew in portent, feeding the already overripe imaginations of those involved with DTF. Enthusiasts used it for drag racing, their speedboats and even rocket fuel. Much to the chagrin of the president it was discovered that his whistle-stop campaigns to Colorado, Nevada, California, Texas, New Mexico, Mississippi and Kentucky had relied on DTF to get them about in the presidential cavalcades. In the minds of the people he had already lost the psychological argument for putting controls on the use of DTF. A low key government enquiry revealed that most military establishments had accounts with wholesale suppliers of the outlawed fuel. With some inevitability the enquiry was hushed up and the report 'lost' in the bureaucratic machinery.

The present government got in with a pledge to sort out the mess, to legalise the supply of DTF in effect, but this had to be achieved through co-operation and licensing agreements. Until that happened the union was continuing to weaken as both the communications and industrial infrastructures began to close down or shrink. Ultimately they broke down completely in many areas. Aviation once the golden egg of transport now faced a bleak prospect as national and international travel slowed down with the shortfall in money and resources. Many poor communities sprang up in the aviation 'bone-yards' using abandoned aircraft as ready-made air-conditioned homes because they were more superior to the shacks they had left behind. The political hiatus with Mexico now laying claim to Texas in the south as the Hispanic population rose to outnumber its counterparts by a staggering fifteen to one and the slowing trade across Pacific Rim and the Atlantic had brought industrialised America to the brink. The whole issue of Mexico disintegrated in grand style when the CIA, in one of its more ridiculous schemes, was caught red-handed in an operation that involved tainting the production of condoms with a chemical agent. It was said at the time that the reagent used had the effect of reducing the strength of the latex to a point where breeding would be the only outcome. The idea behind the scheme was based on a not unreasonable principle, in their minds, to boost the flagging non-Hispanic population whose lack of sexual composure and moral values made them the most likely sections of the community to use them.

The Hispanic community had, up to that point, silently resented the superior attitudes of their fellow Texans for centuries, and it wasn't until the assassination of the first democratically elected Hispanic State Governor by a white supremacist-neo-Muslim-fundamentalist coalition did they show any sign of open hostility towards them. Over the Rio-Grande, Mexico finally got the courage to hold on to its oil reserves refusing to allow any more of its precious black gold to be wrung from them. An abortive raid by Special Forces to capture the pipelines and pumping stations met with such an outcry of international indignation from around the world that the US had to withdraw. Disgusted and in a fit of pique the President got Congress to stop its UN membership payments and cease all other funding. The UN had seen this coming for no other reason than it had happened six times before. There had been a carefully stage-managed convocation at the UN dome where ambassadors exchanged the hard-hitting views expressed by their governments' back home. The Chinese UN secretary-general, Shenyang Li, a gentle, but wise individual noted for his aplomb and unflinching political skill sat impassively as the American ambassador to the UN led up to the formal announcement. Li asked if there was any way that such a valued and respected member of the UN could be persuaded to turn from taking a heavy-hearted decision. The American ambassador looked at him sadly, and shaking his head slowly, said no. Before the conclusion he withdrew with his aides and the UN secretary-general closed the convocation before almost seamlessly moving on to a general assembly. Resolution 597 was proposed and passed with a majority of two-thirds of the nations represented around the world. Britain, Ireland and Australia were the notable detractors not supporting the adoption of the resolution, while China, Korea, India and the Solomon Island Republic registered abstentions.

Not since the heady days of unchallenged trading in the latter part of the twentieth century had the US faced such a bleak prospect. By linking the nations of Europe into a Federal State system the shutters had come down to outsiders. The more discerning Europeans with their wider cultural heritage had cause to celebrate a return to a powerful bargaining position on the world stage; not seen since the days of the rampant colonialism by its larger members two and a half centuries earlier. Japan's new lease of life with its relationships around the Pacific Rim became a key founder in the Pacific Union that emerged from a previously wobbly coalition made up of Oceania, the Philippines, Malaya, Singapore and Thailand. The PU, adding all other countries and island nations except those in the British Commonwealth and Burma. The Burmese having closed their borders for over a hundred years, shutting out an increasingly critical world audience as the military dominated government cruelly suppressed its people, much like the North Koreans before them.

The following day arrived with the presidential entourage leaving the White House for Washington-Dulles late in the morning. The air force had to share civilian bases now including hangars, common flight operations, and the support of Air Force 1. The slender tilt-wing aircraft lifted off from the White House Lawn carrying the President while his wife and his aides, who would be travelling with him, made their way along the congressional underground roadway towards the airport. The aircraft's plasma ignition cutting in with a high pitched crackle as it cleared the treetops. The pilot swung the aircraft around by thirty degrees while simultaneously initiating a gentle climb over the city. Later, President Shaw looked down on a shore line that seemed to drift slowly by as Air Force 1 flew high along the eastern seaboard under the watchful radar envelope of the Air Force's photonic Sky-watch system. Far below the UN council met and ratified Resolution 597 while the President dozed in the late afternoon sun streaming through the window. The great aircraft banked slowly right on the commencement of an avoiding turn to fly around a huge cumulus-nimbus seen towering out of the western sky ahead. Its base obscured by line of cloud far below while the majestic column rose above sixty-five-thousand feet topping out in a mighty anvil at least eighty miles long.

Li paused for a few moments in silent reflection then looked up from the papers on his desk and made the pronouncement. "Resolution 597." He began in a flat, expressionless voice, "has been ratified by the member states and is effective immediately. The withdrawal of the United States of America from membership of the United Nations Assemblies and committees is complete. No requirement will be made to recover funds amounting to $153 billion American dollars in recognition of the long standing service and good will of the American people to the United Nations in the last hundred years. In accordance with the wishes of the Central Committee, General Council and all member states, we give our thanks to the American ambassador." Li nodded towards the empty ambassadorial desk. "For all the work that his country has done. Further, that it is the will of the members of the United Nations to vacate this assembly building at the earliest opportunity."

High above the Atlantic storm layer lashing the sea into huge waves, Air Force 1 slid majestically past the point of no return. The President being briefed by a military aide was distracted when a shiny suit strode into the executive lounge coming from the direction of the mini-communications booth. "Mr President, we have received this communiqué' from the Vice-President's office." The military aide tactfully excused himself as the shiny suit handed the President a slim electronic tablet. He read and then read the message a second time, scrolling up and down the miniature view-screen. "Have you read this Rawlings?" asked the President dourly. "Yes Sir I have and I've asked Senator Burnett to join you. If there's anyone else you want to discuss this with Sir I'll go fetch them?" President Shaw nodded his approval. "You can ask Dr Shivulski to join us please."

"What do you make of it Dan?"

"Well, it seems pretty straight forward to me Mr President. They just decided to move out after we decided to quit on um." drawled Dan Burnett in a rich southern accent. He stood six feet five inches and despite his spare tyre one could still see the hallmarks of a one-time athlete in the huge frame. Michel Shivulski, a broad faced intelligent looking foreign relations analyst pondered the viewer thoughtfully and voiced the obvious question. "What exactly do they mean by vacating the assembly building?" Dan leaned over grabbing a hand full of peanuts. He could see out of the corner of his eye that the President disapproved. "Aw, hell Mr President,

Libby ain't here to see this, it's the first snack I've had all day." He referred to his wife knowing full well that the first lady and she had made a deal to ensure the big man cut down on his intake. "You ain't gonna tell on me now are you?" The President smiled and shook his head. "Mike, what's your impression, what does it mean exactly?"

"I think they're meaning to go elsewhere Mr President, and I don't believe it will be on US territory for much longer."

"That's what I thought Mike. Have Ned Jones call me when we arrive in Paris. Get on to Al Baker and Have him get the details on this. Tell that son of a bitch I need to see it before I leave London. That gives him two days, that should be enough time"

"Yes Sir Mr President." Replied Shivulski who got up and moved towards the comms centre. "Dan, did anyone know about this beforehand. Anyone at all?"

"Can't say that I know the answer to that question. I sure as hell didn't. Shoot, I reckon Al Baker has got one big surprise comin' his way when he gets the message." They both smiled at each other in a secretive smile of mutual understanding. Al Baker ran foreign policy planning for the State Department like a feudal lord. His hawkish stance towards those nations who didn't fall into line with his policies was well known. The turnover of senior staff and secretaries was as legion as his personal preferences, dictated in abrupt personal epithets not only undermining them, but threatened to extinguish enterprising hard work with a resigned lethargy leading up to industrial action by the civil service rank and file. "Burn em" Baker as he was known had provided US foreign policy with a thick vein of arrogance. Woe betide any country, ethnic group or person that stood in the way of attaining the goals of such policies. Alternatively, who simply stood up for their nation's rights where it flew against US foreign policy; which he felt that he owned as a personal fiefdom. He made few friends in Capitol Hill and mostly regarded the inmates of that institution as rather dull and in need of 'educating' about foreign policy. As much as he resented the fact when someone crossed his sacred boundaries he could never see the other side of the coin when the US decided to mobilise its forces to charge into other countries to make a point about their ability to get what they wanted. Now that was policy! Be it a trade agreement or revenge. This time it seemed as though the UN-Section had failed to predict the kind of reaction to the US suspending its membership. Someone was going to get a roasting and they were eager to see how Burn em Baker was going to slope shoulder this blameworthy situation onto the shoulders of his subordinates.

4. CONVOI EXCEPTIONEL

Three and a half months after the Privateer had been settled into number 5 dry dock at Portsmouth she emerged in her new colour scheme. The old pennant number SK 393 MG had been repainted in smart white and black lettering over an orange background. It was a cool evening as the dockyard mateys tied her up alongside the wall in north basin. Her sleek hull and delicate looking carbon-fibre fins merging into one as the carefully painted colours gave the impression of a mono-hull riding high in the still waters. Fred and Chip walked past the old Nelson along the colonnaded rear of the naval museums, their voices echoing through the lofty portals as they chatted about the new sensor arrays and communications outfit, before moving out onto the main concourse beyond the ancient Admiralty Dockyard gates. It was a celebration to mark the eventful refit schedule coming to an end. The refit and paint-job was done at the behest of the Admiralty with no expense spared. The old Camber docks still untouched over the centuries retained one or two red brick alehouses and pubs well known to local seafarers. The seven o' clock ferry to the Isle of Wight slid out of Portsmouth harbour as the small gathering leaned against the taff-rail reaching along the length of the long low balcony overlooking the narrow entrance. The choppy waters slapping noisily against the brickwork underneath. A warm breeze held back the cool maritime air, mixing with the aroma of good food and breathing beers. It was late summer yet the swallows and house martins still swooped up and down gathering insects. Seagulls preened themselves in niches on the granite walls at Dolphin Point, just the other side of the harbour mouth. Holidaymakers in brightly coloured clothing mingled with the more sombrely dressed commuters from London disgorging from the harbour's hover-rail terminal. The four celebrants; Chip, Fred, Nigel and his young Norwegian wife Gry felt the hour was good, very good indeed to indulge in relaxation with fine food and some excellent wine. With the taedium vitae of dockyard life almost behind them they whooped it up into the small, wee hours of the night. With the final bell bringing an end to their festivities they caught a metro-cab near the old slipway, eventually crawling into Nigel's spacious flat atop Portsdown Hill at four o' clock in the morning. The ancient Roman quarry site had left a centuries old white scar in the face of the downs that was a landmark known to every sailor.

The old follies along the ridges of the South Downs had long since been turned into 'executive' dwellings. The Admiralty research establishment had been hived off, first as a civilian run outfit, then as a re-development site with a stunning view when the civilian defence agencies went under. The UPA had negotiated some pretty unique agreements with the local Boroughs. For freedom of access to the beauty spots that were dotted along the private road running along the cliff edge, there were quite a few concessions resulting in better facilities and less costs for providing services. While not truly a societal off shoot it still remained very much within the required definition of a non industrialised urban preservation area.

They sat and talked slouching in a long white leather settee looking through an immense window at the twinkling harbour lights in the distance below. To the left they could see the far off arc lamps around the Hayling UPA while to the right they could see the outline of the distant wall under the lights of the Gosport City UPA. Nearer still, the skyline of the Fareham UPA at the head of the creek, though mostly out of sight, lighting up the night sky. A low cloud base hung above the harbour creating a beautiful tunnel effect with the city lights reflecting off the nebulous fracto-stratus gliding beneath the upper layer. The old Solent City marina lay in darkness behind its gigantic cofferdam, except for the occasional low-level pedestrian lighting giving off a cosy glow in the corners of the buildings and among the vegetation. A Siamese cat walked daintily across the small patio in front of the window and the last thing Meg remembered as she drifted off into a contented sleep, cuddled against Chip, was the automatic light illuminating the tiny garden when the cat triggered the intruder circuit.

The following morning the girls decided to go into Chichester on the hover rail and took the cable car down to the local halt. Two senior naval officers dressed in mufti later called to see Chip and Nigel. Not that being in mufti could actually hide their service bearing and smart hair. Later, Chip's company lawyer arrived and together they all sat down going over the contract with a fine tooth-comb. The supply officer, a commander with a florid complexion and a seemingly good nature brought with him a standard contract for signing. The Commander guided Chip through the tortuous clauses going through the various sub-sections for clarification. The company lawyer being a much younger man and keen to impress occasionally interjected with a quiet commentary on various interpretations, allowing the Commander to continue speaking while Chip grasped the interpretations on the hoof –so to speak. After some brief discussion and a word or two with Nigel, Commander Potterton-Haines then proffered the final page for signature and the two law-smiths signed the business agreement between the Admiralty and Golden Arrow Marine. After a notional cup of coffee and some biscuits Captain Dunham the senior of the two visitors swung quietly into action. He looked at Nigel and the company lawyer and Nigel taking his cue ushered the young fellow out of the front door into the morning sunlight. Blissfully unaware of the true nature of the remainder of the meeting he caught the coastal hover rail to Dover making the connection back to Margate after a sumptuous lunch at one of the terminus' better restaurants. No doubt the expenses would be swallowed up in his client's fee.

"Now gentlemen, I believe it's time we had a brief discussion about the nature of our requirements for the Privateer." He began producing a neatly folded chart from his business case. Deftly unfolding it across the table for all of them to see, noting with envy that the table was made from real wood, a rare commodity indeed! "We require the Privateer to act as an auxiliary between various locations and our Principal naval ports. Notably Portsmouth and Newcastle here and here," he pointed to the chart, "and occasionally up to Rosyth and occasionally round to the Gareloch on the West Coast of Scotland over here." As he spoke Potterton-Haines removed papers from his own business case and opened a large sealed manila envelope handing the contents to Chip. "You will see from the orders that you will ship mainly stores between the bases, occasionally making trips over to Ostend, Rotterdam and infrequently to elsewhere, as the needs arise." The Captain laid out a series of neatly typed schedules and signals manuals indicating some of the more arcane techniques of identification used by naval vessels at sea and when entering or leaving naval ports. "You won't be required to carry any secure communications, so there is no need to worry about more than the normal level of security for yourself and for your crew. Incidentally, now that we've covered the outline of our requirements this is a good time Bob," he said turning to the Commander, "if you cover the details about crewing." The Commander opened another sealed envelope with a pleasant smile on his face handing over two large certificates each bearing the official seals of the Defence Ministry and of the European Armed Services Secretary. Chip flinched slightly as he read them. Captain Dunham beamed appreciably while the Commander congratulated him on being commissioned as a Lieutenant Commander. "I can see that you're pleased and that explains the rather interesting colour scheme of your vessel." He explained. "You will find another envelope in that pile with a commission for your co-pilot Frederick Newman. We found his past very interesting to say the least, so he has been commissioned as a Lieutenant on the General List which gives him a bit of space should he be looking upwards at any time in the future."

"That will please him immensely I think Captain. He has, as you know, got his First Officer's ticket since leaving the service five years ago and has a business degree to lay alongside it. I think he will be pleased to get the Commission and some guaranteed sea-time on which to build his hopes for his Master's ticket down the line. That is excellent news that I will have great pleasure in delivering to him personally."

The briefing continued for another hour with Captain Dunham commenting on the tenor of the role to be played by the Privateer and her new crew. "Your crew will consist of a Sub-Lieutenant, who like yourself incidentally, has several years experience of light commercial vessels such as yours, a Warrant Officer in charge of engineering, two mechanical technicians, an electrical technician and an electronics expert, plus four seamen with sensor and communications specialist training. They're all hand-picked men who can be trusted to be discrete and from time to time you will be asked to take the occasional Marines detachment, but only between establishments. The crew knows there will be a requirement to be dressed as civilian crewmembers, but they do not know the full extent of operations. Please be discrete about your role and further missions, and also, we want you and your crew to act as observers wherever you put into port. It's vital for us to be aware of changes in harbour installations as well as any other feedback you may pick up from the locals."

That evening they had another celebration leaving Fred, who had volunteered to stay behind and show off their proud vessel to their new operations officer Jason Howell and their marine engineering Warrant Officer Mr Leyland Pengelly. The Jolly Farmer on the outskirts of Catherington lay way off the beaten track and outside the influence of any urban or sub-urban law. Once a small village-cum-dormitory for professionals in Solent City region it had slipped back into its rural way of life as legislation destroyed mechanised and traditional farming. Those left behind returned to the old ways of making a living from the land and sold their produce in the clandestine market places where the writ of law had no mandate. Once interlaced with metalled roads and byways, many of the lanes had been ploughed up in the absence of any district or local authority funding to maintain them. Except for main routes in and out of the countryside most travellers kept to the fast inter-UPA roads, the IUPAs, or recognised E roads. As Nigel approached the pub from the muddy car park the nose of a stun rifle emerged from a partially opened upstairs window. "That's far enough. State your business and then be off." rang the shrill voice of a woman from within.

"Ursula, Is that you?" asked Nigel courteously from a safe distance. "It's Nigel Woodingdean. I've bought some flowers for you and Marigold." Nigel added hopefully.

"Oh it's you Nigel that's all right you can come in, and those other people are they all with you?"

"Yes, they're with me. That's my wife and brother and his girlfriend."

"Alright then, Marigold will open the door, just wait a minute."

A few moments later the figure of a younger woman opened the door and stood back with the door handle in hand ready to slam it shut behind them. "Hello Marigold, you're looking well. How's your mother?" asked Nigel looking a little relieved trying to keep a conversation going. "Oh, she's alright Nigel, just keeping strangers at bay you know. She's not been the same since those travellers came through last year and trashed the field down the bottom of the lane."

"There's no end to what they will do. Didn't they break in your cellars a couple of times?"

"Yes about four of them on the inside and six on the outside who they tried to let in. But fortunately Ned was in with a couple of his lads from New Home Farm and let 'em have it." She said this last bit of information in a low whisper. "Marigold this is my wife, whom you met when we last came to see you, this is my brother and Meg, come to join in a little celebration."

"Nice to meet you all. We're not very busy, so would you like a place outside or inside?" enquired Marigold. "Oh, outside I think under the trees." Marigold led the way down the tiled passageway to the rear of the pub and out into the back. A high wooden fence topped with jagged pieces of steel now marred what was once a pretty view of rolling fields and hedgerows, a testimony to their local difficulties. Ursula appeared in the doorway and greeted Nigel and Gry warmly. "I see your back from the big city then." She observed with a smile. She knew perfectly well where they lived, but to her it was still more people than she could cope with other than on market days. Two little imps emerged from the kitchen and rushed over the lawn to where Nigel sat on a rustic chair made from branches and two rough-hewn planks of cherry wood. "Hello Molly, and who's this handsome fellow here –your baby brother, eh?" He grabbed them both under the arms scooping them up to shoulder height as they squealed in delight. "I've got something for you two, d'you want to know what it is?" The children looked wide-eyed at him and Molly plonked a big wet kiss all over one side of his face holding him fiercely around his neck with her chubby little her arms. "Ho, ho, ho! You do then, hey. What do you say Conrad. Do you want to see it?" The little boy became a little bashful and with one arm entwined around Nigel's neck from the other side, stretched out a beckoning hand to Marigold. She took him in her arms and swooped him down and up as Nigel lowered Molly to the ground. Gry slipped Nigel a Small wooden box that he handed over to Molly with a solemnity masking the twinkle in his eyes; he kissed her gently on her forehead. Next came a big paper parcel for the little chap. He walked across the small gap between them and took his prize looking at it a little suspiciously. He stuck out his hand and very seriously, shook Nigel's own hand before turning on his heels to run and hide behind his mother's skirts. "Oh, Nigel you shouldn't spoil them so much." protested Marigold mildly. "Oh, but it's so much fun Marigold, and besides look at their happy little faces."

Chip and Gry knew the story behind his friendship with Marigold and her mother, except to tell it briefly in the background while Nigel and then Gry were making a fuss of the children with Ursula and Marigold looking on wistfully. Nigel and John Kane had met at the Naval Academy and had been friends ever since. Both got their wings as naval aviators and had begun successful careers as multi-role combat pilots, qualified to fly a number of different aircraft. On a black day five years earlier while patrolling the Straits of Gibraltar they gave chase to an unmarked skimmer on the surface that looked like a gunrunner, or perhaps it was smuggling illegal immigrants. No one knew for sure. Their number one was a Senior lieutenant by the name of Merindel who played by the book and who also suffered from a bad dose of his own sense of superiority. On the way down to the surface to investigate John, the number three, had seen the size of the craft using his head mounted visually enhanced optical sensor array and reckoned it was too big and too well organised not be supported by other forces in the area. His number one insisted on a low pass in echelon that turned out to be a fatal decision. Like the sniper in the trenches who sees a light flare in the darkness; takes aim at the second sighting and fires at the third, so did the marksman on the well armed smuggler. John sensing something was amiss pulled a tighter turn as the flight angled across and around the craft and climbing above the other two narrowly avoided the better part of a vicious salvo. When the round struck the fragile fin of his aircraft he knew that he was in trouble. Barely in control he turned his wounded plane towards Gib after a quick call to his number one. At the court martial it was disputed that he heard the call made by John at all.

A small plasma-drive aircraft dropped out of the clouds and bounced the other two as it passed from up above and diagonally across from the back of the formation to the front. Merindel broke and ran for cover in a bank of clouds formed by the unstable air that was common in that area, losing his wingman Nigel, who was frantically trying to locate him. With John out of the running and on his way back to the base at Gib, Nigel had to face both the surface craft and the aircraft unsupported. He launched a missile at the skimmer and pulled a high G turn to get on the outside of the attacking aircraft before it could get a line of fire. The warning system told him a missile had been launched and was locked on to him. Then another, and another. Merindel had pulled a medium g turn and stupidly flew back out the cloudbank the way he had gone into it. He fired at the first thing he saw and flew back into the clouds. The pilot of the attacking aircraft seeing what had happened remained in a tight turn for three hundred and fifty degrees and made off after John's crippled machine. Nigel meanwhile threw the stick hard over to the left, stamped on full left rudder and in a three-quarter roll turned back on himself just as the first of Merindel's missiles flashed past on the right hand side losing its lock on his aircraft. John could see the other two almost on top of him and pulled up in a vertical climb pulling counter-measures options out on his voice controlled tactical controller. The VCTC delivered two charges of explosives into the sky covered in thick wadding comprised of millions of tiny pieces of silver paper and crystalline shards. Climbing into the sun he topped out at twenty-two thousand feet and veered off masking his plasma exhaust and then by reducing his throttle to idle. One missile engaged his chaff and blew a gaping hole in it leaving a huge shining scintillating doughnut suspended in the sky. The other followed him up and finally locked on to the sun as its target. From his position he could see nothing through the cloudbank below and radioed his number one. There was only static on the channel. Changing from tactical to the general frequency he received a mayday from John who was under attack and losing altitude. "Squirrel five, one, one, this is two, I'm on my way. Squawk, over."

"Two this is three, roger." John acknowledged and transmitted his locator emergency code in response. "Three this is two I have you at twenty miles. Turn left missile launch, missile launch!"

The pirate aircraft had launched a missile at John who could do nothing to manoeuvre his aircraft as fast as he wanted to. The VCTC delivered its own two missiles in response, both swinging outward and then around to lock onto the advancing rockets. They engaged and destroyed the threat, but the other pilot knew this would happen and waited until John fired his last missile at him. Successfully avoiding the missile he closed on John lacing his aircraft with canon fire from a hundred metres. John's aircraft folded in a blinding flash and was gone. The chute opened with the seat still intact but no John. Nigel scanned the sensor screen watching horrified at the smear representing John's aircraft fading slowly from view. In cold-blooded anger he used the VCTC to vector his own aircraft in a suicide collision course with the pirate. They closed at over a thousand kliks per hour until finally the VCTC launched a brace of missiles at close range and pulled up the aircraft. His G-suit pressing hard against his body as another high-g turn tried to force blood into the ends of his arms and legs. At the same time both of his missiles struck home reducing the speeding pirate's own plasma-jet to a ruinous boiling cloud of burning fuel and debris. Spiralling down to the surface he looked for any sensor activity to indicate where his number one had got to and saw nothing on the view screen, only the tenuous trace of a second parachute sinking slowly towards the surface. The VCTC vectored him at high speed to the last known position of his friend's machine. Arriving two minutes later he went to manual and circled around looking for signs of John among the floating wreckage of his plane. Waiting for as long as his fuel would allow, he saw the skimmer patrol arriving all too late. He circled round them once and turned away heading for the airfield just ten kilometres away, feeling numb. It was the loneliest flight of his life. Merindel made immediate denunciations of both his flying and that of John's, making a loud scene at the debriefing. The squadron commander sat passively at first trying to gauge the dynamics between the two men. Publicly he announced a board of enquiry would be convened and pulled both men off flying duties for four days. Privately, he was a worried man. He had seen the sensor recordings and that only left the flight recorders in the aircraft to confirm his suspicions about what really happened. When John got back to the UK he went straight to John and Marigold's home. It was more distressing to see her standing there with one babe on her hip and the other at her feet looking gaunt and pale. Ursula had been staying with them for a while. They had been very kind not blaming him at all. All he could say was that they had started a routine patrol and had been bounced by gunrunners in the Straits of Gibraltar. It seemed important to her that he was there when the end came and it tore at his heart when he heard her crying in the kitchen as she made the tea. The rest he would have to hold on to until she was ready to know the full story. By then Merindel had been promoted to Commander and shunted off to an admin desk in a training squadron. John was exonerated by the data on all three flight-recorders. Having been seen to have fulfilled every requirement demanded when in action.

They watched the children playing on the grass with their new toys and listened patiently as Nigel, Marigold and Ursula caught up with 'family' news. With the evening air growing chilly they moved indoors to the private bar sitting near to a freshly lit log fire. The children slumbering blissfully on a large settee as the small group chatted amiably about all sorts of things. Locals came and went in the public bar causing Ursula to come and go periodically. Eventually the time came to say goodbye. They left the children sleeping as he and Gry kissed them goodbye, then slipped out the door to their vehicle. Marigold gave them a fond farewell and insisted that she was quite safe. "Besides, I have the base-station you gave on your last visit. If we really need you I'll give you a call." Waving and calling goodbye they drove out of the park onto the track and slowly down the lane. Marigold waited until they turned the corner and disappeared from sight, then turning slowly towards the house closing the door softly behind her.

The shakedown cruises went well. The new crew settled in quickly and their sub was, as had been said, an excellently well trained individual in skimmer operations with eight years in the merchant marine and coastal waters, who could be left alone in the cockpit as and when the occasion demanded it. Chip and Fred were amazed at how the crew had been trained both technically and in the way that cleaning and maintenance schedules had been introduced without so much as batting an eyelid. The twin power plants ran smoothly and had been finely tuned and balanced for optimum performance. Speed trials had shown the old girl had been given an extra eight knots in the water, due partially to the removal of barnacles and other crud from the hull, as well as, to the engine alignment. At the end of a busy month the Privateer slipped her moorings from North Corner and set course for her home port in Margate. Along the way the relief was almost palpable as they made ready for their disembarkation. As it was, the trip back was uneventful with a following wind and a glassy sea to skim over at full speed. Fred had waved at the Marine sentries still patrolling the harbour while the seamen set to work on flaking down the ropes in readiness to tie up alongside. Meg had arranged for the crew to be billeted in various hostelries in town, so while Chip left Fred and the new sub to work out the navigation for the following day's trip, he and Mr Pengelly went to meet the harbour master. "Ah, there you are Woodie, come on in, come on in. And I expect this one of your new crew is it?" Old Roy Crayford smiled at the look of amazement on Chip's face. "Hello Roy, they haven't dragged you out of retirement have they –where's that young rascal Andy Rayner then?"

"Ah, come in and close the door. That's better, don't want to talk too openly given the queer times we're in, do we, eh?"

"No, quite responded Chip. "By the way this is Leyland Pengelly my Engineer. Leyland this is Roy Vincent the old Harbour Master that used to be."

"Nice to meet you Leyland. I hope you can keep those two out of trouble that's all I can say, never a dull moment, never dull with him and Fred around."

"Well what's to do with young Andy then, you haven't given him the push have you?" asked Chip slyly. "Nothing of the kind, the poor devil decided to go back to the navy. He said they just came round to his house one evening and asked him if he wouldn't mind working for them for a nice fat bounty. So off he's went leaving the missus behind until he knows where he's going and can send for her."

"Well I'm blowed!" said Chip with a conspiratorial grin. "I reckon they'll find him a nice quiet job as the Queen's Harbour Master in a nice little backwater down in Devon."

"Well you might be right at that, but he was a good lad, knows his stuff and then some more. I don't mind telling you, you bein' ex-navy like." He squinted a little at Leyland adding, "and so are you by the cut of your hair."

"Well put Roy, we seem to be in strange times as you say and Leyland has a way with engines that makes him very welcome aboard the Privateer. He has a couple of likely lads with him who work well at keeping them sweet as a nut and we have a new lease of life in the old girl. With that in mind we're clearing our yardarm with you before we catch the tide at four, tomorrow morning. We're making for Rotterdam to pick up some pumping equipment from one of the yards up the Rhine and then picking some stores up from Ostend." The old Harbour Master smiled a knowing look as the last piece of information was offered. Chip handed over his manifest to be registered and a navigation plan giving a brief outline of the Privateer's intended movements. "You'll need special papers to get into Ostend as you probably know, and that will take at least three weeks judging by the current demand. You have little chance..." Chip waved a travel carnet under the Harbour Master's nose dropping it on to his desk. Roy looked at it briefly and blinked. "Where did you get that?" He demanded "It's bad enough having to get one in the first place, but a multiple entry carnet is as rare as rocking horse droppings!"

"There you are Mr Harbour Master, Sir. All is taken care of." announced Chip warmly. "All that remains is for me to ask for your discretion in the matter and not to put it about."

"Ah, right, so that's it then, you must be well connected and up to no good as usual. Well I suppose you ex navy types are all the same. You must know what you're doing, and as for my discretion in the matter of course, that's not a problem. I'll be in the Queen's Head at half past seven, if you take my meaning."

"Ah, yes I almost forgot. This is for you. It should have gone to Andy, but now you're back in the hot-seat you should have it." Chip slipped a bottle of old navy rum out of his bag and put it on the desk in front of the Harbour Master whose eyes lit up at the very sight of it. "An excellent choice of tipple if I may say so." He grasped the bottle with a meaty hand and hefting it lightly he moved it swiftly out of sight, locking it in the bottom draw of his desk. "See you later Roy, until then we have a skimmer to get ready for the morrow." Chip and Leyland rose from their chairs, shook hands on it and left the harbour master's office with a feeling of having accomplished one of life's little pleasantries.

It was late afternoon with a comfortable warm sun pervading the still air around the harbour. By five o' clock they strolled back onboard the Privateer to the sound of music echoing in the depths of the hull as they walked across the narrow gangway. The skimmer was a multi-hull design consisting of a large inner hull supported by two slender outriggers. There was a main cargo deck at the same level as the main deck running along the entire length of the vessel. Designed to maximise the space used for efficient cargo carrying. Below that were a couple of smaller decks that had been converted into crew accommodation. The narrower portions of the lowest deck reserved for the power units at the aft end with compartments for stowage of spares, paint and personal belongings in the for'ard areas. There was a new bulkhead on the main deck separating a small section of the cargo deck immediately below and behind the cockpit.

The new accommodation was divided into four parts. The front section immediately below the cockpit had been converted into a chart and radio room containing sensor array equipment. It would pass for an up-market bridge on any craft being operated by a successful trader. Aft of this on the port side a cabin served as a day room-cum-chart room for Chip. Behind that a small wardroom for Fred and the young Sub. Across a small gangway separating the port side from the starboard side were two other compartments. One containing the sophisticated electronics for the sensor arrays, not normally available to the merchant marine. Aft of that was the small ship's galley and crew room. Below the cargo deck the sleeping quarters had been built in the for'ard part back to the mid-section of the hull, including cladding and soundproofing to reduce the cold and the noise penetrating through the hull. The refit had made for a much warmer atmosphere than the utilitarian austerity afforded by the previous owners. Somehow the Privateer had become alive with a crew, a sense of purpose and a feeling of destiny.

They found Fred in the small lounge drinking coffee and watching a view screen in between filling out a nav-plan for the coming day ahead. The electrical-tech was duty mess-man and seeing them arrive picked up a couple of empty mugs. "Coffee Sir?" He offered. "Yes please, that will be nice." Replied Chip. "Mr Pengelly prefers tea I believe." Leyland nodded and the mess-man busied himself with the makings. They sat down and looked at Fred working away almost absent-mindedly at the nav-plan, putting the finishing touches together with a final flourish of his pen. He looked up and registered their presence with a grin. "All done and dusted boss." He said with the satisfied air of a man relieved of a long chore. "It's always the paperwork I hate, the process is easy in itself. Just remember the bearings and point the sharp end in the right direction." He folded the sensor charts and placed the nav-plan into a folder ready for the harbour master's office later on. "Can I take it Fred that we're all but on our way?"

"Absolutely, no bother at all. The sub is in the chart room just finishing of the computer update and that will be that."

"Good news, how are the troops doing, have the first batch checked in at their various establishments?"

"You'd better see sub about that, but I gather that they should be back any time now for the changeover."

"Mr Pengelly you're booked into the Albert Hotel with us by the way. Hope you will find the view to your liking." said Fred. "It's overlooking the harbour and the landlord is expecting you sometime later this evening."

"Right-oh Sir, I will be mustering the hands at 18:30 for the Captain's briefing and setting the duty watches from 19:15. Sub-Lieutenant Walsh has volunteered to kick off with the evening watch, giving him time for the forenoon. I think he's keen to take her in to Rotterdam and up the Rhine later on." ventured Leyland. "Good man," observed Fred, "that gives us a bit of leeway later on this evening." The mess-man delivered the mugs of tea and coffee and disappeared.

The hands were called at 18:30 precisely without the normal fuss made on most warships. Privateer was rated as an armed merchantman, but there was little external evidence to show it. The weaponry consisted of small-arms and a couple of hand-held gas-laser guided rocket launchers. The briefing was short and to the point. The crew was advised that on the return trip, Ostend could be a little 'difficult' with enforced bureaucracy taking precedence over common sense. Leyland Pengelly stood the hands down and set the duty watch. The remaining hands that had not checked in at their digs were sent off clutching their bags, with strict instructions to muster in the snug at the Queen's Head by half-past nine. Abed later that evening Chip mused silently on the real purposes behind their first trip as a military transport vessel, wondering if it was all as simple as it seemed, presently sleep claiming his thoughts in its unconscious embrace.

Peter Walsh arrived on deck, as the ribbon of coastline became a pronounced shadow thickening in the distance. Overhead a maritime patrol aircraft 'sniffed' them as it buzzed by going down channel. "That's a Belgian out of Leuven." He observed coming into the bridge from the cabin flat. Fred and one of the seamen navigators were up in the cockpit, while Chip and the Petty Officer Electro-tech were discussing the latest advances incorporated in the new sensor arrays. "How do you know that Peter?" asked Chip looking up from the radar viewer. "Oh, the Pilot's name is Matthias Ridderkerke and he's bloody great laugh. Has a penchant for Guinness and loves power surfing if his wife lets him go." The PO looked impressed. Chip looked on amazed. "Are you trying to tell me something Peter?"

"Not especially Sir, it's just that we did mathematics together at Sussex. He got a First and took the Haigh prize for being the best all round. We've stayed in touch ever since. Loves the Brits, can't get enough time over here. Other than that I know if I'm ever in trouble in these waters and he's flying around he'll get me out of a jam."

"That's handy to know, Sir, said the PO. "What does he make of all this fuss over restricting traffic in and out of the UK?"

"Like most people on this side of the Channel I think. A bit of a waste of time." They broke off their conversation being distracted by a low 'blooping' sound emanating from the sensor screen. The coastal outline glowed back at them in a shimmering green prospect with the smearing trace of the fast moving aircraft racing astern of them towards the bottom of the screen. Three new contacts appeared ahead ten miles north of Zeebrugge. Fred looked down through the hatch, looked at Chip, and nodded for him to come up. Chip sat in the jump seat and took the image intensifiers from him. "There's something big coming out of Zeebrugge and it isn't a ferry -looks naval to me judging by the colour scheme on the masts. Take a look at that funnel, it's got boot blacking just below the top."

"Mm, see what you mean. Peter!" He called down through the hatch, get on that view screen and tell me if there's anything coming out of Zeebrugge squawking naval code!"

"Aye-aye, Sir!" The PO moved aside as Peter moved over the display making a few adjustments. "Yes Sir, it looks like the Ghent. It's a Baudouin class Frigate. I'm punching up the data to the auxiliary view screen now. It looks like there's a couple of smaller escorts with her Sir. I don't have actual sensor targets yet, but the SSR is kicking out codes for a couple of small craft as well!"

"OK Peter, keep looking! Fred change heading by ten degrees to due north, I want to give a wider berth to whatever's coming out and move beyond the territorial line. Have the crew fall into their stations." He placed the intensifiers to his eyes again and switched to thermal imaging. There it was now, the telltale smudge of heat rising in a wedge behind the moving vessel as yet unseen. "Petty Officer Bundle, ask Mr Pengelly to come to the bridge!"

Aye, aye Sir!" The PO detached himself from the side of the view screen moving aft out of sight. "Give her another five knots Fred and aim to swing round back on our original heading once we're past the entrance to the channel." Fred repeated the orders and looked at Chip as the numbers on the speed indicator slowly climbed upwards. "What have you got in mind?" He asked, already knowing most of the answer. "I want a good look at her Fred. If we're the subject of this putting to sea then at least we will have the escort between us and the frigate. They may be fast but they will be in the way. On the other hand, I'm banking on the idea that the escort will be a couple of skimmers, they don't have to stay within the navigation of the channel, but the frigate will still have to remain in the navigation before she can manoeuvre freely." Fred smiled looking satisfied. "We're on the same wavelength then." He responded breaking into a grin.

Fred swung down the ladder as Mr Pengelly emerged from the flat aft of the bridge. "Ah, there you are Mr Pengelly. I may need a diversion from you and the men if possible. I want you to adopt a more… shall we say, civilian attitude. We have what looks to be a frigate and her escort coming down the channel out of Zeebrugge, and if they have come to sniff around us I want to give them a convincing display of a less disciplined and less uniform crew. Do you think we can arrange it?"

"Why yes Sir. How far do you want me to go." Came the reply with a bit of a grin appearing on Mr Pengelly's face.

"Ooh, let's not make it too theatrical just one or two minor details. A change of attire here and there, a bit more slouch perhaps."

"I know exactly what you mean Sir. I'll get on to it right away." Mr Pengelly turned whence he came and walking back aft through the flat his demeanour changed from that of a well disciplined seaman to that of a more or less drunken sailor with sagging shoulders and rocky gait. "First class Mr Pengelly, That's the sort of thing. I'll give the word if we have to resort to this little subterfuge."

While drawing level with the mouth of the channel two skimmers emerged at slow to medium speed. Hemmed in by the narrow channel and by harbour regulations they were doing no more than six knots. Behind them they could see the frigate slowly making its way down to the sea. All the displays in the sensor room lit up as the skimmers and the frigate's sensors scanned the Privateer. With the exception of the radar and Chip's image intensifier there was no other transmission from the Privateer's electro-photonic pods hidden down below. She was screened with the latest shielding and when scanned would appear to be otherwise inert. To all intents and purposes she would pass as a civil trader plying the North Sea trading routes between Blighty and the European mainland. Back down on the bridge Chip looked ahead to where he expected to see the other radar contacts appearing out of the haze. He caught a splash of white fine on the starboard bow at about six nautical miles. Thermal imaging mode gave him a clue and he could make out three skimmers in the same uniform light colour scheme. "That's interesting, we have more naval skimmers approaching from the north. Peter, they don't appear to be transmitting squawk codes do they?"

"No Sir, apparently they're running silent, there's no radar or other sensor signatures either." Chip looked at the view screen and took an estimate of the plotted situation from their position between two closing naval forces. "Petty Officer Bundle, any signals from the Admiralty or other information of startling import from the government?"

"No Sir, other than what you've already seen. I'll check the signal computer for any further signals." He moved swiftly to the radio booth and ran through the signal log. "No Sir, nothing new!" He called across the bridge. "Notice to mariner's Peter, anything there?"

"No Sir, I ran through those this morning and there haven't been any updates to NOTMARS since nine o' clock."

"Since nine o' clock you say, what was that about?"

"Just some shipping movements between Den Helder and the Frisian Islands and a tug towing a research rig through the Skagerak tonight."

"Thank you Peter. Let's just sit tight and see what happens." Fred brought the Privateer back on her original course and maintained the current speed. At three miles the small fleet of Skimmers altered course to the inverse of Privateer's giving a calculated two cables closing distance. Walking to the starboard bridge doorway Chip looked back towards the channel from which the two escorts were just emerging. He saw one of them surging forward in a burst of speed rising up on its planes. "Fred, maintain present course and speed. Be ready for changes in course as directed."

"Ready when you are Sir." called down Fred from the cockpit. "Leading Seaman Briggs get down here and get to the bridge con!"

"Aye Sir!" Briggs slid down the ladder and resumed his duties at the bridge console, connected to the cockpit via the audio link. "The other three have accelerated and are now planing towards us Sir!" urged out Peter. "Peter take the helm, Fred get down to the bridge now"! Fred switched to bridge control and shot down the ladder onto the bridge deck with a thud. "Quartermaster, take these intensifiers and keep an eye on that frigate. Tell me what they do next."

"Aye, aye, Sir." The young sailor moved swiftly to the screen door and took up a position where Chip had stood a few moments before. "Petty Officer Bundle, secure all electro-photonic systems and tell the engine rooms to standby for rapid manoeuvres."

"Aye, aye, Sir" The PO moved to a console activating controls and using a microphone. "Laser-cannon Sir!" They firing laser-cannon at us!" yelled the Quartermaster. Chip dashed to the starboard doorway and pulled back the young seaman as a laser guided projectile sailed down the starboard side high over head. "Close that door!" Fred had anticipated the next order and was on the radio immediately. "This is Privateer, sierra kilo -393- mike golf calling warship in the Zeebrugge Channel." He paused before repeating the call. "This is Privateer sierra kilo -393- mike golf calling warship in the Zeebrugge Channel, do you copy, over?"

"Reduce speed to 8 knots off-planes!" ordered Chip. As another two projectiles passed down the starboard side. "The other skimmer is about two nautical miles out Sir and sweeping around to seaward Sir!" Chip could see that he was being bracketed by laser cannon on one side and hemmed in on the other. The other three skimmers ahead broke formation into a wider pattern. Two went to seaward while the third altered course to pass across the bows of the Privateer. "The frigate's turning north Sir and accelerating!" Came a call from the Quartermaster looking out of the aft window. As the gap widened between the skimmers from the north Chip could see his way out of the situation. "Left ten degrees steer 350!" In the background, Fred repeated his calls to the Frigate and was getting no response.

"Privateer sierra kilo -393- mike golf, this is ESNF Waadinxvane, stand clear of the area this is a naval exercise. I say again. Privateer sierra kilo -393- mike golf this is ESNF Waadinxvane, stand clear of the area this is a naval exercise. Do you copy?"

"Waadinxvane this is Privateer we copy, and register a strong protest at the way in which you fired upon my vessel. Do you copy that!" Fred almost shouted into the microphone. The Privateer bucked as the transition from skimming on the planes to slow speed manoeuvring took effect, throwing everyone forward. All of them felt a surge of relief and Fred almost laughed were it not for the fact he was holding on to a stanchion for dear life. "Give him another blast Fred, this is the last thing we needed."

"Sir the other vessels appear to be breaking off on all sides!" shouted Peter over the roar of the unloaded power plants. The skimmer approaching them from the north and between them and the shore slowed going off-planes. Changing course the vessel made directly towards the Privateer. While the vessel cruised past them they heard a dull thud as the door to the deck amidships was thrown open. Somebody emerged on to the deck and was hurling abuse at the patrol craft. "Waadinxvane I say again, this is Privateer we will register a strong protest with the Rotterdam Harbour Master on our arrival and with the ESNF at Brest for the way in which you fired upon my vessel. Do you copy!"

Leyland Pengelly staggered along the starboard waist wearing a red bandanna around his head, carrying a dirty, oily rag in one hand and a half-empty whiskey bottle in the other. He railed at the men on the passing vessel, not only giving a fine performance of a dissolute old marine engineer, but also diffusing the situation completely. The Belgian skimmer Captain looked on in amazement, a smile beginning to crease his face, his bridge crew broke into sniggers and then open laughter as Mr Pengelly walked aft like a man who had urgent need to change his underclothing.

Onboard the Privateer Sub Walsh was smitten with a high pitched giggle while the rest smirked at the charade being played out.

"Privateer, this is warship Ghent, do you copy?"

"This is the Privateer, go ahead, over." Fred snapped back at the microphone. "My Captain wants to know why you are in the exercise area?"

"This is Privateer, and my Captain wants to know why it is not designated as an exercise area, over." There was a long pause followed by a short "Standby." coming from the Ghent's radio operator. "You really foxed them with that one Sir." Ventured the electro-tech. Fred shot a wicked smile. "Yep, it's the simple one's that tend to stop people in their tracks at times like these." Chip turned to Sub Walsh. "Check those NOTMARS again, and while you're at it send a signal to the Admiralty. Tell them the Ghent has fired on us with her escorts, about 25 kilometres north of Zeebrugge light and that we have not suffered any damage. Request any NOTMARS issued since 09:00 today. Classify that as urgent Peter, but not any higher, we don't want someone at the Admiralty spilling coffee all over a nicely pressed shirt."

"Aye, Aye, Sir." As the Sub scuttled off to the radio booth a message came through on the speaker next to Fred's watch station. "Privateer this is warship Ghent, do you copy, over?" The shortened tones of a Belgian accent sounding through the silence of the bridge. "This is the Privateer, go ahead, over." A very cultured Belgian spoke in a smooth and professional voice. His English was almost flawless. "Privateer, may I speak to your Captain please?" Fred handed the microphone to Chip. "Captain Woodingdean here pass your message."

"Captain, my Captain sends you his compliments and apologises for any inconvenience caused to you by this regrettable occasion. He wishes to make his apology to you and asks that you heave-to and make ready to receive a boat alongside." Chip grimaced. He couldn't think what on earth the other Captain wanted. Still, when asked to do something by a warship it was the better option to oblige rather than suffer the consequences of a denial. "This is the Privateer, we will heave-to."

"Thank you Captain. Ghent out." Fred cut the engines while the seamen made ready to take a boat port side-to. The silence was a little eerie at first, especially with the other skimmers slowly circling around them. "Jet boat coming alongside Sir!" called a seaman. "Thank you Baines." Replied Sub Walsh.

Sub."

"Yes sir."

"Make a show of getting Mr Pengelly out of sight just before it arrives."

"Right Sir." In the time it took for the boat to cross the open water Leyland Pengelly had been joined by two of the seamen dressed in equally loud attire standing against the railings looking in the direction of the new arrival. Sub Walsh appeared through the bridge-wing door on cue. "Hey you two. Get that drunken old sailor off the upper deck!" One of them, a Leading Seaman turned away from the oncoming boat and grinned back at him. "Right-oh, Sir, right away!"

"About time too!" whispered Mr Pengelly, throwing his empty bottle into the sea. He struggled at first as the other two men gripped each arm. He made a great show as Sub Walsh waved a dismissive hand in his direction. A few seconds later the jet boat came alongside and a young looking Lieutenant scrambled up the short rope ladder. "Lieutenant Schilders Captain. Captain van Munster sends his compliments sir, and hopes you will accept this gift by way of an apology." Chip looked over the side into the jet boat. On the roof of the small cabin the Belgian seamen had placed two cases containing what looked like bottles of champagne and some beer. "Yes, thank you Lieutenant, I will accept his, er… shall we say peace offering with gratitude. Send your Captain my compliments and my wishes for a good day's sailing."

"Certainly, Captain. Thank you."

The exchange completed, Privateer and her crew made Rotterdam by early evening, tying up alongside, in one of the large basins near the town, on the vestiges of Delfshaven. The duty watch stood by while the off-watch crewmen slid over the gangway for a jolly ashore. Chip and Sub went off to the Harbour Master's outpost nearby to sort out the manifest and other paperwork, while Fred and Mr Pengelly chatted in the lounge awaiting their return. Leyland couldn't help laughing at the special gift for that 'old Chief Engineer' from the frigate's Captain. A tube of stomach pills well known for their effervescent and efficacious qualities to those who frequently over indulged. "Well you have to hand it to him, the man has a good sense of humour."

"I think he was really suckered in by your very good acting style Mr Pengelly. It was the least he could do for us when you think of it."

"I don't think anyone has cause to complain. It was a generous offer."

"I reckon Sub Walsh breathed a sigh of relief when the Admiralty turned up that late arriving NOTMAR. It's no small wonder that that Frigate Captain wanted to sweeten things up a bit."

"The lads will appreciate the beer on the return trip. That was a nice gesture on the part of the Skipper Sir." A low-level buzzer went off indicating the duty quartermaster required the presence of the duty officer. "Ah, that's for me breathed Fred wearily, standing up and heading for the doorway. "Enjoy your run ashore with the boss this evening, Leyland."

Early that evening found the small group of shipmates walking through the built up area of the docks heading towards a taxi rank at the start of their run ashore. The hover taxi deposited them on the edge of Stadhuisplein where at least a dozen street cafés lined the square, where their keen eyes settled on a bar and restaurant that looked a likely place to meet their needs for comfort and relaxation. Here they chatted while sinking Oranjeboom or San Miguel and Oude Bokmar until it became obvious that something more substantial was needed to keep them sober. Wandering off into the evening in search of little more quiet and some food they found a Japanese restaurant off the Lijnbaan where they settled in for a sumptuous meal. At midnight they left the restaurant heading back for a good night's kip back onboard.

What happened next was one of those occasions that every seaman has to accept that somewhere in one port or another they will be the victims of street robbers. Getting 'rolled' by locals was almost traditional as occupational hazards go. The small knot of sailors came under attack by a group of thugs as they hailed a taxi. Disturbed by the sounds of their struggles local worthies phoned the police who arrived too late to catch their attackers, last seen running away empty handed dropping their weapons behind them, leaving their victims somewhat bloodied and injured. A woman police officer ran across the road panting for breath, attempting to arrest everyone in sight in a shrill voice. Sub wiped the back of his head with his hand and as he drew it away everyone could see he was covered in blood. Leyland looked icily at the cop speaking to her in pure Dutch. "Whose side are you on?" He demanded. "Are you going to help us or just stand there waiting for him to bleed to death." The startled cop blinked and spoke into her radio. "Do you speak English?" asked Chip wearily. "Yes of course." answered the policewoman curtly. "Then please arrange for my crew to be taken to hospital. The big man over there has probably a broken leg and is bleeding from two knife wounds. This one has severe concussion, possibly a fractured skull. Leyland acted as interpreter for them in the hospital and later in the police station that looked more like a cross between a public lavatory and a grim looking warehouse. When they got back onboard at four o'clock, courtesy of the local police, the quartermaster and his mate stood stock-still looking goggle-eyed at them saying nothing as they hobbled onboard nursing their wounds.

"Quartermaster."

"Yes Sir?"

"A shake please at oh five fifteen, and not a second later."

"Yes Sir."

"And call out Leading Seaman Tucker, and Mr Pengelly's Petty Officer, Riley. Have them come to my cabin immediately." The two men arrived at the Captain's cabin and knocked on his door gently.

"Come in." Chip stood in front of a mirror in his trousers and bathrobe, dabbing his face with a cold compress of tissue paper. "Well, as you can see, Petty Officer Riley and Leading Seaman Tucker, there's been some problems ashore. Mr Pengelly is in his cabin and is temporarily indisposed for the next few days. Sub Walsh may have a fractured skull. That leaves me somewhat short-handed for the move to the Schiedam, and this is a chance to show me what you can both do. I'm told, by Lieutenant Newman that you're not only a pretty hot navigator, but very good at ship handling skimmers, so tomorrow you're our acting pilot and navigator. How do you feel about that?

"Fine Sir, no problems."

"Good, I'm sure you'll do fine. Petty Officer Riley you will have to take charge of the engine rooms for a while and re-arrange watches until Mr Pengelly can get back on his feet. Again, I don't think you will have any problems."

Yes Sir."

"Remember, if there are problems speak to Petty Officer Tucker who's the Senior PO or come and let me know, two heads are always better than one. Dismissed."

"Yes Sir." Both men speculated on what had happened, but said nothing until clear of the messing area.

"Looks as though they got rolled, poor sods."

"Yep, Smudge said that Sub Walsh is still ashore."

"Wonder what happened to him?"

Chip had a shower and put on fresh clothes. The civilian doctor had put five stitches into his shoulder and covered up the wound pretty well. Wearing a jacket over his shirt hid the bulk of the dressing. Fred appeared as sounds of the hands turning to could be heard throughout the vessel. At half past five the Privateer rocked gently as the tug gently scraped alongside, a crewmen threw over a line attached to a towrope, one for'ard and one aft. "What the heck has happened to you, Chip?" asked Fred in the privacy of Chip's day cabin. His face was beginning to puff out and one eye was closing. "Just bad luck I think Fred."

"...And they got away with it?"

"No chance! Leyland Pengelly just blew the first heavies away until he fell over on a third and young Peter packs a pretty hard punch, but Peter's in a fairly serious condition. It looks like a hairline fracture of the skull, at the very least severe concussion, but we'll find out later today. In any event he may be evacuated as a casualty later, put on a flight home I think."

"Sounds very bad. How's your arm?"

"Just winged me in passing, nothing much, just a scratch. Leyland is going to be out of commission for a while though, relieved of all duties for a few days." Fred looked thoughtful before asking the question that was on both their minds, "You don't suppose it's anything to do with the fact that we're now a naval vessel and there's our unknown cargo that we're about to load, do you?"

"No Fred, we' were just unlucky and got rolled, there's nothing more it than that." He winced moving his shoulder gingerly under his reefer. "It's a small mercy that we have Leyland back." Observed Fred, "we may need some of his mental abilities later on, but for now we've had a couple of people over from the dockyard to measure us up for the jigs being loaded later this morning. Apart from that and the weather breaking I think we should be on schedule to catch the tide this evening."

"OK Fred we'll clew up later for a discussion on that. I gather from the shouting that we're ready to shove off, so we'd better get on to the bridge."

The short trip to Schiedam basin was uneventful. The tug Master made fine work in the strong current that sucked at the skimmer's light hull, turning her round within her own length and backing her deftly into a berth left vacant by a huge carrier that had sailed on the morning tide. This was as Fred had arranged with the dockyard so that the Privateer could slip her moorings and make her own way out of the basin into the Maas navigation without calling for the services of a tug. It was also sound economic sense. With the stern doors of the cargo door wide open like the giant maw of some long extinct leviathan the cranes fed an endless chain of parts, motors, pumps, and finally large pre-fabricated steel sections into the large sloping ramp on the dockside. A motor driven conveyor feeding the goods into the huge cargo stowage along long lines of fitted rollers recessed in the deck. By noon most of the bit parts had been stowed in the lower hold and this had been battened down along with the flush fitting hatch in the cargo deck. By the time the stevedores had finished loading the front end of the cargo deck it was time for lunch, and the ship fell silent for a precious hour of respite.

Chip worked in his day cabin studying the met, looking at a chart that indicated a deep depression was coming their way, with the inevitable strong winds and rough seas in attendance. Looking up at the electronic weather station he pressed a button on its console. Silently it produced a report showing the trends in wind, air pressure, air and sea temperatures and humidity. He was not pleased. Looking at the wind indicator he could see the wind had shifted to a north easterly and checking the barometer he noted a sharp fall in air pressure. He walked into the chart room and scanned the charts, then checked the tide-tables on the 'marine-computed-almanac' (MCA). Fred stepped in looking red around the gills from helping to organise the stowage of their cargo. "Ah, you've seen what's coming then." He said. "Reckon we'll be lucky to get away before the sea-state reaches seven."

"Yes, by the look of it we may be in for a longer stay. Any estimate on the time it will take to finish the main deck?"

"Another six hours at least. I'd say we would be looking at a 20:30 departure if we were fortunate with the weather." Chip looked over to the wind speed indicator again and then out of a window towards the main channel. He could see the water was getting choppy with evidence of foam occurring more frequently as the wind pushed the water in front of it. "It's gusting thirty knots now on occasion, somehow I don't think we can go far tonight." Chip was thinking about Sub Walsh and Mr Pengelly. He'd rather not leave them here unless it was really necessary. In any case a skimmer that traversed the seas down, off-planes made considerably slow progress and although more stable than a mono-hull, such craft had a tendency to pitch rather sickeningly in rough seas. "No, I think we had better play it safe for now Fred. I'll be ashore after lunch visiting Sub Walsh at the hospital and unless I say anything to the contrary when I get back I suspect that we would be better off in port for the night. If Leading Seaman Tucker isn't too busy later on, work him through the long range forecast and an alternative nav-plan for tomorrow at slack tide."

A cold wind kicked up small dust devils that tottered along the streets collapsing as they folded around trams and street corners while he walked briskly from the hospital to the police station. The way the harmonised laws went, the victims of any crime were treated as an accessory to the crime and jailed, bailed and indicted, and generally treated indifferently by the judicial system. All police powers were now in the hands of the Europol bureaucrats who sat in sumptuous offices atop their ivory towers possessing no idea about police work, let alone the law. The police like the legal profession before them were mere technicians. The police Captain was very sympathetic and provided Chip with copies of the reports and charge sheets raised by his officers. "We know this gang Captain, but we are puzzled why they should attack you and your men. Do you have any idea why they should do this?"

"None at all, we took them to be a street gang looking for easy pickings. It's just fortunate that I had my Chief Engineer and my third with me at the time. What do they normally get into jail for?" asked Chip, his curiosity having been aroused. "Oh they are into all sorts of organised crime."

Hailing a hover cab on the corner of Hartmanstraat and Westblaak, he made his way back to the yards at Schiedam. Drops of heavy rain began falling onto the roof of the cab as it sped along heading westwards. By the time they reached the dockyard gates the wind and rain had turned the streets into rivers of running waters down walls and along the pavements into the gutters. Chip dashed into the security office and waited for the rain to abate. After a few minutes he decided to make a run for it to the shipping agent's office not far away. Sipping Oude Geneva in between sips of strong coffee he picked up the completed manifest papers and other documents. The agent's secretary made copies of the met data and finalised arrangements for their departure. The agent sucked his teeth and shook his head. "Not likely Captain. There's a hurricane blowing in our direction, coming in over the Baltic. You may want to reconsider your departure."

"Yes, Mr van Meer, I thought it may come to that. Is any one else catching the tide tonight?"

"Only the Windhover, she's got the size and speed to clear the area before the storm hits us." Chip looked through the windows streaming with rain towards a huge merchantman riding light in the water. Cranes worked overhead like giant matchstick birds feeding their young; dipping and lifting, then dipping once again as they carried cargo up and over her side into the deep holds down below. "A steel castle, she could ride most storms anywhere in the world."

"Yes, she has nice lines and moves fast. They put plasma-jet engines in her two years ago. And now they say she is one of the fastest ships in the world." Chip finished his coffee, thanking the agent for getting the papers in order before taking his leave. "I will have a look at the weather Mr van Meer and may yet revise my nav-plan. Cheerio and thanks once again!" A driver was found and the agent's car took him to the basin where the Privateer was tied up. She was being buffeted against the jetty by the gusting winds and the sound of it whistling through the rigging on the small forward mast made an ominous sound as he made his way carefully across the gangway. He noted how low she sat in the water and guessed that the great barn doors to the main deck would soon be closed. He found Fred and their acting navigator discussing the weather over one of the view screens. They had switched it to met mode and were watching a slow moving swirl of clouds heading south west over an outline of the Southern Baltic coastal region. "Here's the latest met for you two." Said Chip as he walked onto the bridge. "I don't believe we will be sailing tonight, so can you look at the forty eight and seventy two hour forecasts and let me know what the outcome will be. Fred, can you leave that with Leading Seaman Tucker, you can go through it with him later? Any estimate when they will finish loading?" Fred handed the met reports to Tucker and followed Chip into the chartroom. "They should be finished in about half an hour. That makes almost an hour ahead of schedule." announced Fred enthusiastically. He sounded pleased, as well he might. Usually it would have taken longer with Stevedores running the cargo into the ship, but a well disciplined and motivated crew had made their civilian counterparts look slow by comparison. "When does the dockyard restaurant close Fred?"

"At about seven thirty, last orders are usually around quarter past." A cold blast of air pushed its way onto the bridge as someone opened the door to the main cargo deck. Petty Officer Riley entered dripping wet from head to toe. The only visible parts of his anatomy being his eyes and fingertips as the latter protruded beyond the long cuffs of his foul weather clothing. "Loading has finished Sir. We'll be closing the doors in about fifteen minutes. Did you want to inspect the last batch of cargo before we do?"

"Yes, I'll come with you, just hold on before we leave." said Fred. "I think now is a good time to release the duty watch to get cleaned up and go over for something to eat. By the time they get back the others would have finished here and be getting ready to go to the canteen themselves."

"Yes, that appears to be good timing."

"PO Tucker, inform the duty watch they are relieved as of now. They must be back from the canteen by seven o' clock sharp."

Aye, aye Sir." Tucker and Fred disappeared down the short passageway through the door leading to the cargo deck. With tie-downs in place there was still enough space at the back for the cargo they were destined to uplift at Ostend.

Fred went along with the first batch towards the canteen. The small knot of men picking their way through the menu, settling for things like meatballs, spaghetti or schnitzels with mashed potatoes and pickled cabbage. Fred eschewed the licensed restaurant in favour of the self-service area and was amused at some of the more imaginative combinations some of them had chosen. He chose a fillet American, french-fries and a side dish of tomato salad. The conversation was light-hearted enough and to add to their good spirits he thanked them publicly for a job well done in loading the cargo so efficiently. They got back a little early giving the others a chance to get through the rain before the canteen stopped serving food.

Chip went a little later since the restaurant stayed open until nine. Before he left he knocked on Mr Pengelly's cabin door and was received by a cheery "Come in!"

"Hello Mr Pengelly, how are you today after your well earned sleep?"

"Not bad Sir, not bad at all. The old pin's a bit sore though, but other than that I reckon my hand will be alright by the end of the week."

"Oh' yes I forgot you had your work cut out with that hand didn't you. I must thank you for being so good as to put yourself between those thugs and me. They were a pretty mean lot."

"Reckon they were Sir. But they didn't half get a surprise when that first one went over the side like a barrel." Leyland laughed with a twinkle in his eyes. "I must say I was impressed with the way you handled the police, how do you know Dutch." enquired Chip. "Oh, my mother was Dutch, came from somewhere near Gouda. Her father owned a very famous restaurant near there. Ever hear of the Unter den Molen"?

"No, can't say that I have."

"My father was a pilot and for a while he was based at Schiepol before he retired. He took a job flying air taxis out of Rotterdam and the local airfields. He lived near there and it became his watering hole and that's how he met my old mum."

"Well, all I can say is that it was very handy to have a 'native' Dutch speaker working on my behalf." They laughed for a while about the police trying to arrest them and as Chip explained Peter's situation the atmosphere became thoughtful for a while. Two of the men returned carrying a plastic crate containing supper for Mr Pengelly, who managed a whoop of delight when he discovered that they actually got his order right.

The storm struck at eight o'clock that night. The ship heaving and jarring against her mooring ropes and then against the fenders as she came into close contact with the wall. For three days all light craft such as skimmers and the water taxis usually found plying their trade up and down the river were tied up alongside. With the hurricane stalled over the Dutch-German border country they all knew, as good seamen do, that it was going to be a long wait before good weather returned once again. The weather system spread for three hundred miles across the flatlands uprooting trees, lifting roofs and causing immense flooding. Many of the wind-farms shut down temporarily as the gigantic fan blades feathered automatically. During the day and in the evenings Fred, Chip and Leyland visited the hospital. Leyland went with Chip on the second day to have their dressings changed and for a specialist to have a look at Leyland's torn ligament. The agent kindly offered them the use of his car and driver for these trips making it especially easier for Leyland who was still hobbling along with the aid of a walking stick. His wounds were healing well, and apart from the need to report to his own doctor back home he was effectively discharged. Chip's own wound was healing and though he had not spoken about it at all he found the doctor's poking around a very stinging experience.

Peter also looked better. He had his appetite back and was on his feet on the second day of the storm, looking out of the window. The surgeon was not too impressed with his desire to be back onboard, commenting on the fact that if the weather continued to be that awful he would, no doubt, be lucky to make the homeward trip aboard the Privateer. This raised the Sub's spirits considerably, although his thoughts did drift towards that very nice nurse…

On the afternoon of the third day, people were getting a little frustrated with the weather. The wind rattling against doors and windows, stripping off cladding from the sides of some of the older warehouses and dockyard buildings. Smaller vessels jostled at their moorings and as the cold winds cooled down everything, the heating systems were turned on. Mr Pengelly sat in a deckchair outside the control room supervising the process of transferring fuel from one set of tanks to the other in order to maintain an even keel. Someone had stuck a notice on the back of it 'Armed and Dangerous' being a reference to his walking stick and his newly acquired reputation for taking on all comers in a fight.

Goofers appeared on the bridge during daylight hours with some venturing into the cockpit. Music wafted gently through the accommodation areas as did the aroma of freshly ground coffee. Fred enjoyed showing the hands around and chatting to them in the messing area. Facilities onboard skimmers were usually Spartan, but just comfortable, if you were prepared to wait for a shower or a wash basin. Most people had learned to put up with the restrictions of service life, including living out of small tin boxes bolted to the bulkheads. A locker could hold a minimum of personal kit providing it was folded neatly in the recommended fashion. Chip had the luxury of his own cabin with a fitted shower. Fred and the sub shared a small twin cabin, washing facilities and the tiny wardroom. Mr Pengelly had a cabin to himself as the Senior Non-commissioned Officer aboard, and indeed his own shower. The Senior Rates messed in their own area forward while the Junior Ratings enjoyed a slightly large accommodation area in the mid-ships section around the hatch to the lower hold. Privateer had indeed something most skimmer craft were usually devoid of. The crew enjoyed the benefits of a complete entertainment system in their lounge. The low profile satellite antenna hidden inside a tiny radome provided contact with the outside world including audio and visual channels and a recording system that most teenagers would have traded in their hover bikes for. The ship's electrician was doing a course in Cordon-bleu cookery with the crew frequently enjoying the benefits of tasting the fruits of his labours. It amazed everyone that he managed to do anything at all on the tiny three-ring cooker, but he seemed adept at juggling saucepans and bowls. An inter-mess tournament of games helped to pass the time with the ancient game of 'Uckers' becoming the dominant feature as the rain and winds battered the port.

The fourth morning saw an easing of the winds as they backed a little. By mid day Chip and Fred paid their last visit to Peter. He was standing outside his private room with his bags packed. "What's this, where do you think you're going my lad?" Fred demanded in mock tones of disapproval."

"I'm free to go back onboard with you Sir. They've cleared me off their slate."

"Well, where's the doctor then. Let's see what he has to say about it," said Chip thoughtfully. He was secretly relieved at the Sub's progress but still concerned for his welfare onboard, particularly since their homeward trip would be in choppy seas. The doctor seemed to be expecting him and went through as much as he could without breaking patient confidentiality. Apparently, the naval surgeon had approved the decision providing that the 'young Sub' was relieved of all duties pending a full examination on his return to the UK. When Chip returned to the ward he found Peter talking to one of the pretty nurses. "Aha, so that's it." He said as he approached them. Fred sat on the end of an empty bed swinging a leg idly back and forth looked up smiling. "I know, I know, we leave the lad for a couple of nights and look what he gets up to. I don't know. We'll have to think of something to keep him occupied when he's back onboard, a suitable lurk." Fred's mock disapproval didn't go amiss and the Sub smiled sheepishly back at him.

"So that's the reason for your remarkable recovery Peter." Well I must say nurse, er, nurse…"

"De Fries Captain." She added helpfully. "Nurse de Fries, that we are extremely grateful to you for looking after our colleague. He has had a nasty knock on the head I know, but I do hope he has been well behaved during his stay with you. He has indeed made an amazing recovery and it seems that it is all down to you." He teased. "Not at all Captain, he was very easy to look after, and he is very fit I think."

"I think we'll go on down don't you Sir. Peter, we'll wait downstairs at the lift for you. Don't be too long old chap." Peter looked a little flushed as the other two relented and left him and nurse de Fries to say their farewells.

Later that night the storm blew itself out somewhere over the Denmark Strait. By dawn a thin line of golden sunshine creased the eastern horizon with the sun peeping underneath a thick layer of low cloud. By mid morning the Privateer was moving down the navigation towards the sea with a full complement of crew, albeit a little battered here and there. The huge storage tanks of the gigantic oil depots looming out of the fine mist that remained to obscure their view. Once out of the channel they headed along the coast to Ostend shrouded in a penetratingly cold drizzle of rain made all the more worse by wind blown spray that showered the fore peak each time a wave slapped into the starboard bows. The lumpiness of the waves smacking against the hulls created a loud booming noise as she cut a diagonal wake across the soil coloured sea. Sub Walsh sat propped with his feet up on one of the bench seats in the wardroom, facing the view screen. He watched the vessel's progress on the radar occasionally switching it over to the video circuit where the signal from a camera on the bridge looked out onto the slim bows and the heaving waters beyond. Fred took her up to twelve knots leaving the Privateer off-planes in the heavy sea. This kind of weather made a mockery of her forty-five knot capability.

None of the crew sensed the tension felt by Chip and Fred as they approached the Entrance to the Ostend navigation. They hove-to obeying the light signals and following instructions from the Port Authority control centre. Two Jet-Wave ferries emerged from the narrow channel followed by a small flotilla of skimmers. Privateer was number three with another skimmer and a large wood carrying cargo vessel leading the way. Halfway along the channel they followed the other skimmer to the basin designed specifically for these fast low-loading surface vessels. The basin was a miniature of the large container termini that dotted the shores of the European peninsula, providing plenty of room for the multi-hulled vessels to turn the necessary three hundred and sixty degree circle so that they could reverse into the specially shaped loading 'bays' with ease. The Privateer was a Class IV Mark I with a double door rear loading main cargo deck while the Mark II version possessed an additional a double hatch running the entire length of the cargo deckhead, allowing top loading at ports where rear loading facilities for skimmers were non-existent. The advanced lines of the Mk IV a telltale sign of a merchantman designed and fitted for naval use should there be a requirement to fulfill a war role.

As the hands turned-to tying up fore and aft, readying the rear loading doors to receive the loading ramp from the dockside, a couple of cars drew alongside followed a few minutes later by a large hover-rail container being towed by a tractor unit. Three naval types got out of the first car making their way down the quayside, followed by a representative of the Port Authority who had emerged from the second vehicle. They waited patiently until the gangway was moved in to position along the starboard waist and indicating they wanted to come aboard. Chip shot Fred a quick glance as a heavy lump hit the bottom of his stomach. The tractor unit followed the yellow lines marked on the concrete. Deftly following these lines the onboard computer swung the trailer in a huge arc until the far end was pointing directly at the stern of the Privateer. The tug reversing slowly until it reached a pre-defined point and stopped. The automatic cargo ramp on the dock began lowering itself into the locking plate on Privateer's short quarterdeck accompanied by the whine of powerful motors. The upper end sloping into the air over the quay. The Leading Hand standing just inside the cargo deck pressed a lever on a small control panel and the tug began to reverse once more. When the ramp locked into the corresponding locking plate at the back of its low-loader the tug stopped. After a brief pause the floor of the low loader began to tilt in the direction of the ramp and so began the loading process.

They decided that Fred would deal with Jan the Port Authority rep, while Chip received the Three officers of the ESNF in the small wardroom where they exchanged pleasantries until Fred could join them. Ostend was a friendly port, basically because the Belgians are a friendly, hospitable people. Chip and Fred had got to know most of the operations people through their regular visits. The paperwork had been reduced to nothing more than the exchange of a couple of certificates since the European Mercantile Marine Cargo Manifest and Data Interchange System (EMMCMDIS) performed the donkey-work.

The two lieutenants and a Sub-lieutenant chatted amiably with both Chip and Sub Walsh. They could not fail to notice that one of them came with a small document case with the ESNF initials and seal moulded into its fabric. One of the Lieutenants and the Sub were reservists and as such wore the uniform of their national navies; in this case Belgium, while the full-time regular Lieutenant wore the uniform of the ESNF and standard naval hat with the ESNF cap-badge. The badge on his uniform above his breast pocket had upon it the European Union flag alongside the national flag of France. Indicating he was a French speaker. It was one of those quirks that the Union had yet to address, but in the mean time all reservists reverted to their national status and uniform requirements which, as far as the 'locals' were concerned, was a sound method of preserving national identity. Fred had a brief chat with the port representative and agreed to meet with him in one of the local bars that stood close to the Ostend port entrance, if there was time. By the time he joined the others in the wardroom it was getting quite cramped. They sat around the small dining table bolted to the deck between opposing ranks of chairs and the ESNF Lieutenant reached for his case.

"Captain, I 'ave to ask you some questions about your last visit to Ostend when ze port was re-opened for British traffic. I'm sorry." Apologised, the Frenchman. "But zere seems to be a small matter of discrepancy in ze timing of your visit zat shows on ze record in ze maritime register." He withdrew some documents from his case and Chip felt a little uneasy at the prospect of what was about to happen. The Belgian officers remained impassive as Both Fred and Chip shot them quick glances for any sign or hint from them about the 'problem' alluded to by the French Lieutenant. "Ze records show zat you left Margate on ze 28th of September at ze time of ze emergency law closing all ze ports to British mariners. Ze embargo were lifted at ze time of six o' clock on ze next morning, but your entrance into the 'arbour comes at ze time of fifteen minutes after five o' clock.'

"What are you driving at Lieutenant?" Asked Fred getting more than a suspicion that they were going to be set up. "Zis report shows zat you entered ze 'arbour before ze blockade was lifted, and zis, is against ze emergency law zat was still operating at zis time. Ze penalty for breaking ze law in zis case is to 'ave ze ship impounded, and, er, how you say, ze crew fined sixteen zousand, five 'undred EDs."

"What!" Exclaimed Chip looking at Fred who looked equally shocked. "That's ridiculous, it can't be possible!"

Both men were aware that the particular trip in question had been fraught with difficulties because of the closure of the ports and because of the need to get a perishable cargo across before it went off. The agent had said that the merchant would be paying a good price to get the goods across the minute the embargo was lifted. They took it knowing the met forecast was showing a calm crossing with light, variable winds. Ideal conditions for a lightly loaded outbound skimmer to 'shoot' the planes, and back again with a full, well balanced cargo deck. They knew at the time they could pick up a large backlog of cargoes for a good price. By carefully selecting the right cargoes and the right destination ports they could arrange to be back for at least three or four visits to pick up cargoes and deliver them at the elevated shipping prices demanded. They also knew that Ostend was a sore point with the French, and the Germans were also feeling the strain of all the through traffic using their infrastructures, but not profiting from any trade. The opening of the Euro-route and hover rail between Ostend and central Europe meant that large amounts of freight went from the heart of Europe straight to Ostend and indeed, her sister port of Rotterdam. The Flemish speaking nations had always been regarded as the underdogs and ruined by their larger neighbours in long drawn out wars over the centuries.

Now the little fellows were using the system as intended, increasing their trading power bases, prospering their citizens, much to the annoyance of the Franco-German alliance.

"Peter, you're nearest to the viewer console, put up the ship's log for that week if you please." Peter accessed the log giving details of the Privateer's movements down to the last minute. "There, you see that?" said Fred. As co-pilot and navigator for the two-man operated vessel he took particular pride in his work and in his log keeping. "Lieutenant Le Clerq, you can see here that we left Margate at 04:45 passing mid-channel here at the area navigation point CHA at 05:10, then here at the reporting point in the sea-lane GR1, at 05:55. That means we turned starboard on course for Ostend at 05:55 just before the blockade was lifted. We still had twenty-five minutes to run at that point, so how can anyone claim that we broke the embargo?"

"Yes Captain, I see what you are saying. What is your maximum speed?"

"On a night crossing like that with a cargo we can make forty to forty-two knots."

"But zat gives you plenty of time to arrive in Ostend before 6 o' clock."

"No it doesn't, the speed restrictions in the crossing routes don't allow us to go that fast. We can only make twenty five knots, you know that Lieutenant." chipped in Peter, enjoying himself in his quasi-civilian role. Fred was relieved, he hadn't thought of that until Peter had brought up the point. Chip nodded in agreement. "So even if we wanted to, given those speed restrictions we could not possibly enter the harbour before that time. And, of course there was no space at the terminal to take us because of all those other craft stuck in the basin by that embargo."

"So-o, yes I can see zis."

"Then you must be aware, that those vessels had to leave harbour first before anyone could get in. So even if we were ahead of our arrival time. Which we weren't, we could not have entered harbour and therefore we could not have broken any laws. Emergency or otherwise." Chip's logical rejoinder was a perfect defence against the allegation and the French Lieutenant sat and thought for a moment or two, before speaking again. "Captain, may we have a look at the manifest for that trip please?" asked the Belgian Lieutenant politely. "Yes you may. Peter can you bring that up on the viewer, again, please?"

"I see, a container with fresh meat in it, one with Scottish salmon and two half containers of various machine parts and consumer goods."

"Which means what Lieutenant Jaap?"

"Oh, I see, you're cargo weight indicates that your operating speed for on-planes that night would have been reduced to around forty five knots. The sea state was calm at the time of your crossing, but I can see that it became state-4 as you proceeded to CHA here, that tells me you must have reduced speed to around thirty-eight knots or so for safe operation on the planes." Fred positively beamed. The guy was on his side. "Yes, that's about right, and illustrates more clearly that we could not have been any earlier."

The French Lieutenant nodded slightly in mute agreement. He was beginning to see that he had been sent on a fool's errand. Now the tables were being turned on him. He was feeling uncomfortable while Chip and Fred felt they had vindicated themselves and the Privateer. "I understand your situation Captain, and I would be grateful for a copy of your log for zat treep and also for ze nav-plan you filed at Margate Euro-marine?"

"With Pleasure Lieutenant. Fred will you provide the Lieutenant with a full size copy from the console in the chartroom."

"Will that be all for now on that subject?"

"Unfortunately, I must ask you not to leave ze port until I clarify zis details wiz my superiors."

"How much time do you want?"

"About three to three and a half hours I think."

"Let me get this clear, are you placing a holding order against my vessel?"

"Until I give you ze all clear, yes."

"It will take us two hours to load; start to finish. Any delay after that is unacceptable."

"You're log and nav-plan appear to be in order Captain and I hope to let you go as soon as possible, zat is all I can tell you." Fred returned with copies of the ship's movements and nav-plan in question. The French Lieutenant made his exit, not staying for a drink, wisely deciding that after bringing bad news he would best be elsewhere.

The two Belgian reservists decided to remain. The young Sub was keen to have a look around since he had never been onboard a commercial skimmer before. Fred got the Electro-tech to take him around asking him to drop the young man back at the wardroom. He went over to the drinks cabinet and poured a whiskey for himself and the Belgian Lieutenant, and a rum and elderberry smash for Chip. "What was all that about?" Asked Chip as he watched Fred pouring out the measures. "I think they are looking for excuses to make trouble for some people. I don't think it's the navy so much as somebody in Strasbourg playing politics."

"Oh, God, not again." groaned Chip. "We have too much of it back home at the moment, and people just want to get on with their lives."

"May I change the subject Captain?"

"Yes of course, we don't want to get tied up in a political discussion."

"I see from the Navy List that you and your First Officer are reserve officers, recently commissioned. As you see I am also now a reservist. I just wondered if you were like me, an ex-regular?"

"Why yes, I was a pilot in the air-arm and Fred here was in the general service, a fish head."

"Oh, yes, I have heard of this, and you're an airey-fairey, no?"

"Yes, that's right, some people use the term fly-boy, but not so much these days."

"Why did you leave when you had such a great job flying around?" asked the Lieutenant full of curiosity. "Oh, well, you know, it came to a point," and here Chip added carefully, "that I wanted to pursue something more worthwhile back home really. Sometimes it is sobering when you realise that plasma-jet pilot's only have a short career before they either get shot down or pushed into a desk job."

"Yes, as a matter of fact, that is why I left too, about five years ago. I thought I could make more money and settle down. Now I work for a Shipping company in Brussels and spend my time travelling between here, Zeebrugge and Rotterdam." Slowly the penny dropped. "Oh, you are currently working your reserve time and don't tell me you were on the Ghent five days ago?" The Belgian Lieutenant smiled a quiet sort of smile. "Yes I am working my reserve time at the moment, and yes, I was at sea five days ago, but not on the Ghent. I am the commander of the Waadinxvane the ship that fired a missile down the length of your vessel." Chip looked at him and laughed.

"What is the matter Captain. Have I said something wrong perhaps?"

"No, no, not at all. It's very kind of you to come and visit us."

"I have come to apologise for the bad moment I must have given you…" Fred came in and Chip said in a loud voice. "Fred, allow me to introduce Lieutenant, er, er, what is your first name?"

"Hendryk. Lieutenant Hendryk Jaap of the Royal Belgian Navy, erstwhile Captain of the vessel Waadinxvane!"

"Really, so it was you. You know, you gave us a bit of fright there I can tell you Lieutenant, but that's all in the past." He smiled at Hendryk and then joined Chip in laughter, as he too saw the funny side of the situation. "I am sorry, you looked as though you were part of the opposing force, and we actually fired the dummy at the Ghent using you as a radar shadow between us and the Ghent." Hendryk looked from one to another and then, with a sudden realisation, he too laughed as Fred took a bottle from the bar cabinet and poured another round of drinks.

Later, as the doors swung closed down aft and the crew made their way along the cargo deck companionways to the mess or lounge, the conversation drifted cautiously to the allegation of blockade running by the ESNF. "I got the information from the Harbour Master this morning and asked my Commandant if I could join Lieutenant Le Clerq. He seems a decent fellow, but of course he's French and the papers came from the Euro port Bureau in Strasbourg, which as you know is miles from the sea."

"So you think it really is a political deal or even a pen-pusher's slip of the pen?" asked Peter from his corner. "It could be someone with an office boy mentality not owning up to his mistakes, or, yes it could be politically motivated I think." Chip was curious. "Why is that?"

"It's because the Belgians are making money and the French are not. The Germans are the same. Since the routes to the east have been expanded in the last seventy-five years all trade must come through to the west coast of Europe. It's a fact that they don't like very much. We're the little guys, they are the big guys and they are trying to push us around. So, if they can close the ports for a while and make it difficult for British shipping, then they hope to make a profit out of the damaged relations." Hendryk took a sip from his gin and tonic and looked at them thoughtfully. "That is why I took an interest to find out what they would be doing with you today. I don't think Jean-Claude Le Clerq will hold you up. He is probably trying to fix it up for you to go as quickly as possible."

Chip looked more relaxed at hearing the statement. "That's a bit of a relief. How long does this kind of thing take?"

"Oh, he will try to get you out on time, or as close to that as possible. I think with your papers being in order it will be OK." The door opened and the Belgian Sub returned looking pleased. He accepted a drink from the bar and sat down opposite his colleague.

"Well Jan, what do you think of their cargo deck?"

"It's very impressive Captain, I did not believe that so much cargo would fit into a vessel this size, especially a skimmer."

"That's the commercial world for you, instead of building vessels with lots of little compartments stuffed full of people and equipment, we have a fully integrated multi-processor system that looks after everything for us. So we can run with a minimum of manpower in exchange for a reasonable profit."

"It's interesting to see that you're carrying a lot of specialised equipment Captain, Those kinds of pumps you're carrying are usually found in naval vessels, like submarines I think. They have a very big pressure capacity."

"Peter, you're the cargo officer what are your comments on that?" asked Chip neatly side-stepping the quest with a sly grin. "I can't say that I've noticed. It really depends where they are going after we've delivered them. Could be for the Atlantic mining operations, there's a lot of activity in the area south west of the Western Approaches. Other than that I cannot say for certain."

They finished their drinks and rose to leave. "I'll go into the office straight away and see if your papers have been sorted for you. Have someone standby on the harbour frequency Captain and I will have the call made to you when the clearance comes through. Thanks for the drinks, and again my apologies for scaring your crew, especially that Chief Engineer of yours."

"It was kind of you to call and your apology is accepted."

"That's good. Oh, before I take my leave, here is my card. If you have a need for cargo maybe we can be of help at some time in the future."

As they left, Fred was informed by the duty Leading Hand that the cargo was inboard and secured, the cargo doors closed, and the Privateer ready to depart at a moment's notice. He gave the order to single up the moorings and to remove the gangway. The clearance came through with five minutes to spare on the deadline with everyone heaving a sigh of relief. At 22:45 the Privateer made her way through the basin out into the narrow channel towards the North Sea. The weather had cleared somewhat with a stiff offshore breeze raising white caps on the choppy surface here and there. The duty watch went about their business silently as the off-watch crewmen watched satellite entertainment or played card games in the lounge. Leyland Pengelly stirred at about eleven thirty and made some corned-dog sandwiches and a mug of cocoa in the small galley. He finished eating his doorstep sandwiches and hobbling up the flat made his way into the bridge on his walking stick in one hand and his mug of cocoa firmly clasped in the other.

"Ah, Mr Pengelly, welcome to the land of the living. How do you feel?"

"Not bad PO, where are we exactly?" Chip looked down from the cockpit giving his wounded engineer the thumbs-up signs. Leyland acknowledged by returning the gesture. "How are you Mr Pengelly? Feeling better I hope!"

"Yes sir, thank you!"

"How's Sub Walsh doing!"

"Oh, he's much better, thank you. You'll find him in the chartroom poring over some dusty old maps!" Leyland worked his way across the bridge to the chartroom. "Hello Sir." He beamed. "Hello Mr Pengelly, How are you doing? I hear your leg is better?"

"Yes, it is, thank you Sir, mind you, that's minimal compared to your own injuries. Still we have the satisfaction of knowing that we busted up one of their toughest gangs. That can't be bad, eh."

"Well that's true, and I have to thank you for looking after me while I was completely out of it."

"Not at all Sir, just glad we got the better of them."

Five miles off Dungeness the radio op punched through a message to the Captain's cabin activating the message alarm. Chip woke with a start and sat up with that sinking feeling grabbing at his intestines, struggling to wake his aching body. The message came from the Admiralty in London marked 'Urgent, for the attention of the Master Privateer.' He was tempted to turn over and go back to sleep but the years of discipline prevented him from doing just that. He looked at the digital clock on the bulkhead, simultaneously turning on his viewer, cancelled the alarm, selecting the comms screen. With a little more urgency he tapped in his personal security access code and read the contents of the message sheet. It read:

From: C-in-C Naval Home Command

To: Master Privateer

You are requested to proceed to the Port of Harwich immediately. Further instructions will be given on your arrival. Berth C-27, pier 8.

For and on behalf of their Lordships,

Duty Signals Officer: CINCNAVHC

As per common practice the sender remained nameless and un-referenced. Chip always found the security of service types a little frustrating, but a necessary evil in the preservation of information from prying eyes. He reached for the intercom button. "Bridge, Captain."

"Bridge here Sir. Chief Bryant"

"Chief, plot a course for Harwich and inform the duty coxswain straight away of our new destination. Advise me of our ETA. Our berth will be C-27 at pier 8."

"Aye, aye Sir." Chip sat back against his pillow reflecting on the possible reasons why the Privateer had to be diverted to Harwich when they were so close to the yards at Portsmouth. He glanced at the clock again noting the time of 01:15. He was due to take the morning watch in any case and turned over to be awoken once more by the message beeper on his console. "Captain, Bridge."

"Captain here."

"Our ETA Harwich is 03:05, Sir." He felt the changes in the vessel's movement as the coxswain turned to port in a wide sweeping turn. "Thank you Chief, expect a visit from Lieutenant Newman, he's bound to have been awoken by the change in course."

"Aye, aye Sir." Chip felt the hull settle on an even keel with the new heading falling under the needle of the gyro compass, knowing instinctively by the feel of the multiple keels beneath his berth they were in a following sea. 'That's going to be hard work for someone if he's not on auto-pilot,' he mused. Checking the GPS screen he noted the new heading and speed before switching it to standby, set his personal alarm for 2am and drifted off to sleep fitfully, knowing the duty watch capable of taking the Privateer across the Thames navigation area.

He awoke to the annoying sound of his alarm and rolled over to turn it off. Slowly lifting himself over the sill of his bunk he stood up and washed still half-asleep. Heading back along the south coast towards the north east with a following sea in the dark made for a queasy stomach for the inexperienced sailor he mused. Emerging from his cabin a little later he smelled coffee and bacon wafting up the flat from the galley as he walked the short distance on to the bridge. Sure enough Fred was there, poring over the view screen looking at the approaches to Harwich. He selected the overlay and as the numbers came up on the screen he could see where their berth was located."

"Morning Skipper." He greeted Chip with a thin smile.

"Morning Fred, what time did you get up, or do I need to guess, say about ten seconds after we started the turn?"

"You got it in one, the old body clock never fails me, so I decided to get an early breakfast and have a look at the approach plates for Harwich."

"Good man. That bacon smells pretty good to me right now."

I'll have the quartermaster get you a coffee with a bacon sandwich if you like?"

"Yes, that's a good idea, thank you. Now how's that plate looking?" Together they went through a quick brief on the signals, positioning and speed restrictions in the Harwich navigation. "Why Harwich?" Asked Chip half to himself as much to Fred. "It's a free port since they declared themselves a UPA, but I thought it had become run down for decades, particularly since the fish ran out fifty years ago. Look at that huge jetty sticking out from the shore in that basin, that's all new."

"Looks as though they have been busy with their new UPA status grants." offered Fred.

At 02:50 they entered the Harwich control area and proceeded up the navigation with the Coxswain following the approach plates on the view screen in the cockpit backed up by radar sensors. It was an almost straight in approach from the Naze past the old fort on Landguard Point then turning left in a slow turn at 6 knots round the redoubt into the curvaceous Stour navigation. A large dredger loomed out of the darkness, her attendant barges almost full of reeking ooze from the bottom of the channel. Passing down her starboard side they moved cautiously past the disused ferry terminal slowing to just 3 knots in the potential confusion of large shadows looming all around them in the unfamiliar surroundings, slipping quietly into the huge basin behind the old Parkeston Quays. A small boat appeared out of the darkness at the same time that the radio announced the arrival of the pilot boat, taking up a position about a hundred metres in front of the Privateer guiding her along the quays to a position opposite the entrance to a huge basin. The pilot bade them goodnight and left them on a heading across the basin directly towards their berth.

They were astonished at what they saw. Nearly every berth was full of commercial skimmers, almost fifty-five assorted types riding gently in the placid waters. Nearing their destination Sub Walsh, whose curiosity had got the better of him, picked out a naval flotilla partially hidden by the dark outlines of dockside buildings, "Look at that?" He said and people glanced in the direction of the far dock facility. The coxswain swung Privateer in a practised arc and at some invisible point in his mind swung the control column amidships, pulled back the throttles, and engaged the reverse detent on the engine control quadrant before throttling up the engines again. The powerful water jets gradually taking effect with the laden craft moving slowly backwards into her 'slot' alongside the wall. Two vehicles with flashing amber lights on their roofs were waiting for them and as the seamen began tying her up two men stepped out of vehicles. The usual welcoming committee with their electronic tablets waiting to chalk up more revenue in harbour dues and other catchall charges. They left behind two envelopes addressed to the Master.

The off-duty watchmen headed for their bunks with the next watch taking over to commence the morning watch in harbour. Chip retired to his cabin and opened the letters. The first contained new instructions from CINCNAVHC informing him to be ready to leave Harwich in the company of sixteen other craft and a naval escort. Chip was a little disturbed by what he had read and opened the second envelope with a sense of foreboding. It was from his brother in the Portsmouth yards, not from his Portsdown address. He read the letter slowly and carefully. 'By the time you return you may or may not be aware of the changing situation here.' He read. The letter went on to describe the latest political changes made law in the past twelve hours, but not yet made public. His brother briefly touched on the increasing emergency powers restricting the freedom of movement of the population and that all travellers and all commercial shipments were not allowed to move unless they were in possession of travel permits issued by the military or by senior government. In other words, UPA administrators since there were only government ministers above that particular level of authority. The letter went on to inform him that the laws had been ratified by the House of Commons in an emergency session, and that simultaneously, invoking the Parliament Act they side-stepped the need to present the new legislation for ratification by the Senate. 'By the time you leave Harwich the news will break at 08:00 while most people are preparing to leave home for work.' The letter went on. 'The Admiralty has re-called all reservists and therefore as a consequence you will fall under Admiralty Authority regarding the movements of your Vessel, the Privateer. In accordance with the emergency powers you will be directed to join a convoy of vessels scheduled to leave Harwich under escort, for an undisclosed destination.'

Chip folded the letter slowly pursing his lips. 'Bad news indeed!' He thought. He looked into the large envelope and saw another letter inside it. He withdrew the paper and saw that it was another personal note from his brother. He read it twice and was grateful for his brother's thoughtfulness. The girls were safe, but he warned that Meg would be having problems with the broadcast authority when the new broadcast restrictions came into effect with the increased emergency powers. Since they all lived within UPA boundaries added his brother; they would find travel delays and shortages an inconvenience. Only government establishments and the military had cast-iron guarantees for logistical support.' It was what his brother had not said in that letter that worried him. That was not like him. It suggested a pressing need for caution. Chip looked at his clock; it showed the time as 04:26. He leaned over and pressed the intercom button. "Bridge, Captain."

"Bridge here, Able Seaman Beckinsale."

"Is Lieutenant Newman there."

"No Sir, he's gone down aft to the quarterdeck with Mr Pengelly."

"Oh, right, thank you Beckinsale. When he returns ask him to come to my cabin will you."

"Yes, Sir."

"Thank you."

The two men looked intently at the sleek painted shapes of the naval vessels in the early light of dawn. A cold breeze blew over the town causing goose bumps to rise on their skins underneath their shirtsleeves. "I never knew there was a naval yard here Sir. It seems as though it hasn't been here that long by the look of those new buildings on the dock."

"It's a bit funny seeing them here. I wonder how many that leaves in the Portsmouth command area?" ventured Fred. They talked for a while and speculated how long the naval surgeons would give him and Sub Walsh to recuperate from their respective injuries. They heard footsteps coming towards them along the narrow starboard deck and turned to see who it was. "Ah Able Seaman Beckinsale, are you looking for me?"

"Yes Sir, The Captain has asked to see you in his cabin. I was coming down this way and thought I'd take a detour to find you."

"Good man Able Seaman Beckinsale, and thank you." He turned back to Mr Pengelly. "Never a dull moment, you know I've forgotten how it used to be with just the two of us and a complement of four hands. Don't leave without saying goodbye Mr Pengelly."

"Thank you Sir, I'll come and look you out before I do."

Fred knocked on the door and waited. "Come in!" called Chip. As he sat down in the seat offered him Fred saw a very worried man. "Have a look at this Fred and tell me what you think?" Fred handed him the two official letters and waited looking at the blank view screen searching for inspiration. "Phew! What the hell is happening, it looks as though the government or at least someone wants absolute power and they're stopping at nothing to get it."

"OK, we must sort out personal needs first Fred. When this breaks we have a crew with their own families and they are going to be worried just as much as we are."

"Well I'm reasonably un-attached since my divorce, but I wouldn't mind making sure that Mavis and the children are going to be safe." He paused for a moment looking out of the small porthole behind Chip's head. "It's so ridiculous Chip, how on earth does something like this happen?" He demanded. "I've been thinking that myself too. You know that Chief Bryant is doing a college course in political history?"

Yes, he seems quite keen on it as well."

"He was talking about it the other night when we were on the bridge in Rotterdam waiting for the weather to ease up. He said there were two points in history that marked the beginning of the steep decline of democracy in the UK. The first was the repealing of the right to remain silent in the 1990s, and the second was about six years later when the government instigated imprisonment without trial under the guise of anti terrorist legislation. It seems the first change came at a time of political unrest and a failing leadership that responded with censorship. He said it was so bad that criminals were being treated like victims, and that the victims were being treated like criminals; and the bloke who changed the law at the time had failed in his last ministerial job to boot. They made him home secretary and he bungled that too by all accounts. Just like the second guy who made it possible for almost anyone to be held in prison without trial on trumped up charges of being a terrorist. He said the historians recognised that at the time both individuals were men of their times without anything in the way of a vision for the country and as such became the most hated men in the land."

"Well all I can say is that this lot is doing a fine job of making a career out of it." Fred was getting annoyed and they sat there in silence for about ten minutes.

"Fred, we don't have much time before we start to make preparations for the next trip to wherever that might be. It would be a good idea to ask the powers at C-in-C for details about the families of our crewmen. How many are married and so on."

"We could take a look at the personnel files on the private access computer in the equipment room, only you and I have the access code for that."

"Good idea Fred, it's best if you did it with nobody around. Lock yourself in and dig out the information we need so that we can find out who lives where exactly and whether or not anyone needs particular help in getting information about their families."

"The ones with families in the naval ports shouldn't be too badly off Chip, they're all within UPAs and those as you know are protected by law."

"Yes, and you know what they did to the London Borough UPAs when the rioting got bad. They just cut them off and starved them out. I have a nasty feeling about this, and if anything, surviving in a UPA is going to be just as bad, if not worse than it is for those outside their protection."

"What about Sub and Leyland Pengelly? Do we put them ashore here before we sail or take them with us."

"Mm, good question. Technically they should be put ashore straight into the hands of the medics, but without transport and with the way things are going to be as from a few hours from now I am inclined to keep them with us until we get clear instructions."

"I don't suppose they would mind a couple of days more until we arrive at wherever it is we're going. I've just been chatting to Leyland and he's mending well, but we know he needs physiotherapy and a clean bill of health from them before he can return to seagoing duties."

"Right, and that's more or less the same for Peter with his cracked head and those stitches. OK, this is what we'll do Fred. You get the personnel info and sort them out into the two main categories, and I'll get onto the C-in-C and ask for their advice about our two casualties. I need to have a form of words to ask them about the men without necessarily telling them that I know what's coming."

"One other point to consider, if we are going to be at sea when the news breaks at 08:00 it looks as though we don't have much time before we will have to make ready for sea, it's half past four now. I reckon it will take time to assemble a convoy out there in the roads, so we'll be starting at around about six o' clock or I'm my mother's uncle!"

"Good point. I'll enquire if they have a Naval Harbour Master here, and see what I can do to find out. Until then I think we should call the hands at 06:00, and I suspect, we might also clear the decks for this announcement when it comes. Afterward that, I would like you and Leyland, if he is still with us, to arrange individual appointments with the crew to find out if there are problems for them. I'll do your spell up in the driving seat. Who's the duty navigator for the forenoon?

"Leading Seaman Tucker. It sounds as though you've made your mind up about Peter and Leyland staying onboard." Fred got up to leave. "Yes, I don't think they'd thank me for leaving them in a strange port miles from anywhere on the day that the government lurches closer to war on the people."

Chip composed a short message to the C-in-C at Portsmouth regarding his injured crewmen along with an implicit question about leave arrangements for the crew in general. Fred had drawn up two lists indicating those who were effectively unattached and or living at home with their parents, and those who were married living within the boundaries of the naval UPAs. Since the naval yards were within the boundaries of the civilian UPA they enjoyed a special relationship, providing jobs for the masses of civil servants that had replaced sailors at over six times the cost, and for the tradesmen who worked for the private companies contracted to maintain the ships. All of the naval UPAs, in effect, shaped like a half ring doughnut. The ring of the doughnut being the UPA territory with the naval installations and or harbours on the inside bounded by the water. It was half-past five when he joined Fred in the equipment room and sent the encrypted message to the C-in-C. "I see Peter is up and about. I think both he and Mr Pengelly have caught up on years of missed nights. Leyland is down in the Senior Rates mess doodling over the duty rosters for next month. It might be a good time to break the news to them in advance of the men."

"Yes, that's a good idea. Thanks for the tip I think it's best you come along too. When will you be finished there."

"In about ten minutes, I'm just getting the last couple of files out now. Say, about quarter past six?" offered Fred.

"No, I think it's best they know now. Have them muster in the wardroom and let me know when you're ready for me."

"I somehow think that they won't be too worried about losing a little shore time under the circumstances."

"I suspect that the C-in-C wont have anyone around to ask about medical details at this time of day and the other matter can be dealt with on the hoof if I'm not mistaken."

"OK Skipper, see you at six."

At the allotted hour Fred came and knocked on Chip's cabin door and invited him to the wardroom where Peter and Mr Pengelly were seated, looking over an early morning edition that had arrived with the mail. They rose as Chip entered "Thank you gentlemen, please be seated. I hope this wont take too long, but I have the onerous task of informing you about our future situation." Fred sat down at the opposite end of the table. "The information I am about to give you is confidential and is as you might suspect connected with our being diverted to Harwich. We are here as part of a larger fleet and at some time this morning we will be given our orders and a nav-plan to assemble a convoy with the other vessels in the basin, and to rendezvous with a naval escort for an undisclosed destination. The second item that I feel bound to impart to you is one that affects us all, both here on the Privateer and at home." There was a formal silence from the other two as Fred tried to look casual. "The government." continued Chip. "Has decided to increase the emergency powers it wields and at eight o' clock this morning will be imposing a nation-wide restriction on all forms of travel. They haven't as yet declared martial law, but this may be a brief period in which there is a stay of execution for such an order to be made. I can't tell you what this means precisely, except that we are all affected by it, because of our families at home. As far as travel is concerned for us as individuals that brings me to the third point that the Admiralty have communicated to me this morning. All reservists are being recalled, and as from seven thirty this morning we will no longer be a mercantile vessel under contract to the Naval Authorities with a naval crew in support, we are now officially designated an active unit within the Royal Naval Reserve. We are therefore required by their Lordships to revert to our uniform code and to conform to the appropriate marks of respect, etc, etc. Gentlemen, I don't think there is any more to add to that except to ask if any of you have any further questions?" Peter Walsh picked up the newspaper and turning the front page towards Chip held it up for him to see. 'Treachery!' shouted the banner headline in bold letters. 'Government imposes martial law!'

"We just got this a few minutes ago Sir. It seems as though there has been a ministerial leak in Whitehall."

"So it would seem Peter. Well there it is. They couldn't even be honest with the military leaving it until the moment of its announcement." There were a few questions back and forth during which time there was a loud knock on the wardroom door. Fred got up, and moved over to the door opening it ajar. "Yes Chief, what can I do for you?"

"There's a Captain Wiley at the brow asking to see the Captain Sir."

"Oh, right thank you Chief, wait there a moment please."

"Would you like me to escort him to your day room Sir?" Asked Fred

"Yes please Fred, don't hurry I want to finish off here before I leave."

"On my way Sir." Chip turned back towards the other two thinking how easily Fred had slipped back into the grey funnel routine. "Where was I, ah yes, travel. Well, as far as I can tell we may have a slight advantage being active servicemen, but that remains to be seen. However, in light of the fact that we have not made our intended destination and that we are entering a largely unknown situation I cannot honestly put you ashore unless you tell me that your injuries and your general state of health demands it. So, somewhat reluctantly I have decided to take you along with us rather than leave you, shall we say, stranded, in a strange port without much likelihood of making it to a naval establishment where you may receive proper treatment."

"Thank you Sir. I was going to request to stay onboard when I read that headline, but now I am glad I don't have to."

"Thank you Peter, but remember you are still relieved of all duties until you have fully recovered, and that includes an all clear from the first naval surgeon who can clap eyes on you. Now, Mr Pengelly, I know this makes it a little easier for you and the men to be back into uniform proper, but what is more important to me is your wellbeing. If you feel you are able to come along and put up with that gammy-leg for a few days more I would welcome the opportunity."

"I have absolutely no objection Sir. It seems life would be more difficult otherwise."

"Thank you Mr Pengelly, please remember that you are also relieved of all duties until we can get you to some sick-bay ashore. But I would ask you to assist Lieutenant Newman with the task of holding interviews with the crew so that we can get a better idea of their personal situations."

"I'd be delighted to have something to do, and I will liaise with Lieutenant Newman to get things going."

"Thank you Mr Pengelly. Now if there are no other questions I must go and see my visitor."

"No Sir."

Thank you both, that will be all." Peter rose and opened the door for Chip. "Thank you Sub." Chip stopped by the equipment room very briefly to look for a reply to his earlier signal to the C-in-C. As expected there wasn't a single peep from the machinery, so he walked for'ard towards his day cabin.

Captain Wiley was a grizzled old salt with a large mop of greying hair, sporting a voluminous salt and pepper beard to match. He was sharing a laugh with Fred as Chip entered the cabin. "Captain Wiley, a pleasure to meet you Sir. What can we do for you?"

"Well thank you, I'm not too sure that my visit will be too pleasing to you, but I see that there must be some mistake. My information has it that I should be talking to a Lieutenant-Commander Woodingdean and his first-Lieutenant, a Lieutenant Newman, but I see I am in the company of a Captain and a Commander."

"Er, no Sir, we are displaying the rank of Captain and First Officer, well that is what we are until 07:30 this morning." Chip looked at the other Captain more directly. 'Pedantic old buffer' he thought more with amusement than with disdain. "Ah, yes forgive me. There's nothing in my notes to indicate you are in fact a qualified ship's Master, or indeed that you are the First Officer. My apologies to you both." Captain Wiley opened his case to remove two sealed envelopes. "I'm certain you will want to open these sealed orders to find out where you are going Captain, but in accordance with the requirements of the first signal from the Admiralty you are not to open the second envelope until you are under way and at the specified time. I'm sorry for what appears to be a little of the cloak and dagger approach, but believe me when I say that all will be revealed later today."

"Yes, we gathered from the morning papers just received with the mail that things are not looking too bright for the moment." Captain Wiley turned to look at Fred as he spoke. "I see, that is of course the main picture and I have to say it is very worrying for us all. As usual it's the armed forces that are caught up in the middle of it."

"Is there anything you can add to your observation Captain?" asked Chip. "It's rather disturbing for us all since we have just returned from Rotterdam via Ostend, and there's been nary a whisper on the news or media channels."

"Not really, you know as much as I do. You have probably realised by now that the armed services have recalled all their reservists in response to the demand to impose martial law, and of course, that most of the policemen in the country have gone on strike or resigned in protest over the last six months. The assumption being the imposition of martial law has been 'arranged' to deflect the imposition of foreign troops on British soil by the European governing body. You can only take it from there and hope, like the rest of us, that someone has the courage of their convictions to straighten this mess out."

"Thank you for that Captain. As you say, we're all of the same mind waiting to see what transpires."

"Then I must take my leave of you, I still have three more visits to make. What I can tell you is that you should be ready to slip within the hour." Captain Wiley looked at his watch and paused. "Make that fifty minutes from now. All will be clear to you in the next twelve hours or so. Thank you for being patient gentlemen."

At 7am precisely the Privateer slipped her moorings to join a long line of skimmers and other single hulled high-speed transports making their way slowly into the main channel towards the sea. By 07:45 fifty-six vessels rendezvoused with a destroyer, two frigates and four Cutlass class skimmers eight kilometres off Orford Ness. Following instructions the loosely positioned fleet of ships was quickly shepherded into four lines flanked on the outside by a screen of escort vessels. At 08:15 the Admiralty sent a priority one signal to all naval units containing a general synopsis of the political situation, and as encouragement to all those currently in active service their Lordships included in the message a family welfare announcement. Adding that all service families would be brought into the framework of a welfare initiative to ensure their circumstances would not be compromised. Quite what that meant no one could be sure, but a loud debate ensued in the mess-room and throughout the ship.

The hands were mustered in the lounge at 08:30 and Fred informed Chip that the ship's company was ready. On entering the mess-room he could see a lot of serious and angry faces. 'This is going to be a difficult one.' He thought as he moved to the front of the people gathered together. "Thank you, stand at ease, stand easy. If any of you wish to sit down Please feel free to do so.' He waited until the moving of bodies quietened down.

"I've no need to tell you what has happened this morning since the papers have arrived onboard, and no doubt some of the non-duty watch-men were in here when the news broke at eight o' clock this morning. The situation

ashore is serious and therefore the government in their wisdom are now requiring all those who have to travel out of their immediate habitation areas to have travel passes. No pass, no travel. That is the message. However, as servicemen on active duty you will be given military travel permits in due course. In the mean time your service identity cards will be accepted until as such time the government makes a final decision on special passes for servicemen and women. This effects everyone here in this mess hall and I can only say how sorry I am to bring this kind of news to you. You are all good men, hardworking, and with a high level of morale. I can't think of anything worse to happen that would dent that morale. So this is what I am going to do about it. Lieutenant Newman assisted by Mr Pengelly, who has decided to take on this task to help you, will be holding an open forum later this morning from half past nine, through the rest of today. This means that you will have freedom of access to make known any personal difficulties this situation may put you in.

This is not for political discussion or an opportunity to air your views on what is happening outside of this vessel. It is an opportunity to let us know about your families ashore, and any particular needs and anxieties you may have about their circumstances. Mr Pengelly will brief you on the way he is going to run the forum when I have left. It remains for me to say that as far as I can tell we will be at sea for two, possibly three days more. As some of you are already aware we are in need of fuel and therefore, we must put into port in the next six to eight hours or somebody had better come along and tow us. Leave arrangements will have to be re-scheduled and there will be no shore leave during our re-fuelling stop. Please try to remember that a lot of the news you will hear in the coming days will have a modicum of truth attached to it, but that there will be a lot of hype in the content put there to wind people up. Finally, where we are going is something I do not know. As soon as I know I will make an announcement. Until then stay calm and don't let this distract you from the good work you are doing. That is all."

"Ship's company, ho!" The crew all stood up quickly and in total silence. As Chip left the mess-room he could hear the beginnings of a rumble of voices. This was handled by a growling of command for silence by Fred.

5. SLEIGHT OF HAND

The Admiral's car came to a halt at yet another checkpoint on the military highway between Central London and the airfield at Northolt. Travelling in mufti in an unmarked car on a military trunk road had distinct disadvantages in built up areas. However, the uniformed driver and the vehicle's military licence on the windscreen helped to speed up the tedium a little. The vehicle was stopped at the gates of the airfield while air force sentries swarmed over the car giving it a thorough examination, waving it through and saluting the dignitary seated in the back. Although it had been an early start many people were on the move trying to beat the traffic jams.

A Dominie sat on the apron with its twin plasma-jet engines idling. The Admiral boarded the aircraft carrying a large document case and a full-length overcoat draped over his other arm. The mark 43 had a reasonable cabin size, affording its passengers with a decent amount of legroom. Admiral Driver placed the case underneath his seat and throwing his overcoat into the seat opposite sat down looking forwards over a slender wing. A petite WAFOO emerged from the cockpit and approached the Admiral. "Sorry for the delay Sir, our other passenger has been held up, he shouldn't be too long I hope. Is there anything I can get you?"

"No thank you Corporal. I'll wait until we're airborne."

"Thank you Sir." The cabin attendant moved away to the rear of the cabin and bent down taking a peek through the open cabin door. She began talking to someone standing just outside and occasionally he could hear snatches of her voice above the whispering noise of the engines. "Ah, here he is now…" A few moments later Commandant-General Royce boarded the aircraft making his way towards the front seats. "There you are Gerald, have the boys at the checkpoints been giving you a rough time?"

"Yes, bloody nuisance if you ask me, but there it is." The Commandant shrugged his shoulders in a gesture of resignation. "How was your journey?"

"The usual stop-start-stop palaver." Their ears popped a little when the flight attendant closed the small cabin doors causing a small rise in air pressure inside the cabin. "Please fasten your seat belts for take off and stow any loose items under the seats, thank you." The attendant replaced the microphone and sat down at the rear of the aircraft, strapping herself into a vacant chair. No one spoke as the aircraft taxied and lined up on the runway ready for departure. Both men watched the scenery speeding past as the aircraft accelerated and then took off. At about two hundred feet it banked steeply to the right turning northwards. Far below them they could see hundreds of vehicles jamming the main roads and Euro-routes around London just seconds before a screen of clouds abruptly obscured the view. "What will you do in your spare time?" asked the Commandant softly. "Much as anybody else I think Gerald. There's no sense in denying it's a sad day for all of us. I think perhaps, we will move out of the south into a less frantic place to live where we can settle down, build up a nice home business growing roses or something pretty much like it. Marjorie would like to take up a little sailing again, so we'll probably find a small boat coming in handy. Yourself Nigel, any plans after tomorrow?" The Commandant-General looked out of the small oval window as the bright sunshine caught his face. He surveyed the towering cumulous clouds through which they had passed a few moments ago and pondered. "I hadn't really thought about it much to tell you the truth. There's an adventure training school out on the west coast of Scotland that's rumoured to be coming onto the market, I could try that I suppose. Better to adapt to sharpening up these soft corporate types into more useful human beings than slowly fading away in a country estate on the Surrey-Hampshire borders."

"Heaven forbid Gerald, the place is chock-a-block full of withered old Colonels cluttering up parish committees all over the place." The Admiral smiled a genuine smile of relief. He was glad that tomorrow it would soon be over and that he could walk away with his head held high.

Gerald Royce took a longer view and thought he would take both himself and his wife off on a long cruise somewhere, preferably the Bahamas before they disappeared under the sea. "You know they found a colony of reticulated pythons somewhere near Frensham a couple of months ago, and a couple of kids got bitten by baby black widows when they disturbed a nest of them in a suburb of Southampton." The Admiral looked over the top of his newspaper incredulously, lowering it to his lap laughing heartily, repeating faintly 'reticulated python in Frensham.' –"What on earth is the world coming to. A couple of hundred years ago and they wouldn't have survived the journey by banana boat at all. Now look at us. Half the country is turning sub-equatorial while the other half is becoming a giant marshland."

"I didn't realise they had to build storm drains in Orkney and a caisson around Whitby at the turn of the last century," Gerald continued, "they say the rain was at least a quarter of what it is now and they even had snow on the south coast in winter."

"You know, I never thought about that before. Now I realise why there are so many Dutch immigrants. They couldn't pump out the damn polders quick enough when the dykes overflowed. Don't they say that about a third of Holland will be lost to the sea in the next hundred years or so?" quizzed the Admiral. "It's possible. If there's sharks breeding in the North Sea, then I suppose anything can happen, even the fish are beginning to return."

"Mmm." Nodded the Admiral and went back to his newspaper thinking about reticulated pythons in deepest Surrey.

They arrived at Glasgow international airport shrouded in rain. The two passengers catching a glimpse of the Kilpatrick hills through breaks in the broken cloud base. On the way down the aircraft received a buffeting from the air currents over the Clyde until finally they broke through the base catching a glimpse of the shipyards of Clydebank. The rain partially obscuring their view of the terminal buildings that were lit up like a sprawling circus venue in the dull morning overcast. The Dominie stopped along the taxiway to let a small aircraft pass in front of it. The Commandant watching idly as it taxied down a narrow runway through an opening in the perimeter fence into a small apron where a mere half-dozen or so light aircraft stood dripping in the showers.

A courtesy car drove the VIPs to the other side of the terminal building onto a smaller apron where a navy hover-jet waited for them. Raindrops clung like beads to its shiny hull while rivulets ran down from the stubby wings into puddles on the ground beneath. Admiral Driver and the Commandant-General of the Royal Marines sat with their backs to the forward bulkhead watching in silence as the crewman closed the large sliding door. The aircraft rose from the ground like a huge black crow, departing in a low level pass over the main runway and out over Houston and the weapons centre camouflaged from prying eyes. 'It's been empty for decades' thought the Admiral to himself, 'but it has certainly kept the Ruskies and the

Americans tied up thinking it held our latest developments.' They flew over the sagging remains of the Erskine Bridge towards Dumbarton Rock. Nearing the coast the clouds rose to about fifteen thousand feet carried aloft by the winds being lifted by the mountains further west. The dull black hump of Dumbarton Rock came into view, and then it was gone as the hover-jet followed the coast north and west, climbing to pass over the southern edge of Alexandria. The pilot saw the low clouds compacted over Loch Lomond and veered away to follow the ridge of open moorland above Helensburgh. Looking westwards they could see a thick band of dark grey clouds over the Cowal Peninsula. In particular a band of cloud that looked like the lop-sided filling in a sandwich that fell abruptly above the north of the estuary, to a few hundred feet above the waters. The pilot referencing his instruments periodically flew along Glen Fruin in between the ridges on either side. The bottom of the glen was deeply embedded in mist, but the ridges were like the sides of a large roadway directing him towards their destination. The rocky sides naked of trees and grass, looking dismal and wet. They crossed the ridge flying towards Garelochhead when the ground gave way in steep formations, covered thickly with pines, dotted with occasional clearings hewn from the mountainside where whitewashed habitations and narrow forest tracks peeked through the cover as the metal bird flashed by overhead.

They arrived without all the fuss of a fanfare of martial music. A small welcoming committee, the Captain of the submarine squadron, his squadron commander, a Major of Marines, his aide and a small honour-guard, greeted them. The visitors complimented the guard commander for the smart turn out of his men and were then whisked away out of the drizzle in a black saloon. The small cavalcade of three vehicles entered a double set of security gates and turned left into an old red brick building on rising ground. This was his final visit as a serving Admiral and he was coming to say goodbye to his friends. They were guided through the old submarine school building by a Petty Officer wearing a side-arm and a fresh-faced Sub-Lieutenant, past the security desk, up stairs to the Captain's office for a brief stop, where a middle-aged 'Schoolie' greeted them both warmly. Divested of his long overcoat and scarf and with Nigel, his old friend at his side he made his way to the large auditorium up in the roof of the building. He was slightly taken aback at the large assembly of people, but as he walked to the front of the auditorium towards the small podium he realised that he knew most of them by sight, if not directly by name. His farewell address was not overlong, containing several pithy anecdotes that brought smiles to everyone's faces and in some sections of the audience brought hilarious laughter as the Admiral delivered a series of parodies leaving no doubt in the minds of his audience who he was alluding to. "And now it brings me to the sad moment of farewell. I thank all of you for the hard work and determination to keep an effective force of fighting men and ships, well trained and ready. How things will work out in the current climate I cannot say or dare to make comment. I know that the Navy is in good hands and I trust, will be used wisely to restore order to our troubled shores. Thank you gentlemen,"

Two senior captains responded with brief speeches punctuated with corresponding tales of the Admiral's own mischievous behaviour as a Midshipman. Later, mapping his career, by describing his forthright treatment of those who failed to deliver the 'goods', to the bizarre and often rude nature of diplomats and politicians who thought too highly of themselves; receiving a peppery response for their lack of manners. Recounting the story of one unfortunate Commander who was greeted by the words 'Oh you must Driver,' and not 'Commander' Driver, was doomed never to be promoted to any higher rank for the quick rejoinder, 'you must be Smith.' Much to the chagrin of the idiot who stood on his quarterdeck surrounded by bluejackets working hard swabbing the wooden planking, no doubt silently gleeful at the tremendous put-down of the pompous civvy who had left a trail of footprints across their work. Not least of all because the man foolishly compounded himself by announcing in a lofty voice that he deemed himself too important to bring the sack containing the ship's mail. Somehow his feet and trousers got rather wet, while at the same time he was told rather bluntly to 'go back and get it!' Yet, while this middle-ranking pampered oaf of a diplomat complained to the Admiralty about his treatment, the vile individual continued to live a life of total obscurity. The Commander rose to overcome the slur against his good name to attain the highest ranks through sheer excellence and bravery. He being noticed later on at the battle of Hormuz for his quick thinking and professional seamanship proving beyond doubt his exceptional abilities and making a name for himself in history equal to that of Nelson. The briefing ended with a final reminder by the security commander that all present were not to discuss the meeting with anyone until the official announcement was made public on the following day.

****

The refuelling off Grimsby had been a tough experience for the seamen and for Chip and Fred. For Chip because he had to remain in the bridge while Fred and the senior Coxswain handled the skimmer in a 'replenishment at sea' (RAS) operation in a sea that was beginning to get a little lumpy. They went-off planes and slowed to a mere six knots as there was always the present danger of being sucked into the side of the tanker. The risk of a collision combined with the sparks generated where metal scraped along metal could cause the slender fuel lines to rupture and the ignition of hundreds of gallons of spilled fuel. None of the tanker's crewmen had done it before with a multi-hulled vessel such as the Privateer, as the principal owner of the more fragile skimmer Chip was especially anxious. Five hundred gallons went into the tanks in forty minutes while the seamen stood idly by the light jackstay, watching the wires from which the umbilical fuel line had been suspended. The engine room techs, under the experienced eye of Mr Pengelly in the starboard bridge wing, looked uneasy until the fuel gauges recessed below quartz-glass deck plates indicated full. Breathing a sigh of relief they unscrewed the locking collar and swung the dripping end of the pipe over the water. While the techs lifted their tools away, including a large sledge-hammer that was only used in case an emergency break away was ordered, the seamen cleared away protective matting and flushed a small amount of spilt fuel over the side with hoses.

There remained the inevitable shortage of provisions for the crew who was delighted to find out there was going to be a graunch transfer, weather permitting. One of the other skimmers had been stockpiled with fresh provisions and a detailed schedule of those craft needing replenishment had been worked out weeks in advance. The Privateer was fourth in line and was ordered to manoeuvre into position at 17:00. The glass had been falling slowly all afternoon and the weather plate displayed a glum looking forecast for those gathered around one of the view screens. Autumn weather had become unpredictable as the global atmospheric systems changed the seasonal timing and shifted weather patterns beyond previously recorded history. While Buys Ballot's rule still held true like a lot of rules of thumb, the nature of the planet's surface weather now warranted special attention, especially by the three main professional weather watchers; farmers, mariners and aviators. At 14:00 that afternoon the watch-keepers on the radar view screens identified a lone aircraft detaching itself from the mainland. The maritime reconnaissance was on schedule and expected to over-fly the exercise zone later on in a huge sweep of thousands of square miles of ocean. Ninety five miles due east of Sunderland the signal came for Privateer to take her slot three kilometres behind the Kirkliston who was finishing off the transfer of skimmer number three. A signal lamp flashed three greens and one white light in quick succession. "Make your speed 12 knots and bring her alongside the Kirkliston Starboard side to."

"Speed twelve knots, starboard side to, Sir." They closed within a hundred metres of the supply skimmer and reduced speed to match her own at four knots coming off the planes as they dumped speed, pitching nose down in the swell. Ever closer, Fred inched the Privateer until the two hulls were just inches apart, hydroplanes tucked safely in their bays flush with the hull. The sides of both hulls had matting lashed in position draped over the side from the decks above just a few inches from the rushing water.

"Are you ready to start the transfer?" Came a voice shouting through a megaphone from the Captain of the Kirkliston. "Affirmative, commence transfer!" Came the response from Chip.

At the precise moment he agreed to the transfer all hell was let loose. Well, to an outsider it looked as though the crew of both ships had gone mad. While Kirkliston's crew hurled bags, boxes and loose items across the narrow gap between the two moving vessels, the other crew on the Privateer scrambled to catch them as they came across. The gap narrowing down until the two outer hulls touched gently and both ships graunched slightly. The bombardment had reached its most energetic at this point with some of the opposing crews actually handing items from one to another. A large mail sack changed hands in this way. While boxes of food, fresh and powdered milk, potatoes and frozen meat were swung across all around them. The two hulls gradually peeled away and the transfer of airborne objects slowed down until finally they were waived-off by the Captain of the Kirkliston. "Stop transfer!" He called across the widening gap. During the mad scramble the stores had either been thrown through the doorway of the starboard waist onto the main cargo deck or into large sheets of sailcloth that had been rigged as an open collector. In spite of the few inevitable 'losses' overboard, the men had successfully collected a week's provisions and the mail! When the clutter had been all stowed away and the deck swilled down, the mood onboard lightened up with the prospect of receiving mail from home. Chip spoke on the ships' audio broadcast system. "Well done everybody involved in the transfer. I'll be making an announcement this evening regarding the situation ashore and making reference to our current activities with the convoy. That is all."

The glass continued to fall relentlessly as the wind continued backing through east becoming a cold blowing north easterly. White caps became more apparent as the sea began to heave. None of the ships displayed any lights, maintaining their stations by use of radar and GPS. Only the leading destroyer and the smaller frigates maintained a tactical watch on sensor systems while the skimmer escorts relied on low power navigation radar and GPS on the fringes of the convoy for surface targets, and infra-sonar for sub-surface intruders. At 8pm as the hands changed the watch the convoy of skimmers went off-planes, slowing to eight knots as the sea began to lift above force seven.

Halfway through the evening watch Chip made his promised announcement to the ship's company. *"We are to remain within the port areas and not to go beyond the boundaries of the UPAs. That means for UPAs no one can go beyond city limits. The only exceptions will be those small harbours and fishing ports that have no definable boundaries, and where the communities are spread over a wide area."* He looked at the long paper and summarised key points where he felt it was necessary to make appropriate interpretation. *"In relation to our current circumstances the public are aware of a large naval exercise taking place somewhere around the coast of the UK, but given the general situation I think it is safe to say they will have come to their own conclusions about it. Finally, it seems likely that President Warnock will resign in protest against the current measures taken by the government who have exceeded their powers under the current constitution. I want to remind you that we remain servants of that government until they are replaced by a legally, and democratically elected government. Therefore, although we appear to be in a somewhat grave national crisis, it would be best for everybody concerned not to become embroiled in political discussion since this will only serve to make you and all those around you more anxious about their families back home. With that in mind a welfare bulletin will be posted on the notice boards in the next half-hour. This will give broad details of the current situations in the areas where most of us are currently domiciled. That is all."*

Fred breathed a deep sigh as he walked into the wardroom. "So much for bloody democracy then." He picked up two letters addressed to him. Both sealed, but one had been opened. He read the first letter with the earlier postmark where the seal was still intact. His wife and daughters were fine for now, wrote his eldest child, *'...but since mum has to wait for a travel permit to get to work they would be running short of EDs until the problem got sorted out.'* She went on to say that many people were appearing on the streets looking for temporary jobs since a lot of the businesses had closed. Food was still around, but the queues were getting longer every time they went to the shops. *'Mum says the price of bread has shot up from 250 EDs to 450 in two weeks, and there's very little meat left on the shelves in the shopping centres. Her best friend's dad who worked in London can't get to work and they had sent him a video-mail telling him not to go back since the stock exchange was closing down indefinitely.'* She asked when he was coming home again saying that she and her sister were really scared. He folded the letter and looked up at the deckhead with a deep frown. The second letter had been counter-stamped in red ink with the word 'CENSORED' across the front in bold letters. He picked it up getting more and more angry as he thought about it. It was a letter from his former wife written just two days later. He could see that it had once been a four-page letter now reduced to three. Of the three remaining pages, a thick band of black ink applied by hand had obliterated several parts of the texts.

A knock on the door brought him back to the present. It was Mr Pengelly and the Chief standing together outside the door. "May we have a word with you and the Captain Sir..." He turned away looking in the direction of the mess room at the far end of the flat. "It's about the mail Sir, it seems that someone has been censoring the mail and the lower deck is taking it rather hard."

"As am I Mr Pengelly," Said Fred holding up the second envelope. "Alright, but can one of you send one or two of the other Senior Rates along to help them understand and to defuse what's going on down there. "Already in hand Sir." replied the Chief.

Fred found Chip eating a hurried meal in his day cabin while poring over the charts. He folded them up as Fred came in. "You look as black as hell Fred, what's up?"

"It's this." He dropped the marked envelope slowly onto the chart table.

"Yes I know, of the three letters I have, two from Meg and one from my parents, two have been censored." said Chip with barely concealed disgust. "Well, it looks as though the Junior Rates are having difficulties dealing with it and Mr Pengelly and Chief White have asked to see you with a mind to sort it out before things get a bit rough."

"I see. Is anything being done about it at the moment?"

"They've got two of the POs to pay them a visit, and I've a mind to wake Peter and ask him to work it out with Leyland Pengelly as the up-front welfare team."

"Good idea. It's going to be difficult to keep the lid on this. In the meantime I can only communicate with the Devonshire using light signals during radio silence, but I will inform Captain Page and ask him to contact the Admiralty with a view to finding out why this is happening."

"I think we know why it's happening Sir. It's got to stop, otherwise I can see people just walking with their feet."

"These are strange and difficult times Fred. I dare not think beyond next week when the salaries are due."

"Oh no, I'd forgotten about that." Fred looked a little down in the mouth. "Meg says that all small broadcasters are going off-air rather than be pushed around in the new censorship laws that the government have just brought in. So far though, it seems to be all right for her in Margate. Mum and dad aren't affected so much, but dad says they have put a large pontoon across the entrance to the marina. Now if there's anything that's likely to drive him mad it's a threat to his beloved sailing."

"They didn't mention anything about food shortages did they?" asked Fred feeling a little anxious for his estranged family. "No, but I suppose when they wrote their letters they didn't think of mentioning it."

"Melanie wrote saying that the stock exchange is closing indefinitely and that a lot of people are out of work because they cannot travel to work until they get travel permits, and as a result some companies have already folded."

"Fred, I know it's bad, but I think we need to hold on to our own present circumstances, keeping a vision for our future return to our home port. When we have delivered our crew home safely we will by then know a deal more and hopefully, that will include a good welfare package for each of their families, and that, my old friend includes us."

"You're right. Shall I have them meet with you in the wardroom Sir."

"Yes, thank you Fred, that will do nicely. I'll be along in a couple of minutes." Fred left Chip to return to the charts he had been perusing.

The two POs had done really well and when they revealed they had also received tampered mail the crew became less agitated and settled down to a bit of the usual verbal argy-bargy between sailors. "A Bosun's pipe was heard on the main broadcast speakers. "D'you hear there. Sub-lieutenant Walsh and Mr Pengelly will be holding a welfare briefing in the crew lounge in ten minutes time." A cheer went up from the mess-deck and in the mess-room.

The sea took on a dull oily consistency as dawn broke at 05:35 the following morning. Lookouts on the radar had noticed a large target appearing from east nor' east bearing on them for several hours. The SSR plot revealing that it was a large ferry making its way slowly from Bergen presumably, or Goteborg. "Oh that's the Laxi. "Said the duty cox'n in a thick Geordie accent. She'll be arrivin' in time for the passengers to catch the train to London –if there is one, that is." By a quarter to eight the ferry had passed them by at a range of five miles. "Bloody hell would you look at that!" Said the cox'n again. She making a meal out o' that, look how she's ridin' high out the water." The duty watch looked through the spray to see a dark hump rolling along behind a huge bow wave, noting that the ship was riding rather high in the water for a scheduled ferry. Nobody said anything as the truth dawned on them all, that very few passengers or freight had been picked up in Norway for her voyage to Newcastle.

"Signal from the Devonshire Sir." Said the duty radio op as he knocked on the open door to the chartroom. "Thank you." responded Chip taking the flimsy directly into his hand. The message was brief and to the point. The convoy was dividing as and when they would arrive at a point some thirty miles abeam Berwick. It listed those vessels that were required to make port at Edinburgh, and those that would remain at sea for an un-named destination. He noted that SK939MG was still his pennant number, and that they were among fifteen craft bound for the City of Edinburgh. Chip breathed a sigh of relief. He saw the escort would be reduced to a single frigate, the Darlington and two patrol skimmers, the Cutlass and the Rapier. He felt happier now that he knew where they were going.

At 09:12 the entertainment system went 'technical' and died without a peep coming out of it. Since the Senior Electro-tech had nothing else to do at the time he decided to go and have a look at it. He found it was in perfect working order after running diagnostics. The satellite feed had been pulled from the other end was his only conclusion. He went to the equipment room. Normally off limits to all but him, the radio op and the two senior officers, he did some checking and found only the naval channels were functional. Locking the equipment room behind him he went in search of Mr Pengelly, the 'Don' of all matters in engineering. "Mr Pengelly, Sir."

"Yes, PO what can I do for you?"

"Sorry to disturb you Sir, but I think something's happening ashore."

"Oh?"

"Well it's just that we've lost all feed from the satellite except the normal naval channels and the mil-net circuits."

"Have you checked it out?"

"Yes Sir, I spent the last forty minutes checking and double-checking. All the circuits pass diagnostics. There's no feed from the satellite Sir."

"OK, well done. I'll have a word with the Captain or Lieutenant Newman. Does anyone else know what you've been doing?"

"No Sir, I thought it was best to see you first."

"That was wise of you. Keep it quiet for the time being. Let them think it is a fault on the system and I'll see if there's something we can do in the mean time."

"Right Sir." The PO went off leaving Leyland Pengelly with an immense problem. Both the Captain and the First Lieutenant had been keeping watches in between snatches of sleep here and there. Judging by the way things had gone the previous night, the men were becoming alarmed at what was happening ashore, and it wouldn't be too long before one or two people became frantic with worry and did or said something stupid, or both. He had an idea and rang the Wardroom. "Ah, Mr Pengelly how are you today?" Came Peter Walsh's voice. "I'm feeling better for all that sea air. Better than all that physiotherapy they're threatening me with when I get back. And yourself Sir, how's the head?"

"Not bad at all thank you, in fact the pain has all gone and the muzziness with it, it's just the itching in my scalp where all the stitches are beginning to fret."

"Oh yes, I've had some of that in my time. That's a good sign, glad to hear it. Er, may I ask you for a quick chat Sir. It's just that something has come up and we need to put our heads together on this one?"

"Not at all Mr Pengelly, come on up. The other two are elsewhere at the moment."

"Right you are Sir."

Peter Walsh had not been aware of the loss of the satellite link and tried all the channels available on the wardroom entertainment view screen. "Oh dear, it looks as though he's right. I wonder what has happened?"

"If I didn't know any better Sir it looks like a news blackout."

"I had hoped you weren't going to say that, but that is what it looks like I'm sorry to say."

"You may think this is rather forward of me Sir, and I will understand if you don't agree with me, but if I make the observation that both the Captain and the First-Lieutenant have been keeping watches, watch-and-watch about, I would think they're pretty tired out by now. I was wondering if we could take the pressure off them both by volunteering to come back on light duties Sir. We have some work to do if this is a news blackout, but we could help during the daylight hours here and there on the bridge and down below."

"I can understand what you're saying Mr Pengelly, and I must say that I tend to agree with you. I'll have a word with the Captain now that I'm feeling better, and I will pass it by him."

"Thank you Sir. This brings me to the obvious matter of distracting the crew for the remainder of the run to Edinburgh. May I suggest that in our role as welfare committee team members we think about a 'games' evening perhaps tonight? Followed by a knockout round tomorrow evening, depending on whether or not we get shore leave?"

"Yes, that is a good idea. If I take the afternoon watch to relieve the Captain and that means they can use the dogs more effectively to shift the pattern of their current workload. I think Lieutenant Newman could be persuaded to join me on the wardroom team while The Captain takes the evening watch. Yes, I can see that working if I take the middle and forenoon. Oh well, bang goes the idea of day working, but I'm sure they'll accept a break here and there. OK Let's put a contest together…"

The wind backed a little more by early afternoon, easing in strength reducing the spray that had reduced visibility. At half-past three the swell reduced sufficiently for the skimmers to go on-planes and the convoy raced along at twenty five knots, mindful that they could dance rings around the heavier vessels and leave them standing under normal circumstances. St Abb's Head appeared of the port bow as they charged around the east coast of Scotland in perfect formation changing to a more westerly heading passing Fast Castle Head in quick succession. On the approach to Torness there was a flurry of light signals from the destroyer and the escort vessels. This caught everyone's interest on the bridge. The signal op was called up and everyone waited as he read the flickering array in silence. After a while he started to speak slowly. "It looks as though some of the escorts are leaving us. They followed the movement of one of the frigates and two skimmers as they peeled off and raced ahead angling closer to the coast.

"Hey!" called out one of the lookouts. "What's that over there on that point?" All heads turned to see an array of flickering lights on the coastline just ahead and a huge pall of smoke rising above the orange glow of flames. "Looks like something's on fire." said someone else nearby looking through intensifiers. Drawing closer they could see a large industrial complex served by a long jetty sticking out into the sea. Someone punched up the electronic display chart and zoomed in on Torness. "That's Torness power station. It looks as though something's gone wrong there all right." The PO Seaman handed his intensifier to the cockpit where Chip was taking a turn up in the 'gods'. He put the visor to his eyes watching the shore intently for a few moments, zooming in to get a better view. Sharpening the focus and using the phase correction control he could see that a part of the mighty power station was well ablaze. He could also see a lot of tiny figures surrounding one end of the building and what he thought looked like several army vehicles parked near the jetty. As they passed the closest point of approach he caught his breath in response to what he saw. Rioting civilians fighting soldiers in the grounds surrounding the tall building. He put the intensifier to one side and looked briefly at the instrument panel even though they were on autopilot. As he replaced the viewfinder over his eyes something happened. He blinked and momentarily lost all details as the viewer shut down to protect the sensitive photonic circuitry. Removing them from his eyes he saw a huge explosion unfolding from the roof of the generator hall. "What the hell did that!" Someone shouted. All of a sudden the whole scene disappeared as the lights went out in the power station and all along the coast. Chip saw the three naval vessels closing on the jetty and saw them snap on their searchlights, illuminating the scene in a blinding white light wherever the beams fell, blinding the people attacking what looked to be a defensive barricade. Low-pitched sounders emitted warnings from the consoles on the bridge and in the cockpit as coastal beacons and radio repeaters went off-line. These were cancelled almost immediately by the operators who switched the navigation system to raw GPS functionality. The bridge lookout gave a cheer. "That's sorted them out, look they're running away as soon as they realised the navy were coming!" Chip could see that it appeared to be true, but surmised that from their perspective on the shore a whole fleet had arrived to help out the army.

Torness slipped from view leaving the watch-keepers to their own thoughts as the convoy sped ever closer to Edinburgh. Sweeping around Bass Rock the convoy turned west on the final leg of their remarkable journey. By early evening the destroyer broke radio silence and radioed the convoy with further instructions regarding dispersal. At Inchkeith Island the convoy broke formation in an orderly deconstruction into a long line of ships line astern, off-planes. At eight knots they sailed under the twin bridges up the Forth estuary. The destroyer executing a neat turn to starboard coming alongside the jetty at Rosyth in a crisply performed manoeuvre that brought smiles to everyone's faces. "He's no slouch is that one." observed one of the seamen admiringly.

At Grangemouth the remaining skimmers escorted them to the large basin built on the old salt marsh at Skinflats. Every one groaned inwardly, those that knew the place from previous experience. For the place reeked of rotting vegetation in the vilest fashion, when the tide was out. An army of soldiers and sailors swarmed along the dockside peering across the narrowing gap between the skimmers and the loading bays. As soon as the Privateer had tied up a mixed group of soldiers supervised by naval types swung into action. The sailors swung the huge loading ramps into position while others checked the manifests of each vessel, directing the off-loading of their cargoes in consultation with the cargo deck supervisors. The army ran an endless line of vehicles backwards and forwards across the dockside loading containers, chacons and crates onto waiting goods trains. Since the majority of the commercial skimmers were designed to take two large containers side-by-side a lot of cargo was moved very quickly. The Privateer's own cargo deck was emptied in record time, as was the lower hold. Two of the larger fabrications required special handling equipment, so there was a delay until it was found. By nine o' clock in the evening all cargoes had been salted ashore and the skimmer crews looked forward to a well-earned break. As the work petered out the men ashore took time to talk with the crews while they worked alongside them. There had been rioting in several towns and cities, Edinburgh had experienced several power cuts during the day, angry mobs of people had attacked official buildings, looted shops, even attacking the homes of government employees and politicians during the rioting. It was confirmed that there was a news blackout and many people resorted to alternative means of communicating with family and friends.

At half-past nine, Chip addressed the ship's company and told them the official line communicated to him via the chain of command. There was a deal of comment from the younger members and unrest as people fidgeted with anxiety. *"The good news is that we're going home first thing tomorrow. Unfortunately, no one is allowed leave to proceed ashore for what can only be described as for reasons of personal safety. The army has arranged messing accommodation in shed 15 where you will find showers and toilet facilities. Shed 16, which is just over here where we are, is the canteen, which they inform me has been open for business since eight-thirty, and will remain open until eleven-thirty tonight. Breakfast will be served between six-thirty and nine-thirty in the morning. In addition to a mobile recreation facility the army has set up a communications suite so that you can have the opportunity to call your families. Please remember that there are fifteen hundred people here tonight who have all been at sea for several days. Therefore the time is rationed to ten minutes per person. Finally, if the weather improves tomorrow we could find ourselves back in Portsmouth within forty-eight hours. We leave harbour at oh-seven-hundred tomorrow morning. Thank you for being so patient, and I will keep you informed as and when I find out the answers to the questions raised during the last welfare briefing. Now go and relax, get something to eat and come back refreshed, that will be all."*

The following day Fred took the Privateer into the Firth of Forth through the early morning mist. Retracing their previous course he locked in the autopilot then got up to stand behind the pilot's chair allowing the sub to take his place. "There you are Peter. It's nice and flat at the moment so it looks as though we will have a good start to the day." Peter took the helm and settled back in the driving seat enjoying his break from the monotony of the wardroom. "And don't forget, if for any reason you begin to feel dizzy or unwell get someone to take over right away and go below for a rest."

"Yes Sir, I don't think that will be the case, but I promise to step down the minute I start having problems."

"Good man, have a nice time." With that Fred left his place behind the left-hand seat and turning around slid down the short ladder to the bridge deck. "Cox'n, Mr Walsh has the helm."

Aye, aye Sir."

****

Admiral Driver and his companion stood in the huge shed at Garelochhead staring bleakly at the wreckage before him. The Wellington had been gutted and sliced up like a great whale. The old vessel had been mothballed and anchored in the upper reaches of the Tamar for ten years, a lonely hulk. All that was left of her now were the six decks below the waterline from the datum deck to the keel, where the ship's vitals lay. Her engine rooms and boiler rooms, generators and ancillary equipment. "They look huge even in this dreadful state," observed the Commandant-General quietly. "She was Admiral Balchin's flagship wasn't she?"

"Yes, that's right. He took her through the Straits of Hormuz with all guns blazing at the forts on either side. She took twelve missile hits and lost over a hundred of the crew, but in doing so he took out one of the forts and did so much damage to the other that the Iraqis never repaired it. Got her out into the Indian Ocean, patched her up en-route having retrieved her squadrons intact."

"The Saudis gave him the Order of the Palm didn't they."

"They certainly did. In fact so did both the Trucial States and the Iranians. Dubai was able to break the blockade and the oil flowed again in the free world."

"Where were you, on the Prince Regent wasn't it?"

"Yes." Came the quiet reply. He felt it unnecessary to elaborate on the story. He was the only surviving seaman officer after she had received a direct hit on the bridge. Not pulling back for one second he pressed home the attack shooting down several enemy aircraft and silencing the laser cannon in two shore batteries before running out of ammunition. "You know they missed her flight deck time and time again, you'd think they would have learned the futility of sending pilots on suicide missions. Very few survived, and of those who were lost they are all burning in hell by now."

"Why do you say that Admiral?"

"It's simple, their leaders were grasping for power and hi-jacked religion to brow beat everyone into believing they would all go to paradise if they did as they were told, or their families would be imprisoned, which was often the case. The majority of their pilots had been recruited from fanatical groups trained by the brainwashing clerics peddling their mischief. I judge them by the ancient saying; 'by their works ye shall know them,' and they were evil men dominated by black-hearted devils who would think nothing of murder, rape or genocide just to prove a point and to get more power." They strolled in silence along the slipway to the water's edge and then back again. Four huge bronze propellers sat on gigantic cradles awaiting transport. They looked at the debris scattered around, sniffing the smell of burning paint and molten metal as the giant robots cut through her steel bulkheads like hot knives through butter. "Well, at least the re-cycling won't be a complete waste, certainly not after tomorrow."

"Let's hope so Gerald, it's the last thing I could do before I go."

On the drive back through Garelochhead they took the top road giving them a stunning view of the loch and the steep wooded hill sides covered in pine trees interspersed with small clearings where lay white cottages in neat patches of green. They caught a glimpse of the Garelochhead flyer slowly making its way along the old railway on its way above the highland line to Oban, carrying passengers and freight to the outer fringes.

The hover-jet took off from the small parade ground at Faslane just after three. The weather was clear and offered them a fine view of the surrounding countryside as they flew overland to make the connection with their air transport at half-past four to London. "Lieutenant Smythe?"

"Yes Sir."

"Do you still take the eastern route over the loch down to Balloch?"

"Yes Sir, we still do. It's fantastic scenery and sometimes we do search and rescue practice when the weather is too bad out in the estuary. Is that a route you want me to take?"

"Yes if you wouldn't mind."

"Consider it done Sir." The heli-jet climbed over the ridge to the other side where the land fell away slowly across open moorland. The heather was a beautiful deep purple among the withering grasses turning flaxen in the advancing autumn. "We have the time Sir if you want to take the low level route along glen Douglas?" The pilot turned to face the Admiral from his seat in the front of the aircraft. "I couldn't think of anything better, thank you Lieutenant." The jet banked left and they headed in a northerly direction following the line of the hills where they folded sharply in a twist that guaranteed the Rosneath Peninsular would remain forever attached to the mainland. Where Loch Goil met Loch Long in a spectacular junction of steeply wooded coastal borders, again, thickly populated with pines, riddled with deep gullies providing spectacular courses for the many burns to tumble over them as they made their way to the sea below. Following the eastern shores of Loch Long they overflew the railway and coast road closely running together like ribbons through a mottled pattern of brown, green and deep, deep blue. Banking right into the open maw of Glen Douglas catching a glimpse of the railway wagons once more as the long train trundled along the line, shooting the bridge below the entrance to the great open U-shaped pass through the hills. Opening out into a wide semi-marshy bottom, where sheep had grazed for generations along the streams and up to the wire fencing that ringed the old nuclear silos. The pilot flew at two hundred feet above the terrain crossing the narrow road several times where it turned in a hundred places around the deeply rutted courses of the burns feeding the valley and around the tiny crofter's cottages in miniature oxbows. Coming out of the glen they dropped down to the waters of Loch Lomond at Inverbeg, making the turn south that took the small aircraft over the thickly wooded deciduous forest at Rowardennan.

The pilot concentrated on his instruments for a while, initiating a slow climb to two thousand feet, following a line down the centre of the loch. As they approached Luss two smoke trails lifted from the scrub-covered ground from the south. The flight was a VIP taxi ride and the tactical panel was not in use, rendering most of the weapon sensors off-line. The pilot saw them out of the glare of the sun by the merest chance while simultaneously a collision warning system began howling an imminent collision with other air traffic. He shouted a brief warning to his passengers. "Missile launch, brace, brace!" He threw his aircraft into a desperate rolling climb trying to dodge the missiles coming at them. The first missile shot by, but the second caught the starboard wing exploding as it did so. The plasma-jet began shuddering into a starboard turn, having lost all lift on that side. The pilot was screaming something as the starboard plasma drive safeties began to automatically shutdown all systems to the shattered engine. There was a gaping hole in the side of the aircraft where Gerald Royce had been seated chatting idly only moments before. The Admiral sat rigidly in his seat holding his legs that had been peppered with shrapnel, oozing blood. "Admiral! Admiral Driver Sir, are you all right!" called the pilot desperately. The Admiral turned his head slowly around to look at the pilot. Though he could not see properly through the blood pouring down the front of his face he nodded as best he could. "There's no way out of this except to hope that she rolls and comes out flat on her belly as she hits the water!" shouted the pilot. "You'll have to make it out through that hole on the other side of you Admiral. Don't wait for me." The Admiral managed to wipe away the blood from his eyes on the sleeve of his overcoat and saw the pilot flying with one hand on the controls, his right arm hanging limply at his side. He knew it was a futile gesture. He saw the water of the loch through the shattered canopy seconds before they impacted on the water. Using the momentum of his stricken craft rolling in a spiral dive almost like a slender sycamore seedling tumbling in a cross-wind he flipped it over achieving a final flourish as the hull of the aircraft landed flat on the surface in a huge bone-jarring splash.

For a second the Admiral was dazed and his hand was knocked away from the buckle of his harness. Fumbling for the release he fought to free himself as the cold waters rose swiftly from his ankles to his knees, then his waist, rapidly up to his chest. At last he was free, and using the buoyancy the water gave him he headed for the hole in the submerged cabin that was now becoming a death trap. He took one last look at the pilot whose single arm was flailing around in the cockpit, and then he was gone as the nose sank. Screwy Driver used to be a good swimmer, but with a heavy overcoat and burning pains shooting up his legs and thighs he took his time getting through the thin hull. The cold water threatened to take his breath away at each effort to get through the hole. Finally he was through and at the last second the end of his trousers got caught on a jagged piece of metal. He looked up and saw that he was just beneath the surface. Kicking his legs and grinding his teeth he tore himself free. Small air pockets in the cabin had slowed the descent of the aircraft and he knew he didn't have long. Shedding his overcoat he reached for the surface dragging in huge gulps of air on breaking through. Now clinging to the top of the aircraft's skin he began to make his way to the cockpit without any thoughts of his own safety. Through the broken canopy he could see the pilot had managed to grab his oxygen mask, but was failing to move with any great speed. His free hand moving woodenly in the freezing waters. He made eye contact with the young man and knew he was staring death in the face. Slipping off his shoes, Screwy hammered the emergency release of the splintered canopy with the heel of one of them while the other shoe drifted slowly out of sight in the peat-coloured waters of the loch. He was losing any advantage he had as the dying bird began its final slow descent into the darkness below. The pilot looked up at him and at last made a sign, pointing to his left side. The Admiral suddenly realising what the doomed pilot was trying to say. While the cold water began to numb the pain and cause his hands to ache the Admiral swam around the nose of the aircraft until he reached to the left-hand side of the pilot. He could dimly see an emergency release handle and reached down with his tired fingers. The canopy floated off easily under the pressure of the pilot's good hand pushing it from beneath, the final vestiges of air taking flight in a string of bubbles, losing subtle buoyancy. Admiral Driver moved it slowly away by swimming back from the open cockpit. To his horror the nose was now dipping in the beginning of its final dive. Calmly taking a deep breath he dived down and holding onto the rim of the cockpit he reached down, tucking the pilot's lifeless arm into the man's body, pulling it clear of any obstructions. He tapped the pilot's bone-dome three times and pushing himself away from the cockpit as best he could, pulled down the G-Handle. The ejector seat brushing his hand away as it took off for the surface throwing the pilot out of his drowning bird. The Admiral felt he was in a time warp as events slowly unfurled around him. The seat took off at an angle of twenty degrees firing the pilot away from the site of the crash, but out of reach of the Admiral who himself was a long way from the safety of the shoreline.

6. THE MARK OF A TYRANT

The news blackout lasted twenty-four hours. During the morning the Senior Electro-tech, working with the radio op re-programmed the signal processor and switched to the 'free to air' down link systems provided by the 'EuroStar' lunar satellite chain. Leyland Pengelly translated the Dutch/Flemish broadcasts from time to time during the day and there was a general scramble for the lounge when other broadcasts were transmitted in English. As the Privateer made her way around Flamborough Head they had also captured Canadian broadcast channels. The Admiralty transmitted regular bulletins with its normal traffic, but anyone could see from the passive use of verbs that someone was using a lot of words, saying nothing. At a quarter to eleven the hook-up with the UK system was re-established and people crowded into the lounge and mess-room on a minute-by-minute monitoring of the news from home. The usual broadcasters had gone; replaced with strangers who read from heavily censored bulletins with deadpan faces. Lunch time came and went, melded into supper almost seamlessly except for the occasional changing of the watch-keepers as they came and went in synchronism to the inexorable movement of time.

During the afternoon there was a brief announcement that the Chief of Defence Admiral Driver and Commandant-General Gerald Royce had been killed in an aircraft accident on a Scottish hillside close to the submarine base of Faslane. No announcement had been made commenting on the resignations of the Chiefs of Staff earlier in the day. "I guess this is decision time wouldn't you say?" said Fred sitting with his back to the wardroom viewer. They were discussing whether or not to call into their home port of Margate for the night before pressing on to Portsmouth. "Well, since Leyland is using the time to renew his watch keeping ticket up in the cockpit, I can only say that now that I've had time to think about it we should press on to Portsmouth without delay." He held up his hand slowly warding off the rising objection in Fred's countenance. "Yes, I know Fred, but the crew come first since over forty percent come from the Hampshire area, either in married quarters or roundabout in their own homes."

"But Chip, it would only be for a couple of hours to get a change of kit from their digs, while we use the harbour master's phone to…"

"I know, I know, but it is imperative that we have a stable crew for the next trip out. God, their families must be feeling the pinch, and there's no telling that if we put into Margate the local military authorities might want to commandeer us to sort out some local problems. We go back to Portsmouth and I'll see if we can't do a turn-around tomorrow with a skeleton crew to reposition back to Margate. Now I can't do better than that."

"No, I suppose not. OK, I'll get the signal op to start working the welfare schedule at 18:00 so they can contact their families. It was just a thought."

"Oh, I agree with you, and ordinarily I wouldn't hesitate to break the journey, but these are difficult circumstances if not turning into downright dangerous times."

"I'll take over the first dog from Leyland, that gives us a changeover from the morning to the forenoon tomorrow."

"Thanks Fred."

Air-Vice Marshall Crimmond and Major-General Haslet formally announced their intention to resign with immediate effect, feeling the need to vacate their respective headquarters buildings and official residences post-haste. The long expected order to close the harbours and airfields barely twenty-four hours old. "Gone! What do you mean gone?" The Prime Minister fulminated. "Well and truly flown the coup Prime Minister."

"Well, get after them! Go round to their homes and bring them to me!"

"We've tried that Prime Minister, it seems as though they had this planned well in advance and moved out some eight weeks ago."

"What are you saying, that they have disappeared!" roared the Prime Minister jabbing an accusing finger at the defence minister. "It would appear so Prime Minister…"

"Well thank God we got that treacherous swine Admiral Driver and his side-kick Marine. That's at least two problems out of our way. Give me the names of the top brass, because nothing will get done properly unless I do it myself. I'm looking for anyone we can work with, if we have something on them, then that will be better. The more malleable they come the better we can control things and force our way into a more stable position. In the mean time take what resources you need and restore law and order!"

"Yes Prime Minister. I have a shortlist being put together as we speak, that I will give to you in the cabinet meeting this afternoon."

"Very well, now get out of my sight!" hissed the Prime Minister menacingly.

With no President, the chiefs of defence gone and open rioting in the streets he was lurching towards the unthinkable. Without a mandate to rule except the slimmest of toeholds of a majority in the Commons, and implacable opposition in the Senate he can only do one thing. Suspend Parliament and the constitution. A ministerial secretary knocked discreetly and entered the Prime Minister's office holding loose papers in his hand. "Prime Minister."

"Yes, what is it Harvey?" Came the testy enquiry.

"President Muller-Weiss is on line three Sir. He's not very happy and will not be put off any longer… er, his words Sir, not mine."

The Prime Minister ground his teeth and reached for the blue phone on his desk. This is what he had been dreading.

"President Muller-Weiss, how are you today?" The voice was cloying like a surfeit of honey cakes in the back of the throat.

"My health Prime Minister is irrelevant. I am not pleased to hear about the fact that you have extended your martial law to include a complete closure of your borders and a communications blackout for twenty-four hours. Have you any idea what you are doing? Tell me what do you hope to gain by power cuts and curfews when your people are running out of food and water supplies?" The President's stern voice began to rattle the Prime Minister.

"Well, we must use normal methods of controlling the mob to restore law and order President Muller-Weiss. You know that as well as I do. Closing our airports and harbours is just ensuring that the troublemakers don't get away or indeed get support from underground movements from the mainland."

"Very Plausible, but I don't believe it. You have no President, your members are leaving the Parliament buildings in Brussels as we speak and your

Senate is opposed to what you are doing. Can't you see that you've lost the country Prime Minister?"

"I know it looks bad, but until we can isolate the agitators and restore essential utilities we have to impose these restrictions on the people. Even now the military are patrolling our main routes up and down the country, and in a few days the travel restrictions will be lifted as the permits are released. I can predict that in the next seven to ten days Mr President, we will have started things moving back to normal."

"No, that's not possible Prime Minister. You will reopen your borders or you leave me no alternative but to send in police and army units from the mainland to assist you." The Prime Minister flushed deep purple as he fought to contain his rage, barely holding on to the deep fury he felt towards his political antagonist. "No, no, there's no need for that Mr President, You will inflame an already difficult situation. I assure you…"

"You have only until mid day tomorrow. If you do not stop this situation and reopen your borders I will order the standing forces to assist you."

The phone went dead as the European President broke the comms link leaving the Prime Minister hanging in mid-sentence. Warren Atkinson stared at the instrument with undiluted venom and threw it back onto its cradle.

President Muller-Weiss turned to his deputy Holga Augsburger and nodding slightly as he spoke. "It seems as though we will have our little lion by the throat tomorrow Holga. With only a few of their representatives here they have no voice. Please arrange for the army and police to be on forty-eight hour alert, and cancel all leave. I need Ute, can you wait a moment. "He pressed a button on his touch screen and they waited for a few seconds until Ute, the President's private secretary entered the office. "Ute, please ask the Information Minister to call me as soon as possible, and send a message to the head of the Internal Affairs Ministry to call an emergency session of the defence committee for four o' clock this afternoon." Thank you Ute, that will be all for now. Oh, cancel my lunch appointment with the Greek ambassador, he doesn't have much to talk about these days and can wait a few days more."

"Will you be late home this evening Sir? It's just that your wife called to remind you about visiting friends later this evening?"

"No, please call my wife and let her know I will be tied up for a while, but to start without me. I'll be along later." He waited until Ute left the room. "I take it you want an update from the De Agostini Group Sir?"

"Yes I do, please arrange it for two o' clock Holga, thank you. If not make it a working lunch and have them convene say, an hour earlier."

The De Agostini Group was a shadowy name known to only a very select few. The Presidents of the European Union were not necessarily privy to the knowledge of its existence unless they had been selected to join the inner circle. Originally formed by the French, Italian and German leaders to foster closer working intelligence and covert operations designed to maintain commercial and military knowledge on each of the member states. Except for one fact, the other states knew nothing about it. After thirty-five years, the Italian presidency had been terminated prematurely by a Russian Mafia assassination squad and the knowledge had died with the Italian leader, cutting off the Italian connection. Much to the relief of the French and German arms of the organisation because it was long suspected that the Italian underworld had penetrated the DAG organisation.

Otto Sternbaum and his French intelligence counterpart Thiery Saint-Just met in a quiet office above the Königs Café. Thiery had parked his car down a side road off Römerstrasse while Otto took a tram from Horton's towards Leimen, getting off halfway along the wide avenue at the stop adjacent to the little café. The warm smell of cooking mixed with the fragrance of perfume and beer greeted Otto when he pushed the plate glass doors open to step inside. Barbel the waitress gave him a smile waving him through while she served customers at the little glass counter that was, as ever; stuffed full of pastries and torte for which the little café was well known. He made his way through the café noticing the empty seats around the Stamtisch. Striding up the dark stairway two steps at a time he strode quietly along the landing to the comfortable room both he and Thiery used every now and then to carry out the work of briefing and debriefing intelligence matters. No one knew of course, and it was with a sense of amusement that they had been doing this right under the noses of the American intelligence services for years. "Otto, there you are, come on in. I've set up the table and we can start whenever you're ready." Thiery had set up a chess set on a small table while on the larger dining table there stood a large jug of coffee and a freezing bottle of Himbeergeist wrapped in a tea towel. "Nice to see you again my friend, I see we're set for an interesting afternoon." They chatted amiably for a while until the café owner appeared, joining in the pleasantries. She got up to leave and turned in the doorway to speak. "You're just like my poor husband. When he was alive he used to sit in Central Park playing chess with all his old cronies. Still he used to enjoy it in the summer..." her voice trailing off as she left the room and padded down the corridor towards the stairs.

"Orders have been given to put police units on alert for a crossing tomorrow afternoon Otto. We have your Jaeger-Gruppe to thank for doing such a good job in London and Manchester..."

"Not at all Thiery your Marseilles Club has done a fine job in the south and north west. By the way, that was a good idea to take out that power station. I think it tipped the balance in our favour."

"Thank you Otto, it was a good idea by the local group commander who saw it as a golden opportunity. I don't think any of us realised just how much it affected the British government. They thought all their power houses were being attacked and shutdown the railways completely paralysing the last fast means of travel in the country."

"Oh, that was good and Falco is pleased with what we have achieved." Otto poured them both a small glass of the schnapps as Thiery spoke about the successful missions across the UK. "But what of the Americans Thiery? Did any of our sleepers see them at all?"

"Oh yes, but I think your Besonder Intelligence Gruppe have them under constant surveillance."

"Yes, they were pretty active by all accounts penetrating the Britz party and supplying them with money to buy arms and explosives from the US, as also the Irish Republic."

"Ah, yes the US Varmints. Always doing the same things, they never learn."

"We have a new set of orders Thiery, telling us to step up the pressure on the urban commando brigade from this evening for the next sixteen hours."

"Yes, it makes interesting reading. I think they are really going to do it, they are going to send in the army to support the police, my friend, we're going to invade England, what do you think of that?"

"I hope Falco can get our teams out before it starts to fall apart."

They removed several documents stuffed in coat linings and looked at the statistics of a nation's political downfall. Agreeing upon the final details in a thirty-year plan to finally humiliate the British and bring them to heel. "And so the American groups will be compromised by the Alsace teams in London, Aldershot, Edinburgh, Catterick, Portsmouth, Plymouth and on the Welsh borders and the Welsh peninsular."

"Oh yes, that will put the army and the navy in complete confusion. Since they are the only surface forces of any threat value it makes sense to take out their personnel commands and leave behind traces implicating the Varmints."

"I have contacted the cell leaders of our Alsace teams in Scotland and they will be on the barricades in Glasgow and Edinburgh monitoring the Americans. We have a primary group directive from Falco that we must take out the naval base at Rosyth, so I am moving in Alsace three and four under Stahl and Larribon. They make a good team, especially with Larribon's background at the naval academy."

"A good choice Otto. Two eight-man teams should be able to penetrate the perimeter fences at Rosyth and in Edinburgh. Why do you suppose they haven't targeted the submarine base on the west coast?"

"It's not a threat Thiery, look at it for what it is. Three nuclear submarines that they can't afford to use, and a fourth at sea somewhere. None of them can use their nuclear warheads because Europe is too close. There are not enough men over there to get in the way; they will be too busy watching their own fences. So by the time their marines have been deployed they wont have anyone left to make tea, let alone fight a war. No, they are insignificant by comparison."

"They are virtually leaderless now my friend, so it seems we will just walk in and take their country from them." Otto smirked as he relished the thought. "And the Americans can do nothing about it. They have too many problems of their own and the international outcry will ensure they will do nothing directly." Sniggered Thiery.

There was a momentary pause while the Frenchman became somewhat thoughtful. "What is it?" asked Otto, looking across the room towards the door. "Nothing my friend, it's just that we must be careful not to ignore British intelligence, that's all."

"Why do you say that at a time like this Thiery? Is everything in order?"

"Yes, of course it's all in order, but it's MI5, they never miss a trick, and it's all gone dreadfully quiet with them."

"What do you mean exactly?"

"It's just something that I remembered from my days at the training school when we used to do profiling and analysis on foreign intelligence services..."

"You mean those drawn out affairs looking at the strengths and weaknesses of their tactical officers, I remember, that was under Oberst Dortmunder and that one armed Major Keitel; yes?"

"You have a good memory Otto, as ever. Yes, it was Keitel who got us to do the analysis on the second Iraqi war... yes, now you remember."

"Didn't he used to say that were it not for the MI5 dictum of treating ninety-five percent of the verbiage emanating out of the US intelligence sources like something out of Disney world, that the Americans would have covered the world with their own crap by now?" Both men smiled at each other remembering the last days of innocence as young recruits into the shadowy world of 'special operations'. "We used to laugh at that a lot, Otto and of course he was right. But it was hardly a secret then, either, in those days that the only reason why the British went into that war with the Americans was because the Americans threatened to 'pull the plug' as they say on the Trident missile treaty, and get the oil for themselves."

"What's your point Thiery?" asked Otto looking puzzled. "It's just this, that where we can from time to time predict the British to act in a particular way to a particular problem, and the Americans who believe their own fantasies to go out shooting at anything that moves –in any given situation. The British are doing something unusual, and that bothers me."

****

Privateer docked at 20:56 tying up alongside the wall at the Naval Harbour Master steps in Portsmouth harbour. A large coach was parked on the jetty surrounded by Naval Patrolmen. Powerful overhead lights glaring from above brought home a stark reality that fell heavily upon the entire crew. As soon as the gangway went across a Lieutenant Commander and a Warrant Officer came aboard and were immediately closeted with Chip and Fred. A while later a dark saloon arrived through the great archway drawing to a halt between the bus and the gangway. A Captain and a Commander emerging from it carrying small brown document cases headed purposefully straight up the gangway. Peter Walsh was immediately arrested by the Lieutenant Commander and put under open arrest without charge. Leyland Pengelly was relieved by the new arrival and escorted to the wardroom where he too was arrested and charged with attempted murder. The increasingly suspicious crew became ever more concerned to the extent that the duty mess-man could be seen leaning towards the corner of a bulkhead from where raised voices could be heard in the right conditions. Now that the engines were silent he could hear most of the conversation and relayed what was happening to the crewmen.

"Clear off from there. Come on, be about your own business and clear off!" bellowed the Chief Petty Officer. "Able Seaman Rogers come with me, in the galley now!" He gave the errant seaman a dressing down behind the closed galley door, and when he could see the man was in great difficulty asked him outright to tell what was wrong. "Nah, you've got it wrong. They can't do that, surely. On what grounds?" A hard knocking on the galley door disturbed them. "Chief! Chief!" called someone from outside. The door opened and the PO Electro-tech stuck his head around. "Chief, there's a Captain and a Surgeon Commander waiting to urgently see the skipper and there's all kinds of shouting going on in the wardroom. The Chief turned around and looked at the PO and then back at the mess-man. "OK, I believe you, now stay here and keep your mouth shut or you'll get us all in jam."

"Yes Chief."

"Petty Officer, get the first two available men and a leading rate. Meet me outside the Wardroom door on the double!"

"Yes Chief!" The Chief turned to leave saying. "I can't use you lad because you are already implicated. Lock the door and don't come out until I or one of the POs tells you to, understand?"

"Yes Chief."

The senior officers standing on the brow became alarmed when the Chief informed them of a difficulty in the Wardroom. The Chief politely asked the Captain if he wouldn't mind seeing if everything was all right and put himself and his small squad of sailors at the Captain's disposal. "Chief I think we'll take a look, particularly as two of your patients are apparently in the thick of it." The Chief escorted the two men to the wardroom and waited patiently at a discreet distance from the closed door. As soon as the Captain entered the row subsided into an uneasy silence. Shortly afterwards Leyland Pengelly sidled out of the door in the company of the new Warrant Officer, and together they walked down the flat towards the ladder at the far end leading towards the accommodation deck. The Chief had detailed four seamen to watch the gangway and if necessary release it over the side on his order. Waiting patiently in the bridge they watched and waited in the darkness. The PO Electro-tech and the signal op beavered away going over all recent signal traffic trying to get a clue as to what was happening. Sub Walsh emerged a quarter of an hour later in the company of the Surgeon Commander who helped the Sub collect his case from his cabin and escorted him slowly off the skimmer into the waiting car. He left Peter there returning onboard to collect Leyland Pengelly. One of the junior techs volunteered his services and all three walked across the brow towards the waiting vehicle. As soon as the surgeon had got into the front seat the driver drove the car away at a brisk rate and out of sight. The crew had been ordered off the upper deck and out of the bridge for some time and apart from the quartermasters and the small knot of seamen on standby no one else knew what was happening.

An hour later the Lieutenant Commander came out of the wardroom asking for the heads. The sounds of a lively discussion emanating through the opening until he shut the door. "Why are my officers arrested and my crew to be taken away under escort to DQs?" asked Chip for the fifth time. The Captain looked at him bleakly saying he did not know. What he did say by way of a small elaboration was that the order came from beyond naval channels and that meant it had nothing to do with the incident in Rotterdam. "You're quite sure Sir that Sub-lieutenant Walsh is no longer under open arrest, and that Mr Pengelly is also free to come and go without the threat of discipline hanging over him?" Chip's colour was bright red with anger. Fred remained silent, staring at the blank view screen at the other end of the wardroom. "I assure you that the order to arrest both men came from a misunderstanding with the Dutch government. The man who died did so after being interviewed by the police, his injuries and death were inconsistent with the facts surrounding your meeting them on the docks. If you take my advice Commander, just try to forget this happened. The man was obviously put up to taking part in the attack and I suspect he was removed before he could talk to the Dutch police."

"So my officers are arrested one minute and then set free within the space of half an hour without any apology, and now my crew is about to go ashore under escort. What of them?"

"That is a precaution for their own safety, and as I have said the order has come down from outside the naval authorities."

"Has any charge been lodged against this ship and its crew Captain Hamilton?"

"None that I am aware of."

"Are they going to be charged with any offence at all."

"Commander, I do not know. All I can tell you is that every vessel that has returned to harbour in the last twelve hours has had a welcoming committee that took the crews away into barracks under arrest or straight into DQs. The only difference here is that your trip to Rotterdam came to light requiring me to come down to you to smartly undo what was plainly an injustice."

"I thank you for that Sir, but are you telling me that all ships crews are being kept ashore under lock and key?"

"Yes."

"But why Sir?"

"Haven't you heard?"

Heard what Sir?"

"The Defence Chiefs resigned this morning and the Chief of Staff was killed by a rocket attack on his heli-jet as it left Faslane. Both he and Commandant-General Royce are missing presumed dead. The only survivor is the pilot."

"But surely, incarcerating all ships crews is an act of folly. How can this be connected with us, we were all at sea, and we have a major welfare crisis on our hands Sir. We've been at sea or away for almost a fortnight and the crew are desperate to see their families given the current circumstances."

"All I can say is that where possible naval and military families are being brought into the protection of the port areas and military garrisons."

"It looks bad doesn't it Sir." Fred piped up. Just how bad is it?" The Lieutenant Commander entered the wardroom under the suspicious eyes of both Fred and Chip. "First of all Lieutenant commander Tyndale is acting under orders. I hope that you will not bear him any ill will. Secondly, we appear to have a government that is struggling to govern the country without a President, and a Senate that is refusing to work with a government that has no mandate from the people. In effect we have no political or military leadership in this country and a constitutional crisis ranking as high as that which was foisted upon us to get rid of the crown."

"But that means anyone could sail in and attack us with our trousers down."

"We are not into politics Lieutenant Newman, and the whys and wherefores of how we got into this mess are none of our concern."

"Does this mean that every crew and service unit are being held unjustly against their will because of a paranoid government in Whitehall that is about to go under."

"Yes, I suppose you could say that, but I must caution you to be very careful about what you say and where you say it Commander. Several people have already been outspoken about their views and have found themselves either under house arrest or in prison on charges of terrorism."

"But what of my crew Sir?"

"My hands are tied. All captains and their crews are to be escorted ashore to be confined for an unspecified period."

"May I have a private word with my First-Lieutenant Sir."

"If you wish. Please don't take too long, you will only delay the inevitable."

They slipped out of the wardroom and into his day cabin, passing the Chief on the bridge. "Look Fred there's only one hope, it's going to be the Madrid Convention on the Military Contract Rules or we're all confined to barracks while the crew are driven off to prison."

"I see what you're getting at, but hang on a second. This is a merchant vessel under contract to the navy and we own it."

"That's right, and the crew are technically volunteers serving on a merchantman. Now they are subject to the Madrid Convention, and correct me if I'm wrong, but doesn't Article 27 allow for a crew to walk out, effectively demobilising if for any reason the military authorities break their contracts with them?"

"I think you're right Chip. Yes, I'm sure, we're reserve officers and therefore we have the right to resign with immediate effect under the articles of the convention. This is our property, and all the crew have to do is –as individuals, that is- issue a writ or write a letter to the senior officer indicating that the 'service' has broken its contract with them and they are free to leave the service immediately, without let or hindrance."

"Wait a second, what about war?"

"No we're in the clear we are not at war with anyone and not under attack, as such."

"Right get to it immediately, Hold on. Chief!"

"Yes Sir. Is everything all right Sir?"

"Yes and no Chief. I want you to go with Lieutenant Newman to the Senior Ratings mess where he will inform you what is happening. What he needs to know Chief is the response of the Senior Ratings onboard. Then accompany him to the Junior Rates mess and repeat the same after Lieutenant Newman has spoken with them. All I can say to you right now Chief is that we stand between you and that coach, and I do not want any of you to get on that coach. Do you understand?"

"I think so Sir. I have to inform you that I have a small detail ready to cut the gangway free if that is what you require."

"That was very perceptive of you Chief."

"I think I know what's coming Sir, and I'd rather be free to find my own way home than be locked up for something I didn't do."

"Good man, now go quickly while I keep them talking. You have about ten to fifteen minutes."

The Senior Rates were cautious and concerned. Some were on pensionable engagements, others were on short-term engagements, but all wanted to get home to their families. There was a loud rumble of indignation as Fred explained the situation to them and the solution. To a man they were behind the Captain, and were prepared to take their duty stations at a moment's notice. The Junior Rates response came as a livid uproar, but their Leading hands cut across the din with stentorian shouts for silence. When it became clear to them that the First lieutenant and the Captain were going to spring them from the waiting jaws of prison they jumped at the chance to make a break for it.

Within twenty-two minutes Fred returned to the wardroom with his hands full of hastily issued letters of self-dismissal by breach of contract on the part of the naval authorities.

On the top Fred had placed his own resignation covered by a similar document requiring a flourish of the pen from Chip to complete the deed.

"Ah, here he is now Sir. Come in Fred, we were just talking about the Privateer and how we both ended up paying more for her by bidding against each other."

"That's right Sir. I had a nice gratuity and some inheritance, but along came this fellow and he outbid me. Then he had the audacity to offer me a share in the business. So here we are."

"Thanks Fred are those what I have been looking for. Oh yes, is that one on the top all that remains to be signed by me?"

"Yes Sir." Chip took a pen from his jacket pocket and signed his letter of resignation right under the nose of Captain Hamilton. What will happen to my vessel Sir, since the ownership is not in dispute?"

"I have no idea exactly, but I suspect she will stay here indefinitely until you are able to take up your command again or she will be commandeered."

"I see." The Captain did not fail to notice the icy rejoinder he received and nodded sympathetically. "It is trite I know Commander, but I have every sympathy with you." The arresting officer nodded as he spoke. "I am inclined to agree with Captain Hamilton, and if there is anything I can do to help you I would do it, but I can't see a way that makes it possible."

"Maybe there is." said Chip firmly. "I must address the crew and let them know what is about to happen to them. May I suggest that for our best interests and for your safety you go ashore now, and I will talk to my crew? When I've finished I will take appropriate action."

"Thank you Commander, I will see to it that the patrolmen remain ashore for the time being."

"Thank you Sir." They shook hands rather belatedly, the Lieutenant commander looking sadly at the task he was shortly to complete.

Just as the Captain stepped on the brow Chip handed him a plastic folder with all the letters inside it. "Please convey my respects to the C-in-C and to Captain Dunham. Please inform them that our contract has come to an end."

"The Captain looked a little puzzled, then smiled, nodded perceptibly and saluting walked across the brow of the ship onto the jetty. Chip and Fred retired to the bridge and waited patiently for a couple of minutes. The Chief appeared at the head of the flat that backed onto the bridge, calling softly, "Ready when you are Sir."

"When I give the order to breakaway Chief, have the men move like greased lightning."

"A pleasure Sir." Chip smiled a thin smile through pursed lips, his heart beating like a trip hammer. "Can you make the cockpit and get her into a sharp turn away from the wall Fred?"

"You watch me. Nothing will give me greater pleasure than to show this lot how to handle a skimmer properly."

"Keep your head down I can see stun guns and laser rifles."

"No problem" Chip slowly picked up the microphone and made the general call over the ship's main broadcast system. "Do you hear there! This is the Captain speaking." The two officers ashore looked at each other while opening the doors to their vehicle. "Owing to the deteriorating situation ashore the authorities have decided to impound this vessel and remove the crew into open arrest ashore. I know this news will upset you and as the senior officer present I accept your resignations under Article 27 of the Madrid Convention and give the order to breakaway! I repeat Breakaway!"

The small knot of seamen gathered at the brow drew out their knives and slashed the ropes holding the gangway in place, sliding them off, toppling them into the water. At the same time there was a loud clatter from the bows and on the quarterdeck as hatches flew open spewing men with knives and axes. The quartermasters and their mates skidded into the bridge slamming the screen door behind them. A laser round crackled faintly on the other side. Down aft the job was made easier by the nature of the skimmer's construction that shielded the men wielding knives and axes as they hacked away at the stern ropes. Fred hit the engine igniters and did the unthinkable in official naval circles by simultaneously releasing plasma and rotating the engine on the starter. Ordinarily this would set a huge torque on the engine drive shafts causing untold damage, but a seasoned user with a sound knowledge of the technology could sometimes get away with it. The Chief's voice came through on the console loudspeaker giving Fred the precise timing when to hit the plasma injector buttons. The result was an almost explosive surge of energy with flames shooting out of the exhausts for over a hundred metres. The roar was deafening momentarily stunning the patrolmen ashore into frozen statues. Fred allowed the Privateer to move forwards in the water to gain momentum, then swung the control column hard over, executing a tight turn away from the wall. There was a crackle as someone fired a laser rifle and a seaman fell heavily on to the deck in the bow. His accomplice dived for cover behind the screen, began dragging his injured shipmate across the deck out of sight of the armed patrolmen shore side, pushing him into a hatch before following him down. At ninety degrees to the dockside the Privateer presented a small target area to the dwindling fusillade coming from the quayside. Chip juggled the sensor arrays bringing the small tactical panel on line. Almost three quarters of the way across the harbour Fred swung the control column again bringing her bows up in to alignment with the harbour entrance. "Go for it Fred, now!" Shouted Chip as he concentrated on the screen. The skimmer jumped forwards and before they passed the Gosport jetties she rose up on the planes like a proud swan on its take off run. Radar showed a small object in the water at the harbour mouth, making its way slowly across the gap between the opposite shores. "Small boat in the water crossing from right to left, fine on the starboard bow!" The Electro-tech had the bridge watch; called out. "I've got something on thermo Sir, looks like a rope or something across the harbour!" Fred cast an anxious look across as Chip pressed the controls on his tactical display and zooming in. His heart beating fast, waiting for the worst. "Looks like they've put something across the harbour entrance, a rope or chains, I can't tell at this distance Fred. Keep her going a little bit longer."

"Skimmers can't jump booms Chip. Patrol boats can, but we can't!"

"I know, I know, just keep her going and be prepared to take her off-planes on my order." Chip grabbed at the cockpit intensifiers and jammed them against his eyes. He switched to thermal mode and adjusted the phase correction control. "Damn! Looks as though they've got a boat going across it right now. "Bridge, secure all underwater sensors and sound the alarm, brace! Brace! The old submarine base flashed past. "Decision time Chip. Do we or don't we?" There was a long pause. "I don't believe it!"

"What the hell is that!" shouted Fred. "They've blown it Sir! They've cut the boom!"

"Full speed ahead Fred and don't look back!" Chip snatched the intensifiers away from his eyes as the safeties cut in protecting the sensitive photonics and his eyes from serious glare.

The small boat was making its way agonisingly slowly back across the harbour mouth, inch by inch. The crew had jammed themselves into every tight little nook and cranny in preparedness for a collision. Chip reached up grabbing a rope hanging from the deckhead, giving it four sharp tugs. The Privateer's twin sirens gave out four long, shrill warning blasts that would scare the living daylights out of a banshee. As every seaman worth his salt knows, the warning for 'get out of my way for sure as hell I can't get out of yours' is a no compromise final warning to other traffic. The little boat suddenly came to life as the men aboard it started a small power unit. Showing no lights, up on the planes and with blaring sirens the skimmer presented a very wide, squat silhouette to the people in the boat. Scared as hell they ducked as the Privateer shot past them like a bat out of hell with her siren blasts echoing around the harbour. Take her to the right Fred, we'll go up the Solent and out along to Portland." Chip looked down catching a glimpse of the small boat swamped by their passing wake. They 're waving at us Fred. I thought that at least they would have been shaking their fists. "Plasma cannon on the port side Sir!" A bright blue necklace of lights swung out across the water from the old fortress. "Incoming! Incoming, port side three seconds to impact!" shouted the Electro-tech hitting the counter-measures panel sharply. Four small canisters were launched towards the trail of light within a tenth of a second, exploding in the air just ahead of the plasma bolts. The first three dissipated in a pyrotechnic display of pure energy. Behind them the remaining rounds began to penetrate the counter-measure screen. The fourth bolt of plasma spun off landing in the water short of the mark. The fifth kissed the forepeak with a glancing blow, exploding as it fell off. They opened their eyes as the last round shot across the open bows and struck the superstructure between the bridge and the cockpit. The energy bolt shattered two windows in the bridge and bounced up under the cockpit deck where it exploded with a hefty discharge. Fred screamed and sagged forward in his seat where his safety harness held him firmly against falling out of the front of the shattered cockpit windscreen. Chip ducked, and fared a little better, but like Fred was blinded and suffering from discharge burns to his legs. Chip flipped the master control switch and took over as the pilot. "Petty Officer Graham get someone up here and give Lieutenant Newman a hand down." Two of the seamen lifted the limp form of Fred gently down the ladder and onto the Bridge deck. "Medic to the bridge, first-aider to the bridge at the rush!" A couple of minutes later the ship's scribe rushed on to the bridge carrying an enormous first aid kit, accompanied by two large crew members carrying a stretcher.

More laser cannon shot across the face of the dark waters towards them. Again counter-measures went up in the face of the incoming rounds. Again the call for incoming rounds and a time of five seconds was given. Everyone, bracing themselves for the inevitable impact and the scorching heat of multiple discharges. The Chief pushed past the men on the bridge and frantically unlocked the flare box on the bridge wing storage cabinet. While the first round missed its target due to the counter-measures package he grabbed the old style pistol and loaded a magnesium flare cartridge into the breach. Rushing out of the screen door onto the port deck he counted the seconds between each discharge that lit up the counter-measures screen. He held out his pistol arm straight towards the screen as the fourth bolt lost most of its energy in passing through it to fall into the water like a stone. He pulled the trigger and without waiting to see what would happen he flung himself back into the bridge wing, slamming the heavy door behind him. Crouching down on the deck and held his breath. When it came, two thunderous cracks split the air, but the Privateer kept on going without bucking under any impact. Opening the breach he ejected the cartridge onto the deck reloaded the flare gun and went out through the door a second time. The Privateer was now catching the swell as she left the protection of the harbour and dashed across the shallows on her planes. Chip punched up the charts confirming the depth to be only fifteen feet at low tide. Still up on the planes she would have a draught of about two feet when empty. 'Only skimmers can catch us now, the rest will have to round the mud bank.' He thought with some sense of achievement. He took the skimmer round the point hugging the coast around Gilkicker Point into Stokes Bay. "Petty Officer Grey. Any sign of pursuit on SSR?"

"Standby Sir!" There was a long pause as the Electro-tech scanned the viewer on the bridge. "Negative Sir. It looks as though they thought we wouldn't make it past the boom."

"Good, keep your eyes peeled and get some help to clean up the mess. Well done." Another flare went off as the Chief fired yet another buttress defence at incoming rounds fired high over the buildings at Dolphin point. It was a feeble gesture, but nonetheless an indication that at least somebody was still hoping for a lucky shot.

"Chief, come up here will you?" shouted Chip.

"Take the left-hand seat and take a rest, I think you have earned it." Chip looked back at his instrument panel and then back at the dull reflection of light marking out the man's face in the darkness of the windblown cockpit. "Where did you learn to do that Chief?"

"It's nothing really Sir. We used to do that on patrol off Gib. The gun-runners and pirates had some pretty fancy weapons and those magnesium flares have something that sends plasma rounds off in the wrong direction."

"You were on the Gib patrols were you, when were you out there?"

"About six years ago, I was attached to the Skimmer squadron working alongside Europol and immigration." Chip went awfully quiet lost in thought. "See much action there at all?"

"Plenty Sir, we lost a few, but we gave as good as we got then some more."

"Ever come across a large skimmer painted a mottled brown and blue colour?"

"Sure did, we tangled with that maniac four times in three years, and he always got away, but not before doing a lot of damage. How do you know about that Sir?"

"An old classmate of mine had a run in with that particular marauder himself."

"I'd like to have another crack at him, and do it my way. Stuff the rules of engagement, that guy's an unmitigated murderer."

"Seems like we both have a score to settle with him."

"One day Sir, one day I'm going to take him out and that mean boat of his and blow it right out of the water." They skimmed along the placid waters of the Solent towards Southampton water. Lights twinkling away along the shorelines and on hills of the Isle of Wight, but the mainland remained in total darkness except for the giant complex at Fawley. The giant flares a permanent reminder of the energy base for the region.

Looking ahead on radar they could see line upon line of echoes strung along the Solent. "What's that?" Asked Chip more of himself than anyone else. "Bridge, Petty Officer Grey!"

"Yes sir!"

"Get a line on those targets and tell me what they are!"

"Aye, aye Sir!" Fred sat up on the deck of the bridge shaking his head slowly from side to side. "The duty medic had previously cut his trouser legs apart at the seams and tended his burns while he laid there unconscious. Taking a hyper-needle out of the case to administer a pain killing injection into his shoulder and let him come-to naturally. "Where are we?"

"It's alright Sir, we're out of the harbour and belting along up the Solent."

"What. No, not that way tell them no, they've blocked it off!"

"Steady Sir, what do you mean they've blocked it off?" The medic beckoned to the PO who came over and squatted down to listen to what Fred was saying. "They've turned it into an anchorage, there's too many vessels there. We can't make it though them at high speed. The anchorage is full of chains to stop the ships from leaving." The PO climbing partway onto the ladder leading to the cockpit shouted a warning. "Emergency dump off-planes Sir, we're heading for obstructions in the water. Lieutenant Newman says it's a confined anchorage with chains around it across the water. Chip barely nodded as he took the skimmer off-planes and throttled back in one movement. Hitting the reverse thrust control he slowly throttled up again, simultaneously dumping the planes back into their bays to protect them from the immense forces acting upon the slender mechanisms. Fred and the medic rolled over on the deck of the bridge coming to a halt against the foot of the front console. At less than a quarter of a mile they slewed to a halt rocking violently with the nose pitching up and down. Everyone who had a pair of eyes scrutinised the large assemblage of shipping before them. Like a giant carpet an entire fleet of merchant ships had been anchored off in Southampton Water for days. Trapped by the embargo and stuck in an increasingly hostile situation. Slowly the Privateer began picking its way along lines of buoys between which lengths of chains had been slung by the boomers out of the naval dockyards. They had covered about two miles when a warning call from the bridge alerted Chip to the emergence of three targets at the seaward end of the channel. "They're coming this way Sir. Speed about ten knots. That's not very fast if it's a patrol looking for us Sir."

"Understood. Keep your eyes peeled." Chip looked at the viewer and punched in the SSR overlay, catching sight of the codes for three naval vessels. He punched up the register and found three familiar names, the frigate Darlington escorted by the skimmers Cutlass and Rapier. "Well I'm blowed, That's a coincidence!" They were proceeding up the navigation line astern and not making any obvious endeavours to intercept the Privateer. "They must have seen us Sir, but they don't seem to be looking for us particularly."

"No, but they must be doing something. Standby, I'm going to take her alongside this large one here and hide under their radar shadow." Chip took the Privateer into the outer line of vessels and turned the skimmer around on her length bringing her close to the hull of the large carrier. Her own sensors now blind they began to use the under water systems to track the progress of the approaching patrol. At a range of five miles there was a signal beep from the communications bay. "It's the Darlington Sir, their Captain wants to speak with you." called the signal op. "In private."

"Right I'd better slide below. Hold her here Chief and be prepared to back off and run for it in between this line of ships and the one behind us."

"Aye Sir, it will be a pleasure." Fred was still sitting on the deck and looked up as Chip came down the ladder. "I'm all right, don't worry about me, I'll be as right as rain in a couple of hours."

"Good, glad to hear it Fred." Chip disappeared into his day cabin and shut the door. The radio op came through on the intercom. It's scrambled, so it's a totally secure channel Sir."

"Thanks."

"Privateer this is the Captain of the Darlington do you copy?"

"Yes I copy. Go ahead."

"Can you confirm that is Lieutenant commander Charles Woodingdean please?"

"Captain Woodingdean if you don't mind."

"Oh, my apologies, seem to have you listed in the rank of Lieutenant commander."

"I was until I resigned my commission some twenty minutes ago, since that time I revert to my previous rank and this vessel is a commercial vessel no longer under contract to the Admiralty I am proceeding on my way to sea." There was a pause between the transmissions. "Captain Woodingdean I would be grateful for information from you as to what exactly is happening ashore. About four hours ago I was diverted to Portsmouth where I am to arrange to disperse my crew ashore and, as I understand it place my self and my officers under the jurisdiction of the Provost Marshall. Can you elucidate any further?"

"So you are unaware of the recent changes in government at the moment?"

"Only that there is unlikely to be a President for a while, the Senate is suspended and that martial law has been stepped up."

"Were you aware that the Chiefs of Staff have resigned Captain?"

"No, what then is the situation ashore, can you tell me plainly?"

"Not good I'm afraid, every ship that returns to port is being impounded and the crews are being held under close arrest. We just escaped that indignity, but I can assure you that if you dock at Portsmouth or any other port you and your ship will be arrested."

"Do you have any idea why that should be the case?"

"Not really, there is a remote possibility that the death of Admiral Driver has something to do with it, but I don't see how."

"The Chief of Staff, dead. Oh my God when did that happen?"

"Not sure Captain, his heli-jet was shot out of the sky somewhere in Scotland and so far the only survivor is the pilot who is in bad shape. It looks as though the Commandant-General of the Royal Marines was with him in the same aircraft."

"Now I am beginning to understand. It seems as though every vessel that has been at sea for the last ten days or so is being arrested on arrival. That means there will only be half the fleet available to defend our patch. Have you any contacts in Whitehall?"

"None, we were under contract, as I said just now, and the only way I could stop them from impounding my ship and putting my crew in jail was to declare the military contract with the crew voided by the Admiralty board's extreme behaviour. As given under Article 27 of the Madrid Convention."

"My goodness, you're pretty sharp on that aren't you Captain?"

"Well, the alternative is to dock and be thrown in jail. They will offer you and your officers open arrest in the wardroom at Nelson, but when you consider that most of us have been on bone-fide business at sea for the last two weeks. Having little contact with our families, the last thing we want is to be thrown into prison without charge for an indefinite period of time."

"Quite. Thank you for your frankness Captain, I wish you well and Godspeed in your travels."

"My compliments Captain Mortimer, thank you for your wisdom in this matter."

"Not at all Captain, it seems as though you leave me little choice. With my father-in-law murdered like that I can only guess there is a conspiracy theory going around the corridors of power. This means that everyone is under suspicion and that's plainly ridiculous."

"You mean to say that Admiral of the Fleet Driver was your father-in-law?"

Yes. I had no idea until you told me that he was murdered."

"I am sorry to be the harbinger of bad news. My condolences to you and your family, I only found out minutes before we made the breakaway from the jetty. They had patrolmen there with a large bus to take the crew away to jail, and a small transport vehicle for my officers. Were it not for the fact that two of my crew were badly hurt in Rotterdam, and the naval surgeon calling to collect them, I would have had no delay and no inkling until the deed was done."

"I must press on and make a decision." said Captain Mortimer with a tinge of despondency in his voice. Good night, Captain Woodingdean."

"Goodnight." Chip placed the microphone slowly into his holster. A picture forming in the back of his mind. The only connection being, that all four vessels were in Scotland near or at the time the Admiral and the General were murdered. The other Captain was right he thought. If half the fleet was at sea for some reason or other, then the government is using that fact as an excuse for a witch-hunt. It began to look as though the Admiral and the General were the victims of skulduggery by the government rather than by anyone in the armed forces. Seriously undermining the fleet's ability to defend the country against any aggressor – invasion. "I don't believe it!" Chip gasped as the audacious idea gripped his mind in a shocking revelation. "Get me the Darlington on the scrambler."

"Captain Mortimer I am sorry to disturb you, but I think there is a real threat coming our way."

"Can you be more explicit?"

"We spent four days, more or less in Rotterdam and a few hours in Ostend and witnessed several naval exercises off the Dutch and Belgian coast. What we didn't see at all in those exercises gives me cause for concern. We did not sea any ESNF ships at all; they were all Belgian and Dutch vessels. No French or German ships to be seen anywhere. It may be just a daft idea Captain, but when we left Rotterdam and during our subsequent visit to Ostend all the French and German vessels were alongside. I can't explain it, but find the French and German fleets and you may find part of the answer to this problem."

"So what are you saying Captain Woodingdean?"

"Take a look at what is going on around us, we are involved in what is an exercise taking a convoy up the coast to Edinburgh. In the mean time the Admiral and a General are apparently murdered as the Chiefs of Staff resign en-masse. Martial law is stepped up and when the returning ships arrive in their home ports they are immediately arrested and the crews imprisoned. When I entered Portsmouth harbour earlier this evening I saw what amounts to the whole fleet tied up alongside. We have no navy at sea on patrol at this moment. What of the air force? I don't know, but I would hazard a guess they're all grounded, and remember this. During our exit from the harbour tonight somebody sabotaged a boom that had been placed across the entrance. That means the intention is that no one can sail in or out. Even those vessels with crews who may be above suspicion cannot sail out. They have been impounded too. Don't you see; we're paralysed. The European parliament is the only authority now since the UK government lost its mandate from the people, and that means only one thing. European intervention on UK territorial soil."

"You mean armed intervention don't you?"

"Yes, entirely so, but I have no proof of that."

"They wouldn't dare to. I mean it would cause an international stink on a global scale."

"But under the terms of the Copenhagen Charter there is scope for them to 'police' the member states in times of political unrest."

"You're right there I'm afraid. It does look black, and we have so little to go on."

"I tell you what I'll do. We will replenish somewhere safe and watch the western approaches. I can only advise you from what I have seen in the last few days, that if you decided to patrol the Cinque Ports from the Thames estuary to the old Nab Tower." We could either look like fools or end up dead heroes –if you follow my drift."

"Entirely."

"Fare well in whatever you decide to do. For my part I will transmit on broadband if I see anything, and if you're still at sea I'll send you an encrypted message on the MARSAT reserved channels. My radio operator says they haven't been able to shut them down because they are controlled by ESA in Darmstadt."

"Understood Captain. Good luck to you and your crew." Captain Mortimer signed off leaving Chip free to give time to think clearly. "They've slowed down Sir, sounds like they're turning."

"That's encouraging, give them enough time to confirm that report, say two minutes then call me fast as you can." Chip paused thinking rapidly. Four men could handle this skimmer without too much trouble. He walked over to the plot and watched the blank 'hole' in the middle caused by the bulk carrier shielding the low powered radar. "How's the tactical sweep from Tactical Command?"

"It's still up and running Sir."

"Good, stop transmitting radar, go over to Tactco and monitor their progress from that. Let me know when they are abeam Stone Point."

"Aye, aye Sir."

"Slow astern if you please Chief."

"Slow astern it is Sir."

"Take her slowly out along the lines Chief, on a heading of... 245 degrees, at three knots, maintain darken ship routine."

"Course 245 degrees, three knots Sir." The medic returned to the bridge. I've put Lt Newman in his cabin Sir. He's not in any pain at the moment, but he will be very sore by tomorrow morning."

"Thank you for doing that. Is he conscious?"

"Oh yes Sir, very."

"That's a small mercy. Well done. Any other casualties besides Lt Newman and Leading seaman Muggeridge?"

"No Sir, They're both burned, but generally speaking I think they will be up and about in two or three days time."

"I don't think we have that much time. Keep an eye on them and let me know if their conditions deteriorate in any way."

"Aye Sir."

"They have a mile to go Sir, before Stone Point."

"Petty Officer Grey take the Right hand seat. Chief standby for some fast speed changes and quick manoeuvring."

"Aye, aye Sir." Chip followed him up the ladder standing behind the right hand seat occupied by Petty Officer Grey. Right, here's what we're going to do just in case the batteries at Hurst Castle have been warned about us coming. I want the Privateer to emerge at the right speed and location to make it look as though we are part of that patrol led by the Darlington. Exactly, like so using the 'Match Function' here on the navigation console, that's it, now move the red crosshairs over the Darlington like so. That's it. Now use the link command and select manual start. Now when I give the word the Chief here will go over to automatic pilot and press the program lock button up here. The rest is up to the navigation computer and the autopilot."

"Thank you Sir. I've never seen that before."

"Ah, that's because it's a Mk 18 variation on the Admiralty standard. Things are a little different on commercial vessels. Since the government are too mean to spend money on proper warships they kit out their merchantmen as poor substitutes in case of war instead." The Chief manoeuvred Privateer slowly into the narrow space between two rows of anchored ships following his nose on the 'Tactco' display. Chip climbed backwards down the ladder back onto the bridge and took over the navigation viewer from the lookout. "Any sign of change in movement from the Darlington?"

"No Sir. They appear to be slowing down."

"Stop engines."

"Stop engines, Sir." They drifted slowly in the dark as the current took hold. "Get a boat hook on one of those buoys from the starboard bow, we'll just have to sit it out." They watched in silence as the dull red hands of the ship's electrical chronometer eased from two to three, to ten, then twenty minutes. "I'm going to the Wardroom to see Lieutenant Newman. Quartermaster's mate phone through to the engine room and have the Chief engineer come to Lt Newman's cabin."

"Aye, aye Sir."

Fred and Chip bandied about one or two ideas, but the most favourable was to proceed to the Portland container terminal to pick up fuel and supplies. Then on to the Western approaches using Falmouth as a base for the next few days.

"How are the men taking it Chief?" asked Fred. "Not too bad at the moment. They've been sick of the news about things going badly ashore, but if you ask me I reckon they are pretty much grateful that you prevented them from going to jail."

"I'm afraid it's not over yet. We have the possibility of running against the shore batteries at Hurst Castle if they get wise to what we're doing."

"I think the best we can do is clear the upper and lower decks and address the ship's company. I know they will want to know when they can go home and indeed how to get there."

"Yes, I don't have the answer to either of those questions, but I think we must tell them what is going to happen and that we will put together a repatriation program as soon as we have finished our patrol."

"There is a point of order Sir, if I may bring it up."

"By all means Chief Baxter."

"Well, it's like this if we are no longer members of the Royal Navy because we all resigned, we are not exactly acting under any orders or in fact any such system of laws. That's bound to cause some problems for the men. We've all been used to the naval discipline act and follow the code implicitly."

"Yes, of course, and I haven't entirely forgotten that at all, but since you mention it I must address it as best I can."

"Perhaps, the best way to proceed is to maintain the principles of the naval discipline act in spirit as well as in deeds, in that way." offered Fred. "What we are about to do will be more than just a token resistance, and there are all sorts of international maritime laws giving precedence to warships. If we are not a warship Chip we cannot legitimately challenge any suspicious vessel or fire upon a fleet of men o' war."

"Good point, I suppose we ought to cancel our resignations and continue as a naval vessel for a while longer. Chief, how do you think the men will take it?"

"I don't think they have considered the fine points Sir, but it's the only framework most of them know. Except for one or two who came into the navy with previous experience elsewhere."

"Right, it's agreed I'll address the crew and if they accept the idea I will put it into the ship's log that they re-enlisted to a man, and somehow I'm going to get these men home if it's the last thing I do."

"One other point, no one has eaten since last night. We need to organise a proper shift working system if we are going to be at sea for more than four days at a time."

"Thanks Fred, Chief can you organise the roster for mess-men and get someone in the galley right away. Stand down those who have been on watch for more than twelve hours and get replacements for them. Also, please visit the Junior Rates mess with Chief White. Tell them I'll give them a briefing as soon as we are clear of the Solent. Get as much feedback from the men as you can and come and see me once we're out of this hole."

"Aye Sir."

Chip poked his head into the mess room and noticed a number of the crew sitting around. Someone was cooking something on the small range while others were watching the video channel piped through from the camera on the bridge. He was pleased that there was still an observance of the duty watch system that they all adhered to by habit. "Hello Sir, how are things up in the sharp end?"

"With a bit of luck we'll be out of here soon. You might want to watch the Privateer TV station for the next half-hour. Glad to see you you're in good shape in here." He withdrew his head and walked smartly along the flat to the bridge. He scanned the Tactco plot where nothing had changed. It was nearly forty minutes. "Something's happening." Petty Officer Grey had the intensifiers jammed onto his forehead and gave a call from his position in the cockpit. "Thermal shows a small plume of heat coming from the skimmers. That's it, they're beginning to move."

"Standby, lock-on speed match on my command."

"Aye, aye Sir."

"Let them get up to speed first." They scanned the plot, checking it against the view outside the shattered glass windows. A cold blast of air making itself felt as the early morning breezes began to blow. "Steady fifteen knots Sir,"

"Slip the boat hook." A seaman walked out of the starboard bridge door and whistled to his 'oppo' on the forepeak. Making a slicing motion across his throat as he did so. The seaman on the forepeak unhooked from the anchor chain, stowing his boat hook in a rack on steel railings nearby. He scampered along the narrow bows to join the others on the bridge, taking up his station next to the quartermaster.

"Lock on Chief!"

"Lock on!" The skimmer accelerated rapidly in a smooth and powerful surging movement. The escorts were spaced at about five hundred metres from each other as the last one in the line finished its turn and followed the line to seaward. The Privateer under autopilot control with the computer tracking the tactical plot in speed match emerged from the clutter of anchored vessels as seamlessly as if she had been part of the patrol. They maintained a course and speed that must have looked perfect on any sensor display seen by the prying eyes of other radar systems. "Quartermaster's mate."

"Sir."

"Take a message to all compartments. Quietly now, Action stations, we have about ten minutes before we come into range of the shore batteries."

"Message to all compartments, Action stations Sir."

"Good now off you go." Chip watched the lad scamper off wondering how on earth the navy still got away with recruiting boys from their mother's apron strings. "Any emissions on sensors?"

"No sir, just radar and transponder codes that's all."

The gunnery watch on the Hurst Castle laser cannon batteries had distractions of their own to contend with. Armed guards appeared late in the evening under the command of an officious Lieutenant and a Warrant Officer. The Gunnery Chief was relieved and taken away and the men were cautioned that they would be questioned during the course of the night. Nothing was actually said what it was about, and when the killick of the watch on 'A' battery asked what it was about he was barked at for insubordination and threatened with immediate disrating to able rate. The word got round very quickly that something was up, and many of the men felt instinctively that something was amiss.

"Where are you going!" Demanded the Warrant Officer when one of the gunners got up and left his seat. "To the heads Sir."

"Make it lively then, more than two minutes and I'll send someone after you."

The new battery commander arrived in a fast car. He strode into the wardroom and surveyed the small knot of officers gathered around the bar. The glum expressions on their faces said it all. They were not happy. Meanwhile, the gunner with the full bladder dodged past the heads and made it to a phone in an out of the way office from where he phoned the wardroom. "Wardroom, Hall Porter speaking."

"Charlie, this is Pete Singleton, is the boss there."

"Er, what was that, who is this?"

"Charlie it's me Pete Singleton, you're daughter's boyfriend."

I'm sorry there's no one of that name here."

"Charlie stop messing about… is everything alright up there?"

"No I'm afraid he's not here, he's gone away." Pete heard a distant voice in the background demanding to know who was on the phone. He didn't like the tone of it since it sounded like that lieutenant with the bad attitude. "Oh, it's just an enquiry from a lady ashore looking for one of the young Lieutenants who left recently on another appointment." Pete heard the lie and knew something was up. He heard steps coming towards him along the corridor. "Get rid of her." He heard the other man say. "Yes sir, as you wish."

"I'm afraid he is no longer here miss 'Petra' said Charlie, "He's been posted."

"Have they taken him away like our Chief of the watch Charlie?" Hissed Pete risking all as the steps got ever closer. "Why yes miss Petra I will let him know you were asking for him, good night." The phone clicked and went dead. Pete quickly replaced the handset and half-running, half walking on tiptoe scuttled silently towards the heads. He turned on his heels and walked back along the way he had just come, ringing his hands and straightening his fatigues. By the time the Crusher's mate rounded the corner he made as if he was tucking his shirt in and in a bit of a panic. "You the gunner that went to the heads just a minute ago?"

"Yes mate."

"I've been sent to collect you."

"What on earth for, can't a man go for a dump without being hassled?"

"Look, none of your cheek, just get along back to your station and be quick about it!"

"What's going on? All our officers and Senior Rates have been taken away. Is there something going on outside?"

"Just move along."

"Come on mate, I've got a right to know, I'm a voting man just like you, with a wife and kids in Bournemouth. Come on what's the drift?"

The patrolman scowled as he looked at Pete. "Well you're going to find out anyway, but don't you dare tell anyone I told you, OK?"

"OK."

"The defence chiefs have all resigned and a load of brass has walked out with them. That's not all. Someone took a pot shot at the Chief of Staff and that Commandant of Marines who was with him and blew them out of the sky. Meaning, the government has slapped a big restriction order on everyone and everything that moves. It doesn't feel right and they are arresting and replacing every officer and Senior NCO, particularly those who, funnily enough, seem to be connected with the brass in Whitehall, and guess what? I reckon these blokes are moving in to take their place are 'party members' or something like it... Right here we are, and don't waste my time again. You go for a dump in your own time."

"Alright, alright." Pete winked at the naval patrolman and walked into the battery control room with a belligerent air.

"Battery in sight Sir, no energy signatures as yet."

"Thank you, that's a good sign." The small flotilla progressed towards the narrow gap between Hurst Spit and Sconce Point. All the time passive sensors seeking-out those important energy signatures indicating weapons systems being activated. Finally a challenge came over the comms link from the battery commander. "Message to the Darlington Sir, they're asking for ident and disposition codes, they're on a secure channel."

"Thank you, this is it everyone, be prepared for an immediate scramble through the gap." The Darlington responded with her ident and disposition codes as requested, but in a non-secure, open channel mode. There was a long pause from the battery as they drew to within a ship's length of the gap. A query came back from the battery requesting clarification on the Darlington's authorisation to proceed out to sea. There was another long pause, this time from the Darlington's Captain. He responded with half of his little fleet through the narrows. 'Darlington on Patrol as required under Admiralty Instruction 21245/0065, timed at 09:00 yesterday. Darlington maintaining patrol profile.' Came the response from the signal op on the Darlington. "Get me your commanding officer Darlington."

"Standby." Replied their signal op." There was another long pause leaving just enough time for Privateer to squeeze through the gap behind the Cutlass. "Captain Mortimer here, to whom am I speaking?"

"Lieutenant commander Wesel-Etherington Sir."

"I understand you may have a problem Commander?"

"Your Admiralty Orders Captain are more than twenty-four hours old."

"What of it. There is no time limit on my orders to patrol the east coast, except the one noted in the executive order to patrol until relieved on the third day of our patrol."

"Quite Captain, this is the third day."

"Well, whenever the C-in-C pleases, he will signal his intentions soon enough."

"That's not the point Captain, new orders have been issued to all commanding officers to stand-down and for those commanding vessels to return forthwith."

"Orders not issued to me Commander."

"Captain you must put in to Portsmouth."

"I do not believe that a Commander has the rank to make any demand of a senior officer."

"With respect Captain, I advise that you should return to Portsmouth Harbour without delay."

"Unless you can tell me by what authority you are asking me to do that I advise you Commander that I will in no way respond to your request. Perhaps you should begin by telling me what has happened in the last twenty-four hours that has made it imperative for me to break my patrol and return to port."

"Weapons systems are powering up Sir, the battery is preparing to arm weapons!" called the watch-keeper on Privateer's tactical display! "Very good. Standby to go full-speed!" They continued to listen to the dialogue between the shore battery and the Darlington's Captain on the open channel. "My Executive officer informs me that you are powering up your battery. May I remind you Lieutenant Commander Wesel-Etherington that to threaten a senior officer is in itself a serious offence, but to open fire on a vessel without proper rights or authority you stand to face a court-martial." Captain Mortimer was still delaying matters for as long as he could. "I say again, perhaps you should tell me what this is all about."

"Captain Mortimer I am under orders to fire on any vessel attempting to leave the Solent navigation."

"Unless you can verify those orders and where they come from and from whom, you are placing yourself and your career in jeopardy."

"Darlington standby." Captain Mortimer had won, by the time the battery commander got the answers to those questions his patrol would be safely out of the restrictions with room to manoeuvre.

"Weapons firing up Sir!"

"So he decided to open fire after all, he's got to be damn sure of himself to do that." The plasma-jet engines on the Darlington cut-in making her leap almost out of the water by the bows, then she was off with her skimmer escorts in tow. "Look at that Sir, they're way off beam. The duty watch looked in amazement as the laser cannon fire shot rounds in all directions except at the ships passing by them.

"Put it in auto! Put it in auto!" yelled the bony-faced Lieutenant.

"Er, what Sir? Didn't quite catch what you were saying Sir?"

"Put the damn guns into auto mode and fire again!"

"Auto-mode it is Sir." The gun Captain repeated slowly as if he were performing a drill. "Let's see."

"Get that idiot out of here! Go on get out! You're under arrest!"

Leaving the guns of 'A' battery in manual mode the gun Captain turned and faced the bombastic Lieutenant with complete contempt. "Not bloody likely Sir!" You come down here shouting the odds arresting every senior rank and then expect us to fire on our mates down there in our own ships. Here lads I smell a rat, it looks as though someone high up has high and mighty ideas of mutinying!"

"Patrolman arrest that man immediately, remove him and place him in the cells, now. I will not suffer this kind of insubordination!"

"No Sir I will not! I have just witnessed you ordering these men to fire on a squadron of our ships. That is not, Sir, a legal order, and neither is the one you just gave me for arresting a man for carrying out his duty to protect those ships by not firing the guns."

"How dare you!" The Lieutenant made a lunge for the control panel and pressed the automatic targeting button. The other sailors left their positions and brought him down onto the hard floor where he disappeared beneath three large bodies and a hail of fists. "Hookie, can you get on the comms panel and tell them to scram, any way anywhere!"

The leading patrolman walked across the dimly lit fire control centre and worked buttons until he set up the right channel for contacting the Darlington.

"Darlington, Darlington, this is 'A' battery, 'A' battery. Make best speed Captain, I say again make best speed."

"'A' battery this is Darlington, acknowledged. What is your situation ashore?"

"Not sure, all officers and Senior Rates have been replaced by unknown officers. Guns crews suspect mutiny by senior officers, over"

"Understand, what of 'B' battery?'

"Not manned Sir, guns crews are all in cells."

"Do you need assistance?"

"Yes, there is only a PO Crusher here, all the rest have been confined to their messes or taken away in trucks."

"Understood, standby." Everyone held their breath and waited. After five minutes the two escorts slowed down going off-planes, simultaneously the hindmost skimmer drew alongside the first. Looking through their intensifiers the men on the bridge of the Privateer could see the heat signatures of men and their equipment jumping from one skimmer to the other. "My goodness he's going to put a security platoon ashore. Good man!"

"Darlington is calling us Sir, secure Channel, it's their Captain, he wants to talk to you."

"Hello Privateer, glad you could join us for the outbound leg. No time to explain, but I think you'd better make your own way from here. If my men are successful the guns here will be back under the proper authorities within the hour. Understand?"

"Yes Captain, Good luck to you."

"Thank you for the tip-off earlier. I will send my spare skimmer ahead as you suggested. In the mean time use any of your own contacts ashore to find out what is going on. If you spot any trouble coming our way from the Western Approaches contact Captain Passfield at Plymouth. He may be able to help you in some way; his loyalty is unquestionable, Captain. Over"

"Understood, we're pulling out now. May good fortune go with you, Privateer out." Chip put the microphone down and giving the tactical plot one last glance gave the order for full power.

****

"President Muller-Weiss has today decreed a state of emergency in the European State of the United Kingdom. At mid-day today the European Federal Security Council issued an order authorising Federal police units supported by armed troops to move onto mainland Britain." The news announcer on the EuroSat media channel 'Zeitungs International' intoned as the off-watch crew was taking their breakfast. Someone shouted down the flat along to the bridge telling anyone in particular to switch one of the viewers over to the same channel. Sentries on the upper deck remained alert, watching the cliffs around Lulworth Cove. They carried small arms since these were the only weapons on board offering any resistance should there be any attack. Two seamen lay on top of the cliffs out of sight, keeping a watch on the approach road and the fields leading to the cove. Chip had turned in after an exhausting night and morning on the bridge. The crew was absolutely fagged-out with fatigue after hours at a time at their action stations, some sunning themselves in the lee of the main deck that offered them protection from the swirling breezes circulating around the tight little cove. The PO engine room artificer and two of the other techs were replacing the shattered plasti-glass windows while two others welded up replacement superstructure skins covering the gaping holes left behind by the vaporised metal. The Chief of the watch sat in the bridge wing looking at tactical display data while the duty Cox'n sat in the cockpit reading an electronic tablet book, ready at a moment's notice to fire up the engines and head out to sea.

The injured men who could move about lounged in folding chairs or on plastic boxes. Fred escaped the confines of his tiny cabin, lying slumped in a sleeping bag on a couple of wardroom chairs pushed together to make a temporary bed-like structure under the shade of an overhang in the upper superstructure. His wounds in the legs stinging like fury when he moved. The sun gradually bringing colour back into his cheeks while he dozed. By the afternoon watch all was quiet onboard after the repairs had been completed. Chip and the Chief engine room tech did an inventory of fuel and engine fluids, food and other supplies. By four o'clock, well aware of the political situation despite significant gaps in the information and needing to slip away under cover of darkness he was aroused from his thoughts by shouts from the lookouts high above them on the cliffs. "Vehicle coming down the road Sir, fast."

"What kind of vehicle!" He asked, speaking into the radio console microphone.

"Navy Sir, It's a navy staff car Sir. Looks as though, hang on Sir, it's got three stars on a plate in the front Sir."

"Standby everyone, action stations, actions stations. He turned back to the console. Any sign of other vehicles?"

"No Sir, just the one."

"Lookouts, get back to the Privateer as quickly as you can."

"Aye, aye Sir."

By the time the staff car arrived at the top of the steeply turning road that passed down through the ancient cliffs to the water's edge every man jack of them was inboard and ready. The vehicle stopped at the top of the sloping road, then slowly began its descent to the shingle beach. The water was clear and deep with a lovely blue-green colour as the shallows gave way to a deep natural hole in the crust of the earth. When the vehicle stopped the driver remained seated with the engine turning over. A lone figure emerged from the front passenger seat dressed in the full uniform of a Rear Admiral, carrying a silver headed mahogany swagger stick. Placing the stick in the crook of an arm the Admiral lifted both hands to his mouth and hollered. "Privateer Ahoy!" A ripple of suppressed mirth went around the bridge. Nobody moved. Again the Admiral called across to the Privateer. "Quartermaster's Mate, find out who that is."

"Aye, aye Sir." He left the bridge and trotted quickly through the flat leading onto the main cargo deck. Arriving on the quarterdeck and standing with one foot on the low scupper hollered back. "Ahoy on the beach! Who are you."

"Rear Admiral Dunham! Will you tell your Captain that I have urgent business with him!"

"Aye Sir, wait there!"

'Wait there.' muttered the Admiral. 'There's not much else I can do is there?' The lad picked up the microphone and relayed the message to the bridge via the ship's intercom. Chip almost fell off his chair. "I'm on my way." Turning to the Bosun's Mate he ordered the skimmer's small dinghy be made ready to fetch the Admiral.

The Admiral climbed the stern ladder on the wide transom with a practised step. "Welcome aboard Sir. This is, if I may say so, a great surprise. I had thought that you were locked up with the rest of the navy."

"Yes, almost. But by some strange quirk they decided to promote me, I think to get me out of the way and to keep me quiet." They made their way to Chip's day cabin and sat down regarding each other warily. "Just how much do you know?" asked the Admiral bluntly. "Only that just about every senior officer and NCO are under arrest without charge. Quite apart from the huge civil unrest, I'd say we have a country that's falling apart and anything could happen."

"Quite so. When I heard how you made your breakaway from Portsmouth Harbour yesterday evening I had to take the gamble that you would be here. Now look we haven't got long, and there's no time to give you all of the details. Where do you stand with your crew?"

"They are loyal Sir. They resigned to a man, that's presumably one reason why there was no hot pursuit last night. Then to a man, in all good conscience, decided to re-enlist when they realised that we may be the only naval unit defending our shores. Especially, since we have just heard the announcement that the Federal police and the army is being sent in from mainland Europe."

"Good! Yes, they were right to do that, and now I have a job for you to do. By all means proceed through the Western Approaches as guard-ship, but under no account will you engage any fleet that you may encounter. By all means radio what you find, but I want you to sail directly to Gibraltar with my passenger, and you are to guard him with your life."

"Forgive me for saying this Sir, but isn't that a bit melodramatic? After all, I don't even know which side you're on, and with respect, you seemed to have been promoted by the very people who are trying to take over our country."

"Quite right. I do understand your concerns. No I am not on the 'other side' I am as I always have been, interested in the legally appointed authorities of this country, and in the security of this nation. And until someone replaces that authority I shall remain loyal to the principles inculcated in the democratic system that I was first commissioned to serve as a midshipman."

"Thank you Sir."

"Now to my passenger, Mr Jack Keen. You will soon see what is required of you Commander Woodingdean. By the way, where is your First Lieutenant?"

"Unfortunately he was wounded along with two other people last night. We, er, were hit by a broadside of cannon fire making our escape."

"That should never have happened. If he is well enough please ask him to come to the wardroom as soon as he can make it there. I will bring my passenger personally."

On the way out of his cabin Chip sent a messenger to alert Fred, and continued to accompany the Admiral along the main cargo deck to the stern. The jolly boat sped across the clear water as fast as the single oarsman could make it go. The Admiral stepped out onto the beach walking straight to the vehicle where he opened the door for a middle-aged man to step through. He Saluted the distinguished looking gentleman who was dressed in a very well tailored suit of top quality material, a deep blue shirt with a coral pink silk tie to offset the pale head of hair that he carried. The oarsman did not see him at first because the Admiral's form blocked his view. Then he stepped aside as he approached the boat. "Thank you Admiral for your kindness." Said the man in a very cultured voice." He turned and looked at the young sailor seated and holding both oars flat in the water to steady the small boat. The lad gawped, dropping his oars and shot to attention, saluting the civilian very smartly. The man nodded his head forwards in response with a twinkle in his eyes. The boat bobbed a little but the sailor stood firm on strong sea legs. "Thank you." He said. "And who might you be?" He enquired mildly.

"Leading Seaman Briggs Sir."

"You had better sit down Leading Seaman Briggs before you have an accident, don't you think."

"Ye-es, yes Sir." He sat down smartly picking up the oars in the ready position. "This is Mr Keen, Leading Seaman Briggs, I trust you will make his short journey in your boat a dry and comfortable one."

"Yes Sir." With that the Admiral assisted his passenger into the dinghy and then with one foot on the transom and the other at the water's edge he pushed forwards, neatly bringing in his legs to sit in the stern with his somewhat bemused passenger.

"Good Lord! It's the king!" Someone exclaimed loudly peeping through intensifiers. "What!" Came the strangled noise from the duty Chief. "And me in my dirty overalls!"

"Couldn't be better Chief. Pass the word quietly. Get the Quartermaster's Mate down here on the double!"

"Quartermaster's Mate to the quarterdeck at the double." Came the order over the intercom. As the dinghy approached every one became preoccupied with their appearance and positioning on the deck. As the boat bumped alongside two seamen grabbed the bow and stern ropes thrown up at them by Briggs who was white-faced displaying a fixed grin. The man looked positively terrified. As the king made his way up the ladder the small welcoming party stood to attention, the Bosun's pipe twittered and Chip gave his very best academy salute. The pipes died awkwardly as the boy seaman saw who it was for the first time went into sheer amazement. "Gor blimey Captain it's the king, God bless 'im!" Rooted to the spot in abject fear he realised his gaff too late and stood trembling in front of the distinguished looking gentleman turning a deep shade of pink. "Well bless me, so I am, and I can quite see that we are going to be shipmates on this fine little craft of yours," said the king smiling kindly at the boy. "Charming, Commander Woodingdean, quite charming. I don't think I have been welcomed in such an honest fashion for years."

"Thank you Sir. Would you care to accompany me to my Day cabin?"

"Of course, please lead the way." Chip looked at the boy who squinted back at him, manfully holding back tears of embarrassment and shame. As the entourage made its way slowly through the cargo deck a distant wail followed by faint splash could be heard coming from the direction of the quarterdeck. No one in authority dared ask the reasons behind the unfortunate sounds. Knowing sympathetically the kind of rough justice meted out to defaulting boys. The crew kept out of sight except the duty watch at their stations on the bridge. All of them standing smartly to attention while the Captain and his dignified visitors swept through, letting out their bated breath in relief when the moment passed. Excitement rippled around the vessel. The Chief pushing his reluctant lookouts back to their positions on the cliff top, chivvying the tactical watch-keepers to be more vigilant on their sensor equipment.

"…And, so your Majesty, I will leave you in the capable hands of Lieutenant commander Woodingdean, which rather neatly brings me to the next point. Please remove your hat Lieutenant commander Woodingdean, while his Majesty addresses you. This is a serious moment in time, I am sure you will agree, and he has point of disciplinary admonishment to bring to your attention." The Admiral reaching into his jacket pocket to remove two bound letters. "Your Majesty this is for Commander Woodingdean."

"Thank you Admiral. Commander Woodingdean, or perhaps I should quite rightly say, you are somewhat improperly addressed." Chip looked puzzled, but stood perfectly still, feeling a little embarrassed. "I am very pleased to present you with your promotion, you are now Commander Charles Woodingdean, Royal Navy. You will notice Commander Woodingdean that this is a Royal Commission, which I am allowed to grant under the provisions of the Act of Cessation. You are only the third person to receive such a commission in my lifetime, and it gives me great pleasure to bestow this honour upon you. Congratulations Commander on your promotion." The Admiral handed the king a set of shoulder pads bearing the three gold rings on a black background denoting the rank of Commander. "Well done Commander." Chip shook hands with the king, noting its genuine warmth. The Admiral removed a new hat from his bag bearing the traditional 'scrambled egg' on its peak, denoting senior rank. "Well done Chip." He said as they shook hands with Chip grinning widely at his amazing good fortune.

"And now that brings me to a similar impropriety of being improperly dressed before your King. "Lieutenant commander Newman step forward please." Fred was so happy for his friend and ally, his business partner that he almost missed the order from the Admiral. His face suddenly losing its good-humoured grin when he realised that he was being drawn into the inner circle, no longer a part of the scenery. He stood motionless in front of both the Admiral and his King. Chip took Fred's walking stick keeping it temporarily out of sight.

"Lieutenant commander Newman, you have been well recommended to me by the Admiral, as a loyal and capable navigator and ship's Captain in the making. Your long years of service in the Royal Navy before you left to become a merchant mariner have stood you in good stead, and we noticed from your record how determined you are in doing a good job. Your imagination has, I am sure kept you and other senior officers out of trouble and I like that. Well done."

"Thank you Sir." Fred managed a salute without wobbling on his legs. He cast a glance to his left hand in which the king had placed the shoulder pads that bore the insignia of a Lieutenant commander of the Royal Navy. He smiled a deeply satisfied smile and moved back to one side as Chip placed the stick back into his other hand.

"And now gentlemen, here are your orders for the Privateer." The Admiral drew out of his case a large sealed envelope sealed with the Admiralty Seal, bearing the address. Commander Woodingdean RN HMS Privateer. "The first order contains the Commissioning Warrant for Chief Petty Officer White to be made up to Warrant Officer, Second Class, the promotion of Petty Officer, Propulsion Systems Artificer Riley, to Artificer First Class, and your electronics specialist Petty Officer Grey to the Rate of Chief Petty Officer. You will be pleased to note that Sub-Lieutenant Walsh will return, God-willing, to join you a soon as he is able. Unfortunately, the net had already trapped Mr Pengelly within its clutches and he remains confined to barracks in Portsmouth. No doubt, he may find his way back to you once our current situation is sorted out. You are to proceed immediately to Gibraltar." continued the Admiral summarising the Privateer's orders. "And deliver his majesty into the protection of Rear-Admiral Peterson who is due to arrive there within the next three days. You are not to become involved with any units of the ESNF or Royal Naval ships other than the normal exchanges that protocols require. You will find information that you can pass over to your signalman and Chief Petty Officer Grey regarding secure channels, modes of operation and schedules. Give us as much intelligence as you can, but other than that you will observe strict radio silence." The Admiral paused and took a mid-sized envelope out of his case. "These are the papers for your guest Mr Jack Keen. The king smiled. "It was my idea actually." He said. "I thought it had a particular banality about it, to the ears of the uninformed, but reminds me in fact of all the sailors who work so hard, and so keenly to help me."

"That's very kind of you your majesty."

"Mr Keen is a very senior oceanographer working for the Commission for Environmental Protection. Ostensibly he will be travelling with you on an urgent matter at the behest of the European Ministry of Environmental Sciences to resolve the intergovernmental dispute between the Gibraltarian and Spanish governments over the high level of toxins found in Algecieras Bay. Mr. Keen, er, actually Doctor Keen, will endeavour to stay out of sight at such times as he needs to, but otherwise his Majesty has graciously requested that he should be treated as an ordinary civilian travelling aboard one of the navy's vessel's on an important scientific and diplomatic mission."

"Oh, does that mean no marks of respect or deference out of the ordinary Sir?"

"Precisely that." Replied the King. "You and your sailors will have enough on their plates without jumping to attention every five minutes. And besides." A wicked grin came upon the king's countenance. "I think I will rather enjoy the informality of it."

"Thank you Sir, I will see to it that my crew are properly briefed."

"And now Commander, I must leave you and his Majesty for London immediately. Godspeed your Majesty, Commander Woodingdean."

"Thank you Admiral Dunham I am indebted to you, as indeed are all the members of the Royal Family. I wish you Godspeed in return and look forward to the day we will meet again, in better circumstances."

7.   THE DRAGON'S LAIR

"Mr President the situation in the United Kingdom has deteriorated. President Muller-Weiss has ordered in armed police and military units from the mainland. We see that as a military threat to our interests there, particularly our communications network and defence intelligence shield."

"Yes, Bob, I know all that, but there is little we can do. We can't just send a gunboat up the Thames and stir things up; that's out of the question."

"I'm not inferring that at all Mr President, I think we can preserve our network Sir, we have men on the ground who can go into each unit and hold them secure. If matters get to deteriorate where they come under immediate threat we can have them blow the installations and switch our entire operation to satellite and airborne units."

"I agree, that makes more sense, but be sure we have no other agencies on the ground muddying the pool Bob."

"Yes, Mr President, I think that's all been cleared up in the last few days."

"Richard, how many Varmint teams you got in there?"

"Mr President?"

"Don't play games with me Richard, I know very well you have Varmint teams in there. Their trademark is all over the place. If you think the CIA and its other clandestine agencies are beyond my knowledge then think again."

"Yeah, well, Mr President, what do you want me to do?"

"You've done enough damage Richard, that's why I've called you in here today. I'm giving you a warning Richard, and the Congressional Security Committee is howling for your blood, and I am going to give them what they want."

"But Mr President!"

"Don't you Mr President me Richard. For the last two years you have been misleading Congress into thinking that apart from the usual security measures in place to monitor, influence and coerce by the normal methods of moderate covert operations, you have been using Varmint teams to tear apart the civil power in mainland UK. Isn't it enough that we got what we wanted out of the Irish situation a hundred years ago -is it? You have jeopardised our long-term rebuilding of our relationship with the British by letting them fall into the clutches of that grasping maniac Muller-Weiss. I mean he's been making it a point of personal honour in taking the UK out and by annexing the British further into the European Union so far out of our way we'll not get back in there for at least fifty years, you stupid son of a bitch!"

"I am sorry Mr President I don't agree. I have Varmint teams in the area, yes, but no one has been ordered to step up their operations to a full level one agitation offensive, at least not to my knowledge."

"Not to your knowledge Richard?" The president handed over a dossier to his Director of the CIA. "You signed the order did you not authorising Varmint teams one through six to enter the UK and set up cell groups in London, Manchester, Glasgow and Swansea?"

"Yes Mr President, that was about two and a half years ago. We sent them in when the British threatened to nationalise foreign owned industries."

"So why leave them there after the mission to de-stabilise the UK Senate achieved its objectives Richard?" Look here, and here." The President rifled through several pages indicating dates, signatures and key events. "These are all orders issued by you in complete contradiction to what you have been telling us all along."

"No I haven't Mr President. I know nothing about those orders. I haven't sent in Varmint teams with that kind of remit Sir. There should only be two teams over there, operating on totally different briefs, certainly not political agitation on a level like this. Honest I…"

"Save your excuses Richard, we've traced your connections in the field right back to you. Your signature does not have to be on every piece of paper, but if you care to see further down in that pile of doo-doo we have collected, you're in on it right up to your neck. Either way you're out of it. As of now I'm taking you out and you're staying out of my way. You will face a Congressional Committee of Enquiry and I've no doubt that by the time they have finished with you you'll be totally screwed." The President pressed a small button on his desk. Two shiny suits entered the office through a side door and approached the President's desk.

"Yes Sir."

"Remove this, this garbage from my sight. Have him placed under the jurisdiction of the Federal Marshall waiting in the Grey Room. He knows what to do."

"Yes Sir."

"Mr President, you can't do…"

"Come along Sir, you know that's no way to behave in front of the President."

The President spoke into the brief silence that followed the exit of his late colleague. "Bob, I want you to get the Atlantic Fleet out on exercises like we planned. Nothing fancy, mind, just as far as the Western Approaches, you know, round to Reykjavik, maybe a small detachment over to Trondheim for shore leave. That kind of thing."

"Yep, consider it done Mr President, they've been on seventy-two hour standby in any case. I just need to cut the order Sir."

"When the Varmint teams get back Bob, don't intimidate them by throwing them in the slammer. Arrange for them to have a full debriefing and then split them up if you have to, give them the opportunity to retire or return to normal duties. They're all military by the looks of them."

"No problem Sir, but there will be a few civilians with specialist knowledge, perhaps we can take 'em off the Varmint programmes, have them pushed aside into administrative jobs in mundane intelligence, no direct involvement."

"That sounds fine Bob, just do it, the quieter the better, and make sure the next guy doesn't screw it up for us like Richard. Damn it! I hate that man for what he's done to us over the last couple of years!"

"Mr President." The Vice-President spoke. Until then he had watched the unfolding drama with some misgivings. "We're still calling the shots Sir, the European Union does not have the strengths of our own federal system.

I mean their military capability is still fragmented by partisan lines and cannot commit to any large-scale intervention. If Muller-Weiss moves against the British it can only serve to do more harm than good."

"Yep, that's the consensus, but he's actually going ahead with it."

"I don't see how he can sustain any argument for doing this Mr President. The Belgians' own protest pushed them to the brink of breaking away from the union, and I suspect that until they have stronger co-ordination of the police and justice systems the British are going to see this as an invasion. It's psychologically devastating for them."

"Again, you're right, but how does this affect our relationship between the big three in Europe? The French and Germans have the largest territory while the rest of Europe looks to the British for their lead. Threaten the British and you split the EU between two camps, the British and the rest against the Franco-German alliance, with the exception of the Italians who can be bought off any time with their mob politicians. That leaves us somewhat out on a limb doesn't it?"

"I have a meeting with the Secretary of the Security Council later today. Let's see if we can bring a little pressure to bear on the French. What do you say if we move the sixth fleet out of the Aegean and bring them west towards Italy and France, say somewhere near Sicily, that puts us in a position to clamp Tarranto, Marseilles and Toulon."

"Well we need something like this to distract peoples' attention away from our failing economy, so I guess a minor war to preserve our interests in Europe is just what we're lookin' for. Did I hear anybody say anything about the Russians?"

"No they didn't, is there something on your mind?"

"Well Mr President…"

"Now hang on there son, I always get a nasty feeling in my gut when somebody starts up with 'well Mr President' so this had better work."

"As I was saying Sir, the Paris and Frankfurt exchanges have just started rackin' up losses, and the assumption is that when they open for business proper they're going into free-fall, the British are already there. It's rumoured that the European Central Bank is going to slash interest rates by another three percent just to try to save the economy. Everyone is hoarding over there, with consumers holding back on just about everything except the bare essentials. So what I'm sayin' is that we're not far behind them either. The only way out is to pump up our economy, say, is to have the Federal Reserve release a few million dollars to give the country some liquidity. That's the only way to reduce our sliding economy."

"OK, that's par for the course, I don't see what else we can do in the mean time, but why is no one talking about the Russians. What are they doing? Has President Vassiliev come forward in favour of one side or the other? Can their secretive and long standing relationship with the French be upper-most in his mind, or will he favour the British and thereby widen the rift?"

"Mr President."

"Yes Bob."

"It does seem likely they will side with the British on this one."

"How so?"

"They have oil and can trade with the British one to one quite happily, and they need someone like the British with their Commonwealth infrastructure with which to open up foreign trade for materials, since their own infrastructure is failing back home in Moscow they've got nothing to lose."

"So let me get this straight, if we find a bargaining chip based on oil, sunflower seeds or whatever the hell it is that's so important we stand a chance of regaining lost ground with the British."

"Yes Mr President."

"And we can have our foreign war into the bargain."

"Er, not exactly Mr President."

"Aw, now come on Bob…"

"No Sir I'm not sayin' we can't have our foreign war. We need to work on it just an itty-bit more before we can walk in there and start crossing swords with everyone. The chances are that while our Mediterranean and Atlantic fleets are on 'exercises' they will be called on to escort supplies to the British, just like it was a century or so ago. Are you with me so far Mr President?"

"Sure am Bob, all the way."

"Then it's going to get nasty when the European President orders a blockade of the British. He's goin' to want to starve them into submission, but he can't afford to run more than six to nine months. Let's just say that with their economy slidin' like ours it's goin' to be more like close to six months. Somethin's going to break."

"The Russians will be forced to switch sides with the winner, and the British will be close to collapse."

"That's it Mr President, so why don't we rock the boat a little and get ourselves in there early, say interfere with their pipelines in the North Sea. The British will be cut off from the gas supplies on the continent, and be makin' enough oil reserves for themselves, if they've got any sense. The Russians will then decide to join with the French and the Germans and turn the screw on the British. If that happens we're locked out of any real presence in Europe Sir, so we'll have to accelerate hostilities by cutting off the British from their oil."

"You mean we step in at the right moment with a regular supply of stocks to keep the British going"

"Yes, they can't afford to pay us up front. Hell, Mr President, nobody can afford to do that, so when it's all over we'll screw them down with trade agreements they'll never be able to profit from including war loans that will keep them locked into our debt for at least a hundred and fifty years. You get your war and a firm foothold in Europe through the back door using the British."

****

"The navy under the command of Rear Admiral Dunham has literally marched into Whitehall from Parliament Square and is now manning all routes into and out of the Centre of London. Rumour is rife that scores of sailors are in the Houses of Parliament completely surrounding the Senate Chamber and the Commons. No one is coming out or going in. It's an extraordinary day with Londoners telling me that it's the first day for months that peace has finally descended on the City of London. In addition there are reports coming in that the navy is bringing in hundreds of vehicles loaded with provisions, not just here into London, but all around the country. It seems as though the political stalemate has been broken, and the Senior Service has taken the initiative in breaking the blockade

that the government has imposed on the people of this country. The army is co-operating by allowing the navy to distribute food that has been stockpiled in the docks for weeks under control of the recent government strictures, and that Soldiers and Marines with specialist skills are taking over power stations up and down the land. Wait a moment." The news reporter on the EuroSat news-link, paused pressing an earphone tightly into his ear. *"Oh, it's great news for the people of this nation. The navy; a small group of which; have escorted the Prime Minister out of Downing Street and are at this very minute; have been seen heading this way towards Parliament Square. Yes, there they are, look at that, they are not taking him to the Commons Gate, they're going in through the Senate Gate. I can only speculate what is going on in there, in the mean time we wait as a nation with bated breath. Perhaps this is the break we have all been waiting for. With that I'll hand you back to the studio."*

****

'Jack' lay back in his bunk drifting off to sleep with the gentle rocking of the skimmer easing him into peaceful dreams. Chip moved in with Fred in the small twin cabin sharing the small wardroom, using it as an office-cum-operations room whenever their guest was in his day room. The crew walked around in silence whispering conversations among themselves, until it was made known that Jack would prefer it if the men could continue about their duties in the normal fashion. "After all." He said to Chip. "I may be Royalty and the King, but there is no practical advantage to be gained from treating me like an ancient temple in the presence of which one is felt constrained to whisper in case some thunderous god is disturbed from a centuries-old slumber. Dispensing retribution on those mortals who dared disturb his repose." Chip had the word passed along and by the end of the first day the crew returned to a more or less normal routine. The last item in the repair list included a fresh lick of paint over the patched up wounds in her superstructure and along the scorched deck. A new name had been given her by Royal Command. The old SK939MG was obliterated forever, by swift strokes of a wide paintbrush under the steady hand of an Able Seaman, and the Privateer became HMS Royal Oak. The ship's name board made up appropriately by the skilful hands of a Cordon-Blue student chef who was more than a dab hand at artwork with icing sugar. The gold lettering upon a red background tiddlied up in proper naval fashion shone brightly in the afternoon sun. As the king observed, 'a just and fitting name for a king's hideaway'.

The orders came together with a number of authorisations and passes to pick up fuel, stores and whatever requirements they had need of. The letters Patent and the Royal Warrants were acceptable to all authorities cognisant of the reformed constitution and of the Act of Cessation. That the head of the royal family, no longer recognised as the head of the nation, retained various privileges and marks of respect, retaining the title, but no place in the ruling of the nation. That privilege falling upon the President who ruled as an elected political leader, ensuring the balancing act between the Senate and the Commons gave as fair a hand of governance as could be achieved for the benefit of the nation. The Prime Minister representing the popular voice of the people as the elected leader of the Lower House in the manner of a political 'administrator'; during his term of office. Despite the political downplay used to reduce the monarchy to a mere sinecure; no one actually paid any heed to the parliamentary claptrap. He was still their king, and the common folk up and down the land still regarded him as such. They understood his position, and wherever he went the people flocked to see him. A kind and courteous man, with a profound concern for the ordinary people of the nation and for their wellbeing. The act may have removed him from the constitution, but unwittingly it served to emphasise his political neutrality keeping the royal family out of the political spectrum and safely out of any blame for the current ills of the nation. Whereas all officialdom was bound to perform whatever legal requirements had been made upon them in the king's warrants, the population without such constraints did so willingly, and so the monarch had a guaranteed following that no one in all good conscience could deny him. A loyal following that would aid him given the chance. The Admiralty Seal set beneath the Royal Seal of the House of Windsor made it sacrosanct. The Royal Oak was about the king's business and no one should in the least manner interfere with her or her crew.

They sped the short distance to Portland Harbour making the breakwater by dusk. Jack kept out of sight while a reception committee greeted them as they came into the harbour alongside No. 1 jetty. The list of provisions had been handed over to the senior naval officer commanding the detachment protecting the harbour installation and its precious stocks. All around them they could see men working automatic equipment loading freight vehicles and fast hover-rail wagons at the railway terminus. It seemed as though they had been expecting the Royal Oak and watched as the fuel lines snaked across to the skimmer almost before the seamen had doubled up her moorings. Boxes piled high on the jetty were immediately thrown onto the conveyer that fed her stern doors in a non-stop line. Chip and his newly commissioned Warrant Officer went across the brow cutting a pathway for themselves through the melee on the dockside. Further on they found a Captain dressed in action working dress and a peaked cap pulling a large tarpaulin from a mountain of stores. "Captain Brunning Sir?"

"Why yes, I say grab that rope over there. That's it, good show." Mr. White stepped forward and together with the Captain pulled the tarpaulin neatly away from the pile.

"Thank you Mr..."

"Mr White Sir."

"Now perhaps Commander you can tell me who you are and what it is you want."

"I am Commander Woodingdean Sir, the officer commanding HMS Royal Oak."

"I think you will find everything is in order Commander as requested by Admiral Dunham."

"Yes sir, that's fine thank you. I present my papers Sir.' The Captain looked a little off balance. "Papers you say, what's this?" He took a pair of glasses from his shirt pocket and put them on. Carefully unfolding the thick documents Captain Brunning read through the documents very carefully. "Well Commander I can see that you have been busy and you're on an important mission. By Royal command no less. You can be assured of our discretion. Now tell me how can I be of further service to his majesty?"

"Well Sir, we are effectively un-armed only having small arms for our personal protection if required on shore patrols. Have you any laser cannon, missile launchers, or other portable or semi-portable gunnery that you could let me have?"

"Ah, I see where you are coming from. Can you tell me where you're headed Commander Woodingdean." At this point the Captain looked over the top of his glasses and his eyes wandered to the wings on Chip's uniform. I see you're flyer Commander. I knew a Woodingdean once; young chap looked just like you. Were you ever in Gibraltar?"

"Yes Sir I was."

"I remember now, you were involved in that sad mess involving that gun runner weren't you?"

"That was my best friend, we were in the flight that got bounced by his personal plasma-jet."

"Sorry to say it was me that went out to pick up your friend. It must have been a frightful loss for you, you looked absolutely shattered when I saw you two days later."

"Thank you Sir, we still pop in to see his family now and again, the kids are growing up fast."

"Yes, and this isn't getting you what you want. Look come with me and bring Mr White with you, I think I know someone who can help." They followed the Captain to a low two-storey brick building in the middle of the warehouses along the main quay. "Sergeant Conningsby!"

"Yes Sir."

"Where's your Captain Fitzpaine?"

"He's over there in shed number four Sir. They're just starting to move the stuff out of there onto the wagons Sir."

"Thank you Sergeant."

Come along, if anyone can help you, he can." They rounded the side of a large shed and turned a corner passing through the wide gap between cavernous double doors. The sounds of powerful plasma-drives greeted them as they entered the huge storehouse. Royal Marines were busily moving mammoth cargo lifters around laden with large storage containers. "Captain Fitzpaine!"

"Yes Sir!" Called the young Marine Captain turning on his heel in response to hearing the Senior Officer's voice."

"We need your expert opinion on fire power and hopefully you can then provide us with the means Captain."

"That's sounds more up my street than shifting cargo Sir. What exactly is the problem?"

"Allow me to introduce Commander Woodingdean. Captain Fitzpaine, Commander Woodingdean of His Majesty's Ship Royal Oak." The Marines

Captain stood to attention giving Chip a smart salute in typical Marines fashion. "Do I take it you need some guns Sir?" He asked Chip with a smile.

"Right on the nail Captain. We only possess small arms for the moment, but where we're going calls for something a little more substantial."

"Can you tell me where you'll be going Sir, or is that strictly off-limits in this discussion?"

"Not at all Captain, we're bound for Gibraltar where there is to be an international inquiry into environmental problems."

"Not my cup of tea Sir, but Gibraltar, yes, that does present some special problems with the kind of freeloaders and pirates in that part of the world. The French and the Spanish don't seem to care too much. But if you'll tell me what kind of vessel the Royal Oak is Sir I may be able to come up with a recommendation."

"She's a Class IV, Mk 1 Skimmer with twin plasma-jet propulsion, refitted in the last two months with Admiralty standard command & control systems."

"Mm, that would make her a Mk18C by our standards. Any fire control capability Sir?"

"No, none that I know of."

"In that case you'll probably require a small twin laser-cannon mounting on the fore-deck and probably a couple of semi-portables down the port and starboard waists. Mm, being an 18C you probably have an enclosed quarter deck don't you?"

"Yes, you seem to have a grasp of our situation. We could do with a couple of automatic laser rifle mountings there. There's been many skimmer Captain who's complained about the weaknesses that are inherent in that part of their vessels."

"How big is your rear access Commander, single or twin door with an opening deckhead?"

"Twin doors, rear loading, not top-loading, just a few feet where the flare of the doors round over to a flush-fitting bulkhead seal."

"Oh, one of the earlier Mk18s, I know what you mean." The Marine Captain paused for a moment or two thinking on his feet. "I'd say you could fit a hundred megawatt plasma canon in the back there Sir, but you'd need a trained gunnery crew to man it."

"We have the space at the rear of the main cargo deck, but the doors could only be opened, say about a quarter of the way each side otherwise they begin to play havoc with our stability."

"What about hand-held missile launchers. Could your men handle those?"

"We have a couple of trained missile men onboard, but they have been working tactical systems of late, but they can adapt."

"Right Sir. I'll get some of my men to bring down a couple of semi-portables for your mid-ships emplacements, a twin twenty-five for your fore deck, and I'll see what else I've got for your main armament aft. If we can get one, you must have your automatics removed from the quarter deck before you commence firing or you'll fry the little guns with plasma overload, and they are likely to take a substantial part off your quarterdeck when they blow."

"We could do with some hand-helds, Captain Fitzpaine."

"I can spare you a couple of those, say twenty rounds apiece."

"Make it twenty five could you."

"Right, twenty-five, I'll have to confirm with the armoury Sir, but I'll do my best. Look Sir, you seem to be in a hurry and you don't have any men onboard who are trained." Captain Fitzpaine turned his attention to Captain Brunning. "I would be willing to send some of my men with you as a gunnery crew. They need the practice Sir, none of them have had recent practice and they could do with a break from shifting cargoes around."

"How many men will it take?"

"Four men Sir under Sergeant Conningsby, he's been at it for five months without a break, no family to speak of, and he's seen action before. And I can spare one of the Corporals, Corporal Greasby, he's a gun maker by trade, very handy to have around if you need to repair guns in a hurry."

"Are you confident you can spare the men Captain Fitzpaine."

"Yes Sir, can you give me two hours to get both the guns and the men together?"

"Is that all right with you Commander Woodingdean?'

"Absolutely, we have one or two spare bunks, the rest can use a section of the crew accommodation area, and we have some time it seems. You were expecting us?"

"We were told someone would be arriving, requiring a rather speedy turnaround."

"Thank you Captain Fitzpaine, your men shall find us over by number one jetty." Chip turned to face the senior Captain. "Thank you Sir, I am sure this will stand us in good stead."

"Not at all, If you meet those pirates on the surface you give them hell Commander, we have a few debts to pay in addition to your own."

An hour later a small vehicle arrived with two gun-mountings in the back. Four men climbed out of the cab and worked the small crane on the vehicle positioning the larger gun on the quarterdeck and the smaller twin on the fore deck in front of the bridge superstructure. Another crew of workers arrived in a similar truck, this time hauling plasma bottles and welding kits over the quayside onto the skimmer's narrow waist. They began manhandling their equipment down to the quarterdeck where they started to lay rails in position on the main cargo deck. They grabbed some seamen who went through various evolutions opening and shutting the cargo doors until the men had positioned the rails just right, so that a gun could be mounted on the rails and traversed back and forth without fouling the doorways. They quickly tack-welded the rails in place, marked out the holes in the flanges, and then drilled holes in the decking allowing the rails to be bolted in position. The semi-portables were brought onboard and stowed in the cargo deck adjacent to the screen doors on each side of the ship. Finally, they bolted the twin twenty-five Megawatt laser gun emplacement on the foredeck. The Royal Marines arrived in a couple of MPVs unloading their kit, slinging most of it across the narrow gap between the jetty and the deck. They commandeered one of the craned vehicles and slung a small cargo net from the hook. The ammunition was handled expertly by the men who gently lowered three loads into the open side-doorway giving access the main cargo deck. Next came a small bucket brigade along the gangway as they handled a collection of small arms and rocketry safely in pre-loaded stowage boxes onto the cargo deck.

Within two and a half hours the Royal Oak had been replenished, armed and was ready for sea. By a quarter to nine Mr White gave the order to start engines and she slipped her ropes once again heading for the Channel. No ceremony or circumstance, just a quiet run to the breakwater then she was gone. The evening swell over the inky sea did not bode well for their journey across the Bay of Biscay.

Dr 'Jack' becoming the sobriquet they gave the king down in the Junior Rates mess seemed to stick with an inevitable amount of popularity. As the skimmer went on her way the crew returned to the rhythm of life at sea, taking the rolling deck in their stride. The addition of the marines brought out old familiar rivalries with their attendant good-natured banter between the sailors and the boot-necks. Combined teams worked at the stowage of the ammunition and lighter armaments before they repaired to the mess-decks for the usual welcoming. The Corporal being put up in the mess with a spare bunk, while the privates were given a sectioned off area of the lounge for sleeping quarters. Sergeant Conningsby found a place in the Senior Rates mess and was happy with his ration of alcohol out of a keg.

As the night wore on the wind backed causing the sea to rise and fall more deeply as long range Atlantic Rollers, reinforced by the wind, became crammed into the funnel of the western approaches. They went off-planes just before midnight making just fifteen knots in a starboard sea. All eyes were on the tactical plots with sensors trained on the surrounding area for many miles. Those who were off-watch scrutinised the entertainment and news channels for the latest updates on the situation in the UK. All were immensely proud of the navy's apparent role in bringing law and order back to the nation. The Senate had been asked in short order to suspend the government and rule directly until a fresh mandate was obtained from the nation. The Army lifted travel restrictions in several major towns and cities, enabling crucial supply lines to be reopened. The President was rushed back from his private residence in Berkshire and re-instated by an immediate and unanimous vote of the upper house. Naval patrols cleaned out the dregs haunting the Lower House, unceremoniously throwing them out on to the street, mounting a strong guard at every entrance to the ancient building. Rumours had been flying around thick and fast for most of the day. The people were very concerned about the intended 'invasion' by forces from mainland Europe and any news from that quarter became more and more unsettling by the hour.

President Warnock made several attempts through all of the official diplomatic and non-diplomatic channels to contact the European President or his Deputy. He knew they were stalling when, by two o' clock in the morning, no one was available. He left a communiqué at the Presidential-suite and with the Security Council. At four o' clock it was decided to inform 'our American friends' that the crisis was over. President Shaw was mighty pleased to hear it and re-iterated his kind offer of help should his 'friend' in the UK require it. Warnock gratefully declined the offer, commenting on the rather large size of the exercise fleet approaching from mid-Atlantic. Everything was smoothed over and Presidents Warnock and Shaw breathed a little easy.

At half-past four the alarm bells started ringing in long range military observation posts. By almost five the President was informed of intense activity in the Channel ports from Denmark to Belgium. Energy plumes were seen rising above naval installations amidst a lot of activity, while several military airfields gave indications of large transports embarking large amounts of stores and troops –apparently. In stark contradiction to the unfolding events the tactical plots and sensor relays didn't show the same data. All was apparently calm. The local national defence system in the UK had a small number of different feeds; not all of them were native European data links. By the six o' clock news stories began to break indicating all naval units had pulled back, being replaced by line regiments who patrolled in their stead. President Warnock sought advice from his Senate Committee for National Security and sealed the fate of thousands of people up and down the land. A presidential address was scheduled for 06:45 that morning.

"People of the United Kingdom, I have today very sad news to bring to you on a matter of the utmost importance to us as a nation. As I am speaking, units of the European Standing Naval Forces, and the European Standing Army are embarking towards our coasts with the intention of taking over our country. I cannot allow that to happen. I have signed the order mobilising our armed forces to the defence of our nation. To that end the naval units who so courageously brought law and order to our country and who, together with the army re-established our supply chains; have already been recalled. They will engage the large fleet that is sailing towards our shores at this very moment. Supporting them is the Royal Air Force and the Royal Marines units. Army units are now preparing defensive positions along our coastal routes and at strategic locations up and down the country.

I have made contact with our old friends in the low-countries and elsewhere in Europe as to whether or not they will stand down their portion of the military and naval forces fast approaching our country. I have to tell you that I have received no such undertaking. Sadly, therefore, I have to announce that we are at war with the states of Europe

As the representative head of state and of government in this nation I call upon all able-bodied men and women above the age of eighteen to step forward and to volunteer to serve our country in its defence against the aggressor. Who even now is gathering momentum as their army crosses the North Sea from the continent of Europe. You must report to your nearest recruitment office or Territorial and Reserve Units wherever you are, to enlist in this great enterprise." He paused then resolutely spoke the words written out of the constitution almost a century ago. *"God save the King!"*

Dr Jack was asleep; the excitement of the last four days had clearly tired him out. In a way the events had become all too surreal as they unfolded, and he was glad to get away for a while. Chip read the signal that came through a quarter of an hour before the President's address to the nation. It was brief and to the point indicating the nature of the threat and who the threat was, and of course the change in status from readiness to that of a war footing. He could not believe it and squinted at the signal several times while getting dressed. "What is it Chip?" Mumbled Fred who had been disturbed by the signal op knocking on their cabin door. "Serious stuff I'm afraid, are you able to get up Fred and muster all the crew as soon as possible. I must inform the king before anyone else."

"Inform the king Chip? What is it, is it war?"

"Yes my friend, they've finally done it. President Muller-Weiss has ordered in the navy, ground troops and armed police to take over the country!"

"Strewth!"

"Keep the lid on this and rouse the crew with a minimum of fuss, have them clear the lower deck and muster in the cargo deck in fifteen minutes."

"OK Chip, consider it done." Fred waited for Chip to leave their cramped quarters before heaving his wiry frame out of his bunk. Looking down he saw his wounds had started weeping into the dressings around his legs. He ignored the pain as he pulled his uniform trousers over the bandages. 'They'll have to wait.' He thought to himself.

The much increased ship's complement were mustered in their divisions exactly on time and waited in silence for Chip to appear. The ranks of sailors, rocking slowly backwards and forwards as one, while the deck rolled gently beneath them. The king appeared shocked, but shook his head with a dignified air of resignation. "Even now, they dare to push ahead with this unconstitutional step a second time Captain Woodingdean. I thought they would have learned from the discord it made with the people of Belgium."

"Just so Sir. I have the men mustered and I am obliged to inform them before the news is given publicly. May I have your permission to withdraw Sir?"

"Yes of course Captain. If there's anything I could do I would be grateful for the chance to assist you."

"Thank you Sir for your kind offer. The men may want to see you around and about Sir during the day, it may be an encouragement to them."

"That's is a good idea Captain, I would be glad to talk to some of them, I gather they haven't been home for almost a month now?"

"No Sir, they're feeling somewhat out of it at the moment, but they are fiercely loyal and looking for a scrap." The king smiled up at him from his chair."

"And you must go Captain. Please let me know how they take the news."

I will Sir. Thank you."

He ordered the men to break ranks and they assembled around him in a tight knot of humanity, some looking half asleep, others alert and concerned. Standing on an old box he began the awkward task of breaking the news. They all took it in silence looking glum. *"The only good news I can offer at this difficult time is that it was the Navy, as you no doubt are aware, that made the difference by breaking the stranglehold on the country. That it means essential supplies, of food and water and sanitation are back on-line. Our families will be getting back to normality as the days go by. Travel restrictions have now been lifted except for the normal system of patrols and guard posts required when the country is at war. Please register any strong concerns for your families through your divisional Senior Rates, and I will ask for a replacement Welfare Committee to field your concerns. Once again I will do my best to provide answers to your specific questions. Except one, that is, no one knows as yet where we shall be going after Gibraltar. I would like to add that His Majesty is concerned for you all and is aware that you have not been home for some time. He will be seen walking about the ship taking a general interest in us and how we work. You are not at liberty to express your own views on the subject, either political or otherwise. Remember the proper marks of respect, and in addition you do not address His Majesty unless he speaks to you first directly. Thank you that will be all."*

Most of the crew was having breakfast during the Presidential Address as the Royal Oak dipped and skewed in a worsening sea. Rain began beating down on the superstructure and on the decks like an incessant drum beat. Although her central hull was broad and deep like a true merchantman, she was travelling light and tended to wash out across the crest of each wave as it charged into her from the open Atlantic. Seamen rigged storm lines along the decks and inside the main cargo hold as the weather began to deteriorate in a deepening low. The dark grey sky flickered occasionally as the Bay of Biscay began to show her teeth according to legend. The viewers gave off an eerie light in the gloom while the watch keepers patiently observed tactical, weather, communications and sensor plots.

"Herr President!" Came the enthusiastic greeting from Deputy Augsburger. "They are on their way!" The northern flotilla of the Dutch, Belgian, one Norwegian and two Danish frigates will rendezvous thirty kilometres from Gravelines and sail from that point into the Thames Estuary into the Port of London. Riot police units are being flown into the old airfield at London City while the Spanish navy sailed last night bringing the troops we need to Control their remaining ports and cities in the south and western peninsula."

"How long will it take for the Swedish and Norwegians to arrive in the north Holga?"

"They started embarkation at three o' clock this morning, and will arrive some ten hours later in a second wave that is designed to cause a lot of confusion with the English. They are heading for the principle ports of Grimsby, Hull, Sunderland, Newcastle and Edinburgh."

"It's a pity we can't reach their western ports so easily. How do they propose to move once they have taken control of Manchester, Liverpool and Glasgow Holga?"

"Ach, that is more difficult. Edinburgh will be surrounded once the northern Fleet under Admiral Hemke of the Netherlands has landed troops at Berwick. They have fast ground vehicles and will enter the city from the south swinging around to capture the airport. Their navy will be blockaded in the Firth of Forth, and so will be cut if, Herr President, they choose not to stay out of the way. The air transports will use the airfield as a fuel dump and transit camp from where Norwegian and Swedish Commandos will continue their journey to take Glasgow and the Clyde port installations by noon on the second day." The exuberant deputy, pointing several times on a wall map as he spoke.

"General Friedmann did say that by taking these routes here and here the ground troops will be able to break the main lines of communications between England in the south and Scotland in the north, here at Carlisle and just outside Newcastle."

"By the time we have our ground troops in place all the major north-south routes will be segmented at key positions, and the east-west routes will be secured around London until the Spanish fleet arrives on the western Peninsula. Here at Falmouth and over here in Plymouth, while they will either take the port of Bristol or blockade the Bristol Channel if the British refuse us entry."

"Very good Holga, I think everyone has done well. Please inform the General Staff that I want to hold a briefing with them at four o' clock this afternoon." President Muller-Weiss pressed a button on his view panel. "Ute, come please?" As the deputy left the presidential suite the President's leggy secretary entered the room. She was wearing a blue pin-stripe skirt, a sheer off-white blouse with a delicately folded cross-your-heart plunging neckline, revealing just a tiny amount of cleavage of her ample bosom. President Muller-Weiss watched her for a moment as she sat down in front of his desk crossing her legs carefully, notepad and pencil to hand. "Did you get through to General Erbeldinger in Mannheim Ute?"

"Yes Sir, he sounded really grumpy when I told him you wanted to speak with him."

"That sounds like the old devil Ute. What did he say exactly?"

"He said you had no business messing about with an old war horse like him, especially when he is on holiday."

"Ach, so that's why he is difficult to track down. Where is he Ute I must speak with him?"

"He's taking the Kure at some clinic in the hills near Bad Kissingen."

"Good, leave me the details of its address and telephone number and I will contact him myself. Thank you Ute."

"Not at all Sir. May I ask something Sir?" Her pencil dropped from her hand as she spoke, he caught a flash of soft white skin beneath her blouse as she leaned forward to pick it up off the carpet. "Yes what is it?"

"It's just that I have not been home for eighteen hours and I need to go home to rest and get some sleep. So if you don't mind I would like to go." He gave her a casual look as she stood up and smoothed the wrinkles out of her skirt.

"Of course Ute, I am so sorry. Everything has been so distracting in the last forty-eight hours that I have forgotten, even for myself. Please go home and come back tomorrow morning refreshed."

"Thank you Sir, I'll ask if Martina from the registry can stand-in for me if you need anything; she has only just come back in."

"She will do nicely, thank you, now go and get some rest."

The European President moved into a small office off the main suite closing the door behind him. He opened a large ordinary looking cabinet to reveal a completely miniaturised communications panel. From here he could contact any one of his key subordinates at the touch of a button. "Erbeldinger please?" He enquired.

"Wait a moment Sir, I'll get him for you." The receptionist at the clinic located the General in his private suite and connected the call. "Heinrich, is that you?"

"Yes, yes, you know damn well it's me. Why this cloak and dagger approach?"

"Oh, it's not really you know, just precautions. Put the scrambler on Heinrich." There was a slight pause before the old General spoke again. "Well Mr President I see Phase one of Operation Drachonsberg is under way. Phase two is ready to be put in operation at any time."

"Good, Heinrich, that is really good. There's just a small change in the timing I think and then we can wait for the right moment."

"What are you proposing?"

"Let the French move first Heinrich, give them about two hours before you start your Schnell-Commando-Gruppe mobilisation."

"That's tactically a big mistake, you should know that. It will cost a lot of lives if we lose the element of surprise."

"Can you give me two hours Heinrich, that's all I need?"

"Ja, it can be done, but it is as I said, very costly in the number of men we are likely to lose as a result of stalling our initiative."

President Paul van Beek of the Netherlands spoke over the secure comms link to his counterpart Erik van den Baalen of Belgium. "Erik, I don't like it. First you in Belgium, and now our old friends in the UK. We owe them too much."

"Ja, I agree Paul, but there will be reprisals you know that. What about Rasmussen in Denmark, did you get through to him?"

"Ja, he is just as disturbed as we are, but we all have one thing in common, and that is we all have the Germans just over the border, and you have the French too."

"It's too quiet Paul, there's nothing else on the map, I'd say we're being used. There's not a single French or German unit anywhere in the civil or military units on their way over to England. I tell you they are using us Paul."

"Rasmussen says the same thing. I don't think anyone has failed to notice it Erik. The answer is always the same; we're tied to the civil and military accords. So what are you going to do Erik pull out and risk another presidential enquiry? It could cost you and your country a great deal."

"You know Paul, we value our friends. When we were in great trouble they always helped us, even when the French marched across the border seventy years ago they landed a whole army in time to cut them off. 'Just visiting' they said. Le Ramat their president swore revenge. I think the time has come to be counted. I know what I must do. All I ask is that if you decide to join us you make it soon."

"OK my friend I will let you know, good luck in whatever you decide to do."

"And to you my friend."

"We cannot locate the king, Sir. He appears to have completely disappeared. None of his household knows where he is and the royal family is rumoured to be either at Sandringham or even as far away as their Balmoral estates."

"Thank you William, in some respects no news is good news. Please send for Major Anders of the Royal Engineers. He is in London isn't he? And an ADC to his Majesty?"

"Yes Sir, he was until about three months ago when he finished his appointment."

"Good, perhaps he can help us William, but please, be discreet and choose your moment carefully before you inform him that I want to see him. Tell him it is a matter of utmost urgency that I want to see him straight away."

"Yes, of course Sir."

"Good William, now hurry, we don't have much time!"

"William Goodfellow, private assistant to the English President, walked swiftly through the lofty and warmly lighted corridors of the president's official residence with a graceful ease. Used to being both a high-level advisor, secretary and sometimes messenger. He was a familiar face among the powerful and influential circles of national and international diplomacy. Few looked up as he passed by them for they knew he was about the business of the president and only the foolhardy would impede his progress. Only once did anyone ever interfere with him and to that person's cost. The individual concerned was bombastic and totally self-interested lothario of an MP with a minor Baronetcy in his pocket. He chose precedence one day, while driving his vehicle the wrong way down a one-way street, on the pretext that since he was an MP and the other road was blocked he had a right above anyone else to take that course of action. Waving his hand angrily at a London policeman he ordered the copper out of the way insisting on some imaginary authority that even the short arm of the law could not touch him. While the recalcitrant MP was being arrested on the street along came William Goodfellow in his vehicle in the proper direction. Seeing that his intention to pass down the street the wrong way was now blocked by the oncoming vehicle, the wayward individual loudly abused the police officer blaming him for causing the obstruction. William, it must be said, sat calmly waiting to see what would happen. Pushing the policeman aside he climbed back into his vehicle and started to drive it directly towards William mouthing obscenities and gesticulating wildly with his free hand. William sat impassively as he watched the other, much higher vehicle, approach his own. As the front ends of the vehicles connected two burly policemen appeared around the street corner coming to the aid of their colleague. It augured badly for the police as much as for the arrogant politician puffed up with his own sense of self-importance. The police Commissioner was ordered to hush it up, but unfortunately too many members of the public, including a network news reporter and the cat was out of the bag. William on the other hand remained out of the limelight by simply staying calm and unruffled. No mention of charges and fines was made in the press, and indeed, the buffoon received a disciplinary 'ticking-off' from his party secretary. However, imagine his surprise when a higher charge of impeding a presidential emissary was laid at his door. The man was left with no alternative and slunk out of public life with two, rather than one chip on his shoulders.

A friendly and amiable man without the need to press his rank or status, William found his way to Wellington barracks and carefully acknowledging the marks of respect offered to him by the common soldiery, arrived at the office of the Adjutant in double quick time. The Major, he discovered, was across the river in Battersea training a squadron of engineers in the finer points of micro-engine maintenance and repair. William courteously declined the offer to wait in the Adjutant's office and chose to go there directly. He enjoyed the short stroll from the entrance to the park to the military encampment. He eventually found the Major in the centre of a scrum of soldiers, leaning over a stripped down engine. "Major Anders?" The Major looked up and looked directly at William with a pleasant look of enquiry across his face. "Yes, I am he."

"Allow me to introduce myself Major." William produced a small metallic-like business card with the presidential logo in the top right corner. It read 'William Goodfellow, Private Secretary and Presidential Equerry'. Pierce Anders whistled a soft low whistle expressing his surprise and that he was suitably impressed. "Ah, I see, and you want to see me, here, now?"

"If that is not too much of an inconvenience Major."

"Give me a minute to wrap this up. In the mean time you see that smaller bivouac over there, make yourself at home and I'll join you shortly."

"Thank you Major." William was enjoying the luxury of the warm winter sun on his face and strolled over to the Major's tent. He sat down in a studio chair and in the lee of the tent allowed himself the temporary enjoyment of sunning himself in a quiet spot for a few moments. "Right, what can I do for you Citizen Goodfellow, that brings you all the way down to a muddy field in the London Boroughs?"

William opened one eye and viewed the Major with a smile, then closed his eyes one last time. "Tea William?"

"That would be nice but mind you, none of that chemical sweetener you shove in yours."

"Oh, really, and what's wrong with that me lad?"

"Oh nothing much." answered William laconically. "Just a damaged liver and a malfunctioning pancreas after years of exposure to it."

"Oh, I see William, I am sorry to hear that. Are you really that ill?"

"No, but you soon will be if you keep piling it into your tea."

"OK William, now suppose you tell me what this is all about? Or do I need to guess?"

"We have lost someone rather dear to us Pierce, and we don't know where he has gone?"

"That's rather careless of you William." The Major looked intently at his old army friend and pondered his answer to the next question. "Don't suppose you know where he is do you?"

"Not likely old chap. Could take an educated guess though, but who wants to know and why?"

"It's quite simple, we have no Lower House at present, no chance of an election for the foreseeable future, and a war on our hands. Does that ring any bells with you my fine friend?"

"Now look here William I'm a soldier, not some soothsayer or informer. Suppose you get to the point, and here's your tea." William opened his eyes slowly locking them onto the mug wafted in front of him. "Thanks." He took the tea and thought for a moment. "Well it's almost that simple Pierce. It is more constitutionally sound to have a king and an elected Assembly of one kind or another than to have an elected Assembly in isolation."

"You mean you're looking for his majesty to install him in the capacity as the Royal Advisor to the government pending some future elections, and all that constitutional guff?"

"Yes."

"Well, why didn't you say so. No I don't know where he is. How does that grab you?"

"I'm not convinced. Tell me. If I gave you a warrant to find the king to persuade him that he is needed back home to help run the country would you do it?"

"Mm, difficult one that. All expenses paid –with an advance?"

"Of course. So you do know where he is."

"Er, no William, I have a hunch that I know where he is, nothing more."

"We need him here Pierce, otherwise we are constitutionally at an impasse, and that has given President Muller-Weiss and his cronies precisely the impetus they needed to send an armed invasion over here. With him here to work fulfilling the task of Royal Advisor and independent arbiter, Muller-Weiss and his little gang haven't a leg to stand on."

"Yes, that's all very well, but supposing he's been spirited out of the country or something similar, it will take time to find him and to get him back home, and, I suspect, time is something we ran out of at around about five o' clock this morning."

"You're very well informed Pierce."

"No more than usual William, it's in all the briefing procedures for senior officers."

"Humph."

"Look, I'll ask around William. Give me the next couple of hours to finish this off, have a change of clothing and then I'll come and see you."

"That's m'boy. Now tell me, what's with that tiny little gadget thing you were messing about with?"

"Oh, that. It's a neat little toy isn't it? It's a free-piston Stirling engine. Ever so easy to run and operate. They're like the old diesel engines that they used to have aeons ago but now much cleaner to run. No one could get them to work efficiently for literally centuries. Then some chap got their efficiency up to about 30% and they started using them again experimentally. Do you want to have a look? They're so simple with metallised ceramic components and plasma injection cooling systems bolted on; gives them something like 67% efficiency. Just right for small generators and battlefield power sources. I think the navy's invested heavily in the technology to provide emergency power to their smaller ships when the main drive systems fail."

"No, that's alright, really, I thought I recognised it. My old granddad had something like it at home. He generated his own power with it. Very handy during those dark days before they rebuilt the grid."

"A genuine antique eh?"

"Well, look I must be off, but come in mufti wont you, and I'll arrange for you to have as much authority as one can have in order to travel and overcome petty officialdom on the way to finding our quarry. Believe me Pierce, no harm will come to him, not while President Warnock and myself are around to see that nothing can go wrong. Whatever happens, whatever you hear, you must come straight back to us. Do not drop your guard for anyone, especially the politicos on the mainland."

"Fine, I'll see you in about a couple of hours."

"Cheerio and thanks for the tea Pierce. You always made a good mug of tea."

"Thanks William, see you later."

The Adjutant came swinging by in his hoverbat an hour later looking as though someone had ruffled his feathers. "There you are Pierce. -I had this rather interesting character see me earlier looking for you. Did he find you?"

"Yes thanks, did he say anything?"

"No, not a thing, just said he was quite happy to wander off down here by himself to see you. He seemed to have a pretty important looking ID."

"That's William for you. We were Cadets together when we joined up at the academy."

"I see, and now he's a civilian working for the President's Office. He's more than a secretary I'll be bound."

"Yes he is, but I'm never sure what other jobs come under his belt."

"It seems he's pulled a few strings Pierce. It appears you are being re-assigned to a new appointment with immediate effect. Is this something to do with the fact that you were until quite recently the king's ADC, or shouldn't I ask."

"Can't say for sure. Are those papers for me?"

"Yes, I thought I'd bring them personally since they are marked high priority."

"I hope he has arranged a replacement for you. It's damned awkward this. You know we've just received the word, we're moving into the docklands area. The rumour is that there's a planeload of French militia being sent in and due to land in about an hour's time. Our job is to round them up and send them packing." The Adjutant handed Pierce Anders his re-appointment letter to the General Staff, acting as a Presidential Envoy on temporary assignment. Pierce opened the folded letters and checked the contents, scrutinising the new ID and travel permit. He whistled that low-pitched whistle of his. "That lot would get me just about anywhere in the UK let alone anywhere in the Union. Pretty impressive for an old crock wouldn't you say?"

"Old crock?"

"Yes, I thought you knew? He took a couple of plasma bursts in the leg at Ontario Heights. Oh they re-grew the lower parts of his leg in the bio tanks and totally re-built the tissues, even the missing bone, but some of the nerve damage couldn't be healed, so he has a small implant to fire synthetic ones."

"He was over there. You don't mean that fellow Goodfellow?"

"Yes, that's the one. He stopped the American spear head dead in its tracks, he and his Sergeant."

"Well, I'm blowed. He's the man all the fuss was about. They reckon he should have faced an international tribunal for genocide or something."

"Hardly when you think about it. American division held up by two survivors defending Canadian pipeline installations. The truth is James, the Americans, shot half their own ground forces to pieces themselves, while their air force blew up most of what was left. All William did was hold two hundred of them off until Canadian reinforcements arrived five hours later. By that time only two Brits survived out of sixty-five. The Yanks were gobbling with abject embarrassment and accused us of using some secret weapon."

"Whole thing was stupid in the first place if you ask me. Fancy trying to steal gas from the Canadians just because they had run out of their own supplies"

"Well, for all that William left quietly and with good humour. It cost the Americans a Presidential election and he's the only VC for about eighty years, and they gave him his third pip into the bargain."

"Well, I must say, I have never shaken hands with a VC before. What a day it is Pierce, an extraordinary day. Good luck to you. If there's anything I can do to help you just say the word. Now I must be off. Bye"

"Thanks James." The Adjutant walked out of the tent, hopped into his hoverbat and was gone. The techs under their Sergeant were clearing away their specimen engine while Pierce Anders walked slowly out to the waiting transport.

Halfway to their destination the Norwegian Frigate Lillestrom slowed to a crawl. The Captain signalled the flag officer that his vessel had developed engine trouble and was heaving to with the skimmer Telemark standing by in attendance. As the naval force approached the outer reaches of the Thames Estuary the Danish contingent suffered a minor catastrophe when a plasma cell ruptured spewing high energy plasma into the atmosphere in a blaze of sparks and shutdown their engines. The second Danish frigate took the first in tow, heading back for Denmark. The Belgians kept having trouble with their radio systems breaking down until they reached a point where the Belgian vessels executed a neatly synchronised one hundred and eighty-degree turn and facing due east stopped engines in a defensive formation. Shortly afterwards the Netherlands navy peeled away line astern drawing themselves across the front of the Belgians extending the line to the north. The troops onboard unaware that anything was wrong for a while. As the afternoon wore on tactical plots registered the passing of transports on low level approach in the skies. Their pilots apparently, blissfully unaware of the change in circumstances among the surface vessels. Approaching mid-channel each aircraft received imperative instructions to stay out of UK airspace or face the risk of being shot down. As the first transport dispersed towards the old London City airport the tactical systems onboard registered that ground weaponry had locked onto them. Passing through five hundred feet on final approach a salvo of plasma cannon fire streaked past the nose in an upwards arc. Intended as a warning shot the pilot took note, but continued the approach. At three hundred feet a plasma burst took out his starboard outer engine and the pilot broke off his approach by hitting the throttles and pulling up and away from the runway centreline. The two aircraft destined for Heathrow Metro fared none-better. After two missed approaches each, including a Bosnian death-slide, the pilots decide to give it a day. As evening fell the flotilla of ships moved off-station and began a slow journey back the European coast.

By five o' clock that evening Europe had become an armed camp with the Low Countries and the Scandinavian countries mobilising in the north and west. Politicians scrambled for exit routes out of the European buildings in Brussels like rats from a sinking ship, while the population waited indoors with bated breath on one hand and a bottle of Geneva in the other. Messages of support came from all over the place as President Warnock put together the final touches of his national address for the early evening news bulletin. France and Germany remained in apparent calm. There was no mobilisation and no news bulletins about the abortive raids on the British Isles. The Swiss quietly mobilised their army as the population made their way down to their bombproof shelters. All was quiet apparently from the Pyrennees to the Pas de Calais and from the Schwarzewald to the Baltic.

Halfway across Biscay the tactical plots went blank as the EuroSat downlink was pulled by the mainland, and the UK switched to alternative modes of operation. The radio op and the PO Electro-tech loaded the latest codes and 'played' with the system for half an hour before establishing some decoded link data. Limited data was coming through and they could see the plots for the UK and their own locale at the touch of a button. The Royal Oak was travelling slowly in the heavy swell and the torrential rain made it impossible to see much beyond the foredeck in front of the bridge screen. She ran down one slope to bury her slim nose into the face of the next oncoming wave, heaving herself to the crest of that, then shuddering all the way down into the trough behind it. Low power sensors extended the range of their vigilance by a dozen miles or so, while sub-surface information was completely impossible. The hands changed watches for the first dog leaving the off-watchmen scurrying for the small galley and some tea with a welcome bite of food. The Marines had no opportunity to calibrate the guns, and like jack-tar sat out the weather wedged in corners or stretched out in their accommodation areas. Here and there, small knots of men gathered at the small portholes along the upper superstructure of the cargo deck or at the larger windows in the stern-doors. The empty deck throbbed and rattled as the vessel rose and sank, rose and sank. The quartermaster's mate looked a deathly pallid green as he clung to a stanchion trying to time his breathing with the pitching and rolling of the skimmer. The bucket of goo at his feet told its own story.

The king graciously accepted the appointment of two mess-men and the electrician was utterly delighted to be recommended as the Royal Cook for the journey. The king knowing full well their professional priorities ran hand in hand with a ship's domestic requirements, made as little impact on them as he could. Although domestically he was somewhat a late starter in life, his early apprenticeship at the naval college soon came back to him as he changed gear and began to manage his own personal requirements. He was fascinated by the industrial laundry unit built in to a small alcove in the midships section 'tween decks. He received instruction on how to use them from an 'awfully nice chappie' with a beard, who turned out to be one of the engine room mechanics. The lads had a whip round pooling their own resources to present the king with a tub of royal dhobey-dust that was left in a specially made bracket screwed into the bulkhead next to the washing machine. He discovered it, much to his relief and delight noting the primly made out label announcing proudly 'Dr Jack's Dhobey Dust – Hands Off!' He found the tumble dryer quite a novelty enjoying the heat as he pressed his hands against the glass in the door.

The second day brought much speculation as dawn broke high above an evilly compacted mass of swirling clouds. The craft was operating at the limits of her stability and Chip ordered a change of course to bring her head fully around into the rolling seas. The new course would take them widely across the great bay, but as safely as could be managed. The alternative was to turn for the distant shore beyond the horizon with a following sea. The news 'viz' in the canteen only went off late in the evenings when no one was there to watch or when, as now, the signal deteriorated through bad weather. The system struggled to hold its lock onto the satellite chain miles above in space, although some of the men watched it as the signal flicked on for a moment or two, then flicked off again.

There were a number of abortive attempts to land both troops and federal police on UK territory. Without naval support to secure the port of London with their reinforcements of ground troops, the whole situation developed into a fiasco that the media exploited remorselessly. The Belgian and Netherlands' news agencies ran a fully public commentary on the situation for those two nations, making it known that both nations had opted in favour of the British position having mobilised their forces in a defensive move to fend off any interference from 'external' forces. Still there were no words or actions from the European President. Although, one correspondent from the WNA did report that several high ranking officers were notably absent from their headquarters while the defence ministers were also not available in their ministerial locations in the parliament building.

The king suffered seasickness with great stoicism during the bad weather. When he was not resting he scanned the viz whenever he could. At times he tried to follow the tactical and sensor plots as a distraction from the queasiness gnawing away at the pit of his stomach. Seeing the plight of the boy seaman he took pity on the lad and asked Chip to have the boy relieved from duty. The navy not recognising seasickness as an ailment refused to allow any seagoing crewmember any leeway. Chip sent for the boy's 'sea-dad' expressing both the king's concern for him as well as his own. The Leading Seaman tacitly confessed that he had arranged the occasional sub for the boy, but agreed wholeheartedly it was a kind offer to stand him down. The lads in the jungle greeted the news warmly, with the usual banter associated with 'smally-boyz' in the mob doing a man's job. Someone rigged a makeshift hammock out of ropes and a blanket and they shoved the poor wretch inside it with his little plastic bucket. At mealtimes they helped him where they could, leaving him to sort out his bucket and other things, occasionally waking him with a mug of hot sweet tea. Late in the evening a hand appeared clutching a mug of coffee laced with liberal quantity of rum. Although illegal, some still used it discreetly to settle upset stomachs or calm the nerves here and there. With his watches covered by the lads the boy fell asleep assisted by the rocking motion of his comfortable hammock.

Public opinion was definitely very mixed. The official news agency of Europe the ENA slated the British as a rowdy, unconstitutional, ill-mannered lot at the heart of most of the troubles that beset Europe as a whole. Their ranting was tempered by the sympathetic and encouraging new-sheets produced by the supporters of the British, who publicly revived some old scandals over the unbalanced apportionment of grants and the enormous sums of money being pocketed by European civil servants, while revealing some new scandals. Implicating the declining democracy within the European super-state since the President had taken office. In the Middle East some reports indicated that Iran was seen to be assembling its troops and resources in what was suspected to be a possible situation along its border with Turkey.

Later the following day as the Royal Oak slipped passed the north coast of Spain with the Barrosa peninsula far to the east, the President of the United States, and thousands of people around the world woke up to the startling and bizarre world of globalisation. America's largest utility crashed spectacularly from its hallowed place among the top one hundred. Thousands lost their jobs that day as the skies cleared on the western Atlantic seaboard of Europe. The company, Gencat had major fingers in every power utility around the world. Its escalating financial difficulties collapsed finally in the face of falling energy prices that had uncovered undisclosed debts and doubtful accounting. Major European providers owned by Gencat suddenly found themselves naked and exposed, and business crumbled like a house of cards. By the time Royal Oak had weathered the storm abeam the north Portuguese coast the army and airforce back home had stepped in with their specialist units at every power station on the mainland. Their navy colleagues were drafting in nuclear and regenerative system specialists to cope with the few controversial power stations still in service. The lights went out across Europe as thousands of redundant workers from the gas and electricity industries shutdown their works and picketed the gates. In the US there were howls of rage as banks and insurance companies went to the wall. The largest howls came from several of the eastern states that had invested their pension funds in the corporate pie. Insider dealing, incestuous partnership deals and finally, the downturn in available cash in the hands of the energy consumers in both the States and in Europe, where the company had most of its assets, extinguished the dreams of millions of ordinary people.

"Mr President we have a serious situation here."

"Don't tell me something I already know Arthur, or is there something new you have to tell me?"

"It's the damn Russians Sir."

"What?" The President turned pale. "They've offered the Europeans assistance in their current difficulties Sir."

"OK, spit it out Arthur, what are they saying?"

"They've picked up on Gencat's failure Sir, and they're offering a deal with that son of a bitch Muller-Weiss!"

"Damn! That's the last thing we needed. They've beaten us to it. You know what will happen if we don't keep those two apart? We'll be faced with the prospect of a massive power bloc coalescing right in front of our eyes. All the way from the Atlantic to the Pacific!"

"We may be able to stall them Sir. There's the split emerging between the northern countries on the mainland coming out in favour of the British. If we can turn that situation to our advantage and widen the split we may yet have what we want by way of an even wider doorway into the European heartland."

"That doesn't address the problems we have been saddled with at home. We're going to have to get the military involved in this one, just to get the lights turned back on."

"I know that Sir, but can we afford to lose the opportunity before the Russians swing a deal with the Europeans and close the door on us remaining in Europe?"

"We won't have anything unless we get ourselves back on line with the utilities Arthur."

"That's a fact Sir. Look, the British have pulled the plug on their gas pipeline to Europe, they're also self-sufficient in energy reserves for a while, and as long as they're in good relations with the Polish over their coal supplies they will remain buoyant in spite of this problem. The mainland is not so simple. Their utilities criss-cross so many borders so many times, it will take them a while to sort this mess out for themselves. The Norwegian and the Dutch can help the Belgians and the Danes, while that leaves Switzerland neutral –as ever, and Luxembourg undecided."

"There's Spain, and you're forgetting the Balkan states Arthur. You know that the Iranians never forgave the Turks for developing their hydroelectric complex, damming all those rivers and flooding the valleys. There could be a chance there through the back door. Has President Vassiliev made any announcements yet Arthur?"

"No Sir, we only have our intel reports to go on, but it's solid information."

"I see. Well, we'll have to commit the military in providing manpower at the power houses and gas pumping stations, as well as to providing emergency power to farming and out of town areas. That will take a while to set in motion. Hell, that means just about everybody else in the industry is going to have to assist in patching it up. That's going to reduce our capability to backup anything that we do, be it an offer of military support to the British or a defensive action against the Canadians or the TEKs of China and Japan. No, charity begins at home Arthur. Put together some ideas with Bob with this situation in mind to see if we can exploit and push home our clandestine operations in Europe, something that will hold together for a while until we can concentrate on getting our forces consolidated on external affairs. Got it?"

"Yes Mr President."

****

"Captain, this is the bridge."

"Captain here, go ahead."

"We have a three contacts on sensors Sir, making speed in our direction from the west."

"I'll be there in a moment." Chip walked from the wardroom up to the bridge and looked into the primary tactical plot. "Any ident on those contacts yet?"

"No Sir, they may not be on our mode."

"Change mode, that big one looks like a carrier and the two others an escort."

"Tried that Sir, there's no ID."

"In that case keep it on mode sweep and let me know when the plot changes. Chances are they're Americans coming in to join the sixth fleet."

"Aye, aye Sir."

"Signalman!"

"Aye Sir!"

"Scan the Admiralty and US movements list for the last month, see if you can find any movements listed for the US in the Mediterranean."

"Aye Sir."

"Good evening Captain." The king emerged from his cabin a little more cheery than he had hoped for. "Oh, er Good evening, Sir, er, Doctor Jack." The king regarded Chip with a mischievous twinkle and pretended not to notice the slip into formality. "I see the weather has changed for the better, and we will most likely have company just before dawn."

"Yes Sir, it's just possible the Americans are going to be ahead of us as we turn the corner around the bottom of Spain."

"Oh splendid Captain, we shall have a sight to cheer us up after the last few days of beastly news and awful weather."

"We will indeed, would you like me to keep you informed Sir?"

"Please Captain, I wouldn't mind some distraction and I'd like to see what kind of ships they are." The duty signal op approached Chip from the side and discreetly handed him an electronic message tablet. The MT displayed a NOTMAR indicating that the USS Cyrus Vance would be transiting the Straits of Gibraltar en-route to joining the sixth fleet.

"Here's some interesting news Sir, it's the Cyrus Vance with her escort. She's joining the sixth fleet, probably at Syracuse."

"Oh, that was quick. I shall be pleased to catch a glimpse of that one. Let me know when they come into view Captain. Thank you." Dr Jack turned and wandered down the flat on his way to the small canteen. Fred had taken the Pilot's seat a little earlier and was enjoying the freedom of the open sea. His upper torso moving fluently backwards and forwards with the rhythm of the waves. Sub Howell acting as the co-pilot was also enjoying the different view and his first watch as a duly qualified skimmer pilot. Chip climbed up the ladder light of foot and crouched behind him in the back of the cockpit. "How are you feeling Fred?"

"Oh, just fine, with medicine like this I'll be right as rain in the next two or three days."

"Glad to hear it, did the medic get any more splinters out yesterday?"

"I'm afraid so. It's getting to the painful stage now that the skin is healing over the entry points, but with that magnetic resonator our electronics genius built he can tell which one has a splinter underneath it and which ones can be left alone."

"That's a good idea. I wonder how he thought of that?"

"Don't know Sir, but I tell you this he's doing all sorts of magic with the satcomms down in the equipment room. Go and have a look."

"Is it legal?"

"Er not entirely, but since it's more or less war Sir, it doesn't make much difference."

"Touché. I think I will next time I pass by."

"You won't be disappointed."

"Changing the subject, have you seen the sensor plot?"

"Yes Sir. Looks like a flat top coming through."

"I'll have them punch up the tactical data as soon as we can get it."

"Right you are." They eased forward as a large wave lifted the bows in a majestic sweep skywards. Chip waited for the bows to hang momentarily at the crest then, turned on his heel and slid down the ladder before the keel beneath them started its downwards slide.

The two groups met six miles distant at the approach to the Straits. The reason for their apparent speed became obvious shortly before the flat top came into view. She was at flying stations and periodically the distinctive buzz-crackle of powerful plasma-jet engines could be heard as her pilots flew the pattern inbound for their 'home plate'. Chip was somewhat amused at their decision to fly on the approach to a narrow channel that offered limited manoeuvrability, particularly since the sea state was far from perfect.

He regained his perch in the cockpit and watched enviously as the pilots went through their evolutions. "Hey look at that, there's another one being waved off!" called Fred. "Seems like they're getting some refresh time in by the look of it."

"It's amazing how soon you forget the intricacies of military VTOL/STOL approaches," said Chip wistfully. "I'll bet, look at that one there, looks like he's skidding in the air."

Sunlight peeped through a ragged cloud-base that held off the surface by a margin of three hundred feet. Keeping their distance the Royal Oak fell into position early, thus making his intentions known to the Captain of the carrier, and to the Captains of the escorts. While progressing through the narrows three miles abeam and slightly astern, it became obvious that the carrier was having problems getting its aircraft back on to its flight deck. The narrows created a much higher frequency of waves with deeper troughs causing the deck to pitch alarmingly. Out of the gloom there appeared a large liner east bound for the Atlantic. She was huge, deep in the water and fast moving. The rake of her stack and the line of her bows shouted cruise ship. She must have been doing at least thirty-eight knots. The Carrier's skipper was caught with his trousers down, technically, while attempting to navigate the narrows and accommodate the squadrons onboard in their flying during marginal conditions. The carrier furiously signalled the cruise ship to get out of the way. Both the Captain and the Air Commander were spitting venom. "Can't that son of a bitch see what we're doing!" yelled the Captain angrily at the advancing liner. He had two aircraft to go both short on plasma-cell energy generation. The cruiser just kept on coming. With a large whoosh and a shower of blue sparks the penultimate aircraft touched down on its insulated pad on the flight deck while five miles astern the last aircraft rolled out on its final approach. They tried light signals as well as shouting, but to no avail. The liner was fast approaching giving the carrier and its attendant escorts and rescue aircraft little spare room.

"He's got to be thick or stupid pulling a stunt like that."

"Which one do you mean Captain?" Came the voice of Dr Jack. "Oh, hello Sir I didn't hear you coming up. It's the Carrier. He must know that just about every vessel in the Straits runs the risk of being attacked by pirates, that's why they all make a beeline in and out of the Straits at full power. The only hope they have is to outrun them into the open sea and the swell. It slows down the pirates who lose the chase the minute they have to go off-planes, and at this time of day the poor visibility helps them escape their clutches. That Captain is hazarding his ship and his aircrew."

"I see, well let's hope he can get through without causing too much embarrassment." They watched in silence as the last aircraft swept in upon the carrier's heaving stern. "Oh my goodness!" Cried Dr Jack as the little splinter of an aircraft suddenly pitched upwards just before crossing the stern. "He's run out of plasma or something like it!" observed Chip his heart in his mouth. The slender nose pitched up momentarily a split second before the aircraft swerved to the left nose high then dived to hit the sea hard. "Look at that!" Somebody yelled from the bridge below. They saw the aircraft amid a shower of sparks before it exploded, below the surface disappearing in a huge flash as the carrier slid past it. The Captain must have ordered an immediate turn to the left and then to the right. Amid the confusion it put the carrier momentarily on a collision course with the cruise ship. The carrier's bow turned agonisingly slowly back onto its original course while the upper superstructure and masts of the liner passed in front of its snub-nose and then down the starboard side of the flight deck. Those in the lower accesses beneath the flight deck could see far into the cruiser's brightly-lit interior. The stately ballroom, dance floors and restaurants slid by in a silent testimony of opulence. Like a snapshot in a dramatic movie the figures of men frozen by amazement cast a surreal shadow across the enfolding scene. The amplified sounds of the water being churned up in the narrow gap of sea far below them, the closeting of the overcast and the ordinary sounds of the other vessel spoke of another world about to crash into theirs. Finally the moment was gone leaving it to the escorts and the rescue hover-jet to get out of the way and locate the pilot, if he survived.

"Lookouts out on the Starboard side, at the double." ordered Chip on the ship's intercom. "Sir, I will try and keep our distance, but I am obliged to help in the search for their pilot."

"Not at all, Captain, please proceed as normal."

"Thank you Sir."

"Fred bring her round a couple of points, there's just a chance he baled out before the explosion. Bring the speed down to five knots."

"Five knots it is." They scanned the distant sea that lay between them and the flat top without seeing anything obvious. Everyone turned to look more closely in the direction of the carrier, the lookouts straining their eyes, trying to penetrate the evening mist. The signal op called out "There's a chute dangling from underneath the lift sir on their port side aft!"

"Good man!" shouted Chip. Make the following signal; use signal lamp only mind, and ignore ident!"

"Aye Sir."

"Signal is as follows. 'To the USS Cyrus Vance: have spotted a parachute beneath elevator, your port side. Good Luck'. Message ends."

"I don't suppose we'll ever know if the pilot survived." Dr Jack spoke the thought aloud, though it was on the minds of everyone watching the distant drama. "Captain. Equipment room." Blared the mini-loudspeaker in the cockpit. "Captain here, go ahead."

"We have acquired tactical Sir, request your immediate presence Sir."

"Can you put through to the bridge plot?"

"No Sir, it's serious, you need to see this."

"OK PO, I'm on my way." Chip and Dr Jack swapped places in the cockpit and Chip slid down the ladder to the bridge below. Striding into the equipment room he found the ship's electronic wizard surrounded by boxes neatly stacked up across a desktop with cables looping around like a rats nest of spaghetti. "What on earth have you got there?"

"Oh it's a domestic decoder system piggy-backed with one of our tactical boxes interfaced to the comms link decoder box through the tactical processor node Sir."

"I'll take your word for it. What's so important?"

"I've broken into the Eurosat-taclink and the plots are very different from the ones we've been getting, here take a look at this."

"What's all this, it looks as though there's a lot more activity in the Baltic fleet than previously known."

"That's not all Sir. Have a look at the US downlink from their navy's Villager tacsat network. They have it online and we're picking up bleed-through from their antennae on the Cyrus Vance. That's why the viz. is much better at the moment."

"What the hell is all that mess down there. That's Cadiz isn't it?"

"Yes Sir. I'd say the fleet's in if I'm not mistaken."

"There must be nearly a hundred and fifty vessels there. Can you get the SSR data and get this information out to the bridge view screens?"

"It'll take about five or ten minutes to complete, Sir, but if you want hardcopy I can print it out now without it coming on the viz."

"Do it. I need to see what they've got there. Thanks PO and well done."

"That's all right Sir, I thought you wouldn't mind."

"Keep at it, and let me know when you can get through to the plot."

"Aye Sir." Chip held his breath as he read through the list of names coming off the printer. "Foch, Cousteau, La France, Seville, Don Giusseppe, Juan Carlos, all heavy cruisers, thirty-six frigates, fast attack boats, skimmers, troop transports five submarines and two flat tops." The list indicating an impressive collection of firepower gathered for a single purpose. "Get me the SSR printout for the Baltic as well. This is beginning to look like an invasion fleet."

"It does look as though there's something going on Sir."

"Look at this, the Bonaparte, Villiers, the Paris and the Pompidou. Adenauer, Breslau, Brandenburg, Lubeck and the Heidelberg, plus dozens of skimmers and assault craft."

"If you were to ask me Sir I'd say they were going to strike at the UK in a classical pincer movement from both the north and the south."

"Quite; right stay at it, this is all good stuff." Chip picked up the intercom microphone and sent for the signal op. Together the three of them worked on a priority signal to the Admiralty requiring them to break radio silence. The Chief Electro-tech worked out a narrow band compression signal that the radio op had encoded with an almost impossible to break encryption code. Fred was relieved of his enjoyment and together they worked on the tactical plot in the bridge using the electronic tools and the new found gadgetry to pinpoint concentrations of naval forces at other ports like Toulon and Marseilles, picking up an Italian Viper squadron transiting across the western Mediterranean. Presumably, on its way to Cadiz. These were arguably the fastest surface vessels around. The best combination of performance and design, something the Italians always did so well.

"The Americans can see all this, but I wonder if they will do anything with the information to help us?" Pondered Dr Jack who had been roped in to sift through another list of tactical information. The Royal Oak was making heavy weather of the Straits as the radio op broke radio silence in a brief one way communication to the Admiralty. Overhead a maritime reconnaissance aircraft could be heard zooming past looking for a break in the clouds for visual contact. The Royal Oak was positioned just far enough out of the way of the US patrol, but just close enough to be mistaken for part of the action. With her SSR 'squawk box' switched to standby mode there was going to be a question mark over her identity as far as the Americans were concerned, but everyone else would take her to be an American vessel. The Americans had an idea she was a British man of war, obviously, but had no intel on her. Playing the game for the next two hours they ploughed on eyeing each other up while following the same course. Abeam the Rock, Chip brought Royal Oak onto a northerly heading, peeling away towards the apparent safety of the Harbour at Gibraltar. The poor visibility persisted and no one saw anything solid until just beyond the breakwater where the lookouts caught a glimpse of the light beacons and the cliffs beyond.

Chip handed over his precious cargo to the Governor-general who escorted Dr Jack to a waiting hoverbat keeping the façade going all the while. The crew shut down Royal Oak's engines and waited patiently for the leave arrangements. Fred briefed the crew about security and the messing arrangements in the small barracks. Chip, Fred and the Chief Electro-tech went ashore shortly afterwards and disappeared into the naval complex of buildings, sheds and offices, Emerging some time later into a brightly-lit office deep in the heart of the rock itself. There they briefed the C-in-C and his security team, leaving the technical details to the Chief Electro-tech who delivered a set of schematics and a list of instructions on how to build a multiplex decoder interface, handing over a copy of the necessary program code on optical disk.

"You're right about one thing." Observed the C-in-C's aide. "Whitehall has made no mention of this information. Either they are aware of it and protecting their sources, or they are indeed ignorant of what is going on."

"I suspect Sir, that they are probably making preparations for defence as we speak, but as you say, are in ignorance of this information."

"Now that you're here, what are your orders after this point in time?"

"I'm to await further orders Sir. Presumably Dr Keen will either stay here at a discreet distance or be flown out to some other destination."

"Well, all I can do is to thank you Commander for bringing him safely to us. For the time being, welcome to the Dragon's lair. We're surrounded by the Spanish and likely to be attacked on both sides by both the Spanish and the French, so watch this space is all the information and the warning I can give."

"Is the squadron still active at the moment?" asked Chip, an idea beginning to form in his mind. "Yes of course, although they have somewhat scaled down their activities until Spanish have remove their field artillery from the border. I see you're a pilot. They'll be pleased to see you Commander."

"Thank you Sir."

8. A CHASE IN THE FENS

"Alexeyavitch, you are not proposing to agree to OPEC's demands at this moment in time, are you?"

"Boris, you know what will happen if we hold out for much longer, OPEC will make it very difficult for us. We will lose their respect, and after all, we have made enough money for the time being."

"Yes, but to drop the price down to twenty five dollars a barrel will put our prices up and already there is unrest in the provinces."

"I know Boris, but you know as well as I do that they will kill off our markets by undercutting us. We cut production by a hundred thousand barrels a day and watch the price of oil go up again. That puts us in a stronger position to bargain with Muller-Weiss and the British -Muller-Weiss wants more oil, -the British want oil. Let them fight it out and we sit back and make a big profit. Then you can have your Trans-Siberian super highway."

"Yuri, tell Boris how we stand with our gas pipeline supply to the west."

"Boris you worry too much. Since we renegotiated the deal to pump gas from our Siberian gas field to the EU the price has been steadily rising over the last ten years. Now since they are on the brink of war and their utilities have failed they want more gas, and they want more electricity. The price has just gone up, so it is with oil. If we hold back on production the obvious will happen."

"Yes, that's all very well, but the plan calls for a strategic link between our western cities and our energy resources. The old mag-lev railway is costing too much out of our development budget for the link Yuri."

"Be patient my friend, you will see. The situation in the west will provide us with greater leverage in the world markets and we will be able to take off the top layer and pay for a hundred, no two hundred strategic links across the Federation, and beyond that."

"Alexeyavich I have to show you this intelligence report that came into my ministry late yesterday. It shows there are people willing to sabotage the pipeline, why only three days ago someone tried to blow up one of the pumping stations, and you know what that means, no gas for months until we can repair it."

"Yuri is this true?"

"Yes, it looks like it. We think it is the Americans again. They don't want us to use it, so they will blow it up in order to destabilise our supplies to the EU."

"Do you have hard evidence of this?"

"Not yet, but any day now we hope to catch them and work back as far as we can."

"We already have exercises taking place close to the Finnish border, and down in the south, can we spare some militia to go on exercises, ostensibly to guard against a simulated attack?"

"We don't have the budget for that Alexeyavich. Besides, the American steel is beginning to show signs of failing badly in places. It's a long time since they built it for us, and the repair programme has not been exactly kept up to date."

"Boris! What are you trying to do, uh? Make me look like a fool! You know very well that it has taken a long time to walk back from collapse. Now, only now, are we able to make enough money from such things -yes? Then, we can start to rebuild our infrastructure."

"Please, please. Boris, Yuri, this is not the time for that kind of argument. We will reduce production and stabilise the price of oil at a 'comfortable' level. Privately we can set any price we want to. The gas situation is easily understood and we will be able to exploit both Muller-Weiss and the rift caused by the Americans."

"That's true, don't you agree Boris?" Eh, it's quite something when you consider that the manufacturing output of the Americans has fallen into third place and Germany, yes Germany has twenty-seven percent unemployment across the country and they cannot sell their cars. Look, it's falling apart for them too. Both the Germans and the French have reduced their industrial output by nine and a half percent, but we are picking up as they start to use us with our cheaper prices. Boris it's working. Don't you see?"

"Of course Yuri, I see it that is why I want the super highway finished. It will connect our steel mills and factories in the east with our gateways here in the west. It will move our prosperity as our own output picks up with the new demand from the west."

"And of course it will connect our high technology here in the Federation to the east. What could be better? Work together on this and tell me what you have got, then perhaps we can look at some military support to protect our interests not only here, but abroad."

"As always Alexeyavich, you are right. Come Yuri, let us do as he says and draw up a plan of action."

****

Meanwhile, Pierce Anders found himself standing amid the hullabaloo of London's main hover rail terminus. Turn to the right and he could be on a fast transport to the continent, except that there was an armed guard manning an official barricade. Turn left and catch a 'wobbly' to the north of the country, limited stop, cold tea and a headache at the other end. So called the wobbly because with Britain's narrower gauge railway the high-speed definition of the European rail network was marginalised by the peculiar rocking motion that set in once the carriages were elevated above the narrower track. Walking without hurrying he headed for the underground system that would take him to the regional terminus at king's Cross. He was bound to have picked up a shadow somewhere and from time to time found himself pausing outside shop windows looking at the reflections they gave from different angles while he pretended to be window-shopping. The miles of underground shopping malls with their well-lit tunnels, pavement bistros sporting tables and chairs underneath the branches of imitation trees, plastic flowers and so on, gave a kinder prospect to the traveller with time to spare. He caught the 'flyer' to Norwich on a ticket for Colchester, which was not an unreasonable thing to do after all, for an army officer travelling in mufti with the country on the brink of war.

Late in the evening he arrived at the RTO at Colchester's modernised hover rail terminal to arrange for a vehicle to pick him up. He caught a glimpse of a short man wearing a nondescript brown raincoat as he climbed onboard the military hoverbat, and was sure he had seen that raincoat somewhere on a railway platform in London. Seeing his papers the gate-guards waved his transport through into the heart of the garrison itself. If he was right and his shadow was non-military he would be safe for the night in his temporary quarters. He made two personal calls before heading for his room.

At breakfast he was the first to arrive and was careful to blend in as other officers began to wander in to the dinning room. By half-past six he had changed into fatigues before commandeering an MPV. It contained a pile of kit bags and odds and ends bound for a convoy heading out of the garrison towards Harwich. It had tinted windows preventing outsiders from looking in and suited his needs. The convoy left the garrison by another gate taking the old road out of Colchester where he was relieved to find no brown overcoat anywhere in sight. The trip was uneventful and for him it was a relief to find that almost all service personnel were on the move in uniform. Very few civilians were in evidence. The MPV dropped him at the naval base where he found the Queen's Harbourmaster's office. Shortly afterwards he found himself speeding across the estuary towards Felixstowe in a fast multi-hull that the navy used to ferry personnel and their belongings around the two harbours. He couldn't help noticing the growing assortment of vessels and the defensive emplacements in and around the estuarine towns.

In Felixstowe he found the army liaison office next to the station and changed out of fatigues back into his uniform with collar, tie, jacket and peaked cap with its thick band of gold braid along the front of the peak. By a quarter to ten he was seated on the fast train bound for Ipswich where he caught the express bound for Norwich. His brother met him at the station to whisk him away in the direction of the family farm at Horsham St. Faith. He spent the rest of the day around the farm hoping that by doing so any scent of him would be growing cold. An idea that had been fizzing slowly in the back of his mind came to the surface. "Phillip, do you still fly that old contraption of yours?"

"What d'you mean by old contraption? It's a vintage aircraft with a highly respected pedigree." They laughed. "Well, I have an idea and I'm also in a bit of a hurry."

"Ah, is it legal? I ask myself."

"Oh it most definitely is legal Phillip, you can be sure of that. In fact you would be doing a great service if you could fly me to see an old friend who may be in trouble."

"This isn't official business is it? You know my insurance limits me only for pleasure flying."

"Consider it unofficial brother dear, just a jaunt for a couple of civilians going to see an old friend."

"You wouldn't mind telling me just who this old friend is would you. It's just that I've got a nasty feeling in my water."

"Come on then get your maps out and I'll show you."

By half-past three they arrived at the disused airfield just outside Norwich. The long low hangars now rented out piece-meal to the odd enthusiast who still had a dream that private pilots would one day have the right to pay non-commercial rates for their fuels and for parking. Removing the covers he could see the old Tomahawk was painted in white with old-fashioned red and blue go faster stripes leading back from the nose sweeping all the way along the fuselage and up the vertical fin. The distinctive low-winged high T-tail, two-seat monoplane sported a new coat of paint and a brand new airworthiness ticket. Before opening the hangar doors his brother did the pre-flight checks walking swiftly around the aircraft in a clockwise direction. Switching off the electrics, he then proceeded to check the hardware more carefully, under the bemused gaze of his brother. Finally Phillip tested the fuel in the tanks and from the bleed valve in the left-hand side of the engine cowling, idly tossing the spent fuel away on the concrete floor. "Right let's get her outside." He said with firm edge to his voice. They manhandled the large hangar doors until they were just wide enough to accommodate the narrow ten-metre wingspan. The slender wings rocking up and down as they dragged the aircraft without too much difficulty out on to the apron, closing the doors behind them. Clambering in to the interior Pierce noticed the reproduction plastic interiors and the soundproofing carpeting on the floor. Rubbing shoulders in the narrow cockpit his brother went through the checklist and finally locked the throttle into a just cracked open position with the red mixture lever set to rich. He looked around once and then turned the old fashioned key in the ignition shouting, "Clear prop!" The engine choked into life easily and the throttle was set while more checks were carried out, this time on the engine's performance. After checking the magnetos he switched on the comms console and released the handbrake by pushing down on the release and pulling slightly back before allowing the tension in the system to pull the lever forwards.

They wobbled over the edge of the concrete apron onto the grass taxiway. After completing high power checks and making sure that the engine temperatures and pressures were within limits he moved the aircraft onto the runway, advancing the throttle in a single slow movement all the way to the firewall. The single propeller dragged the little aircraft forwards at an ever-increasing speed until at fifty-five knots he gently inched the control column backwards allowing the aircraft to fly itself off the ground.

"Not the same as for your average jet-jockey eh?" His brother grinned at him happily. Pierce smiled back enjoying the experience of being airborne again. They levelled off at a thousand feet on a rough heading that carried them in a north easterly direction towards Fakeham. In less than twenty minutes they turned due east and dropped to five hundred feet south abeam the town. The flat countryside beneath them looking drab and dirty as the dereliction of winter set in. Well on time due to an easterly wind they made their final approach fourteen minutes later as the field near Anmer became visible. Harvey Thorne met them in his muddy old Agri-car. Once they had manhandled the aircraft gently under the protection of a small hangar next to Harvey's vintage Mooney they set off for the farmhouse nearby. Fred cheerfully threw a code lock card at them as they climbed into Harvey's swanky 'town' vehicle stored in a large garage next to his home. The code lock blinked green while the onboard computer ran self-test and sensor checks then turned a steady green indicating the vehicle was ready to drive. "Voice command input activated." Came the computer-generated voice from a hidden loudspeaker. Phil grinned with delight and gave the command to 'drive'. The vehicle moved forwards and got as far as the gate leading from the house and gardens before it slowed gently to a stop. "State destination and preferred route." Requested the vehicle trip program sub-processor. Harvey came running up laughing. "Sorry I forgot. You'd either put in a trip by pressing the trip command button there and telling it where to go or by turning it to manual. The computer will let you take it from here."

"Thanks Harve, we'll take it from here and leave the computer behind." Phil touched the manual button and drove out of the yard waving to his friend. The car handled the road beautifully as they passed along the country lanes. Taking the hairpin bends in its stride as the adaptive suspension and dynamic inflation subsystems adjusted both tyre pressures and suspension for controllability and for a perfect ride. Soon, the massive wrought iron gates came into view as they drew near. Phil drove past continuing down the road for a couple of kilometres. Behind a stand of trees shedding their summer coats of green he turned right onto a farm track of granite chippings neatly edged with coping stones on each side, later taking a right at a fork in the road. They swept around a wide curving route between fields and woodland until they reached a point where the great house came into view. Beyond the gardens tucked away out of sight they came to a gentle halt outside a neatly painted cottage belonging to the estate. Phil backed the vehicle carefully between a small barn and the side of the cottage out of view from the general surroundings. Being relatively flat countryside, the nearby hillocks represented occasional vantage points for prying eyes. Pierce knocked on the front door and stood a couple of paces back from it. He heard footsteps approaching from the inside along the tiled floor that he remembered during his frequent visits as one of the king's equerries.

The door opened slowly and a middle-aged man with greying hair and a slight stoop looked out directly at him. "Major Pierce Anders, what a pleasant surprise. Do come in, you're most welcome."

"Thank you Hilary, it's nice to see you again. This is my brother Philip, and I've come to see you about a private matter." They walked across the threshold and stood by the doorway as Hilary Askew, one time estate manager and advisor to the king on local agricultural matters, proceeded to lead the way down the narrow hall. They entered a neat lounge made cosy by the warmth of a small log fire burning in a mock Elizabethan grate of the second era. "Well, there's no need to introduce my wife to you. Look dear it's Major Anders come to pay us a visit with his brother." Veronica Askew looked up from her book tablet and smiled a kindly welcoming smile. "It's lovely to see you again Pierce do come and sit down and tell us what you've been doing lately. And this is your brother, you're so alike."

"This is Phillip, Veronica. You may remember that I mentioned he farms not far from Norwich."

"Oh, that's right, I do remember there was an occasion when we chatted about your family. Well, Phillip you are just as welcome as is your brother. You're not another practical joker are you? Having one around like Pierce is quite enough believe me."

"No, far from it. I'm supposed to be the serious one of the family."

"Good to hear, now come along and sit down, and tell us what it is that has prompted you to come all this way to see us. Although I think I can guess. It's about his majesty isn't it?"

"As usual Veronica, you are very much on the button, so to speak."

"Well, in that case I'll leave you and Hilary alone together while I make some tea in the kitchen. Can your brother stay with you or does he want to join me in the kitchen?"

"I think I would prefer to join you in the kitchen Mrs Askew. The less I get involved the better."

"Oh, please call me Veronica. Come on then we can have a chat over some fruit cake."

Hilary and Pierce chatted for almost half an hour before there was a tap on the door. "Come in." Called Hilary and his wife came in carrying a tray with two mugs of tea and some slices of cake on a large plate. The conversation stopped until Veronica left the room, at which point they picked up where they had left off. "I can only tell you Pierce that he came to see us about ten days ago and after about an hour he vas visited by an Admiral and the Admiral's young aide. His majesty seemed to be expecting them and after a short while here in the lounge they all left in the Admiral's car. Where they went to I've no idea, but the king did tell us that he was going somewhere safe until all this trouble had blown over."

"Any idea who this Admiral might be"

"Not in the slightest. We seldom see anyone in uniform here except the royal equerries when they come and go on their official duties."

Pierce Anders had met and befriended the Askews during his time as an equerry. Enjoying their company and the freedom to roam the large estate with Hilary who was an excellent manager and an excellent shot when it came to shooting game. A minor peer coming from one of the old families who still retained the right to inherit a title he had met and fallen in love with Veronica one of the ladies in waiting to the queen. The two men had hit it off immediately and their friendship had grown as they established joint interests in fishing, fine whiskey and intellectual chatter as they walked around the fields and byways of the estate. One thing they both shared was a passion for the rectitude of public attitude towards the king and the protection of his person from either scandal or harm. Pierce new it was a mild risk so he broached the subject more directly. "I've been asked by the President to find his majesty and to ask him to come to London."

"What on earth for?" asked Hilary Askew looking a little suspiciously at Pierce. "I don't have much time to explain Hilary, because we have to get back to our aircraft before it gets dark…"

"You flew here? This must be very important for you to do that, but I don't see how I can help you."

"The President does not have a complete mandate to rule without the Commons. With the legislative body now gone the constitution allows for the President to either manage in the interim pending a general election or in a time of crisis jointly with the monarch. President Warnock is, I believe, an honourable man. He sees it as imperative as a bulwark against the increasing threats by the European Parliament to put their own armed police and militia on British territorial soil."

"You mean he wants to avoid an invasion by bringing the king into public life -but what if that plan does not succeed? What if the Europeans go ahead and invade anyway, what will happen to him?"

"I don't know. All I can think of is that the same Admiral whom he knew and appeared to be trusted by the king is our only link, and I must find him."

"Well, if it's any help to you Pierce you should be on the look out for an Admiral who walks with a pronounced limp and an eye patch."

"My God Hilary, we don't have an Admiral that fits the description!"

"I can't help you anymore than that. That's all I know. A very pleasant man, but I would say he was a man very much in pain of some sort given his gammy leg, and the king seemed to know him quite well."

"Well, it's better than nothing. Perhaps I'd better head off back to London and have a discreet look around the Admiralty. Such as it is, these days, but tell me, what of the Queen and the royal family? Are they safe?"

"Ah, that I can tell you. They are quite safe. The Prince of Wales is safely tucked away with an old friend on Dee-side, while Her Majesty is staying at the Canadian High Commissioner's private retreat at Chiltern Park with the three princesses." Pierce felt highly relieved and looked it too as Hilary scanned his anxious face, noting the change in his manner. He knew that Pierce would not betray his trust in sharing such sensitive information. Pierce nodded his approval and spoke softly after a short pause in the conversation. "I'm glad we still have friends that we can trust." Hilary knew of his fondness for Bernice, the youngest of the princesses, nodded silently in agreement before saying. "It will start getting dark soon, but before you go let me give you something." Hilary rose from his fireside chair and crossed the room. He reached for a drawer in an antique dresser pulling it open. Fiddling around for a few moments he appeared to find something, grunting with satisfaction as he pushed the drawer back. "I know that I can trust you, and your intention is to bring him back safely. Take this small medallion. It's not much, but the king gave it to me a few years ago when we had a successful hunt with the king of Afghanistan. If you give this to his majesty it will tell him that you have seen me. He knows you as a trusted aide, but this will give him much more to trust you with. I hope you will understand. You must give it to the king personally. If you fail in your mission to see him then the king is indeed in danger, then send this back to me as fast as you can."

"I hope that I will not have to do that, but I will if circumstances dictate. Thank you Hilary, thank you."

The flight back to Norwich was uneventful, taking a different route back to the aerodrome. Phil didn't ask any questions although he remarked on his brother's brooding silence as they drove back to the farm. "I can't tell you any more than you probably know or can guess. What I will say to you is that if I need your help at any time in the future I know that I can count on you."

"Thanks brother. I said it before and' I'll say it again. The less I know the better, but yes, give me call when you need me. Right, time for a quick bite to eat and then I'll give you a lift back."

"I'd better change and get my bag packed. I can catch the eight thirty and be back in town before I'm missed." He grinned at Phil.

"No, you can stay as you are, I'm taking you all the way in to Colchester. You can catch the hover rail from there and if anyone sees us who is inquisitive enough to find out, they will only come to the conclusion that you have come to see your brother during a spot of leave. How about that?"

Frost was in the air as they left Phil's little family tucked up in bed behind on the farm. Waving goodbye to his sister-in-law Anna, they headed off into the night. They made good time, being waved through the various army checkpoints around Norwich. From thereon it was an almost clear run south to the outskirts of the tumbledown remains of Diss, a long forgotten market town now abandoned by the population as the drive for the safety of the UPAs attracted people away from it. Two minor checkpoints at crossroads along the way slowed them up momentarily until at Diss they ran into a long queue caused by a double roadblock at the conjunction of two major routes. Soldiers walked slowly along the line of waiting vehicles, occasionally chatting with the drivers as they answered the inevitable questions about how long it would be before everyone got through and how were things elsewhere. Pierce spoke to a tall rangy looking Corporal as he passed by. On discovering that he was talking to a serving officer he snapped smartly to attention and directed Phil to pull out and drive directly to the barrier. He radioed ahead giving the soldiers at the checkpoint advance warning. In a few seconds they were through and on their way again, leaving the long tailback behind them in the receding glare of the overhead plasma-lights. Again they made good timing down the road expecting to pick up the next checkpoint at Earl Stonham. Pierce started to doze off and from time to time opened his eyes to see where they were.

"That's odd." He heard Phil mutter as he slowly woke up. "What's up?" He asked rubbing his eyes with his hands. "It's those vehicles in front. They're slowing down. There's no checkpoint here; it's still about two to three miles before we reach it. Must be an accident." They looked out from the comfort of their vehicle as they saw distant figures caught in the lights of the vehicles in front. There was an occasional flash of blue as they drew closer, finally slowing down to a crawl. "This is odd. Look there's about four policemen up front and they're checking people out, one either side. They must be looking for someone."

"Phil, turn around, now!"

"What do you mean?"

"Just do it. Slowly and without any fuss. Make it look as though you are not bothered with waiting." Phil looked at him with amazement on his face. "Phil this is not a legal check-point. The police have no authority to do this under martial law. They're probably not policemen either. Look at those cars beside the road. Four policemen Phil -in six cars, look there are four more in that second car? No, there's something fishy here. Otherwise they would have overhead lights and the usual flashing beacons and signs. No just turn around and drive back the way we came without making a fuss of it."

"OK, whatever you say Pierce. It may be as you say." His brother quietly turned the car around about four hundred yards from the barrier secretly hoping no one would notice as they slowly gathered speed, while Pierce zoomed the scale on the vehicle's positioning system. "Take the next left here towards Mendlesham." Just before they turned off they could see the lights of a fast moving vehicle catching up with them. "We're about 20 kilometres away from that last checkpoint," said Phil hurriedly. "They look as though they are determined to catch us whoever they are."

"Don't use the foot brake Phil, pump the handbrake and turn you headlights of just before you make the turn. With a bit of luck that hedge at the bend in the road will mask your side-lights."

The country road ran directly away from the main road and he didn't want to test out his theory about the hedge if he could help it. Sure enough the other driver brought his vehicle into a sliding turn down the narrow road. They danced a merry dance along the lanes startling foxes and other night prowlers as they sped past. Just outside Gipping Pierce took them through a sharp left turn beyond an earlier junction bringing the vehicle to a stop inside a field behind a hedge. His brother killed the engine turning off the lights. A few moments later they heard the approaching vehicle at high speed. There was a squealing of tyres and an audible thump as the vehicle connected with the bank at the roadside in its turn along the other road. Phil started up the engine and drove back onto the lane with a pounding heart. "What is it you're involved with Pierce?" He asked shakily. "I'm trying to find the king and take him to safety Phil." Came the quiet reply.

"Looks as though somebody doesn't like that."

"Well now you know the sooner we part company the safer you'll be."

"Agreed, until then we stick together."

"Right."

"Right."

They headed for Old Newton twisting and turning around bends and corners as fast as they could go. Going up a small rise they could see the lights of the other car momentarily as it sped along the other road on a fool's errand. By the time they took the left fork to the village Phil caught a flash of light coming towards them at an oblique angle from behind. "I think they've seen our lights Pierce, and they're coming back this way to catch us up."

"OK, take the left fork once we're through the village towards Haughley. There's a railway crossing there. It will be quicker to pick up the main road to Bury."

"Bury, why Bury?"

"There's a major intersection halfway along it, and where there's an intersection like that there's bound to be an official check-point, and I want to see how official or un-official these people that are chasing turn out to be."

"Here we are, left?"

"Yes, go for it." Pierce reached behind his chair and dragged his large bag over to the front. After a few seconds of unravelling his belongings he withdrew his sidearm and checked it out. "You really think it's that serious?" asked his brother through gritted teeth. "Very serious."

It was their turn to suffer a set back as the railway crossing loomed in front of them out of the darkness from around a bend. They sailed across it with the brakes on hitting the road hard on the other side, skidding violently, lurching towards a sharp left-hand bend and into the muddy bank opposite, coming to a sickening halt. His brother, dazed and breathless looked across at him hopelessly. "Can you get it re-started Phil?" He punched the re-start button on the console once. A pool of red indicators remained illuminated. He hit it again with his fingertips. Some of them went out while others coloured green turned on. Two amber lights came out of the reds that had been on. "Hit the over-ride." hissed Pierce. His brother obeyed instinctively with the engine bursting into life raggedly. He reversed it off the bank and put it carefully into forward drive once they were back on the road. "Hurry, they'll be on us in a few seconds!" Called Pierce as his brother gunned the acceleration. The vehicle shuddered and lurched forwards but did not increase speed very fast. "The dynamic drive has gone Pierce, it's slipping, it's no good the suspension leveller has had it. We probably ripped the hydraulic lines from the pump, there's no automatic recovery like in those military vehicles of yours."

"We'll have to ditch it Phil. Here. Stick it in the gateway to the field over on your side." They drove into a muddy field behind a balding hedge. "I can hear them coming!" Yelled Phil. "It's no good Phil you'll have to make a break for it. It's only a hundred yards or so round the bend down to the main road. Leg it down the field and see if you can get through to the lane down there. I'll try to delay them. It's about four miles to the first checkpoint near Woolpit. Raise the alarm if you can, now go!"

"What about you?"

"I'll be alright. They won't be expecting anyone to take any defensive action, but I intend to slow them down. Go on off you go!" They could hear the chase vehicle belting around the bends in the lane down which they had just come.

Pierce had a half-hope that whoever it was they would make the same mistake and hit the bend as badly as they had done a few minutes earlier. He ran half-crouching until he was a few yards from the bend behind a young oak tree in the opposite hedgerow. He lay down beside the tree under the hedge and waited. The noise became louder. He caught a bloom of powerful headlights as the vehicle lit up the roadside verges in its twisting and turning down the narrow lanes. Finally the large vehicle hit the railway crossing and took off at the front end. Engine roaring it flew into the same place as they had just done and came to an abrupt halt. Pierce timed his shots to coincide with the heavy landing. His first round caught the front tyre that ended up mashed against the ground when the vehicle stopped. The second caught the rear tire a glancing blow, passing through it to penetrate a vital part inside the vehicle's machinery. The driver attempted to start the vehicle two or three times. On the fourth attempt the engine coughed into life and then died almost as suddenly as the noise had begun. The driver kept the ignition alive over as the monitoring system told its sad story.

"No go Guv, two flat tyres and fuel starvation. Could have dented the fuel tank when the back end hit the bank as we bounced."

"Get to it you other two and see how bad it is. The auto repair system might hold for one of the tyres, and there's a spare under the back end!" Two heavies got out and wandered to the back of the vehicle in the dark. After much fumbling around they got the back opened up and emerged holding a spare wheel. "Falcon this is Redhawk do you copy?" the first man spoke into a comms unit. There was a long pause before he called again. "Falcon, this is Redhawk do you copy." Pierce was curious. He moved away from his hiding place crawling slowly towards the broken vehicle. Again the man called into his comm. unit and waited. He threw it onto the dashboard in annoyance and climbing out of the car he watched the others working on the wheels. "The back one is self-sealing Guv, but the front one has had it, look here, there's a big hole right through it." The driver got out. "The fuel line seems to be giving a problem, but I'll pump it around the other side, see if that can bypass the problem. The system is running it now in maintenance mode."

"All right, come here." beckoned the other man. He shone a light on the front wheel and motioned for his companion to be quiet, dropping his hand from his mouth to his side to indicate that he should take something out of his tunic. The other man did so casually while the one whom was obviously the boss walked over to the other side of the vehicle where he quietly alerted the other two men removing the other wheel. "It's no good Guv, we've lost them by now. Anyway suppose it wasn't that bloke on the run from Colchester, we'll never know... er right Guv, right you are." They quietly laid the wheel down and made as though they were going to the back of the vehicle to fetch something while surreptitiously feeling for their hidden weapons.

Pierce failed to see the subtle movement of the driver in the dark, but he recognised the two oafs emerging from the other side had changed their posture. Reading their body language he looked for the other two and only found the 'governor' standing stock still while staring intently at a point that gave the impression he was looking at the vehicle, but wasn't. He could no longer see the driver. Moving quietly away from the hedge he sought the safety of the darkened field rather than become outflanked by the driver whom he assumed was creeping along the shadows of the roadside. He was fortunate to have made the decision. He used his weapon's built-in night-sight locating the driver as he did so, standing close to where he had just been lying. The two heavies fanned out with their boss walking slowly along the opposite side of the road. Pierce let out his breath slowly and evenly as they stumbled upon Phil's broken cuddy. He watched as they warily signalled what they found leaving Pierce Anders in no doubt that they had rumbled the fact that their quarry was now running on foot. "Nah, Guv, they've probably done a bunk by now. If we can fix the new wheel in place we might be able to catch them before they get to the next checkpoint. "Pierce knew his brother was probably walking fast carrying a mild concussion. That meant he was in no state to evade such a pursuit by four armed men running him down from behind. He watched as they all walked back to their own vehicle. The driver looked inside leaning over the console instruments. "The system is up and running with full fuel pressure."

"Right, let's get on with it, we must stop them at all costs. I must get hold of them tonight!"

In the darkness Pierce stood up crouching low and ran back across the muddy field towards the road. His breath rising like steam in a trail behind him. He made it to the oak tree and rapidly crawled along the foot of the hedge to his previous position. Burying his nose and mouth in his clothing in order to mask his heavy breathing and hide his breath that would otherwise give him away.

The henchmen watched as the driver reversed onto the road, then clambered back in to commence the chase. "As they did so the boss-man's radio burst into life. "Redhawk this is Falcon, do you copy?" The boss motioned for the driver to wait a moment. "Falcon this is Redhawk, go ahead."

"Status report Redhawk, we heard your call earlier?"

"This is Redhawk, our men are on the road to Bury and we are in pursuit. We intend to cut them off before the checkpoint east of Bury. Both are on foot."

"You say there's two of them Redhawk?"

"Affirmative, the vehicle registration is as follows…" Pierce fired two shots in quick succession. The first blew a hole in the hand of the boss man whose howl of pain could be heard loud enough to wake the dead. His second shot took out the front offside tyre. Running forwards towards the car with the hedge between him and his quarry he crouched low keeping to the darkest shadows. He had to somehow get back to the fork in the road to disable his pursuers and make off after his brother. The dunderhead twins in the back threw themselves out of the vehicle firing their weapons wildly in to the night. The driver looked out of the vehicle and back at his superior trying to make a decision. In the dull glow of the rear lights Pierce could see the outline of the largest goon and took careful aim. The man went down with a severe burn to his knee, writhing in agony on the wet grass beside the road. His pal from the back seat ducked out of sight behind the vehicle and waited. Pierce knew that he was exposing himself but needed to give his brother time.

Reaching the junction undiscovered, he could see the four men trying to cope with their distractions. The driver killed the lights plunging the country lane into immediate darkness. Pierce seized his chance to cross the road some fifty feet in front of the vehicle and roll over into the ditch on the other side. The buzzing of a high-powered laser rifle on charge could be heard clearly now as he began worming his way through a gap in the other hedgerow. That could only mean one thing. They had night sights and they intended to kill! He drew closer and through the hedge he could hear the boss man cursing and shouting in pain. Alongside the front of the vehicle he could just make out the bulk of the other dunderhead hiding by the car. His friend was still writhing on the grass in front of him. He held his breath as the goon with the rifle moved stealthily upwards and forwards. In doing so he placed the night sight to his right eye and scanned the hedge across the road in the general direction where Pierce had been about two minutes previously. He began to sweep carefully and deliberately, occasionally letting his breath out. Pierce could see the steam issuing from the other man's face and kept working his way back up the lane in the direction of the railway crossing. He was close enough to hear the man mutter a curse after finding nothing during his initial sweeps using the night sight. "He's not there I tell you. He's moved off. The shots came from that tree down the road."

"Well if you think he's gone down there, then you'd better get after him and quickly." hissed the driver menacingly. "Right on Guv, but Wally's had it, took a couple of rounds in the legs, you'll have to get him in the back of the car."

"So I hear, now get on with it!" He hissed again.

The remaining dunderhead slowly backed away from the vehicle and made a sweeping pathway that curved towards the shadows on the opposite side of the road from the tree where Pierce had originally made his first attack. Pierce continued back along the original road until he reached a point where his line of sight made a tangent to the bend in the hedges. The rifleman was at the other end of the tangent giving Pierce a clear side-on view. The dunderhead was widening his sweep backwards and forwards. He must have found a residual trace of body heat for he was now swinging the gun towards his left down along the hedge towards the junction and the road in front of the car. Pierce took careful aim and with a clear bead on the weapon fired his own. There was a howl of pain as the goon stood up dropping his rifle to the ground.

"There's one of em now. Hell he's behind us!" Shouted the other dunderhead who had been writhing on the ground a few moments before. There was the sound of a heavy laser pistol discharging and as Pierce turned to run up the slope around the bend he felt the searing pain of a strike against his right thigh. "I got 'im! I got 'im! Came the triumphant calling from the man on the ground. Pierce hobbled at a fast pace gripping his thigh with his right hand to suppress the pain. Out of sight he could hear the engine of the vehicle being throttled up and guessed the chase was on. He made heavy going for about a hundred metres before the vehicle could be heard coming up the lane behind him. He reached the crossing as the lights caught him in full view. Hearing the impact of the rounds spitting on the ground in the narrowing distance behind left him in no doubt they were gaining on him furiously. He was running out of options and had nowhere much to go for cover. Wet and cold he pounded across the tracks and was almost at the other side when disaster struck. The wet sole of his boot made slippery contact with one of the steel safety rails and his foot turned beneath him in an agonising wrench. Pierce went down heavily with a meaty thump right in front of the advancing vehicle. For a second it stopped. "Go on, get the man, you can see he's down, just flatten him!"

Pierce, clutching at his ankle, sat up ignoring the pain of the burn across the side of his thigh saw the danger, feeling a deep vibration in the ground as the vehicle lurched towards him. Lifting himself up on one leg, he leaned over the edge of the track toppling forwards onto the hard earth on the other side beneath the level of the concrete hover trough. As the battered ground vehicle closed upon him at speed he caught a glimpse of something huge and dark swooping down on him blocking his view. There was a huge bang followed by the sound of tearing metal with sparks showering in a long trail along the tracks. A hover train had silently hurtled towards them without any of them noticing a thing until it was too late. The carnage left behind in the aftermath of a half-mile journey of destruction was beyond description. A fierce fire ensued engulfing the wreckage. In the confusion Pierce slipped across the railway at the rear of the train using the night to swallow up his presence.

He met his brother at the junction of the Bury road a few minutes later. His shadow detaching itself from the black hedgerow as Pierce hobbled along. Phil looked in better shape than did his wheezing sibling staggering along beside him. "By heck! You're looking the worse for wear. Look at you all covered in mud up to your eyeballs!"

Pierce looked at himself in the moonlight and grimaced. "I must look an absolute mess." He agreed tiredly. "What happened back there?"

"They chased me as far back as the tracks and as fortune would have it they drove right in front of a train."

"That was one hell of a bang. It must have woken every household between here and Bury."

"They didn't stand a chance bro.', they were so fixed on the idea of running me down that they forgot to look out for themselves." His brother nodded silently. "Look," gasped Pierce a little easier, as his breath began to subside, "I can't wander around like this, let's get back to that transport of yours and see if we can do something to get it going again before the hordes descend upon us. At least I can get changed into some clean clothes that won't arouse any suspicions."

Together they walked back up the road and found their vehicle where they had originally left it. Being a farmer Phil was adroit at solving problems by either fixing them or by bypassing them one way or another. With the pressure of discovery now a thing of the past he took a mere twenty minutes to solve all the problems flagged by the computer system. Those that were un-fixable had been by-passed leaving the knotty problem of the crooked suspension system and the torn hydraulic lines. The auto-jack was used as a ram between the suspension arm and the under frame to push the front leg forwards, releasing the wheel wedged in position against the rear of the wheel arch. Emergency repair tape held spliced lines together and with a little spit he managed to fit the hydraulic line back over its inlet pipe before using more glue band to seal the edges.

They finally got the plasma injection circuit to run and started the engine after two abortive attempts. Easing the vehicle out of the gateway, Phil headed down the lane into Haughley. Turning the lights off he steered cautiously and quietly through the village, noticing that the lights were on in several of the cottages. As they passed out of sight several villagers emerged all bearing arms. For them in the days of lawlessness and disorder it was commonplace to go abroad in small, well-armed groups for safety. They usually shot first and asked questions later, but on this night they would find themselves doing other things.

Taking the back roads Phil got them into Ipswich without coming across any patrols or checkpoints. Pierce caught the last train from Norwich wearing his spare uniform, walking with the aid of a stick they had culled from one of the hedgerows. The station was very busy with uniformed soldiers embarking and disembarking from the train. Phil left Pierce to settle down in his carriage apparently well camouflaged amongst all the other uniforms. He drove out of the hover rail terminal and headed north along the Euro route towards distant Norwich and home. At the major fork in the road he found that he was quickly waved through along with other traffic, as the troops cleared the way for emergency vehicles. Indeed, all the checkpoints had been left abandoned as the soldiers were seconded to help at the scene of the emergency. He arrived back at the farm weary and all done in. Leaving the transport in a barn he slipped quietly into the spacious kitchen to be greeted by his wife.

****

9. CRUISING THE MED

Chip and Fred scrounged a lift to Gibraltar airfield from a passing hoverbat. The young Corporal was only too pleased to see fresh faces around the base. "It's not been the same since they started to drive up the anti a few days ago. Most of the shipping has either been boarded and searched or escorted into Algecieras."

"You mean they have set up a blockade?"

"Yes Sir, since the day before yesterday. Didn't you know?"

"Apparently not. It must have been the bad weather, we had no trouble arriving this morning."

"Maybe they've decided to take a day off." The hoverbat dropped them off at the mess where Chip went striding up the steps onto the front porch two at a time, through the double doors into the wide hallway, heading for the lounge.

"We need to ship those spares from our bases in Cyprus back here to support the squadron's operations. In return they need provisions for at least six weeks if they have to withstand any local pressure from the islanders to leave. The Greeks are a friendly lot, but with the non-aligned countries putting pressure on them as well as our ex-pals in Europe on the Greek mainland we can only expect trouble."

"Do you expect them to blockade their ports at all Sir?" Chip looked at the charts as he spoke. "Not entirely," responded Captain Ansty, "but the Russians may cause some local difficulties since they control the harbour installations at the Larnaca freight terminal. The real problem may come from the Turks who may use our own situation as an excuse to invade across the old green line to get at us. That would mean instantaneous war between Turkey and Greece that might give us enough time to regroup the garrison and airfield resources into well defended installations while the locals are otherwise occupied." During a slight pause in the conversation Chip picked out a detail on the chart laid out on the table before them.

"There's a small bay here at Dekelia close to the power station where I see there is a jetty running out from the shore. That might be better for us than trying to go through the commercial installations. Our loading ramp has a fair degree of flexibility and we don't have to park ourselves at a container port to shift cargoes."

"Even better. It's all man-made around there with concrete anti-erosion holding the coastline together. The last time it was dredged was about a year ago, and you see that sandy bay here immediately to the west, it has a small restaurant complex specifically catering for the soldiers and their families. Up on the hill there, overlooking the areas are the senior officers' married quarters, so you may well find yourselves under some scrutiny, no doubt." The C-in-C of Gibraltar gave a wry smile. "Yes, that sounds perfect. It's in the base and so will keep prying eyes to a minimum and it is on the main road so all the stores can be got in and out in one operation without to much faffing about. Good. Any other questions?"

"Er, yes, what is the precise nature of our return cargo?"

"You will be pleased to know that you will be carrying two Cheetah Mk Is crated along with six engines and other engineering paraphernalia, and sixteen tonnes of plasma-gel in drums."

"I need to have their weights for our Load Master to work out their disposition on the cargo deck Sir, does anyone have those figures available?" The Admiral pulled a face.

"I think we can have them sent to you. Does any of that cargo represent any problems to you?"

"We have enough room for the crates given that they have appropriate dimensions to fit through our stern loading doors. We don't have the capability of adjusting our main deckhead in the way that the later variations in our class of vessel can. As to the plasma-jel is it literally in jel or pellet form?"

"We don't know, but again we can get that information to you. Do you have any preference?"

"It is safer to carry the pellet form Sir because it is more stable. The gel is, I'm afraid, more likely to break down given the vibration and movement of the vessel through the surface. When that happens, spontaneous detonation is inevitable. In addition, if we have to face opposition involving weapons discharge the gel will have to be jettisoned or we will all go up like a giant firework."

"Ah, I see. Well I'll get my people on it straight away. If we find that you have to pick up your cargo in gel form are there any precautions you can take to reduce the likelihood of spontaneous or manmade detonation?" There was a slight pause before Chip spoke. "Mm, the only known method of stabilising gel is to smother the drums with a continuous spray of cold water. That would require a re-assessment as to where best to stow the drums. At the moment it is my intention to use the lower hold which is partially below the waterline. If on the other hand we have the gel form there is no other choice but to put the drums on the main cargo deck, and we would then have to reposition some of our Marines who have their accommodation there."

"Do you have much space for them elsewhere?"

"We could utilise part of the lower cargo hold, but the main drawback will be that we have all the explosives stowed above the crew quarters and machinery spaces. There would be no margin for safety and little chance of my crew making their escape should anything go wrong."

"I see, then it is problematical for the safety of the ship and her crew. Prepare to get under way before dawn the day after tomorrow and in the mean time I will see to it that you get the information you require."

"Thank you Sir."

Chip and Captain Ansty departed for an early lunch leaving the C-in-C and his remaining staff to continue with their own discussions.

Back onboard the first loads of fresh provisions had arrived by transport and the Sub called the hands to turn-to on the loading. Using a small conveyor that dropped the cases, crates and sacks onto the main conveyor at the stern the crew quickly stowed nearly a tonne of fresh and dry provisions that could last them for some time at sea. During the afternoon and for the remainder of the following day a steady relay of transports arrived to disgorge their flatbeds into the open maw of the Royal Oak's loading bay doors. By eighteen hundred the crew had been given leave to be ashore for the evening, but to return onboard by one o' clock in the morning.

The flat calm of the harbour was mirrored by a glassy sea shimmering over a gentle swell as Royal Oak made her way silently past the mole on her auxiliary engine. Unlit and without obvious signs of departure she had singled-up and finally slipped with only two seamen working the ropes on the open decks. There was no farewell party or noisy activity. Just two men ashore to slip the ropes from the bollards who gave a quiet wave as they strolled back to their dockside hut for an early breakfast. Outside the mole by a mile the plasma engines kicked in and the crew settled down to the prospect of a long journey on the planes. It was always a pleasing experience to be on the move with the knowledge that soon another destination would be added to their list of places visited. Dawn lit up the top of the distant peak of the rock in a golden hue as the last bastion of civilisation and safety slid over the horizon behind them. At half-past nine the Marines began gunnery practice, testing themselves and their weapons thoroughly. In the afternoon they began the first of two days training for the ship's crew as it sped along in open waters. The laser cannons were in tip-top condition with the small installation on the quarterdeck proving to be a deadly addition. In addition to the laser and plasma weapons the traditional weaponry of shells, grenades and bullets had been included in the armoury, much to the delight of everyone. During the second afternoon two of the seamen heaved a large empty drum over the side as the skimmer cruised slowly on the dark blue sea. Chip and Fred watched the target practice that ensued, as did the rest of the off-watch crew. The lasers vaporised large sections of the drum above the surface as the cannons were fully checked out in action. A final shot despatched the drum to a watery grave as the laser round seared the surface of the sea at the waterline. Every one completely absorbed by this exciting distraction waiting for the final wave of testing using the solid round weapons. The ship's crew were delighted to become involved in the gunnery activities and fired happily at several more targets under the supervision of the Marines Sargent and his corporal. The other Boot-necks busy loading empty magazines with fresh ammunition. When the solid round firings began all of the available crew was given an opportunity to fire these older weapons. The loud bangs followed by a second's worth of silence before the sound of each round striking their distant target was more satisfying to the ear than firing the latest laser rifles. 'Bang, silence, clang!' The Marines were careful to point out that there was always the danger of a solid round bouncing on the surface of the water, hitting the target only to rebound and bounce back towards the point of origin. That is, striking the bearer of the weapon or someone else nearby. The topic of conversation for many hours after the practice had ended was centred on the effectiveness of one type of weapon over another, and many a bet was made between those of differing points of view.

Chip and Fred worked slowly through the tactical plots, now fully integrated with their augmented functionality, tracking the movements of previously unrecorded targets. Principally, there was an increase in military flights emanating from the French and Italian bases along the northern Mediterranean shore. The Adriatic ports came under scrutiny as previously active plots indicated several enclaves of shipping, and then suddenly blanked out. "It seems to me that they're running without their transponders and avoiding initial detection." offered Fred. "It sounds about right. Let's see if the Yanks have kept their Tacsat channels open?" Speculated Chip half thinking aloud. Fred keyed in the access codes and the display changed to pure video mode. The screen went momentarily blank for a second. It lit up with a colour panorama of the Earth from a height of six hundred kilometres. Using the controls Fred quickly zoomed into the Adriatic region. "There they are." crowed the Sub jubilantly. "Looks as though they have got a couple of big ones in there, with about a hundred or so smaller craft."

"Let's have a look at the eastern end of the Med., I want to see if there's anything waiting for us." Chip ruffled through a small pile of NOTMARS as he spoke. "There's a carrier with a couple of escorts Sir, look at that." The three of them watched in silence at the small naval force sailing through the Aegean. "Presumably making their way to anchor off Athens," said Fred, moving the view to centre on the carrier itself. "Judging by the formation they're at flying stations, that should be interesting for them." chimed in the Sub. "I thought the Greeks had kicked them off their base after they found out the Yanks had been behind the riots in Corinth and Athens. When was it, ten years ago?"

"That's right Sub. Observed Fred joining in the discussion." It was an object lesson in how not to interfere with your friends. The last link in the chain reaction that cooled off the previously strained relationship between Europe and America, you might say." There was a long pause. "Zoom out a bit number one, I want to see a bit further south and west. The southern toe of Italy and Sicily came into view after a momentary blank screen. "That must be the USS Chelsea down here at Syracuse. You can see her escorts anchored off here and here." Observed Chip looking at the fatter form of a heavy cruiser with its wide snout and curving bow.

Later that evening the daily report was transmitted to Whitehall fully encrypted, containing compressed data on all the satellite intelligence they had captured so far during their journey. During the day they had made good progress at an average of forty -eight knots. Given the outbound cargo they were carrying it was excellent progress. At night they slowed to thirty knots for safety in case they came into contact with waterlogged objects like tree trunks, containers, or other paraphernalia dropped overboard from other vessels. A narrow beam forward-looking audio receiver-transmitter sensor fitted under the bows and its associated 'squawk box' kept on the bridge (popularly called the fart-box, derived from its acronym FLART) kept constant watch for such obstacles. In other circumstances the transmitter could be switched off and the device used purely as a listening device. The fart alarm, providing an audible alarm and an approximate range of possible sub-surface conflicts in front of the keel. Twenty two hours later with the Balearic islands far behind them and with Sardinia some ninety miles beyond their horizon on the port quarter, Fred noted the auto-pilot kicking-in to change their course. It was the morning watch with Fred up in the cockpit monitoring the course that would take them south of the Sicilian coast in the narrowing waters between the island and the African coast of Tunisia. The instruments casting a dim glow over him and the duty coxswain. At about ten to three the fart alarm trilled loudly making everyone on the bridge and in the cockpit jump. "Range is five miles sir." Said the Coxswain clearly, checking his instruments, noting with satisfaction that the computer had placed a red blob in the appropriate place on the ship's head marker on the plot in front of him. "Right Cox'n steer ten degrees to starboard and bring her round to one, three zero degrees."

"Starboard ten degrees, one, one zero." There was a pause while the cox'n made the necessary adjustment to the autopilot. The 'pooper' stopped sounding off as the bows swung round on to the new heading. Fred left it there for five minutes. "That should be enough." Fred observed as they saw the red marker move off to the left. "That will give us almost three miles clearance abeam, bring her back onto a heading of one, two zero and hold her steady on that."

"New heading one, two zero Sir." There was a short pause as the skimmer responded to the command inputs from the cockpit. "Heading now one, two zero Sir."

"Officer of the watch, equipment room."

"Officer of the watch, go ahead." Responded Fred.

"We have a faint signature definition Sir, I've made it available on the bridge tactical plot. I think you might want to take a look at it."

"OK PO, I'll be down in a minute." Fred scanned the navigation plotter and the instruments, and then quickly turned his gaze back to the plotter again. He extended the sensor range looking for any surface vessels. "Nothing there Cox'n, I wonder what our techno-wizard has got for us now?"

"Bound to be something requiring miles of cables and dozens of flashing lights." They grinned at each other in the gloom as Fred got out of his seat and stepped over the top of the ladder.

"The infra-red doesn't pick up anything at all, but as you can see, with the composite plot and the improved filtering we have a number of targets moving through the straits of Medina here, but look over here Sir." The Chief Electro-tech fiddled with the controls on his gadget producing a display of the Mediterranean where Royal Oak was currently bowling along. "There, that target is not detectable on infra-red or on radar. Even if we program new chirp parameters there's no measurable signal. However, the composite reveals that seventy miles off the African coast we have a definite signature moving towards us."

"I see what you mean. Are those targets in the Straits over there being masked by the land mass echoes?" Fred squinted at a faint trace on the black face of the tactical display screen. "Yes Sir, but as you can see, there's nothing to mask that target coming along the coastline down here." The PO tapped the plot with the blade of a very small screwdriver to emphasise his discovery. "Normally we should be able to see it on all tactical sensors, but not normally on the navigation radar until it is within range."

"How did you do this?" There was a slight pause as the technical wizard thought about his answer, but Fred stalled any reply. "I shouldn't ask, I reckon I'll be here until dawn. OK, that's very good. Can you tell me speed, range and bearing of this unknown target?"

"Speed and distance are approximations given the sporadic nature of the returns we are getting but the bearings are no problem. I suspect that as we get closer the plot will firm up. At present the target is making about eight knots and is two hundred and fifty miles away from our present position."

"I see, and your assumption being that this is a naval vessel of some kind?"

"Yes, ordinarily naval vessels will have some degree of protection designed into their superstructures and hull to deflect sensors and absorb interrogating transmissions as much as they can, but what makes this peculiar is the almost total lack of signature definition. This vessel does not want to be found under any circumstances."

"What do you think?"

"Could be a spy ship Sir, possibly a Russian or even a yank, they're the only ones who could afford to get away with it. It could be a French-Israeli derivative, they have been at the same game for long enough through collaborative agreements."

"How do you know all this?"

"Ah, part of my murky past Sir, working in the defence industry."

"Right. I understand. OK, let's assume this is a possible hostile and log it into the tactical system for the duty watch to keep an eye on. Thanks PO, that's pretty impressive."

"Thank you Sir."

With dawn breaking on the second day of their journey the skimmer was running at a pace, throttled up to forty-five knots and racing ahead into the Sicilian Channel. At a quarter to nine the augmented sensor arrays on the Royal Oak detected aircraft movements heading their way with the result that Chip ordered the ship's company to fall in at their action stations. "They are American aircraft judging by their ident markers, but I'm not taking any chances given the armadas gathering in this neck of the woods." breathed Fred rubbing his tired eyes after his interrupted rest from the previous watch. "You're probably right Sir." agreed the Sub. "But we'll know for certain in about four to five minutes."

Three 'Rattlers' buzzed them in a wide sweeping circle at about five hundred feet, moving off in a north easterly direction once they had finished reconnoitring the Royal Oak. Climbing into the blue skies their wingtip vortices leaving small trails of vapour squeezed out of the atmosphere as their stubby little swept wings cut through the atmosphere. Chip looked longingly at the small formation until they became no more than tiny specks in the distance. "You don't suppose the Italians will take any action against us during the uprising Sir?" Everyone on the bridge looked at the able seaman that had ventured to voice his thoughts. "That's not certain for sure; what anybody is going to do at present, but it does look as though the French and Germans, along with the Spanish may be preparing to make political 'meat' out of our own misfortunes. I think it is a good idea to trust President Warnock and those who are helping him to put the country back on an even keel before anything serious happens, don't you?"

"Yes Sir." The conversation died leaving everyone with unspoken private thoughts on the matter. The sun was up, the sea was a deep blue and the spray sparkled like jewellery as their narrow wake cascading behind them, fell into a wide pathway of churning water. "They're coming back Sir!" warned the tactical plotter scanning his display. Chip walked over to the tactical display and watched the plot slowly as three symbols moved swiftly across the screen. Two of the aircraft made a tighter descending turn eight miles to the south west of their position while the third Rattler appeared to maintain a flight level of ten thousand feet on a wider turn behind them. "That's the lookout over there. He's just making sure no one will jump them during their next manoeuvre. If I'm right they're puzzled about our lack of ident marker and those two are coming down for a closer look at us."

"A photographic run maybe?"

"A good possibility. Let's see, fifty miles, at about three hundred knots, say nearly ten minutes. Sub!"

"Sir."

"Detail off a couple of the techs to rig a temporary structure on the roof, they have about five or six minutes at most before those incoming aircraft have clear visual contact on us. Something uncomplicated, which looks like an aerial or a weapon, but with a sack hastily thrown over the top of it. Catch my drift?"

"Yes Sir, no problem." One of the 'electricians' dashed off to the galley where he commandeered a couple of large empty cans from the waste disposal. The junior Electro-tech disappeared into the radio workshop to emerge shortly afterwards with a reel of cable, a broomstick and a large roll of HBM tape. The boy had been sent down aft for a roll of cod line and two large rolls of paper towel. In record time the small team of subversives had erected a makeshift aerial and associated yardarms that had the two shiny cans fixed onto the ends vertically upside down. The cod line vibrating in the wind as the skimmer sped along in the morning sunshine. The base of the broomstick was rammed home inside an empty ringbolt recess in the roof some five metres behind the main mast aft of the cockpit roof. Although somewhat rickety in appearance they finished the job and clambered down as the lookouts made visual contact with the approaching fighters at extreme range. "Look at that!" Shouted the port lookout as he followed them in with his intensifiers. "Bloody hell, they're really low!"

At about twenty feet above the sea the two Rattlers hurtled towards the skimmer from astern, passing down her port side at a range of two hundred feet. Chip stood just behind the lookout and scanned the aircraft for signs of other activity in the wing-roots and fuselage. The leader's aircraft he could see had a small opening that his wingman did not. Tucked tightly into the space directly behind his leader's starboard wing, the second aircraft looked so close that those on board felt they could almost reach out and touch some part of it. "Well done everybody!" congratulated Chip above the din. "Let's see what their intelligence techs make of our makeshift broomstick." The two aircraft peeled off across the bows at about two miles eventually rejoining their lofty compatriot at ten thousand feet. With the lighter side of their situation in mind the crew stood down from action stations forty minutes later as they transited the Malta Channel. By noon the skimmer and her crew sped into the unrestricted waters of the central Mediterranean.

10. THE BLACK PIRATE

At 16:40 in the afternoon some two hundred and eleven miles from Malta the warm afternoon air permeated the atmosphere throughout the entire vessel, and those off-watch lounged on the starboard and quarterdecks basking in the heat unaware of events around them. On the southern horizon just beyond visual range a low black shape followed an intercept course. "Here Chalky, what's that blob out there?"

"Don't know, looks like another skimmer."

"Reckon she must be about ten miles away."

"Ask the lookout Bill, they know what's out there."

"Aw, it's gone, bloody sunlight's a bit strong."

"Kenny's the gadget whiz kid ask him."

"He's off-watch."

"He's on the quarterdeck poking around one of those laser rifles with his screwdriver." As the crew chatted the whiz kid ambled slowly towards them emerging from the top of the ladder leading down to the quarterdeck, wearing a towel around his middle and a pair of flip-flops on his feet. "Hey Kerry, did you see that other skimmer over there coming towards us?"

"No, can't say that I did, where?"

"You can't see it now, it's in the sunlight right now."

"Right, another skimmer you say?"

"Looks like it. Low on the water at present."

"And I suppose you want me to have a look?"

"You're the man Kerry."

They grinned at him in light-hearted fashion, looking at his flimsy attire. "Pick up the phone and ask." As he spoke the PO Tech wandered to a small phone box on the starboard superstructure and opened the lid. The two conversationalists sniggered. Within ten seconds action-stations alarms went off throughout the Royal Oak sending the crew scurrying to their appointed places. Some of them darted into their accommodation to pick up appropriate clothing. "What is Sub?" All the bridge crew were scanning the surface for visual contact with the bogey, and none could see anything through the shining orb of the sun and the intense reflection of sunlight on the water. "No idea Sir, Someone sunbathing on the starboard side says he saw a skimmer at about eight miles and wanted to know what it was, but we have nothing on sensors."

"Hell, this could be a false alarm Sub."

"There's no sensor contacts Sir." flustered the Sub acutely aware of impending embarrassment, but a possible visual sighting of another vessel. I felt…"

"Relax Sub, let's see what we can see, eh."

"Yes Sir." There was a long pause redolent of a lazy Sunday afternoon under a hot sun, belying the rising tension as everyone strained to see what was out there. "There, over there, bearing about forty to fifty degrees!"

"I've got it." Fred called. He swore. "It's shifting like a damn rocket Sir. He simultaneously picked up a microphone and spoke into it. "Guns crews at the ready we have an unidentified target bearing down on us fast bearing approximately forty degrees on the starboard side, out of the sun." Chip nodded his approval then changed the filters on his image intensifier and looked again sweeping them slowly into the glare of the sun. "It's the Benghazi pirate!"

"Is there still nothing on the Tac scanners?" checked Fred.

"No Sir, nothing."

"Where's the Chief electro-tech?"

"He's closed up in the equipment room Sir."

"Equipment room, bridge."

"Equipment room."

"We have visual contact with a solid target and nothing on the tactical plotters, we need that data now."

"The equipment is running fine Sir. All tests show all functions are operating."

"Stay at it I want this problem resolved."

"Aye, Sir."

"Range on my visual scanner is five miles Sir and closing rapidly."

"She'll open fire from the starboard quarter to draw out fire and lock missiles on our gun emplacements. That's his style. Guns crews hold your fire until ordered otherwise."

"We may be able to get her up to fifty five knots." offered Fred from the centre of the bridge.

"Make it as fast as you can Fred."

"Right away Sir."

"The beat of the skimmer's plasma driven hydro-jet engines rose significantly as the vessel rose higher on the planes at the faster speed."

"He's got enough space on his side. Look at that, we're as far away from land as one can be in this part of the Med." Fred nodded as Chip noted their predicament. "Well, we're not a merchant skimmer my friend, we are a fully armed warship and I intend to see him off or send him to the bottom."

"Have you anything in mind?" Fred asked a little cautiously.

"How fast can we make turns and close with him as quickly as possible Fred?"

"At this speed we have a two mile turning circle. If we dump speed the steering gear will have a greater effect for command inputs. Say if we dump speed down to about forty knots we can shorten that turning circle and bear round with a good compromise between speed and manoeuvrability."

"Right, this is what I propose. He obviously thinks this is a merchant skimmer judging by his intention to attack. He may be a little surprised at our speed, but possibly that we have a light cargo. He will give chase and draw our fire as I just said, so he wont expect us to do a fast turn and attack. We must turn this situation around to stand a reasonable chance of making our destination with this cargo."

"Sounds a very reasonable prospect Sir. I'll go along with that. If as you say they will draw our guns and target them at the beginning of the engagement, then our stern gun can be brought into play later as a nice surprise."

"Good, let's commence the plan."

"Range if you please Sub?" called Fred.

"Four thousand visual Sir."

"Thank you." Fred then spoke into the microphone. Standby bow gun. Standby Starboard guns. Stand-fast Stern gun." He paused momentarily and glanced at the tactical display. Equipment room I need that tactical data now!"

"There is no tactical on this target Sir. It must have blanking. I'm completing a composite link Sir. Should be through in the next thirty, ...there, you should have the composite on your screen, it's the purple cross on your screen."

"Thank you." Everyone breathed a sigh of relief.

"Guns on auto!" Chip gave the order.

"Range Sub?"

"Three thousand eight hundred Sir."

"Thank God for good Christian measurements like yards."

"What Sir?"

"Never mind Sub. Now! Speed to forty knots ten degrees to starboard." The skimmer's movement was rapid while the heavy load dampened the worst of the instability problems caused by the unusually abrupt command inputs. "Starboard guns open fire!" The immediate weapons release set hearts pounding and the crew braced themselves against incoming rounds. "Sargent Conningsby, where is he?" called out Chip across the bridge. "Abaft the after derrick Sir with a portable." Came the Swift response.

Leading Seaman Bryant take a message to Sargent Conningsby."

"Yes Sir."

"Break out missile launchers and be prepared to engage the target as it bears around in the turn, and enemy aircraft attack is extremely likely. Fast as you can Bryant!" The leading seaman dashed down the flat into the accommodation area, through that and along the cargo deck until he reached a heavy door in the side of the superstructure.

The pirate vessel rode low in the water representing as small a target as possible. The vessel had been gaining on the Royal Oak until she had performed the remarkable manoeuvre. The low profile and angled, highly sloping superstructure gave away her lines as a heavily modified skimmer re shaped as a sneak attack vessel. Chip marvelled that he had not noticed how small a target she had represented even during his last brush with her in the Straits of Gibraltar. No wonder her Captain could afford to be so cheeky! The Royal Oak's semi-portable laser guns on the starboard side made little difference to the hull or superstructure. There had to be some kind of special coating, there was no other reason for the rounds to be deflected like that.

The suspicion had long been held that the pirate vessel and crew had come into being, courtesy of yet another twisted CIA strategy to train and equip local subversives with a view to destabilising middle-eastern oil producing nations. The Libyan centred Arab Nation being the prime target. Yet, once again, the subversives taking the initiative and their booty along with their training began to harass the shipping lanes looking for rich pickings from non-Arab nations, turning the tables on their treacherous benefactors. The fantastic vessel was getting a hugely deserved reputation for unmitigated violence and bloodletting.

"Bow guns open fire." The big guns manned by its Royal Marines crew, spat furiously at the attacking vessel. The pirate Captain taken momentarily by surprise showed that he was still very much on the ball, turning his vessel and chasing the stern of his victim. He successfully drew the fire from the starboard guns and noted with satisfaction as the bow cannons stopped firing having reached the end of their lateral movement. "She's coming around the port side, ready with the guns on the port side. Hold fast on the quarter deck!" The pirate fired a long shot at the stern of the Royal Oak. At the same time both the port and starboard guns raked the blackened vessel from stem to stern as she passed across the profile of the large cargo deck profile. The starboard guns ceased firing as they came on to the target, shortly followed by the cannon fire from the bows. "Chip watched the pirate as it drew closer. Steer to port fifteen degrees, full ahead both. Cox'n steer to cross her bows ahead!"

"Port fifteen, full ahead both, steer across her bows."

The pirate vessel concentrating its firepower on the Royal Oak's for'ard gun emplacement struck her guns with several scorching rounds, melting the metal screen in a shower of molten sparks. The acrid smell of burning paint and slag steel quickly invaded their sense of security within the confines of the bridge. A marine dashed from the forward shelter with a sledgehammer, followed by another burdened with a fire extinguisher. The hammer rose and fell twice as the Marine knocked off a large section of metal that had wedged the gun to a standstill. The other Marine was seen checking the gun mechanisms. Another laser round seared the gun emplacement causing serious damage. Both Marines fell to the deck seriously burned. "That was our main hope for getting out of this alive." Chip said somewhat distantly looking up from his tactical display. "Sargent Conningsby at the port waist, permission to fire missiles, Sir?"

"Permission granted. Aim for her bridge, you can just make out the darkened glass panels. Then take her at the waterline."

"Roger Sir, firing missiles."

"What the heck, we're slowing down, watch your speed Cox'n!"

"She's slowing down Sir, I'm losing control, steering is not responding!" There was a high pitched whooshing sound as the Marine missile crew fired their weapon. At less than a thousand yards the projectile crossed the gap in the blink of an eye. Everyone on the bridge held their breath, the side guns still firing at the pirate vessel and the pirate's main guns turning the forward laser cannon to slag. The missile entered the superstructure just below the deckhead and slammed into something solid just behind. "Well done the Marines!" shouted Chip with his hope for a successful encounter growing. Huge holes appeared in the superstructure as the detonation disintegrated plasti-glass reinforced windows. Fred and Chip were well aware that the main armament on the pirate's foredeck had not been silenced. Giving rise to a strong desire to keep the concentration of action against the enemy's major armament. With fire billowing from the pirate's bridge they had problems of their own. The skimmer was in danger of sliding into a dangerous roll as her speed fell off drastically with her steering locked in position. "Port engine stalling Sir, starboard is in the red, no jet drive. Request shutdown of Starboard engine Sir?"

"Is it completely stuffed?" asked Fred suddenly feeling very exposed. "Yes sir, we took a long shot of laser cannon in the stern, looks as though the jets have gone and the plasma drive safety has been shorted."

"OK shut it down, how's the port engine for continued service."

"I need to send a man over the side to check out the ejectors Sir, and the steering gear. We have a fire in the steering gear compartment."

"How long Mr. How long?"

"Ten to fifteen minutes Sir."

"OK Mr. See to it." Fred took the decision and called up to the cockpit. "That's all Cox'n. Stop engines, wheel amidships if you can and get yourselves down from there quickly!"

"Sargent Conningsby!" Called out Chip – fire at will!" Chip ordered over the ship's main broadcast sound system."

"With pleasure Sir."

By coincidence the second missile struck the pirate at the waterline with a crumpled sort of thud. There did not appear to be any reaction for a while. "Airborne target Sir, faint but just detectable, range fifty miles and closing fast!" Another round of laser fire struck the Royal Oak a devastating blow, this time the cockpit collapsed under megawatts of sustained laser fire. The Cox'n and his mate went white when they saw what might have just happened to themselves. "We can take it from here Cox'n. You're a marksman. Get to work with some of those rifles and choose your targets carefully."

A loud whoosh announced more missile fire, this time from just in front of the bridge screen. The missile struck home on the pirate's main gun exploding loudly against the rim just above the deck. The gun looked as though it wobbled and appeared to continue functioning, but then a large fire appeared from a hole in the deck immediately below the mounting. Secondary armament on the pirate skimmer took out the semi-portable on the portside, leaving its crew in a bad way. Acting-medics appeared and carried off the injured men within the superstructure of the cargo deck.

"Ten minutes." snapped Chip coldly. "What?"

"Sorry Fred, that aircraft will be here in ten minutes, within missile range in about four minutes."

"Fred looked blank for a second."

"OK Fred you deal with the armaments I'll get Conningsby on to it. This is my thing – dealing with aeroplanes." Fred nodded. "Sargent Conningsby."

"Conningsby, here Sir."

"We have an aircraft approaching from the south west. It will be in missile range in just under four minutes. Set up one of your launchers immediately and open fire at will. I want four rounds of missiles."

"Four rounds of missiles Sir, at the approaching aircraft."

A laser round took out the aerials on the roof and the mainmast could be heard crashing down. Burning debris rolled off the roof onto the main deck. "Incoming!" called the tactical plotter, brace, brace! The Royal Oak shook and whipped from the bows to her smoking stern as a missile struck the bows of the starboard hull, entering it from the gap between the main hull and itself. The missile detonated causing the bow section to lift out of the water. Another missile from the Marines struck the pirate vessel down by the waterline at her stern. The planes auto-retracted as the Royal Oak teetered on the water dumping her hulls into the briny. The cause and effect of dropping the shattered outrigger's hull below the surface was an immediate flooding of the outrigger. A serious fire had taken hold in the outrigger now suddenly extinguished by the inrush of the Mediterranean waters created a large black cloud of acrid smoke.

Chip was aware of missile fire somewhere near the stern. The pirate vessel crossed in front of the Royal Oak bringing her secondary armaments to bear on the bridge. Everybody on the deck now!" yelled the Sub. Instinctively, everyone ducked or flattened their bodies against the deck. A missile struck the heavy door on the starboard side passing through it like a water jet through a snowflake. The 'TAC' plotter who had simply ducked and leaned against the front of the bridge watched transfixed as the thin missile shot across the bridge towards him. He dropped to the deck terrified with his eyes as wide as a cat's in a car's headlights at dead of night. The missile slid through the air and corkscrewed into the plasti-glass windscreen where the terrified plotter had just been standing seconds previously, exploding as it passed through the glass issuing a deadly hail backward into the space in the bridge as well as causing murder outside. The 'TAC' plotter was unharmed, but found his friend the Bosun's Mate slumped on the deck with his clothing stripped from his bare and bleeding back, burned and smoking. Fred had dived into the Chartroom with the helmsman and two of the other plotters. Chip lay motionless on the floor, blood pumping from a nasty wound under his uniform. The motor had detached from the main body of the missile and could be seen gyrating and twisting in the air outside above the foredeck, spilling burning fuel and gases in a wide swathe across the whole area in front of the bridge. "Oh! ...Oh! ...Oh." Came a voice from under the debris of shattered glass as people began to move, the voice trailing away. "Those not injured quickly -man the wheel and somebody check the tactical plot." ordered the Sub. Two seamen stood up slowly stumbling towards their stations shedding debris and glass splinters as they moved.

"Ouch! ...Ouch! ...Ow!" Someone began to whimper softly under the wreckage and to cry openly. "Boy! Where's the boy? Anyone seen the lad?" Those who were standing idly shook their heads. Mounds of rubbish lifted as other bodies emerged from underneath. "Looks like the skipper stopped one Sir." The radio op bent over another mound of scorched clothing spurting blood from a severed artery. Removing his own shirt he wrapped it quickly over the wound gripping it tight in a vice like grip to staunch the flow. "Ow, ooh." There it was again. "Guns crews maintain firing. Command is moving to the after conning position." Fred had crawled out of the chartroom and rising to his feet saw the complete mess, and ordered the evacuation of the bridge. "Sub, take all those who are fit and able down aft. I'll transfer the con from here then join you. Watch out for that aircraft and its missiles, he's a nasty piece of work, now go quickly!" He reached for the nearest microphone. "Medics to the bridge. Medics to the bridge!"

"Ow, ow."

"Whose that?"

"It's the boy Sir, I think."

"Find him, there's not much else we can do here."

"I'm trying Sir, but my legs won't work." Fred looked down receiving a nasty shock. A deepening pool of blood oozed from the man's back and leaning over him Fred knew he would never walk again unless there lived a miracle worker and surgeon combined. "Sorry Bryant, you just stay still and I'll see to it."

"OK Sir, I can still use my... hands..." Mercifully the leading seaman passed out where he lay.

Fred located the boy where he lay under a pile of rubbish in the bridge wing in front of the armoured door. The blast had him thrown hard against the door, head first, followed by a large section of plasti-glass windshield. It had severed the back of his head from the back of his neck to the top. His right arm had a double compound fracture above and below the elbow, and one of his knees lay at a peculiar angle. The medics arrived in the form of one of the off-watch engine room POs two of the seamen and the ship's writer. "One of you over there and attend to the Captain. Bryant is unconscious and bleeding internally. Careful, his spine may be severed. Someone help me with the boy. Petty Officer Graham helped Fred lift the boy gently out of the rubble of glass and metal fragments. "OW! ...Ow!" He squealed like a babe as they carefully turned him over and laid him down on his side in a clear patch of deck. "OW! Ow!"

"Easy boy, let's have a look at you, there, just hold my arm if you need to." The PO was one of those older professionals who had been promoted and busted a couple of times in his chequered career. The boy was about the same age as his youngest, and being a father he felt for the dreadful dilemma facing the youngster. "OK Martin, I'm going to have to turn you over in a minute. Get you off your arm." Can you hold him, there, Sir while I put a dressing over his head, before we move him."

"Right you are." Fred was numb with shock as he realised that he could see the back of the boy's brain, his hands becoming sticky with ichor. Holding him as gently as he could while the PO removed the plasti-glass shard from behind the boy's shattered skull. The big Seaman deftly pushed the loose bone back into position and started to bind the boy's head with a shell dressing. "Ok Martin, you're head is nearly finished. You cry all you want. There's many a man here that would. Good lad, hold tight now." He quickly inspected the lad's twisted frame with gentle probing fingertips running over his torso and limbs, nodding silently as he did so. "His back's OK Sir, and I don't think there's any more damage other than those we can see."

They lifted him gently, holding his head and neck carefully in position. "That's a good sign." Breathed Graham quietly, "No other signs of bleeding, looks like head, neck, one arm, one leg. "OW! Ow!" The boy vainly held back the tears and started to blubber quietly. "There now, that's your head sorted for now Martin. Hold on a second and I'll sort out the pain for you." Fred took off his jacket rolling it up into a bundle, handing it to the PO who in turn gently tucked it under the boy's severed head. Reaching into his bag the big seaman took out a hypo-injector labelled morphine. Lifting the boy's shirtsleeve on his good arm he pressed the injector against the warm skin, leaning backwards to look at the boy, noting his other injuries. "OK Sir, I'll take it from here with one of the others. I reckon you'll be needed elsewhere."

There was a pause in the gunfire as Fred nodded, standing up to look out of the shattered windows. "She's on fire, burning like a Roman candle by the stern. That's a good thing!" He looked down at the boy seaman in time to see his body sag as the morphine derivative took effect. "Well done PO." He moved across the bridge checking controls and viewers looking for what was working and for what had been trashed by the exploding missile. Taking a final look at Chip's unconscious form between two of the medics, he then rushed through the flat down into the cargo deck and aft towards the emergency conning position. With the boy now unconscious the burly Petty Officer splinted his broken arm and dislocated knee as quickly as he could. All the time, clearing away the rubbish as he worked gritting his teeth. The ship's writer was cleaning the burned and lacerated back belonging to the Bosun's mate, peeling back charred clothing that had run molten into the man's skin in patches. "PO, I think we need some morphine over here, I can't work any further without causing so much pain." He looked up from the boy now swathed in bandages and passed the hydro-spray to the Writer. The effects of the morphine told its own story as the Bosun's Mate finally stopped shuddering and visibly relaxed. Gently, layer after layer of burned clothing was peeled away until they could take the shirt off his back. The lad was left cushioned between a collection of jackets and rolled up charts to stop him from moving, until they could get him in a more conventional stretcher.

"Bloody hell! Would you look at this?" One of the seamen attending Chip had found a large slice of plasti-glass inside his arm buried half into the muscle. "Alright, keep it down, just stick to the facts without the melodrama." Petty Officer Graham growled with concern looking over to the young man who had turned a deathly pale. He looked over his shoulder towards the other side of the bridge. "Careful with that. You might have to check out the blood vessels for damage first before taking it out."

"It looks as though it's severed the artery. What do I do now?"

"You're a seaman aren't you Eddie? Tie up the artery about two inches either side then remove the glass. We'll think about sowing it together when I've finished here."

"OK."

"Right, let's get this chap comfortable lying on his stomach." Together they lifted the Bosun's Mate carefully onto a couple of blankets snatched from the messdecks and laid him down. "Right, the boy's the most seriously hurt, let's get him out of the way and into the wardroom as soon as the stretcher bearers arrive." Graham walked over to the other two working on Chip. You haven't used any morphine yet? Good. Did you check his head for signs of injury?"

Yes PO, he's got a nasty bump on the left hand side, that's probably why he's out cold."

"Fair enough. You let me in there and standby with the hydro-spray in case he comes round."

"What did you use for the ties Eddie?"

"Wire wrap from the instrument room."

"Oh, that's novel, let's have a look." There was a momentary pause as he rifled in the medical bag. "Where's that pair of scissors and the knife?"

"Incoming! Brace! Brace!"

"Not again!"

"Steady lad, let's keep going."

The loud banging of gunfire could be heard as rounds peppered the decks and upper superstructure, followed by the sound of an aircraft passing low overhead very fast. Glass flew around everywhere as bullets penetrated the metalwork finding more targets between decks. Somebody somewhere outside screamed in agony and then the sound died almost as suddenly as it had begun with a strangled gurgling. Graham steadied the hand of the Writer who had come over to assist. "Yes, you can see it jammed across that blood vessel. Listen, has anyone got any tubing, Scribes see if there's anything in the medical kit?"

"What is it you're after?"

"It's simple really, if I take out the glass he's going to bloody well bleed to death. So before we remove the ties, let's see if we can get a bit of tubing inserted between both ends where it's severed and sow it all up."

"My mum used just trim the ends off and tie em up when she did the cooking, couldn't we do the same PO?"

"Have we got anything to sow him up with?"

"Not in the medical kit, but there's bound to be some silk thread or something in somebody's housewife."

"No time for that, have you got any more of that thin wire?"

"Yep, I've got miles of it here, it's got some kind of insulation on it."

"That will have to do, give it here." The huge fingers of a seaman's hands are capable of surprisingly fiddly jobs. Using a medium sized pair of scissors the hard hands worked slowly around the torn artery leading into the arm, snipping away the rough edges. The upper section required a quick snip straight across in order to 'finish' off the end. "Now scribe, you have the dainty hands of a woman, sow those ends together in as close a stitch as you can, just like your dear old mum." Licking his lips slowly the writer commenced the devilish job of inserting the hair-like wire into the tough meat of the artery. Millimetre by millimetre they worked around the rubbery tube until both halves were tightly joined, looking like an elbow patch in a shirtsleeve.

"How can I tie it off?"

"Ah, that's easy. A series of bights then slip the end of the needle through like you would finish off a button."

"Oh, I get it." They worked in silence with the young scribe's tongue wrapped around the left side of his upper lip in deep concentration. The deck heaved as the skimmer was struck heavily on the port side. "Damn!"

"Keep going, I'll see what that was."

The PO stood up slowly looking about him carefully. Taking a peep through the broken windows he could see the pirate ship alongside burning fiercely in the stern and amidships. The boot-necks were running along her decks in a well rehearsed routine, shooting at any pirate that showed his face or lobbing grenades into hatchways or holes in the metalwork caused by the

Royal Oak's missiles. Close on their heels came the rest of the boarding party in their working blues carrying an assortment of small arms. "We've got a boarding party across, good for them!" Ducking back down again he concentrated on the job at hand. "Neat job Scribes, now let's get those ties off and see what happens. "Take the one off that end going into his arm. Then we can loosen the other one to see if your fancy piece of stitching will hold." The noise of battle seemed to fade into the distance as they watched the repaired blood vessel taking the gradual increase in blood pressure from the heart. "Looks like you did a good job there, just a wee bit of blood, but what do you expect with a seaman and a scribe for a pair of medics. Good lad, now lets bind it up all up, not too tight mind, just tight enough to close the wound and stop all that other bleeding." Holding Chip's arm gently while the scribe wound a long bandage around and around, Petty Officer Graham took stock of their immediate surroundings. All five wounded sailors were more or less taken care of, but the boy, he was in a bad way. "Give the Skipper a shot of morphine then come to the wardroom." Leaving the rest of the temporary medics in charge of the other casualties they walked into the wardroom where three other casualties had been laid. "He's looking bad PO, can we do anything for him?"

"No I don't think so. Make sure he's comfortable and don't let anyone move him for now. Stay with him and if anything happens give me a shout. I'm going down aft for a stretcher."

The heavy knock had been the collision between both vessels as they vied for best position from which to bring their armaments to bear. "It's obvious they're running her from a command centre deep in the hull somewhere. We've taken out the bridge and have several successful missile shots into the centre, but she is still going."

"Her steering gear's all gone Sir, and look at the way she's moving in the water. I reckon she's holed and taking water."

"Engine room! When can I have that power!"

"In another two minutes Sir, the Port engine is coming online!"

"I haven't got two minutes Mr. I need propulsion now!" The pirate vessel had drawn away with the Royal Ark's boarding party onboard fighting furiously to get below. "I think you're right Sir," yelled the Sub over the rattle of the small arms. "As long as we remain close to them their pilot dare not try to use any of his missiles!"

"Good, but here he comes again with his guns. Where's that other rocket launcher? What the hell is going on down there?"

Throughout the whole encounter so far not a single pirate had been seen emerging from the ship. Small arms fire sent a wall of destruction from hidden orifices in the superstructure. The pirate crew could not be drawn. "Sub. Get for'ard onto the main deck. See if you can find that other rocket launcher. We must stop that aircraft before it comes within range. Get them to launch two rounds of missiles, two missiles per round, each pair five seconds apart if you can do that we might stand a chance!"

"Aye, aye Sir." The Sub squeezed through the wreckage of the heavy door and dashed out onto the fore deck where he was confronted by a scene of carnage surrounding the laser cannon emplacement. The cannon had been reduced to slag with major pieces of it sagging or blown off and strewn across the deck alongside the bodies of the marine gunners. "Medic! Medic!" He shouted twice. Walking around the smouldering cannon he found the blood bespattered rocket launcher lying to one side and picked it up. Gingerly making sure it was safe and good enough to use without taking his head off the first chance he got to fire it. He was surprised to see it was not badly damaged in any way and that a round was already in the spout. "Sir!" called someone. There was a pause as he put the launcher's sight to his eye. A voice approaching from behind replied at length. "OK Sir, I've got it, we'll sort them out."

Two medics tended to the Marines as the Sub slowly walked around the other side of the slagheap that used to be the main cannons. He heard more than saw the plasma-jet aircraft coming in for another strafing run. Taking his eye off the sight he swung his head around until he could see his target. "Well, in for a penny, in for a pound." He swung the rocket launcher back into position and found the target momentarily in his sights, pulling the trigger. At first nothing happened and he stood there nonplussed. Suddenly he was rocked backwards as the missile launched itself skywards directly at the raider.

"Anyone know how to load this thing!" He called out blindly. "Yes Sir. I do." The Cox'n took a missile round out of the ammo box. "Stand with your legs apart Sir, one more behind the other to steady yourself when she fires." The Sub did as he had been instructed. "I'm releasing the breach now Sir. Hold her tightly with your hand away from the firing mechanism. Show me your firing hand Sir." The Sub swung his arm out sideways indicating that his hand was not on the trigger. When I've finished loading

259

the weapon I will tap you on the back of the head and move away. You will then be free to fire the weapon." The Sub nodded. He felt movement and heard the scraping sound of another missile being fed into the launcher. "Hold it!" The Sub had inadvertently moved his hand in towards the firing mechanism, but held it clear having been given the warning. "OK, Sir." He felt two gentle taps on the back of his crown and saw movement off to one side. He saw that the pirate jet had swung off to avoid the closing missile, giving him a clear view of its belly. Without thinking he fired directly at the fast moving target and noted with satisfaction that this time he did not get pushed backwards off his feet. "Reckon he's got enough to keep him busy for a while Sir. Would you like to have a crack at his bows? I don't think we've done enough damage yet?" The Sub turned to look at his loader. Fine by me Cox'n. Looks as though they've taken a chunk out of you though."

"That's why I want to sink him so bad. They got the boy, and I'm ready to go over there myself and tear them apart."

"Give me another round then and we'll work on that."

"You're on Sir."

Together they went through the drills loading, tapping the head, and firing until they had stitched four more missiles along the waterline of the enemy's hull. The deck suddenly lurching between them as the engine room brought the port engine back into play. The Cox'n caught the Sub as he tottered backwards and together they managed to stay upright.

A Marine appeared from one of the bridge wings and ran along the deck towards them. "Do you need a hand Sir?"

The Sub looked at him for a moment. He was burned about the face, had an arm in a sling and was all bloody and torn down one side. Don't mind me Sir. It's what I'm trained for." The Sub hesitated, then decided. "Yes, take over for me, I must get back down aft. Load for the Cox'n!"

"Right Sir."

"Cox'n, how would you like to have a go with the last five rounds?"

"It'll be a pleasure Sir."

"First priority is that aircraft. Knock it out of the sky, then if you've any spare rounds, just keep blasting away at the hull."

"You bet."

"Good luck!" An explosion tore apart the sky then another, as both airborne missiles found their mark. The jet was reduced to a shower of pieces falling from an evil looking fireball some five miles distant. "About time too, that one damn aircraft has done us more harm than the whole of that skimmer put together!" yelled the Marine above the din. "OK Boots, lets knock the hell out of that bat boat over there or whatever it is!"

Royal Oak headed for her adversary turning aside at the last moment to come alongside. Fred, grabbing his radio to recall the boarding party. For some peculiar reason there was a pause in the weapons exchange as she drew alongside. The men jumped across the narrow gap, some of the casualties were blindly thrown across for welcoming hands to catch them. The Corporal waved the all clear in the direction of the conning position and the helmsman turned away from the burning pirate vessel. A single missile round shot across and buried itself into the hull of the black vessel just below the bridge.

"Cease Firing! Cease Firing!" bawled the marine Sargent. "We're not achieving anything with that small arms fire hitting us from within the ship unless we can force an entry somewhere, we must withdraw before we run out of ammunition." said Fred disappointedly to those at the emergency command centre. There was mute agreement and a nodding of heads. "I think we've done enough damage to put the pirate out of commission for a long time. He's lost his air cover and will be damn lucky if he gets back home before he sinks." observed Sub confidently. "Sub, assist Sargent Conningsby with the ammunition count, I'll take her from here."

The Pirate vessel receded into the distance slowly, wallowing in the rising swell as both vessels backed away cautiously like two leviathans licking their wounds after a fight that neither of them could win. "Helmsman, set your heading to one, two zero degrees half ahead port. Cox'n, well done with that rocket launcher. I want you both to keep that pile of junk out there covered from a position up on the roof until we're a safe distance away. Sargent Conningsby, have a guns crew standby on the quarterdeck while we are at short range. I wouldn't mind betting they'd take a last shot at us in the dark when our back was turned"

"Aye, aye Sir."

The casualty list rose to ten wounded, four seriously, three including the boy critically. Petty Officer Graham and his first-aid team did a sterling job patching up the battered crew. He slipped quietly into the wardroom to take a look at the boy. He was still very white, looked clammy and his breathing came in shallow breaths. "I don't know how long he can hold out Sir." He said quietly, biting his mouth to hold back the tears.

"No, it's really beyond our skills. It's up to the Maker now and our engine room crew."

"You don't suppose we could break radio silence and get him and some of the others airlifted en-route do you?"

"It's worth thinking about. I reckon that most people would know we are here anyway, especially after all that missile firing having taken place."

"We'll be finished with the hydraulics on the planes in about ten minutes Sir." Said the Chief engineer poking his head through the curtain across the door. "Good news Chief, and well done in getting propulsion back, that was in the nick of time."

"Pleasure Sir."

"There will be a briefing at half-past seven in the lounge, please be there."

"Will do Sir."

The boy stirred a little with a hiss of breath.

"The morphine must be wearing off."

"That's the trouble with these cheap derivatives. Given the real stuff he would be safely out of pain until we could get him ashore."

The boy coughed and stirred again. "There, lad hold still. We'll have you ashore soon."

"I have to report the casualty list to the first Lieutenant, so I'll make the recommendation to get the three casualties air-lifted if we can, before the daily report is sent out."

"Thank you Sir."

Fred looked at the list with a heavy heart. With Chip barely conscious and out of the frame for at least the next twelve hours it fell to him to make the decision. After a quick conference with the radio op and the whiz kid, the Royal Oak broke radio silence using a narrow beam low power transmission encrypted beyond normal levels of encoding. The message sent to the C-in-C at Gibraltar noted tersely the destruction of the enemy aircraft and the serious damage inflicted on the pirate vessel, adding that it was believed to be sinking. The casualties: two dead, ten wounded: one seriously, three critical. Finally, Fred requested immediate evacuation of the casualties.

The skimmer required careful handling on the planes with one engine and her damaged hulls. The increasing swell added to the technical difficulties without the use of her stabilisers. The duty Cox'n had a high workload with the autopilot tripping out and with constant demands to trim and re-trim the balance. Royal Oak received a flash message from the C-in-C that the evacuation had been granted. She was to hold position until help arrived.

By nine o' clock the weather began to worsen accompanied by lightning flashes every few seconds from beyond the eastern horizon. Dark clouds blotted out the stars leaving the reduced crew on duty with an intense feeling of loneliness. Spots of light rain could be heard landing on the deck and upon the canvas sheeting that shrouded the gaping hole where the cockpit used to be. At half-past ten the radio op had contact with a flight from the Rock and relayed the message to Fred who was using his cabin as a makeshift operations centre. After holding position for nearly an hour and a half the cox'n was relieved to shut the throttle to idle giving her enough thrust to hold her way against the oncoming waves.

Martin had started to cry again as they gently moved him. Everyone wanted to lend a hand as the pitiful bundle of life so nearly snuffed out was manoeuvred along the companionway to the open foredeck. The large transport helicopter had dropped two medics and a surgeon to assess the casualties. The Fresh faced doctor looked at the boy before they moved him and shook his head slowly. "How long has he been like this?"

"About four hours Sir."

"You did a good job PO, let's see if we can make some minor improvements." As they lifted him the boy whimpered once and then stopped abruptly, sagging in the stretcher. A medic stopped what he was doing and looked at him quickly lifting an eyelid looking for vital signs. He lifted his eyes coming into eyeball to eyeball contact with the large PO. "We have a resus unit onboard the chopper, let him go PO." A portable radio hissed on the medic's shoulder as he spoke into the microphone and let go the button.

"Roger that, resus ready, give him number two, we already have number one."

"Everybody move, we have a crash team emergency, this one is next to go up!" People moved out of the way as the stretcher party careered the rest of the way out onto the deck. The winch-man had already lowered the steel-framed stretcher with two deck hands holding it steady on the deck. Swiftly, but gently they lowered 'Boy' into the cage and frantically waved at the chopper. "You bring him back safe you hear me!" shouted one of the hands -almost with tears in his eyes. No one looked at each other straight for several minutes afterwards as they continued to load up the basket. A second chopper that had stood off at a mile now swooped down to take the remainder. Chip, although groggy stayed onboard. The surgeon had recommended evacuation, but understood the compelling reasons for his patient to refuse. Three casualties and Chip remained onboard. The surgeon and a senior medic who had become aware of their immediate needs indicated they were remaining with the Royal Oak. With their noisy visitors gone the peace fell like a heavy weight upon the souls of those who mourned. The Sub took the evening watch until midnight when he was relieved by one of the Chiefs and the duty watch taking over the middle. The Cox'n himself took over the helm peering over the instruments with his one good eye while the duty Bosun's mate took the navigator's position at a small navigation console that had been rigged up by the techs nearby. With just under halfway of their journey completed they had a lot of time and sea miles to catch up on. Those who could slept the sleep of the dead while the surgeon and his medic cut, cauterised and sewed through the night. Working on those whose lives and livelihoods rested on their skills; severed limbs, a ruined hand, a couple of feet and a torn artery, a ruptured spleen. At one in the morning the stabilisers were fixed and brought back online. The effect was immediate and welcomed by all. Now they could go on-planes and cruise at their maximum speed with a generous helping of smooth motoring.

For sixty hours they pressed eastwards to their destination, with the techs working non-stop to bring the electronics and mechanical systems back into a semblance of working order. It didn't matter that there were cables and hoses lying on the decks or hanging from the deck-heads in loosely secured runs. Every run of cables collectively restoring the operational life-blood of the vessel. Early in the second evening an Admiralty tug met them off the coast of Cyprus, whereupon Chip, slumped in a temporary chair in his shattered bridge, refused the tow, but gratefully received the mail. Their arrival at the small dock on the edge of the garrison town of Dekelia signalled the end of such a troubled voyage. Not a single member of the crew stepped out for a run ashore that night except for those bound for the British Military Hospital. The small restaurant and 'kebabery' in the sandy bay next to the dock providing a welcome change with its brightly coloured tablecloths, wholesome food and warm atmosphere beckoning with all the safety of a womb. Back onboard, seeking the security and the solitude of their companionship won through difficult and frightening circumstances they rested in quiet conversations, slept deeply or paced through the empty companionways trying to forget. Outside on the jetty armed soldiers stood guard and shivered a little in gently falling rain under the glare of the powerful overhead lamps.

11. RECKONING

Boy died alone without the loving care of his mother's arms to nestle him as he slipped away on his journey into eternity. The Spanish had invaded by land as the French hit the rock with a continuous bombardment from the sea, reducing the town and harbour to rubble over a period of ten days. Those who could walk fled. The hospital staff were rounded up, and then frog-marched across the empty void of no man's land into La Linea, to disappear from view. The Spanish soldiers cared nothing for the patients. An arrogant Colonel shrugged his shoulders and many of the casualties were dumped out in the open. They stripped the place bare concentrating on setting up a command centre and heavily armed soldiery manned every window and doorway, peering out from behind piles of sandbags. The British held on and on, much to the growing ire of both the French and the Spanish who hated the British with a fervour buried in history. Only the insistence of a short wiry Major prevented boy's immediate execution by having his life-support torn from the lad. "Colonel Castellino, he is a boy, look, he is just seventeen. He's as old as my own boy and your own Carlo and Crezus. We don't make war on children or people in hospital do we?"

"Leave him there then, if he lives or dies it is in the hands of fate."

"Is that why you shot that doctor Señor?"

"Major, you will carry out your orders to the letter, is that understood!"

"No Sir, we do not fight a war against civilians or children." Spat the Major with rising indignation, watching the Colonel reach for his pistol. "No Colonel, it would be very unwise for you to try this." The Colonel stopped with his eyes level with the snout of the Major's own handgun a short distance away from his head.

"You dare to countermand my orders! I'll have you shot for this!"

"I don't think so Colonel, the matter is already taken care of. Sargent Manuel, you can bring in the Colonel's escort now." called the Major over his shoulder.

"Si, Señor." Replied a voice from beyond the doorway where both men stood eyeing each other. "A lesson in military conduct Colonel. Even the men are disgusted with your lack of humanity. You order the murder of wounded and dying soldiers and children because you have no strategy to overcome the problems facing you."

"You'll pay for this, I swear…"

"When this is over the regiment will decide Colonel Castellino who is in the right. I will trust the regiment." Three men came into the room with weapons drawn ready to use them. "Please, Colonel, go with your escort. The General is expecting you already." The two men eyed each other severely for a moment. The Colonel a peace time officer with a larded penchant for pomposity, self-importance and cruelty versus the Major from an aristocratic family with a reputation for professionalism. "Please leave your gun where it is."

"Don't you think that I need it for self-defence, there is a war going on outside!"

"Not where you are going Colonel. I insist."

With the Colonel and his escort gone he walked quickly to the hastily put together radio room. "Corporal, inform Red Dust that the deed is done. That is all. Let me know if Red Dust replies."

"Yes, Sir. Message to Red Dust, 'the deed is done'.

"And get me the British Commander on the radio when you have sent the message." The Corporal looked at him sideways at first, but did as he was told. He knew, as did all the enlisted men that the Major was not one to be argued with or to mess about. "The British commander Sir."

"Thank you Corporal."

"This is the senior officer of the European Standing Army Forces in Gibraltar. Is this the Officer Commanding the British forces?"

"You seem to be in error Major, we are your allies and you have invaded sovereign British Territory."

"Who is speaking please?"

"Captain Hadbroke, Royal Navy."

"Captain Hadbroke This Major Bardella. I give you my compliments and wish to inform you of an offer of a cease-fire to take care of your wounded. We have a number of your people here in the hospital."

"I see Major. Please standby." There was a long pause before the British Captain came back on the radio. "Am I to understand it that you are offering a temporary cease-fire in order for us to collect our casualties?"

"Yes Captain, that is right."

"You must know that we have limited facilities here to look after hospital cases Major. Don't you people understand the terms of the European Act of Union or the Geneva Convention in matters relating to prisoners of war and casualties?"

"Yes, we do Captain, we are not permitted however, to evacuate across the border at this time, and therefore you may wish to do something yourself."

"I see. Just what do you propose Major?"

"We propose one hour under the white flag to allow you to collect your wounded."

"To commence when?"

"I can arrange it in fifteen minutes."

"Do you have a list of casualties?"

"Yes, my Lieutenant will give you the list over the radio and if you accept we can arrange a cease-fire fifteen minutes after that."

"And what about your French colleagues at sea Major?"

"General Corte has negotiated this proposal with the French Admiral commanding the fleet, and he has agreed to abide by reasonable terms for a temporary cease-fire."

"Standby Major." Captain Hadbroke looked over to his Admiral and sighed almost sadly, "It's very odd, very odd indeed."

"They're up to something, and it doesn't bode well for us."

"May I suggest that we look at the wording Sir. The Major said that the French and that presumably means the Spanish as well, are open to any reasonable agreement for a temporary cease-fire. We are snug and safe here for several months, but after three, nearly four days of pounding away at the town, and the garrison they now want to offer us a temporary cease-fire."

"What's your point?" Asked the Admiral "Well, it's that they are either up to something or they know something that we don't. Something that is to our advantage and they are stalling for time."

"Yes, that sounds more like it. Is there a political flavour to this?"

"Not entirely Sir. The political situation is as we pretty much suspected all along. I'm not altogether sure how the local situation here can reflect on the general situation in Europe with regard to either the French or the Spanish. Both were our allies until they attacked us at the beginning of the week."

"Maybe President Warnock has brokered a deal politically and those people outside are in fact under orders to do their utmost to dislodge us before the deadline; which we apparently don't know about."

"No, I don't think it's that. We'll have to go along with it, but keep our eyes peeled."

"Alan, get back on the radio, tell them that we agree in principle to a temporary cease-fire for the purpose of picking up our casualties, for one hour only."

Three hours later the cease-fire took effect. The former patients who had survived the attack on the hospital had been transferred to the harbour in lorries and loaded onto a landing craft provided by the French navy who promised immediate care and relief for the suffering. The wounded seamen who could walk took Boy's body and wrapped him firmly in the sheets on which he had lain. No one was allowed to relieve them of their burden, even to the extent that the French seamen who reached out with willing hands to take him over the side onboard ship were pushed aside. Stiff with pain and seething with anger and pride they bore him gently across, carrying him to a place of rest on the quarterdeck and sat down watching over him rather than leave him as a nameless heap of jumble amongst others. Armed sailors pushed their way across the steel deck and prodded the men from the Royal Oak who remained resolute in their watch over the boy. It had become, like so many tragic things in war, a point of honour. The kid had always tried hard, and took the hard life that he had with a helping hand offered now and then when the endless ribbing stopped. His sea-dad took it hardest of all, though he was far away, still on the Royal Oak -hopefully in their minds; they had made it to Cyprus.

A French sailor swore and raised his rifle butt to the head of one of the British sailors. He lost the argument as three tars took him out by grabbing him and flinging him over the side. They sat down in silence surrounding boy, as others rained revenge on them. A French NCO shouted something obscene and they stopped beating their prisoners. A Commandant appeared who seemed to know a little English and spoke to the British seamen. He saw a killick and noting its bearer spoke to him in simple halting phrases asking him why they did not leave as they were told.

"Any of you speak French?" Asked the Leading Seaman."

"A bit, more like Franglais though, said a stocky Cornish seaman."

"Tell this officer what those dago swine did to the boy, and tell him this. If they can murder a boy in his hospital bed, then they can murder us where we are now, but by God there will be a price to pay when the time comes!"

"Vous Frenchie et les espagnol a tue la jeune garcon. Notre garcon a la hospital mate. Il etait blesse, et vous smash him, il est mort maintenant. We look after him now, that was our last order from the Captain."

"He is a boy you say?"

"Yes."

"You are all from the same, er, place… er ship?"

"Catches on fast." observed one of the ABs sarcastically. The Commandant ignored the interruption.

"So he is young boy you must take care of, yes?"

"Yes."

"But unfortunately he is dead. Said the French Commandant in a softer voice"

"He's dead mate because you and the Spanish took his life-support away and left him to die alone! You bastards!" The seaman stood up boiling over. "Shut up Smudge and stay down otherwise those stupid Frenchies will lay into us for keeps. Sit down, and do as you're told!" There was a pause while Smudge looked in the face of authority with searching eyes. He returned to his crouching position next to boy and the others.

"How good is your English Sir?"

"I think you could say I understand most of what you 'ave said up until now."

"Then know this, we will stay with the boy. You see when we left the boy in that hospital he had a chance to live. He was a fighter Sir, with the back of his head blown off, but he was coming back no sweat. Then along comes this Spanish Colonel, a friend of yours, and lines all the doctors up and shoots them. Do you understand that?"

"I understand."

"Then he takes the civilian nurses and hospital workers out of the hospital and marches them over the border into Spain. Now see, this is where it gets really bad for the boy and us. They just unplugged his life-support and stole it. They left him to die and us outside in the yard for three days with no food or water. "Can you believe that?" The Commandant looked at the angry killick without any expression on his face as he paused for breath. "No I don't suppose you do. Well, we're here to see he doesn't get any more bad treatment. We're going to get him home, or see to it that he gets a decent burial like any man is entitled to. Call us his honour guard, but by God, if you treat him with no respect then we will finish the war here for you if you push us!"

The killick sat down to muttered calls of 'Here, here.'

The Commandant spoke rapidly causing a wall of French sailors lined up along the quarterdeck to reposition their firearms in the non-aggressive position. He left the armed guards and headed towards the radio room. 'Things are getting away from us.' He thought just before he spoke to his superiors in the French battle fleet.

Shadows were lengthening as their transport vessel pulled away from the jetty, the sun slipping below the horizon at the end of a shocking day. High above them the sound of a bugle call could be heard ringing among the lofty

271

granite outcrops, washing down through the evening air onto the empty streets below. It was the last post. Evocative, sad -yes, but delivered with such a strength that was the embodiment of defiance and that defiance was almost palpable. Palpable too was that long silence as the last notes drifted away leaving them to their thoughts and to the close bosom of night.

After five more days of bombardment with repeated attacks by Spanish ground-forces the beleaguered 'rock apes' had the feeling they were going to hold on to their long-held piece of granite. They had been spurred on with the news that a combined French and Spanish armada had been persuaded to turn back by a fleet twice its size, made up of representatives of six navies supporting the Royal Navy. A blockade of the Skagerak and Kategat by the Swedish and Norwegian navies supported by Danish torpedo boats effectively sealed the fate of their French allies, unfortunately giving their German co-conspirators a political pathway of denial, since their fleet never left the safety of their harbours. The American sixth fleet made slow circles in the Gulf of Aserte, while other vessels dallied in and around the North Sea between the Faeroes and the southern tip of the Scandinavian peninsular while their diplomats attempted a media war falling slightly in favour of the British, but barely so.

What really made the news was the political bombshell spread on the front pages of La Monde, The Times, the Frankfurter Gemeinshaft and so on. *"British prisoners beaten up and murdered during casualty evacuation!"* accompanied by photographs taken during the evacuation of casualties at Gibraltar. *'Franco-Spanish coalition of forces butcher POWs!'* shrieked the New York Times. In full view, the quarterdeck of the landing ship could be seen with French sailors using rifle buts on bandaged British sailors. Photographs showing the British matelots being forced to their knees while bags were being forced over their heads by their French captors were underlined by the words *'As if Spanish butchery was not enough!'* further underpinning the tragedy behind Boy's death at the hands of the invading Spanish army. The papers identified the men as crew from HMS Royal Oak, a specially adapted high-speed transport vessel, etc, etc. The political pressure was being piled up with every hour that passed. Italians read the La Figaro with the dreadful pictures supplemented by snaps taken of the Spanish civilians, and a few British medical staff held in wire cages out in the open, where none were allowed much food and denied washing facilities and sanitation. It was a media field day where the gazettes demanded answers to questions by the hundred such as; *'Why are they being treated like this? Where is the Geneva Convention? Under whose authority are they doing these things? Have they no pride? These are civilians and prisoners of war. 'Not since the American brutalities in the old Afghan and Iraqi wars and at Guantanamo Bay has anyone seen such unbridled torture and ill-treatment of civilians and prisoners of war.'* On and on it went for days. As it did so many thousands of ordinary people across the European Union questioned the validity of going to war in the first place. Had it not been what the British had said all along? Keep out, it's their problem that the British Parliament had failed, and no one else's.

President Vassiliev was more than delighted in being an independent supplier of oil. Russia could broker its own deals without the tedium of the tribal squabbling that stultified OPEC. Not only had they diverted gas and electricity supplies into Western Europe at extremely accommodating prices, but also the deals over petroleum and strategic oils sent the cash registers spinning like Catherine wheels as the Roubles kept tumbling into the Russian exchequer. "Now Dimmer, now is our chance to push the Turks into thinking they can get back into the underbelly of Europe. The Greeks cannot hold them back, while we in our position of, shall we say, supportive 'friend' to the European Union in their little argument amongst themselves, can step in and take the Dardanelles for our own."

"Da, da, it is ever as it used to be. Perhaps they will stop fighting each other and rush to help the Greeks. It is, after all, in their union declaration."

"It doesn't look that way Dimmer, we think that they will be so busy sorting out the political differences, and you know that Muller-Weiss is now fighting for his political life, if not for his country's pre-eminence in European politics." voiced a tall thin strategic analyst.

"Do you really suppose we could get away with this. One wrong move and we could be facing the combined wrath of the European Standing Forces and the Turks."

"You will see, the timing is critical admittedly, but we will have control of the Dardanelles, and the Greeks will be very happy to get their Constantinople back again after so many centuries."

"As long as the English king can be, shall we say, apprehended before he can come out in support of President Warnock. If that happens Muller-Weiss has no other course of action but to withdraw."

273

"Precisely Boris. As usual you have a grasp of the situation. If that little puppet can be found and be made to disappear the situation in Europe will continue to be unstable."

"So it all hinges on your little ploy to upset the islanders of Aphrodite." The analyst spoke again. "But Mr President, the value in all of this comes like so. The Greeks already have Macedonia as far as Pristina in the north by the treaty of Vienna. Albania does not control its economy with the result that economic migrants swell the local populations across its borders with Greece and Hercegovina. As always they have moved into neighbouring provinces and demanded autonomy. Well, not for some time, the Greeks have managed to repatriate most of the Albanians, and of course the Italians have done so from the Terra d'Otranto centred on Brindisi. It pressurises the Albanian situation, and it is always possible that there are a few hotheads around who are looking for the right moment, a few weapons, and some cash, to start a fight. With a full scale uprising in the north in Macedonia, the Turks will take the opportunity to seize control of the island if they believe there are boatloads of Albanians heading that way, including a reasonable number of Armed Greek soldiers. They will not be able to resist the need to 'safeguard' their slender hold in that territory."

"So the Turks attack the Greeks, the Greeks are caught between the Macedonian Albanian situation and the Turks, while Europe struggles to cope with their own war leaving the pathway clear for us to assist the Greeks and push back the Turks to the other side of the Bosperous. If it fails because the European situation improves, what then?"

"Not a difficult problem for us Mr President. We pull the plug on our Syrian aid programme when a few Iraqi missiles go astray into Iran, and of course we must honour our treaty with Iran, Sir," the analyst gave a wry smile as he spoke. "And the final piece of the jig-saw fits into place with a Kurdish uprising in the disputed border region where, shall we say, yet again, over enthusiastic Turkish soldiers will pursue the Kurdish insurgents deep into Syrian and Iranian territory."

"Do you plan that we get involved in the conflict in this secondary theatre?"

"No Mr President. We shall remain a discrete distance, but nevertheless we can be seen to be giving Tehran moral support."

"Remind me never to buy a second hand car from this man." Joked the Minister of Defence with a huge grin.

"It looks as though it will work after all...."

****

Brigadier Malling was a little uneasy. The morning was hot and the garrison commander had requested an early meeting straight after lunch. His married quarters were pleasantly dark and cool while the overhead fans beat a gentle breeze in his study. The maid could be heard preparing lunch in the kitchen while his driver could be heard whistling as he polished the car. The 'houseguest' next door had caused a bit of a stir arriving after dark one evening a few weeks previously. He walked across the hallway into the dining room, along the long mahogany table lined with chairs. Turning right he wandered out onto the patio where Bougainvillaea splashed bright vermilion across the rear walls of the house, mingling riotously with the vines that hung from every spar on the pergola above. He looked sadly at the dried up patch that was an excuse for a garden as the hot sun turned the last vestiges of soil into sand, expunging all life from the plants that his wife had set into flower beds a few weeks previously. He sat down in a cane chair lifting a newspaper from the platted cane table and waited. Presently, the butler appeared with a tray on which was placed a large bottle of gin, a bottle of tonic and an ice bucket. "Thank you Mario, I will serve myself."

"Thank you Sir."

"How's your boy Mario?"

"He's getting better Sir, the plaster will come off next week."

"I'm glad to hear it. Has he missed much school at all?"

"Perhaps, you know, but his mother likes to keep him at home and make a fuss of the boy. Like every mother does."

"Well, at least he is in good hands. Mario, please sit down for minute, that's it, over here."

Mario slowly sank into one of the chairs sitting bolt upright. "Oh, sure Sir, he's always being spoiled by his mother."

"Now I know that the accident has caused you a few problems and my wife and I have talked it over and we have come up with a decision that I would like you to hear."

"What do you mean exactly Sir?" asked Mario with unmasked curiosity in his voice.

"That lorry driver who hit your boy cannot be found, and you know how difficult it is to trace some people. He gave a false address in Larnaca didn't he?"

"Yes, Sir he is not a good man."

"Well that does seem the case. Now here's the thing. We understand how difficult this has been for you and we have a gift for you and your wife. We understand that here in Cyprus you are a very caring and protective of your children. Please accept this gift as a private gift from both my wife and myself to you and your wife Helen, for your boy."

"What is it Sir?" Asked Mario looking at the white envelope held out by the Brigadier.

"His medical fees Mario, I hope you will accept this gift." The Brigadier was only to well aware of Cypriot pride, and had done his homework well, knowing his butler could not afford the medical fees to complete the treatment needed for the recovery of his son. "But Sir…"

"Mario, please, I am well aware of the work you do in your village to help others, and you know, I think you are a man who prays a lot. Here is one answer to your prayers. The good Lord gives us enough money Mario, it's really his money, and we would like to share it with you for this reason." Mario was silent. The Brigadier had perhaps, taken the wind out of his sails. He wasn't poor, but neither was he that well off that he could settle the medical bills out of his modest pay packet. "I… I… I don't know what to say Sir, this is a very generous thing to do…"

"Now don't you try to wriggle out of it Mario, we're very fond of you and your family, and you are very good at your job. We're proud of you and very grateful for the way that you have looked after us since we arrived."

"I don't know how to thank you enough Sir. I am truly very grateful. You and your lovely wife are very kind and gentle people, thank you Sir." The front door bell saved them both from embarrassment as Mario jumped up like a scalded cat, stuffed the envelope carefully into a pocket and walked swiftly through the dining room towards the hallway.

Dr Keen looked down from his lofty perch through the acacia fronds towards the sandy bay, noting the presence of the new arrival partially obscured by the jumble of rocks and concrete down by the dock. His life would be idyllic were it not for the circumstances that surrounded him. Rubbing his greying beard in a wide sweep of his hand between the open thumb and forefinger, he pondered his chances of wandering down to the dock alone without being noticed by one of his bodyguards. The Brigadier living next door was a quite a card really, but hadn't much idea about the effects of living under virtual house arrest on a fugitive VIP. Sipping a gin and tonic idly, he came to a decision and had a desire to try out the little restaurant on the edge of the bay just across the road.

"Costas! Are you there?"

A distant reply came from the kitchen. "Yes Sir, just coming."

"There you are Costas. Have you started lunch yet?"

"Mr Applethorpe was about to start making it Sir."

"Will you tell Mr Applethorpe that I will not be needing lunch today Costas."

"Yes Sir, will you require the car Sir?"

"No thank you Costas, I have made alternative arrangements."

"Very good Sir."

Costas, the most trusted and well respected Greek butler and man's man in the British army smelled a rat, and smirked to himself. 'He is going to do something silly,' he sighed to himself as he walked quietly into the spacious kitchen. "Jim, he doesn't want lunch today after all. He has made alternative arrangements."

"Right you are then. I'd better put the fish back in the fridge for tonight. Has he decided to go to the Officer's Mess for lunch?"

"No idea, he seems quite relaxed really, doesn't want his car." Jim Applethorpe thought for a moment. As a dedicated professional chef he had the best qualifications and experience to serve the weird and affected palettes found in the army social set. However, for the likes of Dr Keen who had a fine sense of manners and an un-affected palette he was sometimes unsure of the changes that had taken place in his daily routine as a master chef. True the Doctor had a good nose for wines and a wide taste, but in reality loved the wholesome produce to be found in the local markets, intermingled with good British fare from time to time. Jim didn't much like being a minder either. He liked his important guest, and like Costas it was both a pleasure and an opportunity for him to display his talent. "I'll ring the mess and warn them just in case."

"Don't worry Jim I'll do that. By the way, what time is our lunch going to be?"

"Give it another half hour Costas. Sardines and your style of salad, how does that grab you?"

"You are really learning our ways Jim, I am beginning to think you will become a Greek cook in your own taverna one day."

"Get out of here! Otherwise you'll get no tsasiki today!" Came the grinning reply.

"Followed by water melon if you're a good lad…"

Jack slipped out of the patio window into the warm shade under the pergola; he went around the side of the house and out of the front gate. The guard hut at the bottom of the access road leading to the main road was out of sight round the bend, so no one from there could notice his progress. Crouching to get through the hole in the chain link fencing he pushed through the sparse undergrowth walking to one side as he negotiated his way down the slope through the bushes and on to the dusty ground at the bottom. The sea breezes carrying the sounds of children playing in the soft sands at the water's edge. Approaching the road he caught the aroma of Greek cooking on the same gentle winds, relaxing him even more as he looked forward to a little light relief. 'Now what was his name?' He thought to himself, 'Chip ah, Woodingdean. I wonder if they have a phone in there.'

Chip was sitting in a deck chair on the quarterdeck under an awning twitching the fishing rod that Chief Grey had loaned him. "Well I'm blowed if there's anything down there interested in my bait. You had any luck Sub since I've been away?'

"Not much Sir, at least not during the day, there's plenty of larger ones about in the evening when the tide's in." The Sub-lieutenant smirked. "When the tide's in? When the tide's in? Where did you do you learn your navigation that's what I want to know?" They both laughed enjoying the sunshine and doing very little. With half the crew on leave in Cyprus, a few still undergoing rehabilitation at the military hospital, the rest who were fit continued working tropical routine taking it easy while the army technicians under the supervision of dockyard mateys carried on the repairs to their injured skimmer. A phone went off close by in the rear of the cargo deck, "Get that will you Sub." drawled Chip as he sunk further into his comfortable position, his knees becoming even redder under the powerful middle-eastern sun. "If it's for me tell them I'm not available until this evening there's a good chap." The silence that followed in the next ten seconds made him suspicious so he opened an eye cocking it in the direction of the phone. "It's for you Sir." His heart sank. "Is it important sub?" He rubbed his arm as a twinge of pain hit him while changing position in his chair to get a better view. "Yes, Sir, It's Dr Keen."

"Oops! I'm right there Sub. Tell him I'll be there in a second." He took the phone from the outstretched hand and paused before answering. "Commander Woodingdean Here Sir." He said politely. "Is that you Commander?" Will it be alright if I call you Chip, you know it isn't so formal then?"

"Why of course Sir. Is there anything I can do for you."

"Yes, I would very much enjoy the pleasure of your company for lunch, and perhaps your first lieutenant if he can come too."

"Why yes Sir, that would be very nice."

"In that case I'm not very far away, perhaps you can come to the little restaurant just a few hundred yards away in the sandy bay next to where you are?"

"You are here Sir. Well, that's very nice of you to ask we'll be along very shortly. Er, would you prefer us to be out of uniform Sir?"

"Yes, I think that will be just perfect. It's a lovely day for a light lunch and to be in a cool place, with good company. I look forward to seeing you in a quarter of an hour."

"Yes Sir, thank you."

"Goodbye." Chip swung the phone back to the Sub who had remained at a discrete distance out of earshot. "Sub. Find Lieutenant Commander Newman he is to be dressed in his best casual civvies for lunch with Dr Keen and on the gangway in five minutes. Five minutes and no more!"

"Yes SIR!" The Sub was impressed, very impressed. The skipper was being invited out to lunch along with the first lieutenant. 'Boy wait till I get home!'

Actually, Dr Keen had caused a bit of a stir. The restaurant owner and headwaiter recognised the king as soon as he walked in, and almost staggered into the food counter at the back of his little establishment. "Quick!" He blurted to the girls as he held onto the furniture for dear life. "Whatever that man wants you give it to him and you treat him like a VIP!" He whispered urgently, hastily wiping away a spot of grease on an otherwise clean surface. One of the waitresses looked in the direction of the older man approaching them and turning back to her boss stuck her tongue out at him before striding cattily away towards the new arrival. Something made her look back just before she reached him, and the terror in the old man's face looking at her from behind the counter caused her own heart to miss a beat.

Pellegea, one of the older girls managed to overtake her from the other side, and spoke before she could turn around. Maria nearly bumped into the man coming up short. "Good afternoon Sir. Would you like a table for one?" She heard Pellegea ask him. She could tell he was different by the resonant tone of his voice and by the well-spoken manner through which she could hear his very good English. "Not exactly, may I have a table for four please, perhaps not too far from the window?"

"Why of course Sir, over here, please sit down." She heard Pellegea say in her best English. "This is Maria, and I am Pellegea, and we will be serving your table."

"Thank you Pellegea. This table looks very fine to me. Maria woke up in time to draw back the chair for the gentleman and assisted him to be seated. "Would you like something to drink Sir while you are waiting for your, er, friends?" He looked at her pondering on the decision. 'Oh my God, what have I said,' thought Pellegea to herself, beginning to panic. "No, thank you. I believe I would like to wait for my friends. May I look at the menu?"

"Yes, Sir." Maria stretched out her hand slowly to the grey haired gentleman with the dawning realisation that she knew him and also knew that he was a well-known figure, but couldn't place him. The king looked at Maria, Maria looked at the king, and Pellegea looked at Maria. The king looked at them both quizzically for a moment and instantly all three burst into embarrassed laughter. The girls more in sheer relief, and the king, who saw the funny side of their situation. He motioned the girls to come closer and whispered conspiratorially. "It's alright, just relax and let us enjoy a rare moment of freedom."

They left him quietly with smiles on their faces looking at Giorgio their boss, their faces lit in high colour, their eyes bright with curiosity. "Giorgio grabbed Pellegea by the wrist as they disappeared out into the kitchen at the rear through the hanging fronds in the doorway. "Georgio, who is that man, I know him, I tell you. He's very famous isn't he?"

"When Maria has finished at the table in the corner get her and Anastasias to come here immediately. Go now, it's very important!" For one minute he was completely speechless until they came into the kitchen. He spoke quietly and quickly. 'That man is the king of England. So don't mess things up." Maria's mouth dropped open and Anastasias looked through the brightly coloured fronds and gaped. Giorgio, suddenly aware that his highly successful restaurant was suddenly entertaining the king of England, felt a twinge of regret for his 'greasy spoon' establishment. 'In another life, another time perhaps, in better circumstances… "He just wants to be free." Maria interrupted his thoughts. "What's that Maria, he spoke to you?" Pellegea answered for both of them. "He just wants us to relax, Georgio. He told us it was for him a rare moment of freedom. She looked away through the fronds with a rising empathy for him. "Pellegea, you will take over that table exclusively, and Maria you will help Anastasias and Helen with the other customers. If you need any help Pellegea, then ask for Maria. Now go! We have other customers coming in." The girls were flattered, where Anastasias just shrugged his shoulders and continued serving the tables and clearing up without any fuss.

The saw him sitting at the table next to the window looking out to the sandy bay, and the families playing and lazing on the sand. Turning around to face them as they approached the table he greeted them warmly. "Gentlemen, how nice to see you both again. Come and sit down."

"Doctor Keen, Sir, how nice to meet you again. Thank you." They sat down. "May I introduce you again to my colleague Frederick Newman?"

"Of course you can. And please call me Jack or indeed Dr Jack, whichever, I will not mind."

"Thank you Sir, most people call me Fred."

"It's a pleasure Fred. Now, let's see what we have here." The king nodded gently towards Pellegea who handed Fred and Chip their menu cards.

There was a growing awareness in both Fred and Chip's minds that the king was feeling uneasy staying at his safe haven on the hill. It was quite a surprise for them to learn that had been viewing them almost every day through his intensifiers, and that had exacerbated his position, albeit a pleasant one. The king felt keenly that it was time to be going home for the good of his people and for the safety of his country. As they talked in lower tones Pellegea, occasionally with the help of Maria, served them faultlessly. The wholesome Greek food was to the liking of their guests and it pleased her that they chose a fish mese' for the main course and some Commanderie to wash it down with.

A helicopter droned heavily over the background noise while crossing the bay, temporarily drowning out conversation. In the near silence that followed the gentle hum of conversation drifted effortlessly as other parties dined in the lazy atmosphere of an early Mediterranean afternoon. A child came rushing by jostling Pellegea and rubbing shoulders with her honoured guests as he trotted past. The lad fell on the floor in front of the king and howled. Pellegea was mortified as the king bent forwards and lifted the mite onto his feet. "There, there little chap." He crooned softly; looking at a pair of bright, shiny blue eyes that held him with a slight touch of suspicion. "Now let's have a look at that knee, oh let's make it better, there how's that?" The king rubbed the red looking knee and the child relaxed a little. "There you are, better now?" The child nodded and Pellegea warmed to the humanity of her 'special' guest. The little boy's mum came towards them from the table where she had been sitting and apologised. "I'm so sorry." She announced. "He is so quick. Thank you for taking care of him."

"What's his name, he's a lovely little boy?" Said the king beaming, and handed the little chap over to his mum.

"This is Alastair, my little terror." replied the woman, placing him on her hip. "Oh, yes, I can quite see that. You're going to break some girl's heart one day with those good looks of yours. Glad I could help." He said waggling the boy's chubby little hand affectionately. At that moment the woman locked eyes with the king and she stammered. "Well... thank... thank you for taking care of Alastair." She walked away a little flustered looking back only once. "Oh dear said the king softly, I don't suppose she recognised me do you?"

"Possibly Jack, but I think she's trying to work out who you are." Chip replied softly, trying to look nonchalant. "Well.' Said the king, "let's taste the ice-cream before we go, I'm not going to change my intention of having a good lunch with a pair of stout fellows like you."

"That's very kind of you to say so Dr Keen. In fact I think I'm going to enjoy a nice ice-cream sundae."

"That's the spirit, come on Fred name your fancy."

As the lunch drew to a close they became aware of a gradual silence descending in the little restaurant as families decanted onto the beach. The few who remained had twigged to the fact that here they were in the presence of someone special. Perhaps encouraged by the fact that unbeknown to the little trio enjoying themselves there was a 'presence' outside the little establishment.

"Oh I say, look at that." murmured the king looking out of the window. Chip who sat facing the king alongside Fred turned discreetly. His heart sank. There in the little car park stood a couple of open topped MP vehicles stuffed full with MPs, and a staff car. "The game's up Dr Keen, you have been found out enjoying yourself out of hours." Joked Chip with a smile. "How about taking the back door and walking back to the house with me gentlemen? I could do with a little company." Chip smiled conspiratorially looking at Fred. "Anything to help."

"Good fellow, let's pay the bill and be off." Pellegea watched in detached amusement as the king fought off the polite desires of the king's luncheon guests to pay for their delightful repast. The king drew out a small wallet, and paying the waitress handsomely the three of them stood up to leave. Pellegea was flummoxed; she did not know what to do. As her distinguished guest passed her by she gave a quick courtesy, as did Maria standing slightly behind her. "That's very kind of you." Said the king raising his index finger over his mouth in a sign of secrecy, tiptoeing towards the back kitchen. Giorgio panicked at first, but when Fred explained what they wanted he let them pass hoping no one would notice the 'mess' in the kitchen.

The three co-conspirators emerged into the bright sunlight facing the road on the verge of the sandy bay. Stepping out of what little shadow there was from the building they sauntered across the road. "Aha!" called someone suspiciously. The king's shoulders sank in mock disappointment and he half turned to look at his accuser. "Brigadier Malling, how pleasant a thing it is to see you, I fear." The king smiled a wicked smile in the direction of the Brigadier. "I guessed as much, er, Doctor Keen. Did you enjoy your lunch Sir?"

"Absolutely splendid Brigadier, and in the most pleasant of company."

"Can I offer you a lift at all Sir?"

"No thank you Brigadier, but I dare say that I'm forgetting my manners. Brigadier, this is Commander Woodingdean and his first lieutenant, both of the Royal Oak." Having completed the introductions with some amusement they joined the king as he headed for the small valley, walking towards the bushes and saplings on the lower slopes below his eyrie. The noises of the resort receded into a blanket of silence as they walked across the hot sand. "It's very soporific in the afternoons, I sometimes get the feeling I could stay here for ever with the different smells and the sounds of life going on around me at a leisurely pace." Sighed the king as he trundled up the slope beginning to pant in the heat from his exertions. "It's rather nicer than sitting on my quarter deck waiting for the tiddlers to take my bait Sir. Very agreeable indeed."

"Brigadier, I have come to a decision, and I would like to discuss it with the three of you over drinks."

"Yes, Sir, I would like to hear what you have in mind and perhaps, be of service to you. May I first make a phone call to the Provost Marshall, it's just that he's probably falling on his sword, or at least making out his resignation and I wouldn't want to lose a good man because of lunch."

"Good Lord!" The king stopped at the threshold to the hole in the wire fence. "I didn't stop to think of that." He grinned at the Brigadier. "Will you give him my assurances that I would prefer it if he refrained from doing that, after all, it's not expected for someone like me to er, shall we say... make a run for it." They all chuckled softly at the thought of an embarrassed Provo Marshall sweating under his collar waiting for the executioner's hand to fall –like so many of his own victims.

****

Pierce Anders sat in the jump seat all the way across the Atlantic, captivated by the controls and instrumentation in the slender cockpit. "So you see Major, the stupidity of late twentieth century thinking. All that bureaucracy and, dare I say it, high level gin-swilling that went on crushed the life out of aviation for several decades. It killed off all but the rich, the supply of pilots into the airlines dried up within a few years and legislation sunk all but two of the world's biggest manufacturers"

"So what you're saying is, that the bureaucrats were responsible for the crash of the airlines because they were passing laws they didn't understand?"

"Yes, basically that's it. The rot started really badly in the nineteen eighties and got worse from there onwards. What ultimately happened is that they fell into the trap of being controlled by the airline industry, and by then the political duffers who were more interested in scoring points didn't even realise they were being taken for a ride under a snowstorm of high-level PR that completely fooled them. They couldn't see that every time there was an edict passed by the Joint Aviation Authority, people were being forced out of the sky and training companies were going out of business. Therefore, when Argentina attacked our oilfield installations in the South Atlantic in 2118 we had, by that time, insufficient pilots and next to no training facilities outside of the big airline training schools. Our air defence had been taken away right out from under our noses by a series of blunders one after another."

"But even so, the eight hundred seater was a bit of a marvel wasn't it?"

"On paper only, you have to remember that the Americans fed them the bait way back in 1997, by producing a canted feasibility study on super-liner transports. The Europeans fell for it hook-line-and-sinker. Almost went bust and the Yanks clawed back their losses in the aviation market almost over night. After that it just remained a pipe dream fantasy."

It was half past six in the evening local time as the plasma-stream military jet arrowed across the eastern seaboard of the Canadian continental landmass, over the thickly wooded coast of Labrador. The golden hues of the sun mingling with the early dark of night separated by a layer of brown as the sun sank below the atmospheric envelope.

Far below them the island of Anticosti settled like a dun coloured anthill in the blue and slate grey waters at the entrance to the mighty St. Lawrence River. "This is where we wave good bye to our friends up there." Said the pilot looking for a moment at the airframe of a large passenger aircraft some two hundred feet higher and a quarter of a mile in front of them. "Why do you bother doing it this way?"

"Oh, it's simple really, we don't want the Americans to see us, so we tag along out of sight to sensors in the air or on the ground. With the cloaking device switched on we can then drop out of controlled airspace as though we were never there, and no one can see us at all. Clever stuff, eh?" Pierce smiled. "Normally, we'd drop you off at the base in Moncton, but the Americans have a lot of 'snoopers' in that area."

They followed the St. Lawrence all the way down, keeping Quebec, Montreal and Ottawa well clear to the left of them. Then dropping down to cross the Ottawa River high above Bryson and the Madawaska River south west of Renfrew, into the lowlands. A hundred minutes later they were cleared for a straight in approach to the forward tactical fighter base at Guelph. It was pitch black as they touched down with the pilots using their night vision headsets. The near silent plasma-jet military aircraft engines fitted with hush-kits and other gizmos sped along the runway losing speed slowly until they reached a distant taxiway. The 'Nigel' in the right hand seat throttled back to idle before engaging reverse thrust, and slowly opened the throttles up again until they had reached walking pace. Turning off the runway they headed towards a large hangar fronted by a wide apron on which were parked numerous military jets of all descriptions. A batman appeared and waved them on towards the hangar where they were finally waved to a halt and shut down. "Right Major, you stay with us until the rest of our 'passengers' are off-loaded, then you're to come with us as aircrew for the debriefing where we will part company."

Following a positive lead given to President Warnock's private secretary and assistant William Goodfellow, Pierce had made his way across the Atlantic to look for his king. William told him privately in a discussion that took in Chelsea Gardens and the Embankment as their office in the broadest sense. He remembered what his old army pal had told him as he made his way to the 'pick up' after they debriefed the aircrew and scanned the defect log. The black MPC was parked in front of the air-crew pick up point where Pierce waved a discreet, but cheery goodbye with a 'see you in a couple of days' flourish. Grant Speedwell met them at a government 'safe house' where he briefed Pierce on the situation 'on the ground'. "You will notice a lot of defensive emplacements in the area leading up to Niagara and on the US side of the border. The situation here is tense, but under control. Both sides have long and frustrating border checks, so you will have to sit it out. Your Canadian-American identity is possibly the best combination you can have right now, so don't be too bothered about it when you're over there. One other thing, we only know you're here for a special, that is to say non-military activity. Now what that means is, that you have next to no protection if they apprehend you. When you give the word that you have got what you came here to get, use the code word just for that situation. If you're on the run and want us to come and get you, with or without whatever it is you came here to get, use the other code word. Does this make any sense?"

"Very easily. No problems."

"OK, so if you're in a jam get to the nearest exit point and we'll come and get you out."

"Fine by me. Are they nervous just at the border, or is the civilian population sensitive to this situation?"

"Well, let me put it to you this way. They didn't thank us for pushing them back when they decided to steel our gas and oil a few years ago. They just think they've got a right to do what they want, to almost anybody, but what hurt them the most was when some skinny runt of a kid held back an entire division and whipped their asses long enough for the Canadian Cavalry to arrive. And he was British, so I guess you'll have to watch yourself a little bit." Pierce said nothing just shook his head in mute acknowledgement of what he was hearing.

"Right now Mr Ellis Perkins, your business trip to Canada is about to end, here's your customs papers, slips, exit form and temporary pass issued by the US Commandant-General. In case you didn't notice, the border area on the US side is now officially a US military zone, and will be for some time. You're business associates are waiting for you in the next room where you'll spend a couple of hours together so they can brief you on your activities in Canada for the last three days. Oh, incidentally, there's been more terrorist action in New York, your hometown. There's a military presence there, but as usual it's not up to much. Guess you Brits know how to handle it better. Right let's go and meet your buddies."

The two hours of intense brief left him a little worse for wear. Not a man for the cloak and dagger stuff, he felt the tedium of having to cram a myriad of facts, figures, and the seemingly pointless data to cover the wrinkles in any man's life. Eloise was his secretary with whom he was romantically linked. A good looking, auburn haired woman with a good figure to match. Although he knew that Eloise was not her real name. George Eastman who was a heavier individual, balding, wearing a crumpled suit and fashionable glasses that didn't quite suit him. Gerry La Fargue who was their manager and the 'business brains' in the engineering design company they were all billed as working for.

The following morning found them driving along the highway towards the Canadian border opposite Niagara Falls to the north of Buffalo. Passing around the bay approaching Hamilton they could see coastal defences stretching far into the distance. Just beyond the conurbation of Hamilton they could see the straggling necklace of high barbed wire fencing snaking across the countryside marking the beginning of the military zone. Concrete gun emplacements and patrol vehicles increased rapidly as they approached the first checkpoint on the way in. Canadian army units who were armed to the teeth accompanied the Mounties manning the first checkpoint. Pierce saw the heavy barricades lying by the side of the road with huge mechanical movers parked behind them, ready to jostle them into place by pushing them across the highway with their incredible brute strength. Soldiers were in position manning foxholes, armoured vehicles and so on. Although very much in evidence the soldiery seemed to be quietly going about their business. Their passes were scrutinised one by one against a checklist held by one of the Mounties. They were waved on to an open area by the road side where soldiers armed with up-turned convex mirrors on long poles silently walked around their vehicle checking the under-body for signs of hidden weapons and more importantly, hidden explosives. Pierce's new identity had transformed him into a typical North American male working for a commercial company on a business trip. He looked the part with his hair brushed differently, open necked shirt with the collar stud hanging off to one side, and loudly coloured casual trousers right down to his expensive and inappropriate choice of footwear. 'Ellis' and Eloise sat in the back seats in front of a pile of PR materials; specimen artefacts and suitcases piled up in the luggage space behind them.

With the first checks completed they breathed minor sighs of relief as they passed along the peninsular between Lake Ontario and Lake Erie. Huge earthworks had been thrown up all along the ground effectively dividing the peninsular into several segments all facing the actual border way off in the distance. The second checkpoint lay behind two such giant earthworks where, once again, they were 'checked out' including having to vacate the vehicle which was subjected to a thorough internal search. This time their inquisitors were army personnel who quickly and effectively completed their tasks, getting the answers they required in a very short space of time. On arriving at the exit to the second point they were given a handful of documents and told to have them duly completed by the time they arrived at the third and final checkpoint in the canal-zone.

George Eastman and Gerry La Fargue kept up a long conversation, occasionally breaking it to make one or two observations for the benefit of Ellis in the back. Under ordinary circumstances he would have dozed off in the warmth of the vehicle, particularly since he had spent most of the last fourteen hours travelling to get there. Tension was just below the surface and he knew that this was the easy part. Once in the Canal Zone on the other side he would have to face potentially unfriendly troops and officials. "You see that strip there up ahead Ellis? That's all mined with stun mines. You tread on one of those it wont kill you, but you'd wish you were dead anyway."

"What do they have here Mk 5s or Mk6s?"

"A variation on the Mk 6s I think. Very effective though, although the US still produce those nasty little anti-personnel mines under licence from the Pakistani armament manufacturers just outside Karachi."

"They were banned by the UN Commission for the conduct of war and the welfare of the common soldier weren't they?"

"Absolutely right, and incorporated by the Geneva Convention of 2026, but they prefer to inflict casualties with steel splinters or ball bearings that tear them apart. Reckon it costs an enemy more in resources that way."

"Ellis, when was the last time you carried a weapon?"

"About thirty six hours ago, why?"

"Shoot, that may be a problem. They have some pretty good 'sniffers' on the other side, better than ten parts in five million. But you've had a shower this morning and freshened up, yes?"

"Yes, I don't think that's too much of a problem though, is it?"

"Hope not." They sat in silence now as the final checkpoint was reached. George pulled over into a long queue at a lay-by where they started the inconvenient task of completing the sheaf of forms the soldiers had handed them earlier. Hoardings blocked the view from the highway on either side so no one could see what was going on beyond the ribbon of the highway. All the cafés and restaurants along the way had been closed or taken over by the military leaving no eating or rest room facilities between Hamilton and St Catherines.

They passed under what looked like a bridge, but they could see through the vehicle's sunroof that it was in fact a screen consisting of large sheets of hoarding bolted onto an intricate structure of steel scaffolding. No one could look east towards the border and neither could the Americans look westwards from their look out posts on the eastern bank of the falls. The convoy they had been assigned to began moving off slowly towards the bridges over the canal. Once across they turned south towards the checkpoints opposite Buffalo. Passing through one of the innumerable chicanes constructed of large concrete blocks forcing all vehicles to turn sharp left, then sharp right, they gradually became aware of a huge pair of twin towers dominating the skyline. They turned southwards on a converging course towards the canal with a sense of foreboding.

"That's the Potsdam Gate," said Gerry softly. "They named it after the large towers that the Russians built on the outskirts of Berlin to stop anyone from stealing a train to make a break for freedom."

"It's impressive," said Ellis passively, "we've heard about it back home, but what did they hope to achieve by building a gateway like that?"

"Propaganda mainly, but now they hate it since President Stevenage called it the Potsdam Gate. They realised they had made one of the biggest propaganda mistakes of the century."

"Well, when they grabbed the canal they claimed they had the freedom and the right to protect their trade routes. What they wanted to do was to supply their war effort via the Great Lakes. So they figured that if they could grab the whole of the Niagara Escarpment between Lake Huron and Lake Ontario they could control the whole navigation, but they needed the St. Lawrence, and that required them to push their border all the way to the banks of the St. Lawrence. That's where it got nasty. They stirred up the French separatists against the government, and while they were embroiled in a civil war with the authorities the Americans grabbed the territory from the south bank of the St. Lawrence to Nova Scotia, and the rest is history. They built the gate as if it were a gateway to freedom on their side, but it turns out they miscalculated, that's when the Brits and the Commonwealth stepped in to help us, the Americans lost face big time. We got our territory back and they ultimately lost the propaganda war as well as the war itself."

"I can understand now, why the UN has moved out lock stock and barrel to Geneva. They had to after impugning the American President," thought

Pierce more to himself than to his travelling companions. "By the way, don't ever call it that in front of an American. They don't like it either, makes em mad as hell, especially if you tell em you're from Montreal.

Not a tree nor a bush or a rabbit hole had been left in the Canal Zone. Both sides had been stripped and covered in armoured pillboxes, heavy gun emplacements, trip wires and the general paraphernalia of war. Their final checkpoint was more a formality of gathering together a convoy of vehicles one the eastern side of the bridge over the Niagara cliffs. The river boiled in turmoil unnoticed far below them on its way southward into lake Erie.

They entered the Potsdam Gate to be greeted by 'squaddies' bawling at them, gesticulating with arms flailing in abrupt right angled gestures difficult for most people to understand. The convoy was directed towards a narrowing funnel of concrete blocks by a line of soldiers with flags. Ellis looked carefully around him noticing the apparent 'front' while in the background soldiers lounged about smoking cigarettes idly talking among themselves. "Get out of the Vee-hickle and stand over there!" Bawled a Sargent to Gerry who was the driver. "Gerry cupped his left hand to his ear in a gesture of 'Say that again' towards the soldier. "Goddamit! How many times do I have to say it? Get out of the Vee-hickle and stand over there! Now move!" The vehicle was searched thoroughly, the engine, luggage spaces, glove, box, etc, etc. At the second checkpoint at the exit point of the military zone on the eastern outskirts of Buffalo they were randomly selected for yet another detailed search under the scrutiny of a middle-aged Captain. At one point a soldier indicated that he wanted to have a close look at the occupants, by searching them individually. There was an intimidating moment as one of the soldiers showed signs of wanting to search Ellis more closely. Eloise deftly placing herself between the approaching soldier distracted his attention giving Ellis time to move away. He changed his mind motioning her to open her handbag. She clung onto to it raising her voice with indignation. "No, I won't how dare you go into my handbag! Stay away from me! How dare you!" Alerted to the rising fracas the Captain told the soldier to back off. "Sorry ma'am, he ought to know better. Please take your handbag over to where the Corporal will search it. Thank you." The female Corporal took the bag and searched it properly muttering under her breath. "Sorry Ma'am, he's a little bit difficult to manage at times." Eloise took her bag without saying anything and left the search area heading towards the car. George was climbing into the driver's seat when Ellis chose his moment and joined him in the front passenger seat while Gerry moved into the rear. Eloise climbed in and they were waved on.

Where it had taken thirty-five minutes for them to pass through the Canadian zone it took an hour and a half of direction, misdirection and harassment by the US military before they were able to make it to the customs checkpoint. In a totally different atmosphere of near silence where the polite request for passports and customs declarations seemed a world away from the one they had just left a hundred metres on the road behind them.

The rest of the journey through the militarised zone on the US side was made difficult by the desire by the locals to look good, but their ineffectual use of manpower created alarming and sometimes comical confusion. Once out of the zone they stayed on the interstate without stopping until just outside Syracuse. They stopped for 'refresher' and some coffee at an IHOP before going on. Ellis was tired, and although he looked like a company rep who'd just had too much partying the night before he was beginning to feel that dreadful sucking feeling as his body and brain desired a temporary shutdown. As ever the people were genuinely pleasant and helpful totally belying the fact that there been a vicious war between them and the Canadians with the Brits just twenty years earlier.

Ellis looked puzzled as they chatted quietly in a corner out of hearing from other travellers. "Hey, Ellis, said Gerry. "You look as though you're worried about something?"

"Not really, more puzzled you might say. Why were those soldiers ripping out those Montreal window stickers from some of the cars in our convoy?"

"Oh, that, that's just their way of tryin' to keep a lid on things. Montreal wasn't exactly something to shout about as far as they are concerned. It was a disaster for everybody. Hell what they did to that place was awful. They just bombed it from the air, to take out the city's defences and flattened it."

"So much for their deal with the separatists, they just wanted the strategic advantage and used them to get where they wanted to be, leaving them completely exposed," added George. "Yes, it wasn't a very bright idea to murder the residents, but I seem to remember it cost them a President and ultimately the war."

"Too darn right it did. Thanks to the Brits". Eloise chimed in quietly. "Since that time we've had the moral as well as the actual victory."

"Does that mean that as far as the ordinary man in the street goes, they have no problems with that or is there still some tension there?"

"Sometimes I'm not so sure either way." She replied. "I'd say most of the people want to get along with life and forget about it, but there's quite a few who hold a very hawkish point of view. They're the ones who can't except defeat at any price, who want to run private armies and start the war over. Mostly some die-hard politicians and some ex-military people usually. Otherwise we're still pretty friendly."

Ellis awoke on the outskirts of New York as they sped along one of the expressways alongside the river. Eventually they took a turn into the myriad of city streets and headed for the centre of the city. They crossed Times Square at 45th Street threading their way through road-works, past hotel guests squeezing their overfed frames into limousines in the middle of the street up to 6th Avenue. Eloise bade her farewell for the time being and made for her five o'clock appointment with the hairdresser on the corner where they dropped her off just as the traffic lights turned red. Ultimately, they swung into 5th Avenue and went around the block until they drove into the underground car park of an apartment block close to the City Library. The apartment was on the fifth floor above the street from where they had a good view of the small park and the street that lay alongside the library building. Eloise joined them at half-past seven looking very posh in her new hair-do and a lovely dress that hugged her ample figure. The men had made use of their time resting, bathing, watching the television, and chatting to Ellis about some of the intricate knowledge that he, as a temporary denizen of the city should know about. They went downstairs in the lift and walking out onto the street hailed a cab that whisked them away into the evening for their dinner at an expensive restaurant.

****

US President Barclay T. Shaw sat in the Oval Office surrounded by his chief aides and by two secretaries of State: one for foreign affairs and the other for Security. "Dan, I don't believe this war in Europe is going to help anybody, and more to the point it was inappropriate for the US President to be visiting the French on the eve of their attack on the British. It has put us on the wrong foot don't you think?"

"I'm more than inclined to agree with you Sir. In fact I think Muller-Weiss set this whole thing up."

293

"Well it certainly has frozen us out of any immediate possibility of getting back on good terms with the British government."

"We-ell, we've sorted out the foreign policy planning group. Finished reshuffling one or two people around and thought you might like to think about appointing a new face now that chicken-shit director Al Baker has been gone for a coupla months."

"I'd like to see Dr Michel Shivulski in there, Dan, what d you think?"

"He's a good choice Mr President. Well connected and he knows what's going on, doesn't stand for no nonsense and I sort of guess that those staff problems over there will come to an end, so we won't experience any serious lapses in our policy reviews in the future."

"Good, have Linda fix up an appointment for him to see me tomorrow over breakfast, that's the only time I have spare."

"Now gentlemen." Announced the President, "The war in Europe, or shall we call it a 'little local difficulty' over there? How do we get back the ground we have lost over there and protect our foreign trade in Europe?"

"Well Mr President. The Norwegians have lodged an official complaint regarding the close proximity of our Atlantic fleet to their territorial waters claiming that we violated their international boundary..."

"Yes, yes we know all about that, so I repeat the question. How do we get back our lost ground?" There was an ominously long pause.

"We wait," replied the Foreign Secretary. "Wait?" What do you mean by 'wait', is that it; just wait."

"That's the recommendation. We let our Atlantic fleet stooge around Iceland for a while longer. Keep a presence, but keep them well away from the main spotlight, and we just let this war come to a 'natural' conclusion. The EU that will emerge will be weaker and we can be in a stronger position to negotiate better tariffs with the splinter groups on a national basis rather than in a head on with the combined bargaining power of the whole of the EU."

"How do we do that."

"We need to find a key that would first of all put us back in favourable light with the British."

"A key? What sort of key?"

"Well, we're still looking at the prospect of blowing their off-shore pipe-lines from the gas-fields. The oil is almost played out, so it really doesn't matter about that, since the Russians are on the verge of a second agreement with the British, we still can force the issue there a little bit more…"

"Daniel, you've got Something on your mind, spit it out."

"Mr, President." Spoke out the Secretary for Foreign Trade. "Before he does there is the trade option of cutting our agreed export rebates. If we continue to use the scheme to offset taxes in the manufacturing industries…"

"Bryan, we've done that before to off-set the cost of exports to Europe, can we afford to do it again given our situation here?"

"I think the question is can we afford not to, or at least go some way to mediating our situation in Europe. Their trade commission keeps banging away that we're unfairly subsidising exports. Now unless we want another trade war with Europe, we need to loosen our posture a little bit with them, or we will find ourselves facing stiffer tariffs, and our export markets will begin to dry out. If we back off from our position we will be seen to be 'aiding' them' through their current local difficulties, otherwise we will lose what little we have left of both our grain and beef export markets to the Russians and to the Canadians."

"It will cost our producers more Bryan, and lose votes."

"I know that Mr President, and the Europeans need the cash, it's a case of either we cut our subsidies however well we may disguise them, or we lose the markets and our exports fail driving down our balance of payments."

"You mean they'll bring down the shutters to US imports -completely? Can they do that?"

"Yes they can. They have enough energy and grain, including beef and raw materials coming in from the Russian Commonwealth system and the Chinese autonomous States, that all they have to do is call 'foul' and walk away from us."

"Mr President, if I may cut in here?"

"Go ahead Dan, you might as well finish it off and ruin my day."

"It don't seem as bad as all that. It may cost a few votes, but I think I have an idea that can help put us back into good favour with the British and maybe guarantee a more positive relationship for both of us."

"What are you suggesting?"

"Well, we do two things. One, we go ahead and blow the pipeline..."

"Dan!"

"I know Mr President, just hear me out..." there was a slight pause as the President nodded with a sigh of impatience. We blow the pipeline, but implicate the Germans. Our intelligence reports tell us the French are about to do the same to us. However, Muller-Weiss has left the French high and dry. Has there been a single German soldier or police unit near the UK since this fracas started? No, so we make it a little hotter for the krauts. Point two Mister President, the key. The key is running around out there somewhere. If we can find their king and bring him back home safely you can ride the protests over the easing of our export rebates. The Brits will be falling over themselves with gratitude in a blaze of publicity that will guarantee another term in the White House. They will no longer have their constitutional crisis. Muller-Weiss and his cronies wont have a leg to stand on, and we come out of it looking like their best friend. It's a simple as that, and we exploit the situation using the British as a base from which we can negotiate better terms to trade with Europe."

"Hell, Dan, nothing's that simple."

"Shoot, I reckon we all know that, but that's the key we're lookin' for."

"Anyone care to comment?" Invited the President."

"It doesn't ease our oil situation, and we must have a long term solution to our supply problem, or we risk disintegration, starting with industry. There's our communications infrastructure, which is already creaking badly, and if we haven't got the energy to fuel both industry and our economy we just won't make it."

"Bryan, I want to talk about that later, but I have a liking for what Dan has been proposing and I think we should take make that an urgent matter for discussion as a priority. Does everyone agree?" Nods and grunts of approval carried the idea forwards unanimously.

****

Ellis sat back in his seat pondering briefly on his next moves. Since his contacts had dried up in the Big Apple his only recourse was to head for Washington to tap into the security and intelligence communities for more information. George and Gerry had been helpful, and Eloise had come up with some interesting 'feedback' provided by a drug dependent CIA agent working on foreign nationals at the New World Trade Centre complex.

Eloise sat next to the window watching the twinkling city lights peel away as the small regional aircraft lifted into the skies. Then they were gone in an instant when the aircraft shot into the cloud base above New York like a needle through muslin. Once 'on top', the moonlight lit up the tops of the clouds far below, while shining through strands of cirrus-stratus high above like a powerful torch through lace curtains. They relaxed and chatted about all sorts of things, enjoying the luxury of being away from the stresses of the office environment of the past few days. They had a good laugh, somewhat discreetly, at the expense of one tired looking Federal Agent in the Metro Deli on 45th Street, who seemed to have reached expiry point. To avoid further contact with him they slipped into the deli merging in the queue just out of sight behind the door. While Ellis had his back to the door at the far counter in the back of the deli, surrounded by other people, Eloise leaned in through the plastic curtain hanging down over the cooler as if to choose a salad or a cold drink. The man had walked past looked in, missed seeing them and hurriedly departed down the street. By then the queue had moved on and shortened, so they indulged themselves on bagels. She had a Nova on butter, while Ellis preferred an egg and bacon with butter. They walked slowly back to Times Square towards their lodgings not bothering about being 'rediscovered' at all. He had been around for two days and since they were warned all foreign aliens could expect to be tailed at some time during their stay in the US, they walked up the street unconcerned.

The following day they dined in a cosy little Italian restaurant on 46th Street. Sometime during their fulsome meal Gerry had noticed a potentially more sinister tail sitting at a small table near the door at the bottom of the stairs. They continued as if nothing could disturb their enjoyment. The food was delicious and the wine superb, a good Chianti. The man took a side order and sat there drinking mineral water, watching the group quietly as customers came and went through the door close by. It was a simple trick really. As they approached the door Eloise had stumbled knocking the man's glass as she steadied herself on his shoulder. The water spilled out over the front of his shirt and trousers amid her shocked protestations of apology.

George and Ellis kept on walking while Gerry went through the pose of a mildly despairing if apologetic partner, the other two quickly disappearing through a set of double doors on the other side of the street. Gerry apologised once again and left the establishment, hailing a passing cab.

Later they clewed up at the flat opposite the library and chewed the fat over the last two days. "That guy was not FBI." said Gerry firmly. "And he's carrying a weapon."

"No, he's not FBI agreed Eloise, I don't think he's from around here, not a New Yorker that's for sure, more mid-west. Could be services?"

"Well, I think it probably wraps it up here for a while Ellis. If your leads are cold then perhaps we'll move onto the exhibition in Washington tomorrow."

"Does that mean they're onto us?" asked Ellis looking very concerned.

"No, don't worry about it." George said confidentially. "I think it's unlikely, more probable because we gave that Fed the slip yesterday."

Washington looked drab. Years of neglect, the war, and social deprivation all conspired to make even the institution and government buildings look stressed, slowly decaying like crumbling refugees out of Honeker's Germany a hundred years gone by. The high fencing partitioning the Federal Highway out of Dulles no longer served to make the distinction between the Federal route and the City route into the City. It was a protective barrier designed to keep beggars, muggers, thugs and other undesirables from making contact with foreign visitors and the better off. The old beltway was now a cracked and pitted racetrack encircling a huge ghetto of Washingtonians trapped by circumstances, much like their President, but much poorer, within the inner suburbs. They stopped off in Reston for a half hour to check some details at the 'office' then headed along the beltway to Tysons Corner. They disgorged themselves out of the air-conditioned MPV and piled into their rooms at a shabby motel next to the old highway out of town. It's a bit like Marseilles or Shanghai." Remarked Ellis. He had never been to Washington before. "Well, they're not as rich as they used to be." Gerry noted. "They have to pay for the same things we do at the same prices, guess it hurts them and their economy."

"We have the same back home, but those who can afford it get out and go into the UPAs."

"Is that working still?" asked Eloise showing interest.

"No, not really, some are well off, but most of them within the older bigger cities are really falling apart like we see here."

"Why did you set them up?"

"It's before my time, but it was economics that started it, and the social engineering laws that more or less forced people to abandon smaller settlements because the authorities could not support police services and organised crime began to take over."

"Sounds really bad over there."

"Yes it has been worse though. The euthanasia laws made it harder for people to stay alive, so those who could afford it moved into those areas where the local administration refused to adopt the edicts."

"We heard about that. So what do people do now?"

"Those outside the UPAs are mostly farmers or factory workers without any protection from the Department of Social and Community Affairs. So if a farmer fell of a tractor and broke his leg the likelihood of him receiving medical treatment would be assessed according to his age and the cost of making him well again."

"You mean they wouldn't treat him?"

"Not if he was deemed to be too old or the treatment too costly."

"That's awful. We still have insurance over here; at least, some of the better companies honour their policies. Others keep changing the rules to take the money off people, without providing enough cover. So does anyone get medical care at all in the UK?" George asked. "Well, it's better for some in the UPAs with their clinics. The Doctors and nurses are not tied to a checklist provided by the government. They treat everyone on their own merits and where people are dying they will provide hospices and palliative care."

"You mean they don't even do that over there?"

"Yes, it's as simple as that. The government system still taxes people to the hilt for things like medical care, but have imposed such stringent means testing that allows only a very few ever to qualify for any healthcare.

Refugees mostly because of international law, otherwise, none of the population."

"That's terrible!" George replied with genuine dismay. "So what does this checklist do for a patient Ellis?" Asked Eloise "It's part of the law requiring a doctor or a Chartered Nurse in the absence of a doctor, to assess a patient according to predetermined criteria. If the patient has a lot more ticks down the right hand side of the list than the left hand side, the patient gets to the next stage, which is the stage two assessment."

"What happens then Ellis." Asked Gerry who was beginning to feel a little indignant. "Oh, it's the means test. So sick people will normally get through to stage two, that's the point where most people get refused treatment because of their socio-economic background, or if they do get authorisation it's for very little. You know; a single parent from the wrong side of the tracks will get nothing. For example, if that person is a woman and she just happens to be pregnant, they will coerce her to have an abortion, and that includes at full-term." Eloise grimaced. "What happens if the first assessment goes the other way?" She asked. "That's the point where the patient is refused treatment anyway."

"God, how awful." Replied Eloise expressing her disgust. "Does anyone get treated at all?" She pressed. "Oh yes, the politicians have complete access rights to the state healthcare system, and that includes the state paying for private care. They've got index-linked salaries and pensions, and that doesn't change whether or not the country's economy is doing well or if it collapses. Like now, where we have something like twenty eight percent of the population nationally who are unemployed, they just keep playing with the figures and paying themselves out of the money they cream off in taxes while the rest starves. They've made themselves bomb proof."

"What about you, you're military aren't you? Do you get the same treatment?"

"No Eloise, we get exemption, partially because we have our own clinics, and they give us a thirty year safe period after retirement where we can't be refused treatment."

"But you said it was part of the euthanasia law. How does that correspond to euthanasia Ellis?" Eloise was looking cross when she spoke. Ellis was taking a shine to her. "It's just the way I described. You either get treatment or you don't. The medical profession no longer has any say in the matter. A small government department handles all decisions relating to life and death. Unless of course you are well off to live in a UPA that has a declaration of devolved government and hence no euthanasia law."

"But does that mean anyone can be excluded under any circumstances?"

"Oh yes, absolutely. The medical and nursing professions have always been taught to evaluate a patient under the three cardinal rules of State-Welfare, ailment and age. Age comes first, then income and last social background. So someone may be young, healthy and pregnant, but has a poor social background and not married. As I said just now, the assessment would be abortion based solely on economic and social background."

"What would they do to someone like that?"

"They call it counselling, but everyone knows its professional bullying. Way back when this was being taught in the twentieth century, the medical staff had no authority, but would find any means possible to get someone like that to have an abortion."

"What if they didn't want to?"

"It would be emotional blackmail and threats, even telling them lies just to get them to abort."

"Sure sounds inhumane over there." Mused George. "Well," continued Ellis, "when the economy collapsed in 2117 it hit the country hard, mainly because the population was shrinking, society had fragmented so badly that people founded the UPAs, and the earliest constitutional reforms included proper care and welfare in the UPA communities. No more abortions, no more expensive counselling and care for emotionally and mentally scarred young women, and in fact young women who could go on and get married and have children without expensive fertility treatment. Those other couples who genuinely could not have children got the chance to adopt."

"Hey Ellis, how do you know all this?"

"I did three years at medical school and decided I didn't like it, so went into engineering."

"You sound like a handy engineering type to have around when someone gets hurt.' Gerry observed with a grin.

Ellis slipped into the British Embassy just before nine o' clock in the morning. His contact met him in an inner sanctum, then momentarily ushering Ellis to follow him to a stairway behind a cleverly disguised doorway. Opening a door at the other end of the room they mounted a staircase and walked down three levels to a more secure area. As discussions became more detailed written reports and pictorial information gave way to film clips, the dispositions of personnel, and assumptions as to who was last to see the king, where and when. "Finally, we located this gentleman here. You see, just here, how he is partially obscured by that sign on the right over there. The king climbs out of his hover-bat and makes his way over to the back of the lodge. Mr A. N. Other greets him, shakes his hand and they move off." Ellis -now Pierce since he was back on home-turf, recognised immediately the lodge at Sandringham, but said nothing. "Have you any idea who that person is?" He asked the intelligence staffer. "It's just that whoever it is, is known to the king for him to have met like that and shook hands. A family friend, someone like that."

"Well we've looked at it from that angle and eliminated all regular 'friendships' outside of their immediate circle. That leaves two possibilities. But before we go any further I want you to look at this." The screen was filled with a large image of both Pierce and his brother entering the lodge at Sandringham. "Guess who we found making a surprise visit?" Smirked the security operations chief. Pierce smiled back. "So you have me on record as well, eh?"

"It's hardly surprising, but don't worry we had been advised by a mutual friend that you might turn up and to leave you two alone."

"That's very thoughtful of him. I'll have to thank him next time we go for a drink."

"We do know of course, about your interesting little téte a' téte with the others on your way back later that night. In fact it will be some time before we can identify all of them, but we did know this man." The image on the screen switched to a sharp close up image of the man they called the Guv'nor. "You do pick up some pretty rum characters when you go walkabout Major."

"Who is he?"

"Piluis Donver to be precise. A very slippery character until his untimely demise five weeks ago. How you managed to survive any form of attack made by him is quite remarkable."

"Oh, why do you say that."

"He is, er, was a nasty piece of work. Originally trained by the European Intelligence Agency, he went underground some ten years ago emerging with another identity. This time as an agent provocateur up in the northern UPAs back home, then vanishing as quickly as he appeared. We think he was hired by the US later on and was still working for them, until he met you that is, as part of their covert operations in the UK and on the European mainland."

"You mean one of those dirty tricks-cum-assault teams? Peppermints or something?"

"Almost, Varmints to be precise. William did brief you well?"

"So what are the findings so far?"

"Well, having fed all the junk into that giant computer back in Cheltenham we applied all the known associations and peripheral links we could think of. Judging by the movements of people in and out of the country, including the President of the US of A, we can surmise that either he was smuggled out on Airforce one, or somebody somewhere is holding him with a view to completing their intentions of invading us."

"What does that boil down to Sir?"

"It looks like this Major Anders. Either we find him quickly or we might find him dead and the UK annexed as a new province belonging to our old enemy across the Channel."

"How much time do we have?"

"I'd say about six more weeks before the political chicanery settles down and the ESA is launched in a second attack on Britain."

"Do you have any alternative theories about the king's whereabouts?"

"None that we can think of. It's a question of finding the right connection between the right moment with the right person, and then we may find the key to unlocking this mystery."

"So there is a possibility that he is in Europe somewhere?"

"I didn't say that, it's just a possibility, but we have no proof that is the case. He may also, be in hiding somewhere back home but I doubt it. He above all knows the constitution and how important it is for him to get back home quickly. None of the movement correlation algorithms we've run points to Washington, New York or to the US. You've been on a bit of a red herring, but you might be able to pick up something from one or two people at the Pentagon. We can have you on a temporary detachment here if you like. Going in on a more or less liaison footing, is that something you want to follow up on?"

"Yes, I would like to follow up on what remaining leads there might be if, for no other reason than to eliminate them from my list."

"Good, come back tomorrow morning and we will have your papers ready. It's unlikely to blow your existing cover, and it remains for me to ask you if you would like to go out as yourself or work your way back to Toronto the way you came in?"

"I'm afraid it's going to be the way I came in, otherwise it leaves loose ends this side of the border."

"Quite."

****

Rear Admiral Dunham had flown out from Blighty in a civilian fast jet converted into a two-seat reconnaissance aircraft. The pencil slim avian took off at half-past midnight climbing fast towards the upper atmosphere where the pilot held it in a fine balance between falling out of the sky and cruising along at high speed. The dim glow of the instruments providing the Admiral with enough light to see by other than the star lit heavens above. Gibraltar was in the hands of the Spanish and French while the Italians patrolled the waters between Sicily and the African coast. By the time they crossed the coast of England they were already at cruise altitude on the edge of the aircraft's performance envelope. The pilot's flight plan had been approved as the most sensible and expeditious route to get to their destination. They flashed across the night sky over Belgium and Luxembourg in the airways before their controllers had been aware that 'something' had transited their air space. The Germans with their routine efficiency followed a passing dialogue with the young lieutenant who was grinning all over his face as their trusty steed flashed over the borders of Germany, into the Eifel control sector. Then out of their sector back into France and back into Germany again, sliding effortlessly into another sector very briefly, as they sped through the southern tip of Germany where France, Germany and Switzerland met. At first losing interest as the aircraft was headed beyond their borders of responsibility, then asking more demandingly for flight plan details; for a flight plan not filed with any civilian organisation, but again too late for effective dialogue to take place. This was a dash across Europe in the best spirit of adventure. They were talking to their Swiss counterparts trying to get ahead of their radar contact as it flashed across the dark shape of the Bodensee far below them into Austria. Flying a straight line into Italy then, turning east to penetrate the Austrian border again before hurtling across the next international boundary into the mountainous region of northern Slovenia. Here the republic's antiquated air traffic control system almost missed them as they bounced across the southern border with Hungary across its fat underbelly. The French and German controllers had long forgotten about their 'unknown' by the time the Hungarian sector controller lost them on radar, sliding over the boundaries again about a hundred and fifty miles as the crow files, north of Belgrade. It was breathtaking and the Admiral smiled at the audacity of the young pilot's daring plan. The Romanian airforce scrambled when they picked up the 'chatter' from other sectors giving a general call to the un-planned aircraft to comply with requests for flight plan and intentions. They sped on across the southern skirts of the Pannonian Basin turning to the south east to 'stitch the border in a line fifty or so miles from Timisoara. From time to time the Admiral could pick out the great ribbon of the Danube illuminated by moonlight peeking through the cloud breaks below as they closed with the next turning point, where three more countries met in a fold in the earth's crust. They were gone once again, speeding southwards, in and out, in and out. First one country, then the next, back and forth. "The Bulgarians usually shutdown their air traffic control system at night, so there will be no more than an emergency watch on the ground." Commented the young 'renegade' as he prepared for the next sector. The aircraft responding smoothly to his voice commands as they aced it across the European peninsular. Finally, taking the long line south across Bulgaria from abeam Sofia to the border with Greece, staying well clear of the sensitive areas of Macedonia. Going hell for leather they shot across the narrow strip of rocky land that was Greece between the mountains and the sea across the wide reaches of Strymonic Bay, skirting the Halkidiki peninsular poking into the northern Aegean like a huge udder. The Aegean shone like a black leaded stove under the moonlight. From their lofty perch the two men could see over a wide-ranging panorama of mountains, islands and the sea beneath a bejewelled canopy of stars. Steering well clear of the Turkish border and following the airway they shot down the middle heading for a turning point that would eventually take them across the ancient island community of Rhodes. "So far so good," the Admiral observed with growing respect. "It's not quite over yet Sir, we've got to keep a sharp look out for the Turks. They are very twitchy about their airspace, so we may pick up some chatter or they may even scramble an aircraft given our current situation." The tactical display remained blank and the en-route frequency remained relatively quiet since there was little or no traffic at that time of night. In a final graceful descent they swept down towards Cyprus, the island of Aphrodite. The 'jet-jockey' touched down in style in a beautiful greaser along the runway, letting the nose drop slowly as the air speed bled away to nothing. "That was two hours and ten minutes, a fantastic run Lieutenant. I'm very pleased with the outcome."

"It was a pleasure Sir. I thought it would be a good idea to get you back on the ground early enough for a bit of a rest or a spruce up before breakfast. The flight canteen does an all day breakfast twenty four hours a day if you feel peckish Sir."

"That's very thoughtful of you, but I must continue with my journey. Another time perhaps Lieutenant." They climbed out of the cockpit and clambered down the small ladders fitted to each side by the ground crew. An aide took the Admiral's leather satchel while guiding him to a sleek looking hoverbat. "We'll go in this Sir, it's the quickest way to get to our destination." The driver held open the rear passenger door, closing it gently on its seals after the Admiral had seated himself in the comfortable padded seating. How long will it take Captain?" Admiral Dunham asked. "Not long Sir, about forty five minutes in a straight line across country."

"Across country you say?"

"Yes Sir, it's the shortest and the quickest route. It may be a little bumpy in places, but our driver knows the route well." The vehicle's console emitted a subdued glow from the front of the vehicle giving an eerie quality to the final stage of his journey to visit the king in his temporary residence.

They arrived at the Brigadier's house at ten past three where the two men talked quietly over a jug of hot coffee. The house servants not yet in attendance allowed them to talk more openly without interruption. The Admiral was not surprised at hearing about the recent caper at the kebabery and informed the Brigadier, who looked relieved at the news, that he was there for the express purpose of returning the king back home with all haste. "The situation is getting worse by the day." He said. "The French and the Spanish are building up their forces to the south west, while all the indications are that the Germans are amassing their troops in training camps in Bavaria, at Baumholder and in the Turingen Forest. They've lost confidence with the French, but it is projected that they will make their strikes along the east coast and strike inland, while the French and Spanish fleet cover the Western Approaches."

"Will our neighbours continue to withdraw their support or join them?"

"There will be sanctions made against them, but it depends how far Muller-Weiss wants to take it. He's lost face politically and must press ahead with his chosen path or resign. That will throw more confusion into the melting pot because Augsburger will be seen as a continuation. That is to say, the Germans are perceived to be the cause of the problems causing division, so it is a remote possibility that an emergency plenary session could be called to replace the Germans with the next President in line. That interestingly enough puts the European Parliament in the hands of the Belgians."

"You mean all change."

"Almost certainly, but for now, we must get the king back home to assist President Warnock and defuse the situation. The French and Spanish fleet will probably dissipate on some flimsy excuse that it is an 'exercise' while the Germans get off almost free from actual involvement, leaving the French with egg on their faces over the recent attacks."

"Have you found who's behind the attempt to kidnap the king?"

No, but going by what the Captain of the Royal Oak put in his report, the raider was determined to press home his attack beyond the point where he should have broken off and made a run for it."

"You should have seen the mess she was in when she arrived. By all accounts if it hadn't been for their second officer they would have ended up walking the plank."

"It must have been a tough scrap, but I am grateful for such an enterprising commander. Had he not had the experience he wouldn't have given it a second thought to stop off en-route to pick up a few cannon and some Marines."

"Peter, how are you going to evacuate the king back home?"

"I was very much impressed by the way I arrived this morning, and it tempts me to send him back the same way. What do you think, can we give him an escort?"

"I think we should perhaps defer our decision on that until we have referred to the OIC of the local Squadron, Group Captain Evans. He will be able to give us the best data available. Would you like me to arrange a meeting later this morning?"

"Yes, that would be helpful," agreed the Admiral. "But timing is of the essence. I understand the Turks are up to something on the mainland, which is rather uncomfortable news. Have you seen any signs here on the island?"

"We're waiting for something to happen, but the impression is that they look to be building up towards making a grab for the island if and when, Greece becomes embroiled in our war at the other end of Europe."

"Does any of your local intelligence on the island back this up?" The Brigadier nodded while the Admiral paused to take a small folder of papers from his satchel, handing them to the Brigadier who shuffled through them slowly for a few minutes without a hint of any expression on his face. "That bad?" He responded, eventually breaking the silence. "How long can you hold out?" Asked the Admiral in a matter of fact manner as if they were discussing a fleet regatta, not an impending war. "We've consolidated our resources so that if we have to fall back we have a smaller, but well defended number of positions within the jurisdiction of our sovereign bases."

"Well, Dickie, the tacticians are saying the Turks are planning a strike against the island with the intention of pushing the Greek population into the sea. We are seeing a slow build up of troops and munitions just outside Balikesir and at Corlu in the north."

"That could be a feint, but it still poses a threat as a genuine second front. If I can get estimates of their size and strength, the kind of units they have supporting the front line, I would be in a much better position to understand our present situation here."

"How long can you hold out with a full scale invasion on your hands?"

"Without support, about three months. Less if the attack on the island included us as a target."

"You may have to hold out longer if our situation at home deteriorates into a war with France and Spain. We may completely lose Gibraltar for a time, and of course we have no guarantee of providing you with supplies with the Straits blockaded."

"We will have to stand down our commitment to the UN peacekeeper force."

"That is already taken care of. By this time tomorrow we would be using our current situation with the European authorities as the reason for withdrawing from that particular activity. The Greeks will complain of course, but if their own intelligence is any good they will know the reasons why. It also forces them to deal with their own situation, allowing the UN to pull back after a day or two of hostilities."

"Do you expect intervention by the US at all Peter?"

"Not entirely. They are currently standing off in the Gulf of Serte watching the action from a discrete distance. If there is a problem at this end of the Mediterranean it will be a while before they can expect reinforcements to arrive."

"This business with the king. Why did they send him out here in the first place?"

"You can imagine that with a fair number of Senior officers in favour of the government's desire for absolute power we could trust no one to keep him safe. So we got him out in the nick of time. There were two European and one of our government inspired special forces units waiting for a chance to grab him. He who holds the king holds the board, and it isn't over yet, Dickie. Someone in the ministry is leaking crucial information to the other side. The persistent attack on the Royal Oak has got several people very worried if the reason for it is to be believed."

"It's going to be tough at this distance, but whatever you want Peter, you have my full support."

"Thank you Dickie. You hold on here and try to broker a reasonable peace with the locals without getting involved with their conflict, unless of course, you become a target yourself. In that case send me word, and we will try to help you. But I cannot stress enough, it all hinges on getting the king back home."

The warm deck underfoot was pleasing as many of the officers and crew spent their rest and recuperation lounging barefoot in the hot sunshine, being lulled to sleep by the gentle slapping and gurgling of the wavelets rocking the hull of their craft. Some worked on pet projects in small cubby holes down below 'tween decks in the cool morning until the hot air forced them on deck to laze and chatter before lunch and then go for a taxi to take them into Larnaca or beyond. The Royal Engineers had done a good job repairing the badly torn cockpit, superstructure and hulls. The smell of their ship and the accompaniment of the running machinery worked its homeliness into them to which they gravitated with an instinctive familiarity of the womb. An army bus collected them for meals three times a day, and a welfare bus occasionally dropped by to pick up the odd group of sailors looking for a ride into town or to one of the resort hotels along the way. Two of the marines were building canoes in the main cargo deck, while small groups of sailors were building huge kites. Each group vying with the next to produce the most exotic design that would fly in the ship's kite flying competition at the end of the month, three weeks away. Others were building model boats. Fred and the Sub had gone off to the officers club to enjoy a day's sailing and a midday barbecue. Chip had invited his Warrant Officer to join him for a chat over coffee on the quarterdeck, so that they could keep abreast of repairs and the state of the engines. They were poring over a pile of reports and the master schedule when instinctively both men noticed a sudden silence throughout the ship. Looking at each other they both heaved themselves out of their comfortable deck chairs casting a careful look about them. A Bosun's pipe twittered two pips urgently over the main broadcast system. A long pause followed before the same signal was repeated throughout the ship. "I think we may have a visitor Sir, a VIP." The engineer walked to the port side and leaned over the railing squinting along the side of the skimmer in the bright sunlight. "Oh, bloody hell Sir, It looks like that Admiral from Gibraltar, a General, and, er, our, er passenger!" Chip moved like greased lightning under the awning through to the cargo deck, arriving at the brow just in time to see the VIPs stepping onto the gangway. All those on deck and in view stood to attention as the king, Admiral Dunham and Brigadier Malling walked slowly across the intervening gap between terra firma and the ship. The pipes twittered and fell endlessly while Chip greeted them one by one with a crisp salute as they stepped onto his craft. The army stewards who had been assigned to Chip and the wardroom rushed about for a mindless minute of terror, removing debris, swiftly tidying away the papers, magazines and books strewn across the makeshift bunks and in the armchairs. By the time the

VIPs arrived in the wardroom all was apparently in order with a fresh pot of coffee brewing peacefully on the bar.

After the formalities and a light discussion about recent Euro-centric world events, the stewards withdrew leaving them to their private discussion. The Admiral removed more papers from his bulging satchel putting them on the table. "These your majesty are the latest government reports that you asked for, and I have included the strategic assessment in which of our defence analysts have given the different options that could transpire."

"Thank you, I will go through them with great interest, but tell me. How are the people at large?"

"The community as a whole is faring much better Sir, now that the travel restrictions have been lifted for several weeks and the distribution of consumer goods is getting back to normal. The UPAs in the poorest areas are breaking down, while their counterparts who are better off are faring reasonably well, with a softening of the barriers between the two groups beginning to emerge. I really think that this unfortunate situation, hard as it may be on the people, is bringing them together in a new spirit of community. I would suggest that since we have started conscripting people into uniform in the face of recent events, they are finding themselves preparing for war with a new sense of freedom in spite of recent hardships."

"How is this war going to be paid for Admiral?"

"In a nutshell, we have sufficient reserves for about a year, no more than that in terms of timing. Already the Russians and the US are making independent gestures of aid in the form of oil, and from the Russians energy transmission through the grid networks across the low-countries. Although we expect them to hold back on offering an arms deal until they deem things are turning bad for us. The Americans however, have included a hint of early support in that dimension by their language. In the main, the exchequer under the Chancellorship of 'Clipper Browne' hoarded some five hundred billion Eurodollars…"

"Wha-at!" The king looked utterly amazed. Do you mean to say that for all the last eight years of telling people they had to pull in their belts, higher and higher taxation and all the poverty that meant, he had not spent so much as a sous on any of his social reforms?"

"Yes. It was literally a 'war chest' to finance their take-over of the government and the security network of state police and informers, and the like to suppress all political opposition. The details are not clear yet, but the next move after having complete censorship of the press, was to have exploited the situation like a saviour arriving in the nick of time. While miraculously opening up the food distribution chain and easing travel restrictions a little. It was their intention to impose a special police brigade alongside the normal civilian police, but reporting directly to the Prime Minister."

"What about the presidency and the process of democracy?"

"All to be swept away by political reform. He would step up to become the President, while scrapping the office of Prime Minister, effectively ruling over a one party state through a reformed Senate or Presidium"

"Now I understand why you felt it was safer with me out of the way. You may not know this, but the Queen and I had an invitation to attend a private luncheon at the Guildhall. It was only by your timely intervention that we did not arrive there. Do you think that was a ruse to get us there and keep me prisoner?"

"Yes Sir, that was almost certainly the case. With the press being censored and some of the new police units in position in London it would have strengthened his hand considerably. We only just realised what was going on when a ministerial aide tipped us off. The rest you know Sir, and what we propose Sir, is to get you back home as quickly as possible."

"What has changed?"

"Well, from what Dickie tells us there may be some local difficulty here on the island. The Turks look to be massing troops and armour in the border region north of the Dardanelles. That could very well mean a major conflict here on the island. The way things work in the Balkans Sir, is never very clear to anyone, even the protagonists, but we're somewhat concerned that the Macedonian province is becoming politically unstable as more and more Albanians move into the region demanding political autonomy. But the primary reason Sir, you know already, it gives President Warnock the legal base that he needs to maintain a constitutional transitional government with which to go forward and hold free elections."

"I'm glad we agree Admiral and I would like to take my leave of this island as soon as possible." Both the General and the Admiral looked at each other with almost unconcealed relief.

"Commander Woodingdean." The king turned to Chip who was adjusting his sling unobtrusively during the conversation. "How near to completion is the Royal Oak?"

"I have an estimate of three of four more days before we can bring the crew back onboard and commence work up Sir. We only need to fine tune our engines and tweak our new sensor systems, and crew replacements will be arriving the day after tomorrow."

"Can you dispense with the formal work up and do your 'tweaking' as you say while under way Commander?"

"Ye-es, I suppose we could, but may I ask the question Sir, would it not be faster to fly you back home?"

"Well, yes it would, I have to admit..."

There was a dull thud outside the vessel followed by three more. Everyone looked up with an unspoken question written across furrowing brows. "Excuse me Sir, but that sounds like artillery fire. I will see what is going on, by your leave your Majesty?"

"Yes, you're not holding exercises today are you Brigadier?"

"No Sir, I must admit that this sounds ominous." Chip scrambled out of his chair and into the flat where he met the Chief of the watch in his capacity as officer of the day. "What is it chief?"

"Parachutists, Sir hundreds of them dropping down over the hills. The gunfire is coming from about ten miles away. They are shooting at what looks to be civilian targets!" Together they strode onto the bridge heading for the large windows. "Here, give me those intensifiers for moment?" Chip clambered up the recessed ladder to the roof over the cargo deck and scanning the ridges he could see transport aircraft disgorging hundreds of parachutists into the air. "The General joined him and shouting to his driver seated in his staff car called the driver over with his communicator.

"Right, Commander I've seen enough here. It looks as though the Turks have stolen a march on us and have started their invasion. I must be off. My suggestion to you is to get your crew back onboard as quickly as possible and get out of here."

"Right Sir. But we have no decision about how his Majesty is going to get back home."

"That's none of your concern now Commander. You must prepare to move as soon as you can."

"I will Sir." They clambered down the ladder, hurrying back to the wardroom to tell the others what was happening. "We will have your butler pack some of your things to travel with Sir," advised the Brigadier, "but we must get you off the island as quickly as possible. I am needed at my command HQ. Admiral may I suggest that after you have dropped me off you should escort his majesty to the airfield and prepare for immediate departure..."

Eight of the crew had spent a week in cheap lodgings above a bar in Larnaca overlooking the sea. The coast road out of town being more open with cool zephyrs blowing away the heat and the fumes kicked up by passing traffic. Others had strolled off for a walk around the harbour for some exercise and for a 'recon' of the bars in the harbour area. The harbour smelled like any Mediterranean port; of sweat, rotting fish, diesel oil and a mixture of dust and pine trees all wrapped into one large stench. They had found a bar near one of the old quays and were idly watching a small freighter being loaded while having breakfast in the morning sun at one of the pavement tables, the derricks nodding and dipping like giant insects drinking from a puddle. The first salvos sounded like distant thunder at first, the wind coming from the opposite direction masking the sounds effectively. The barrage drew closer and a telephone jangled inside the shady recesses of the bar. The waiter moved into a corner to answer it, jabbering away in Greek, while the men became aware of a change in the ambience as women rushed about scooping up tiny children, rushing indoors with their squealing charges, bolting their doors behind them. Traffic stopped momentarily with drivers, standing beside their vehicles gaping. Two of the lads got up and walked to the edge of the sloping pavement looking eastwards along the curving bay. "Look at that. What's going on?" They crossed to the other side of the road with a growing sense of concern. "It must be an exercise or something."

"But they're firing real ammunition aren't they?" They could not entirely see the distant view with all of the aircraft and parachutists because of nearby buildings blocking their view. They crossed back over the road as the local population began to dissipate with increasing panic. They called out to the barman. "Hey Achilles, what's going on?"

"I doan' know Mr Roger, I think someone is shooting a beeg gun at the airport."

"At the airport! Why would they do that?"

"I doan' know. I think you come indoors now it's safer for you."

They moved from their pavement location into the coolness of the bar and waited. Two of them elected to stand watch on the beach while the others used the phone to get to the base to find out what was going on. The line was busy. Someone ran upstairs to get a personal communicator, but for some reason it wasn't logging on to the network.

Forty minutes later there were huge explosions in the harbour with large columns of smoke starting to rise into the atmosphere. The barkeep started to close up his establishment and made a waving off motion with his hands in between moving his furniture back into the lounge. "You go now it's better, get your things and go back to the base!" The other three wanderers returned from the harbour at a half trot. "It's a bloody invasion I tell you, there's a couple of big destroyers out there and a whole fleet of skimmers, all banging away at the installations!" They all ducked instinctively as a large explosion tore the air apart. "Get your things as fast as you can and get down here!" A Leading hand barked in their direction. "I reckon there must have been a general recall. Any ideas about getting back?" asked someone else. "Grab a vehicle and make a dash for it along the coast road." suggested another voice. "Sounds like a good idea. Any more suggestions" They all nodded in agreement. "Right you two get the first vehicle you can find and get it back here."

"Sounds like heavy gunfire at the moment, there's no small arms as yet." ventured a Marine. "Whatever it is it's coming our way, so let's not hang about." They waited for a few anxious minutes until their colleagues could be seen returning with an acquired vehicle. "Here they are. Right get into that, throw your bags anywhere! Hey, you guys on the beach, get aboard!"

The commandeered vehicle was a battered MPV with a cracked windscreen and broken sunroof. They lurched forwards as the driver hit the throttle hard in a fast exit from the town. Five miles down the road they ran into a Cypriot roadblock manned by heavily armed soldiers and police. A long tailback of vehicles had gathered along the road. But the local population was not about to turn around, resulting in a series of heated arguments characterised by wild gesticulations of the arms, terminating with the steel of rifle barrels being poked into ribs or up nostrils as tempers became more and more frayed. Just as the driver of the vehicle in front of them threw himself back into his shabby pick up they noticed an air force hover bat approaching the barrier along the road from the other side. A section of the barrier was moved away letting the hover bat through, a small union flag fluttering from one of the aerials. They waved it down, with the driver in RAF fatigues slowing enough for a quick exchange of information. "What's going on?"

"It's the Turks, they're invading the island! You'd better get back to your units."

"Our ship is in Dekelia, can we get through?" They ducked as another explosion, this time in the hill country, thundered in the warm air. "No mate! They seem to be surrounding the town, they've almost cut the road off about two miles further on."

"Where are you going?"

"Across to the airfield, that's about as safe a place to be right now."

"There's not much hope of getting through the town, there's a couple of destroyers shelling the harbour and what looks like an invasion force of small craft heading for the beach."

"There's a way round that, if you don't want to try it back there follow me." With that he slowly moved off to the other side of the road allowing them time to make a decision. They quickly made up their minds leaving the commandeered vehicle in the line of traffic in the road, sprinting across to the waiting MPV. The driver almost smiled at the incredulous response of the locals, driving away smartly before anyone could do anything about it. By going around back streets and along the byways the driver took them out of the town towards the base at Akrotiri. The hover bat was in surface mode for most of the way until they were within a few miles of their destination. Once 'out' of the restrictions of built up areas and far enough from the action the driver hit the hover mode and they shot along on a levitating cushion with the wheels retracted. The sovereign bases were shutdown tighter than a drum taking half an hour before the guards would let them through the outer defences. Once they got onto the base they were pretty much left to their own devices, while the afternoon drew on and the invasion pushed forwards with growing momentum. The force built up as Turkish soldiers swooped down from their strongholds in the north and from sea born carriers they penetrated into Limassol and Larnaca. At Nicosia they met stiff resistance particularly, after destroying a UN peace keeper observation tower and a checkpoint by bulldozing their way across the green line, so called because a century ago someone drew the defining line of demarcation across a map in green ink. The airfield was strafed and bombed leaving no chance for either side to use it for fixed wing resources other than hover jets and choppers. The town nearby was party to viscous street fighting between the retreating Greek army and the invading Turks.

"We can't stay here. Either we scrounge a lift on a military transport or we make our own way back to Dekelia."

"Let's split up and do some digging around. Give us a couple of hours to move around in. Say, to find alternative means of transport or, take what we need and move out under cover of darkness. What do you say?"

"Sounds good." Everyone agreed at the prospect of a little skulduggery.

The Greeks were caught in a vice. The Albanian interlopers began an insurrection in Macedonia by slaughtering a large number of the populations in some of the small provincial towns, while Albanian militias drove a two pronged attack directly across the border. Within forty eight hours the General commanding the Greek army on Cyprus was forced to conclude that he was not going to get any support from the government in Athens, and began consolidating his troops in a small number of strategic positions along the western end of the island. He began by holding Paphos for as long as possible and by commandeering anything that would float or fly to take his men off the island. The Turkish invaders were sealing off the island ports, firing continuous barrages into the towns reducing them to rubble, forcing out the inhabitants. In desperation the Greeks turned to their allies for help. Turkish spies on the ground got wind of this and the artillery up in the hills on the escarpments above the coastal belt began pounding the airfields. The king of England and a High Admiral were forced into crawling in the rubble that was once a Royal Air Force air base. The rounds that had nearly snuffed out a king instead destroyed his only hope of getting off the island by air. Together they emerged from the wreckage of the small terminal building staring at the burning wreckage of the only aircraft capable of doing the job safely. It's pilot lay crumpled up on the pitted runway convulsing and choking. The two men stumbled over to him gently turning him on to his side so that he could breath without choking on the vomit pouring out of his mouth. "Over here!" Over here!" desperately shouted the Admiral above the roar of exploding shells. Above them a defending squadron flashed overhead simultaneously discharging their missiles at the Turkish gun emplacements. An armed military escort of Air Force MPs dashed over to both men surrounding them completely in a human shield. "Get him up, quickly get him up and out of here to hospital!" bellowed his majesty to the Sargent of the Guard. Grabbing the stricken pilot from where he lay they half carried; half dragged him along as they raced with the king to the security of a small bunker.

Brigadier Malling sent one last urgent message to the Turks to stop firing or to suffer the consequences. There being no response within the designated deadline he gave the word to unleash the kind of terrifying reply that made the British army a legendary foe. In two hours of unrestrained action the Turkish artillery in the hills were wiped out. Invading ground troops were cut down in their hundreds by a wall of laser cannon and solid projectile rounds, while their airforce units fell to the ground like burning leaves from a fired tree, lighting up the early evening gloom. When the British forces ceased firing the remnants of the invading army slithered away into the night abandoning their positions. A brittle peace ensued during which the thunder of the day's retaliatory action reverberated around the corridors of power in Istanbul bringing fear to government ministers and to their military advisors. Too proud to admit their error of judgement the Generals recommended an all out offensive to remove both the Greeks and the British in a 'once and for all' roller coaster for domination.

Whitehall had been prepared for the diplomatic outcry issuing an immediate reply before the ink was wet on the Turkish complaint. Both the British and the Greeks were caught up in the same trap for different reasons, both were fighting fires at different ends of their supply lines and some sacrifices had to be made. With half their forces tied up at their Thracian border with Turkey. The remaining half was stretched to the limit in Macedonia and in the home country. When the sirens went off all the male population were immediately called up, while the refugee families they left behind began blocking the roads from the outlying regions, heading into the main population centres in a dash for safety. The wily Turks knew this and waited until the civil panic blocked all the major arteries from the countryside into the large towns and cities, knowing full well that the Greek army would not be able to move, becoming bogged down. The eastern Mediterranean bonfire was about to explode as the Turkish invasion of Cyprus became the match to ignite a huge conflagration across 'middle earth' where Europe met Asia and where Africa's brooding desert hid lustful eyes turned northwards in eager anticipation of rich pickings.

12. RUNNING THE LINES!

Chip's final trip to the physiotherapy clinic had its comical moments. While the world outside was in complete uproar, here he was sitting quietly at an exercise station pulling weights up to his shoulder. The crew had returned to the Royal Oak, even those sailors caught up in the bombings of Larnaca and Akrotiri. Everyone ashore was talking about a rag-tag bunch of sailors and a couple of Marines who paddled their way across fifty miles of sea, hugging the coast by night, hiding during the day, until they reached the safety of the UK base in Dekelia. It wasn't good propaganda for the Turks who had claimed they had the island completely cut off from any counter attack by the Greeks. The Turks found a moderate voice in their government who urged caution, since the British and Greeks were technically allies in the greater scheme of things in the European Union. That meant they could call on the ESA and the ESF to bring down a mighty army on their heads if they continued to attack British sovereign bases. The Brigadier had bought his garrison some time, so they repaired the physical damage as best they could and dug-in waiting for the expected second attack to start. The Turks played a waiting game in the north winding up the enraged Greeks into lather by taunting them from the safety of their border barricades.

Even though the power station's lights had been switched off since the first raids on the base at Dekelia, people still found their way to the little kebabery in the bay. The crew never wandered far from the ship as she lay tied up snug in her little rocky cove. Georgio had the girls place candles on the tables just before sunset, their flames giving out a warm glow in the taverna during the evenings that followed the first day of hostilities, giving it a safe and cosy womb-like atmosphere. The men sat outside after their meals, some on the chairs others on the sand, others paddling ankle deep in the shallow water as they chatted far into the night. Chip, Fred, and the Sub sat on the small patio under the awning speculating about coming events. Chip offered a snippet of long awaited information. "Tomorrow we get our replacement 'engines' and then we can see what kind of man we've been allocated. They tell me he's a whiz on plasma-jet marine engines having influenced the design of those new inter-coolers we've got."

"Let's hope he knows what to do when it gets a bit hot, eh?" Mused the Sub, a glass of beer in hand. "The current holder of that honour has really done well, hasn't he?" summed up Fred quietly. "Yes he has. Although he's altogether a different character from Leyland Pengelly, he damn well knows his stuff alright." Chip silently wished for Leyland's large as life presence among them. The big man knew how to 'liven' things up, and keep people going with a bright sense of humour and a wicked grin. "You know, Mr White has also done extremely well for someone who was effectively promoted in the 'field'. He's a little cautious but nevertheless if he hadn't whipped his seamen into shape they would not have held together so well during our moments of trial."

"That was the second promotion board he sat for his Commissioning Warrant, any idea why he didn't get through the first time?"

"I checked up on that." informed Chip. "They told him he was too young."

"That's not fair, they know damn well if it's down to promoting a snotty to a Sub they are usually younger than any of their NCO counterparts, still he got a well-deserved promotion and it goes to show that people do better under real conditions."

"A good decision by all accounts"

As conversations slowed to silence at the end of the evening the men made their way slowly back to the ship in small groups, perhaps to make a final cup of coffee before turning in for the night in their comfortable bunks. The detachment of marines would be returning onboard tomorrow morning, and that meant more new faces to fill the gaps carved into their ranks by the pirates. Some of the stragglers stopped to chat with the soldiers guarding the small dock and their floating home knowing that from the morrow their routine would be back to normal with a full day's work ahead of them. The only relief being the daily trips to and from the mess halls for their meals.

The Admiral commandeered 2 seats on a transport aircraft leaving within the hour after the cessation of the first attack. The men on the ground had filled in the large craters with monstrous earth moving equipment, and with muscle using spades and shovels. Being surrounded by casualties and medical staff had made the king a little uneasy. That both he and the Admiral had 'stolen' places badly needed by such men, but the Admiral allayed his fears in politely insisting that to delay his return would result in hundreds if not tens of thousands more casualties. The Load Master directed his extra special VIPs to the front of the large cargo hold where they could hunker down on a couple of canvas seats in front of the only heat available. The Turkish commander had 'apologised' for the enthusiasm of his troops during their overrunning of the island, and was not slow in coming forward in agreeing to allow the British bases to function as normal, without interference. Plans to evacuate casualties and service families began almost immediately. Diplomatic clearances having been approved for evacuation by boat or by aircraft. A wise old general back home flew-in the paraphernalia of war on the transports designated to take out the evacuees on the return flights. The airways literally buzzing with transports flying up and down the length of the Aegean, across mainland Greece to Thessalonika. Into troubled Macedonia en-route to overhead Graz before entering German controlled airspace over the Black Forest, skirting France in a wide berth via Stuttgart control and onwards to Belgium then over the choppy waters of the North Sea and home.

Three transports had already been despatched to take off the wounded. The king reflected on the desperation and insanity of war as the aircraft lined up ready for departure. After a long wait that made seconds feel like half an hour the aircraft throttled up for its take-off run, bumping along as the wheels encountered the hastily patched up holes in its path. At last they were airborne and looking through a small window in a side door they watched the ground slide effortlessly away at a crazy angle as the big metal bird crabbed sideways in a stiff sidewind. They watched in silence as they flew in a south westerly direction out over the dark blue sea below, climbing ever higher. They joined the airway just south overhead Paphos with a gentle turn locking onto a heading that would take them far above the island of Rhodes. Greyness began to swallow up features on the ground as the last probing rays of daylight turned to gold, suffused with the blood red of sunset. The island slipped from view in a sea of darker grey, and then they were gone, just a trace on radar sensors otherwise unseen by human eyes.

"Anyone alive over there!" roared a booming voice across the brow. A startled Bosun's mate popped his head around the doorway. "Bloody hell! It's Ivan the Terrible!" He whispered deafeningly. Someone out of sight muttered an oath to the accompaniment of receding footsteps running into the distance along the internal deck plates. "Good morning Sir, did you want someone to give you a hand with those bags?"

"Yes please young shaver, who's the officer of the day?"

"Chief Grey Sir."

"Chief Grey now, is it. What's he been up to?" The young man was about to answer when he was interrupted. "No, I don't want to know, it's bound to be no good, no good at all." Two hands appeared and gawked at the large be-whiskered figure rolling across the gangway, across the brow. Turning smartly to face the quarterdeck giving a snappy, but respectful salute Leyland Pengelly, Sub-Lieutenant, Royal Navy touched base with the deck and felt at home. "By heck, what have we got here... Sir?" The Chief emerged with a pleasurable surprise on his face. "Glad to see you're still around Chief." Came the genuine reply. "I hear you took quite a beating in getting here."

"Yes, we put up a good fight though, beat the swine to a stand-still."

"That's the main thing. The price is never worth it though, it's the result that counts."

"Yes Sir, we did take a few casualties."

"We all heard about the lad back home. I never did like propaganda but I think it woke people up to what was going on when they saw that story in the press."

"How's it going back home?" Two steel boxes were deposited around them and a grip followed, being thrown from one end of the gangway to the other and deftly caught before set down on top of one of the new containers. "I'll have them put your stuff in the hold by the flat until we can sort out your accommodation." Leyland heaved a small sigh, beginning to feel the heat of the mid morning sun. "It's better than when we left, but I will tell you more later. I must pay my respects to our leader." A wicked grin crossed his face and they both laughed amiably.

The wardroom was empty as was the chartroom and the lounge. He caught a glimpse of one of the hands trying to slip out of sight, and after a pleasant grilling the 'skate' informed him that there was a heads of departments meeting on the quarterdeck. "Nice to see you back Sir." offered the skate meekly in mitigation. Ivan shot him a suspicious look easing it off with a smile. "Well thank you. It's nice to see that some things don't change." Everyone knew that 'Ivan' was back, and many were encouraged to hear his voice booming in the cargo deck. Emerging onto the awning covered quarterdeck a few minutes later he was temporarily blinded by the sunlight dancing on the waves like molten honey rippling down a slice of toast.

Chip looked up and for a moment looking puzzled, then rising to his feet with a genuinely warm smile, greeting Leyland with a loud announcement. "Well I don't believe it!" Everyone swivelled their heads to look at their visitor. "Congratulations!" Greeted Fred impulsively, and the meeting was abandoned for about ten minutes while everyone welcomed him, asking questions about home and other things. "Gentlemen, gentlemen, can we resume our meeting please." called out Chip with a good-natured smile. "We have about twenty minutes or so to discuss the remaining points on our agenda, and I suggest that we continue our welcoming in the wardroom immediately afterwards." They all sat down. "Leyland, come and sit beside me in this spare seat, if you don't mind?"

"A pleasure Sir." He boomed and walked around the seated throng.

"...So that's it gentlemen, we will slip tomorrow night as planned, once we have successfully completed our trials around the 34th parallel we will return to take up stores and inform the authorities here that we have returned to the fleet. In accordance with the Garrison Commander's requirement we will begin our patrol round the island. As long as our presence is noted it will serve as an indication to the Turkish government that we mean business if they want to take further action against us. One last thing, mail goes off at 16:00 tomorrow afternoon, be sure to let everyone know. Thank you"

They all listened in silence while Leyland Pengelly told them of events as they unfurled after leaving the Royal Oak at Portsmouth. He had in fact been arrested the following day in his hospital bed, but since there was nothing the authorities could do they left a naval patrolman guarding the doorway to the ward. The young sailor wasn't happy about it at all, and had taken the earliest opportunity to find out from Leyland what was going on. Together they pieced a more or less correct picture of the situation and while the guard went off to check one or two things out, he had a quiet word with the Ward Master. A craggy white haired gentleman with thin features and a large hooked nose jutting out from a florid complexion. After phoning around it became obvious to all that a political situation existed and a coup d' etat was in fact in progress.

Leyland could be pushy to say the least and hobbling along on his crutches he might have misled others into thinking he was a soft target, but he managed to find a few loyal Petty Officers and ratings not yet caught up in the net. Together they went around to the cells and relieved the sentries of their weapons if they proved to be disloyal. With the junior ratings freed and under firm orders to remain quiet and disciplined the sailors guided by Ward Master Hammond, and spurred on by Mr Pengelly rounded up the guards outside the Senior Ratings mess liberating all the men with the most authority in the navy. Those who resisted were hustled out and banged up while the raiding parties of loyal sailors led by their NCOs sketched a plan to take the more heavily guarded wardroom and spring the commissioned ranks free. It was not an easy task since their final objective was approached via an open space on either side.

The Chief GI, 'God bless his cotton socks,' they all muttered loudly, came up with an idea to march a squad of men to the wardroom under the guise of a relief party to change the watchmen. So bold as brass and under the gaze of an accompanying officer he did just that. As soon as the grateful guards had been relieved on the outside they were marched back by a Petty Officer into the arms of the waiting loyalists. Many of the men were confused. They had been browbeaten by commissioned officers to perform what had been illegal duties, so as more men were 'taken out' peacefully, the picture began to get clearer. Finally, they sprung the wardroom by overpowering the armed guards standing in the wardroom reception and beyond in the lounge and dining rooms. The hall porter finishing it off by clubbing a treacherously obnoxious Lieutenant Commander with an antique shell casing that had been used as an umbrella stand. Having freed the captains and commanding officers of several warships, they wasted no time in gathering their crews and wresting back command of their ships, making ready for further action. Leyland formally handed over his part in the release of the prisoners to a grateful Captain who ran the naval barracks, retreating along the darkened pavement to his hospital bed in the company of his enthusiastic Ward Master. "And the rest is history." He concluded.

"Any news of Peter?" enquired Fred.

"He's well and has suffered no brain damage from his fall in Rotterdam. The last time we spoke he was being appointed as a liaison officer working with the Belgian and Dutch navies. Probably on some kind of combined defence strategy as an interpreter. He sends his regards and his regrets at not being with you on the journey out here."

"How did the boy's parents take the news about their son's death?" The question was the last piece in a giant puzzle that had not yet been completed, a small but exceedingly important piece in the minds of his former shipmates. "Not good." Came the serious reply. "The media coverage had almost ruined their family privacy, but the Admiral gave orders that we were to either give him a full naval funeral with all the dignity allowed, if they permitted that to happen, or that they should be allowed to bury him in accordance with their wishes. In the end he had a really nice funeral carried to the church resting on a gun carriage with a full honour guard. There were so many flowers from people all over the place, it smelled beautiful…"

"How many of our casualties managed to go?" asked Chip quietly, looking very serious. "All of those released by the French and who could walk. One of the lads fought like mad to leave RNH and they let him out under the watchful eyes of one of those starched little nurses to chaperone him." Chip nodded appreciatively as the 'new' Sub was offered a refill to his beer glass. "Those Frogs treated them better once they found out what had happened ashore, but it was touch and go after the press got hold of it."

"You mean they weren't going to repatriate them?"

"No they weren't, none of them. They had the wounded under armed guard in some small naval clinic in Toulon while the rest remain to this day as POWs somewhere on the mainland, either in France or Spain I believe. Then some old Admiral told them to behave and do the sensible thing. So they sent the injured men home from the clinic on a plane, and the Frogs retired their Admiral, likely on account of his political cheek, thereby embarrassing themselves even more."

"Well, I think that's enough for one day Leyland. Glad to see you back fit and well."

After lunch Chip and Fred briefed Leyland for two hours on the current programme that included a short 'historical' on the damage sustained by their trusty vessel during the encounter with the pirate. The refit included larger accommodation to cater for a larger complement of crew, an engineering officer, gunnery officer and a detachment of marines. There was also a Medic on the list, who was not available until they returned home. The cargo deck was now some thirty feet shorter at the forward end as the flat was extended with messing facilities. By far the biggest changes had been the addition of armour plate and improved firepower. "Tomorrow night we will commence with the balancing of the power units and then speed trials. Late in the afternoon we will do some weapons firing to test our guns. We must be finished within a schedule covering forty-eight hours, and be prepared to ride with out-standing problems or defects, fixing them on our patrol. Any questions Leyland?" enquired Chip looking at him quizzically. "Not really Sir, the 'black magic' of the inter-coolers will not require much calibration, but I would like to inspect the hull sometime this afternoon or first thing in the morning."

"Not a problem, although Chief Riley has been down with the divers twice to inspect the damage and then the repairs."

"I see you had to repair the bow section and one of the stabilisers."

"Yes, the army did well by us on that one. They hoisted the front end up while we were loaded down with ballast in the stern, then propped her up on sheer legs for a week until they pre-fabricated new hull sections for both, then just welded them into place."

"For a small dock and a slipway they have exceeded their limitations." Said Leyland with admiration."

"What prompted you to get involved with the inter-cooler project?"

"Well, I had some spare time you might say, and paid a visit to one or two friends at the training school over in Gosport. There was some development scientist, trying to push them the wrong way. Absolutely stupid notions about implementing a good idea, so I asked if I could see what the problem was since it was about time, in my view, they let a real 'engineer' have a look at it. It took five minutes and two sheets of paper. Poor man, his little chin was wobbling because he had to go away to rethink his methods."

"What will they do for us precisely?"

"Reduce heat loss in the system and improve efficiency, and lower our heat signature to about zero point one above ambient anywhere in the world."

"Pretty handy against heat seeking weapons, if only we could reduce our heat emissions from just about everywhere else." thought Chip out loud. "True, but there is a solution in the pipeline developed by one of the research engineers at the Admiralty Propulsion Research Centre. His transfer equations show that it's possible to shift heat around away from the hull and other hotspots while using the ambient water temperature to stabilise an entire hull. Unfortunately he hasn't been able to work out how to do the same thing for a ship's superstructure." Chuckled Leyland.

"I leave all the techno-chatter to you Leyland, you know best."

Late that evening the Gunnery Officer arrived dressed in flying kit carrying two large holdalls that he heaved onto the quayside from the army hover bat. Lieutenant William Cavendish MacBrayne of Menteith walked easily across the gangway towards his latest appointment, sighing as he did so with a contented sigh of relief, the duty Bosun's mate returning his salute as he stepped onto the deck of his first sea appointment. The hover bat hissed gently in the background as it reversed back down the jetty disappearing into the darkness. "Good evening Sir." greeted the Bosun's Mate. "I can call someone to meet you?" Chief Riley appeared through the doorway at that moment in the role of OOD, saving the Bosun's mate the trouble. Escorting MacBrayne through the bridge the Chief took him to the wardroom, where he made his entry to the amazement of the three members lazing around reading papers and playing a noisy game of chess. Forgetting that he had been wearing his flying overalls, boots, and scarf tucked inside around his neck, he made a pretty sight. "Well, who have we got here?" Demanded Fred looking up from his three day old copy of the London Telegraph, grinning from ear to ear. 'In for a penny, in for a pound' thought William and introduced himself loftily as "Lieutenant William Cavendish MacBrayne of Menteith, late of one eight six Squadron, Royal Naval Air Station, Culdrose," a generous smile working itself across his face. "Hells bells Lieutenant, that's a wicked entrance at this time of night. What can we do for you?" Fred noted the wings sewn onto the breast of the visitor's flying overalls. "I'm you're new gunnery officer Sir." announced William a little seriously while reaching into his kneepad to remove his letter of appointment. Fred took the documents and indicated for the new arrival to sit down. "Why a naval aviator Lieutenant?"

"Ah, yes, I can see where you're coming from Sir. It's because I'm a missile expert in addition to being a pilot, and you've been fitted with an aircraft missile system cannibalised from a Zed-6A that had an unfortunate 'accident' while on a training exercise a few weeks ago."

"Now it makes sense. Have you literally flown in?"

"Yes Sir, I scrounged a lift on a prowler that was short of a navigator. Been on the go since nine thirty this morning."

"Let's get you something to eat then we'll go and see the Captain. I've no doubt he will be keen to have another pilot around."

"Can I postpone the food until I have reported to the Captain? It's that I have some urgent dispatches for him, and would not feel comfortable sitting on them for any longer than is necessary."

Chip was, as predicted, very pleased to see another pilot. The newcomer noted the golden wings sown onto the sleeve of Chip's jacket hanging on the outside of his clothes cupboard. Having finished their introductions, William handed over the dispatches and departed with Fred for a light meal, leaving Chip to read through his papers. Locating an on-duty mess-man in the small mess hall they repaired back to the wardroom to begin the less formal introductions to his new shipmates over drinks.

Royal Oak slipped out of the tiny dock at 11:30 reversing her engines. The army guards waved her off silently in the dark as she ran slowly backwards in neutral for a full cable's length before the powerful twin engines were applied to ease her forwards, at the beginning of the long journey in front of them. Turning gracefully under a cloud-scudded night sky she disappeared into the darkness heading directly out to sea. With only sensors in receive mode the tactical lookouts relied on their specialised tacsat links developed by Chief Grey. They had waited until the Turkish destroyer patrolling the southern coast of the island had retreated slowly out of immediate danger, slipping out of the 'net' for their rendezvous with the 34th parallel.

Fred wove a pattern of lazy 'S' turns while en-route getting a feel for the controls after lying alongside for so long. As the eastern sky greyed a ragged dawn far above the Levant, Chip climbed into the newly armoured cockpit to spend a much valued hour driving the skimmer around. First on planes then off-planes, noting the changes in the critical speeds when the planes would automatically retract or when they would refuse a command input to deploy if the speed was too slow.

"Right Fred, let's get those new figures into the computer and placards in the cockpit and in the conning position on the bridge."

"We have lost some of the sensitivity through all that extra weight of the armour plating. That means we need to reconfigure our fuel consumption at some later point if we can book a stint on the measured mile off Portland."

"Yes, we'll get a good idea if we punch the new figures into the computer to recalculate our performance envelope and fuel burn using the GPS."

"I reckon we may have lost quite a bit in terms of range say as much as two hundred, maybe two hundred and fifty nautical miles."

"That's something for our engine expert Leyland can do for us."

They began their sea trials with several attempts at running a measured mile for different indicated speeds. In doing so they quickly reassessed the performance of their engines and hull configurations for a given range of operating parameters. By four o' clock in the afternoon the contingent of Royal Marines began testing their weapons while the seamen gunners began test firing their main armaments. In the evening the sensor arrays and the tactical systems operators were put through their paces as computer generated scenarios challenged them to a three hour dual of wits and nimble fingered electronic warfare. By the following midnight most of the results were showing, at a brief glance, that most of the gunners were a little rusty, and manoeuvring was sluggish in the lower part of the performance envelope. "My calculations show that if we changed the angle of attack of the planes by just over half a degree we could in fact increase our forward speed to compensate for the extra weight we are carrying in the hull, especially that armoured fish tank of ours above the bridge."

"Wouldn't that take a bit of time Leyland?"

"Certainly, about four or five hours. All we have to do is slacken off the guide tubes and locking bars and use a heavy maul to knock them forward a little, using a template."

"That simple."

"It would be worth it, if for no other reason than to stop her 'mushing' in the turns and for increased stability."

"Can we do it ourselves or do we need support?"

"We can do it ourselves. The planes have been refurbished so there's no crud on them yet, and no corrosion on the fittings. Should be tolerably easy, providing we can scrounge some diving equipment."

The following day they practised fast manoeuvres, slow manoeuvres, fire fighting, damage control and their rescue at sea procedures. By tea time at half-past five the tired crew looked forward to night firing exercises before they turned north for Dekelia. Periodically there were false alarms, where the tacsat images indicated moving targets passing within thirty or forty miles of their area of activity. Approaching Larnaca Bay from the so' south-east the tacsat images revealed the presence of a large fleet of ships manoeuvring close to Famagusta in the bay beyond Cape Grkeko to the east. In particular, three fast targets detaching themselves from the main group on an intercept course with Royal Oak. By the time they were abeam Fig Tree Bay Royal Oak had sped effortlessly past the headland at Cape Pyla and into the territorial zone of the British sovereign base. At one o' clock on a pitch-black night they slid into the little basin shutting down the engines with an air of accomplished satisfaction. The monitor screens had worked very effectively in the infra red mode providing clear pictures of the narrow entrance as it glided closer and closer. The seamen wore wrap around helmets as did their counterparts ashore who; working in total darkness; saw everything in almost true daylight with just a little flatness in the colours. The only limitation to the new night working headsets on trial by the navy, was perhaps the bulkiness of the design.

The new galley and three chefs produced a wholesome choice of meals including donner kebabs, Greek salad and tzatziki with chip dips, or an Anglicised version of fish mese', or for the more narrow-minded palate oggy and chips with mushy peas. The late 'dinner' had been the idea of the new 'Guns' and Chip recognised immediately the traditional flying fraternity's propensity for an all day breakfast or something like it. He willingly agreed, since the combined work-up cum shakedown cruise had included getting back to Dekelia without provoking the 'twitchy' Turkish patrols. After a long day the crew were pleased to be sitting down to some of their favourite foods before heading for their bunks. Fred and Chip passed a few private comments about the changes to their possession and admitted wryly that the inclusion of a proper galley had been the best addition to date. Their previous existence of providing specialised high speed cargo services between Margate and the low countries seemed almost a century past in time, perhaps, a lifetime. "Maybe we could open a Baltic route, who knows?" Said Fred wistfully as they gathered their thoughts and took stock of where life's many twists and turns had put them. "You know Fred, I'd like to get a little plane. Nothing fancy, just functional and capable of small to medium sized cargoes. A sort of air courier service taking in the Low Countries and the Baltic as you say, or maybe across Biscay to northern Spain." Fred savoured his Commanderie looking deep in thought. "Ye-es, a sort of feeder into the main business of shunting small numbers of containers and smaller heavier cargoes on regular high speed routes. Could put a landing pad on the roof I suppose…"

"A pipe dream to hold onto Fred when this is all over. I must say I'm rather looking for an opportunity to get home. We all need to see our families again. We haven't had any mail for weeks."

"Didn't Admiral Dunham say something about the post office having been taken over by activists involved with the coup?"

"He said it would take at least three months to sort out the mess." There was a tap on the door before one of the duty Stewards opened it a crack to announce Chip's dinner would be ready in a couple of minutes. "Will you join me Fred, we haven't exactly had time to have a chat for a while?" Fred accepted the invitation and for a couple of hours they held an impromptu board meeting of Golden Arrow Marine. "You know." said Chip finally. "We are paid under our agreement with the Admiralty, but I'm concerned that the contract doesn't apply when we are working under the direction of his Majesty the king."

"You mean that the Admiralty might not pay their rent?"

"If that's true under such circumstances..."

"First thing we do is Give our bank manager a ring when we get back home."

"Then who pays us for our contracted services?"

"Probably the king. I don't know."

"Looks like we'll have to ride this one out until we get back. Mind you, perhaps our electronic genius could work something out for us, and we could find out tomorrow maybe..."

In a blaze of sensor and communications transmissions Royal Oak slipped out of her dock at half-past eight the following morning. A distant Turkish destroyer alerted by the meaty signals handed out on a plate by the British began shadowing them as they turned south-east along the peninsula at the beginning of their patrol under clear and sunny skies. The water turning a deep blue as they left the shallow greens of the shelving sandy bottom beloved by small children and snorkelling adults. Forty minutes later Royal Oak slipped from its 'shadow' rounding the point of Cape Grkeko. After about an hour the 'panting' destroyer finally caught up with Royal Oak some six miles off the rounded hump of Cape Elaia, as she began her run along the 'tadpole tail' shaped peninsula at the eastern extremity of the island. The destroyer was effectively shooing the British skimmer away into international waters. Rounding the point at a discreet distance between the two of them, the destroyer Captain took his vessel in the channel of water between the Kleides islands and the mainland. The ship's company was not closed up at action stations being fully prepared as they went about their duties in protective clothing carrying their steel helmets with them. The seamen on deck and the bridge watch keepers enjoying the 'leisurely cruise' at twenty-five knots in a light and steady swell. The watchful eyes of the lookouts catching the distant glare of reflected sunlight on the tops of the huge apartment blocks and hotels littering the island's numerous tourist resorts. Long range sensors picking out the receding coastline of the tail as well as the Syrian and Turkish mainland below the far horizon kept them informed of the conditions that lay ahead. The augmented tacsat system providing further intelligence offered the system operators no evidence of hidden 'nasties' in the seas around them. Apart from their 'shadow' six miles astern it could not have been a more perfect day. Fred headed to the chart room with a sheaf of reports under his arm, tapping gently on the door before entering. Chip looked up as he went in. "Fred."

"Yes Sir."

"Were you serious about that idea of putting a landing pad on the mid-section?" Fred shook his head and grinned. "Only half joking really. It seemed to satisfy your desire to get back into flying, and meet up with our business goals. Why, you didn't take me seriously did you?"

"You know what they say, 'many a strange thing happens at sea'." Chip smiled stretching his arms out wide after spending many hours shuffling papers and monitoring their progress on the bulkhead mounted display. Fred put his papers down on Chip's in-tray as his Captain groaned at the sight of yet more work. "It would require us to strengthen the roof somewhat, add a bit of fire-proofing and all that?"

"Maybe, maybe not. There's a spot just where the after mid-section of the roof meets the last section before the doors. There are three ribs in that area designed to strengthen the join and cut down vibration in the superstructure. All we would need to do is put a thin sheet of titanium or chrome steel on top of it, put some anti-skid paint down, and voila! You have a landing platform for a small hover-jet. We have the beam up there for people to get out either side. The only other addition would be to add a ladder on each side leading down to the port and starboard waists."

"You might want to suggest it to the General he might agree to putting one on top there for more pressing reasons. Hey, that means we could get it done for free." They both laughed at the idea of approaching the serious looking General for the resources. "Fred, it could work. Have a word with Leyland and see if he can come up with anything technical to reinforce our argument."

"You are serious."

"Yep, it's about time I got back into the air. That young gunner has got me all envious I can tell you. Just walking onboard in his flying kit brought it home to me that I have not been on the inside of one of those things for far too long."

"Are you game for it? I am if you are?"

"Yes, alright then. We can hammer out the details when we get out of this little lot and when our time's our own. Bet you Fifty EDs it can't be done."

"You're on Fred, just you wait and see. I can almost smell those dollars coming my way."

By late afternoon the little fleet of two were rolling along the northern shores off Kyrenia in the face of a gathering wind. The flags aloft on their small masts standing out stiffly, cracking and shaking as each new gust drew a shock wave of sound from the curling ends of bunting. A small flight of gulls soared and skimmed over the face of the sea while little streamers of foam detached themselves every so often as a crest of water gave up an offering to the winds above.

"Aircraft approaching from the north Sir. Range about a hundred and fifty one miles, bearing green 085."

"What height Guns?"

"Looks to be climbing Sir, probably on take-off out of Konya."

"Give me the profile when you have more details please Guns."

"Aye, aye Sir."

Chip looked at the Fortin barometer swaying gently backwards and forwards in its gimbals, then out through the armoured plasti-glass window towards the exposed facets of the high mountain ridge that ran along the north edge of the island. He began to feel a little uneasy at the thought of being hemmed in by the distant peaks on one side and by the change in the weather. Looking at the plot he could see the build up of the Turkish presence on the island by the number of red coloured spots clustered together in the next big bay around the point ahead, Morfou Bay. Drawing abeam the tiny island of Glykiossita the profile of their journey began to change.

"Two surface targets moving out of the bay ahead Sir. We have them identified as patrol vessels, possibly skimmers."

"Keep me informed." Chip stood up from his paperwork and walked over to the door where he picked up his flash-proof gloves and helmet before passing through onto the bridge. "Sub, when we reach this point here, in about ten minutes from now, I want you to sound action stations. Just a precaution." The young Sub nodded and returned to his concentration to the plots in between visual scans of their own physical location.

The jarring sound made by the alarm sent men scurrying to their action stations in an instant, their hearts pounding with excitement as adrenaline pumped into their systems at accelerating levels. Chip was standing looking through the forward windows at the distant headland.

"Off-planes, full ahead both when you're ready Cox'n. Starboard ten heading 260 degrees." The Cox'n repeated the orders pausing as he waited for the right moment to throttle up as instructed. "Number One. I want to take us out of the potential bracket between the destroyer and the oncoming vessels…"

"Vessels identified as Skimmers Sir. Range eighteen miles, weapons systems are powered up Sir."

"Right-ho Guns." The atmosphere notched up in tension as they waited for a proper view of the approaching craft to appear through the visual monitors on extended telephoto range. "The destroyer is staying on its present course Sir."

"Thank you Sub." Chip and Fred worked on a solution to put the destroyer on the inside of them and behind, so that they could not be bracketed by the other three ships in any combination during what might prove to be evasive manoeuvres. "We have the advantage over them for about a minute." came back Fred coolly. "As long as they remain in skim mode on-planes they will have to transition before they can manoeuvre at speed in this swell without coming unstuck." They waited agonisingly slow minutes before any change in the disposition of units around them emerged. "Airborne target now eighty miles Sir, same bearing, now level at ten-zero."

"Thank you guns. Power up anti-aircraft weapons at sixty miles. I want to give them a warning, not frighten them into doing something stupid at close range. Is that understood?"

"Understood Sir. Power up at sixty miles."

"What is that destroyer doing, surely if they were going to do something like attempting to stop us he would have tried to keep us in the frame."

"It might be something entirely different Sir."

"What do you suggest Fred?"

"Changing of the guard Sir?"

"That's a possibility. Hang on a second. Chief Grey, the minute those two skimmers go off-planes I want to know immediately, can your underwater sensors handle that?"

"No problem Sir."

"OK, Fred you were saying?"

"Look at it this way. You're on station down here to the south and west. Your turf so to speak." He tapped the tactical plotter with a stylus where the outline of the coast and their near neighbours on the water were displayed at close range. "You've followed a cheeky little beggar like us around the island to the other side. It's not your patch, and you need to get back to start your patrol before nightfall. So these two bogeys coming in are probably his relief."

"I'll bear that in mind."

Leaving the white arc of their wake spreading out slowly behind them the Royal Oak sped away from the destroyer, her bows began to pitch and skew like an old scow as the sea came into them from a ten-degree angle on the port bow. The destroyer kept on its former course, its bows gently nodding in the swell. "The other two vessels have changed course to intercept Sir. CPA in twelve and a half minutes."

"Thank you. How far away is that aircraft guns?"

"Seventy two miles Sir!"

"What's its ground speed?"

"Two hundred and fifty knots Sir."

"That gives us nearly seventeen and a half minutes until it is overhead our position."

"One minute to the sixty mile deadline Sir."

"Thank you Guns."

"Close down the cockpit Cox'n and get down here as quickly as you can."

"Aye, aye Sir."

"Look at their approach, one slightly head of the other in closed right echelon. I want you to swing around when I give the order and we'll go down the leading vessel's port side providing us with enough cover if they are intent on doing us damage. By the time they have sorted themselves out we will have about five minutes to run clear before we have to deal with that aircraft."

"One thing at a time, eh?"

"That is it in a nutshell." Chip indicated to Fred that he wanted him to take over the conning from the bridge position.

Spray rattled and gurgled as they continued to charge through the oncoming swell. The monitors showed the other two skimmers racing towards them in a stern sea. The sunlight was beginning to shine in their faces as the huge golden disc moved inevitably lower on its long journey towards the western horizon. Donning sunglasses the bridge crew had less of a strain on their eyes.

"Powering up anti-aircraft weapons system Sir, Target range is sixty miles, time to overhead fourteen minutes thirty eight seconds!"

"Fred, I'll give you about three to four cables before we manoeuvre, on my mark."

"On your mark Sir." The seconds ticked away as the men juggled with figures mentally racing against the computed resolution to their constantly shifting situational problems. "Destroyer has activated its weapons Sir."

"About bloody time! Thank you Sub. Engine room!"

"Engine Room here."

"Mr, er… Leyland, what's is our new limit on the planes given our current configuration and the adjustments you made yesterday."

"Can you be more precise Sir?" Queried Leyland

"We're doing twenty two knots Leyland, I want to turn into the incoming sea. What's the white-arc limit on our planes in extended mode."

"Ah, I see, you want to pop them out, that would be about two or three knots for a one degree change in angle. You should therefore limit your speed to about eighteen or nineteen knots, say eighteen in a swell like this sir."

"Thank you Leyland."

"Bridge, sensor room!"

"Bridge, go ahead Chief Grey!"

"Augmented tacsat is showing faint target echoes in the bay ahead Sir. Nothing definite, could be echoes from the surrounding mountains or genuine targets."

"Patch through to the starboard monitor on the bridge."

"Aye, Sir patching through now."

The other skimmers had grown from mere blobs on the water into two distinctive aerodynamically shaped vessels racing closer, white spray shooting up in shimmering walls of water as they nodded and dipped like a pair of porpoises.

"Range to the Skimmers Sub?"

"Five thousand yards!"

"Standby Number One." Fred nodded and splayed his feet a little further apart. "Turn left five degrees, heading 245 degrees." Fred repeated the order as the Sub shouted a warning. The second one is crossing the stern of the lead boat Sir!"

"Damn!" The new course placed Royal Oak on a reciprocal course to the approaching vessels. The sudden change in position meant that the other skimmers were changing positions relative to their quarry. Left echelon instead of right echelon. At a closing speed of something in the order of forty-five knots there was not much room or time to make a decision. "Fred, bring her around to pass down the starboard side of the lead boat!" Fred manoeuvred his pride and joy in a beautifully crafted turn to port keeping his eye fixed on a large space immediately in front of the lead boat. "Destroyer is changing course towards us Sir!"

"Thank you Sub."

"Guns, where's that aircraft."

"Twenty miles to run Sir, descending, zero weapons on-line Sir."

Everyone gawked as the bows of the lead boat and its squat flat bridge slid past the bridge windows on the starboard side a cable's length away. "Just three more seconds and we've done it," muttered Sub dead pan.

The narrower Turkish vessel slewed around in an avoiding turn almost too late. The bad timing of the turn coinciding with a trough opening under the nose just as the planes auto-retracted. For terrifying seconds it up ended her stern tubes while burying the nose and the starboard bows in a steep dive. "Reduce speed to eighteen knots, turn right heading 250 zero degrees. Standby to go on-planes!"

"Eighteen knots!" Warned Fred who was watching the speed indicator closely. "On-planes!" Shouted Chip watching the other two skimmers now sliding astern through the windows. The planes snapped out biting deep into the crest of an oncoming wave holding the bows up momentarily longer before dipping into the face of the next wave halfway up the slope. "Increase speed to twenty-eight knots, maintain present heading!" Chip paused taking another look through his intensifiers noting with a sly grin that the second skimmer Captain had turned in a wide arc to keep away from his wallowing friend in the other skimmer, giving himself room to manoeuvre to continue the chase. The effectively empty hull, devoid of heavy cargo had given the wider Royal Oak an advantage over the hounds chasing her as she rose on planes and supporting structures designed to carry more weight than the combined total of the smaller Turkish vessels behind her. Her bows were literally flying from wave top to wave top as Fred finely tuned the throttles to match their speed to the frequency of the oncoming sea.

"Signalman, radio that aircraft on channel 243 and tell him to clear away or he will be fired upon!"

"Message to aircraft. Clear away or be fired upon Sir." As the signal op muttered into his microphone the lookouts smiled among themselves at the acute embarrassment of the Turkish skimmer captains. The second skimmer had slowed down visibly to help his patrol leader. There was a palpable change in the atmosphere among the bridge crewmen when it seemed the chase would be given up.

"Aircraft does not respond Sir."

"Keep trying until he does. Guns, Where's that aircraft?"

"Range nine and a half miles Sir, level at four zero. No weapons signature!"

"He would have fired by now if he had any hostile intention," said Chip looking at Fred and to William. He swung around looking for the destroyer catching a fleeting glimpse of it some distance beyond the two skimmers.

"Standby to engage aircraft!"

"Locked on Sir!"

"Fire on my command!"

"Skimmer giving chase Sir!"

Sure enough, when Chip looked back he could see the other Skimmer had completed his 'investigating' turn around the other wallowing vessel and sheared away from it hard on the throttles.

"Aircraft at five miles Sir!"

"William, unlock targeting, fire one missile wide and ahead of incoming aircraft!"

"Unlocking target sensors, firing wide." William tightened his finger on the pistol grip. A loud hissing sound was heard momentarily before the roar of the plasma rocket engines cut in when the missile took off from its platform in front of the bridge screen, leaving a trail of white exhaust gases behind like a blanket of acrid fog. "Visual contact with the aircraft Sir" Shouted the Sub. "Looks like a reconnaissance prowler."

"Thank you Sub."

"Target aircraft changing course Sir!" shouted the gunner urgently. "Look at that, must have scared the holy shimmolies out of him!" Chip risked a quick peek at the aircraft noting it's sudden change of course ninety degrees to the right with a satisfied grin. "Where's that destroyer Sub?"

"Behind the skimmer giving chase Sir!"

"Good, Round the point Number One make a beeline for the other side of the bay."

"Guns, lock on to target aircraft and standby for another missile round."

"Locked on Sir!"

"Signalman make light signal to Turkish destroyer. Message as follows. 'Thank you for the escort today. Sorry I cannot stay with you. Must dash home for tea.' Message ends."

The incredulous signal op repeated the message and walked out to the bridge wing taking his place at the aldis station.

They rounded the headland of Cape Kormakitis commencing their dash across the bay. The lookouts met with the astounding view of an invasion fleet anchored in the bay. In the distance beyond they could see the intensifier images of landing craft at the beaches. The change in course across the bay bringing the sea more from the starboard side started to rock the hull of the Royal Oak. The sun now shone fully into their faces making it more difficult to use visual means without shades. The long-range visual system shut itself down protecting the sensitive eye of the camera from damaging overload. The plot indicating that the destroyer's new position now lay further behind than before, and that only the skimmer was now in the chase. "Take her in a little closer Number One. I want to have a good look at what they've got." Fred switched his navigation console to include the chart overlay as he turned the skimmer to port in a gentle turn, noting the rock formations pinpointed in red on the chart. "The other skimmer has changed course to intercept Sir," called one of the lookouts. "Have the aft guns crew standby to put a shot across his bow, one round only on my command!" At Chip's command William muttered into his microphone the appropriate order. The plot indicating the second skimmer trying to run a line on the inside of the Royal Oak to place itself between the bay and themselves. "This is what it's all been about. They didn't want us to get too close and see what is going on." confirmed Fred, the realisation dawning on his face. "Well, we gave them something to think about back there." William chuckled. "Right, hold your course. Cox'n take over from the First Lieutenant at the helm."

"Aye, aye Sir."

Fred picked up a set of intensifiers and walked over to an aft facing window, training them on their 'tail'. "If he's not careful he'll do some damage, the idiot!" The irate and embarrassed skimmer pilot was slowly losing, making 'rough weather' of the task set before him. The narrower vessel was proving to be less stable in the deepening swell than its quarry. Shorter and carrying less weight it nosed into the waves continually rolling like a drunken man in the cross-sea. The lighter structures in the hull and planes suffering under the enormous pressures of the impacting waves. "Range now twelve thousand yards to the other skimmer Sir."

"Good, how's that aircraft doing guns."

"Climbing away to the east Sir."

Chip nodded "Thank you William, there's a chance we can get out of this situation by the time we turn the headland at the other end of the bay. Then we shall see how badly this skimmer wants to catch us up, if he's a mind to."

"If he has any sense he will slow up."

"The other Skimmer is moving up Sir, looks like he has sorted himself out."

Both Fred and Chip looked at the tactical plot where the target blobs indicated a change in status, course, speed and closing speed as applicable. "Thank goodness the destroyer is going back." Noted the Sub extending the range of his monitor as the larger vessel slid over the edge of his viewer. "I'll get Chief Grey to send off the visual data once we've got all the pictures."

"Yes, do that Fred, please. I think the Brigadier and his people will be interested to know. Looks like they might be assembling a fleet with which to break the siege at Paphos. At least they can slip a warning to the Greek commander, but I don't suppose it will help them much."

"Weapons lock Sir! The skimmer's initiating weapons."

"Which one?"

"The one nearest to us!"

"The fool!" hissed William in disbelief.

"One round William, across his bows, if you please!" The laser cannon kicked as it delivered a scorching round in the direction of their closest Turkish pursuer, followed by a huge burst of steam erupting from the sea close to their bows. "Holy Moses!" shouted one of the seamen plotters. "All vessels in the bay have activated their weapons Sir!"

"Recommend firing Chaff Sir!"

"Go ahead William, three rounds!"

"Skimmer still giving chase Sir!"

"Fire another round across his bows William!"

"Take her out of here Number One! Set speed to thirty knots and make for the headland past Kato, keep us three miles from the shoreline as we make the turn, I want something solid between us and that fleet in case someone else has any ideas at popping-off any more missiles."

"Signalman, make signal to OIC Cyprus, plain English." The signal op looked a little amazed, but said nothing. "I am under attack from Turkish patrol three miles west of Cape Kormakitis, Morfou Bay. Returning fire: estimated strength 45 vessels at anchor, with 2 in pursuit. Message ends." The laser cannon hissed and whined as the recoil sent a small shaking motion along the length of the Royal Oak. Another plume of steam burst skywards. "Incoming! Brace! Brace!"

"Rapid fire stern guns at will!" A muffled popping followed the familiar whining hiss of laser cannon fire.

Chillingly, a missile rose briefly from the starboard side of the pursuing skimmer, locked on to its target as it left the launch tube on the beginning of its fiery journey across the comparatively narrow gap between the two vessels. It settled at a point some two metres above the surface at three hundred and sixty miles an hour. The rattle of small arms fire adding itself to the cacophony of war from down aft. Chip stood watching the missile's approach with the naked eye, following the discolouring trail of gases. He saw it fleetingly rear up and inexplicably shear off to the right passing away into the sun.

They dashed along towards the broad Tillirian coastline approaching Kato at the end of a thirty minute chase across the wide bay, costing the crew of the Turkish skimmer time and distance as their smaller craft continued to make heavy going.

"William get more chaff into the air and target that skimmer as he comes around the point."

"Weapons arming Sir. The skimmer's got another missile up the spout!"

"Do it now Guns! Fire!"

"Missile away Sir!"

The snout of the Turkish skimmer appeared around the blunt headland in pursuit of its quarry. The missile fired by Royal Oak left no time for evasive action. The outgoing delivery shot close to the surface unseen by the Turkish crew looking into the glare of the late afternoon sun. If they knew about the missile's presence there was no obvious indication as it slammed home into the main hull causing it to disintegrate from the inside. Rounding the point they could see the front end bite deeply into the swell as the craft slewed around sickeningly with the failure of the planes on one side, throwing its stern high into the air. They watched in horror, as if in slow motion, it careered sideways in a slow roll inexorably turning the craft onto it's topsides, sliding along upside down. The ancient mountains brightly lit by the late afternoon sun standing in mute testimony to the latest tragedy on the waters far below.

"Range of the other skimmer Number One?"

"Three point six miles Sir!"

"I suspect he will stop to give them a hand. I want everyone to be on the alert. If they can hide a large number of vessels from us in a bay like that, then there may be more elsewhere on the way back home."

"Cox'n, set autopilot range at twelve miles and engage."

"Autopilot to twelve miles and engage."

"The ships in the bay have powered down their weapons Sir."

"Good! That proves a point if anything. That skimmer pilot of theirs got too close to us for them to take a comfortable shot at us, or they didn't want to be discovered."

The sun slid down further, edging along from the starboard bow to shine fully along the starboard side. In the almost peaceful silence that followed the lull after the engagement Chip kept the pressure up to perform vital tasks before the next round commenced. Signals had been despatched to Brigadier Malling informing him of their brief engagement as a defensive measure, and the visual log of the shipping they had seen anchored in the bay. He included a request for all information regarding Turkish naval vessels and their dispositions along the coastline between their current position and Dekelia, especially those blockading Paphos and Larnaca.

"The other skimmer is slowing down Sir, looks like he's stopping to assist the other one." Sub broke the silence of everyone's private thoughts. Long shadows cast themselves along the port side of the ship as they continued in their helter-skelter run away from danger. Chip came to decision after conferring with Fred and his gunnery officer. "Cox'n, bring her round onto a heading of two six zero and bring us down off the planes if you please."

"Sub; take over the bridge. When she's settled in the water set course for Mazaki Island, make your range six miles and take her back up to twenty-five knots. I think we will give Chrysochou Bay a closer look. We've had enough surprises for one day."

Fred watching the instruments as the Cox'n brought her speed down to the twelve knots speed datum required before going off-planes. In response to the autopilot adjustments made by the Cox'n, the speed dropped off further as the hulls settled lower into the water, while the auto throttles gently compensating for the slowing process built up the speed until she was back at the middle of her white-arc operating range. Chip sat watching the tacsat data looking closely for any signs of weapons activity from the fleet.

"Two friendlies approaching at four hundred knots Sir!"

"Which direction Sub?"

"From Troodos. Identified as Zed-6s weapons armed Sir."

344

"Keep a good lookout everyone! We're not out of the woods yet!"

"Well done William, that was a pretty good demonstration of your missile system. Thank your guns crews for me."

"Thank you Sir, I think they will be delighted to hear that you're pleased."

"Number One, the same applies to your crews down aft. I'm sure they have probably thought about it by now, the fact that they were in the enemy's sights when they launched the missiles. They have done very well indeed."

"Thank you Sir." I'll get the galley's crew to distribute some refreshments to the men, if I may, and let them know we won't be having any formal meals until we arrive at Dekelia."

"Good. I want to see you two in five minutes for a council of war. We have many miles of potentially hostile waters to patrol tonight before we get back."

A signal arrived from the Brigadier confirming constant air cover for the rest of their journey. The bronze and golden hues of the early evening passing into night with the men remaining at their stations sipping hot drinks and munching biscuits, patiently waiting for any news. Some sitting on the deck where they worked, the adrenaline receding from their blood vessels leaving them with a burden of tiredness. The message also warned them not to proceed closer than thirty miles around the western side of the island because the invasion forces were knocking the hell out of Paphos, and would 'take-out' unauthorised units within range. Leyland appeared as the new range of forty miles was set on the autopilot, and he met with the others to report on his part of ship. The journey home became stretched as they reduced speed in a gathering storm. The air pressure fell with clouds compacting high above them blotting out the stars. Some one hundred and fifty miles later they tied up at just past midnight. Chip and Fred having been summoned to an intelligence de-briefing walked across the brow while the 'troops' made ready to tuck into their long awaited victuals. Leaving behind them the aroma of wholesome food they clambered into a waiting hover bat as large drops of rain splattered themselves to destruction on the warm concrete road, and they were driven away at high speed.

The senior intelligence officer, Colonel Renton, confirmed what they already knew and then some more. The Greeks were hard put to it to find the manpower to relieve their garrisons on the island. The fly in the ointment being their EU membership and hence the alliance with other EU states – like the UK. Being pressed in Macedonia and facing the mainland border with Turkey in a massive concentration of troops ready to counter any insurgence by the Turks, it was going to be very unlikely that they would be able to resist for long. It was then that the bombshell was unleashed upon the gathered briefing. The meeting was interrupted by an urgent phone call from the deputy OIC. The silence among the members of the armed forces gathered in the bunker was oppressive while he delivered the depressing news that the Czech Republic, Austria and the Swiss had declared their airspace closed to all British movements except scheduled flights. "The German and French foreign ministries are expected to announce their own measures in the very near future." He intoned in an almost expressionless voice.

Fred ruminated in silence about the significance of the possibility that the Turks had a cloaking device and let the thought go as the seriousness of the wider situation outweighed it by a clear majority of reasoning. As soon as the Colonel stopped to draw breath a tide of questions erupted from the thirty or so representatives crammed together in the small briefing room around a highly polished oak conference table. Having called for silence the Colonel continued his intelligence report announcing that the current situation would add further delays to the logistics of their situation since all traffic would be required to circumvent the growing area of prohibition. "Needless to say gentlemen, without our supply lines we are faced with a number of difficult choices." Responded the Colonel finally. "Thank you gentlemen that will be all for the time being."

Most of them knew by then that they were on their own. The French and the Spanish were blockading the Straits while the Italians ran patrols up and down the Mediterranean Sea looking for British stragglers. A few British freighters had run foul of the patrols, but nothing significant was done to them other than escorting them to the nearest Europort Controlled Harbour for impoundment. The Cyprus garrison was isolated in an unhappy environment growing ever more hostile as time slipped by. The meeting ended at the ungodly hour of a quarter to three in the morning. Pale and haggard men stood up sagging on their feet making their way out into the muggy night air to the transports waiting to whisk them away to their different units. As Chip and Fred moved to make their own exit the Colonel's assistant Captain Ockham approached them indicating discreetly that they should enter the sanctum sanctorum of the Colonel's office.

After a pause of a ten minutes the Colonel appeared with a sheaf of despatches under one arm. Motioning them to sit down when they stood up as he entered the room, the Colonel informed them that Brigadier Malling had wanted to speak to them personally. Chip felt a little harassed like a low time pilot being summoned to the control tower after some misdemeanour. Almost expecting a reprimand for the day's shooting match against the Turks he waited with bated breath. Indeed, immediately after his arrival in concert with a Major of the Royal Engineers and a Group Captain Engineer from Akrotiri, Brigadier Malling announced that very subject as the first item on the agenda. There was no 'ticking off' or other form of admonition. "I'm well pleased that your excursion not only divulged some badly needed information about the Turkish navy's disposition, but also in that it gave them a useful demonstration of what they may otherwise construe to be our capabilities at sea as well as on land. We expected Famagusta Bay to be the first place they would build a beachhead, but now it's obvious they can sweep across the island fanning out in all directions. In that respect Commander you did a good job today."

"Thank you Sir, although I'm bound to admit to some luck in the matter."

"Nevertheless it made them stop and think, and that little skirmish of yours may have brought us a little more time now that they have seen what your vessel can do. I just thank the stars that you're not a bloody pirate."

"Ah," interrupted Fred, reminded of his small problem over the cloaking device. "That's probably an appropriate place in time to mention the fact that we encountered their fleet in Morfou Bay after only the flimsiest indications on our sensors."

"Oh, yes." Responded the Brigadier brightly. "These two gentlemen are here to discuss that little difficulty of yours, and I felt it best they came into the briefing early on in order to hear what happened. Group Captain Barnes and Major Griffin have an interest in electronic warfare and I want you to arrange to meet with them tomorrow so that you can go over the details more closely than is necessary here."

"It's just a thought Sir, but two things occurred to me as we were driven over here. They didn't exactly appear on our tactical monitors, and perhaps more interestingly, they did not activate their weapons systems until the weapons exchanges took place between ourselves and our Turkish friends in the skimmer patrol."

"Your point being?"

"If it wasn't the terrain giving us added difficulties, and I have no reason to believe that is the case. Then they must have some type of cloaking device, and it might just be that while making themselves transparent to standard sensor detection, it renders their own systems blind to what is going on around them."

"How did you make that conclusion?" asked the Colonel.

"It's just because none of the vessels in the bay did anything until after the exchange, and then when they powered up their weapons systems none of them did anything except power them down again."

"That could have been a coincidence when they saw their own patrol was dealing with you, could it not?"

"True, but what fleet commander would do a thing like that unless he either didn't know who was out there firing away, or he found out when the cloaking device was de-activated long enough to do a sensor scan."

"May I ask why your augmented sensor system did not give you any warning that they were there?" The Group Captain asked, sitting back in his chair with one hand on the table, covering a notepad pad, the other in his pocket.

"Is that common knowledge?" Chip asked the Brigadier.

"Only among the specialists in electronic warfare, so you may speak openly."

"The EuroSat system went off-line three days ago, as you are probably aware, but so did the American system at about one o' clock yesterday afternoon. They have closed the portal to European users, since none of our access codes allows further entry into the tactical links."

"I see your point. That could make life difficult for the rest of us since we are using local battlefield systems." Replied Major Griffin quietly. With the second and shortest intelligence de-briefing over, the Group Captain and the Major left after exchanging details with Chip and Fred. "I'll be in touch later today Commander to make an appointment to come and see you with Major Griffin. Say lunchtime, I want to be meet your officers if I may, and one other gentleman who seems to be re-writing our designs."

"Oh, that must be our Chief Tech, Grey." Replied Chip. "Shall we agree to one o' clock unless I hear otherwise during the morning?"

"That sounds about right for my diary." Responded the Group Captain. "How about you Roger?" "That's a lot easier all round I think. I'm not too far away from the dock where the Royal Oak is tied up, so I can walk from where I am down to the ship." The two men left the bunker on their way back to their bases, and in the short lull that followed the Brigadier's mien changed to a visibly graver countenance. "Captain Ockham would you mind leaving us for a few minutes. I'll call you back when I've finished here." There was a brief pause as the Captain nodding politely left the room closing the door discretely behind him.

"What I am about to tell you is known only to myself and to Colonel Renton. Firstly, we are confident that this base and its personnel are beyond the reach of those people who want to make things difficult for us to achieve our goals. There is a concerted effort to undermine the operations of British forces in Europe as they are being brought to bear in the defence of the realm. That effort, gentlemen is furthering its cause by using every device at its disposal; from legalistic and defensive bureaucracy driving procrastination into the record books, right through the spectrum of subversion to out and out thuggery and murder. While we can guarantee to a point the loyalty of our own forces on the island, for the very reason that we are so far out of reach, we cannot vouch for the credentials of every person arriving on the island since hostilities began. One of our recent arrivals actually being detected by an old school friend of the man he was trying to impersonate. Since that time, we have rounded up several people with inconsistencies to their backgrounds, and we are now confident that we have nipped in the bud an attempt to infiltrate our ranks. It is for that reason I introduced you to both Group Captain Barnes and Major Griffin. Having met them you will know who they are and that they are above suspicion, and I leave it to you to adopt a more cautious approach when dealing with people that you have not been in personal contact with on some earlier occasion."

Now, as you can guess, we daren't risk sending this next piece of information home even by the most securely coded messages because we believe someone deep in the organisation is screening all intelligence communications." Chip looked from the Colonel to the Brigadier and then to Fred. "How does that involve us Sir? All my men are loyal to the king and I will personally vouch for them with the exception of my gunnery officer and the replacement marines."

349

"Your marines are not a problem since they have been on the island for almost a year, but your gunnery officer is an unknown quantity isn't he?"

"Ye-es." said Chip slowly. "What do you know about him Commander?"

"Only what he has told me, that he's a Zed-6 pilot on detachment because of his expertise with the Zed-6 gunnery system that the airforce people here on the island fitted to my ship."

"Do you have any reason to doubt how a pilot, like yourself, I have to add, would know about the particular variation of armaments on a converted cargo carrier?"

"No, although his appointment papers appeared to be in order."

"That is precisely the point I am making. Although I will now disabuse you of any fears that you might have regarding Lieutenant William Cavendish MacBrayne of Menteith."

"What do you mean Sir?" Asked Fred beginning to get annoyed at the late hour he was being asked to think over such things. "Just this. We can vouch for Lieutenant MacBrayne, but there will be others with whom you must be on your guard at all times. The reason for this is perfectly clear, as I shall now illustrate. Colonel Renton will now provide you with a piece of this jig-saw puzzle."

"Just so, and to start with this won't take up much more of your time. You were right about that possible security leak on the whereabouts of your passenger on your outbound journey to Gibraltar. We know of at least two groups of people looking for the king with a possible third party now becoming embroiled in the pursuit."

"The danger we face is growing more acute each passing hour. The longer it takes his majesty to get back home, the easier it becomes for our adversaries to attack us." continued the Brigadier, "and for that reason I have to tell you that the aircraft carrying the king back to the UK has been lost."

"What!" Chip's involuntary outburst went unheeded as the Brigadier continued in a low and commanding voice. "We know the pilot had turned around on the advice of other aircrews currently heading down the airways across southern Europe. They were the last transports to get through before they were closed. The alternative route across the Balkan Peninsular and over the Carpathian mountains into Poland via a ninety mile strip of the

Republic of the Ukraine is the only other option the pilot had providing he could find a place to set down and pick up more fuel. We know he had enough fuel to put down safely back here with more to spare." The Colonel stood up and walked over to a plasma screen on the wall. A few seconds later a relief map of the Balkans lit up the wall in sharp focus. While the Brigadier spoke he adjusted the view zooming in to include just Greece and Macedonia. "We know that someone fired upon the aircraft before it crossed the border with Macedonia heading back into Greek airspace, disabling at least one of its engines."

"So he's still alive then?" Asked Chip with visible relief

"We can only assume that he is, nothing is certain Commander." Replied the Brigadier looking briefly at his watch. The colonel continued his briefing pointing to various places on the electronic wall map with a large pointer. "One of the other ferry pilots en-route from RAF Lyneham bound for Akrotiri reported seeing an aircraft fitting the description to have been hit by a missile somewhere near the town of Strumica north of the border. He tracked it for several miles finally losing it in failing light somewhere in the mountains to the north of Thessalonika. The nearest habitation is Kilkis. The Thessalonika radar controllers have no other information, even though their warning systems are high up on the mountain peaks overlooking most of the terrain. As you can see, it's pretty wild and rugged territory, not good for a forced landing. However, there is an unconfirmed report made by one of our commercial airways Captains that on his let down into Thessalonika he saw a military aircraft below him as it passed through his landing light beams with fuel streaming behind it. Apparently, going in the direction of the Halkidiki Peninsula and then presumably, over the Aegean. The airways Captain declared an emergency and the Greeks scrambled two of their fighters. The pilot of our aircraft meantime had made plans of his own. They actually made a forced landing here on the eastern side of the Gulf of Thessalonika. Just a few minutes ago we were informed that they made a forced landing in the flat region of agricultural land between the foothills and the sea about ten miles south of the airfield at Thessalonika, at a disued private airfield. The Greeks have rescued all our own casualties and others without too much difficulty. There is no sign of the king or his companion Admiral Dunham. Where they are now is anybody's guess. They have simply 'disappeared' off the face of the earth."

"It's going to be a tall order Sir if you're asking me to find them?"

"Yes, I realise that, but we might be able to help you there," replied the Colonel a little testily, turning to face his audience. I think that Brigadier Malling will answer that question."

"Well, as you can imagine this is an embarrassment for all concerned. The Greeks are getting twitchy about the fact that an undetected aircraft had apparently penetrated their airspace to crash only a few miles from their second most-busiest airport. They, like us, would prefer it not to have happened at all. While the diplomatic arguments are raging, the Turks are beginning to smell a rat and that could hasten our demise here on Cyprus. The Greek government has graciously conceded to allow us to remove our casualties and the medical staff on humanitarian grounds at the earliest convenience. The flight crew and one or two male passengers over the age of seventeen remaining behind at the pleasure of the Greek government."

Chip sighed with an air of resignation at the inevitable logic of the Brigadier's summing up. "They need their diplomatic 'token' of disapproval, as you can imagine. You will therefore be the instrument of evacuation from Thessalonika and proceed with assurances, given by the European President himself, that none of the blockading ships will interfere with your passage through the Mediterranean and round the corner back to the UK."

"I don't suppose that's all of it Sir, is it?" Asked Fred tiredly, he was beginning to feel ragged at the edges with fatigue."

"No it is not." Confirmed the Colonel abruptly, apparently not the only one feeling tired. "We have six days to spare before you are due to pick up your passengers", continued the Brigadier. "In the mean time you will sail for the Aegean tomorrow night when no prying eyes will be able to see you leave -and I mean just that. Make the most of that six days Commander; take as long as you need to dally in and around the islands, en-route to Thessalonika. The Greek government is content to let us send a vessel, without an escort, and by the way they are not sending any escort of their own, So make good use of that freedom to find his majesty before anyone else does."

There followed a short dialogue of questions and answers before the inevitable questions arose over tactical matters. The only word the Brigadier offered was that 'help' would be available when they needed it. Otherwise they were to proceed as ordered in a packet of sealed documents handed to Chip by Colonel Renton. The Brigadier left shortly after the private briefing, signalling the return of Captain Ockham who escorted Chip and Fred to the door on their way out.

It was twenty-five minutes to five as they stepped into a cool hover bat waiting to take them back to their ship. Both men were too tired to talk, struggling to stay awake using the distractions of the changing scenery to do so as it flashed past, occasionally revealing new military emplacements along the way. Chip secretly grateful that his sealed orders were not to be opened until he was at sea contemplated the contents of other letters accompanying those orders in a large manila envelope. Exhausted, they walked across the brow and turned in. Rain began to fall in sweeping curtains pushed along by strong gusts of wind from the north. The falling rain hitting the roof hard created a sound like the roar of a powerful engine as large drops smashed against the roof over the cargo deck. "Landing-pad." Smiled Fred to himself as he drifted off to sleep.

13.   LOSING TIME

Euro President Muller-Weiss and his deputy Holga Augsburger seldom travelled together. It was a matter of common sense and good security protocol. They met in the old Bunde administration building in Bonn with two of their top ranking Generals and Admiral Shaeffer of the Bundes Marine. Apart from the security surrounding them the only other people in the building were the archivists working to preserve the mountain of documentary evidence produced by a Government every moment of every day. The mighty Rhine no longer a threat to a nation's hidden history since all the records had been removed from the basement a century earlier. General Friedmann looked sourly at his President while the others stared in disbelief at the hard-line the General was taking.

"Drachonsberg cannot go ahead as planned under the circumstances. Can't you understand that! The blockade of the fleets at Bremerhaven and Wilhelmshaven killed any idea of Drachonsberg continuing as planned, we can achieve the same result if we use airborne troops. "Herr General!" Muller-Weiss shouted, trying to regain his composure. "Heinrich, that is not good news. Where is your Schnell-Commando-Gruppe?" Are they all running around in the dark too? All shining like little glow worms in their little wooden huts. Is that it?"

"What the President means Herr General is that using airborne troops is politically insensitive to our situation. The rest of the member states would see such a move as an invasion of 'shock-troops' and that would be disastrous for the European Presidency and for the country to be seen in such a role."

"Then without ships how are we going to push ahead with your plans to pull down the British and their friends in the Low Countries? Tell me that?"

"The French are getting impatient with us." Joined in the Admiral with all seriousness, "they are becoming suspicious that we did not intend to join the fleet in the North. If we wait any longer they will go ahead without us or withdraw."

"They cannot withdraw Willi, they are already committed too deeply, but it will threaten our alliance if we delay any longer." Came the swift and exasperated presidential reply. "That can only mean one thing, we fight our way through the blockade extending our operations to include the Hollanders and the Belgians as legitimate targets on the grounds of what? Interfering with lawful execution of Federal edicts? General Gotha, tell him what this will do to our country." The younger General began to offer his advice. "Please, consider the weight of evidence that we cannot do any more, the situation…"

"Enough!" Shouted the German President of Europe imperiously, already aware of the rumour that the European Commission was looking to distance itself from the Presidency, since failure was not an option acceptable to the Commission. General Friedmann walked to the edge of the concrete balcony and leaning on the concrete balustrade announced his final verdict in a tired voice. "You want a war, go and fight it yourself. In five minutes the population will be running scared for the borders trying to get out of the way before it lands on them, while the rest is looking for you to do something about it. No, you must abandon this crazy scheme and declare martial law on the English before it blows up in your face. They will respond naturally enough, saying they have already done this and have things under control, that will make shaky ground for us to move on the British"

"He's right of course." agreed the Admiral reasonably with a slight tilting of his head to one side. The President looked at him with a harsh staring glance that could easily freeze a rodent in a rat trap. Augsburger nodded in silent agreement. "What do you say General Gotha? Do you agree that we cannot continue Drachonsberg?" The European President was beginning to conclude there was no point in continuing his line of argument so aggressively. "It's a hard fact Sir, we cannot proceed that way unless we get our men onto the fleet at Kiel and push through the Norwegian patrols in the Skagerrak, that would add a week to a schedule that's already a month overdue. Any further delay is a serious threat to achieving our goal."

"Is there any chance at all that you could tilt the balance in our favour while we are fighting this mess?" Asked Augsburger "What have your DAG teams come up with so far Heinrich?" asked the President beginning to calm down.

"Only that the English king is probably not at home. Probably abroad somewhere. In Canada or the US."

"No, not in the US," denied the Admiral, "my sources say he is not there. A British agent has already made contact with one of their sources in the Pentagon, close to the Security Committee. He found nothing, so we conclude that they are also looking for their king."

"Ach, so, I can see where this is going. Heinrich, suppose you collect a small team together, widen the search. Yes, yes of course," said Muller-Weiss thinking on his feet, "and have them focus on finding where this wretched fellow has gone to earth. In the mean time gentlemen, I know that you are right. We have to start clearing up this mess, and at the same time try to win back some credibility with our French allies."

"I think I may be able to help you there." offered Admiral Shaeffer. "The simplest way, and probably the best is to adopt a less militaristic front. We can decant our Federal Police units and our troops from Wilhelmshaven and Bremerhaven to Hamburg over night. What if we disperse our fleet between those two ports and Kiel, by sending elements of both those fleets through the canal? The Norwegians would think that we are going to take them around the northern route, but in the meantime we move our men and equipment from Hamburg in the merchant fleet. They have plenty of skimmers. There must be at least a dozen or so loading and loading in the docks each day. They are very fast and effective, yet would represent a more acceptable means of transport, and we could have our force out into the North Sea before anyone knew about it."

"Herr President, General Friedmann." interjected Augsburger in a more enthusiastic tone. "This is just what we want. Our allies will bring their forces in naval vessels with all the negativity attached to their intrusion, but at the same time our sensitivity in the choice of transport would appear a little more germane to the business of federal intervention than outright invasion. So the Norwegians complain when they see they have been tricked, by then it is too late!"

"Ja, I understand that clearly. So we can kick-start Drachonsberg back into life after all, eh General?" He smiled a winning smile in the direction of his recent adversary General Friedmann. Then prepare your regiments for embarkation from Hamburg. "Sehr Gut, Herr Praisident." Came the unabashed reply leaving the President of the European Union with the uneasy feeling that he had been out-manoeuvred all along by the wily old General. "How long will it take?" He asked keeping his composure carefully intact once again. "Thirty-six hours, not more than that before we can sail."

****

"Wilma have Senator Richardson come in will you."

"Yes, Sir."

The short, rangy looking Senator stood up from his chair on hearing the President's voice over the intercom and walked into the Oval office with his two assistants.

"Good morning Wyatt, take a seat won't you, gentlemen."

"Now let me see." The President paused momentarily as he rifled through a small pile of papers on his desk. "Ah, here it is. Yes, let's face it Wyatt we have a difficult problem here with i-Mart going down. Can't anyone of its competitors pick it up? It would sure make things easier if they did."

"Only piece-meal. There's not much they can do since they are all suffering from the same problems."

"That's not what I expected to hear. If a major supermarket chain goes down because it can't supply the market, then a lot of people are going to be left high and dry come Saturday shopping, aren't they?"

"That's an overly simple picture Mr President. This is a warning that the transport infrastructure is breaking down. Do you have the US Institute's study of American Transportation and Distribution report to hand Sir?"

"Not immediately, but I seem to remember that it made some pretty sweeping statements about the reduction of competition down to about four or five large operators, leaving just enough for a few small fry to pick up business at local levels."

"Well, they predicted that difficulties in the economy and the high taxes on preferred fuels were slowing down deliveries of all consumer items for more reasons than just consumers tightening their belts."

"Yes I know all that Wyatt, consumers buy less, the supermarkets drop their prices, things start moving again."

"If this was just a recession I'd be inclined to agree with you, but it isn't. It's more serious than that Sir, with the haulage companies going out of business at the rate of nearly twenty a week. The people can't buy their food because we have a transportation problem. Hell, if the Texans start buying their food wholesale from over the border that must tell you something about the situation down there and the same is beginning to happen in the mid-west."

"How long has that been going on Wyatt?"

"About three weeks now, you can see a line of Mexican trucks on the highway all the way on up from Laredo to Nacogdoches in San Antonio, to Austin, Houston and Fort Worth."

"I'd like to ask who authorised that, but I guess I've no need to ask."

"Suppose you give me the rundown on what's happening out there and summarise what you think we should do about it."

"Well, it's kinda like this. We are faced with a failing transportation system. The producers can't get their products to the markets and the consumers who are already being coy about their spending can't get the supplies they need. So the producers are going out of business at the rate of about six thousand a week on average. It's that simple Mr President. With less products getting to market, fewer deliveries and agricultural output rotting in silos going nowhere, because we have a shrinking haulage fleet. I'd say the report was right in its assumptions and we've reached that point in time where they said we'd be in trouble. We're going to have lots of hungry people on the streets looking for food, looking for gas at the pumps and all because there's no delivery."

"How wide spread is this problem Wyatt?"

"All the southern states bordering Mexico have made other arrangements for supplies. That includes genuine gasoline that we can't produce in the same quantities any more. The Pacific states are suffering the worst, although California does show signs of developing local initiatives, you know communes and that sort of thing, co-operatives handling just enough for their needs, but nothing to match the depth of the problem. Alaska is just becoming a wasteland again with the majority of people remaining being posted there to man the military bases. Very few civilians want to be there and risk being cut off. The mid-west is showing signs of fragmentation with shipments of almost anything heading out west being hijacked before they get to the West Coast."

"You mean people are actually stealing lorry loads of food?"

"Not just food. Anything they can get their hands on and sell on the black market for money or for food."

"Not drugs or other contraband?"

"There's always going to be criminals mixed up in that kinda situation Mr President. It seems as though the only people capable of surviving out there are the hillbillies, the mountain people and the Goddamn Indians!"

The President looked out from behind knitted eyebrows as an aide involuntarily cleared her throat in rising embarrassment. "Sorry Mr President, I forgot you're part Cherokee."

"That's alright Wyatt I know what you meant. In fact I think you're right. Such people have been self-reliant for centuries, holding on to their survival skills while the rest of us have been drawn into the net of supply and demand without learning those skills needed to survive. I've got the picture and I've had a look at the report, so I can see where you're coming from. What I want are your recommendations. Can you give me a clue as to what's on your mind?"

"Cut taxes on preferred fuels, accept the fact that most people are using local alternatives and lift the restrictions on its use."

"You mean legalise that stuff?"

"What I'm saying is lift the restrictions for now, let those people out there in the hard-pressed communities do their own thing for a while and review the situation later. It will help people to move around, get to work and to their local supermarkets while the haulage companies get moving again, so the economy will start to recover. Additionally, subsidise the procurement of trucks through to commercial vehicles weighing a ton or more. That way the hauliers can replace their ageing fleets and keep up with modernisation. It's the only way forward Mr President."

"Yes, but where's the money coming from Wyatt?"

"Reserves, Mr President, otherwise we not only lose the transport infrastructure, we lose the ability to remain a strategic power on the world stage."

"That's a powerful statement coming from you."

"I know it is, but look at it this way, with our transportation problems, food shortages and the fall in manufacturing output we can't afford to ignore the signs, and, by the way, our military capability is suffering the same problems as the civilian population. Why there's hardly a day goes by without some military transport lying by the side of the road broken down. If we can't get our tanks to war or our supplies to our troops at the front, wherever they may be, because our military transport vehicles are old and out of date, and don't have a compatible supply of gasoline. Then we are not going to get the results we wanted. The same applies to the airlines. Most of them have just abandoned their planes leaving hundreds of aircraft on the ground with nobody who can afford to run the businesses to keep them in the air."

"I know, we can't exactly blame the Generals for allowing the commands to make their own arrangements for fuel, even if the majority are using non-preferred varieties."

"It's not in my book to pass judgement either Mr President. I think they've showed extraordinary patience and aptitude in being flexible about our situation."

"Well, I see we still have a problem with Chicago and Detroit. Since the war with the Canadians we've had to rebuild entire cities and an industry that has no factories left to speak of. If only the railhead at Chicago hadn't been wiped out it might have been different I suppose, but we have to deal with that in the present day."

"Milwaukee isn't far off completion, can't they start production soon?"

"Lack of investment. The corporations are holding onto their money trying to ride out the recession. If we give them any funding for development they'll simply snap up the money and invest it in gilt-edged securities until things get better."

"That's right, the 'English solution', rob the poor taxpayer and pay the rich corporations and watch them get richer. That's what they taught us at Harvard Mr President, or rather I should say, how not to run a country. However, I have no desire to inculcate the policies of despair. By accepting these recommendations we may be in time to slow down and even prevent total economic collapse, if not I can see that the Institute's findings will start becoming a reality in three months, with widespread unemployment, industrial and social decline in every state."

"So you're saying we aim some more of our spare capital right at the point where its needed through appropriate subsidies, and encourage re-vitalisation that way rather than by direct financial involvement?"

"Absolutely, Sir."

"You know, it's the darndest thing, but I asked the question why it is the Saratoga kept breaking down and no one could give me a direct answer. She's back in Syracuse with a main bearing overheating, and the damn natives have insisted that we do not fly off our squadrons while she is alongside the wall."

"Maybe the navy's suffering similar problems with substitutes instead of the right kind of oils to go into the grease, that kinda thing?"

"Could be Wyatt. It just seems that we can't get anything we want any more. Can you imagine it? The Eye-talians telling us what we can or cannot do?"

****

"What is it William, you're looking disturbed?"

"President Warnock, Sir, I have very disturbing news for you, and it presages our worst expectations."

"Come and sit down William and tell me about it."

William Goodfellow sat down facing President Warnock feeling tired for the first time in ages. Up until now all the challenges he had encountered had been met and overcome. Some of them ending in quite remarkable and successful conclusions, while others had ended quite differently than expected, but quite suitable and acceptable under the circumstances.

"The aircraft carrying the king has been lost Sir."

The president looked blankly for a moment as the news gradually sank in. "You mean you've found him William, and now he's gone again?"

"It's as I've said Sir," remarked William sadly, "the aircraft he was travelling home on has vanished and was found after having made a forced landing in northern Greece. Except to add that Admiral Dunham was with him as well. They were not found at the scene of the accident,"

"Does the absence of any information regarding our two VIPs allow us any hope for their survival William?"

"It gives me an indication that they were either not on the aircraft, or if they were, they managed to get away before the local authorities could detain them."

"What is being done to find out where they are?"

"Firstly, we have negotiated the repatriation of our casualties..." The President's eyebrows shot up at the word casualties. "Casualties I should say, being evacuated from Cyprus and the medical staff looking after them. However, President Stakis wants his pound of flesh and the Greek authorities have detained a small number of male civilian evacuees for questioning."

"This sounds quite unreasonable William. Why would they want to do that?"

"I suspect they don't want to inflame the Turks into stampeding across their border on the excuse that we are helping them in their own struggle –at least, not yet."

"Ah, so what you're saying is that by holding one or two, possibly more of our evacuees they are biding for time?"

"I think that is the heart of the matter Sir."

"William, I don't need to tell you that we have next to no time left to find the king. Army intelligence is telling us that the Germans are up to something, but nobody knows quite what, while the French and the Spanish are taking turns in exercising off our western approaches. We need another month or two before we can get the systems in place to hold a general election, and I don't have to tell you that the European Commission is desperate to bring us down."

The president looked across at the highly polished table in front of William where sat a crystal glass image of the goddess Europa riding a great bull, the symbol of the European Union taken from ancient Greek mythology. Looking at the image for the first time in a new light as it reflected the sunlight in a myriad of rainbow colours, he felt a sudden urge to pick it up and hurl it through the window of his inner sanctum. He felt too a burning hatred welling up from within at the thought of the dreaded Commission. 'How dare they!' He thought wildly. 'The whole damn lot of them. Un-elected yet all powerful, dictating policies to grind us down. Dumbing down national laws in a frightening way, removing the rights of veto, freedom of speech and opposition as they smother us with political correctness, tying us up in knots as they force us to abandon the yard-sticks of society, questioning morality, ethics and self-determination. While robbing us of the power to stop them without accountability to anyone for what they are doing!' He sighed looking around him and out of the window, his face beginning to redden with the onset of hypertension.

"Are you alright Sir?"

"Yes William, thank you." The president turned and looked at William feeling a little defeated and tired at the day's news. "It's just the thought of losing the race at the final hurdle. If I didn't know any better William, I'd say off-hand that if we could find a way to break with our political masters in Europe I would do it and the devil take the hindmost."

William seldom saw his superior looking so angry yet so sad. The president continued voicing his thoughts. "The Dutch Leader of the House of Deputies has remarked that the Socialist Economic Alliance of European Ministers is pushing for more punitive and restrictive measures once this fracas is all over. We lost the right to veto a long time ago, but now opposition leaders are deeply concerned that any political dissent whatsoever will be put down by the Commission using the SEA as the instrument of their will. I fear we have opened up some festering sores William, and unless we can resist these latest moves, we are going to have to make our own minds up about where we stand in the Union as a whole."

"That would be very unfortunate for us all Sir."

"Well William, back to the king. Is there anything we can do?"

"Fortunately, I have someone in transit at this moment who will be making contact with our own people close to the situation. There are a number of other people working to help us in this matter Sir, and I've no doubt that whichever way the news breaks we can trust them to have done their best."

"Keep at it William, we're rather desperate you know. Admiral Dunham has become an unwitting figurehead in our recovery plan, and it would be a bitter blow to all of us if he and the king were both lost to us."

"There is one other thing Sir." President Warnock tilted his head to one side. "Oh?"

363

"EuroSat capability has been denied us for the last six hours. Although our forces have been using some alternative means, they now report that the Americans have 'pulled the plug' on their own satellite facilities. Our access codes no longer function and our forces are now effectively fighting blind."

"That is not good. We expected the EuroSat link to be broken at any rate, but why the Americans? What are they up to?"

"I've arranged a briefing for you this afternoon Sir at two o' clock, with Admiral Hayward and one of his aides. I've also sent a note to the American embassy and re-scheduled your meeting with the Trade and Industry Secretary, Lord Hawthorn, until after you have met with the Ambassador Schuler"

"Hayward, wasn't he on Admiral Driver's staff before the Admiral was killed?"

"Yes, indeed. Has a very keen grasp of the situation and has done remarkably well in building up good relationships with the right sort of people, so if anyone knows what can be done he's the man to tell you."

"Very well William, I see you've been your usual thoroughly efficient self." The president smiled wanly at his friend and secretary. "Bear in mind I have a meeting with the leaders of the opposition parties tonight at the Guildhall, so I don't want my revised schedule to go beyond half-past five."

"I've informed the Admiral that you have a pressing engagement late this afternoon, so he's bound to keep it short and simple."

As the impromptu morning meeting ended in the presidential office at the old houses of Parliament, Royal Oak was making her way slowly though the waters of the southern Aegean. 'Crawling' in fine weather was always a good option, it saved fuel, the men went about their duties in a more relaxed atmosphere, and people generally worked better. The night dash across an oily swell beneath a sultry cloud base gave little cause for enjoyment as they skimmed around in a wide circle for the Dodecanese, threading their way carefully in between frequent Turkish patrols. Turning northwards around the western tip of Rhodes she slowed after ten hours of 'steaming' at high speed, greeting the only Greek patrol to meet them with a hearty message of felicitations just before daybreak. Dawn caressed the sky with nebulous fingers of gold in the clouds hanging high above, as the duty chefs crawled from their bunks down below. It was five o' clock, the duty watch sat or stood around on the bridge drinking hot sweet kai, watching the occasional raindrop plopping against the plasti-glass windows, waiting. The changing pitch in the high powered engines not going unnoticed by the wary denizens snoozing in their 'nests' tween decks. Day one of her journey to evacuate the casualties began with a quiet repose like a calm before a gathering storm. Ordinarily, the journey would take a night and somewhere in the region of half a day to transit the rock-strewn waters of the Greek Islands at high speed. Chugging along at ten knots, off-planes, they hovered between night and day with the prospect of an uncertain future ahead of them, hoping the news that they were on their way home would hold true. Before the dark pile of Rhodes had dipped below the far horizon on the starboard quarter they had struck the white ensign from the masthead with due respect, raising the hated blue and gold flag of Europa in its place. Not pausing to show any mark of respect or courtesy to the shameful pennant as it was shot disdainfully to the masthead in haste. Now Royal Oak would pass as a nondescript member of the ESNF without let or hindrance. Few except those who knew the protocols would question the missing marks of nationality and assume that she would be native to those waters.

Six and a half-hours later and twenty eight miles from the western edge of the tiny island of Sirna, the starboard engine began growling like a trapped tiger. The stern lifted slowly in the swell and the growl took on a life of its own as the swilling waters threatened to flood the stern tubes where the back pressure increased alarmingly. Coughing one more time in a rasping hag-like sound and with a final shaking roar, the engine died in a long-winded grumble like a farting whale. Royal Oak slowed to a crawling five knots as the hands began filing into the mess for lunch. Leyland Pengelly breezed through with an oily rag in one hand bearing the doomed countenance of an engineer bearing grave news. "What's up Sub your precious engines blown a gasket?" Chided Fred as the engineer entered the bridge making for his Captain's day cabin. Politely knocking on the door, he entered as he was summoned; beaming like a naughty child once the door was closed behind him. Fred was summoned to the inner sanctum and together they raised three glasses of finest old Plymouth in salute to the Royal Oak. "Down the hatch!" they all muttered, and continued as if the world had fallen apart in the depths of the engine room.

She made one signal on a general Euro-Navy channel, indicating her situation and the Captain's intentions to temporarily heave-to, slipping in the conflicting details of another vessel's ident code on the message identifier.

Going in a straight line it would take her some seventy-nine hours to limp into Thessalonika. As it was they began to follow a deceptive pattern through the Cyclades beginning when they reached the staggeringly deep waters around the ancient chaldera at Santorini thirteen hours later. The weather remained sultry and oppressive with occasional flashes of sheet lightning illuminating the distant skies to the north. Athens at half-past one in the morning is not a good place to be on the streets in a thunderstorm.

By half-past seven on a grey and misty morning Sub took the helm as they passed abeam Sikinos, avoiding the islands and rocky outcrops. A single pulse on a tight beam of electromagnetic energy transmitted by their personnel locator system, using a pre-determined ident code, emanated in the ether around the skimmer in an ever-increasing circle. The low power of the mono-pulse, sufficient to activate any sensitive receiver in a hundred-mile radius, bounced among the many islands reverberating silently with the wave steadily advancing over the region. "If they have one of those personal survival beacons." Colonel Renton had observed. "Then there's a chance you may find them before our 'friends' on the other side do." Ahead of them in a straight line lay the distant Euboea Channel and to the far right the busy Kaphereus Channel, neither of which was an option open to them as they made their way slowly northwards. The display on Royal Oak remained passive not receiving any returned signal from a personnel transponder.

The second day of their tour would take them on a course to a point equidistant from the islands of Siros, Kithnos and Yioura. Providing the Greek navy kept their focus of attention around Athens and the channel leading to the myriad of islands belonging to them almost touching the Turkish mainland, they would be fortunate to escape detection. Any aircraft spelt immediate danger and for this reason the crew rehearsed their parts in a subterfuge that would be brought into play if reconnaissance aircraft ventured within distance. Eleven hours later they ran into a fishing fleet running without lights as night fell upon a blustery evening. Dinner was temporarily postponed as they turned away from the little fleet of ships that appeared to be making for the island community of Panormos. Stragglers saw them passing by in the gathering gloom and began waving to them enthusiastically; bringing a mild panic into minds of one or two people standing on guard in the bridge. "Come on Chief, let's go out there and wave back at them." Chip and Chief Grey left the comfort of the bridge for the starboard side just outside the bridge, standing there with smiles on their faces waving casually at the fishermen in the last two boats. Hearing voices calling out greetings faintly across the water, they gave one last final wave before returning to their safe haven and disappearing in the screen of darkness. "Thank goodness they haven't cut off the civilian GPS channel, I don't think my dead reckoning by night would be half as good as this without it." muttered Guns doing his turn as duty pilot. "That's only the beginning William." Chip said softly. "Bring her round William onto a heading of three four five and plot a course to take us through the channel there with Andros."

William quickly set to work in plotting a new course on the navigation console adding the new information to the database being followed by the computer. The autopilot responding to the new command inputs almost immediately. As the crew stood down heading for their overdue victuals Royal Oak made way for the narrow gap between two islands of granite to emerge clear on the other side nearly two and a half-hours later. Another mono-pulse interrogated the region as the evening of their second day drew to a stunning close with glorious sunlight igniting the high cirrus miles above them, giving way to a beautiful indigo night sky laced with a myriad of stars.

At nine o' clock in the evening, after a quick bite to eat, William disappeared into the equipment room and finding nobody there slipped a small flat packet from his trouser pocket. Quickly scanning the equipment racks in the subdued lighting he found what he was looking for and slid a piece of equipment out of the rack on its runners exposing the cables at the rear of the unit. No one had noticed him going in the equipment room since it was off to one side in the after part of the bridge complex, and he knew by days of careful observation that he would remain undetected as long as the watch keepers were busy at their various tasks. He quickly pulled out a long flat cable plugging the loose end into the little package he had brought with him. He then plugged the other end of the package into the rear socket from which he had originally moved the cable. Working in the subdued lighting he fumbled it a couple of times finally pushing home the package with a faint snapping of sprung retaining bars. Silently he pushed the unit back into the cabinet on its runners hearing the sprung catches click the electronic equipment safely into place. Moving furtively, William crossed over to a small console where he stood typing swift instructions to a hidden computer buried in the heart of the equipment room technology. Just as he pressed the action key he heard a slight noise outside the equipment door, and sitting down quickly he tapped more keys causing the computer to display a composite video from a passing satellite. The door opened a crack as someone held a conversation just outside the door. The conversation finished and in walked Chief Grey holding a mug of tea.

"Hello Sir, you shouldn't be in here." William had heard his voice just above the whirring of fans and the air-conditioning, and pretending to be absorbed in what he was doing looked up slowly with a look of busy concentration on his face. "Oh, hello Chief, what's up?"

"You shouldn't be in here by yourself Sir. Is there anything I can help you with? This is a restricted area."

"Yes, I'm sorry Chief, it's just that I had an idea and I wanted to try it out before I told anyone else, save the embarrassment if it failed." He looked at the Chief a little quizzically. "Tell me what you're trying to do and I'll see if it can be done. How about that Sir?"

"Well, I've done some of it already." William turned to the screen and sitting back in the chair he showed off his achievement.

"That's very good Sir, where did you get that from?"

"Ah, Chief, it's always been there, but no one has ever bothered to try the civil aviation downlink from the old Galileo system."

"How on earth did you know about that?" William gave a secret smile of relief as the Chief took the bait and was hooked. "It was supposed to have been switched off decades ago when Galileo-ten got singed by a solar storm about fifty years ago. I used it a few times myself, for real, when I was a commercial pilot. It's very helpful when the local system fails and you're flying in areas that have no backup, like the Pacific."

"Does the Captain know you can do this?" asked the Chief in amazement. "No, as I said, I wanted to try out my theory before making it known."

"That's really ace Sir. We could do with this information out on the tactical system."

"Good, then I'll tell the Captain straight away and ask him to bring the information up on the tactical displays."

"That's fine Sir." William got up and walked to the door. "Nice little caboosh you have here Chief." He observed casting an eye around the room making sure that he had left nothing un-done." Closing the door behind him he moved silently along the back of the bridge out into the flat leading to the accommodation. Chief Grey turned up the lights and moving around the equipment room slowly he checked out that all was well. The pattern of lights and sounds seemingly unchanged, he shrugged his shoulders moving back to the console where he fiddled with the controls looking at the satellite images and the GPS overlay. He couldn't get it to work properly making the assumption that the operability had to be different from what he knew to be the normal methods of using navigation and tactical systems.

It was a dilemma for any Captain of a man of war. Go too far out and risk being seen and possibly being mistaken for an enemy, or hug the coast to avoid sensor detection and risk being seen by someone ashore with an enquiring mind; either way; ending with the same result.

Chip had turned in at ten o' clock that night quite exhausted while the skimmer 'patrolled' the eastern shores of Andros in darkness. Occasionally the moon peeked out from the ragged breaks in low flying fracto-stratus. Otherwise, they had to rely on the lookouts with their intensifiers and sharp eyes. Fred didn't want to disturb Chip from his slumbers. "After all William, he's been on the go for almost eighteen hours. No, What we will do is get Chief Grey in here and have him show us what this new gadgetry can do for us. I'm quite happy to use this information without the need to go any higher. Particularly if it's what we need and can give us advance warning of what is going on out there in the real world." The telephone rang in Fred's cabin as he was speaking to William. "Yes Chief Grey, what can I do for you?" Fred paused looking puzzled as his caller spoke. "Where are you?" He paused again listening intently. "I will be with you right away." He placed the phone in its receiver and standing up moved to the door. "Come on William, this concerns you as well." A few seconds later they stood behind Chief Grey who sat hunched over the console in front of them. "I'm looking at a GPS plot and moving map display of the area Sir. "I've done something to the display Sir and it looks like I can filter out the cloud cover and see the surface..."

"How is this done?" Asked Fred and suspecting a technical prologue wouldn't help him understand any better he followed up by saying. "Skip the technical stuff please Chief and tell me what your main points are." insisted Fred mildly.

"Two surface targets coming our way Sir! One from over here on the right Sir, and one closer over here on the left, see, in the channel turning south."

"Right thank you Chief, punch that through onto the tactical console if you can?"

"Yes, no problem Sir."

"William, get us in close to the shoreline otherwise we'll be like sitting ducks in this moonlight. I'll wake the Captain."

Chip rose immediately and walked barefooted onto the gloomy bridge, wearing his trousers and a light vest. "Watch those soundings over there." He said indicating to Fred the shallow water and rocks below them as indicated on the charts. How far are we from the shoreline pilot?"

"Half a mile Sir."

"That's not going to be enough." Chip and Fred shuffled the chart around looking for a better prospect.

"There," said Fred. "In there, that little cove tucked in behind the headland where it turns into the island."

"Got it."

"What do you think?"

"Good enough for our needs Fred. As long as the EuroSat network remains denied to everybody we have an advantage over the rest of the crowd. Let's stick her in there and shutdown the engines."

"I'll send a runner to get the men to action stations."

"Good idea, let's hope we wont need it." Chip mused optimistically.

Royal Oak vanished under the protective shadow of a roaring great cliff and into a shelving bay under an outcrop of granite. The engines fell silent as they nosed into the bay with the Cox'n at the helm turning her nose seawards in a slow arc. Though they themselves were lost from view, the sensors in passive mode began to receive minute telltale signs of other vessels approaching nearby. The distant thrum of powerful engines could be heard as a Greek patrol vessel skimmed along the coast about three miles distant. "I hope they don't use their night vision systems or we've had it," muttered William. No one answered him as they waited in the dark hoping that their profile would merge with the rocks around them. "She's turning our way!" hissed one of the tactical operators. "What's the other one doing?" asked Chip softly.

"Just coming out from that small island, range eighteen and a half miles." Came the reply from out of the dark

"Speed?" demanded Chip urgently.

"Fifty knots Sir."

"That gives us a little over half an hour…" Fred halted in mid-sentence as a sharp change in the engine pitch of the nearby patrol craft distracted him.

On the quarterdeck men sat on the deck below the level of the all metal sides out of sight from prying night vision systems that could detect body heat from a long way off. Wild sage and rosemary suffused the still air in the little bay, completely at odds with their current situation the peaceful air with its aromas relaxed them evoking distant thoughts of bright sunshine cool beer and nothing to do. They stiffened as they too heard the urgent changing in the engine noise not far away. On the bridge the lookouts confirmed that the skimmer had turned away almost abeam their little cove and was heading out into the open sea towards the island of Vrakhonisis at break-neck speed.

Without tactical data supplied by the EuroSat network they were stuck with the problems of not being able to identify their targets at long range. Until then they could only see two targets in their vicinity, both likely to be Greek patrols. "They're closing with the other target Sir. Estimated time to intercept is twelve minutes."

Chip's reply was interrupted by the desperate call. "Weapons powering up Sir!"

"Who! Where?"

"The other incoming vessel Sir, It's got a weapons lock on, no… weapons firing!"

"Incoming Sir! Two minutes and ninety seconds to impact!"

"They can't possibly know we're here!"

"Send up Chaff!" shouted Fred. "We don't have the time to do anything else!"

"Do it!" Responded Chip urgently. "Out over the bay, otherwise it will strike the rocks above us!"

A marine silently dropped a round of chaff into a mortar tube firing it directly from the port waist. The charge lifted it four hundred feet into the air before it burst into a hundred thousand pieces of flimsy metallised plastic. Without the fiery trail of a rocket-launched charge to give them away it was their only chance of protection. "The skimmer has powered up it weapons, Sir, target lock engaged, missile launch Sir!" There was a dreadful silence as men watched their dimly glowing screens looking for a hope that might never come. The fiery trail of a rocket motor hurtling skywards on its journey momentarily lit up the nearer of the two craft. A lookout shouted. "It's not coming our way! They're firing away from us!" Chip and Fred pored over the tactical plot not yet believing their luck, looking for clues as to the identity of the two patrol craft. "Permission to power up weapons Sir?" begged William. "No Guns. Leave them as they are!"

"Sir?"

"No weapons!"

William stood agitated at the dimly lit fringes of his weapons system desperate to power up and loose off a few missile rounds. Missile approaching nearest vessel Sir, fifty seconds before it passes!"

"You don't suppose they're firing at each other do you?" suggested Sub grasping at a straw.

"What do you mean Sub?"

"You know, one of them is one our side, Greek, the other Turkish?"

"Just a merest chance Sub, we will find out in the next ten seconds." Fred replied. They waited in silence counting the seconds with only the inner sound of pounding hearts accompanying their thoughts.

"Incoming has passed the other vessel Sir. One minute forty five seconds to impact."

"That's the answer to our question number one, we won't be making a dash across the channel tonight."

"Incoming missile has lost lock Sir!" It's veering off course, going across the other side of the bay."

"It's the chaff!" confirmed Fred with great relief, "It's gone for the chaff, and now that the chaff has all but hit the surface it's missed us!"

William and Fred grunted as they hunched themselves down onto the bridge wing deck while looking at the small point of light indicating the vapour trail of hot exhaust gas pushing the rocket along. It lifted up about two hundred feet scaling the high granite cliffs and then exploded in a fiery plume of fury as the warhead detonated against the solid face of a crag high above the sea. Another flash lit up the sky to seaward and they slung their viewers around to a point far in the distance.

"Missile lock Sir, the nearer vessel is launching another missile!" A second flash of light, then a loud roar could be heard as the sound of a detonation reached their ears. "Hold everything, I think Sub is right!" said Chip calmly, "We've walked into a firefight between the locals. Number One, have a messenger relay the message to the ship's company and tell them not to power up any weapons unless expressly given the order."

"Aye Sir." Fred detailed one of the seamen to bear the message throughout the ship, starting with the crews closed up at the armaments and the marines closed up with portable laser rifles and rocket launchers.

Gritting their teeth throughout the whole exchange they watched as for an electrifying ten minutes the two vessels threw missiles and laser cannon at each other. The furthest vessel, which they assumed to be a Turkish marauder, had slowed down taking two missile hits, while their adversary had a narrow escape when a second missile bounced along the upper deck before splashing harmlessly into the sea over the stern. The distant vessel was on fire but her gunners were still firing her guns with deadly accuracy. They hit something vital causing an immense explosion to tear the hull apart on the port side near the stern, a telltale flicker of blue green giving a hint of an immediate disaster as raw plasma spilled out of a damaged engine conduit. The furthest vessel heeling over sharply by the bows dove into the waters with her stern pointing to the stars high above on the beginning of her death dive to the bottom. The nearest vessel rocked violently as the stray plasma field blew her stern apart into a trillion pieces of atomised metal, skin and bone. The night sky lit up for miles around and then a split second later the darkness collapsed around them leaving her with her stern section full of water dragging her slowly down.

"Mayday received on emergency marine channel Sir. ID is a Greek vessel, sinking, no other communications Sir. Standby for position report." There was a breathtaking pause. Sub and chip scanned their screens for clues looking for other surface movements in the area –finding none. It's coming from the nearest vessel Sir, range six and a half miles."

"Signal op!" called Fred urgently, "any sign of a reply to the mayday?" Fred looked at Chip in the darkness. They both knew that technically they had to respond if no other vessels were around. The pause grew longer as they watched the signalman go through his routine of testing the airwaves and as the tactical lookouts did what they could with their limited systems. "No reply to the mayday Sir."

"Right. Looks like we have our hands full. Any news of the other surface vessel?"

"Under water sensors indicate she's sinking Sir, definitely beneath the surface."

Cautiously Royal Oak nosed out of the small bay into open waters, moving as a darkened mass across the water Chip kept her off-planes to reduce her signature to any snooping sensors passing overhead in the heavens above. The only transmission being her navigation radar in acknowledgement of their somewhat awkward circumstances. Covering the intervening distance between the stricken Greek vessel and the hide-away in the cove in less than half an hour they found a shattered skimmer floating low in the water, with men swimming around a partially inflated life raft trying to get in it. Leyland and his Chief stood silently watching the hull as the crew steered their vessel close to the wreck. "She's down by the stern which tells me the aft bulkheads are holding if she's a type forty-seven Sir."

"I don't know if it's worth the attempt Chief. It really depends what time we've got and how the Captain wants to play it."

"Mmm." Came the thoughtful response as his Chief swept his gaze over the midship sections. "I reckon it's worth a quick once-over Sir. They don't seem to have any pumps going. Maybe we could pump her out, patch her up a little and tow her into one of their little harbours."

"We'll see, let's wait for a decision first, but you may be right. The stupid idiots just love abandoning their ships without trying to stop them from sinking, and this looks like a classic case." It didn't take long for the answer to arrive.

"Leyland, I want you and the Chief to go over with a couple of your men and see what you can do. We'll finish picking up survivors, but I want a damage report on that skimmer in ten minutes."

"Aye, aye Sir."

The Greek skipper and two of his officers had remained onboard. One of Mr White's seamen had trained a small lamp on the Royal Oak's masthead illuminating the Union Flag hanging there. Another manned a small but powerful searchlight shining it in the water looking for survivors. Although their Captain was relieved to see them, he and his officers were very cautious and very suspicious about the presence of another ENSF vessel in their territorial waters with an all English speaking crew. Leyland and his team came onboard very quickly and while he did some explaining to their Captain his men went into the lower spaces looking at the structure of the vessel for signs of damage, probing the lower sections for leaks. They quickly discovered the engine room was impossible to enter since the plasma stream had fused the large hatchway from which only a small leak was draining a minimal stream of seawater. Lower down, the decks were awash with water which was rising slowly up their legs. The crafty 'stokers' found the occupants had broken basic rules of ship protection when they discovered an open hatchway leading down to the deck below. It took three of them to overcome the pressure of the water coming up from down below, but with the hatch finally closed it meant that the water would not flood all the way up to the main deck above. Silently they watched the water level and were satisfied in noting that it had stopped rising, moving quickly on to inspect other areas below the main deck.

Leyland reported back to Chip that all flooding had been stopped, but emergency electrical power was needed to get the pumps going since all the skimmer's gensets were under water. She was indeed capable of staying afloat and it was worth giving them a tow to the nearest shore. "Three hours maximum." Came the reply to Chip's question about how long it would take. That would take them until just before dawn. "We could pump her half out," said Fred hopefully. "Then tow her while pumping out the remaining water. If we beach her at a decent speed it would lift the bows out of the water and maybe when they get a diver down it would be an easier task for them to patch up the holes in the hull and then pump her out fully."

"Well, we've technically blown our cover, so let's do it. We might get some good will out of this in the long run." A portable pump was sent over while a party of seamen in a small boat rowed around the hull of the skimmer hammering wooden plugs into holes in the hull above and below the waterline. Within fifteen minutes the pump coughed into life spewing a wide jet of water over the side through an armoured hose. With the hull slowly rising above the water more wooden pegs were hammered home as eager fingers probed for holes torn in the hull by shards of steel. The electricians worked quickly to isolate power lines that were submerged or broken; rigging emergency couplings to badly needed services around the ship. Slowly their efforts brought back the doomed ship 'Elekta' from her watery grave breathing life back into her shattered body. By half past three in the morning they began the tow towards the distant shore. The dilemma being that they could not risk being seen in such a position in broad daylight, neither could they be seen helping the Greeks so openly which would cause an immediate war between the British and hence the Union as a whole, and the Turks. The mission they were on quite separate from the diplomatic fire and counter-fire that would be heaped upon their heads.

They held a conference with the Greek Captain, explaining their reluctance to be seen towing his ship in broad daylight. He understood the wider ramifications, agreeing to their proposals perhaps, because he was grateful to be alive and that his crew had been given medical treatment for their wounds. He had lost six of his crew, mostly in the engine room, including two seamen who had been blown off the quarter deck never to be seen alive again. His engineering officer had survived the attack by simply being elsewhere on the small craft sorting out an auxiliary pump in the forward section of the hull when the missile struck home initiating the plasma explosion. The only comforting thought for Chip had been the side effects of the plasma explosion that meant most naval and military units within a 60-mile radius would be temporarily blinded until their sensors recovered from overload. Royal Oak had only one sensor working in passive mode together with her satellite system when the explosion tore apart the ether, but their temporary loss only made a small dent in their otherwise clandestine mode of operation. By the time they beached her in the cove she was riding four metres higher in the water and getting easier to pull along. The bows scraped up the sandy bottom lifting high enough to clear part of her keel from the white gravel. "We can't risk crossing the channel until tonight, it's out of the question. William, when we move back to our old position under the rock face I want you to take a party of men with Chief Riley and help those Greeks pump out the water and patch up her hull if possible. Those of the Greek crew will go with you, and take along that young Sub of theirs. His English is slightly better than the others."

Sub-Lieutenant Korpoulis mopped his brow on the greasy sleeve of his overalls, waist deep in seawater. The pumps were just holding their own against the influx of water flowing into the lower decks and he watched ribbons of water flickering in the light of his torch, cascading in graceful arcs down into the dark pool all around him. During the following day the British proved themselves well capable in their emergency repair operations; while seamen cleared out a lot of debris and hammered more plugs into holes, the engineers worked their way around the hull bonding patches into the torn metal. Stopping only to fabricate patches fashioned from scavenged materials taken from the shattered stern section. The Greek sailors quickly learning from the British tars what was required of them, began hammering plugs alongside their rescuers, clearing out more of the debris and assisting in the repair work translating the Greek logos on the pipes and cables requiring repair. Cleverly and with great care Leyland's team slowly restored the power from her own generators allowing the electricians and electro-photonic systems to re-initialise the skimmers communications and computer systems. Using three emergency generators in tandem they developed enough power to activate the planes in a strategy facilitating repairs to the lower hull beneath the waterline. Cleverly and slowly, Leyland's team, having removed power from the starboard planes activated the planes on the port side, lowering the huge steel 'wings' onto sections of lumber placed in strategic positions on the sand. The hull began to heel over exposing the rents in the metal skin caused by cannon fire and by missile attack. The sailors swarmed underneath with repair materials not bothering with the wooden plugs while on the far side of the hull water began pouring slowly back out into the sea. By mid-afternoon they begun the same process on the other side of the hull until finally the Elekta was ready for 'launching' in the shallow waters. Slowly turning her around and by sunset they beached her stern in the sand.

Chip gave them until eight-thirty to complete the work of strengthening the bottom and the bulkhead of the last section of the hull for'ard of the vaporised engine room. Without structural strengthening to support the weakened areas the pressure of the seawater under for'ard movement was deemed likely to cause a catastrophic failure and she would sink like a stone. The seamen had brought her anchors up the beach burying them deep as they could into the sands of their secret cove. It took a difficult fifteen minutes for the Greek Captain to accept the principle of flooding the forward section in the bows in order to lift the stern out of the water. Between them Chief Riley and the Greek engineer persuaded him it was the only way they were going to get him and his vessel back home in one piece. Working quietly as they could under awnings to protect the glare of their cutting tools from shining outwards and being detected, they cut away more pipes, cables and engine parts that remained of the engine room systems. Having removed the dead weight and drag components that would impede her progress in the water they set to work reinforcing the damaged sections with any usable scrap, under the hot afternoon sun. By nine o' clock they re-launched the Elekta much to the relief of the working parties. The Greek Captain looked unhappy with his vessel lying nose-down in the water, the evening shadows not able to hide the unusual attitude of his charge. While the engineers cleared away their tools and the seamen collected a mountain of wedges and cordage with other paraphernalia, the engine room techs pumped out the forepeak until there was enough water left to balance the hull without the weight of its engine room. By ten o' clock they pulled her out of the bay heading north along the island towards the Kaphereus Channel.

The Greek Captain quickly agreed to the plan suggested by Fred and Chip, that the Royal Oak would tow him into the main channel using the darkness as cover, transmitting a general Greek ident code until a patrol came to investigate. At such a juncture Royal Oak would slip her tow and silently 'hand over' the tow to their own people while making a diplomatic withdrawal. With her ident codes transmitting a distress signal indicating she was under tow the Elekta made sedate progress into the heavily guarded channel heading towards the ancient city of Athens. The communications channel became alive with jabbering Greek demands emanating from other patrol craft, swiftly turning their attentions on the newcomer making her way slowly towards them along the blunt snout of Andros. Under a gibbous moon the Royal Oak seamen quickly hauled in the tow ropes flaking them down and stowing them away in silence. They had remained completely darkened throughout while the Elekta rode with her lights turned on and an additional jury-rigged light signal indicating that she was under tow. The Greek Captain kept up a simple dialogue with the engineer who remained on the bridge of the Royal Oak throughout the short journey. His responses in Greek giving the impression to anyone using the same radio channel that both ships were Greek. They came alongside briefly to drop off the engineer then shearing away Royal Oak made for open waters, returning the way she had come.

Once around the Kefitevs peninsular they transmitted their mono-pulse signal waiting for any sign of a response in the silent darkness where, two hundred and seventy miles ahead of them, lay their destination. Apart from the duty watchmen all of them headed for their bunks after such a strenuous day. Pleased that they had had a chance to demonstrate their skills in bringing an almost total wreck back from a watery grave. They all knew the Elekta would probably be scrapped, but her systems would provide vital salvage in the war going on around them. The difficult thoughts keeping Chip awake probed his mind as subconscious accusations of failing in their mission ran riot. Emerging from his cabin at three in the morning he shuffled into the little pantry and making himself some kai wandered onto the bridge where the comforting glow of the instruments lulled his aching mind. Before them on the sensor display glowed the echoes of the southern tips the Sporades islands and beyond the inky blackness of the open waters of the Gulf of Salonika, and no hope of finding the wanderers from the downed aircraft. Even their crawling pace of five knots conspired against him allowing no mitigation for losing a day's worth of effort in their search. 'Could they stretch fifty four hours?' He wondered as the imminent dawn of day four of their journey bore down on him like a dead weight. Again, the mono-pulse went out just past the forty-five minute mark. Again, they waited in that interminable silence with bated breath, then let it out in disappointment as nothing appeared on their sensor panels. Chip wandered into his day cabin where he sat motionless in front of a panel watching world news events patched in from an Indian communications satellite chain.

The news from home was not good. Switching occasionally from channel to channel he built up a picture from the mosaic of foreign broadcasts transmitted in English. They gave every indication that the European Commission had given the go ahead for police action to be taken against the British. Everyone knew about the combined fleet exercises in the Western Approaches, and about the marshalling of police and militias in preparation for another demonstration of the Commission's authority. French units were being deployed in Belgium for onward despatch to the UK mainland, but as everyone suspected they were there to bring the Belgians to heel. The Dutch and the Danes resisted any such incursion of their territorial borders arguing the Commission had no authority beyond seeking permission to do so, and that permission not being granted they should go elsewhere. Having blocked the way for the Germans to cross over the Maas to the south, the Luxembourgers remained impassive as large bodies of men and equipment passed through their capital on their way westwards from the northern towns of Germany. Many hoped this was just as it looked while others feared it could take on the proportions of an army of occupation within minutes.

The only ray of light that anyone could see was the counter-point in the news where reporters observed that Germany was taking a softer line by dispersing her naval transports away from her North Sea ports, 'returning many of them to their base in Kiel.' The Spanish occupation of Gibraltar had become a secondary issue in the face of mounting tensions between the British government and the Commission. President Warnock was viewed as a man up the creek without a paddle facing a hopeless situation while desperately trying to rearm his country's defences pitilessly run-down by the onslaught of legislation from the Commission. Other reports had varied opinions on the outcome of the Balkan 'war' over Cyprus, noting the ominous build up of Turkish troops on their border with Greece, and the tired old details of the Albanians yet again stealing everything they could, including Macedonia. How the Greeks would fare if the Turks and the Albanians attacked in unison, and how the rest of Europe could respond to the threat to their southern flank. The US had sent six more vessels to join their Mediterranean fleet including another aircraft carrier, the USS Martin-Luther king. Some speculating that they were coming over to protect Israel, others that they intended to join the British in a show of solidarity. The other news contained local items of interest, some American foreign service broadcaster was running a commentary on the lava flows in Northern Wyoming in the context of the dangers to wildlife and the farming communities, etc, etc.

Skiropoula loomed ahead as the hands went for their tea following a beautiful day's sailing across a calm sea. William set course for Psathoura wishing he could stop off at one of the little islands on the way specifically, on one of the beautiful beaches. Day five would dawn long before they reached the tiny island and with it the last vestiges of hope that somehow their quarry had either been 'dropped' by their failing transport or had made their escape this far south. William was a worried man occasionally casting his eyes towards the equipment room door expecting trouble. "Course set for Psathoura Sir, ETA 09:30 tomorrow morning." He said with an air of finality. "Thank you William." Said Chip, deep in his own calculations absorbed by the few options left open for further action. Twenty-two miles along their track, ten miles east abeam the tiny splinter of Skantzoura, a sensor alarm went off jarring everyone's thoughts. It was almost eleven o' clock. "Submarine Sir." Came the alert. "Thirty two miles on our starboard beam." It was delivered in a near whisper making everyone smile. "Show me?" Said Fred who had until that moment been scanning the dark shore with his intensifiers. "There Sir, just coming round the point between Skiros and those little islands." The operator pushed some buttons and bracketed the target with a strobe following up his actions with a magnified plot of the distant location. "It's not going very fast Sir, it's creeping round that headland." They watched slowly as a tiny rotating symbol turning at high speed indicated the computer was working to identify the hidden vessel from the terabytes of data stored in its tactical memory web. "No match? That's not right Sir, I'll run it again."

"Leave that for a moment, and give me the target depth, speed and heading, I want its CPA and anything else you can give me."

"Yes Sir, coming up now on the main console."

"It's on an intercept estimated at ten point eight miles ahead of us on this track."

Chip was already there in front of the panel looking at the magnified plot. "We are well within range. The trouble is; whose is it? Either way we could be in trouble."

"Depth is ten metres, coming our way, speed ten knots. That puts her at the right depth near enough to launch a torpedo." passed on Fred.

"Leading Hand!" called Chip. "Sound action stations!"

The weary crew hardly believing their rotten luck tumbled out of their bunks, some rubbing their weary faces while others, taking advantage of the crammed ladders, paused to put on their anti-flash clothing. "Doors opening Sir!"

"Cox'n, standby to increase engine speed!" Came the order from Fred. "Planes on auto at eight knots."

"William." Said Chip as the gunnery officer appeared. "We have no anti-submarine capability, so unless it comes to the surface your guns are going to be a little impractical. Have a word with Sargent Conningsby and see if you can come up with anything that could make a lot of noise in the water, that sort of thing."

"We've got rocket launched grenades Sir, they could make it a bit difficult, especially if we can land some of them in the water on top of them."

"Good, see what he can do, in the mean time, leave your guns crews closed up, we may need them yet." William walked to a nearby comms box picking up a telephone handset, and began talking into it, then returned to his gunnery console. Minutes ticked by agonisingly slowly. "Target speed is increasing Sir. Now passing twenty knots, range now twenty seven miles"

"Keep it coming!" urged Chip looking at Fred.

"We seem to be attracting a lot of attention these days, do you think someone's on to us?"

"Submarine now passing thirty knots Sir." Chip nodded in acknowledgement. "Must be a newk! Has to be, plasma plants can't drive a sub at that kind of speed, the acceleration is colossal!"

"Fred, what are the chances of a newk running the channels of the Aegean just to sink local shipping."

"About next to zero I'd say."

"And what are the chances of someone with a brand new boat or an old one with a sophisticated box of tricks powerful enough to mask their fingerprint doing the same?"

"Again, zero."

"I think we've run out of luck Number One."

"I'd say we've got less than ten minutes. They know we're here and by now they think we don't know they're here, so he's coming in close to make sure."

"Thirty-eight knots Sir!" chimed a tactical operator.

Chip nodded and looked at the chart overlay on the screen. "If he goes any faster he'll run out of manoeuvring room. He paused for a second glancing at the plot weighing the fast running data in the balance. "Turn left heading two seven zero, maintain present speed. Number One, we're going to make a run for it behind that island, just for the moment we'll let him think we're just ambling along in that direction."

The lazy turn to the west gave the advancing submarine an almost clear sound print of their engine noises. Both engines running at five knots still made enough of a racket to trigger the sensitive fields of any underwater sensor for miles around. Watching the red dial face of the backlit gyrocompass swinging round Chip waited gritting his teeth until they settled onto their new heading. "Now Cox'n full ahead both engines!" Royal Oak leapt forwards causing everyone aboard her to lurch backwards where they stood. Siting in his chair Chip let the motion push him firmly into the comfortable upholstery. Watching their speed indicator he ticked off their speed in five-knot increments until they reached thirty-five knots in less than a quarter of a mile. Passing towards forty knots he stopped counting.

"Torpedoes in the water Sir!"

"Two Sir, just two!"

"Forward sensors are activated Sir!"

"Torpedoes are locked on Sir!"

"Right, thank you. Lookouts keep your eyes peeled."

They dashed along under a clear evening sky leaving a huge tell tale wake of foaming sea behind them, dazzling in the raw moonlight. "Time to impact nine point four minutes!" "We don't have enough time Sir!" shouted Fred from across the other side of the bridge. Chip plotted a course tight around the island feeding each step into the navigation console knowing full well that the skirts of seawater around the island hid jagged granite just below the surface. He pressed the update button waiting for a solution to appear on the tactical plot. "Nine point six minutes to the turn, nine point six in the red!"

"Damn it we're out by four minutes!"

"Leyland! Screw down the safeties!" shouted Chip into the engine room comms box. "I want everything you've got in the engines!"

"All the way Sir?"

"All the way!"

"Aye, aye Sir!"

"William! Get those grenades in the water now. Every ten seconds, they're the only countermeasures we have!" William gave the order to fire over the comms box link with the marines on the quarterdeck. The bridge crew cheered by the eager response in the tone of the veteran Sargent's voice coming back over the loudspeaker. "Commence firing, dead astern, narrow pattern." No one heard or felt anything as the first pattern flew skywards with a huge plopping sound like a giant sucking back on a gigantic lollipop. The first two grenades swept upwards into the night in a huge arc, where they seemed to hang at the very limit of their upwards motion. Unseen they began their plummet to the sea, their streamlined casings giving them deadly precision to land at the orthogonal with the surface. The fuses detonated at the same depth as the rapidly advancing torpedoes. Fred balanced the nav data in his mind coming up with a dangerous alternative. "We could do a sliding turn on the planes Sir, drop a couple of grenades over the side as we do it and hope the torpedoes will slide past. They haven't got the turning circle that we have."

"We'll have to wait and see."

"Range to the island Pilot?"

"Seven miles Sir!" The solution leered back at him in red. Three point four two minutes to impact.

Unseen, the torpedoes jinked in their courses losing their target lock as the first grenades went off. The only noise on the bridge being the rattling of the superstructure as the engines red lined it down aft until the tactical operator yelled, "Torpedoes no longer locked on Sir!" Both went wide in their search for their lost target taking up precious seconds until they passed beyond the curtain of noise to re-acquire their original victim. "Torpedoes locked on Sir!" Everyone's heart sank. "Six miles to the turn Sir. Time to impact..." The plotter paused as the numbers altered briefly on the display, "...exactly two minutes."

Still the solution leered back at him in red figures. 'Ten seconds' he thought to himself despairingly, 'those grenades gave us ten seconds.' Again another curtain of sound spread out in the water behind them. This time the torpedoes were much closer and passed through the noise losing their lock for only eight seconds. "Continuous fire William short range if you please!" William passed the order and the marines began firing their grenades into the water at close range, while their Sargent interpreting the situation in his own mind summed it all up by proceeding to drop grenades by hand into their wake. Another long pause as time ticked relentlessly onwards.

Chip checked the speed indicator against the computer and was pleased to note they were dancing along at sixty knots. Then back at the solution still tauntingly red. They had gained a measly twenty seconds or so grace, but there was still too much water between the skimmer and the turning point ahead. Another and then another series of under water thuds went off as they hurtled ever forwards across the glassy surface. The moon silently watching the doomed skimmer as it raced with death to the imaginary turning point in the darkness beyond. He looked again at the speed indicator, cross-referencing it with the rev counter scale on the dual engine control panel. Instead of an estimated time to impact of fifty eight seconds he saw the figures rolling as the computer re-shuffled the dynamics in its digital labours to finding a solution. One minute thirty-three seconds! Thirty-five extra crucial seconds to run, only half a mile left in which to live and then it will be all over. More banging, and yet more banging as the frequency of the grenade launchings increased. On the quarterdeck the marines were working like men possessed. Three miles to run or thereabouts. "Thirty seconds to impact!"

A huge explosion lifted a ragged waterspout half a mile beyond their transom. The vision rose in a huge boiling destructive tide of foam accompanied by the roar of a torpedo warhead tearing water and air molecules apart. "Hooray!" Somebody shouted out in the darkness on deck. The underwater sensors temporarily themselves shut down protecting them from overload. "Torpedo has lost lock Sir!" called the tactical operator. "Number One, standby for a high speed turn!"

"Standing by for high speed turn Sir!"

Chip hated the thought of putting his ship in danger. Quite apart from the risk of damaging the ship was the ever-present danger of rolling her over, and the noise that such a manoeuvre would make could easily cause the freely running torpedo to acquire lock onto Royal Oak in an inevitable showdown of firepower. A sliding turn meant that she would literally be skating while turning on her beam ends momentarily out of control like a hovercraft in an unexpected gust of wind, or a novice skater turning backwards on the ice, wobbly and uncertain as to the outcome. The torpedo was running wild with its telemetry and onboard systems blinded by the death of its companion, having crossed the wake of Royal Oak it headed on a gently divergent course towards the tiny island. "Look!" exclaimed a seaman lookout at the stern. "There it is, you can just see that faint trail of white in the moonlight!" Everyone stared hard, but not everyone saw it. "Visual contact Sir, range about one thousand yards off the port quarter!" Chip and Guns leapt to the port bridge wing with their intensifiers in hand. Sargent Conningsby grabbed one launcher team and together they manhandled the launcher to point in the direction of the torpedo. "Cease firing!" Came the order from William and they disappointedly watched as their only shot in the new direction took to the sky.

Together they ran a dangerous course to the granite ahead, already living on borrowed time speeding relentlessly towards their turn, the moonlight mocking them in the remaining seconds of grace. "Sensors back online, torpedo still running wild Sir." Came the call.

"Thank you lookout, everyone stay calm. The clock ticked dispassionately on to the moment of truth, the engines staying a fraction above red line whining in the background as the hull vibration continued to shake everything loudly. Sixty seconds to go, 'tick, tick, tick'. A voice out of the darkness called, choked and started again. "Range to... Range to turn Sir." Another pause as the numbers whirled silently in their electronic throne. The numbers turned to orange and Chip waited not seeing the subtle change in status. "Eighteen hundred yards, orange Sir, no immediate solution!"

Chip glanced up at the figures hardly daring to hope. Fred and William looked ahead searching the dark patch of water for signs of obstacles that would indicate rocks standing in their way. The Cox'n standing legs astride strapped in to the helm position ready for the fateful order that would either send them into a fiery hell or slide past death while cocking a snook a the grim reaper's scythe as it missed the mark. 'Just under a mile.' The thought flickered through the minds of everyone on the bridge.

"Visual contact with the torpedo's wake Sir!" confirmed the port lookout.

"Thank you, well done!" Replied Fred. "Range to turn." called the Cox'n. "Twelve hundred yards, thirty seconds." Chip got out of his chair tearing himself away from the figures that no longer made any sense. The stark reality of a torpedo running in the water past them in close proximity and the dark mass of the headland ahead called for more immediate attention. He checked their speed. 'Seventy knots, way to go Leyland!' he muttered to himself. Still the second hand of the clock ticked on, the figures remained orange adding a final context to their situation. "Torpedo has locked onto us Sir, range one thousand yards!"

Fear like thick treacle slid over their minds as hearts now sank to the pit of each man's stomach jolting them in their guts, holding on to something solid as if that would guarantee a measure of security against the inevitability of the imminent collision while they raced on. Royal Oak 'flew' across the water yet again in a desperate one to one against the warhead. "Range to turn six hundred yards, fifteen seconds!" The numbers screamed red as the equations crunched out the solution of the damned.

"Torpedo beginning its turn now Sir!"

"What?" Fred's mind locked in to the figures as the triangle of speeds spewed out numbers he could barely catch and hold. "Range to turn?"

"Three hundred yards Sir." Replied the Cox'n "Range and bearing of target?"

"Eighteen hundred yards Sir, closing fast!" The computed solution glimmering deepest red in defiance. Chip watching the forward sensor array made his decision. "Now Cox'n, make your turn now!"

"Brace! Brace for high speed turn!" William shouted into the comms box system, his voice reaching every compartment and crewmember. "Wheel fifteen degrees to port Sir!" Called the Cox'n as the starboard bow planes lifted momentarily into the air, then bounced along the surface as its counterpart began to bury itself deeper into the jet black waters of the night. The stern planes just held them together as they part skimmed, part flew and part skidded into the turn. The tactical computer blinked out deferring its final crimson leering solution of death, then blinked on again smugly. "Solution in the orange Sir!" Called the tactical plotter holding onto his bowels for all he was worth. "Bring her right two points Cox'n!" ordered Fred. "Right two points Sir!" Looking to maintain as much forward motion as possible rather than bleed too much off in the turn Fred, balancing the turn by the pitch of the deck beneath his feet more by experience than by exact science. The planes remained on the knife-edge of their performance envelope as the heading came round to within ten degrees. None of the lookouts could find the torpedo track in the water, their turning had caused the moonlight to shift and they were done, standing silently watching for any small clue that would signal their demise.

"Torpedo range..." The tactical plotter never finished his sentence. A huge explosion erupted alongside them buffeting the air and water into a spectacular fountain of shimmering white. A shower of rocks rained down on the water where Royal Oak had been a split second before in her madcap turn around the splinter of earth looking for shelter. The moon slid behind a veil of icy cirrus as if hiding its face in shame for its coldly mocking indifference upon the scene below. In the darkness the hidden enemy listened to the sounds of death waiting patiently for any indication of life beyond the moment of execution. There were no more detonations from their quarry's pitiful armoury, no more engine noises or other sounds apart from the sound of debris falling back into the cold sea. Sensors gave no hint of electronic signatures, no vibrations in the ether to trigger the alarms. The hunter's single periscope deflecting the triumphal moment to the watchful eyes below the surface as he saw from the comfort of his control room the reflection of the craft caught in the momentary glare of the torpedo's initial detonation. No sign of wreckage or traces of life the hunter turned slowly down the channel with her periscope telescoping back into the depths, then she too was gone as her commander took her down into the hidden depths of the nocturnal sea heading south.

Skantzoura is shaped like a small nematode creature in mid crawl, like a lazy 'S' written in childlike handwriting. While its northern headland faces Northeast, its body twisting around to the south and a tail twisting in the opposite direction to the south-west. A seven and a half nautical mile twist of land almost worthless in advantage as things go, but precious to somebody enough to stake their flag and nationhood upon it. The skimmer nestled in the bay hidden by the shadows as the sun began to rise in the east. Lookouts posted in the hills above watched for signs of other craft finally switching their intensifiers to day mode once the light of day shutdown their night vision systems. Royal Oak lay beneath them inert upon the waters, her bows facing south and west in line with the contour of the shoreline. At night the lookouts had been served by runners scrambling up and down the face of the hill, by day the signalmen waved flags at each other under the strict imposition of radio silence. The men onboard crept around careful not to knock things together as they went about their duties. An early morning breeze bringing a chill to those watching from the hilltop as much to those below them working to clear debris from the decks. Lookouts onboard watched the distant islands for signs of surface craft whether they be fishing or one of the Greek patrols that frequently passed through the islands.

William arrived at six-thirty, a trifle early to take the morning watch, wearing the same clothes he had worn all night. His anti-flash clothing hanging from his belt and steel helmet propped up against the now inoperative navigation console. He sat in the high chair surveying the view out of the windows to the south and across to the distant islands. His thoughts wandering to the extremity of the previous night's experience and how he had toyed with the idea of activating that 'box of tricks' using his gadget hidden away in his cabin.

Leyland appeared at seven preparing to make an exploratory dive around the hull. He left the engine starter keys in their places on the 'hazards' keyboard and locked it, handing the key back to William. By the time he had finished his inspection everyone was up and about finishing breakfast or lounging in the open air waiting lamely for the sun to rise above the hill. The lookouts changed hands at eight o' clock with the tired looking hilltop watchers returning wearily smelling of earth and wild herbs. Chief White chivvied the goofers from his beloved decks, roping in several stragglers to help his men get rid of the rubble and dirt strewn along the port side. As Royal Oak bumped gently against her fenders nudging the rocky side of the island, Chip held a council of war. He suspected, though he never said as much; that the previous night's action had been the result of a concerted effort to remove the Royal Oak; and that only meant one thing. A stool pigeon somewhere in the camp, back in Cyprus, as the Brigadier had pointed out, or perhaps, onboard his ship. Privately, Fred doubted there could be a 'stoolie' onboard, but both he and Chip agreed to keep an open mind on it. The fact of the matter being that their erstwhile adversary had been waiting for them, and had sprung the trap that had given them no chance of survival.

The council of war, such that it was had not much to offer in the way of options. It was day six and they had run out of time in their search for Admiral Dunham and the king. They had effectively just less than thirty hours to make the trip to Thessalonika as agreed by diplomacy. If they were later than that, then nobody knew for sure what action the Greek authorities might take. Chip planned a course of action that would take them through the islands at a modest though respectable speed of twenty-five knots on the planes. "They know we're coming so they will be looking out for us, and if they are looking out for us in the role as 'friendlies' they are hardly going to start a shooting match, are they?" Agreed Fred as he continued his part of the briefing. They would then proceed at a more respectable speed of thirty-five to forty knots across the open water towards the Cassandra Peninsular. Just off the coast they would develop engine troubles once again. "Shocking maintenance standards down there." Said William shaking his head from side to side in mock disfavour. "Just because it's my watch, again!" Leyland smiled back at him out of the corner of an eye, as William became aware of a heavy pressure being exerted on his foot. "Oh, sorry, was that your foot? Deary me, I must be losing my sea legs." apologised Leyland with a sly grin lifting his foot away. Chip noted the almost unobtrusive banter and was thankful that the morale among his officers appeared to be high. The skimmer was relatively unscathed with nothing more than a few minor dents in the hull and superstructure received from falling rocks. Their sturdy craft was running like a completely well oiled machine.

At 07:45 they powered up their systems and slipped their moorings heading directly for the scattered islets and the channel beyond. In half an hour they traversed the waters passing close to the island community of Halonnesos. Still flying the lone flag of the Union they made sure that they were seen from a distance of five miles. The cluster of buildings and the prominent little basilican roof of the church glinting in the sunlight passed by almost wistfully in its peaceful surroundings. At 08:20 Chip noted the autopilot, changing course to the accompaniment of the rising reverberations of the engine room as the pre-programmed speed settings jiggled the auto-throttles. Shortly afterwards he observed the attained speed of forty-five knots and returned his attentions to the chart laid out before him. The sensor arrays in conjunction with the old Galileo-10 satellite kept them reasonably informed about other surface movements. The reduced electronic data providing only ident codes from which the database sub-routines could only determine basic information about the nature of each contact. Tactical data from other systems being drawn into the navigation plots as a backup until full restoration of the EuroSat network could be achieved. The mono-pulse search signal went out into the ether with the plotters painstakingly scanning their displays eagerly looking for any signs of a reply. "Transponder code received Sir!" urgently called one of the plotters. William dashed over to look at the plot as the signal faded and disappeared. "Where was it?" He asked waiting for a response from the plotter. It was only a single return Sir. There must be something wrong with our equipment, I'll run diagnostics."

"Where was the target?" Demanded William, getting exasperated.

"It's just an estimate Sir, but it looks to be somewhere here on this bit of coast line."

William looking at his watch made mental calculations, quickly expanding the view on the navigation display. Fred and the Sub were lounging in the wardroom off duty; the Captain was in his day cabin looking through NOTMARS and approach plates for Thessalonika. He could just make it back to his cabin on the pretext of visiting the heads. At the point of making his decision the techno-wiz kid emerged from the equipment room, heading down the flat towards the accommodation. He looked quickly at the doorway of the equipment room and then out towards the fo'csle. Chip emerged from his cabin walking over to the tactical plots. "Where's that transponder burst William?" He asked. "I was about to come and tell you Sir, it's located somewhere on the peninsular we think. It was only a brief detection before the computer could get a lock on it."

"Keep her steady, we don't want to alert anyone else to what we're about."

"Aye, aye Sir."

After forty-seven minutes, at twenty-five minutes past the hour of nine, they reached the rocky headland of the peninsular where the engines coughed and spluttered in a convincing display of impairment by some hideous fault within the onboard machinery. Royal Oak crawled close to the shore a cable's length from the rocky coast of the Cassandra Peninsular. The high tops of the steeply wooded hills shimmering in the morning sun as the deep blue waters gently rocked them. One hour and forty minutes after they had begun the final leg of their journey, the crew waited patiently with the skimmer chugging along at five knots. This time there would be no skulking with minimal sensors, now they were a British man o' war on a mission running with a sick engine, weapons systems on standby and all else warmed up ready to go at a millisecond's notice. Chip surveyed the chart and gave the order to take Royal Oak around the headland into the wide bay between Cassandra and Sithonia.

Taking regular sightings from a radio mast on the spine of the peninsular, they travelled slowly along the coast keeping a distance of two miles from the rock-strewn shoreline. Abeam the mast where a shallow fold in the high ridge dipped down towards its neighbour she slowly turned towards the shore of Cassandra. Chip looking at a distant view of a small community of houses high above in the hills. A splash of colour off to the right looking like the high slanted side of small cruise ship docked in a hidden basin. He took a squint at the chart overlay noting they were on course for the tiny cove in which was depicted a small jetty. Slowly they entered the placid waters, crossing the strong currents that lay just outside the entrance. Turning to port they found the jetty hidden behind a steep rocky outcrop. A small steamer painted garishly in blue and yellow was tied up alongside. Chip shook his head pursing his lips in frustrated and contained anger. "That's all we needed." "Alright Number One, let's turn her around and we'll come alongside the end of the jetty starboard side to."

A broad strip of sand protruded from the sea all away around the cove, where olive trees and grass met the division between land and sea. Rusting vehicles left under one or two trees and occasional piles of empty boxes bleaching slowly over the years were mute reminders of nearby habitation. An earthen track led alongside the cove to the jetty, its far end disappearing into the trees where a metalled road began beyond green verges and high grassy banks. They had arrived. The scent of pine trees and grass penetrating their senses as flies began to probe the atmosphere in search of fresh pickings for the day. On the jetty empty boxes lay alongside, old fishing nets and the paraphernalia of a once tiny fishing community; now rusting gently into oblivion. Under the nearest trees were faded wooden racks where equally ancient water-scooters were stored in the shade. Patches of oil added to the rich aroma of tarred wood, wild sage and the smell of the light dusty earth. Twice more they had sent out the interrogative transponder pulse. The first one drawing a blank, like others before it. As they proceeded up the coast within the bay, just before they turned her in towards the little harbour they sent another one. A clear signal was received by the sensitive transponder array high up at the top of their stubby little mast. Committed to the turn they calculated the need to close in on the signal and balancing the need to maintain discreet presence the skimmer put in to the little haven with a monumental sigh of relief. For once things looked as though they were going ahead as planned.

Admiral Dunham had no way of knowing who or what had triggered his emergency locator. The injured marine acting as their guide since their exit from the scene of the forced landing, had spent many daylight hours working with it while they were holed up. Travelling by night he had guided them past checkpoints here and there. Ducking for cover as convoys and patrols came by. The Corporal openly admitting at the time that he knew who they both were, offering his services as a trained soldier of the sea and SBS Squadron member. The Admiral, ever watchful against the opportunistic and unwanted attentions of self-seekers had grudgingly accepted the man's logic when he had first received the offer of help. "Well Sir, it's like this." He had said pointing out the obvious. "And no disrespect to either of you, but how long do you think two middle-aged gentlemen without hunting or survival skills are going to make it out here? I've been out here for over a year and I can live undetected for months." The king nodded in silence in the gathering gloom on the airfield. The Admiral blustering somewhat, pointing out the plasti-cast on his left arm and the bandages on his leg. "That's a flesh wound some Turkish blighter gave me, and it's healing nicely thanks to the stuff the medics gave me, and my arm was due to have the cast taken off yesterday, but that's not going to hold me up." The king tactfully pointed out that technically the young Corporal was right to insist, and in any case they ought to be moving if they were going to escape at all.

He guided them through the fields and dusty tracks along the coast. Finding hideaways in barns or small field huts as they slowly trudged across country. The soft brown earth sometimes sandy sometimes not, appeared well cultivated and looked after. From time to time they were forced to make their way slowly through the hilly countryside in order to avoid settlements where large villages or industrial complexes increased their chances of detection. The first two days were hardest as the two older men began to show signs of fatigue in combination with wear and tear. Their shoes beginning to chafe and their inappropriate clothing beginning to make them itch as they sweated away the days under cover. Their resourceful guide stole boots and clothing for them, food from the fields and garden plots along the way. Water was a frequently needed commodity and he was reluctant to let anyone drink from the local streams for fear of chemical and organic contamination. The king snored loudly during the day sometimes requiring a discreet nudge when field workers came by. During the early evening on the second day of their march the Admiral asked him what he was intending to do and waited patiently for a reply. The Corporal's response was as simple as it was direct. "Get a boat and sail out of here." The Admiral pondered this knowing full well the potential loss of opportunity to save their country from the gathering wolves. "But." He added. "It's not for me to decide Sir. You tell me what you want to do and where you want to go and I will guide you." Came the simple offer. "What do you recommend asked the Admiral, we need to get the king home as fast as possible?"

"Sail across to Karitsa, just a couple of miles up the coast from there and hitch a lift on the old road to Larisa. There's an airfield at Larisa, but it's an old crossroads as well. When we get there we can take our chances at the airfield Sir, or if it doesn't work we can hitch down to Athens or take a transport, anything to get you to our Embassy down there." The Admiral pondered some more and agreed tacitly that it was a reasonable course of action to get to the town on the other side, but cast doubt on the success of getting on an aircraft at such a strategic airfield.

They waited two days before they could cross the narrow defile that separated the peninsular from the mainland of Halkidiki. At the bottom there lay a stinking canal through which small boats could navigate, mostly pleasure craft and the like. Soldiers guarded the only bridge across the gap, making it extremely difficult for them to move around. The rest was a

Godsend for the older men who had become acclimatised to several years of sedentary life behind desks and in comfortable drawing rooms.

The Squadron Leader who piloted their fated aircraft had given them a map, a spare compass and the location beacon. The map, he explained, would only give them outline information with key topographical and demographic information, since it was really an aviation map, although the presentation was more accurate than other forms of roadmap. Before he left them to supervise the unloading of the casualties he told the Admiral that he had been instructed to initiate matters by activating the beacon using the number code set up by pressing the miniature buttons on the unit. He gave the Admiral the ident code for the king's flight and asked the Admiral to restrict the use of the beacon to a few selected times during the day and night. In the dark neither of them could see that it had been damaged by the rough ride of the forced landing. Sometimes the Corporal would see the power indicator illuminate only to see it wink out as he pressed the transmit button. The first night by the bridge he offered to steal one from the Greek soldiery, but the king was a little against the idea of getting involved in any violent action if the Greeks put up any resistance. He could see the young Corporal was frustrated by this, and sought to mollify him by saying that if the Corporal was caught two VIPs would be hard put to it to do anything else, except to give themselves up. The Corporal had watched the narrows for long enough to know that few people came to their boats except the fishermen who parked their more powerful craft towards the entrances at either end, mostly at the western end of the canal. He selected a boat and during the night prepared it making sure it had a properly working set of oars and rowlocks. It was agreed that he would set up a diversion to distract the Greeks while the Admiral and the king ran down some greasy steps to the waiting boat below and rowed across to the other side. "But how will you get across?" The king asked. "I'll swim across once I've made my way back out of their way."

They had taken their time in getting across the narrow channel. Had anyone stopped them they would have passed for two old Greek gentlemen worn out by working the land sneaking back home after an illicit night's drinking with their pals in some off the beaten track taverna. As it was, Corporal Wesley gave them enough time to cross over and clamber along the other side to the western end to hide among the boats. He found the small wooden hut that the soldiers used for relaxation and to cook their rations. It was empty, but the fire had been banked up giving off an encouraging glow. Silently creeping in through loose boards at the back warped by years of sunshine and salted air. He fanned the burning embers until they became hot, placing a metal can among them into which he had poured some evil smelling turpentine. With watchful eyes he kept guard on the outside while fanning the flames with his good hand. He heard the turpentine beginning to boil and left the hut the way he came in. White fumes began pouring out of the top of the can wafting upwards in the heat thrown up by the fire. For several minutes the brew continued to fill the hut with its evil smoke until the spirit reached its flash point with spectacular results. There was no explosion or noise to speak of, just a quiet whoosh as the smoke laden air in the cabin ignited. The sudden flash of light drew the attention of all the soldiery who by now realised it was their tea hut that had caught alight. Panicking in case the owner would come out and beat them for turning his shed into a pyre, they rushed to put out the flames.

Making their way around the end of the canal they slipped unseen across the rocks and on to the dry earth of the fields skirting the houses there. Along the main road garages, restaurants and tavernas could be found. Here their enterprising escort nabbed food and soft drinks along the way. Sometimes a hotel would provide rich pickings. He surprised them all on their fourth night appearing in their hideout holding up three bottles of San Miguel in his hand, producing three donner kebabs from within his shirt. Sometimes there was no alternative except to climb back up the steep slope to where their little road met the highway where shear cliffs prevented any passage to all but the nimblest of goats. Pressing onwards down the peninsula the tourist traps became more frequent and although a seemingly endless source of plunder they also posed the greatest threat to their progress. Walking silently across the main road to the eastern side of the peninsula they discovered the old road following the coast. While the highway cut a more or less straighter, wider pathway across the higher lie of the land, they had the advantage of keeping to a much easier route and out of sight of the fast moving traffic. It was flatter and sometimes they walked next to the glimmering white sandy beaches while at other times the road meandered through the small villages perched between the rocky slopes and the sea. From time to time they would see other late night 'stragglers' wandering along the road, old couples out for a stroll, the occasional cyclist balancing old age and gravity in a slow dawdle, hovering between falling off in the white dust and catching their feet in the spokes. The king thought it fantastic that all they needed to do was grunt in reply when greeted by the friendly Greeks. As long as no one wanted a conversation they were safe.

Five kilometres north of Polychronos they had a serious run in with the authorities. Walking silently along a tree lined promenade dotted with tavernas bearing brightly coloured menu boards written in English, they were rounding a corner when a dog started barking at them. A Greek patrol came around the corner in the opposite direction before they had time to get out of sight. Quick as a flash their streetwise companion spoke to the Admiral in an over familiar voice. "Come on dad, how about some fish an' chips before we turn in? Granddad, how about you?" The shocked king almost lost control of his bladder when he realised the cheeky Corporal was addressing him in a far too far disrespectful manner! "Now look here!" He retorted, to be interrupted by no less a person than the Admiral. "Well, that's not too bad an idea. I must admit I could do with another beer before I, er, get me 'ead down..." the Admiral's voice trailing away as he tried to distract their utterly disgusted liege-lord. Actually realising that no common or garden Greek soldier could possibly tell a cockney accent from another. "Come on granddad." perked up the Admiral taking the king by the elbow. "Let's get some fish an' chips, or perhaps you'd prefer a just another beer to whet your whistle." The king stared helplessly at the Admiral as Corporal Wesley made way for them, then at Wesley as the Admiral led him resisting somewhat, up the short terracotta tiled stairway leading to the forecourt of their chosen eatery. "Beer, have you gone mad?" stammered the king. "I don't... oh dear." He paused, catching sight of the advancing soldiers and understood their dilemma. "Well I suppose a beer would go down very nicely, thank you." They sat down at a table next to the street behind a low patio wall. The king looked at his feet while the Admiral stared out to sea wishing he were as small as a sand hopper, while Corporal Wesley grabbed the menus passing them around. "You tried that Greek salad yet granddad?" He asked the king impertinently, secretly beginning to enjoy his new found acting ability. "It's really very nice. Here, I'll get the waiter. Garcon! I say in there. Garcon! Service!"

The soldiers' voices could be heard as they spoke among themselves. The rhythmic beat of their footsteps an ominous tattoo as they walked closer and closer. A waiter appeared looking completely amazed. "Hello, Sir." He said in a guttural voice. We close in ten minutes, it's curfew in haff an 'our."

"You take plastic?" Wesley proffered a credit card and waved under the waiter's nose.

"Yes Sir we do, but we close in ten minutes." The waiter replied flatly. "Curfew comes in haff an our."

"Can you give us fish and chips to take away please?" Insisted Wesley.

"Oh, OK, you want take away, here, look at the take away menu pleeze." The waiter took the menu from Wesley turned it around and gave it back to him showing the relevant details of the take away menu. The soldiers drew opposite, somebody laughed and one of the soldiers stopped to lean over the low wall. "Hey English, you'd better hurry up its curfew in half an hour!"

"Yeah, OK, thanks!" Replied Wesley. You guys want a beer?" He offered. The king shuddered slightly, quietly passing wind as the Admiral, with eyes bulging tried to look at the menu while a burning sensation tore at his bladder like a thousand pound pressure hose about to explode. "Where's the toilet please?" Whimpered the Admiral who tore off into the indicated direction inside the establishment. "No, not tonight English. Thank you." The man's voice trailed away into the darkness as he caught up with his companions.

The waiter carried on totally unaware of the hidden drama lying beneath the veil of British urbanity. The king fidgeted uneasily as they ordered different foods and some bottles of water. He looked relieved when the Admiral returned looking much better. "Might I make the suggestion Sir that we avail ourselves of the washing facilities, it has been sometime since any of us have used any, and I think you will find it most refreshing."

"A good idea." commended the king, finding the power of his speech returning. "We have placed our orders, so you might like to place your own. I won't be long." The Admiral settled into his chair saying. "That was very cool behaviour on your part Corporal Wesley. I can't say how much I appreciate your ability to blend in. Well done."

"Thank you Sir, all in a day's work."

In fifteen minutes they left the taverna to the cheery farewells of their host, hugging their meals as they walked uneasily to the end of the promenade, vanishing in the comforting shadows once more. Five minutes later they climbed the steep road leading away from the beach towards the highway. An army truck sped by going north as they crossed the road into a sandy gully between tall rushes on either side. The soft sand underfoot deadening their footsteps while the dense growth quickly blanketed all sounds from the road. They walked in silence for a while, following the meandering gully until it widened out into a very wide track between deeply gouged banks of brown-black sun-baked earth. In the gloom small groups of buildings appeared surrounded by olive trees and outhouses. About two kilometres further on they found a workman's hut on a raised plateau of dry earth tucked into a dark hedge. Wesley handed the Admiral his food and worked his way around the hut in an ever-decreasing spiral until he was satisfied that there was no one nearby or indeed, anyone else inside it. They crawled into the hut and made do with what they could find. The fitful moon light occasionally lighting up the hut without penetrating the gloom. Wesley found some old sacking and draped it across a large hole in the front of the hut. The only sounds being made were the chomping of their jaws as they ate the food hastily prepared for them by the little taverna.

The king refused to move at first telling them that he had had enough excitement for one night. After a while he relented and making their way back to the road the two older men waited until Wesley crossed over and checked out the streets on the other side. A truck roared around the bend from the south and they watched it heading north past the bus stops, straight across the road junctions without stopping, receding into the far distance. Halfway down the street they had clambered up only an hour before they turned off to the right back onto the old coast road. Having cleaned themselves up at the taverna they felt much better with a stiff evening breeze keeping the cloying heat off their oppressed senses. They trudged silently past houses large and small, surrounded by low walls and railings fronting well manicured gardens and shrubs. A few lights peeked out from behind storm shutters telling them which houses were occupied and those that were not. So it was that tripping up in the occasional pothole and covered in dust they emerged on the outskirts of the next village. The sound of a vehicle coming towards them made them jump and seizing the opportunity Wesley shepherded them into some scrubland alongside the road. In the gloom he could see the vehicle coming and crouched down in the burned grass as it passed by slowly. It stopped a few yards away waiting. Wesley heard a noise coming from behind and, signalling to his companions to lie flat, he rolled over lifting his head slowly until he could see above the grass. He froze. Sinking slowly to the ground he signalled for the other two to remain perfectly still and quiet. Two soldiers appeared at the end of a narrow track that ran all the way along the wall of a house bordering the scrub. Beyond them he could see a line of olive trees or acacia as the ground rose more steeply into the near distance. The soldiers approached talking among themselves. They heard the chink of metal rubbing against metal, the swish of uniforms as they brushed against the grass fronds. A greeting was made to someone in the truck, and lifting his head in the other direction Wesley saw the two men clamber into the back of it. He looked over to his right and observed another group of black shapes walking along the road towards the truck. 'Must be the night shift clocking off.' He persuaded himself hugging the ground.

Twenty minutes later they heard the lorry moving off. Wesley risked another look and for several minutes watched in silence, slowly moving his head from side to side, using the periphery of his vision where the eyes are more sensitive, scanning all directions for signs of patrolling soldiers. He imparted his strategy to the Admiral while at the same time gently nudging the inert body of his king who lay face down snoring gently into the dust. He went ahead up the incline along the wall. A dog barked somewhere nearby, but he continued padding along the dirt pathway in silence. The footpath led up to the main road again where on the other side he could see nothing but a vertical rock face cracked and pitted with age. To the south there seemed to be no break in the geological surroundings. About two hundred metres in the other direction he could see an entrance between two white pillars. He went as far as the entrance and in a brief shaft of moonlight saw a large wooden shack up on an escarpment under some trees. He looked at the establishment within the gates adorned in white and surrounded by more of the typically manicured Mediterranean gardens that they had passed earlier. Slipping in through the gates he half ran half walked to his left in a crouching gait up to a small tiled stairway leading to a pergola that stood above the level of the ground on a small mound. Looking up the slope he saw another block higher up the slope and a narrow gap between the side of the closest building and its boundary wall. It spoke 'trap' and he edged backwards towards the stairway. Cutting across the front of the gardens below the front entrance he saw the upper level shadows cast by an overhead canopy under which he found a veranda across the front leading around to the side of the house. He found the large swimming pool and skirting across the open space of its entrance began to make his way up the steep tarred driveway towards the tree-line.

Forty minutes after completing his reconnaissance of the area he returned to the lower scrub-land between the houses, and together with his charges, they retraced his steps onto the higher ground. The hut was partially hidden by tall sun-dried grass affording them some cover as they wove a path through the gnarled trees. Another shaft of moonlight broke through the nebulous clouds giving them a resplendent view overlooking the pool. Feeling hot and bothered it was quite natural for them to have the desire to go and bathe in the crystal clear waters.

By the time dawn streaked the clouds above a cold easterly wind sprang into life gradually lifting the surface of the deep blue waters of the bay into small white horses. At noon the wind was steadily beating across the road ruffling the water in the swimming pool below. A dog started barking somewhere near the house and a man appeared at the rear next to a steep loading bay leading an Alsation on a long lead. Wesley followed them with his eyes through a narrow gap in the planking as the man led the dog into a small white MPV, and clambering in after it drove off towards the south.

He caught a glimpse of a large sign at the front of the building, regretting his hasty decision to hide in their particular lodging. The Halkidiki Peninsular Hotel lay in full view below them with its neatly laid out gardens, primly edged pathways, and a sizeable swimming pool. Using his intensifiers he scanned the verandas and the dining room beyond the swimming pool. Two older teenaged boys emerged at half-past seven and began to hose down the terracotta tiles on the veranda floor, clearing away rubbish and detritus left behind by their dwindling number of guests. Eight rooms remained occupied by stubborn visitors, mostly British, as they determined that war or no war, they were going to finish their holidays one way or another! The white MPV returned with the man and no dog. The boys began unloading trays of food from the luggage compartment at the rear. The Admiral woke soon afterwards noting that despite the warmth in the hut he was beginning to feel the chilly drafts penetrating the knot holes and cracks in the wooden planking. He watched in silence as Wesley sneaked out of the hut heading for the dense undergrowth under the trees high up on the ridge behind the hotel, taking the transponder with him. The idea being that once on the higher ground any signal received from a search party's transmitter would stand a better chance of being detected by the small device. Promising to be back by midday he left them in the relative safety of the hut. Crawling and climbing he made his way over the fold in the hill to find a small level patch before the ground rose steeply again in another rocky outcrop. The air was a little warmer here as the combination of undergrowth, acacia and pine trees provided adequate shelter from the steady wind pushing upwards from the shoreline. A silence enveloped him as he padded along towards his goal.

The king awoke hungry and stiff from the previous night's excursion through the village. They lolled against the sides of the hut talking in low-pitched voices for about an hour. He brightened when the Admiral informed him that Wesley had gone to try out the little locator beacon promising to bring food and drink back with him. The Admiral shifted his vantage point so that he could take a look out across the bay. Passing slowly along the shore in front of them, about a mile out to sea, a huge galleon with its sails furled, and with the Jolly Roger flying from the masthead slid by without a sound. The brown-black hull trimmed with yellow paint, large square windows, and a classic fenestrated stern made him laugh softly. The king, being concerned for his welfare asked him if everything was 'alright'. The Admiral pointing to the crack in the wall of the hut invited the king to have a look. "I say, you don't suppose he wants to get us home in that do you?" queried His Majesty. The Admiral started to laugh and for a few moments they both 'lost the plot' as they giggled hopelessly at the thought.

The sound of approaching voices shut them up pretty quick. From somewhere down in the front came young voices talking. A man emerged on the veranda and shouting in their direction began a short conversation with the unseen people lower down the slope. The Admiral recognised the tones of a man shouting orders and unsure of the outcome felt obliged to ask the king to prepare for an immediate evacuation. Higher up on the escarpment hidden from their view, poked the green tiled roofs of a private house. The two boys emerging into view made a beeline for the hut. Following an almost invisible path in the long grass they walked past as the two occupants dithered inside. Their voices carrying across the short distance between them. One of them picking up a branch threw it angrily at the side of the hut making the king jump like a hare startled by a fox. The king slipped off-balance falling sideways grabbed out to hold onto something. There was a loud crash as the king and a large grass-cutter crashed to the floor of the hut. The king groaning rolled over rubbing his side. The boys looked at each other and ran over to the hut flinging the door wide open. In the bright sunlight that dazzled them the king and his escort lay momentarily blinded.

The boys who were almost as scared 'toughed' it out shouting at them in Greek which neither of the two men understood. "Do you speak English?" enquired the Admiral softly. One of the boys broke away from the door shouting urgently in Greek across the pool below to the hotel. The man appeared on the veranda demanding to know what the boy wanted in a strident voice. Disappearing into the house for a few moments he emerged trotting across the veranda with a shorter, burly individual in tow carrying a broom handle. More shouting across the pool as the men made their way around the front of the enclosure towards the near end. The Admiral stood up helping his majesty to his feet as he clutched his side. "You wait pliz, my father comes!" said the older looking youth. The Admiral nodded. "How bad is it Sir?" He asked the king softly. "Just a scratch I think, I winded myself more than anything else."

"What you doing here in my house, pliz?" asked the man bluntly. He was red faced with dark sun tanned skin beneath a short mane of greying black hair from beneath which he shot stern grey eyes.

High above them Wesley tinkered with the beacon jamming the case together and wrapping a loose wire across the small cell inside. He pressed the on button, but his thumb slipped with sweat releasing it almost immediately. "Damn!" He cursed his luck as he tried again in his precarious position perched halfway up a tall pine. This time balancing with his elbow hooked around a handy branch, pressing the button more firmly with his index finger. For a moment or two he could see nothing in the bright sunlight, but for a second or two he was sure the small display registered a 'hit'. Climbing down the side of the tall tree he moved along to another ridge across a small dell. Just below the high grass he caught sight of a wide un-metalled road winding its way up the slope towards a flat area among more pines and bushes. Looking back he caught occasional glimpses of the bay behind him. Making the topmost part of the high ground he saw the dark blue of the distant sea in front of him. It could only be the Gulf of Salonika. Passing between the pines draped occasionally with plastic bags into which resin oozed he climbed onto a small platform of rock, and with a hopeful wish pressed the on button once more. The small sounder beeped twice indicating a received signal from a distant transmitter. Looking up into the face of it as he held it aloft he watched despairingly as the power indicator rapidly ran down to zero, whereupon the small display panel went completely blank. Noting the time he stared at it for a few seconds before switching it off and stowing it haphazardly into a small shoulder bag. Carefully retracing his steps he made his way along the ridge and back down towards the Halkidiki Palace Hotel. Up here bees buzzed in the warm air and the open spaces on the top of the peninsular beckoned to the heart of an outdoorsman. He scratched idly at the skin of his forearm just poking out from the top of his cast as sweat ran into the mildly chafed skin, mentally working out his next moves to 'acquire' provender for himself and his distinguished companions.

The Admiral and the king were escorted from their hideout to the side door on the veranda. The man told his two younger escorts to stay with the two interlopers while he went away inside the dining room. Crossing the white marble floor he became distracted by a deep resonant voice of a woman to the accompaniment of her sandals slapping against the stone floor. A plump woman of a certain age and with a classic pageboy fringe fronting short black hair appeared as he motioned her to follow him. Nico spoke rapidly to her in his native tongue as they emerged onto the veranda pointing at the two senior gentlemen standing against the low wall of the patio. She looked at the two dishevelled men looking as if they had spent a night on the tiles, covered in flecks of straw, streaked with dust and looking very sorry for themselves.

"My husband says the boys found you up in our shed?" She asked in a rich mellow American voice, with more than just a hint of 'east-coast' –possibly New Hampshire bur. The Admiral nodded. "I'm afraid we were."

"OK, you guys in some sort of trouble maybe?" She asked pragmatically looking directly at the Admiral then shifting her gaze onto his quiet companion. "Yes, we, er, had an accident and lost our way looking for help…"

"An accident you say?" She interrupted staring intently at the silent one.

"Are you both OK, I mean, is there anything we can do?" She asked turning to look at the Admiral with equal intensity. " Er, no, there's three of us and our driver, er my son has gone to look for help."

"I see." She said with a deep furrow forming down her forehead. She was being bugged by something and didn't like being lost like that. "Say, do you want to clean yourselves up a little bit, you look kind of messed up." Nico looked on passively, following the conversation in English a lot better than he could speak the language itself. His wife Bronwyn, pointed to the older man's shirt where flecks of blood mapped the contours of an ugly wheal beginning to show where the blood was welling through broken skin. "Do you need to go to hospital with that?" She asked the king who inadvertently rubbed it with the palm of his hand, wincing as he did so. Bronwyn went white as the king sat down on the wall, for despite several days of growth she recognised his famous head through the stubble.

That's what was bugging her, she didn't know who he was, but knew he was famous. Turning to Nico and his three companions she gave rapid directions. Nico questioned her twice and then escorted the two men inside the hotel passing through the bright dinning room into the wide lounge beyond. The youths and the other man with the broomstick went their separate ways. A few guests were milling around the reception talking to the concierge, while two others sat in the porch waiting for their lift into the village. Bronwyn spoke to the young girl behind the counter who quickly rummaged for two keys, and hardly stopping at all she led them up a short flight of steps into a cool dark corridor. The king was ensconced in room 8 while the Admiral was put in a room opposite across the corridor. After quickly showing them their rooms she left them to get on with their ablutions, promising a late breakfast would be ready for them in an hour. Walking behind the highly polished marble counter she called out to her husband who was hosing the geraniums in the flowerbeds and pots just outside the front door.

"Alex, you take the guests in to Polychronos. Nico, I want a word with you!" Nico turned off his hose and came inside. Alex appeared from behind the double doors leading to the dinning room and caught the keys belonging to the MPV that Bronwyn threw at him.

The guests rose from their seats following Alex down the steps to the MPV parked outside. A heavy truck roared past on its way north as a small group of cyclists shouting gaily at one another headed south, turned down the narrow footpath towards the old road at the bottom of the hill. The guests had left the entertainment screen switched on in their haste to get into the MPV ahead of the crowd in order to get good seats. Bronwyn's first reaction was to have called the police, but the two old men did not look the 'type' to be of any bother. 'Still." She thought. "There is the accident, perhaps they should be told?" She decided to wait until the foundlings or the younger man's son could tell them where their car was before doing anything, otherwise it would look a little weak.

Nico rustled up some breakfast while Bronwyn helped the receptionist Anita with the paperwork. Nico's sister appeared with a tray of coffee cups, leaving one on the counter for the receptionist she and her sister in law went up the short stairway and into the bar overlooking the lounge. Sitting in their favourite place by the back door she confided in 'nita that she thought one of the strangers was quite famous. Anita who had not seen them was not convinced and said that she would wait until they emerged. Bronwyn sat smoking and listening while her eyes wandered, as a woman's eyes always do, over the furniture noting the papers strewn on the settees and coffee cups left on the various tables. As she prepared to get up and work through the lounge with 'nita her attention was caught by a news flash on the video channel. Although the sound was turned off she could make out the large lettering at the bottom of the screen as a news announcer silently made his announcement. 'English king dies'. Her hand flew to her mouth and grabbing the controller she turned up the sound to listen, hissing at 'nita to be quiet.

Her heart went to the pit of her stomach. 'It's him!' She screamed inside herself. 'It's the king of England here in my hotel!' Anita clucked quietly in her chair beside Bronwyn as the news story unfurled. "Oh God!" She groaned. "How awful!" Anita shook her head muttering something sad in her own language. 'Oh, that's the other man with him!' Good lord he's an Admiral of the goddamned fleet!' She jumped up from her seat shaking her head, walking along the bar to the steps; she crossed the lounge taking a closer look at the pictures on the screen. The propaganda story told them that the king of England had been killed while trying to flee the British Isles. Pictures of a salvage vessel flashed across the scene hoisting wreckage out of the sea. However, no details of where or when this was supposed to have happened were given.

Alison Railton walked through the doors of the hotel during the second wave of announcements pausing between the threshold and the counter as her ears pricked up on news from home. Her green uniform trimmed in peach matching her uniform blouse accentuating her shapely figure as she turned to face the view screen up on the wall in a corner. Standing in silence Allison had a sense of foreboding for her family and friends back home. She promised herself that as soon as the current tour was over she would take the British Consulate's advice and leave the country before either the Turks or the Albanians invaded. "I'm so sorry." She said involuntarily, turning to greet Allison. Allison stared back not knowing what to say. Just stood there shaking her head slowly from side to side. They heard quiet footsteps coming down the stairway and turning instinctively all three women gazed at the innocent faces of the king of England and his escort Admiral of the Fleet Peter Dunham. With eyes popping out of her head Allison slid onto the floor as she fought to stop herself fainting. Nico, who had been leaning against the dining room doorframe looked from the viewer to the men and back again, rushed over to catch the girl before she banged her head on the cool marble floor. The king smiling bleakly watched the remainder of the news flash as the Admiral stood woodenly by his side. As the moment passed and noting that everyone was looking directly at him he began by announcing. "News of my death, it seems, has been greatly exaggerated!"

"So it is you!" said Bronwyn in her deep voice. Anita smiled a kindly smile towards the king and speaking softly to Bronwyn she gave a timid curtsy pulling gently on Bronwyn's elbow. "Oh yeah." She said, nodding her head deferentially remembering her manners. Nico stood there open mouthed holding up the dizzy Allison in his arms.

"So my Lord. What can we do to assist you." announced Nico in his best English.

"Nico," said the king with a pleasant smile. "A little of your breakfast would be an honour to my empty stomach."

They patiently waited on their celebrity guests, and somewhat conspiratorially, they asked to speak with both men after breakfast. Bronwyn jabbered away urgently in Greek to Nico and Anita behind the closed door of the small kitchen. Telling them to keep quiet, surmising that if it was an assassination plot gone wrong it would be best for them to keep quiet about their visitors and help them on their way. Allison sat slumped in one of the chairs sipping spring water out of a bottle. Eventually plucking up the courage to enter into the dining room and speak to the king. She apologised profusely before offering her services by way of her network of friends and contacts to help in any way possible. They saw the point about transport and agreed that her new knowledge of the roadblocks and checkpoints would be most helpful. She nearly laughed when they told her their plans to sail across the gulf and make for the airfield or Athens, noting that without passports they stood every chance of getting shot. She offered them a chance to catch a boat to Crete where it would be safer for them to make an attempt to get back home. Either that or she would try to smuggle them back onto the mainland and onto a charter flight back home.

By that time the Pastouris family had rejoined them in their discussions kindly offering the use of their large van in which Nico and Alex ran back and forth to Thessalonika for provisions. Nico got up and closed the door as the noise made by the boys cutting the grass began to drown out the conversation. Ever practical Bronwyn announced that several British guests still remained at the hotel, observing that so far the security of their guests remained within the family and with Allison. "What about Aphrodite?" Asked 'nita quietly. "She can't go home until we're sure she won't talk." Bronwyn translated the question following it up with rapid Greek to Nico. Anita ushered in the receptionist through the glass doors, bidding her to be seated next to Bronwyn. Looking timid and a little nervous she listened intently while shooting glances at the king. She brightened visibly on being told that she could stay overnight in one of the small rooms. The final arrangements ensured that both men would use their private apartment at the back of the hotel while other guests remained in the hotel. Otherwise they were free to use the facilities with the discretion that their current situation allowed for.

Wesley returned in the early afternoon to the surprising picture of the king and the Admiral sitting by the side of the pool. He knew something was amiss long before the hotel came into view when he sniffed the air laden with pollen, straw, wild sage and freshly mown grass. He guessed it was serious, particularly when he saw the grass had been cut. Somewhat relieved, he remained cautious to the last, worming his way as close as he could get before sauntering out into the sunlight wearing a pair of red overalls that he borrowed from the washing line at the back door of the hotel. "Everything alright Sir?" He muttered as he walked past them. "Come and sit down Corporal Wesley." Said the Admiral politely while the king grinned mischievously at him over the top of a magazine. "Well, I can't say that I don't need a bath and some decent food Sir." Was all he said feeling slightly miffed, and after a polite pause he brought his news about the transponder working and its activation by a distant transmitter using the special ident code. "There's no doubt about it Sir, someone is looking for you. The signal was fairly strong, but the power has run down, so I need to get replacement power cells for it." The Admiral excused himself taking Wesley into the hotel to introduce him as their 'assistant'. Following the scam of the previous night they kept up the conspiracy that they were father, son and grandfather on a family 'bender' for the week. Allison had driven back to her office in Thessalonika to prepare duplicate papers giving them false identities and addresses. Since Wesley was far from famous he was given one of the free rooms downstairs along with the other two and could use the hotel lounge without restriction.

The cold breeze became stronger as William, Sub and Leyland with two of his engine room boys walked up the steep road past large houses built into the steep cliffs. The road snaking around in narrow curves before joining the main road. The road signs were a little confusing showing Golden Beach to the south, Polychronos and Zafira to the north several kilometres away. Wearing the regulation uniforms of the ESNF they waited until a passing army lorry and escort vehicle came around a bend in the road, heading north. The NCO driver of the escort greeted them with a smile asking them in broken English what they were looking for. He was quite concerned that their ship had broken down and agreed to take them to the small harbour twenty kilometres along the road. In fact he offered to be their driver and told them he was on patrol for the next twelve hours. He was bored and could do with some action he said. Looking at their ID cards briefly he waved them into his vehicle. Squeezing into the narrow seats they watched in silence as they drew away from the little cove. The Sargent having struck up a conversation, chatting continuously to William as they bowled along the highway. At noon they drove past Polychronos where the highway skirted the large village on their way to Zafira. It was comforting that they were waved through roadblocks and checkpoints at major intersections without much more than a cursory glance. Slowing down as the highway took them through Zafira, the lorry behind them turned off at the traffic lights. The sailors casting casual glances at the empty tavernas, restaurants and bars along the pavements. They continued for a kilometre until the next set of lights where the driver turning right headed for the sea. Following a couple of quiet back streets he took them to a small boatyard.

Leyland sighed inwardly gazing across the small yard littered with rusting machinery and ancient mono-hulls peeling in the sun. The soldier led them through a building to the other side of the boatyard where, on a wide concrete slipway, stood five large 'booze-cruisers' in various states of repair. 'This is much better.' Thought Leyland as they went through a 'pretence' for something like forty-five minutes to an hour's worth of sorting through engine parts. They decided to have lunch in one of the back street bars rather than risk the establishments on the main road where passing patrols may take an interest in their uniforms. Back at the boatyard they continued their search for the 'right parts' while the rest of them went walkabout looking for alternative transport. They found an old pick up at the back of the yard and after a little haggling with the owner they had themselves a deal. Leaving Leyland and his crew to faff around they headed back to the main road crossing at the intersection towards the hills above the town. Passing by the almost empty bars a second time where they stared back at a few old men seated at tables. Ancient shepherds and mariners playing chess and drinking ouzo, while their womenfolk dressed in black, stumbled around the shops wearing headscarves tightly knotted under their chins to keep out the gusting north-easterly wind sweeping the dust into miniature whirlwinds around them.

Sub activated the transponder once they had gained the relative seclusion of the upper road running between tall pines. They could see the Sithonian peninsular behind them to the east and woods and trees around them to the west. "Got it!" hissed the Sub. "Let me see!" demanded William snatching the hand-held device ungraciously from his hand. It's a very strong signal, they can't be that far away." Handing it back to the Sub he made a mental note of the estimated range and bearing. "About twenty kilometres south of this position." the Sub observed getting rattled at his superior's lack of manners. "Right Sub let's continue in this direction for a while and take another fix." Sub waved on and their driver duly drove off heading towards the top of the peninsular in a westerly direction. Turning and twisting, the road defying both the geology and the lie of the land led them through small hamlets, past lonely houses and alongside farmyards where no one was to be seen. At a quarter to five he activated the transponder again looking at the display. For a moment or two nothing happened, then it lit up dimly as a received signal produced a second location. "Got it," confirmed Sub triumphantly -this time holding firmly onto the box. He took a chart out from under his tunic and recalling the two signals from the device's memory plotted the lines until they intersected with each other.

From his perch above the hotel Corporal Wesley snapped the new cells into his hand held beacon switching it on as soon as he closed the case. Although cracked and now on its 'way out' as a serviceable unit the display indicated an interrogation pulse had been received with an alarmingly strong signal. Shuffling carefully down the dusty slope covered in thistles and scrub that snagged on the skin of his bare legs, he headed for the hotel careful not to draw too much attention to himself, even though, he was a 'normal' guest –to all intents and purposes. His story was quite plausible, someone taking a break while recovering from a couple of nasty injuries. He enjoyed the pleasant company of the English guests, looking forward to having a drink at the bar with Bronwyn as evening fell. If he was curious about her knowledge and wanted to find out as much as he could about how to get off the peninsula, she was equally curious about them being in Greece, and not actually dead as reported on the world news.

The friendly Greek family owned and managed the hotel, kept a spotlessly clean and comfortable establishment. Bronwyn dealt mostly with their English-speaking guests while sometimes it was a team effort to handle the Poles and other nationalities coming from central Europe. "Tomorrow the wind will get better and we will have good weather for at least two or three weeks." Nico had commented seated outside the back entrance to the bar. The other guests had thinned out as the majority either walked into Polychronos or waited on the steps for Alex to drive them in the MPV. The wind had indeed died down with the evening air becoming warm and scented once again. Sitting under the shadowy eaves with just the lights from the bar inside glowing dimly outside helping to diffuse the image of a family gathering sitting in the gloom without disclosing to the casual eye any hint of their facial identities. Nico had pulled the plug on the viewer so nobody could see the news, having stuck a notice across the screen written in the style in which he spoke his English; 'No TV She is broke' and everyone left it alone. They chatted quietly as the Admiral and Wesley sought the answers to many questions about where they were and the chance of either borrowing or hiring a boat that could take them to the mainland. They paused as an army transport sped past the entrance to the driveway of the hotel carrying the hunched forms of a patrol, presumably on their way south to take up their night's duties, the whine of its engine decaying into a distant drone over the night air.

Wesley had left the beacon turned on after advising the Admiral that it was probably the best way of monitoring their current situation. "After all Sir." He said with sensible logic. "Whoever it is knows the restricted code and is careful enough not to broadcast the locating beam very often. I think that could mean they are likely to be 'friendly' Sir." The Admiral agreed and during the early hours of the evening while both he and the king enjoyed the meal set before them of Greek salad, fish, boiled potatoes and green beans. Wesley sat quietly by the bar with the tiny hand held wrapped in a pullover on the table in front of him. Nico spoke of a small boat on the way down to Golden Beach as he handed him a beer. "There's a small harbour there and the Captain." He smiled. "Is quite eccentric, they all call him the crazy Captain, but he's a good seaman. Maybe he can take you if he is not now called to the navy." Wesley drained the bottle Nico had just given him. "You want another one?" asked Nico.

"Oh yeah." Bronwyn chimed in. "He's got a small ferry, used to be a time when it ran between the islands, now he uses it for tourist trips across the bay. We could certainly try to find him." Wesley got up and went to the bar as Bronwyn went to fetch another beer from the cooler. "Boy you must be really thirsty!" He nodded sitting down on one of the tall bar stools. They started chatting amiably about this and that until eventually the king and the Admiral joined them and began to press Nico and Anita for other information. "So you're a Marine, huh?" Bronwyn asked him casually. "Yes, 'fraid so, a Royal Marine."

"Oh." She smiled at him. "A 'Royal' Marine, sorry I didn't realise the distinction." She said innocently. They talked about family back home and general topics, but inevitably returning to the current situation in Europe and at home in England and in Greece.

He discovered that her old man was a submariner and they both drank a toast to the 'silent service'. They agreed the Union was beginning to make it hard for ordinary folk to live. Where once people could look forward to a better hope for the future; better education, healthcare, job prospects and a wider share of the benefits the union offered. It had passed its effectiveness as more and more meaningless legislation and taxation burdened them in Greece as much as it did in England. Perhaps with less hopelessness in Greece, where the people had not been out of touch with the land or lost the knowledge of how to look after themselves. He told her that in the UK, millions of people of all ages felt trapped in a 'system' that promised much, took everything, but gave very little in return when it came to honouring pledges. She talked about the orthodox division of Greece and how, at the insistence of the Commission, the European Parliament had been forced to raise sanctions against Greece who refused to accept the authority of the Catholics who the Commission had appointed to be the representative religious body for Europeans. Where Bronwyn sympathised with the Orthodox rebuff on the grounds that it was they who had founded or 'planted' the early church in ancient Rome. Wesley pointed out the only true reason for doing this was for power, adding that the union had adopted the German government's habit of taxing the people with a church tax that officially was split evenly between the recognised religious groups. However, in reality they made a good 'screw' out of administering the funds before it ever got to the registered organisations. Bronwyn never realised, commenting that 'they wouldn't get away with it back in the US because it was 'unconstitutional' among other things. They chatted until about a quarter to nine when the phone rang in reception.

Anita padded over and picked up the phone responding in a rapid high-toned voice to the caller. She called Bronwyn over, looking concerned, darting glances in the direction of their guests. "OK, now we have a little problem." She announced as they watched her walk back across the bar. "That was the Poseidon and they're telling me the soldiers are going through the hotel checking all the guests out, and if they are not at the hotel they are checking their registrations and identities, you know passports and stuff."

"Oh, dear" groaned the king softly. "I fear we have brought you nothing but trouble." They quickly denied that and imparted their plan to overcome the 'local difficulty' while Nico fetched the MPV from the side of the house. With Anita standing by the phone the party of fugitives sat in the van waiting. Alex sat in the driver's seat as Nico explained in his Pidgin English what they were going to do. The family owned another hotel a few miles down the road above Polychronos. They would wait until the concierge telephoned them to let them know when the soldiers had driven out through the gate of the hotel. Alex would then drive them in the opposite direction and take them to the hotel where they would 'hide' until it was safe to return. The phone rang twice, but each time after a heart-stopping dialogue nothing happened. Finally it came, and Alex drove out of the gates heading south. About halfway to their temporary address they saw the small convoy of two MPVs heading their way and watching them covertly held their breath until they passed. In the distance behind them another military vehicle appeared, approaching at high speed.

William sucked his teeth in frustration as yet another 'trip' along the highway brought meagre results. Sub was sure the signal had come from just outside Polychronos, but according to his own reckoning it was far more likely to be somewhere nearer the town centre. The NCO driver was getting tired and in order not to raise any suspicions they asked if he could let them off at the exit road leading down to the harbour. Having built up a good speed along the straight section of road the last thing any of them wanted to do was to become stuck behind some slow MPV. Pulling out after the patrol had passed them going in the other direction, they overtook the MPV and it load of passengers. "Bloody tourists." Muttered William as the NCO smiled thinly. "They bring good money Sir." He observed. "Without tourists we would not have much to live on." Wesley took a peek at the passing vehicle noticing the occupants wore blue shirts and black berets instead of army fatigues. Alex waved at the driver as the military MPV overtook them. His friendly gesture acknowledged by a wave from the NCO. Roaring past them as they approached the Poseidon's gates Alex slowed turning off the highway, onto a steep driveway that zigzagged up the escarpment through terraced lawns edged with flowerbeds and lofty pines. They stopped off to one end of the building clambering out of the van from where they were politely ushered into a roomy basement beneath the long stairway that led to the main entrance above them.

Back onboard Royal Oak the duty hands were preparing to slip and make way for Thessalonika. When they compared their bearings with those taken onboard by the comms unit on the bridge they were amazed to find the crosscut of the last signal was only a few kilometres away. "They have got to be moving around Sir." Insisted the Sub. "It stands to reason, that all the time we were getting a transponder signal strength of 3 while we were roaming the hills this afternoon, by this evening we found the signal to be strength five in the vicinity of Polychronos."

"No more time Sub." responded Chip shaking his head slowly. "We must be in Thessalonika by midnight or face the prospect of waiting there indefinitely if the Greeks use our late arrival as an excuse to renegotiate the hand-over of casualties." Chip caught William casting a furtive look at the equipment room door and turned away speaking with a hard edge to his voice. "We must not risk losing our arrival time or blowing our cover here. "Thank you gentlemen, that will be all."

"Sir, have you got a minute?" Chief Grey emerged from the equipment room holding something small and black in his hand. "William stood over the other side of the bridge in silent alarm when he realised what was coming. They went back into the equipment room where the gadget whiz kid showed him the little black box that William had secreted at the back of one of the cabinets. "I found it back there, Sir during one of the maintenance routines. It passed the diagnostics without being detected, but when I carried out a physical check as required for a loop-back test I found this dangling behind it." Chip looked hard and cold under the dim lighting of the equipment room. Walking back to the door he turned up the lights and walking back to the centre of the compartment he took the box from Chief Grey's hands. "Any idea what it is?"

"No Idea Sir, I don't even know what it does." Chip looked at it closely fingering the short flat cable dangling from one end. "Show me where you found it?" Together they peered into the cabinet where the Chief pointed to the back of the equipment rack. "What does this equipment do ordinarily?" Asked Chip rather more abruptly than he had intended to. "It's the radar processor. It takes the raw sensor signals and processes them into computer format before distributing it to all of the sensor and tactical displays as normalised video input."

"Can you be a little less technical Chief?"

"Sorry Sir, it converts the raw radar and transponder signals into computer signals that gives us our navigation and tactical plotters the data they need to have in order to navigate and to visualise the tactical solutions required for weapons, and so on."

"Could this interfere with that capability?"

"I don't know Sir. It could do. What it means to me is that an unauthorised piece of equipment has been placed in this equipment room without my knowledge."

"Quite." Said Chip as the discovery threatened to unsettle him. "Is there any possibility that it could be a locator of some kind?"

"You mean such as a beacon telling people where we are like that submarine?"

"You're very astute Chief." Chip said clenching his teeth.

"It could be Sir, the other single lead coming out of the side was connected to our transponder, but as far as I know the transponder has been working without a hitch." Chip stopped in thought for a moment. "What kind of signal does it produce I wonder, any idea?"

"None, it's a complete mystery."

"Right, this what I want you to do Chief. Try and get it working and see if you can analyse the output signal. If I understand you correctly that box of tricks takes our received signals and transmits something up the spout, yes?"

"Could be Sir."

"That doesn't sound too good Chief, please keep this conversation between ourselves. I will inform the first lieutenant and I hope to have your report as soon as you can work out what it does. Thank you Chief."

Chip returned to the bridge in time to overhear a discussion concerning the transponder beacon. "We've received another signal Sir, full scale, indicating they are within five to ten kilometres range."

"Sub, do you reckon you can put that cross-cut precisely on the ground?" As the young Sub opened his mouth the transponder alarm on the tactical display went off and leaning over it they could all see the locating beacon had been switched on and left on." At last!" said Fred with a great feeling of relief. "It has to be them, nobody else would be that cautious."

"The bearing cuts across the highway here with our last cross-cut indicating that they are close to the highway by Poly, er, 'Poly-whatsitsname'."

"How far is that?" Asked Chip "About six kilometres Sir." reported William.

"Where's that nice Greek Sargent of ours?" Chip enquired pleasantly. "He's in the Senior Rates mess having a pint and an oggy." Replied the techno-whiz with a sly grin. "We couldn't exactly send him home on an empty stomach."

"Can you ask him to come and see me, I'd like to thank him personally for the tremendous help he has been to us, and Chief, on the way up sound him out to see if he will do another quick favour for us, will you?"

"A Pleasure Sir." The Chief disappeared down the flat into the accommodation. "Sub I want you to take Chief White and a couple of the hands and go directly to that point on the map, no messing about, ask that Greek driver of yours to take you to precisely that spot and go and find out who or what is there. You have until half-past ten. When we sail, with or without you. Is that clear?"

"Yes, Sir."

"Engines, can we comfortably make fifty five knots or more if we need it Leyland?"

"Not a problem Sir, if anything our mad dash the other night blew away some of the cobwebs and those little beauties are humming like a bowl of custard on bed of ice-cream."

"Quite," Grinned Fred "I'll have to try some of that one day."

"Right, we all know what we have to do?" Everyone nodded "Guns, I want to see you in my day cabin in twenty minutes so that we can go over the magazine audit."

"Yes, Sir."

"Right let's get to work everybody, we slip at twenty-two hundred precisely!"

Venus Theodrakkis was a beautiful young woman of twenty-seven. She often slipped down to the boat to get away from the empty house when her papa was away. Sometimes her aunt would stay with her; sometimes she would be too busy to keep her company. Venus was a free spirit, adventurous, gifted with a quick mind and a warm sense of humour, but careful to have kept her virginity through three tempestuous relationships. She spurned her suitors much to the annoyance of her mother when she was alive, and to her father's despairing soul, she had little time for the cultural excesses imposed upon her by her Greek heritage, despising those who kow-towed to the traditional place and behaviour imposed upon them. Her suitors wanted her for their own selfish reasons expecting her to accept their physical advances while at the same time expecting her to be the submissive and dutiful woman during their courtship and subsequent marriage. She was sure life was too short to be told what to do because it had always been done by countless numbers of other young women over the centuries. She had been standing in front of the long mirror in the small cabin admiring her body after a nice warm shower. Her jet-black hair falling over a pair of flashing grey eyes, draped over the pale olive skin of her shoulders down to the middle of her back as she had dried herself off. Her breasts firm and gentle not flopping about like some of the women her age. Patting her flat tummy and thankful that her careful diet and regular exercise had kept her slim and attractive. She had been startled when Royal Oak swept slowly into view that morning, and hid while the apparently large vessel entered the tiny harbour executing an effortless turn before tying up at the end of the jetty. Quickly dressing, filling her bra with her ample bosom, she moved around the upper cabin and wheelhouse crouching down, occasionally peeking over the bottom of the windows to see what was going on. She watched slightly puzzled as a small group of sailors walked down the jetty to the road nearby, catching their voices on the wind as they passed down the side of her father's boat. At first she didn't understand what they were saying, but when she spied the small flash of a national flag on the shoulder of one of the sailor's uniforms she realised they were not Greek but British crewmen.

She was not sure of herself and wondered why it was she had decided to hide. Shortly before noon she reasoned that since it was her father's boat and her father's jetty she had every right to get up and walk out without feeling like a victim. Emerging from a wide teak door on the main deck Venus proceeded to the gangway and walked across to the jetty. Slowly at first, then more assertive in her posture as she walked towards the strange ship. She could hear the burr of machinery and the sounds of human activity onboard and drawing herself up to her full height she called out in the direction of the bridge. A noisy pump stopped somewhere inboard leaving her standing in near silence. Again she called, causing someone to poke a head out of a door in the side of the vessel's sweeping bridge. "Hello." She called out. "What are you doing here? This is my father's place. You must not stop here." She felt stupid when she realised this was a warship full of brawny sailors and she, a mere slip of a girl was telling them not to park on her father's jetty. A young sailor had appeared and told her he would get the Captain to speak to her. She waited patiently until two officers arrived and came on shore where she stood. They invited her onboard to explain, but she politely refused. The Captain looked quite young and good looking, but his first officer looking very distinguished with a touch of greying hair at the temples and wide shoulders spoke to her in such a way that made her heart miss a beat. They for their part behaved impeccably trying not to let their eyes stray too much for the young lady wore a pair of stretch-slacks and a close fitting sweater, clothes that displayed the fetching curves of her femininity with a casual grace. She could see that he deferred to the Captain from time to time, but she could also see he was the one who was the 'fixer' when he began discussing terms for a few hours anchorage until they could repair their engines. Venus liked the sound of his voice, and soon found her thoughts straying off the subject as Fred; that was his name; Fred began to talk of other things. She remembered telling them that her papa would be back later that evening or tomorrow morning, and that they could discuss berthing fees with him then. She dallied there talking longer than she had intended and walked away slowly turning around several times as she strolled along the jetty.

The big house stood among lofty pines and acacia on the edge of the cove. The undergrowth and high canopy serving to keep the old house cool under the protection of their shady boughs. Venus skipped up the short flight of stairs through the front door into shade of the hallway, moving quickly up the broad staircase, upstairs to her room she sat down in front of the dressing table mirror that had been her mother's and began looking into it deeply. Her aunt would be dropping by on her way to pick up her papa from Thessalonika and then they would know whether or not her father had been offered a commission in the Greek Navy. She knew it meant trouble for all of them if a war was started, but she had other things on her mind and was content to leave things as they were until the moment of truth. The afternoon passed slowly, as she moved around the cool interior of the house, not caring to feed the growing hunger as she went from room to room feeling a restlessness growing within her. At ten o'clock in the evening her aunt appeared in the company of her papa who greeted her warmly. She had dressed for the evening in a cool skirt and blouse with her hair tied back in a ribbon of deep blue with light blue stars dotted about along it. Auntie fussed about as Venus pestered her papa for news of the family in the city and waited just long enough for her questions to be answered before the big one. 'Yes!' She thought as papa told her that he had been offered a commission of Commander and was to report to the naval academy for refresher training in three days time. Not thinking about what she herself was going to do or how she would live without her papa to bring home an income. 'Still,' she thought, 'I've got my job at the apotheka and I'll be just fine.' Lost in her own thoughts as she and auntie prepared a late supper she suddenly remembered to tell her papa about the English boat tied up at the jetty. Her papa was quite concerned and leaving her with auntie strode off into the night carrying a powerful lantern.

Just as her father turned the bend in the road she remembered something rather important and telling auntie who was in the kitchen where she was going, off she dashed in pursuit of her sire, catching up with him a little under halfway around the cove to the jetty. The skimmer looked huge by comparison to the old ferry, but nevertheless its long, wide body and shallow draught belied its hidden strengths and speed. Together they hailed the bridge and William waved them onboard coming to greet them at the brow. He escorted them to the little wardroom where he left them with an old engineer who kept them amused with small talk until the Captain arrived. She heard her father refuse any commission for their use of his little jetty and duly obliged they were offered a drink, before parting company. Venus kept a lookout for the tall, distinguished officer, which meant she was not paying much heed to William, who was trying to ingratiate himself upon her. Venus remembered that the Captain of the boat had said they would be leaving soon to pick up survivors from Thessalonika. During a long conversation between her papa and the Captain the first officer came in and introduced himself cordially to his guests. She tried to be interested in talking to William, but all she could do was cast furtive glances at Fred. "Oh, by the way." suggested Fred at some point in time. "Maybe the Commander could help us Sir. It's just that I was looking at my watch and thinking of Sub. He should be here any minute, but if not…" He left the unspoken question to Chip.

The Commander was delighted to be able to help in the future and at twenty past ten both he and his daughter left the ship, Venus slipping her hand in the crook of papa's arm as they strolled along in the cool night air.

Sub was getting frustrated. The natives were giving him the run around, he was sure of that, but there was little he could do. Back on the highway they drove south again skirting the village and around the bend onto that straight section of road where the driver hammered the accelerator. It was five minutes past ten and they needed fifteen minutes to get back to the ship. They sped past one of those tourist hotels and as Sub turned to say something to his WO it suddenly dawned on him. "Stop here!" he had shouted at the driver who slammed on the anchors causing them to skid in a long squealing slide past the gates to the hotel. Inside the hotel Wesley picked up the sounds and assuming a shunt was imminent looked out across the lounge from the bar to the roadway through the far window. He saw an army MPV slide the full length of the high fence to a stop and then slowly reverse back towards the open gates. Without a moment's delay he disappeared into the rear of the hotel heading for the 'private lounge' upstairs.

Guiding the two older men through the trees up the slope to the escarpment at night was not so easy. He left them out of sight at the base of a gnarled old olive and headed back to the hotel for a 'look-see'. From the side of the hotel out in the shadows he crouched towards the back entrance to the bar and listened intently at what was going on. To his amazement he saw a British Sub-Lieutenant, Warrant Officer and two seamen talking to Bronwyn and Nico who were doing their best to disguise the fact that they knew English. 'So they weren't Greek Army then.' Thought Wesley and made one of the biggest decisions of his life. Bronwyn saw him approaching from across the reception as he walked the length of the bar. Wesley pointed to his shoulder indicating that he knew from the shoulder flashes the men wore that he knew what they were. "We er, have an English guest here he can talk to you." Bronwyn announced and indicated by pointing to the advancing figure of Wesley. "Are you having trouble gentlemen?" He asked, quietly enjoying his moment of anonymity without paying court to the stuff and nonsense of 'yes Sir, no Sir' every so often. Having once entered into a dialogue with the young Sub, he more or less attempted to engage with the WO who would have a more sensible demeanour, and what's more his eyes weren't so close together as the Sub's. "You're after a couple of old geezers, eh? They go AWOL or something?"

"No, they're relatives of our Captain who promised to drop in on them whenever he could."

"Oh, so you mean he's here now?"

"Yes, he asked us to look them up whenever we were passing by."

"Is yours a big boat then?" He asked knowing how the word 'boat' grated on the ears of just about every sailor from Portishead to Pernambuco and beyond. "Not that big actually, but she's nice and comfortable, like." Replied the WO. "It's just that they've been onboard before and liked it so much they, particularly the older gent, said that they'd love to come aboard anytime we were in the area. Have you seen them at all?"

"There's so many old Brits out here who have retired. Some of them might have moved down here recently. You can see them most evenings down in the square in one of the pubs or tavernas. "What's your boat called?" He said noticing how the Sub winced a little at the word 'boat'.

"Royal Oak."

"That's a nice name, where have you been then?" Wesley knew fine well that was not entirely a fair question, but he was very surprised at the frankness of the answer he got from the Sub. "We are on our way to pick up the survivors of a recent air-crash outside Thessalonika." Wesley almost flinched as he heard the news that meant his mates were being taken off back home. "You look as though you've been through the wars yourself?" Sub observed. "Oh, yes, came down here to get some convalescence." He paused momentarily. "You know, come to think of it I did see a couple of old geezers down in the village near to the old church on the beach. You wait here and I'll go and ask my Uncle Albert if he's seen them recently."

"If you wouldn't mind being quick we have to get back to our ship pretty sharpish?" urged the Sub.

Wesley raced upstairs out on to the back landing through the door and up to their hideaway under the trees. Arriving in a state of huffing-and-puffing he broke the news to the other two seated against an old olive tree. "Royal Oak!" The Admiral almost shouted while the king cheered softly. "Sir, we ought to be on our way."

"I totally agree with you. Thank you Corporal Wesley, you have done extremely well," said the king warmly, barely pausing for breath. Walking as fast they dared they followed their young guide back down the escarpment and into the back of the hotel. Walking carefully into the landing and silently down the stairs he paused at the heavy doorway at the bottom so the Admiral could poke his head around the door to look down the long passageway to the reception. Wesley suggested that they move around the side of the building out of the view of the guests while he manoeuvred the shore party back out towards the transport. "Sorry gents. "He grimaced with hidden glee at the prospect of what was about to happen. My uncle says he may have seen two older guys in the Poseidon taverna the other night. They may have been Brits because he noticed they were eating kleftico and chips." He grinned at them apologetically indicating that the shore party should accompany him, into the hotel.

The king and the Admiral stood quietly in the shadows under the roof of the patio from where they could watch the front door of the hotel and the army transport without being seen. As the shore party left by the steps Wesley smiled at Bronwyn and whispered 'thank you'. She whispered back that it was fine, and wished him good luck. Anita smiled and sighed with relief. As the shore party gathered on the dimly lit concourse they heard a voice off to one side. "Sub-Lieutenant Metcalfe." They all turned to see two distinguished gentlemen emerging from the balcony into the light above the front doors.

All of them rapidly snapped to attention while the Sub gave one of his best salutes. "Thank goodness we've found you Sir, and, er, Doctor Keen isn't it?"

"Well done Sub. Can we get out of here as quickly as possible?"

"Yes of course Sir, it will be a bit of a squeeze, but that's the least of our worries, the Royal Oak sails in ten minutes and we've barely time to make it to the jetty."

They scrambled in after the Admiral and Doctor Keen. Wesley waved at Bronwyn and Nico who had come to watch by the front doors, blowing her a farewell kiss. Nico waved back as Bronwyn asked. "I wonder if we'll ever get to see them again?" Their driver looking more tired than before, was glad to hear that he was on his last run for the night. He hit the accelerator sending the MPV off like a rocket down the highway. Sub sat in the front passenger seat and broke the strict regime of radio silence. "Beehive one this is midget six."

"Midget six this is Beehive one." came back the instant reply. "Beehive one this is midget six we have the stores and are returning."

"Roger Midget six understood."

The Sub clicked off his radio as they sped around the next bend on high ground, looking through the trees and bushes down towards the dark water in the bay. Warm lighting from many houses flashed past as the locals whiled away their evening in quiet relaxation not knowing a king was passing through their midst. At four minutes to ten they sped around a twisting chicane on the final leg of their rescue mission. The driver slammed on the brakes of the MPV, startled by the carcass of a large army vehicle lying sprawled on its side across the road in front of him. Soldiers milling around, shouting and gesticulating frantically for the driver to stop. Another stores vehicle swung slowly up and down with the major portion of its front body overhanging the rocky edge of the escarpment. Crash barriers lay twisted and broken among the wreckage of the two trucks as the soldiers on the road, some injured, removed two inert bodies from the mess. There was no room to manoeuvre, so the British sailors assisted the Greeks in giving first aid to the injured soldiers. One of them was beyond help died quietly, surrounded by his grief stricken comrades. They managed to get two of the soldiers to act as policemen using torches on the approach to the bend from the other side. That way they could minimise the onslaught of any other vehicle into the field of wreckage. Together with the British tars who had found ropes and a few planks in the wreckage, they man-handled the up-turned lorry back onto its wheels, then using this as a battered tug they hauled its teetering twin back from the edge onto the road and onto an even keel. The MPV and their driver disappeared into the night with four casualties in the back, while Sub broke radio silence reluctantly one more time giving Royal Oak the signal for an unexpected delay.

Walking slowly and quietly along the highway for the remaining three kilometres they reached the steeply sloping side road through the trees at twenty-five minutes to twelve, knowing there was no need to hurry back. Through occasional breaks in the trees they caught the lights of Royal Oak sliding over the water leaving Cassandra Bay for Thessalonika in the north. A feeling of loneliness crept over them when they lost sight of her passing around the distant headland. They walked in silence down the twisting lane until they reached the fork at the bottom. Two figures walking in the opposite direction came out of the darkness towards them from under the trees. The old Captain and his daughter were expecting them and inviting them home led the men quietly through the tall cool grass verges towards their home.

14. DARKNESS CLOSING IN

The Spanish generals argued among themselves while the French contingent bemused by their antics watched helplessly, shrugging their soldiers in typical Gallic style, they stood up to leave the conference chamber. The strategy meeting had cut to the baseline very quickly; who was going to pay for the extended disposition of troops and their naval transports currently plying the waters of the Western Approaches. Tempers were fraught as both sides took stock of the delays imposed on them by the bureaucrats in Strasbourg. Something was wrong, and the French were seeking reassurances while the Spanish argued the toss on a few thousand EDs and a regular supply of chorizos. President Warnock of Britain had issued a warning that any attempt to land either police or troops on his laughable little island would be taken as an act of war. The brass had laughed it off; the Spanish scoffed at the idea having recently grabbed Gibraltar in the most viscous and unprovoked attack not seen for centuries, conveniently forgetting the British garrison under the rock had yet to be winkled out. The French enjoyed the prospect of carving up the English, but like a frustrated mistress needed the assurances of her lover that he was still there for her, she dallied while the Germans appeared reluctant to make such a commitment. American ships steamed around the edges of the North Sea and at a discreet distance in the Western Approaches. Arguments had gone back and forth as the Spanish accused the Germans of duplicity, an argument that looked increasingly suspicious with the absence of any representative from the Germans. At nine o' clock in the evening they were hammering out minor problems in the supply line management of men and materials when a senior French aide appeared, papers in hand, in concert with a Spanish aide. Both men presented their senior officers with decoded signals that both men read patiently in the silence that ensued. The French General announced, "Messieurs, Je vous present la guerre!" The reaction was as swift as a mouse being despatched by a rodent vaporiser; all voices spoke at once. The French General savoured a moment of silent contemplation while his colleagues kept up a Babel of noise around him. The Germans in typically abrupt fashion had given the code word for the advance and the time and date to commence operations against the

British. It was agreed that there was no necessity for a heavy patrolling of the Mediterranean, since there were no significant British units in that theatre. A token low-key presence in the form of a few Italian and Spanish gunboats supported by two 'knackered' French destroyers out of Toulon was seen as an ample rear-guard.

****

The White House stood in leafy splendour when the President returned from a fishing trip in the Florida Keys, facing his heavy responsibilities with an opening discussion on the spiralling European situation. As the generals filed out of their meeting place in the distant Old World the President of the US was in the throes of receiving no good news in particular. "Henry, you're the expert. How much time do we have to get our people out of the region and back home?" the President asked his Secretary of State for Foreign Affairs. "Two weeks, a month at most. Then there are the civilians to repatriate Sir, all over Europe. Anywhere between the Black Sea and the River Shannon." The General Secretary of the Security Committee seated in a comfortable armchair made his own silent calculations based on his intimate knowledge of international field of operations. "So it's the usual bulletin recommending that all US citizens make their way home or move completely out of the European region."

"Same old message every time."

"Do we have contingency plans for dealing with people contaminated with radiation or any other form of toxic poisoning? -In case they go newk, I mean."

"I believe Senator Garmin heads up the committee for that sort of thing Mr President, but with that in mind I'm meeting with him later on this morning to discuss it with him."

"Fine Henry, let me know what he says. Now if you'll excuse me I have to address more urgent matters with the Security Chiefs."

"OK Sir, I'll send you a draft of the PR as a follow up."

"Wilma?" The President of the United States pressed a button on his office intercom and called for his secretary. "I'm here Sir."

"Have Dan come in now please."

"Hello Dan."

"Good morning Mr President." Dan nodded politely to his political acquaintance seated in the armchair.

"Sit down Dan and tell me what is going on in Europe."

"Well," drawled Dan slowly. "It looks like a hornets nest right now, since the British emergency blew up in their faces. The Germans and the French are keeping the lid on their civilian populations and are moving fresh troops into key areas. You know, roadblocks, sealed districts, civilian disaster teams and opening rescue centres for those who will be contaminated with radiation, and putting up emergency accommodation for those who have been prevented from going home in contaminated areas, and so on."

"I see, there's no doubt about it then, it's expected to go nuclear?"

"Looks like it's the only way them Brits can ensure their sovereignty."

"What about the Rest of Europe?"

"Not convinced about the whole issue at all. The Low Countries are getting more sympathetic towards the Brits than before, since they reckon it wont be long before they all go the same way towards losing their own sovereignty. The Scandinavians are talking of resurrecting their old Free Trade Association in favour of trading under the old banner like they used to."

"How about the rest of Central Europe Dan, I hear little enough about them?"

"Not really an issue Mr President, they're too absorbed in their own cross-border disputes. The Czechs are in real trouble with the Austrians since they bought into that risky Russian nuclear programme with the Austrians claiming they will be caught in the fallout, suffering more than most since they are immediately downwind of the installations just over the Czech border. The Poles are havin' a hard time preventing refugees from charging across their borders. The latest I heard on the way in, is that the German population is now passing east into the west Czech Republic and Poland."

"So where does that leave us? Do we pull our teams out?"

"Not entirely." Came the relaxed response from the occupier of the armchair. We pull them back as far as safety will allow, out from immediate danger of exposure."

"So you do think there is a possibility it will turn nuclear. Then what Jim?"

"We wait."

"You're not telling me something. OK Jim, what's this all about?" He turned to face his other advisors who sat as if lost in silent contemplation.

"You knew about this Dan?"

"Only in the last coupla hours Mr President."

"What else do you want to tell me?"

"One of the Varmint Teams went missing about a month ago…"

"You crazy son of a bitch! Does the Vice-President know about this?"

"Hardly Sir, we…" The president lifted his hand cutting the Secretary short in mid-sentence. "Wilma, where's the Vice-President today?"

"He's in town today Sir, visiting the Veterans Administration Hospital on a PR meeting." Came her neutral reply over the intercom. "Get hold of his Secretary and have him call me as quickly as possible please Wilma." He released his finger from the intercom button. "Let's start from the beginning, how did this happen?"

"We don't have the full details yet Sir, but they were an intelligence gathering group, not strictly speaking acting as agents provocateur, working out of Berlin and Brussels. Then one night nothing, they just disappeared off of the face of the earth Mr President."

"How long have they been missing Dan?"

"About three weeks Sir."

"Dan, if you persist in doing it this way I'll make it tough for you. Tell me how long ago, what they were doing, what your people are doing about it, and if it's not too difficult, why this happened at all?"

"Three weeks today Sir, we don't know where or what happened to them, and as to why, none of the other agencies can offer any ideas."

"No gossip among the intelligence networks Dan?"

"No Sir, not a whisper."

"This looks bad Dan, wouldn't you agree?"

"Awfully bad from where I'm sitting Mr President."

"What is being done about it?"

"We have three Varmints out there looking for them and a team of SOE trained Rangers working in isolation on some other leads. I assure you..."

"Cut the crap Dan, we both know that losing an entire team in an intelligence network means the network is compromised. Either that or somebody is playing a really deep game for big bucks. Now suppose you stop being coy and tell me what they were doing prior to their disappearance."

"We-ell, it looks like they were tapping into the French communications link between some fancy new military outfit's headquarters and Paris. In the process of hooking up their own tap they found a sophisticated eavesdropping network piggy-backed onto the lines coming out of the European Parliament buildings, and that's about all we know for now. But I'll admit that it has an unsavoury smell about it."

"Yes, Wilma, what is it?" The President spoke into his intercom irritably, as it beeped cutting across his train of thought.

"Mr President I am sorry to interrupt you, but Senators McCallum and Henderson are both trying to reach you urgently."

"Can't it wait Wilma, I'm really very busy right now."

"Senator Henderson says, and I quote 'tell that son of a bitch if he doesn't want to see me to turn on his TV and watch the Hunter-Fox News Channel, the news is breaking all the way down the east coast."

"Fine Wilma." He said wearily. "I'll watch some TV."

"Give me a moment gentlemen, let's see what's so important on TV?"

They went into an anteroom where the President picked up a remote and spoke into it. "TV on, channel H F N." The TV came on immediately. He spoke into the controller a second time. "Volume three." Scenes of devastation were evident as the viewer portrayed what looked to be a major flood in full spate. They watched in silence as a news broadcaster plied his trade live while cameras panned in and out from various locations. An unexpected earthquake of enormous proportions had shaken the

Adirondack Mountains in up state New York with tremendous ferocity, measuring eight point nine on the Richter Scale. The cameras revealing the horrendous sight of damage caused by floodwaters smashing through towns and villages on the banks of the Hudson River. Landslides and mudslides adding to the picture of tragedy as whole settlements were swallowed up. "What the hell happened?" Asked the President, more in the way of a personal question than to anyone else assembled with him in front of the view-screen. Finally the truth was evident. The Moriah dam was wrecked by a devastating quake and a hundred-foot wave was proceeding down on Schnectady at a speed of seventy miles an hour. "This should not be happening!" announced the newscaster emphatically. "The IGS in New York has said that given the volume of water and the tremendous speed something else is going on in order to have this happen. The floodwater should ordinarily dissipate in a wide front as it finds valleys and other lakes to empty into…"

"Dan, we have to find those men before there's an 'incident' in Europe, you know what I'm saying?"

"Yes Sir, Mr President, we've got all available people working on it, and I'll get back to you just as soon as I can."

"Very well, now if you'll excuse me I have to speak with our Colleagues from New York and Vermont.

As the President's men singled out of the door hidden pressures in the earth's crust continued to squeeze the Adirondack range ever closer towards the Green Mountains to the east. The fold in the landscape being pushed higher causing the bottom of Lake Champlain to rise, emptying the contents of that ancient pool into the lands lying to the south. Toronto and Buffalo shook as the ledge of rock below the thundering waters of Niagara Falls rose momentarily then fell to a point six-inches lower than where it had rested before. Large amounts of lethal volcanic, sulphurous gas leaking from the bottom of the stricken lake rose through the waters lying in deadly silence on the surface like a blanket of death to be blown by the winds towards many flattened lakeside communities.

****

President Warnock remarked to his private secretary that he got the impression somebody somewhere had walked off with a large amount of the defence budget. "Why look William, all these movements to the north, trainloads of men and equipment. What's going on?

"It's the build up of our eastern defences Sir, you might remember how long it took us to dislodge the rioters from their strangleholds on the power stations all the way from Humberside and across the border. Without consolidating our defences we can assume that the ESA will attempt to land either at Berwick or Dunbar, capturing the roads to and from Edinburgh and the industrial areas on the north eastern coastal strip."

"It's quite outrageous William, it's almost as if someone is financing a private army!"

"Well, it is almost that in a way Sir, since we were forced to run down our traditional garrison towns and naval installations."

"That brings me to another point William, where is all this steel going to? I mean I know we are building up our navy William, but don't the other two services need steel as well?"

"Why, yes of course Sir. It's just that with the running down of the steel mills and without the coal to smelt iron we've had to rely on the Polish pits to provide most of our energy supplies, as well as, our own gas supplies. Now that we have cut off the European pipeline to the mainland we can divert the excess gas and oil production towards our rearmament programme, and overcome the difficulty with the Commission's blockade of our Polish coal."

"I see William. I suppose you're right, but you will tell me if there are any doubts about such things."

"Why of course Sir."

"Now William, I have some sad news to impart to the nation. Vice-President Augsburger has informed me personally that we have seventy-two hours to stand-down our armed forces and receive a European Parliamentary task force to take over the duty of policing this nation. Will you please make the arrangements with Dyke House for a national announcement at six o' clock tomorrow morning."

"I cannot tell you how sad I am that we have not yet found the king Sir." I still have hope yet Sir…" The President held up his hand slowly in a tired gesture, cutting his secretary short. "I know William, I know. We seem to be fated to suffer every humiliation that these un-elected bureaucrats in Strasbourg dream up. I know that most of us want to be ruled by those whom we elect in fair and democratic elections, and I fear the system has gone far too far the other way. It seems now that nobody can stop it, because the Commission is un-elected and the Ministers have no power over the Commission."

"What will you do Sir?"

"I suppose they would want my head on a plate William. Vilify me publicly as a rebel no doubt, and put me under house arrest, and when it's all over try to win the people over by a gesture of leniency by commuting whatever sentence they pronounced."

"I pray that will never happen Sir."

"Me too William, but I think it will take a miracle.

****

There came an urgent tap on his door. Chip worked under the softer glow of his desk lamp out of preference. The harsh glare of the main lights in the deckhead made his eyes sore more readily. "Enter!" He called to be greeted by the senior signal operator. "Sorry to disturb you Sir, we have just received this flash-call from London." Chip took the plain brown envelope addressed to him and glancing up at the clock on the bulkhead opened it by slitting the leaf with his thumbnail. The message was short and to the point. 'President Warnock has been invited to stand-down all British armed services by nine o' clock in three days hence. You are commanded by their Lordships to return to Portsmouth Naval Home Command under full speed, reporting you current disposition.' He sat down wondering how he would manage as a myriad of thoughts crowded in on him all at once. His reply to the Admiralty was as equally terse. 'Alongside at Thessalonika embarking casualties, stores and provisions under the diplomatic agreement to proceed with same unhindered.'

They had made it with fifteen minutes to spare before midnight, being met by the British Consul and a party of soldiers who immediately placed themselves between the population and the skimmer gently riding at her moorings -all lit up. She lay berthed under the great tower where the fast city road ran alongside the seafront overlooking the great wide sweep of the Bay of Thessalonika. The Consul had explained that this was the closest point to the hospital complex where the British casualties had been put.

During the stay at the little haven on the Cassandra Peninsular the crew had rigged lines across the large cargo deck from which they hung large canvas sheets as partitions, giving some privacy to their prospective passengers. Although not normally heated, the Consul had arranged for industrial heating units to be purchased and provided for the comfort and well being of the patients during their journey. By one o' clock they began loading provisions for the journey while a fuel barge came alongside being towed by a small tug. Having finished their replenishment by half-past two they waited quietly for their human cargo to arrive. At first just the reflections of flashing blue lights could be seen bouncing of walls and windows, then shortly before three o'clock in the morning a convoy of ambulances came down the hill into the large road junction behind the tower. They turned right into the fast one-way traffic system going the wrong way by prior arrangement with the police department who ordered the road to be closed off for the occasion. Sixty-three casualties in various states of immobility, accompanied by five doctors and seven nursing staff were embarked onto the Royal Oak. Some of the casualties were hooked up to drips and other medical paraphernalia while a very small number hobbled over the ramp with limbs swathed in casts or bandages. By four-fifteen the embarkation was completed, but no movement on the promenade could be seen to help slip their moorings so they could not proceed. A few hundred onlookers were kept away by barriers a hundred metres distant from the berth and everyone waited in silence. After one or two discrete enquiries by Fred he discovered that no one was any the wiser concerning the delay. He was at the point of eliciting further information from the Consul when a large black private vehicle came speeding along the route taken by the ambulances. The windows had been blacked out with a heavy black tint, so no one could see who was inside.

A tall middle aged gentleman, with a hint of a thickening waist climbed out of the car with the door being held open for him by a security guard. Accompanied by an aide who had got out from the other side of the vehicle he walked quickly over the ramp onto the cargo deck of the Royal Oak making his way forwards through the makeshift hospital towards the accommodation area leading to the bridge. Careful not to get in to any one's way he arrived at the forward door to the accommodation area to be stopped by a sailor guarding the door. "Who are you?" Came the enquiry. "I want to see your Captain."

"Sorry he's very busy, Sir, but the first lieutenant is available." A flustered Consul appeared from behind pushing through the crowd like a man possessed. "Excuse me Sir, I'll deal with this. Let me through my man!" He shouted impatiently. The three gentlemen in front of him turned, the distinguished looking man in the expensive suit and silk tie regarded the Consul in a dismissive fashion shaking his head slowly from side to side. "Turning back to the guard he spoke once again softly, in impeccable English. "Tell the Captain that king Constantine would be very happy to speak with him." The poor sailor of no distinctive rank would have melted ordinarily had he known, but held to his guns resolutely. I will have someone inform the Captain." The king looked utterly nonplussed then began to laugh softly. 'How is it that a king has to wait on the say so of a mere sailor?' He thought, and found no fault in his mild predicament. The Consul at the rear of the party was making his presence felt by pushing to get through. The king's guards holding him in check as he flustered and bellowed to be heard; like most socially challenged government officials on foreign assignments. One of the bodyguards threatened him with becoming another casualty if he didn't shut up and the Consul walked off to find another way onto the bridge. "Chief Riley, can I have some assistance please. The Chief had been checking the engine controls on the bridge and was returning to the safety of the engine room in readiness for their departure. "Yes Able Seaman Locksmith, what seems to be..." he paused in mid-sentence, nodding. "How do you do Sir, you want to see the Captain?"

"Yes please."

"How many in your party Sir?" asked the Chief, looking at the gathering looming over the AB in the doorway. "Just three of us Chief." He said with a twinkle in his eyes. "Come this way please Sir." The king of Greece followed smiling inwardly; led by the Chief who wore blue overalls and his peaked cap at a jaunty angle. They followed him across the bridge to the Captain's day room where Chip and Fred were in discussion over a chart. Chief Riley knocked on the door politely announcing in a soft voice. "His majesty the King of Greece Sir." If ever two men looked as they had been caught stealing apple pie it was at that moment as King Constantine the fifth of Greece walked through the doorway. Well known on the world stage as a scholar and as a keen oceanographer he had succeeded to the throne of his forefathers, one of whom had won it back from the republicans because of his stand for the Greek Orthodox Church. Under constant threat of public harassment or assassination, either, it was suspected, by the Commissioners who hated anyone who defied them. Or by the waning republican movement whose socialist policies had almost destroyed the country once hailed as the cradle of democracy, he walked a tightrope between the political factions, supported by the democracies of the British and the American peoples. A king who genuinely loved his people he never exploited them, being among the first to appear on the scene of any major festival or tragedy as an interested and compassionate man reigning alongside a parliament modelled on the British 'mother of parliaments' as a quiet and effective arbiter.

Good evening Captain." greeted the king pleasantly. "I see you have almost finished your work here and ready to depart."

"Yes Sir. Ready to leave as soon as we have finished loading."

"Good, just a moment please Captain." The king turned and spoke to his bodyguards standing in the open doorway who retreated as the king closed the door behind him. "I wanted to thank you personally for a favour you have done for my people Captain."

"Oh, what favour would that be Sir?"

"I believe you have had a little trouble with your engines in the last few days, have you not Captain?"

"Ye-es, we have as a matter of fact had some problems in that area Sir."

"Well, I am grateful that you decided to stay a while and fix them at Captain Theodrakkis' little harbour."

"Ah, I see Sir, yes he was very helpful to us."

"I am sure he was and I can assure you Captain, I am very grateful for your help in sinking that submarine for us. It has been hiding out among the islands harassing our shipping for several days. However, that is one thing, but there is another that I think I can help you with."

"That's very kind of you Sir, may I ask what that would be?" Fred couldn't help feeling that as this dialogue between his friend and the king proceeded along its courteous way, it was going to lead them into revealing their true reasons for spending so much time in Greek waters, and it wasn't the weather either! "Do you have all your crew onboard Captain Woodingdean?"

"Er, not entirely Sir, we had to sail promptly in order to get here before midnight."

"I am aware of this Captain, and of course how your men have helped us again this evening when there was an accident on the road to Polychronos. My family is very grateful to you and your men for helping our soldiers and

433

for saving the life of my son Phillip who was hurt in the accident." Chip looked surprised while Fred stared straight -ahead not daring to breathe. "I see you are little surprised Captain, both you and your first officer, but there it is, your men have been of great help to me and I would like very much to help you on your way by doing you a favour."

"Oh, that's not entirely necessary Sir, they responded in the only way they know how."

"You're too modest Captain, but I think you will admit if not to me then perhaps, to yourself, you are in a hurry to get back home are you not?"

"Yes indeed Sir, the situation is deteriorating and we have injured people aboard who also need to get back to hospital."

"Well said Captain. I won't keep you in suspense any longer. Your friends are waiting for you in the house of my good old friend from the naval academy. You see I know who Dr Jack Keen is, and of course his friend Admiral Dunham. I know how important it is that you get back home as quickly as possible, so I wont delay you any further. Let your first officer come with me now so that we can fly together to identify all your people for sure. And I want someone who can identify this man." The king held out a photograph of a man dressed in the fatigues of a Royal Marine. "He says he was on the transport with the king when it crashed here. Have you seen him before." Both Chip and Fred looked at the picture shaking their heads. "No Sir, he's not known personally to us. May I suggest that we ask some of his injured colleagues here onboard?"

"That is a good idea Captain, one that I would appreciate, for all our sakes."

"I'll get William to do it." Said Fred, he's more or less finished loading duties by now."

"Yes please number one, tell him to get back here as quickly as possible." Fred left them to talk as he walked briskly down aft, catching a glimpse of William among the melee of people and swaying canvas partitions. "Would you care for a glass of sherry Sir?" Chip asked, thinking of something to say and with which to break the ice. "Yes, thank you Captain, I would like that very much." Replied the king.

Fred returned shortly afterwards and the three men chatted briefly sipping the fortified wine until a polite knock on the door was heard. William entered ushering in a Marine Corporal of the 42nd Commando who made his way into the cabin on crutches. He positively identified Corporal Wesley as a member of his commando unit who actually disappeared at the time the other two gentlemen walked out of the aircraft. "He's one of the best Sir, knows his way around if you know what I mean. Took some shrapnel in Akrotiri among other things Sir, that's why he was sent back to Blighty."

"Good, well done Corporal, and thank you."

"Have you found him Sir?"

"Indeed, I think I can safely say we might know where he can be found. Now I will have to ask you to return to your ward. You have been very helpful. Thank you William." The two men left the conference closing the door behind them. "Well, Captain, I think I can be of service to you. Think of it as a small token of my appreciation for what you have done for us in the last three days. If you will allow me to fly your first officer down to Polychronos, to formally identify all of your crewmen, you understand, I will provide you with one of my officers to act as liaison on your trip through our waters. What do you say Captain?"

"Thank you Sir, we will depart without delay, just as long as it takes for my first officer to get into some appropriate attire." Chip looked at Fred wishing secretly that he could go on that flight instead. "I'll only need a moment to take a wind-proof jacket and a tooth brush Sir."

"Very well, it is agreed." smiled the king appreciatively. Lieutenant-Commander Dmitriou is waiting in a staff car outside and he will act as your guide and liaison officer. Now Captain one other matter. Doctor Keen is an anxious man I believe, as is your Admiral Dunham. It would be in their interests to have them flown home before your country is attacked again would it not?"

"Indeed Sir."

"I will be accompanying your first officer so that I can meet your Doctor Keen and make arrangements through less well-known channels to fly them both home."

That's very kind of you Sir. I believe my first officer, who is known to the king, will impart that news discretely when they meet."

435

"Oh, so you know the king?" Constantine turned to Fred looking at him squarely. "Yes Sir, both Commander Woodingdean and I have been of service to the king for some time."

"That is surprising news, but also comforting to know that you will not be strangers. It makes my task a little easier to know that he is among friends."

"Entirely so Sir." confirmed Chip with a nod.

"Then until we meet again in Polychronos Captain in say two to three hours?"

"Thank you Sir."

"Thank you for your sherry Captain, a most pleasant custom. Good night."

A short and stocky officer strode quickly aboard immediately after the king drove off in his MPV. Fred clambered in to the second vehicle and was whisked away into the night in hot pursuit of the king's car. Almost at once the harbourmaster notified them on the harbour frequency that Royal Oak was clear to proceed on her way, and at 05:00 on a cool dark morning she slipped her ropes heading for the open sea. Once clear of the harbour they went on-planes as the Cox'n took her up to fifty-five knots over a calm surface. The liaison officer remained at a respectable distance once the necessity of communications with the Thessalonika port authorities was over. Clearly impressed with her speed and the way she was being handled the Greek seaman watched with undivided interest. The patients in the cargo deck only aware of the noise in the roof of the great 'hall' felt just the motion of the skimmer as she rose and fell ever so slowly in the gently rolling sea.

Dawn had crept upon them before they passed along the great splinter of land of the Cassandra Peninsula, quickly skirting Poseidon Head en-route for the sweeping turn along its southern most tip into Cassandra Bay. Far away in another world, the German Bundes Marine transmitted the order to proceed, and while Royal Oak prepared to follow the computer plotted course around the headland. Twenty two thousand armed police and soldiers dressed in militia fatigues began their journey across the North Sea hidden in the bowels of a merchant fleet. Hugging the coast each skimmer left the terminal at ten-minute intervals until they reached the Dutch border, then heading off into the Channel they sped towards a pre-arranged rendezvous out of sight of land. The French Admiral received a signal two hours later initiating a sudden change in the disposition of the fleet 'exercising' off the Western Approaches. One flotilla detaching itself heading north-west as the other headed for the narrowing confines of the English Channel between the peninsular of Cornwall and the French mainland. The EuroSat tactical networks being denied to all except the French, Italian and German naval and military commands within the ESF umbrella.

****

New York faced the onslaught of the muddy water wall fast approaching its environs. Two tremors already shaking the city earlier in the day giving some warning of continuing geological activity below the rocky shelf on which the city was built. Some of the waters diffused into the flatlands here and there, but more surges piled the water high as the lake in the north inched ever higher. Poughkeepsie and Newburgh would lose half their riverside conurbations to the unstoppable tide as it raced down the gully between the Catskills and the peaks of the Taconic Range. To the north the Richlieu river and countless streams dried up, the mighty St Lawrence slowed imperceptibly as its banks edged apart while beneath the waters its bottom puckered up in ridges and troughs initiating new and deadly currents along the navigation. The Ottawa River now backing up slowly while Montreal shook gently in a slow and lamentable slide into the mud at the beginning of a million-year journey sideways and downwards. Far to the west Wyoming shook as Yellowstone Lake began to boil in a sulphurous discharge of super heated gases bursting through the bottom. A giant blister of land rose one hundred and fifty feet into the air as the enormous pressures beneath the crust below the mountain ranges sought to push through an ancient plug of basaltic magma hundreds of feet below. The Seminoe reservoir damn developing micro-cracks along hidden pathways following pressure hotspots, jumping from one to another as the concrete structure went beyond its design limits. Settling down as the shock waves ceased in the eerie silence covering the land for hundreds of square miles. The North Platte River turning a filthy colour as it wound its way around the northern flank of the Laramie Mountains.

15. DON'T LOOK BACK

William hurriedly passed the communiqué from the Chiefs of Staff without closing the door of the President's suite behind him. President Warnock didn't need to ask; he felt sure this was the moment of truth where he would discover how devious the Commission had been all along. "I can see from your face William that you bring unhappy news."

"Indeed Sir. I am sorry to say that the Chiefs of Staff have become aware of moving naval forces coming our way Sir, and in accordance with protocols they have put our armed services on red alert." He handed the President the communiqué and continued speaking. "Can I take it Sir that you wish to proceed with the civil defence plan immediately?" There followed a long pause as President Warnock read and reread the intelligence summary a second time, and the recommendation to mobilise the whole country immediately. "Yes, thank you William, without delay. I will want to see the war cabinet assembled within half an hour. In the mean time I want to talk with the chief of staff in the Absence of Admiral Dunham."

"Right away Sir." William strode into the ante-room to the secretary's desk where he found the relevant communications lines. Speaking briefly to a distant voice on the other end he patched the line through to the President, and returned to the Presidential office to await further instructions. He was banking on hearing from Admiral Dunham as soon as possible, but all he could tell was that wherever he was it was somewhere on his way back.

The attacks came at strategic points along the eastern coast while the naval flotilla blockaded the ports between Dover and Falmouth. The second flotilla dallied long enough until the tides were just right then proceeding up the Bristol Channel and into the Irish Sea they blockaded the industrial ports where, with no local naval or military presence to speak of, they sailed unchallenged into the Port of Bristol. The mixed flotilla of French and Spanish vessels disgorged hundreds of militiamen in the uniforms of the hated European Police Battalion -the EPB. These were the 'police' who overran Brussels, Ostend, Ghent, Antwerp and Charleroi when the Belgian President refused to allow his parliament to pass laws given down by edicts from the Commission. The challenge could not have drawn out a more effective demonstration of the Commission's awesome hunger for power. Having challenged the Commission by denouncing them as lawmakers without a mandate to govern, he questioned the authority of any edict handed down by the Commission as being thoroughly illegal and un-democratic. Industrious Belgium, so often caught up in the political intrigues of its largest neighbours buckled under the strain of the Commission's fury, but had lit a lamp in so doing. It was the brave Scousers who marmalised the first cohort that dared to set foot on English soil. Two tugs rammed the first vessel pushing her onto the treacherous mud banks of the Mersey where many seamen have lost their lives. The second was so damaged that it stood no chance of making it in or out of the port of Liverpool. When trying to make an exit from the treacherous channel the Scousers threw grappling irons across the narrow gap of water, and in spite of heavy casualties they dragged the burning vessel into the middle of the harbour and proceeded to sink the tugs around her until she keeled over.

Port Talbot fell without too much difficulty to the Spanish brigade. The Taffs having been fooled into believing that the enemy ships were heading for Cardiff. With the industrial complex falling into enemy hands they had lost precious ground as the invaders formed a shaky bridgehead. The pugnacious Bristolians fired up as much by their local beer as by the resentment of the 'foreign Johnnies' who had made their lives so difficult, attacked with surprising ferocity. Having run down their port and their livelihoods by mendacious trading agreements favouring French ports, they began to let off over a century of super heated steam. Falling steadily backwards the Bristolians bloodied the EPB time and time again. They lost the key objective of the railway link at Temple Meads and for a bloody half an hour they rained hell upon the French and Spanish militiamen until a regiment of infantry arrived from Gloucester. No one had ever seen such uniforms before, their insignia were different and although fairly young men led by equally young NCOs and officers they fought like professional soldiers. The line held, and as artillery was brought to bear on the invading forces and on their ships in the harbour, a split began to appear in the invading ranks of soldiers.

The east coast raids beginning at dawn were more deadly and significantly difficult. The meagre naval forces, although reinforced with greater numbers of fast patrol craft and skimmers, lacked sufficient numbers of heavier, sterner vessels like destroyers and frigates. Leaving the rump of England well alone the German EPB Brigade attacked the Humber and the industrial strip between Cleveland and Blyth, while other units made for Berwick and the Firth of Forth to capture major coastal communications and blockade Edinburgh.

The south coast saw the bitterest fighting as French ships in the main supported by Spanish auxiliaries sailed into stiff resistance. The British navy scoring early successes with their intelligent mines sinking three destroyers and a transport vessel loaded with militiamen of the EPB long before the invading fleet could get into position to off-load their soldiers. The islands of Jersey, Guernsey, Sark and Herm were annexed immediately to the nearest French Department of administration. Since there were no nationality issues it meant that they lost their independence to another indifferent rubber stamping bureaucrat in some distant French office building.

Captured civilians were dragged off to interrogation centres and treated badly by the EPB units who had managed to establish footholds. Some of the militiamen seemed surprised at the aggressive reception they had received, and when told that they were an invading army they could not believe their ears. Through interpreters they got the message that the Brits were quite happy to sort out their own problems without any interference from them. The soldiers believing the orchestrated propaganda fed to them in a daily diet of canted news reporting and military briefings did not believe them. The EPB hustled many of the fighting population down to the docks, imprisoning them in the warehouse district. Captured EPB men were bewildered by the strange uniforms and by the strict military conduct of their captors. They could not see that they were invaders, but policemen doing their duty. When shown the civilian dead and through interpreters they were told that since these were English dead on English soil killed and mutilated by French and Spanish troops, the message began to sink in. "It's the firing squad for you!" Said one NCO to a young Spanish Captain who went white with fear as the soldier pointed his finger at him and with a cocking action of his thumb gave the universal sign for shooting a gun.

During the second night of raiding the Royal Navy sent out patrols to harry and break down the invading fleets. Two destroyers and a frigate was all that could be spared to provide a protective shield around the oil and gas installations remaining in the North Sea. Overhead, British aircraft fought dogfight after dogfight with attacking fighters in an unevenly matched contest. "What we need said one Air vice-Marshall is an aircraft carrier or two or better still more aircraft!" Still the raiding parties came and casualties were high. The whole situation was turning into a mess as newly formed British regiments began to snarl up the roads and block the invading EPB at every key target.

President Warnock put the phone down on the European President while he was speaking. He had no doubt that the Commission's agents were listening into the conversation on the other side of the Channel. "Who rules Europe?" He demanded of Muller-Weiss. "You or the Commission?"

"President Warnock, you know very well..."

"If it's you, then what you are doing is unconstitutional since you have no vote from the Members to do this. If you say it's the Commission, then you are admitting to a conspiracy by allowing un-elected civil servants to pass laws without a mandate! You must pull out now, and send your 'bully boys' home, or we will destroy your little army and you with it. Is that clear!"

"President Warnock you don't seem to understand the gravity of your situation..." Click, went the phone with a defiance all of its own. Enough was enough. "Gentlemen, you heard that he had nothing positive to say, and in the face of it we need to make every day of our six month campaign count." The war cabinet looked at each other nodding in silent agreement while the meeting continued to rumble on noting successes here and there, failures and disasters in other places. The capture of Brighton and the hover-railhead to London was alarming to say the least, as reports from local commanders on the ground began to tell the sad story of home defences stretched to the limit. Shoreham harbour and airfield had been taken in a lightning raid that saw the destruction of the power station and the naval reserve unit's 6 berth yacht. Everybody knew about the yacht, since that was the entire hardware the naval reserve unit had in the way of seagoing craft. Owned and operated by the navy for well connected local politicians and high ranking reservists with nothing better to do. It was not so much a loss as a total disaster for the south coast defences as the socialist motivated nightmare of dumbing down everything had rolled on for decades.

Pierce Anders had returned empty handed, as William knew he would. In fact his mission had been more a process of successful elimination that William would not admit to anyone even in private. He looked bleakly at the facts as they lay before him on paper and getting up from his desk he carried the brown paper envelope containing his friend's intelligence report to a large safe buried in the rear wall of his office. Pierce returned to his unit in Chelsea Barracks busying himself in catching up on the current situation and on the disposition of the troops in the London area. A little over a week later Pierce was in the thick of it with his army group facing an uncertain future with raids taking place to the north and to the south and south west. A call went out for reinforcements to push back insurgents along the south coast, requiring, among other things, a squadron of engineers to support the lines. Pierce and his men snaked out of London crossing the Thames at two o' clock on a miserably soaking morning, with their almost silent convoy of hover bat vehicles swishing into the Battersea enclave leading into the inner UPA of Clapham. Only a minimal security watch patrolled the enclave in view of the national emergency. The guards in brown and orange combination uniforms waving them through without fuss or formality as they sped up the hill towards the old common. Not following the road but arrowing straight across the green sward that once was home to a thousand displaced Londoners during the revolutionary years of the counter-unionist uprisings more than a century earlier. Following the old A23 until its junction with the E23 to the south coast where the high-speed hover-link to the continent of Europe lay at Peacehaven. At the far limit of the UPA they continued through the high walled encampment and electrified fencing without so much as a glance backwards. Their mission to move into the hill country of the Weald national Park and to wreak as much havoc with the enemy's lines of communications wherever and whenever they could. "At Balcombe." William had said. "We will arrange for a little accident where the railway viaduct crosses the little valley on the way south to Haywards Heath. The French will make every effort to re-open the line from Brighton once they have cleared the debris away from the Pyecombe tunnels. The front line running from Lancing to Moulscombe with bridgeheads established at Pyecombe, and along the E27 between there and North Lancing."

"It's either a feint," pointed out the General, "or it will be part of a two headed attack on London up the two major routes of the E23 and E24. Either way you will be heavily involved in sabotaging their efforts to secure either of those routes and the surrounding countryside. We will have transport standing by to take you out of there as quickly as possible. Your Captain Greasley will report you as missing presumed dead, so there won't be any loose ends on that score. While the others push forward to close the routes out of the coastal strip controlled by the French, no one will pay particular attention to another VTOL movement in the area. It is vitally important that you get kitted up in your headgear and flight overalls before anyone can see you and recognise you for what you are. Is that understood Major, otherwise your cover and our carefully laid plans will be all for nothing."

Heading southwards they glided across the Streatham Plain which was once a thriving suburban community until bombed out of existence by drug barons trying to enforce a 'gangland republic' with the old UPA boundary of the Streatham Complex. Then razed to the ground by a vengeful government - their 'brothers' in socialism, who, facing a general election on the party propaganda of 'cleaning up Britain', recognised that government was more than just for absorbing taxes for the twin purposes of indulging in MPs salaries and over-inflated pension rights. Realising these had to take second place or they would lose the election for sure, the reaction was swift and certain with a ninety five percent death rate guaranteed for anyone left within the confines of the complex.

A huge nature reserve and open heath land with rides, lakes and recreation areas inter mingled with serene gardens of remembrance was all that was left as a legacy of a once ancient and thriving Saxon village. Soldiers waved them through while Pierce mused on his pre-meditated demise somewhere in the dank woodland valleys of the high Weald. Someone would start shooting as they laid charges along the viaducts at Balcombe and Wivelsfield. A bugle would sound; smoke bombs would fall to order all around them creating confusion. He was to head towards the sound of the bugle and where he would find cover with a stick of special-forces soldiers. They would provide him with his flying kit and take him to the waiting aircraft. Hardly noticing the quarter-mile no mans land areas on either side of the Euro Route he mentally rehearsed the drill until the convoy came into sight of the Purley Gates. All the land between Banstead and Warlingham had been sequestered by the government decades previously in a breathtaking heist that made Genghis Khan look like a babe in arms. The huge thirty-six square mile lower middle class ghetto had been flattened and remodelled to house a few hundred measly high-ranking politicos and their squirming civil service chums in a high-class reservation dotted with dachas in idyllic surroundings. Regular soldiers who were based at the small garrison at Kenley a few miles away manned the gates; just outside the high fencing of the reserve. He noted the concrete emplacements as they swept past the slip road leading to the entrance of the privileged few. There was also a small airborne counter-insurgency group permanently stationed at the dilapidated air force reserve airfield. The construction of the Purley Reserve had neatly obviated the pressure to plough up the old airfield in favour of building local authority housing. Instead it now fed the constant need to ferry the self-oiling wheels of power to and from the inner city hover-port at Westminster.

Pierce had often wondered what it was like to live in such a place, especially with the Euro Route ploughing straight through the middle of it, albeit in an expensively built cutting hand-crafted by labour service gangs of men and women who were registered as poor or unemployed. Where decades of Middle-English politics had once ruled with an ever-increasing padding of blue coloured sleaze, paving the way for social and moral decline; the socialists refined the sleaze as central control had cranked out more policies to politicians possessing ever-decreasing power. His father had been a boy when the labour service gangs had been in their heyday. "That was the time." His father had told him. "That everyone realised the spin-doctors had become the 'political force' responsible for policing and controlling not only party policy, but as their power grew government ministers and civil servants were drawn into their web of fear, until they became the power for bullying, deceit and intimidation. Everyone lived in fear." His father went on. "Of being denounced by a relative or a friend as either guilty of some petty crime or of the stigma of being unemployed. Once committed to a labour service gang it would be five years before anyone could break free."

He thought fleetingly of his father's stories as the convoy took them through the countryside, of how clandestine refugee escape routes whisked people away through secretive and devious routes across the Channel to secret locations on the continent where they would emerge months later claiming political asylum. Saw also, in his mind's eye, the old scars on his father's hands and arms received during the many beatings he had suffered during his time in a labour service gang. When asked about it by his two sons he would remain silent on the subject. His mother once alluded to the truth during a time when his father lay dying in hospital from unseen scars on the inside of his tortured body. It had been rumoured that a family friend had denounced him for voting for a local opposition MP, and the first thing anyone knew about it was when he was called into his boss's office to be told his job was redundant. It just so happened that a passing Labour Service Investigation Team was 'passing by' and picked him up. Two days later an LS patrol car called at the house and he was gone for nearly six months before they found out he was living and working in filthy conditions in a tin mine restoration project down in Cornwall. Despite the threat of reprisals a national paper long associated with the crusade for political reform and a return to the principles of a justice system, ran a week long campaign highlighting his father's case. Denounced by an unknown informer of some 'unspecified' and undoubtedly, false accusation, imprisoned unlawfully, and beaten left to die without any recourse. Since this acutely embarrassed the political incumbent of both the constituencies where he lived and in the town of Redruth where he had been forcibly taken, it had been decided to make him a special case and release him. The fact that it served the propaganda machine was not missed by anyone.

Returning to face his old boss a year later, his father found that the poor man had been denounced a few months after his own demise. The new boss came as no surprise when he found out his name. The son of a dishwasher turned petty hotel manager; the worm had spent his life furthering his career in a personal campaign of bullying colleagues and of character assassination. In such a way he rose through the lower ranks of industry until one day he screwed up. Someone did a little delving into his background to find that, Lo and behold, he had glossed over the fact that he had invented his academic background. Knowing full well that the trail leading to his accuser lay beyond the knowledge of the office nematode, and delaying the opportunity to denounce the fool for what he was, Pierce's father left with a smile upon his face. One day he would find out, that was one thing he was sure of.

Once over the Merstham Valley interchange they were skirting Reigate City limits as the rising landscape took them over the hill on the south side where they caught their first view of genuinely open country. The tactical arrays picking up countless military IDs on the ground and in the air overhead as men and machines were driven and flown-in to face the southern onslaught. The Grinstead-Crawley Airport-UPA providing an outer perimeter fence that left a ring-fenced Gatwick airport like the hole in the centre of a hollow doughnut. A security system within a security system, Gatwick took most of the international traffic on its three runways since Northolt and Heathrow had been scaled down to take only VIP traffic in and out of London. Hover patrols buzzed overhead along the E23 while military convoys ran up and down its length. At Handcross, high on one of the many ridges of the denuded anti-cline they caught magnificent view across another of the many valleys, plunging down the hillside gathering speed, to climb yet again the ridge on the other side. On the final helter-skelter south the land opened out into rolling countryside between Bolney and the South Downs. The men in the convoy remaining silent as they rushed down the slope into the meadows of Sussex witnessing the bright flashes of light and hearing the dull thump of explosives as they drew closer to the front line.

A Spanish regiment of EPBs attempting to circumvent the blockade at Pyecombe to outflank the native defenders had stormed the hills above Brighton only to find the wide flat top of the Downs left undefended. On speeding across the hills in a wide front they ran into carefully concealed British army units at Saddlescombe and atop the great Dyke. Aerial support was being challenged by ground artillery dug in along the high ground above Shoreham making it doubly difficult for the Spanish and French units to move forward. Infantrymen armed with rocket launchers ruined enemy planes as they attempted to land or take off. One bomber making a spectacular dive into the harbour after a jubilant Pongo made the interloper pay for his arrogance with a well aimed missile up his tail pipe. Following the back roads tucked into the very edge of the north side of the hills the advancing column cut across country until they reached the narrow streets on the approaches to Ditchling. Following the winding country road around the high granite walls of the Rural UPA, they began their final leg up the steep track towards Beacon Hill, a superb vantage point high above the Sussex countryside. The thud and whine of powerful laser cannon could be heard as they crawled ever upwards towards the summit. Driving towards Falmer along the top of the broad sweep of hills they could see a line of emplacements stretching under the trees. Far away to the south west they could see enemy units outflanked and retreating back towards the coast, occasionally catching glimpses of the coast at Shoreham along deep furrows in the rolling hillside. "Boy, are they making a mess of that place!" Said one of the Corporals in the back looking through his intensifiers. The driver drove into a muddy chalky field following a newly-made track down the hill towards the east where a command post had been set up high above a narrow defile. The convoy fanning out in a defensive array along a hedge, disembarking troops in the gloom under a low layer of broken clouds. The rain had stopped falling for a while but a cold sea breeze blew over the hills from the coast. While the artillery in the east and the blockade in the west kept the EPB assault at bay on the rift in the hills north of Brighton, the engineers went to work in the muddy fields on the following morning. Laying charges and setting telemetry controlled detonators with skilful hands until every vulnerable point between Washington and Clayton had been mined. Other engineer squadrons performed the same tasks along the South Downs laying down a barrier designed to hurt, frustrate and whittle down the invading forces at every turn.

The recovery operation did not take place as Pierce had expected. For two days he watched with bated breath as his men worked their way along the railway from Clayton northwards to the cuttings beyond Haywoods Heath and then to the viaduct at Balcombe. A call came from division HQ for repair of the communications bunker at Washington. The generator installation had been taken out by a calculated shot over the hill leaving a large hole in the southern command's communications infrastructure. With the raid at Newhaven nothing more than a holding operation in which the attacking force had been well and truly boxed in, it was a matter of time before they capitulated. In the mean time fresh troops were being released for the build up prior to re-taking Shoreham. Threading its way between Fulking and Bramber it became obvious to the men in the small convoy that French snipers were working the hilltops way above them slowing them down. Sniper fire became more frequent as air cover struggled to nail the culprits. It was twilight when they arrived and began the task of replacing the destroyed plant and bringing the command node back into operation. Upper Beeding saw vicious fighting as the invading EPB battalion sought to charge north and capture strategic roads through the countryside beyond. The banks of the Adur being littered with the broken bodies of soldiers and their weapons as bitter hand to hand fighting ensued. Its chalky waters turning crimson in places as dreadful wounds leaked away from the living into the river. The decaying old convent taking a direct hit, bringing an agreeable finality to centuries of tyrannical education, collapsed into burning rubble, the sparks rising in congratulatory showers as the tinder dry beams spat and crackled forth with pent up wrath. Back at the command tent a large explosion went off close to the parked convoy taking with it a large section of the metalled road on the outskirts of Washington. The tiny village was to become a name synonymous with valorous conduct as the raiders tried and almost succeeded to outflank stiff native resistance.

In the melee following the explosion dense black smoke made the situation more difficult for the men to take their bearings. A bugle went off to one side of the road near the top of a steep embankment and off to their right they heard the blood curdling screams of an infantry attack sweeping towards them. "Move them out!" yelled Pierce. "Captain Greasley, get them out of here now!" Pointing with his arm outstretched Pierce indicating for the column to head directly for the main interchange. Another explosion almost burning the air and another bugle call, then he was surrounded by thick smoke. He fell back towards the slope and began to climb up the chalky bank unseen from the road. Pushing aside small thickets of thorn bushes and winding his way around trees he stumbled into the waiting combat group before he realised they were there. "OK, Sir?" asked a burly Sargent who was squatting behind a very prickly gorse bush. Pierce, nodded briefly, was led at a cracking pace to a small knot of trees and bushes in a narrow defile in the chalk. Behind a high bank of coarse grass covering the chalk downland he swiftly donned a set of flying overalls over his khaki uniform. Scarcely having time to fit the flying helmet over his head the combat group taking him by the arms rushed him quickly over the crest of another high bank into a hidden valley. He gasped at the sheer audacity of the plan. Hidden in the deepest recesses of the hill country lay a perfectly shaped valley with a long flat floor where, in between two strips of crops, a short runway had been laid out, a small hanger peeped out of the bank surrounded by blackthorn and scrub. They dashed down the slope into the valley with the sounds of the skirmishing soldiers and firearms diminishing into silence as the sides of the valley muffled out all sounds from the world beyond its borders.

A sleek plasma-jet fighter lying hidden under camouflage came into view as they ran along the front of the hangar. The group of soldiers dividing itself into two with two men bundling Pierce into the aircraft, while the larger group of four released the camouflage from around the small aircraft. The canopy began closing around them while the pilot started the twin plasma jets. Pierce heard the last of the safety harness buckles click into place just when the canopy was latched and locked into place by one of the soldiers. Almost immediately afterwards the Sargent banged on the side of the aircraft twice giving a wave of his arm indicating the camouflage was out of harm's way and that the pilot could proceed. The pilot nodded returning the thumbs up sign before hitting the throttles controlling the plasma injection circuits. Pierce watched with detached anticipation as the little wings moved forwards over the grass strip. There was a sensation of gathering speed and the growing 'whooshing' sounds as the plasma field injectors did their work. Within fifty metres they were airborne, hurtling towards the far end of the strip. Using ground-effect the pilot hugged the valley floor then, pulling back on the stick at the last minute he shot the aircraft over the treetops towards Storrington. Once over the main road and into the open country they made a tight turn to the north gathering speed all the time. They kept low, down to two hundred feet, a few minutes later passing the old monastery spire at Cowfold at six hundred knots and throttling back in a broad sweeping turn to the north east, crossing the bumpy Sussex terrain alongside the E23 at Warninglid.

The pilot set them down in the meadows under the high wall of Holmsted Manor, the military nerve-centre of the south coast defence operation. Hovering gently between two large fighter-bombers they sank slowly earthwards onto the soft grass while the ground crew waited patiently for the signal from the batsman to cut engines. With the whining engines slowing to a standstill they swarmed around the jet laden with tools and other paraphernalia. The pilot motioned to Pierce for him to vacate the cockpit and he clambered out as a hover bat came into view between the lines of aircraft. The pilot shot him a farewell as he prepared to talk to the ground-crew attending his aircraft. Pierce waited until he was sure the hover bat was intended for him. "Hello Sir, will you please come with me, the General is waiting to see you." Pierce nodded and returned the salute, even though he felt awkward wearing the bone-dome. The driver took him up the bank to a gravel roadway leading them around the front of the building, then across to the other side and through an old converted stable yard-cum-garage, through yet another gate into a second meadow where three large bivouacs had been erected. He drove around the perimeter under tall limes with spreading branches until they reached a medium sized tent with armed guards posted around it. Pierce clambered out of the vehicle and the driver headed off to another part of the field once he was clear.

Major-General Haslet stood tall and erect at his map boards locked in discussion with three other senior officers when an orderly officer gave the news of Pierce's arrival to him. Having curtailed the meeting he left the map room for another part of the tent sub-divided by several sheets of canvas into small briefing rooms. He had been totally exonerated of any complicity in the attempted coup by a grateful President, returning to his military duties during the final hours of the demise of the old government. His part in the plan to restore the country back into a democracy was perhaps, more directly linked to taking an active role in the defence of the realm while the politicians made good use the time he and his colleagues bought so dearly with the lives of his soldiers.

He met the General alone, but the ever-present hand of his friend William Goodfellow was plain to see, in the nature of the work he was being tasked to do. "You job Major is to bring the king safely back to us…"

"He's alive, that is good news Sir!"

"Yes, we have the solid nerve of our friends in the navy to thank for his preservation, but I must warn you this will be no easy matter. Our mutual friend in London asks us to be especially careful of the old guard who are still seeking to influence the outcome by stalling the elections and if necessary, by removing his majesty from the equation altogether. You must trust no one unless personally known by you to be trustworthy, and who can help you if you get caught up in any adverse situation. Believe you me Major the old guard have been found to have penetrated almost every nook and cranny of authority, both in government as well as in the military. There are an unknown number of people who are still working to stop us, and I am able to tell you that the second part of this operation will require you to remain just as anonymous; as you will be held in-communicado for most of the time. Operationally speaking, of course."

"Yes Sir, do I have any means of communication at all?" asked Pierce.

"The fact is Major you are personally known to the king, and those in whose care he is currently residing are as trustworthy as you. In between us; that is me, you and the king and those immediately around him are several groups of people who would not like to have him come back home. In that group I would place other international interests looking for an opportunity to negotiate a king's ransom." The general paused before continuing. "Only a very few people know that the king is safe and well. An even smaller group knows where he is and you will be party to that knowledge shortly." Pierce nodded in silence. "When did you last have something to eat?" asked the General as an afterthought.

"Not since we stopped on the road at the Dyke blockade Sir."

"Ah, in that case I'll take you over to the canteen. Come with me."

Walking out of the tent into the night they strode towards the old manor house, Pierce carrying his helmet under an arm. On the way across the dew soaked grass the General slipped him a small packet telling him to keep it out of sight for the time being. They entered the old entranceway stepping across the black and white marble tiled floor and into the panelled hallway with its oak panelling and wooden floors. The General led the way to a side door at the bottom of a wide stairway leading to the upper floors. He took the narrow staircase to the basement in a rapid advance downstairs coming to another door at the bottom, which he opened, entering onto a small and homely cafeteria. Over a very early breakfast the General asked Pierce about his movements during the past few days seeking clues to the strength of the enemy, their tactics, their weaknesses, and so on. Pierce answered as truthfully as he could, giving due thought to some of the fighting he had seen by day as well as by night. "I'm sorry we can't offer you a place to sleep." Apologised the General as they walked out onto the gravel drive outside the front door an hour later. "You will have plenty of opportunity though on your flight to your destination. That's all explained in the packet I gave to you earlier. Your quarry will be waiting for you and I suspect will be relieved to see you personally. Your instructions contain a few signal codes that will be meaningless to all except a very few people. Use them wisely Major Anders, and then only if you have to. Make your way down that pathway to the left through those bushes and back down to the aircraft in the lower meadow. You will find an armed scout and its pilot waiting to take you. Good luck Major and be sure to be back within thirty-six hours."

"Thank you Sir, goodnight." Responded Pierce respectfully giving the General a smart salute. The General returning the salute walked off into the darkness. Minutes later the little scout took off while the General returned to his work in the great tent. Pierce settled back in his seat as they crossed the county line into Hampshire climbing through thirty thousand feet, following a course that would take them on a diverging path across the coast of the Axe river valley and beyond into the Western Approaches. His bone-dome tilting forwards sometime later as sleep overtook him. The pilot grinning silently to himself reached behind his passenger's chair to get a packet of sandwiches from the seats in the rear. The outline of his face reflecting the dull glow of the instrument panel lighting in front of him while munching on his in-flight snack.

****

Aromatic smoke curled lazily towards the high rafters of the boat-shed as dried driftwood mixed with sage kindling crackled and fizzed energetically causing brief shades to dance about the walls like dervishes spinning across the rough planking. Venus Theodrakkis sat on pile of old crates topped with sacking and dreamed romantically. The British seamen had left the house before dawn in response to a radio message they had received from their ship. Shortly afterwards a sleek, fast combat helicopter had shot around the mouth of the tiny harbour bringing the man she had wanted to see. Her father was there on the jetty to greet the aircraft as it hovered just inches from the ground while depositing two men. Fred, removing his flying helmet looked towards her as she approached him from behind her father's solid frame. The roaring blades pushing a hard cushion of air against the onlookers, revealing her lovely figure as her skirts blew back against her torso and limbs. Fred did not know it, but something just went 'ting!' inside him like the gentle chime of a small bell that he had once heard long ago, now suppressed in the years since his ex-wife had deserted him for another. The aircraft vanished into the night sky as soon as the crewman onboard closed the side door. Walking back to the boat shed Fred briefly took stock of the past few days, particularly the last four to five hours. They had gone through so much and come out of it alive; he could scarcely believe their good fortune. Still there was much more for them to complete before the long adventure was over. Returning the Sub's salute he greeted the men pleasantly motioning for them to remain where they were seated or lounging around the fire. He briefed the shore-party indicating that they were due to be picked up by Royal Oak in a couple of hours. Venus looking across the fire towards the focus of her desire, not hearing the words as he spoke to the other British sailors. The warm apricot and orange light adding hidden gestures to their surroundings. It hadn't dawned on her that she might never see him again until much later.

A little later an army patrol came down the steep road and onto the jetty. The Greek Liaison officer who replaced Commander Dmitriou during the exchange with the chopper emerged from the dark in combat uniform to speak with them briefly, informing the soldiers that all was well, sending them on their way. Lieutenant Roussoss spoke very good English and was enjoying a lively conversation with his British counterparts. Fred eventually left for a breath of fresh air and a quiet pipe. His habit returning to him as the pressures of living on the knife-edge of war returned to un-settle his mood.

"My father smokes a pipe." Ventured Venus as she caught up with him on the grassy perimeter of the jetty. Fred half-turning looked to see her emerge out of the gloom of night. He had not heard her soft footfalls on the thin green carpet of grass. "Is it something that all sailors have to do?" She continued. "Perhaps." Replied Fred feeling slightly amused by her remark. "I keep telling him it's no good for his health, but he never listens."

"No I expect not," said Fred with a slight smile. "He nearly always burns his jacket and his pullovers are covered with tiny holes and burn marks where the wind has blown the tobacco onto it." Fred removed the small 'Windjammer' pipe from his mouth and laughed as he tapped it on the rocks emptying the remains of his previous indulgence into the crannies. "What will you do when the war is over?" She asked pensively. "Are you going to be here in the Mediterranean for sometime?" She followed up immediately, wishing she had not given herself away so easily. Fred reached for a small pouch and said that he did not know for sure. "Were you always a sailor?" She asked stepping closer. "Always, ever since I was a boy and ran away to sea."

"You're not like my father." She observed. "No, I expect not." Replied Fred scratching the back of his head with his free hand. "He's been a seaman all his life, even when he left our navy. That boat is all that he has left now..." Her voice trailed off. Fred looked at the dark outline of the ferry resting peacefully at its berth. "Is that since your mother died?"

"Your very perceptive Commander." replied Venus a little too stiffly for her liking. Still, he had touched a nerve. She softened a little. "And very wise. How did you know?"

"Is that why he takes those summer trips with all those tourists?" pressed Fred ignoring the question for one of his own. "He has always loved the sea." She said looking across the top of the rocks towards the waters of the bay hidden in the dark. A cool breeze ruffling her jet-black hair. She tossed it gently back into place when the wind temporarily caused it to drop across her eyes. Fred began to pack tobacco into the pipe bowl as he cast his gaze aloft noting the distant stars in breaks between the clouds. "I am not sure when we will come back. I've always wanted to explore the possibility of a Mediterranean trade route I must admit. But until now we've not had the time."

"Is that what you were doing before the war?"

"Yes, we own the Royal Oak, and one day when we are free to do so we will return to our business of importing and exporting cargoes across the sea." There was a long silence as they stood side by side at a respectable distance. Fred unaware of what was happening to him as he chatted easily with the Greek Captain's daughter.

"I hope you come back." She said quietly. 'There I go again!' She admonished herself for yet again exposing herself so obviously. 'Why did I do that?' She asked herself.

"It's a nice place you have here, and the weather is very agreeable. It would be nice to do that."

'Ooh!' She thought, 'he's not listening.' As the answer he proffered was not the answer she was expecting.

Fred leaned down behind the rocks and lit his pipe. During the pause she tried to see the outline of his face in the dim light of the flame. He was standing once more looking towards the darkened hillside and the old house that stood a little way up the side of the hill. "Look." She said pointing to a distant light on the other side of the cove, touching his elbow gently with her free hand. "That's my aunt's house over there. I expect she will be coming soon to get Father and me out of bed." Fred did not move. He felt her warm fingers slip into the crook of his elbow momentarily and then they were gone as he drew his attention to the distant light, suddenly feeling very lonely as they left his arm. "Does she always look after your household?"

"Oh, yes, ever since I was ten years old. She came to live nearby when my brother and I were children. She's my father's sister and had no children of her own."

"That was a brave thing to do." Fred observed, "looking after someone else's children."

"Oh, she's alright. Her husband is some businessman in Thessalonika and his business became like children to him when they found out they couldn't have any of their own."

"Really, what does he do?"

"Oh he's an agent dealing in nuts and olive oil. I suppose anything like that really."

"It's sad. A man should have children of his own." Quite why he said that he didn't know. "I think he would be a different man if they did." She offered up wistfully. "More than likely." Fred agreed. They continued talking as the clouds thickened above them heralding an overcast sky for the coming day. Finally turning once more to immediate matters upon hearing approaching footsteps, the Greek Captain appeared with the Sub in tow breaking into their private reverie.

"Your ship is coming in about twenty minutes." He announced as they approached. Fred immediately checked his timepiece. 'Was that really the time?' He thought counting the passing minutes in his head since he had wandered out of the boat shed for a quite breath of fresh air. It felt to him as if time had stood still while making small talk with Venus. "Good Lord! So it is!" He exclaimed. "Thank you Sir." The old Captain caught a glimpse of Fred's pipe. "Oh, so you smoke the pipe?" He asked.

"Yes, would you like to try some of my tobacco?" The Captain grinned while fishing a battered old pipe from out of his trousers pocket. The two men stood at the edge of the jetty puffing away in silent appreciation with Venus standing between them feeling nonplussed and slightly indignant that her conversation had come to an end. She slipped her arm into her father's, standing close to him with her head resting against his shoulder. "Papa, I will never understand you." She sighed. He patted her hand lightly with his while looking at the remaining stars peeping through the vestiges of clear sky. Fred stole a look at the two of them and almost jumped to find Venus looking up at him. Almost innocently she slipped her other hand into the crook of Fred's arm, standing between the two men feeling truly at ease for the first time in a very long time since her dear mama had passed away.

The rendezvous finally shattered anyone's hopes of meeting again as Royal Oak appeared, large as life, around the headland at the outer reaches of the harbour. Venus had held onto her father tightly as the waters filled the widening gap between the departing ship and the jetty. Fred giving a parting wave of his hand as they turned to face the open sea once more. Venus suddenly felt very small and very much alone. No longer sliding among the shadows in stealthy expectancy of being discovered by an unseen enemy Royal Oak raced out of the harbour and was gone. They clambered up the rock pile to wave her off, hearing the change in the timbre of the engines as she went on-planes. Then she was just a distant thrumming in the darkness. Fingers of grey etched the sky with dawn's light as her head touched the pillow. Smiling secretly to herself she turned over and drifted off to sleep. Her kind papa would tell his faithful sister to leave his daughter for the morning while he sat in the kitchen pondering the great events unfolding around his own country. Deep in his heart he knew the day he had hoped would never arrive could not now be very far away. It made him feel old, and with the fussing and gentle chiding of his sister over breakfast it made him feel all the more somewhat older. His sister looking at him for a moment in between her often times censorious chatter saw him looking wistfully at her over his mug of coffee and sighing gently in a deep almost forlorn sigh. He wasn't paying attention and she knew it, but something about that look and that sigh gave her a subtle premonition. She turned away raising her eyes to the ceiling to another part of the house where lay her niece in blissful slumber.

With the duty watches re-shuffled to allow those men who had spent all night up and about time to get to their bunks, the Royal Oak now set course for the gates of Hercules far to the west. Her diplomatic passport agreed and almost 'set in stone' William, who had volunteered the first four hours, now paced the bridge occasionally looking at the navigation sensor plot in passing. He successfully argued that having spent most of the night in the duties of load master he was in no condition to climb so soon into his bunk. Chip retired to his day cabin once they had cleared the coast and made sure the tactical plots were relatively clear of immediate targets. The sea was rolling gently and keeping their speed down to a comfortable twenty-five knots for the comfort of the temporary hospital patients they carried, Chip settled back into a dreamless sleep. With the exception of his close friend all of his shipmates slept deep and dreamless slumber. Fred remained on the edge of consciousness aware of a jumble of deeply disturbing pictures and emotions as occasionally he saw himself talking to Venus in the cool night of a distant garden. Outside the dawn revealing a grey and oily sea covered with a low blanket of deeply compacted cumulus. Their Greek escorts arrived at the entrance to the Kaphereus Channel fanning out in a wall of high-speed defence against the hidden dangers of lurking enemy vessels, on or below the waters. True to his word, the king of Greece had arranged priority for the Royal Oak to make passage through the Corinth Canal. The clearance being handled by trusted members of his staff so that as the Royal Oak approached the outer reaches of the navigation to the ancient city, they were directed through without the hindrance of other vessels in her path. Elsewhere, silent hunters waiting for their quarry beyond the Sea of Crete turned away, disdainfully aware of missing their chance high above the densely packed clouds. Heading west the small flight of aircraft made good speed for their home plate, having been denied even a visual sighting of the intended victim. Their satellite enhanced tactical sensors blinded by thickening clouds and heavy rain.

The ninety-mile journey through the mighty Gulf of Corinth in concert with her escort gave them precious advantage in time. Once clear of the mighty mouth standing at the entrance of the cusp between the mainland of Ellas and Peloponnesus they met their final escort at the narrows of the gulf of Patras heading for Zakinthos. Once beyond the Ionian Islands they bade a grateful farewell to their hosts facing the open waters alone in the gloomy dusk of their first night of the journey home. Exhausted seamen slept or gathered in their crowded mess deck for long discussions and relaxation in between the process of falling into step with seagoing watches. Each man vying with the next to strike up a liaison with any one of the eight female nurses who had eventually arrived onboard before their departure from Thessalonika the previous night. Many of the patients were gladdened by the prospect of moving about on the quarter deck for a breath of fresh air, and many too were deeply touched when on the first day out during their journey across the gulf, the King himself came to visit the makeshift hospital. The men appreciating his presence amongst them, and his personal interest in their welfare. The Admiral was kept busy out of sight in the equipment room, exchanging signals with the powers back home. Many of who were glad to have him back in harness to consult and to make vital strategic decisions. The Admiral was relieved to hear that two significantly well placed moles had been found out and removed. One of them in the army defence committee while another had been uncovered only after significant damage had been done to the air force's strategic defence plan for the nation.

By nine o' clock that night two things happened to dispel any complacency they might have felt over their diplomatic status. A heavily encoded signal arrived for Chip informing him to prepare for a transfer at sea sometime in the middle of the morning, requesting the position of Royal Oak. The signal was un-signed and given their current situation the request was not normal since that information was already in the hands of the Admiralty. Fred and Chip met to discuss the last twenty-four hours, and as a parting shot Chip slipped the signal across to Fred for a second opinion. "It's a bit out of kilter if you ask me." Responded Fred. "Surely they would know that by way of the Admiral here onboard?"

"My thoughts entirely," agreed Chip. "I must confess to having my suspicions. Right Fred, I think we should ignore this for the time being until I can meet with the Admiral." The second thing occurred towards midnight when their augmented tactical displays jumped back into life causing immediate alarm. The duty tactical plotters reporting several targets converging towards them from the south, one of them large enough to be a carrier. Several aircraft became noticeable in their vicinity, spelling an end to their brief period of confidence in diplomacy.

At eight fifteen the following morning a grey smudge appearing on the starboard bow, heralded their landfall with the southern toe of Italy. The Coast of Calabria having been the largest feature growing in size on their radar sensor for some time. Ninety minutes later as they were proceeding into the Straits of Messina two aircraft began closing rapidly from the south. The targets giving clear indication of a flight leader and wingman in tight echelon formation. The flight ID was clearly American and their intention was unknown if not definitely suspicious. Flying the Union flag and in union territorial waters Chip had the signal op send out two signals in quick succession. The first signal offered a warning to the Italian authorities at Reggio of a probable attack. The other warning was sent to the approaching aircraft advising them of the consequences of violating international boundaries. "Tell the Americans we have informed the Europol authorities." The signal op sent the voice message while the action stations alarm sounded in the background. Men rushed to their places of duty and covers were rapidly torn from their places over the cannons. The Admiral emerged from the equipment room and waited patiently, watching the plot for any sign of change in the flight path of the threatening aircraft. "Belay firing Commander! When you think about it we are bearing the markings of a hospital ship aren't we?"

"Why yes of course we are." Chip had realised the significance of any warlike posture presented by any vessel bearing the marks of the Red Cross in a white circle. "It's just a precautionary measure."

"Leave it to the locals from now on. They can deal with it." The Admiral did not miss the significance of a warrior's trait in Chip's approach to always be on his guard.

Far to the stern two slivers of metal dropped below the ceiling of low clouds for a few seconds, then disappeared in a lazy chandelle to the left as they swung back up into the compacted cumulus. The radar plot telling the complete story of their abrupt change in course away from the coast. "That seems to have satisfied their curiosity for the time being." William observed brooding from his position at the weapons console. "It tells us that while we have cloud cover they need to confirm our presence here by more conventional means." noted the Admiral. "Look here and here." He continued, spelling out the obvious. "There are two US carriers in the region. One here at Syracuse, that will be the code for the Saratoga. She's in dock with a seized main bearing, and that will be her replacement the USS Martin Luther king steaming along the coast of Tunisia."

"Their submarine systems are not capable of determining the fingerprint of skimmer class surface vessels, and that leaves them pretty much in the dark." Mused Chip. "It also tells me that they are not receiving MARIS data."

"A good point Commander, it seems as though our European friends have trimmed the Marine Information System data to exclude non-European users. Can your specialists confirm that?" enquired the Admiral. "Yes they can, almost immediately I should think." Fred volunteered by walking over to the equipment room and entering the dimly lit compartment, emerging a few minutes later with a wide grin on his face. "You should see what they're doing in there he observed. They've built a complete composite on top of our augmented system array. The Chief will have it ready in about two hours, but in the meantime he says the EuroSat tactical and information data network has stopped transmitting data to all British and non EU member states."

"How's he getting the data?" the Admiral asked. Chip looked away saying nothing for a moment. "I'd rather not say for now Sir, if you don't mind."

"Ah, fine, just as long as he keeps it coming. For the time being I must get back in there and talk to London."

"Would you care to accompany me to the chart room Sir?" Chip said innocuously, I have something to show you that may be of interest to yourself."

"Why, yes of course." Once in the Chartroom with the Admiral Chip retrieved the small gadget that had been found in the equipment room. "I think you should know we found this piece of equipment in our sensor array systems, and no one knows how it got there." Admiral Dunham looked at the small box passively on the outside with his mind racing rapidly in thought at the endless possibilities as to what it could be. "Does anyone have any idea what it is."

"No Sir, although it seems to be some kind of integrator that sits in between the sensor receiver and transmitter arrays."

"When was it discovered?"

"Sometime after our arrival in Dekelia, so it could have been put there at any time during the refit, right up to the time we sailed for Thessalonika."

"Is there anyone onboard who could have done this? Someone other than your Chief Technician?"

"I can vouch for all the crew Sir, as you probably know Sir they volunteered to a man."

'Anyone new to the ship, apart from our passengers?"

"William MacBrayne is the only newcomer who has appropriate access at specific times. Other than that Sub-Lieutenant Pengelly returned during our last week of refit just prior to our sea-trials..."

"You can exclude Leyland Pengelly, I've known him for some time, and about his recent escapades from his hospital bed. Lieutenant William MacBrayne you say?"

"Of Menteith Sir." added Chip wryly.

"What kind of officer is he?"

"A pilot like myself Sir. He was sent over as a gunner from Yeovilton."

"Why on earth did they do that?"

"The guns were cannibalised from a wrecked fighter aircraft, and he was the only available man who had experience with the type of armament. There's no one else on board who, except myself, could have done the job without training, and there was no time to train people after the Turks began their attack on our bases." The Admiral suddenly realising his earlier observations on the bridge had probably been superfluous in the company of two experienced pilots. He pressed on. "Now I understand. Well, it worries me, but we have more important things to do for now. We may find out what this is at some time in the future, or we may not. I suggest the best thing you can do is to keep it in its hide away and try to forget about it until something falls into place."

"Yes, that's how I viewed it."

The journey up the Straits was uneventful. The Italian navy providing a brace of patrol skimmers to escort them through the busy narrow waterway until they rounded Punta del Falo where a destroyer met them. Dr Keen kept out of sight in Chip's cabin during the difficult time of transferring pilots while the Admiral busied himself in Chip's day cabin with the work of running the navy's defence strategy via tightly secure tacsat links to London. The close proximity of the other naval vessels in the escort providing sufficient 'cover' for the frequent traffic on the up-link. The Admiral suspected that the American warfare officer onboard the carriers had reported an increase in tacsat traffic in the area, prompting the reconnaissance flight from the Martin Luther king. He made a mental note to keep his responses to the constant stream of data down to an absolute minimum once the destroyer dropped astern on the completion of its escort duty.

460

By midnight the Royal Oak cleared the western extremities of Italian influence and with a final send off over the radio where the Italian Captain wished them good luck, they were on their own again. During breakfast at seven in the morning the tactical plot buzzed a sub-surface warning indicating that a submarine had been detected on sensor arrays. The distant target echo producing no ident marker on the display. The fingerprint database routines performed three rapid searches in the main system finding nothing. The supplemental database produced a probable US prototype Washington class boomer out of Portsmouth, New Hampshire. The tactical plotter initiating a history algorithm watched the plot as it reduced the scale to include the whole of the Atlantic Ocean from the US coast to the western Mediterranean. Saw the red line indicating the course the boat had run since leaving her home port. Noting the 'sniffing' around just off the west coast of Scotland before heading around the rugged coastline of Ireland on a wide sweeping arc towards the Straits of Gibraltar. "Ah, ha!" Said the plotter recognising an unauthorised intruder into the European Mediterranean zone. "Possible friendly Sir, US submarine, designated Washington class. Putting data up on the main screen now."

The Sub clicked on the auto-strobe producing the data for an instant targeting solution. Selecting the update function he pre-set the minimum distance that he would allow the submarine to approach before the system automatically set off more alerts. Admiral Dunham noted the latest information as it appeared on the wall screen in his temporary accommodation.

There was no warning. The interloper appeared from the west coming directly out of the sun as the Royal Oak made progress in an oily swell fifty miles south of Cape Spartivento. The lookouts had no time to shout a warning as the aircraft racing past them at low level turned sharply skywards leaving a hollow crater in the water where it's twin engine exhausts gouged out a boiling cauldron. Sounding action stations the whole ship went into a frenzied dash as watch keepers and day-men alike scrambled to their posts. Pierce Anders straining against his harness caught a fleeting glimpse of the grey painted vessel skimming along as the pilot half-turning his aircraft put it into a steep climb. He sat back resting his bone dome against the seat waiting for the next manoeuvre to be executed. Once in the clouds the pilot levelled off briefly before turning his steed around in the opposite direction. With the engines now slowing they began a more dignified descent through the white out until the grey-blue waters began to peep through the ragged fronds at the base of the clouds. The pilot activating a control sent a single transmission in high level code on its way through the ether. The ident code of his aircraft duly received by Royal Oak's tactical filters changed the tenor of the men standing by in tense expectation of war. The Admiral shook his head pursing his lips went straight into the equipment room and gave a quiet order to the senior signal operator. The brief exchange of coded signals causing no change in the warlike posture of the men on the bridge. "Still no target data Sir!" confirmed the tactical plotter. The navigator kept sweeping his sensor array functions for different modes, finally giving up with manual modes returning to full automatic in disgust. "Nothing on navigation sensors Sir!" Came the confirming report.

"Something's amiss. We have a solid target…"

"There' Sir!" Interrupted a Bosun's mate. "Two points off the Port quarter Sir, just under the clouds!"

All those with intensifiers turned to look. "As I was saying, we have a solid target and now a visual contact with a target, but we have no target data." He paused. "William have your guns crews go to standby please, he's lowering his undercarriage. The Admiral appeared out of the equipment room walking to the centre of the bridge. "Heave-to Commander if you please we have a visitor coming aboard."

"Cox'n, Heave-to, and maintain stabilisation. We don't want our patients to get sea-sick, do we." Ordered Fred, being party to the Admiral's spoken order.

Their speed fell away as the plasma-jet made a slow approach towards them. The planes finally auto-retracting as their threshold speed diminished beyond their capability. The deck crew jumped into action with their aircraft recovery and transfer equipment in preparation to receive a visitor. Pierce reflecting with detachment on the final details of his journey on the broad hulled, high-sided craft now rocking to a standstill below them. He thought it looked awfully small and waited patiently as they transitioned from horizontal to vertical flight mode. He saw the pilot breath a sigh of relief as two men appeared clambering onto the broad high roof behind the mast. Realising that he was expected to climb down onto 'that thing' he prepared himself mentally for what would be a hair-raising experience. An audible sound announced the canopy release had freed the plasti-glass dome which was confirmed as the automatic lifter tilted it up and backwards giving both of them a feel of the rushing air around them, even though they were now only travelling at about five knots towards their rendezvous. "I will touch down your side," announced the pilot. "So you should only have to step out onto that roof." He paused. "In theory."

"In theory." Repeated Pierce totally unconvinced, hearing the slight humour in the pilot's voice. They slowly crawled across the sky until the roof was slightly below Pierce's side of the aircraft. Then edging it in slowly the pilot moved over the roof to drop down gently on its starboard undercarriage. A crewman hooked the undercarriage with an earthing rod, then the pilot instructed Pierce to disconnect his comms line before alighting onto the roof of the Royal Oak. "Tell them I have only fifteen minutes waiting time, then I must leave no matter what the outcome."

"Understood." Came the final reply from Pierce before he unplugged the audio link to his head set, then he was gone, scrambling down the side of the cargo roof and onto the deck of Royal Oak where he was greeted by a tall Lieutenant and two ratings carrying side-arms. William indicating to their visitor with hand-signals that he should accompany him forward into a nearby hatchway while the din of the aircraft's engines drowned out any hope of spoken communication. Pierce followed William through the hatchway and along the flat leading into the bridge. There he turned towards one side before knocking politely on a closed door with the titular designation of its owner emblazoned across the simulated oak-wood finish, 'Captain'.

Pierce's first impression was that he had stumbled into the domain of a fiercely independent individual with a careful eye for protocol and not afraid of danger. The Captain had greeted him very formally and asked bluntly what it was that made it so important for him to stop his ship un-announced on the high seas. Pierce smiled back patiently as Chip weighing him up took the sealed packet from his visitor. "Please sit down Major Anders, I see you come with a Presidential Communiqué addressed to the king. What makes the President think that such an auspicious person as the king would be onboard my otherwise unlikely vessel?" Chip asked his visitor firmly. "First let me explain that I have only fifteen minutes before the pilot has to turn back, with or without a response to whatever is in the letter. Secondly Sir, I can only relate to you my small part in this mission as a late equerry to his majesty, and as such I remain loyal to him as much as I do to the current government of our country under President Warnock's leadership. Who is attempting to bring about the wishes of the people for a democratically elected government by first fulfilling the constitutional requirement of an interim government in which the king's blessing is an important requirement."

"So you personally know his majesty then?" Chip could only admire the man for his outspoken courage, and for laying his cards on the table so openly at the very beginning. "Yes, indeed Sir, for three years I worked with him and, I believe, remain in good standing." Chip paused momentarily. Then calling for William had the visitor escorted to the wardroom.

Chip went to the equipment room and asked the Admiral to join him. The Admiral seemed relieved when he looked at the covering letter from William Goodfellow, Private Secretary to the President. "We've met," added the Admiral. "He's loyal and a good friend of both the President and to the king. I think we can trust this Major Anders. If he comes with the approbation of the President's personal secretary and is a former ADC to the king, he comes with a fine set of credentials indeed." Chip accompanied the Admiral to the king's cabin, entering in response to the call for them to enter. The two senior men quickly discussing the letter sent by William Goodfellow to the king; came to a momentous decision. "Commander, I will return to England with the Admiral and Major Anders in that small aircraft." The king paused noticing the serious look of concern on Chip's face. "Come now Chip, I have enjoyed the good company of yourself and of your crew. You have cheerfully provided me with safety and with your ample protection, and if I may say so, with your enthusiastic company in the most difficult circumstances. This is something that I must do, and I can promise you that I will be waiting to hear more about you and the Royal Oak in the weeks ahead. Where is Major Anders for I must see him quickly before I am to be rushed off in that tiny bubble circling around us?"

"He's waiting for confirmation that you are aboard Sir, in the wardroom."

"Then let's go and meet him." said the king making his way towards the door.

The reunion was warm and friendly with the young army man genuinely relieved to find the king alive and well. "How much time have we got before I must depart?" asked the king finally.

"Just under ten minutes Sir." Responded Pierce. "I have flying kit here for you and for the Admiral."

"Oh, how is that?" demanded the Admiral pointedly. "I saw no reference to myself in your letters of despatch Major Anders."

"My apologies Sir." Said Pierce fishing out a second packet from a pocket in the knee of his flying overalls. "My first duty was to establish the king was onboard and to accompany him home. But William did say that in all probability you would be near to the king and made provision for the aircraft to accommodate all of us."

"William you say, Major?" asked the king momentarily pausing. "Of course, Goodfellow and Anders! Observed the Admiral, pleased that what had been bothering him had finally come to the surface." The Admiral clearing his throat opened the letter to read the contents quickly and thoroughly. "Right." He announced. "I must collect my things and be on my way. There have been some developments, as you are probably aware." With that he excused himself from the small gathering and taking his flying kit with him headed back to the equipment room.

The little scout came racing up to the skimmer's position with something like seven minutes left to spare. Five people stood on the roof three of them in flying kit waiting to be picked up. A Bosun's pipe twittered feebly against the rushing sound of the jet engines while the Captain, First Lieutenant and the officer of the watch formed a small knot of officialdom wishing them a hearty farewell. The king gave a warm wave of his hand after returning the salute then they were gone leaving them in the near silence of their surroundings as the scout lifted away and shot off into the skies above. The sudden change of atmosphere with the departing dignitaries left the crew feeling a little lonely as the vessel began to make way again, in the face of oncoming rollers fanning out from the Atlantic gap between the two landmasses of Europe and of Africa in the west. Sub had noticed with satisfaction how the planes had locked smoothly into position at around nine knots. He loved to tinker with the refinements of ship handling in manual mode. The steel grey painted hull climbed majestically out of the waters gathering speed towards the west.

The first detonation struck the point of the bows just on the waterline as Sub turned back to look at the nav plot. With action stations sounding and the skimmer letting the Mediterranean Sea enter into the hull, the weapons systems cut in to auto-defence mode. A defensive screen of rockets shot out from their launchers, and while the forward guns lay somewhat canted a second explosion went off nearby as another missile or shell missing its mark splashed harmlessly into the sea exploding on impact. Bullets struck them with deadly force penetrating the superstructure from stem to stern. A seaman on the bridge managed to activate the emergency control console before slithering to the deck in a growing puddle of his own blood. Shouting orders and filling in the gaps the senior sailors grappled with the problems associated with a surprise attack, not knowing whether it was by a naval adversary or an airborne attack -or both. The tactical plot zoomed in as the systems scanned to find a target. The only possible threat appeared to be the large red blob on the display representing the Carrier force steaming along slowly to the south of them. Another explosion and William joined them on the bridge. Chip looking at him severely as he rushed over with his trousers open at the waist, while tucking in his shirt. The man had plainly been caught with his trousers down and Fred smiling, even in this tough moment of extremity, wondered how William Macbrayne of Menteith would explain this piece of drollery in the event that they survived the attack.

The radio operator was sitting down on the deck bleeding profusely from several splinter wounds to his upper torso and arms, repeating over and over the message given to him by Fred. "This is the hospital ship Royal Oak, stop your attack immediately! I say again…" William looked helplessly for tactical data and finding none shot his Captain an anguished look. "Going over to manual Sir, we have no tactical data!"

"Very good Guns, make it so!"

"Lookouts, anything!" called out Fred desperately waiting for a reply. "Cox'n, bring her around to one, eight zero and increase speed to thirty knots!" The Cox'n repeated the order making the adjustments on the autopilot finding with some relief, that she was answering the helm. Down below the damage control party found complete mayhem under the bows into the forepeak where a long gash in the hull had left the nose open to the sea just on the waterline. Slowly she recovered sufficiently as the hull rose beyond the gash spilling the water and debris out into the open sea. Frantically placing mattresses over the hole and then wooden shoring behind them they plugged the large opening as she accelerated to high speed, approaching thirty-four knots a vibration began to make itself known as they ploughed over the top of the seas nose heavy. The damage control team threw down large hoses connected to emergency pumps that sucked greedily at the murky water now filling the bows up to their waists. With the Mediterranean no longer leaking inboard the pumps were visibly reducing the mass of water. At thirty five knots a high frequency vibration began to shake the hull with every component rattling in sympathy throughout the skimmer. "Bridge, engine room!" Blared a loudspeaker.

"Engine room, go ahead!" answered Fred.

"Looks like asymmetrical retraction is imminent!" Leyland Pengelly made the fateful pronouncement on the planes with the solid voice of conviction. "I'm sending two of my hull technicians up there now."

"Thank you Leyland, how much time have we got?"

"Not long Sir, say about two or three minutes before retraction."

"Damn! Chip swore. A missile slicing through the air bounced across their view through what remained of one of the forward windows. "Its' an aircraft Sir!" shouted the starboard lookout. "I can hear an aircraft somewhere on this side above the clouds!"

"Why can we not see it?" demanded Chip. "For the second time today we seem to have lost our tactical ability to see our targets!"

A missile launched from the port waist left a smoking trail behind it while simultaneously a laser cannon started firing. "Aircraft passing overhead starboard to port Sir, still no tactical!" shouted William. The distant sound of cannon could be heard and the sea nearby became stitched with miniature columns of water as rounds worked their way relentlessly across the surface of the sea towards them. Everybody down!" Shouted Fred as the cannon fire ripped into them diagonally from the bows on the starboard side across to the port waist on the other. The Cox'n looking up at the vacant cockpit fleetingly in time to see the windows and seating erupt into splinters, dimly grateful of the protocol to stand down from there in time of battle. "Incoming!" yelled the port lookout. "Brace for impact! Brace! Brace!" The sound of rapid firing increasing as the Marines opened fire with everything they had at their disposal. The rocket screen seemed no match against the unseen assailant's onslaught. A split second of silence then an almighty bang as the missile struck home beneath the stern, lifting it two metres higher before it sank ominously deeper into the waters.

"Damage Control report forward section please Number One?" Demanded Chip." The skimmer suddenly lurching on its port side as the hull went disastrously asymmetrical, threw them about the bridge like a collection of rag dolls. Fred never answered the call. His body thrown into a tactical plot with such violence breaking three ribs and knocking his head on the bevelled edge of a plotting table had sent him reeling unconscious to the deck. William staving his arm against an equipment panel tore his shoulder, broke the arm with an audible snap, as the lookouts fell to the floor. Chip remained strapped in his Captain's chair, although his legs fell out from under him as the Royal Oak slewed around in what seemed to be a death-blow dealt by the unknown aircraft. Chip was aware of being the only one capable of taking any action on the bridge. "All guns fire at will, follow the sounds of the aircraft engine. "Sub-Lieutenant Pengelly to the bridge!"

More cannon fire stitched the hull finding soft targets in the cargo deck. The screams of dying men, rising in terrible foreboding as the once placid hospital became a charnel house. A female nurse lay almost headless, bleeding to death having fallen victim to a round penetrating the roof, the round carrying on to strike an injured marine where he lay in his sick bed powerless. Sporadic fire from the guns' crews kept a futile barrage of laser and solid rounds in the air around their stricken vessel. Leyland appeared in his white overalls; quickly taking on the duties of others rendered hors de combat, the big man stepping over the spreading ichor with some tact. "Bows section sealed off Sir." Came the only piece of good news from the forward damage control party. "Not much damage down there, but we're still pumping out the bilge!"

"At last, something is working for us!" Exclaimed Chip. "Sub, what's the matter?"

"Its Lieutenant Menteith Sir he's conscious, wants to speak with you."

"Not now Sub there's more important things to think about."

"I think you should listen to him Sir, he says he can save the ship."

"Does he now. I wonder how he can manage that?"

"Bridge, engine room!"

"Engine room, Captain, go ahead."

"We're taking on water through the stern, she's down by a meter Sir."

"Do what you can to keep the engines running. Where's the aft damage control party?"

"We've lost them Sir. I've sent half the control room crew down to sort it out and get a pump rigged, we need to plug the outside with canvas before we can slow down the intake of water."

"Do whatever it takes Chief, we must move, what's the maximum speed we can do?"

"No more than about fifteen to twenty knots Sir."

"That's not enough Chief, but it will have to do."

"Aye, aye Sir."

"Bosun's Mate, take a message to Mr White. Tell him we need to rig a cofferdam around the stern ASAP, take as many men as he needs. Look lively now!"

"Yes Sir."

"Leyland, tell them to stop pumping in the bows, we need to counter flood the weight of water down aft."

"Already done Sir."

"Thank you Sub."

"Incoming missile! Starboard side! Brace! Brace!"

Chip shuddering held on to the arms of his chair in a desperate act of self-preservation. Leyland took a pair of intensifiers from the cold fingers of a dead seaman in a single move heading towards the port bridge wing. "It's a Zed-6!" He gasped. Just seen it fractionally below the clouds!"

"Hold tight Leyland!"

The Techno-whizz emerged from the equipment room dragging the sobbing radio op slowly over the threshold. A large wound gaping in the man's side revealing the gruesome sight of his intestines poking through his shirt. A Bosun's mate took off his own shirt and wrapping it around the man's torn body held the vital parts in place, laying the man down in the prone position on his other side. Footsteps could be heard on the upper deck as men scrambled to get out of the way of the rapidly incoming projectile. Nothing happened! The whoosh of a chaff dispenser and the rattling sound of automatic gunfire conspiring to lure the projectile away from its target into the pathway of a swarm of fifty rounds of ammunition, ending its flight of destruction in a blinding flash a cable's length from the hull.

"What now?" Chip closed his eyes his mind racing for an answer. 'God, how I wish I was up there now!' He was angry, absolutely livid. His ship was a sitting duck and there wasn't a blind thing he could do to stop his enemy from finishing him off. More cannon fire, yet more footsteps as desperate men ran to dodge the rounds as they sought to steal a life here, a life there. More rounds loosed away as the seamen and the marines fought to make a lucky hit somewhere high in the clouds. They wove a brave pattern in the water trying to dodge the weaponry aimed at them. "Whoever is up there is determined to finish us off!" observed Leyland coolly. The planes had been retracted allowing them a meagre twenty knots as the engine room had said it would. Getting slower in response to the helm it was just a matter of time and they all knew it, as they grew heavier in the stern.

"Well, William we seem to be in some difficulty today, but I hear you can save the ship." Said Chip leaning over a slumped William who was clinging onto a shattered stanchion, taking in huge gasps of air. "Its in the equipment room Sir. I put it there. It was me."

"What? You, William, you put that black-box in the equipment room?"

"Yes." He gasped in pain. Sub, clear off, I must talk with the Captain in private." The Sub looked at both men and Chip looked at him nodding silently as more gunfire shook the hull. "What is it William?"

"It's beyond top secret Sir, that's why I am here really." He coughed as a spasm of pain caught him in a vice like grip causing Chip to wince. "You're a pilot, you must have been aware that some covert intelligence operations used specific aircraft, and wondered how they came back instead of being shot out of the sky?"

"Yes William, but what has this got to do with us?"

"It's an electronic cloak Sir. Just have the Chief put it back in and enter the following activation code. The software will do the rest."

"Do what William?" Chip was damned if he was going to let him get away without telling him point blank what would happen. Glass flew around them as more incoming rounds struck the bridge fenestration from behind. "It will completely hide us Sir. We will become invisible to all tactical and non-tactical sensor arrays. Only visual sightings will discover where we are. If this aircraft loses us and intends to sink us he'll have to come out of the cloud base to finish us off. He won't be able to do it any other way." William coughed again then gave him the access code for the cloaking device before falling silent gasping for air and nursing his broken arm, the compound nature of the fracture barely hidden by the thin sleeve of his shirt. His face pale behind the ruddy cheeks suffused with blood through the effort of coughing.

The techno-wizard walked into the damaged equipment room stepping through cables dangling from the deckhead and acrid smoke curling through holes in the deck. The skimmer shuddered as more rounds raked the decks from bows to stern, catching many off-guard. The casualties in the cargo deck growing by the minute at each pass. Overhead lights flashed and flickered around the darkened room as the Royal Oak wove a pattern of manoeuvres exposing the damage to the ship's hull as it twisted and turned.

"Steering gear failure Sir." Came the message from the control room confirming the last possible hope for Royal Oak to dodge her attacker as a past event. "Thank you Chief," was all that Chip could say, "see what you can do, in the mean time keep the engines going at all costs."

"Aye Sir, we can keep her running at twenty knots without too much difficulty." Chip looked at the nav plot seeking a way out of their predicament, but there was nothing left he could do except steer by using the throttles asymmetrically. They had worked their way south of the thirty-eighth parallel without any hope of immediate rescue. "Signalman, make signal to the Admiralty and to the Senior Officer Euroports Mediterranean."

"Sir."

"From Hospital Auxiliary Royal Oak. We are under attack from unknown aircraft, position as given below. Badly damaged and sinking. Request immediate assistance to evacuate casualties, medical personnel and crew…" Chip read their position from the nav plot in a monotone voice dreading the finality of his message. "Send this in open format, no encryption, understand."

"Yes Sir, open format, no encryption." Chip wanted people to know what was happening, and if that pilot had any heart he would break off his attack or otherwise be uncovered as a fully motivated murderer without a conscience.

"Incoming missile three points off the port quarter Sir!" a lookout yelled. Chip unstrapped himself from the chair restraint and walked to the bridge wing holding his intensifier to his eyes as he got there. The edges of the broken glass playing havoc with the auto-focus. The techno-wizard walked back onto the bridge. "Brace! Brace!" Came the strident call as yet again the crew and its failing hospital list faced the prospect of yet more carnage. "Someone give me a lanyard or a rope please I have to hook up a bypass cable!"

Somebody cursed as they caught a glimpse of the incoming missile. "Range about four miles Sir!"

"Thank you!" Replied Chip. The remaining Bosun's Mate handed over his knife and lanyard to the Chief before jamming himself into a corner between two bulkheads at the back of the bridge. "Aye, Sir!" More laser cannon and gunfire caught their ears as the deck and guns crews continued their defensive barrage. A hand launcher fired a missile from somewhere down the port waist and Chip could see the two marines loading and firing a second round. Willing them to succeed he saw the smoke trails heading off towards the incoming missile. Daring to breathe a snatched breath he watched agonisingly as the weapons hurtled towards each other almost in slow motion. The blood pounding against his aching temples. The first one passed wide and commenced a wide sweeping turn in seeking out its quarry, lost its lock on the target and headed into the clouds out of sight, four seconds later the second missile slammed home in a roiling black cloud of flame and destruction. Chip thought he heard the sound of the aircraft's engine accelerating away at high speed and waited hopefully to hear the first missile hit their enemy. No such luck, a loud explosion lifted their hopes briefly until it was obvious from the falling debris some miles away that the attacking pilot had dealt with it decisively. Not enough debris to be an aircraft.

They waited in the silence that followed with nothing but the blood pounding against their own eardrums as a tattoo heralding their inevitable end. The lookout's cry came far too soon than expected as dazed men hunkered down in response to the shrill call. "Incoming! Port side! Brace! Brace!"

"How many does this bloke have for God's sake someone shouted through the smoke. The smell of blood lending its sour presence to the other smells waging war with their senses. Again Chip scanned the awful gap between the sky and the sea looking for the herald of his nemesis. Watched in dread as the next salvo from the marines' hand launcher missed the mark unexpectedly and ran in long curves to follow its predecessor into the clouds above. The Sub shouted for the chaff dispersing rocket screen to be launched, not knowing if these had expired or if the launchers were still intact. Nothing happened. A faint cry went up as the missile clawed its way in a closing arc towards the centre of the hull a metre above the waves.

Unbelievably, the missile passed to the shattered stern, then around it and away across the open water on the starboard side on a blind vector, exploding two cables downwind.

The techno-whiz walked slowly through the equipment room door looking directly at Chip nodding and giving him the thumbs up sign. Chip looked at him with nerves as taught as steel cables. "Well done Chief. Now it's our turn." Turning to the Bosun's Mate he gave the order. "Pass the message to all hands. Any one still able to fire a gun or a hand launcher muster on the upper deck!" Stragglers came out of every possible nook and cranny. Those not involved in damage control came up on deck to be presented with the weapons they had been trained to use by the marines on their outward journey. William staggered to his feet wiping blood from his mouth on the back of his shirt-sleeve, activating the twin cannons mounted in front of the bridge. "If he gets out of this alive he will be the luckiest bastard child ever to be born." He growled.

"Yes, quite William, but do your guns work?"

He tinkered with the controls with his good hand getting a green light at each touch of a button until one light came on amber. Cursing softly to himself and shaking his head from side to side he informed Chip his guns could not be used in automatic mode. "But by God Sir, I'll fire them in manual and the devil take the hindmost!" He announced through clenched teeth. "That's the spirit William, we'll make him pay for this…" The sounds of laser cannon fire from directly outside the bridge cut him short as turning he saw the distant shape of a Zed-6 skimming the waves straight towards them. Firing in manual mode because his weapons could not lock onto the cloaked skimmer below, the pilot pulled up almost too late, the air above the deck crackling with the suffused smell of burning metal and ozone. Two rocket launchers firing independently sent missiles chasing after the bandit as he pulled up in a vertical climb for cloud cover followed by a hail of rounds from the rag-tag collection of small arms fire bursting from the crew. Two heavy bangs went off as William sent heavy rounds into the sky from the deck guns for'ard. Chip held his breath in the ensuing silence as the Petty Officer on deck called the order to cease firing. The distant sounds of the aircraft racing away could be heard nearby.

A thump could be heard followed by a ragged cry as men cheered. "That's got 'im!" Someone yelled. "Let's see if we can give him some more!" shouted another voice from further down the deck. Many oblivious to the smoke and to the crazy angle the decks were taking due to the flooding down aft they waited patiently to administer punishment to the hated enemy who had smashed their home to glory. Chip and the sub could only watch, noticing grimly the red back of the PO's shirt as blood seeped from innumerable wounds between his neck and waist, standing erect with his legs apart swaying gently to and fro as the swell lifted and dumped the hull into the water. Receiving a careful tap on the back of his head from the handler as the next missile was rammed home ready to fire. Smoking debris fell through the cloud about two miles away, not enough to be a whole aircraft, but enough to indicate damage had been done. From out of the cloud base came the Zed-6 trailing smoke from one of his engines, firing a long burst from his cannons. No one moved watching the death pattern of cannon fire creeping ever closer. Chip and William knew exactly what the pilot was trying to do. This was his last pass before breaking off his attack and heading for home, a long shot before pulling up out of range of the weaponry assailing him from below. The past fifteen minutes had seemed like an age in which men had died, others had been reborn, and the fates had cast their dice upon the gaming tables of Valhalla. "Take this!" Hissed the bleeding man as he squeezed the trigger launching his missile. William's guns burst into action giving the signal for all the small arms fire to commence flailing the air for a chance of downing their combatant.

The missile struck the failing engine with a loud thump sending the fighter spinning off to one side. The pilot wrenching his controls to compensate for the asymmetrical power now forcing his craft over on one side and around in a tight arc. One of William's rounds smashed through the fin reducing it to tatters as the aircraft rolling over length-wise nosed towards the grey waters in a bunt. With barely enough air space between the little craft and the water its pilot succeeded in half rolling the airframe back towards normal, ejecting at two hundred feet in a direction away from the stricken skimmer. Another ragged cheer went up and died as tired men sagged with relief at the sight of their adversary falling into the sea. The aeroplane died in a huge splash and was swallowed up without a trace. The sight of a small canopy falling slowly to the surface being all that was left to show there had been an enemy. "Cease firing!" Came the order from on deck and Chip felt the moment had passed, leaving them to face the prospect of patching up their ship and of facing the horrific casualties that there would surely be.

"We have partial steering Sir." announced Leyland in a matter of fact voice. "And the water has been pumped out of the fo'csle. "May I have your permission to direct the damage control parties from down aft?" There was a long pause before Chip, turned to face Leyland who was all spattered with oil, blood and the charred remains of burnt paint that had burned though his white overalls down to his skin beneath. He had not had the time to realise the prospect of hidden casualties down below in the engine room spaces. "Please, and thank you for your sterling work here on the bridge. Let me know how long before we can be under way?"

"I will Sir." Leyland headed for the flat leading to the cargo deck cum hospital heading for the hatchway leading down to the depths of the shattered hull.

"Sub."

"Yes Sir."

"Did you see where that pilot went into the water?"

"I think so Sir, he's about two miles away on the port quarter."

"Good, steer towards that point Sub. I want to find out who that pilot was and who he was working for."

"Aye, aye Sir."

"William, how are you feeling?"

"Bit rough Sir I'm afraid, but I can get by for a while longer."

"We need to talk, but first let me thank you for what you did."

"Thank you Sir."

"I'm going to ask you to stand down for a while in order to get that arm fixed and your ribs looked at. When we pull that pilot onboard I want you here in the bridge at those guns of yours just in case."

"Understood Sir."

Chip looked at his watch noting the time at 07:58. He was shocked that it had all happened in such a short time. "Bosun's Mate?" Bosun's Mate!" There was no one to answer his call. A signal op appeared from the starboard bridge door stripped to the waist, mopping his hands on the tail of his shirt. They saw the blood as the signal op shook his head from side to side slowly while looking at Chip and William. "If it's a message Sir I'll take it. He won't be taking any more I'm afraid." Chip thanked the man for his voluntary attitude before passing the order for all able bodied and uninjured men to stand fast at their guns. The rest were to stand down and assist the damage control parties, but for the badly wounded the medics would be dealing with them directly. He looked away beyond the shattered plexi-glass to a point between the sky and the sea not daring to think about the charnel house their enemy had made of the cargo deck.

Royal Oak answered her helm like a bee stuck in honey, taking an age before the bows came around towards their opponent floating somewhere ahead. Chip went into the equipment room to find the leading signal op and the Chief tech clearing up considerable damage. Walking carefully over bodies and debris on the deck he went back onto the bridge noticing for the first time that his friend had not been where he had originally fallen. Not daring to think the unthinkable, he went walkabout visually checking the damage, talking to the men as he went along giving them an encouraging word as he passed by. He stumbled into the wardroom tripping over rubbish on the floor. He found a surgeon and a nurse leaning over the inert body of Fred lying on the table. A bottle of plasma hung from a bracket giving him vital fluids as they operated on him, throwing swabs onto the carpet trying to save his life. The surgeon looked up at Chip locking eyes with him for a moment, then he looked away to concentrate on the gaping cavity in Fred's torso. "How bad is it?" He asked fearing the worst. "He'll live just as soon as we can find the tear in his artery. Do you know his blood group by any chance?" Chip was taken aback at the gruffness in the surgeon's voice, but ignored it in consideration of the fact that he was not able to dwell on the subtleties of protocol in the face of dishing out life and death decisions with his hands deeply crimson with blood. "He's A rhesus positive. I will let you have some of mine if you need it."

"We will, can you get someone from the medical team to hook you up as soon as you can, this chap's going to need it immediately if he's going to survive."

Chip turned away closing the door behind him, noticing the white stockinged feet of a nurse protruding from underneath a sheet covering her body from the head to her calves. The door clicked shut as losing his temper he sought to go out on deck and escape. Walking slowly down aft on the upper deck he could not fail to notice the gentle incline towards the stern. Reaching the ladder leading down to the small quarterdeck he could see the sea lapping a foot or so just below the brim of the stern combing. He walked down feeling leaden inside, reached the deck and walking around to the great stern doors saw that they at least were intact. Climbing up the port ladder two steps at a time he saw the damage inflicted along the other side of his vessel. Large ragged holes, broken windows, soundproofing material that hung in great swathes from every entry wound in her huge cargo walls. Taking one of the after doors he found his way inside his cargo deck wincing at the tragedy of human life snatched away in battle. The survivors helping the injured, the injured helping the badly wounded and the few medical staff who remained on their feet desperately stemming the tide of life that ebbed away from the many injured people strewn upon the deck and on blood soaked cots.

The hardened steel deck had resisted many of the solid rounds with devastating effect. They had ricocheted along the deck or bounced around the great cargo hold inflicting multiple casualties. Walking for'ard he reached the companionway down to the lower decks having noted the damage above water he was now about to find out the truth below it. Passing back to the control room he could not fail to notice the quietness of the men as they covered up more bodies than he could equate for those who were alive.

The hull rumbled from deep down and he heard raised voices coming from the machinery spaces. Leyland was booming into a microphone on the end of a long curly cable as Chip arrived. "Leyland!" How is it?" He had asked as his engineer cocked his head to one side listening out. Leyland lifted his hand in a mute call for silence, waiting for something. A muffled voice came over the loudspeaker from the other side of the control room. Leyland was watching a small view screen showing what seemed to a flooded compartment. "It's Riley Sir, we'll know in a second or two what's amiss."

"He's diving in the steering gear compartment?"

"Yes Sir. He's about forty feet beyond the engine room door almost at the transom."

"What's he doing?"

"Assessing the damage to the stern at the moment. He reckons we can wedge the smaller holes and use splinter boxes to cover some of the others, but the transom may not be so badly damaged as we first thought."

"Assuming its bad news how long have we got?"

"About an hour until we can shore it up, but it's the steering gear that seems to be the problem."

"Will counter flooding the for'ard section be of any help?"

"If we could move both people and as much equipment for'ard of stanchion twenty-six Sir, we could hold off the flooding. What we need to do is remove the torn canvass once the sharp metal jags have been cut away. Then we can seal the stern as much as we can. Maybe we can weld some patches in place. She'll be right as rain then."

"What comes first?"

"Getting more pumps down here and plugging the holes as we go along, say about four or five hours worth, then we can see a bit more clearly from that point."

"We can reduce speed now that we have rid ourselves of that aircraft."

"Keep her at about three knots for the time being Sir. With both engines unscathed we will have power to spare for the after pumps as well as additional lighting. But we need to stop at some point to weld the plates in situ." Leyland paused looking awfully tired. "Let me know when you're ready for that."

"Aye, will do Sir." The detached voice of the diver came over the speaker as Chip made his way out of the control room.

Once back on the bridge he found the sub and a lookout peering at the tactical display with a proximity beacon blooping in the background. "What is it Sub?" He asked. "It looks like the Martin Luther king has launched two aircraft in our direction."

"There's a chance that submarine of theirs picked up the sounds of our conflict and told them something was going on." Whirling round, Chip walked quickly into the equipment room to find the Chief tech. He ordered the cloaking device to be switched off immediately and the memory buffers to be erased. "We don't want them to start nosing around. They are bound to be suspicious once we suddenly reappear on their sensor screens."

Ten minutes later Commander Hal B Pinko and his wingman Lieutenant JG Frankie Bartolomeo flew a careful pattern at a tangent to the Royal Oak's position, emerging from the clouds at three thousand feet. On observing their down by the stern attitude and the copious damage topsides, the flight commander radioed home plate informing the Squadron Commander he was going to offer their assistance since the vessel appeared to be sinking. Pinko called the Royal Oak on the international distress frequency receiving a terse reply to go ahead with his message. The offer of assistance was politely refused on the grounds that Italian units of the ESNF would be expected soon to lend assistance. When Pinko informed the vessel below that no other ships were in the area he was told to standby. Pinko informed them he intended a slow pass down their starboard side, and that he would be obliged if they did not fire on him.

Chip's temper reached breaking point when it was confirmed the Italians had not responded to their earlier message. 'If the Admiralty can reply all the way from London, where were the bloody Italians!" Exploding with exasperation he decided that his casualties had more chance of surviving if they could be transferred to the carrier. In a one to one with the carrier's Captain they agreed to lift off their casualties and transfer them to the carrier, and to return them to the UK. Chip declined any immediate assistance for his vessel in the immediate future saying that a full assessment of his situation was currently in hand. As he spoke the engine slowed to idle leaving the skimmer to coast towards the downed enemy pilot.

Cutting short his conversation with a reference to calling him back later Chip left the equipment room as the inflatable boat slipped its ropes and shot towards the billowing chute a hundred yards away. Six men armed to the teeth sat ready to loose off rounds should the pilot offer any armed resistance to rescue. The two American jets passing down the other side of the ship as they came around the front of the canopy that hid the pilot from view. The pilot was floating face up in the water unconscious of the activity going on around him. With little care for his well being he was dragged over the side and dumped with cold contempt onto the wooden duck boards. Six armed men secretly hoping he would do something hostile, one of them giving the order to ease off, reminding them it was an inflatable boat after all! One of them laughed at the thought of blasting the pilot to hell and causing their own plight of sinking as they did so. It broke the tension and they chuckled while they had the freedom to do it before turning for home aboard the Royal Oak. On the way back they saw the bows lifting higher out of the water than normal due to the flooding stern.

An hour later the first of the choppers arrived to take off the casualties. All spare hands set to work carefully hooking up the stretchers, saying a kind word now and then, waving farewell with a considerate 'Cheerio mate, see you back in Pompey.' Others looking bleakly at the silent ones being hoisted up and away from the charnel house and mess that had become of their home. A tearful farewell by a young doctor to a wounded nurse, who was left with a stump where once her left arm had been, lifted away unconscious in the gusting down-wash. A string of four helicopters came and went before there was a lull in the rescue. The sensors showing that the carrier was still three hours away.

Leyland was considering his options sourly as the exploratory dive into the engine room came to an end. The plasma jets could work quite happily under water down to a depth of ten metres or so. "If we could get some flotation and more scrap metal we could finish the job and be under way again inside five hours Sir." Came the hopeful appraisal from Riley. "Send a runner to find Mr White, and let's find out if he has enough spare canvas left. In the mean time we can recommend that we stay at this speed." He paused, thinking that it would be a close run thing. "It would be a pathetic disaster when you think we baled out those Greeks just a few days ago." Riley nodded thinking of the bitter irony of that happening. "I'm off to have a chat with the Captain. I'll leave you to get the work started. Liaise with Mr white and the Chief tech if you need to rope in extra hands."

Aye, Sir."

16. BITTER HARVEST

The analysts had confirmed that American steel was floundering badly. Around the world governments had closed the ring of trade agreements tightly in a noose leaving no way out. Just as they had inflicted a mindless trade war on the Japanese in the nineteen thirties over a century ago, now the American government was reeling under the burden of failing industries and closed marketplaces. With nowhere to trade and with increasing political pressure the hacks on Capitol Hill began baying for punitive action.

At the same time the 'Council of Twelve', the High Presidium of the European Union upon whom rested the awesome political power of more than a third of the world's political muscle issued a decree indicting those countries that had allied themselves to the British rebels. Warrants went out for the arrest of the Prime or First Ministers of those nations. The Commission was exacting heavy fines on every rebel nation, sweeping aside their protestations with the threat of occupation if they did not comply. The moderate voices of reason had failed with the Commission ever out of touch with reality.

Peppino di Napoli, the reformed Mafiosi and political mole had risen through the ranks of international politics with amazing good fortune. His first major appointment as Italy's foreign trade minister: taking place only two years later, after his first appointment as under-secretary. From there, using his connections to pull strings, he won for himself, and his criminal colleagues political clout as well as a financial mountain of fabulous wealth. Smiling to himself feeling warm and smug he left the Council Chamber heading for his gigantically apportioned offices high above on the thirty-fifth floor. The final battles were being fought as the pieces of the mighty jigsaw were being lined up before dropping into place. Political opposition back home knew that they did as they were told or face the stress of nasty little dirty tricks campaigns to besmirch them, or, if that did not work, a car accident here or a drug induced heart attack there would soon remove them from public life. Nobody could prove anything, but it was known that from among his friends and associates a staggering number of people had 'died' over the years. With outside help from their friends in the US and latterly in Russia, the European Union of organised crime had infiltrated the heart of Europe's power base through the labyrinth of its banking operations. Knowing full well that money is power is more money and more power, the corporate raiders of old began to fade out as the criminal underworld began to take over, changing their spots, getting educated and wearing expensive suits, adopting the language of high finance and political strategists alike. Instead of the old mentality using the entrapment of key individuals at high levels they now moved in, taking over with the knowledge contained within their ranks. No more the grubby street-wise peasant stock with a soulless desire to make money any way they could, but a burgeoning middle-class criminal culture. The stock exchanges bearing witness to the influence the new tribe exerted as previously unheard of traits began to emerge. Small companies disappearing like they hit a brick wall, others just staying small while in reality their funding was enormous by all other known measurement methods. Banks ruined by so called rogue traders who had been manipulated from behind the scenes by unknown grey suits in respectable Manhattan.

Almost gleefully he could see the giant scissors in his mind's eye cutting the chains to the drawbridge of fortress Britain. It was only their stupid pomposity and class-ridden social system that had allowed them to escape the full impact of mob control. 'But now.' Peppino thought to himself. 'We wait only two or three more weeks before they fall like a house of cards.' Seated in his huge black leather chair he viewed the political agenda of the high council comparing it with the objectives of the cadre of 'les unconnue', the secret ones. The four men he tele-conferenced with later that day representing each major mob enclave around the world. The US (unstable as it was with its petty in-fighting), the Japanese-Korean federation (strict, disciplined and demanding), South America (formerly the 'shining path'), and Russia (up and coming but always struggling), and finally the fifth member of the golden pentangle, Europe. The media had oftentimes leaked interviews, and expose' after expose' without really exposing any thing more than the tiddlers in the field of mob rule. They had talked of the success of the British campaign over the years, and were enthusiastic in their agreement to shift the multi-billion currency laundering operation to Frankfurt once they had Britain in the bag. "After all," observed Takamura the head of the Japanese clans, "we have complete control over their telecommunications infrastructure and of their finance ministry. What more could we want?"

"The British are finished breathed Valentin Fuertado, the Don of the Russian connection. "They'll be nothing but a backwater, a pimple on the anus of Europe!" He chuckled gleefully. Emilio Murato, the clever Corsican, who had run the South American clans for forty years looked unmoved, his face filling a segment of the huge conference screen. "I don't believe anything until it has been achieved. Believe me, these people may have soft politicians, but they are a tough nut to crack when you threaten their country."

"Emilio, you're too sceptical. We have them tied up with so much legislation they can hardly move without passing wind before someone is running for the rulebook. Like the Germans before them, they will go down very soon. Our institute of Social Affairs has completely undermined their democracy with political correctness."

"What do you know of democracy Pepe?" asked Takamura rhetorically, "your country has never known democracy. You are totally disorganised. It's the only way any of us can survive. It's the same in Russia." Peppino di Napoli shook his head. He had heard it all before. "Political correctness is the natural corrosive of democracy, wait and see. The British have it like the plague. They can't last for much longer, supposing they win? Where will they go? How will they bargain against the irresistible powers of enforcement of the Commission? Tell me that? We run the Commission from here at the very heart of the union in the Presidium. Anyone who stands against us will be crushed by economic sanctions long before we take such military enforcement like this. The Germans are on the brink of economic collapse. Just a word from this chamber and the truth about their national budget will cause such a political landslide into national poverty that no one dares to talk about it. The French, my friend, are so much in debt that they know when it happens the whole world will be upon them howling for repayment. No, the British are small beer my friend, on the edge of ruin and falling into the pit as we speak. Then we will expose the Germans and the French for taking most of the grant money out of the money box and bingo my friend, Europe will be ruined, and that's where we step in to fill the gap!"

"Yeah right." Sneered Carlos Ritzio, head of the US contingent. "And where's the cavalry?"

"In your pocket." said Takamura coldly. "That's why you've got three hundred and seventy five million to rub under the noses of your President and the Senate. You buy him off with that money and save his political butt over US steel, and we make sure that he or the Senate doesn't go charging in to rescue his good friends in England."

"There, I told you so. It's really going to work this time." Peppino rubbed his flabby hands together smugly, breaking the connection.

****

The gloves were off as far as William Goodfellow was concerned as he saw the casualty lists coming in from around the country. The new regiments had quitted themselves well and with only one 'missed' opportunity where French paratroops had taken Bath after brutally attacking the civilian population all was well for the most part. The raids on London never materialising the way they had been expected, had been nothing more than a testing of the waters for the enemy. Carlisle falling unexpectedly to German airborne troops was an unexpected sting creating a major headache for commanders on the ground in the north. The north-west communications routes had been lost as a consequence with everyone expecting a follow up operation to grab the Tyneside towns with the inevitable linking up of the invading forces along the passes through the Cheviots. News of the king's whereabouts was far from forthcoming with the late arriving news of the Royal Oak's final message that she was under attack. William sat in silence despairing of a happy resolution to the multiplicity of his goals. 'No one could be that stupid.' He thought to himself. 'That the arrival of the king could put an immediate halt to the hostilities. It would however, make the Commission's case less tenable and eventually unsupportable if, and only when the general election could be held to install a new government.' He kept reminding himself of the possibilities as the stream of news poured in to his office from his own intelligence sources.

While he toyed with the idea of informing President Warnock of the potential loss of the Royal Oak, the little jet made its rendezvous with a tanker high above the western approaches. Both aircraft were cloaked requiring first rate navigating skills on the part of the jet-jockey sitting in the left-hand seat next to Pierce. They had sat mesmerised as the pilot, jiggling his controls, inched the umbilical onto his fuel port at the third attempt. Effectively blind to external events and unable to communicate with the outside world both the king and his escort Admiral Dunham had nothing better to do than sit and observe. Totally unaware of the drama that had unfolded far behind at their point of origin, both men were speculating on the conditions awaiting them back on the ground in London. Very slowly the pilot eased back the throttles just enough to withdraw the fuelling probe from the umbilical. Once clear of the tanker they climbed in a gentle climbing turn to the northwest leaving the jet tanker far below. The king dozed held in place by his safety harness while the Admiral noted the southwestern coastline of England sliding beneath the wings of the aircraft. Wide gaps appearing in the clouds below looking like giant fingers drawn out across their path pointing towards a distant hub of compacted shadows far to the northeast. Lyme Bay's stunning mix of undulating cliffs and rocky foreshores giving way to broad green downlands of the hinterland beyond. Following a pre-determined flight plan the little scout raced high above the hills towards Boscombe before gently turning left towards Greenham. From there following the southern contours of the Chiltern Hills until Pierce could make out a slender finger pointing into the sky from the densely wooded hills ahead below them. The pilot pulling back on the throttles allowed their chariot time to slow down, dipped the nose ever so slightly earthwards in a descent that took them over the old E40, where applying power again, they turned onto a south easterly heading almost into the sun. Maintaining two thousand five hundred feet above the land, details of the surface became almost completely recognizable. The mast at Stokenchurch now sliding harmlessly into the haze behind them as they passed across the cutting in the chalk hills. Following the ribbon of highway with his eyes as it swept in loops through the hills, Pierce could see a tiny bridge way ahead of them, beyond that he could make out a small town. On the right a small green area beyond the sweeping valleys falling away to the right. The pilot rapidly making changes to his aircraft's configuration crossed the highway again with the undercarriage rumbling into position beneath them.

The king began stirring as the noise awoke him then it subsided into near silence when the throttles were drawn back even further. Making a turn to the right Pierce caught a flash of gold as the late morning sunlight flashed from a golden ball atop a spire on a grand old building situated in parkland. The narrow strip of green had become much wider and within its boundary he could make out the dark grey strip of a runway. The features slid by looking very close now as they descended even further, the pilot turning gently to the left over the derelict community of Freith. A one time open prison for social undesirables now a blot on the landscape gradually returning to nature. Pierce followed their progress without further reference to the map he had been using. The pilot turning for final approach made small adjustments to the controls to line up on the centre line before speaking into the radio. With the nose slightly down and balancing the approach on the throttles they arrived over the threshold with the short grass strip between the fence and the runway rushing up to meet them. Gently pulling back a fraction on the stick the nose raised a little as they began the flare for a more conventional landing just beyond the piano keys at the runway boundary. They kissed the deck in a gentle greaser with the nose held just off the runway until their speed fell back allowing the nose wheel to touchdown halfway along the tarmac surface. Applying reverse thrust the pilot slowed down the scout in a roar of undiluted energy reducing their forward speed to a mere crawl. "Well Sir, this is where I must take leave of you. May I wish you God speed for the remainder of your journey and for the coming days ahead of you?"

"Thank you Peter you have been an indomitable friend. I will be in touch no doubt very soon, and may I also wish you God speed."

"Thank you Sir, I leave you in the capable hands of your pilot and Major Anders. Goodbye."

A batsman had waved them to a spot in the middle of the apron well away from the car park beyond the perimeter fence. The Admiral unleashed his harness straps and lifting himself out of the confines of the back seat, climbed over the hatch combing and was gone from view. They watched him being met by a couple of navy types in uniform with whom he shook hands and as the canopy was drawn over them saw him being driven away in a hover bat bearing navy markings. The king sighed; stretching out in the back in the additional space afforded him by the departing Admiral. The pilot re-jigged his aircraft for an immediate departure as the aircraft taxied back out to the runway. Neither of his passengers could remember much about the final leg of their journey over London, except to remark upon the damage they had seen and the fortress like nature of its inner defences.

They landed vertically in Parliament Square right outside the ancient doors to the houses of Parliament. The down draught rattling the fraying timbers bending treetops sideways as they dropped down towards the small courtyard. A guard of honour was there to meet them, hastily reassembling as the engines wound down to an almost silent thrum. Pierce Anders saluting in finest fashion as his friend the king climbed out after him to the accompaniment of the old national anthem. A beaming President Warnock stepped forward from a small knot of dignitaries greeting the king personally before escorting him to the assembled Senate within the hallowed halls. Pierce following on behind at a discreet distance. Approaching the Senate Chamber he found the doors had not been opened for him as one might expect. Before anyone could account for this inappropriate oversight Pierce

Anders came to the immediate rescue of the king, and in so doing covered the embarrassment of the President and his small entourage. "By your leave your majesty." Taking the large knife strapped to his calf and lifting it up backwards by the hilt he rammed it home on the highly polished escutcheon beneath the ornate handle. One, twice, and finally a third time. Not realising the significance of what had taken place an armed guard opened the door to scold the perpetrator who had committed the awful act of disturbing the peaceful business of the Senate. His face crumpling in astonishment at the august assemblage with the king at its head. "His majesty the king waits without!" Pierce announced solemnly. "Bravo." said the king softly in an appreciative tone. Such was the secrecy of the day that no one knew of his arrival. Turning deeply red and motioning to a second, unseen person, the doors swung open as the Sargent announced in a parade ground voice; "'is Majesty the king!" All rose as the king slowly advanced into the chamber for the first time in his life.

In fifty-seven minutes the king was accorded a warm welcome and briefed on every subject right up to the last minute of the war. Finally, the senate pausing to see the royal seal of the house of Hannington applied to the cooling wax upon the great document that not only permitted the interim government to continue under the king's royal care and patronage, but which later became known as the Act of Sovereignty. For within its precepts were to be found the charter ending British membership of the European Union; in one stroke the instrument that brought constitutional rectitude under one set of internationally agreed rules, brought to an end the impropriety of foreign government upon the heads of the British nation. A full-throated cheer went up in salutation lasting for nearly a quarter of an hour. For many of the assembled worthies felt the breath of freedom for the first time in their lives, and it smelled good, barely containing their sense of joy in respectful silence as the king stood to leave the chamber, heading for the small media studio two stories above. The king's broadcast went out over all the national networks at three in the afternoon. The international networks getting hold of the story shortly afterwards. "What a day this has been." Said the king standing in front of a large window looking down on old Father Thames. "Here today, gone tomorrow. This morning we were in the middle of the Mediterranean, and this afternoon we are in London as if nothing had happened in between."

"It does feel like that I have to admit." Said Pierce as rain rattled against the glass in a buffeting wind. The president and Vice-President of England stood around them making small talk with aides and senior ministers.

William Goodfellow had arrived at the convocation a little earlier giving him enough time to chat in private with his old friend. Pierce felt dismayed at the news of Royal Oak's situation and felt somewhat at a loss at how to tell the king. For although he had had very little to do with the ship, William told him there was 'history' with the king and the vessel. As Pierce made his way across the reception room to inform the king, William headed towards the President to impart the same dreadful news. A polite silence fell upon the gathering stifling conversation as swiftly as any given signal might have done. The king held up his glass of sherry contemplating the mellow brown-red contents. "Major Anders." He said quietly. "I give you the Royal Oak, I trust that she and her faithful crew will find favourable winds and calm seas." Lifting his glass to eye level in a moment of peaceful reflection the king announced "The Royal Oak, may God truly bless her and those who sail with her."

"The Royal Oak." Pierce replied quietly. The king seemed genuinely upset, wiping away tears welling up in his eyes, returning his gaze to look through the broad window at Londoners hurrying through the rain beating against the glass. A world away from the scenes of carnage he had narrowly escaped from during his stay in Cyprus.

17. GATHERING STORM

Around the world gasps of apprehension filled many a face. Politicians and analysts alike rushed into media studios to give their opinions about the chances of Britain's survival in the face of the gathering wrath about to fall on them from Europe. On that fateful day when evening sunlight filled the sky with gilded broken clouds. As once more the golden orb sank beneath an apricot and ginger sky, bidding farewell until the following dawn, a message received on William's personal communicator turned the glorious view of Father Thames bathed in gold into a forlorn mirage, fracturing hope as a stillborn moment stole across his heart. "William, you look pale, what is it. Not more bad news I hope?" President Warnock had stood at the same window for sometime, enjoying a rare forty minutes of relaxation. The king had left with his young aide in tow, and the tone of the early evening had changed as hope began to run high among the different threads of conversation wafting around the room. "It's the Americans Sir, they've blown the pipeline from the North Sea."

"What! Are you sure William? This has to be a mistake!"

"The pipeline is blown Sir, there's no mistaking that, but as to who is responsible for doing it we have no other indications at present."

"How soon before we know?"

"Not long Sir. Air patrols are in the area and will be dropping divers down by now. A couple of skimmers are attempting to run the blockade in the Firth of Forth and will arrive at some time tomorrow morning with a contingent of Marines."

"Get me the Trade and Industry Minister immediately please William, and someone from the Defence Board, I want a strategic overview on top of all the other information. This puts us in a bad way I fear."

As William Goodfellow began the task of pulling people together, Royal Oak floated on a pitch-black sea with the huge silhouette of the Martin Luther king looming high above them in the darkness. The American

489

Captain had earlier taken a decision that would enable the smaller skimmer a chance to get home. One of her escorts had come alongside to deposit technicians and materials with which to aid the crew in their repairs to the stern and steering gear. The crew had gone around slapping on elephant patches to cover the myriad of bullet holes with the usual high strength foul smelling adhesive while the qualified ships divers took it in turns to patch up the holes under water. Even better, the aircraft carrier hooked up high pressure air lines fed from her much larger battery of machinery, and slowly but surely they raised the stern with floatation bags lifting it higher and higher until the bows hung low in the water. Careful not to over-stress her keel they kept the hull just as high as they needed during the next phase of the repairs. The steering gear had then been cut away and hauled up onto one of the side decks of the carrier near to one of its vast workshops where the smiths and artisans began to strip it down and rebuild the broken mountings and pipes.

Given the strained relations between their two countries Chip was quite amazed at the extent of their willingness to repair his vessel at sea. Ordinarily it would have been a tow to the nearest harbour with all the attendant legalities of salvage. Her Captain had been polite and very positive that he would prefer to see them back in the water fighting, rather than end up as prisoners chained to the wall in some stinking harbour basin. It seemed plausible enough and Chip was willing not to have to rely on any of his erstwhile European neighbours for just that reason. With their hospital ship status almost literally blown away, the American Captain offered to take the wounded to the UK, so while the engineers and technicians beavered away both captains sought consensus from higher authorities. By three o' clock the following morning the stern repairs were completed, and the steering gear, rudders and stern tubes all rebuilt. Still riding in the water nose down, the men from both navies worked tirelessly in shifts encouraged by their senior NCOs to exacting standards of workmanship. The new steering gear was gently offered up to the hull underneath the stern where divers had earlier marked out the final placement of crucial pipe ends and supports. Then, the buoyancy bags were deflated allowing the stern to sink back into the water. The crew of the Royal Oak switched their efforts to the counter-flooded bow compartments, emptying them out with high-pressure pumps. In spite of the awful casualties the actual damage to Royal Oak had been surprisingly light. Were it not for the steering gear taking an indirect hit when the first missile exploded beneath the stern, they could have kept going, but at a snail's pace. The hole in the bows was nothing by comparison, being easily managed by straightforward repairs once the water had been pumped out.

By dawn a haggard looking Leyland Pengelly walked onto the bridge smiling thinly to himself, the younger Sub had turned in after completing a twenty-hour shift leaving Chip and Mr White to cope with the day shift. The skies were beginning to show signs of clearing in the upper layers, and bearing mind that with both captains anxious not to be caught in *flagrante~dilecto* by passing satellites, Leyland switched on the engine control console watching the lights checkout with a satisfied "Aha." He looked up and announced "Engine trials in ten minutes, providing of course the seamen and the electricians can finish patching up the fore peak. Mr White, have one of the Cox'ns checkout the cockpit controls please."

"Aye, aye Sir."

"Well done Leyland." Said Chip relieved and grateful for a favourable turn in their fortunes. Both men looked at each other from beneath hooded eyes, intuitively recognising the unspeakable pain behind the 'thousand year look' they bore while they exchanged vital information couched in pleasantry and mutual regard. At least they had something in common with the crew who moved like veterans in a world where only veterans could survive. The huge shape of the carrier was disappearing fast into the early morning haze towards the eastern horizon. The other escort destroyer was nowhere to be seen. Making no promises the Captain had indicated coincidental air cover for them as they approached and went through the straits. Otherwise he would be in danger of blatant political misdemeanour if his task force were to be found escorting them openly.

The Royal Oak's logbook showed that she proceeded under her own power a little after nine o' clock. Of course the engine trials were simply the first hour or two of her long journey homeward. All patches and repairs held-good. The steering gear performing perfectly once the calibration and trimming had been completed. Crucially they headed into the swell through five knots watching engine temperatures and pressures as the hull neared the auto-sequence threshold of nine knots that would extend the planes into the water. At nine point four nine knots the planes extended into the water lifting the hull clear. A wide clearing turn of three hundred and sixty degrees to the left and then to the right was made in which the crew re-calibrated their compasses, locked in their servo-repeaters and adjusted their laser ring-gyro trim. With seven hundred and forty nautical miles to go before they reached the open mouth of the Straits of Gibraltar, Chip passed the order to set course. It was a quarter past ten and if all went well they would reach the Atlantic Ocean in a little under sixteen hours.

Although on a war footing Chip was certain of two things. The ESNF commands may well have ignored their distress call deliberately. Secondly, they still bore the Red Cross markings on their sides and on the roof, and he was going to use them to his full advantage -come what may. In his briefing to the crew he thanked them all for their gallantry and for their hard work. He wanted them to know that as far as everyone onboard was concerned they still had their unique status of diplomatic immunity and he was going to play that card all the way if need be to get them all home safely. Although protocols demanded they should all maintain a proper day working routine he was giving all hands with the exception of duty watchmen a make and mend for the remainder of the day and for the next two days providing both the weather and the enemy held back. "I don't think there is any doubt in my mind or yours that we are now at war with Europe, and as such the ESNF or the land forces in the guise of the ESA are our enemies," concluded Chip.

A hundred and eighty eight miles down track the sensor array detected a fast flying aircraft approaching them from astern. The target's particulars were all there in plain view; a US helicopter was racing towards them at a height of three thousand feet like a bat out of hell. Onboard sat grim faced men with a mission on their minds. They hove to at four o' clock on Friday afternoon while the chopper dropped a line towards the roof, edging closer. The message had said very little, but as requested by the American Captain, they hove-to in the rolling seas to receive a personal delivery. First a small grey sack was shimmied down the line into the hands of a waiting seaman who passed it along to another standing nearby. Next a metal stretcher appeared on the hoist with someone sitting upright inside the metal framework. Fred with his ribs and arm all strapped up, with powerful painkilling drugs coursing through his veins sat erect returning the salute given him by the winch-man. Slowly but surely he reached the roof of his beloved skimmer and with the help of the seamen unlatched the straps that held him in position so that he could climb out. No sooner was he out did the chopper shear off, winding in the stretcher as it bore away. Fred gave a final wave to the winch-man.

With the aid of two of the ratings Fred laboured slowly down the ladder with the breeze flapping at his trouser legs as he stepped onto the deck of Royal Oak looking tired and pale. "What's this Number One? Asked Chip mildly, concerned at the apparition that stood before him. "You can't get rid of me that easily you know!" Half-joking Fred met Chip with a warm handshake and speaking softly said. "We need to talk." Chip made way for his wounded friend as they walked through the doors and along the flat to his day cabin. "Drink?" Chip offered. "Coffee will be fine."

"Anything strong in it?" Offered Chip further, not sure whether it was painkilling drugs or something more sinister in Fred's demeanour. Fred shook his head. "They patched you up pretty well I see. How are the rest of our casualties Fred?"

"In better shape than they were a few hours ago. But tell me, how are you here in this neck of the woods heading along at a cracking pace when last I heard we had no steering gear to speak of?"

"Our American friends did well by us. Without them we were only a couple of hours away from crawling into port with our tails between our legs. Put it down to Leyland if you will, it was his idea, and the sea was kind enough to remain calm to enable us to carry out the operation from start to finish." Chip explained briefly the idea about the flotation bags and the generous work done by the American sailors in patching up their leaky stern and repairing the steering gear. "We are working up to full operational capability by sometime tomorrow. Just in time for our dash up the Channel."

"I don't think so." announced Fred very seriously. First, there is a large armada between us and Blighty situated in the Bay of Biscay. Secondly, before I give you Captain Mahaney's letter, I have to tell you that since late yesterday the Americans have technically entered the war on the other side."

"What!" Fred held up his good hand to signal that he wanted to continue. "It looks like they sabotaged our North Sea pipelines by blowing up a major pumping station out in the North Sea. Captain Mahaney was good enough to tell me of this development during the morning. He's a good man Chip, said he didn't personally believe it himself, but that in any case it didn't matter as far as he was concerned. He will rendezvous with the Saratoga tonight; she's on her way to the US; and will transfer our casualties onboard with a view to bringing them back home by the quickest route. This letter is for you from Captain Mahaney, and he has included some other information for us to look at contained in the mail sack." There was a knock on the door as a steward returned with a tray of coffee and biscuits. During the brief pause in their conversation Chip opened the letter

493

from Captain Mahaney and carefully read the hand-written note. 'Dear Commander.' The letter began.

'By the time you read this note your loyal First Officer would have informed you of our current situation. I have made the order for your casualties to be transferred to USS Saratoga for the purpose of sending them home in the quickest way open to me. Whatever the outcome may be, and no matter where we stand across the divide that may have been cruelly set between us, I remain confident that we stand together against the common enemy, the sea. I wish you and your stout ship bon voyage and trust that the good Lord above will turn his face to smile upon you as you journey home.

Mahaney, CJ, Captain USN, USS Martin Luther king, 9th June inst.'

Chip whistled softly. "He's no fool that one, very cool. He could get into a lot of trouble for helping us in the first place, I suppose. Now this."

"He has the measure of us I think. He was aware that we were out there all by ourselves batting on a dodgy wicket under the temporary label of being a hospital ship. Said he wasn't very much surprised that no one else responded to our mayday." Chip pursing his lips together in thought got up and looked out of the window. It was one of the few remaining windows left intact. "What else has he sent over with you?" He asked with his mind dwelling on something else. "Tactical data and such like. You know corroborating evidence. Oh, and some other information that might be helpful to us on our way home." Together they went through the small amount of material sent by Captain Mahaney, looking at recordings taken over the last thirty-six hours. The un-edited data showing salient facts on the navigational plots for an area covering a wide area around the Royal Oak at the time of her battle with the unknown aircraft. The damning indictment that several patrolling French, Spanish and Italian naval vessels were in the area and did not respond to her distress calls was plain to see. Chip looked up from the viewer noticing his friend looked very tired. Beads of sweat glistening on his forehead as he fought to stay awake. "I think we need to get you into your cabin Fred, and get you rested for a while. I swear you've turned a whiter shade of pale. Then we'll talk again later about the next leg of our journey later this evening."

"One more thing." said Fred a little more urgently. "Our friend Lieutenant William Cavendish MacBrayne of Menteith, I vaguely remember we had a problem with his security status…"

"I am surprised you were aware of it judging by your condition at the time. It's all in order Fred, we had a long chat about it during the first night when we had time to sit and think about our own safety after the attack was over, and it was apparent no one was coming to our aid. He's a special ops pilot and his reason for being here was in fact completely genuine. He'd banged out of a jet during one of those early confrontations and had been waiting for the all clear from the medics before getting airborne again. In the meantime someone pulled a few strings to get him over to us in Cyprus to give us a little additional covert support from the inside."

"You mean he's a friendly spy."

"No, far from it. He's special ops and has a way with guns and gadgets so they tell me."

"Ah, so you've been in touch with London."

"While you were away it has proved to be an interesting time. We are following our own noses under strict radio silence. I'm not taking any more chances. Not with that black-hearted pilot aboard..."

"You mean you've got him, he's alive?"

"Alive my dear Fred, and banged up in the hold where he'll be the first to 'get it' if any more of his friends are out there to cause us more grief."

"Any idea who he is?"

"Not really, the man is still unconscious and I've not seen him yet."

"Might be a good thing if you did." Came the tired reply.

Fred wanted to continue the conversation, but Chip decided he had taxed his friend and colleague long enough. Placating his protestations with a mild threat of pulling rank he led Fred out of the day cabin towards the wardroom. A cold breeze whistled down the flat as gaps in the emergency glazing let in cool sea air piling up against the bridge screen. The Cox'n giving Fred a cheery wave from his seat up in the cockpit as Fred looked around before heading down aft. "We should have the remaining windows sorted before the end of the dog watches." Observed Chip as they made their way into the accommodation area. We're also using the time to change our silhouette just to add to the confusion." Chip knocked on the wardroom door before opening it to make way for Fred. He stood momentarily at the door waiting for the banter to start before closing it. "By heck!" Boomed

Leyland. "You two make a right pair of winged chickens. If you don't mind my saying so Gentlemen!" William and Fred regarding each other momentarily before grinning sheepishly if not pained to observe that they were both strapped up and looking very much the worse for wear. Leyland moved a couple of chairs together so that Fred could sit down and put his feet up. "Reckon we need to requisition more chairs Sir, the rate we're going," said Leyland smiling at Chip. "Sub, I leave it to you to act as policeman and nursemaid, and dare you tell a single joke until they are much better or I'll log you as a danger to the welfare of your fellow officers!" Chip left smiling at an innocent looking Leyland Pengelly who was himself smirking at his good fortune at finding a couple of soft targets for his irrepressible, yet under the circumstances, discrete humour.

The oncoming watchman found the Chief Tech slumped over the tactical display console in the equipment room. He had been working non-stop for almost three days rigging emergency cables and repairing, as best he could, the shattered systems comprising the navigation and tactical arrays. The ships communications system was fortunately lightly damaged and although ready for action Chip had decided to maintain radio silence on their approach to Gibraltar along the underbelly of Spain. He was despatched to the Senior Rates mess for a good long rest and told to leave the remaining work to the combined efforts of the senior radio op and the junior electro-tech.

Chip was aware that they might have a good chance of rebuilding some of the tactical equipment if the spares down in the stores situated in the lower hold weren't ruined. The techs salvaged an encoder-decoder and spare reels of cable from the store, together with additional fittings with which to make up replacements for the broken and melted items left strewn among the rubbish. Most of the evil black soot had been washed away from the room, but there was still a trail of it across the deck of the bridge where men had paced back and forth in the process of repairing and cleaning. "Look at my bloody deck, they've made a complete shambles of it moaned an able seaman in disgust at the state of his part of ship. "Myers!" growled a Petty Officer. "Just be thankful you've still got a deck to clean, there's time enough to tiddly it up when the work is finished. Until then you can go and get some kai for the duty watch. Get to it you skate and look lively!"

"Yes PO." The skate disappeared down the flat grasping six mugs in his hands. "Typical bloody H branch. Never stop whining. Can't think why we got landed with him."

"Spare hand, mate. Every time there's a war on they have to leave their cushy little number behind and join the real navy. He got shipped out from Blighty just before the Spanish put up the blockade at Gib."

"Next thing we'll have 'im swinging the lead just to make sure we don't hit anything!" The laughter rippling around the bridge proving a reasonable litmus of the easing tension among the Senior Rates and the watch keepers. A good sign that would soon infect the whole crew as stress levels fell. The smell of cooking had been wafting through the bridge while they had been hove-to, giving them something wholesome to look forward to, including the normality of sitting down to eat at a table. Pot mess was one thing, but eating it out of a mug for two and a half days with a couple of buttered wedges and some sultana cake had not been conducive to maintaining the normal cycle of events, weighing heavy in the stomach as the food became compacted.

During the night attempts had been made to get some of the media broadcast channels via their downlink decoders in the communications processor. Chip was eating spaghetti Bolognese just before midnight savouring the Mediterranean herbs, not missing the irony of its origins for a second. Everybody's timing was thrown askew by the past few days, and while some slept heavily at odd times of the day, being active at night, others struggled to rest having reached an average that left them hovering in the twilight halfway between sleep and wakefulness. The zombies would usually fall asleep halfway through a meal or walk around in a dazed condition. The news was not good, and it was a grim reality that without a tactical system they could run into some serious trouble in a few hours time. Chip sat reading and re-reading the American Captain's letter, taking a sip from a glass of Chianti in one hand while holding the letter in the other. On the one hand he just could not believe his good fortune. On the other he was hopeful that he could count on the verbal offer of coincidental assistance as they came ever closer to the Spanish coast. The thought that the pirate vessel upon whom they had inflicted so much damage, measure for measure, as had been meted out to them came foremost in his mind when he contemplated the chart strewn upon the far end of the table. The intelligence report had suggested that it was just one vessel in a well-tuned operation designed to plunder vessels along the major routes in and around the Mediterranean. He checked his watch for the umpteenth time noting the progress as miles away to the north on the starboard quarter the Balearics began to slide further away.

A gentle tap on the door disturbed his thoughts. "Come in!" He called.

"Sorry to disturb you Sir." apologised Mr White sticking his head around the door. "I thought you should know we have got tactical up and running with some pretty hairy plots coming in from the eye in the sky."

"What did you say?" replied an incredulous Chip grasping at the words spoken by the Warrant Officer.

"The tactical system is up…"

"No, no Mr White, that last bit?"

"You mean the eye in the sky?"

"You're a genius Mr White, a bloody genius. Who's the duty signal op in there at the moment." asked Chip grabbing the letter from the table.

"The Leading Signalman is taking a turn Sir."

"Good. Let him know I will be over there directly. Thank you Mr White."

"Thank you Sir." Chip read the letter again with a fresh understanding of the message within the message. *'…I wish you and your stout ship bon voyage and trust that the good Lord above will turn his face to smile upon you as you journey home…'*

"Of course! The eye in the sky… the good Lord above, he's giving us a hint to use their own system. How stupid of me not to spot it earlier!" Finishing off his late dinner with great enthusiasm he headed for the door on his way to the equipment room.

With nearly five hours to go and with the plot looking very unstable due to the necessary calibration having not been done, and because the signals had been shut-off to British units, there was not much to see. The leading signalman jumped at the chance to find something better to do while the duty tech began the final stages of the calibration. The first tactical command information chain remained closed to them even with the right access codes being applied. The second one took a few moments to 'wind in' as the complex synchronisation process cranked around until there was a signal match within the system clock circuits. The word 'Lock' appeared briefly at the top of the blank console when the tactical system processed the first data packets to be received. There it was in beautiful colour, a full tactical plot as the satellite, miles overhead, churned out a constant data stream of information. Changing aspect ratios and so on, the operator produced a full screen plot of the eastern Mediterranean, leaning over to the console he typed in the command to fire up the distribution system that would relay the information to the remaining panels throughout the ship. "Well done," praised Chip. "How long before the calibration is finished?" He asked. "Not long Sir." Came the answer from the tech. "I can do it with live data, since it is self-calibrating, more or less. Say in about forty minutes. But you can use the data for reasonably accurate target bearings now, if you needed to."

"Right, let me know the minute you've finished it."

"Yes Sir."

"Well done the pair of you." Chip walked out into the bridge to see the duty watchmen gathering around the one remaining tactical display. "You can use the one in my day cabin if you have to Mr. White."

"Thank you Sir. All we need now is the augmented overlay and we can then see what's below all this cloud."

"Very good Mr White, see to it that they get to work on getting the overlay data as soon as possible please."

"Aye, aye Sir."

Chip disappeared into the day cabin to finish his glass of wine in one gulp before sitting in front of the tactical display to adjust the controls, bringing up a segmented display showing both the navigation and the tactical plot information. Far behind them he could see several unknown vessels moving in the great sea. Two targets interested him. A large and a small target coming their way several hundred miles to the east. The tactical plot confirming his suspicions that it was the Saratoga and her escort destroyer. With just under five hours to go before they commenced the run he needed to appreciate all the facts now at his disposal. With an ETA in the straits at about half-past four he was not looking forward to making the run to Cape St. Vincent in the face of Spanish patrols meandering up and down the Gulf of Cadiz. Although it would still be dark it was a disquieting thought. With an increasing swell being felt under her keel, it was unlikely he could maintain their present fifty-knot speed. The tactical plot showing clouds clearing in the eastern part of the Mediterranean being pushed north and west in a huge circle. He knew they had to get clear before dawn and under the remaining clouds while the giant Catherine wheel of a weather system slowly spun the covering blanket out of their area.

The idea came at that point in the night when all souls are dead in their sleep. He was half-asleep in his chair in front of the plot when something woke him into full alertness. A change in the sound patterns around him, nothing definite. The swell had shifted, and he felt uneasy. Leyland had shrugged himself awake some minutes earlier and was making coffee and a cheese wedge when he felt the tremor in the hull. His pasty-faced visage and bleary eyes transforming him into a life-like resemblance of an ancient cartoon character known as Yosemite Sam. Looking around him sniffing the air, he placed the coffee jug gently down onto the hob, locking it back into place. Leaving his cup he walked slowly out of the galley into the flat as Chip, emerging from his room spotted him hovering in the flat with his head cocked to one side. They had a brief exchange as they walked down aft to the big door leading out onto the cargo deck. Leyland headed for the engine room as Chip walked back to the bridge where he cast his experienced eyes over the instruments glowing dimly. Nothing showing that anything was amiss. Until suddenly the proximity alarm broke his concentration with a shrill screeching. "Obstacle in the water five miles dead ahead, called one of the lookouts. Time to impact six minutes."

"Cox'n turn five degrees to starboard, and initiate collision avoidance on autopilot."

"Aye, aye Sir."

Chip was quietly grateful the crew had become so well connected in their duties, and realising he would be technically interfering stood at the back of the bridge watching the computed plot as it was fed automatically into the autopilot. It suddenly occurred to Chip that such a hazard might cause intense damage to the carrier or her escort if they did not have the same forward looking sensor arrays as those fitted to high speed skimming vessels. All but the old ekranoplanes who literally flew in ground effect above the surface of the water were in danger from running into such things. "Mr White." Chip called softly, "Try and get a profile of that object in the water, it might be big enough to do serious damage to that carrier coming up from astern."

"Aye, aye Sir."

"Sub, I'll be in my cabin." Sub turned and nodded politely, turning back to watch his console display. Once in his cabin Chip glanced at the tactical plot noticing the patrols along the Spanish coast bore the hallmarks of a two-way stream of traffic between opposite ends of the Gulf of Cadiz, with fast moving craft disappearing in the old harbour. As time moved on he could see that only three patrol craft remained in the area.

Two nautical miles from the mystery object it became obvious that it was a huge size, more than likely a steel container washed overboard from a merchantman in rough seas. Chip ordered the go around as the idea formulated in his head. William was sleeping upright in his chair when Chip awoke the slumbering pilot. "It's more comfortable than rolling about in my bunk." He assured Chip. "Sorry to wake you, but is your black box fully operational Guns?"

"Yes, I think so, although it has not been tested since the equipment room fire."

"William can you put it back in place and be ready to switch it on at my mark?"

"You have something in mind Sir?"

"Yes William, perhaps our ticket through the Straits and a helping hand to our American cousins."

"I must point out Sir that I have sole discretion over its use, and it is imperative that neither the enemy nor our, ah, American friends must get wind of it."

"I had more or less thought that would be the case. So this is what I am proposing to do with it…"

William agreed and with the aid of the roused Chief techno wizard they secretly installed it back into place while the duty men were given forty minutes leave to have a drink and something to nibble on. Simultaneously, the Royal Oak closed in on the mystery object until the proximity alarm gave a hundred metre warning. A small boat was put into the water and a crew of two marines and two seamen shoved off slowly towards their quarry. Using hooded torches they found it by observing a peculiar flatness in the water when the swell passed along the object. It was a huge steel container as suspected. Royal Oak nudged closer in until the seamen on deck could pass a hastily rigged danbuoy with a flashing light beacon on the top of it down to the men in the boat. Quickly and expertly they attached the danbuoy to the object, held in place by a powerful magnet. With a wave of his arm, and torch in hand in the direction of the bridge the leading seaman activated the beacon and locked the mast of the buoy into its upright position. Back in the equipment room William activated his black box and waited patiently for confirmation that Royal Oak would be oblivious to all except optically aided surveillance systems. Scrambling back onboard the men secured the boat and its engine while the Royal Oak left the area back on course.

Mr White had marked the position of the submerged container on the electronic chart noting they had one hundred and seventy four miles to run. The computed time indicating that they had three and a half hours to go before entering the Straits. Chip checked his watch noting the time approaching twenty to one, putting their revised ETA just after five o' clock in the morning. He wished that he had more time to tow the huge danger into the mouth of the Harbour at Cadiz and leave it there for some unsuspecting patrol boat to founder against, but time, as he was well aware, was not on his side. Long range sensors on the Saratoga followed Royal Oak right up until the moment she hove-to alongside the container. As far as her navigating officer was concerned she was dead in the water. "Oh ho. Look's like they've got a problem." After a few moments the plot confirmed his suspicions and he rang the Commander's cabin on a direct line. A few minutes later a small conference began concerning their next moves in passing through what was a war zone, in which they were regarding themselves as strictly neutral.

At four am the crew had been shaken out of their pits and duly fell in for action stations. Each crewman collecting from the galley a mug-full of hot drink and a brown paper bag containing breakfast. The infamous tradition of a hard-boiled egg accompanied by a bacon and sausage sandwich. The last forty-six miles began to screw up the tension as the advancing coastline notched up another range marker on the displays. Running with weapons systems on standby did not help the growing feeling of exposure as the smell of land permeated the darkness on the deck outside. The two patrol boats were still very much in evidence on the other side of the narrows. Lightning flickered occasionally in the clouds high above the mountains to the north. The last of the rain that had beleaguered the Mediterranean for the past five days now fell in a blast of sand laden wind coming up from the northern Sahara. Apart from the small task force some five hundred and twenty two miles astern the patrol boats were the only other craft moving about. The Captain of the Saratoga was looking at the facts. "We've heard no alarm from them, and there doesn't seem to be any transponder alarm either. For all we know Lieutenant they could just be having problems with their engines. No Gerry." He addressed his Executive Commander. "I don't think we need to send out a patrol, not in this neck of the woods and certainly not until our dawn patrol. To fly an extra patrol would look out of place, and we must at least leave them to their fate for the time being."

"I concur Sir," nodded the Commander. "However, if they really are in trouble there has to be a contingency plan. We saw how their last mayday was completely ignored by their late friends in the ESNF."

"I agree, and we shall have to wait until we find out what is wrong with their vessel. For now, we proceed as normal."

The Coxs'n adjusted the autopilot while his co-pilot scanned the darkness for any signs of movement. All the ship's company who had survived the previous action were at work. Some of them totally unscathed working with the silent persistence required of them alongside equally determined and obstinate shipmates, who, standing on crutches or with an arm or a head in bandages, turned-to unflinchingly. Waiting for the gods of war to throw more dice. Her wake subsiding to a mere ripple compared with the twin-mountains of foam that had borne them all the way from their near-demise south of Sardinia. Removing every physical possibility of a sensor trace in the enemy's camp Royal Oak rose majestically into a more strategic posture as the throttles were pushed to the firewall. On the high mountains there would be many eyes peering at them through the darkness, totally blind, except perhaps for the unwanted glint of moonlight to reveal their presence, they hoped they would be safe. The minutes ticking by relentlessly. A set of red numbers flashed up on the tactical plot indicating a vessel powering up within the mole surrounding Gibraltar harbour setting teeth on edge. A large destroyer could be seen moving through the outer harbour towards the open sea, heading straight towards them. Someone muttered an oath in the darkness while others using intensifiers probed the night. Raindrops clattered noisily against the wooden panelling and the rigid replacement glass. A nebulous grey surrounding them as they passed along through the shower in the narrow gap of water midway between the two Spanish coastlines.

The Spanish forces had failed to get their hands on the plethora of sensor arrays and communications equipment on the Rock. Before burying themselves beneath their natural granite fortress, the survivors of the early raids on British soil smashed everything that could not be taken within in the labyrinth below the mountain. The Spanish garrison tried desperately to dislodge the multi-force army opposing them from within the mountain. The brave contingent of soldiers, marines, airmen and sailors defying even the best efforts of the Spanish parachute brigade. Even the French brigade failed. Although casualties mounted up on either side, they were far more severe for the invaders from the mainland. In one riposte to the General now commanding the attackers, the Admiral reminded him that of all the most dangerous of men to give arms to were his band of a thousand sailors. A figure slightly over calculating, "And that can only mean one thing." Added the Admiral with a serious overtone in his voice." "You will die to the very last man!" Even the Marines feared Jack with a loaded weapon! The Spanish general shook his head in disbelief. "We have them totally surrounded and cut off. Yet these bastardos, still they fight on!" Every day and every night British snipers took a grim toll of their careless assailants from over a thousand different vantage points on the rock. The Spanish sensor aerials working away silently rotating, while men in large trucks sat in front of their displays gnawing on chooros and sipping chocolate, seeing nothing to disturb their wellbeing. A moment of panic as a break in the clouds revealed a small black dot on the silver sea far below.

A watch keeper taking a break to relieve himself against a retaining wall that surrounded the old tourist car park saw it for a moment before the rain swallowed up the vision before him, a small dark smudge on the open water of the Straits. Opening the door to his surveillance crew he sat down quickly scanning his display, going through the ranges, changing parameters, "There's nothing there!" He raised his voice calling for his lieutenant. "Hey Lieutenant, Señor, I've just seen a boat out there, but I can't see it on my display."

"What do you mean Garcia?"

"I went out to go for a leak Señor and saw this boat in the middle of the channel, but she is not here on my display." Come, show me this boat Garcia." They left the trailer and walked to the retaining wall looking out as far as the eye could see. "I don't see anything Garcia. What do you think it was?"

"I don't know Sir. A boat, going fast. Towards the sea, that way." He pointed towards the Atlantic. "Was it a big boat Garcia, a long boat, short, wide. Was it tall, did you see any guns on it?"

"No it was a long boat not high, like one of those fast container boats that ride on the water."

"You mean like a water skiier Garcia?"

"Si, Señor like a water skiier."

"Are you sure Garcia?"

"Sure, I'm sure. I see it with my own eyes Señor."

"Alright, I believe you Garcia. Let's go back inside and check the schedule. It could be the Rodriguez, she is due out at about this time." They tried to raise the Rodriguez on the comms box without any luck. Twenty minutes passed before the young Garcia decided to have another look-see beyond the steel walls of his trailer. Out in the Bay of Algecieras he found the large black shape of the Rodriguez heading for Cadiz. 'No!' He thought emphatically to himself, 'That is not the one I saw.' He walked back to his position unhappy. "Señor, it is not the Rodriguez, I am sure of it. She is out in the bay. The ship I saw was far into the Straits."

"I hear what you are saying Corporal Garcia, but without radar contact there is no confirmation." His supervisor walked over to him. "Look at your plotter. See, here is the Rodriguez, now extend the range so." They watched in silence as they concentrated on the different ranges. For a few seconds each. "See there is the American carrier with her escort, she's due to come through here later this evening, perhaps tomorrow morning early. Now look at the EuroSat overlay."

"Si Señor, maybe you are right and I am wrong. There is nothing there because of the clouds, we cannot see the surface."

"Look, we cannot contact the Rodriguez, Miguel, because of the sand in the atmosphere, we can talk to Cadiz, but not to the Rodriguez in full view. That's nature at work. Perhaps you saw the shadow of a cloud, eh?"

"No Señor, it was not a cloud."

"Miguel, is this what you saw?" The Lieutenant asked, placing a recognition book on his subordinate's small desk open at a large plate showing several silhouettes of a large class of warship. "Si, Señor, it is like that one there, maybe not so tall, but similar."

"That is the Rodriguez, Miguel. She is a fast destroyer, they all go on skis."

"Maybe Señor, but the one I saw was not the Rodriguez."

"Perhaps not Miguel, you're tired. Keep a good watch on your radar and leave the ship recognition to me, eh. There's a good fellow."

"Si Señor." Corporal Miguel Garcia sighed as only a hacked-off Hispanic soldier would do, with an expressive tilt of the head to one side and a hand lifted in resignation, so passed a fleeting opportunity for the enemy to deal with the Royal Oak, still on her tortuous journey homeward bound.

The Rodriguez came within seven miles of Royal Oak, leaving the battle weary men on the skimmer shrouded in silent darkness, fearful of discovery, holding their collective breath. William longed for an opportunity to personally launch a missile right up its stern pipes, contenting himself with looking at the solution. Then, the heavy destroyer curled away along the coast of Spain towards distant Cadiz. "Tell me William, do we still have our towed array in the hold?" queried Chip out of the gloom.

"Somewhere Sir, I seem to remember seeing it partially crated up. I think we used the wood to plug a lot of the holes we collected."

"How long would it take to check it out?"

"I'll find out. What exactly does it do?"

"Ah, I can leave that to Mr White, he's the UWV man amongst us. I'm sure he'd like a chance to use it." Fred was seated behind his command plot-display looking at the traffic when he overheard the conversation. "It's a bit like a torpedo on the end of a long rope William. You can take 3-D scans of the sea bottom or pretty pictures, and, more to the point, when fitted with a rack you can drop mines -like a fast minelayer."

"Blimey! Why didn't anyone tell me about it? I just thought it was a bit of superfluous kit that no one else wanted for his part of ship. Hell... you don't mean to say we're carrying mines do you Sir?" Chip nodded with a grin emerging on his face. "That's exactly what I mean William. Jump to it, we haven't much time."

"Absolutely, I mean yes Sir."

Chip, Fred and William were later to be found referring to the Admiralty chart for the Southern coast of Spain. In fine detail on the map spread before them they discussed the problems associated with getting in and out of the approaches to Cadiz, around the headland, drop a string of mines, and then turn around to shoot off into the dark before being seen. "What are the chances of us being seen and challenged?" asked William thoughtfully, being mindful not to expose the cloaking device. "I'd say that if we kept just far enough apart from that ship out there, what is it? The, er, Rodriguez," observed Fred, looking up at the tactical data, "then we might get a chance to follow him all the way along Cape Trafalgar and across the mouth of the bay. The rest is a matter of dropping the mines in the channel as we pass along. All in a day's work, so to speak."

"Any other objections gentlemen?"

"Only that we have to be certain that our cloud cover remains absolutely tight or we lose the whole initiative, and stand to take another beating, this time from the shore batteries out on the spit." noted Fred. "I've got the Sub looking at the meteo-data coming in from the US, so we'll find out for sure in a few minutes."

"So, as long as the cloud base hangs together, and with the majority of their fleet out in the Bay of Biscay we stand a good chance of pulling this off. Agreed?"

"I see those patrol craft have just turned in the direction of the Rodriguez, Sir." said one of the Tac plotters. The war council looked at the plot in silence watching the red symbols moving slowly around in the direction of the larger ship. "That answers that question. Looks as though they're all going in for breakfast."

"Towed vehicle is fully deployed Sir." Squawked a voice from an overhead loudspeaker. Fred motioned for William to acknowledge.

Changing to a converging course with the Spanish destroyer, Chip gave a succinct briefing to the assembled Senior and Junior NCOs who could be spared from their action stations. The word passed quickly among the rest as they imparted the message throughout the vessel. "We're going to blow Cadiz!" Was the buzz, even though they knew it meant that some unlucky warship or a transport vessel might get it and possibly sink. Accelerating slowly to match the destroyer's speed they cruised along at sixty knots a few miles astern while destroyer's escorts 'covered' her bows about two miles ahead on either side. The sky remained savagely dark with the occasional flickering of lightning over the mountains. Lookouts on the Rodriguez did not see anything at all. Tucked up in their warm stations at the side of the large battle-bridge they chose to gaze forwards and a few degrees off to the side where the most danger lay from collision with their escorts. A passing shower of dense rain shrouded them in streams of water flooding down the windscreens, adding to their sense of comfort inside the vessel, but making it harder to look at anything except the navigation display. Careful not to be silhouetted against the distant lights onshore their 'shadow' slid easily over the pock marked waters using every advantage the low visibility provided. So confident were the Spanish authorities that the distant war would not come home to roost there was no imposition of a curfew or a blackout. Lights were twinkling everywhere from coastal towns and settlements. A red symbol flashed on the display giving the warning of a vessel in the harbour about to depart. Following it with his heart beating fast the watch keeper whispered a quiet alarm. "Vessel moving in the harbour Sir." Although the noise within the bridge was loud, the silence among her crew shrieked of tense nerves. "No Ident Sir." All looked intently at the small symbol as it separated from the dull outline of the harbour ahead moving into the channel. "Bloody hell!" gasped William. "I'll never get a chance to take a swipe at them at this rate."

"Hold your horses Guns, it may not be as bad you think. It could just be a tug going out to escort her into her berth." Everyone sagged inwardly as the common-sense answer eased the adrenaline flow. "Second target powering up Sir." Again the dreadful wait as the seesaw of fate rocked backwards and forwards.

Dawn was creeping up on them as they observed the first escort making the turn into the Cadiz navigation, followed by the destroyer itself before the second escort followed them both into the bay. This was their most difficult time, five miles astern and with the lights of the ancient town looming over the top of the headland lighting up the clouds hanging far above like a photographer's white umbrella, reflecting it in a wide circle for miles. Flying the Union flag and with their hospital decals masked by grey painted hoardings, they hoped that any observer would take them for one of their own. The two targets inside the harbour were now stationary as the larger ship manoeuvred into the navigation on its way into the defended port. "Make ready to lay your mines Mr White." Called William as the point of no return had been reached. "Ready to lay mines Sir." Came the quick response from the command station down aft. Halfway along the spit of land the order was given. "Reduce speed to twenty knots." Again, the Cox'n easing the autopilot controls in preparation for their fast mine-laying mode. "Sir, the other tug is stationary just inside the headland." Again, everyone, looking closely at the plots. Again, that sinking feeling in their vitals as the unseen fates twisted the screw down harder, sitting there like a loaded gun waiting to blow away their hasty plan to avenge their crewmates languishing in Spanish military prisons. Agonisingly it turned slowly after the last escort heading down the navigation. As Royal Oak drew close to the end of the spit of land the town of Rota came into view on the other side of the bay. Although some six miles distant its lights bringing dread to those who saw them. "Hold fast everyone, we're out of range, the bloom cannot reach us here." Fred informed them. Less than four miles from the enemy coast and a third of the way along their six mile dash William gave the order as they reached the marker on the tactical plotter. "Drop mines!" Unseen beneath the hidden waters the subsurface vehicle's bomb bay already open began to drop its payload at precise intervals taking into account the speed of the tow and the currents in the water around it. A few tiring lookouts may have seen the crest of a wave thrown up momentarily and been forgiven for thinking that's all it was. The inner harbour revealing itself to the naked eye and to those with intensifiers on Royal Oak who looked down the throat of the enemy's stronghold and laughed inwardly. The navigation lights and signals blazing away as if war never existed. "All mines laid Sir." Came the final message. "Good, retrieve the UWV and secure." Replied William casually belying the fact that it had taken six and a half minutes to traverse their target.

"Cox'n, set course to auto-pilot and hold your speed." ordered Chip feeling the sweet smell of success for the first time in days. Following her pre-set course Royal Oak sheared away from the coast in a curve that would lead them directly to the distant cape of St. Vincent two hundred and fifty miles down track. Dawn cracking the sky as they beat along at fifty-five knots dangerously too close to the coast for comfort, soon they would fall below the horizon, out of sight of land. At ten minutes past six they had turned towards the empty horizon, and now a lookout posted on the bunker on the tip of the land finger jutting out into the sea saw a ghostly silhouette rushing away at the far end of the bay. Idly looking at his watch noting the time, then lifting up his intensifiers concentrated on following the dim outline just ahead of a lighter patch of sea; it wake. He thought he saw a large blue flag flying from a masthead. Yes, there it was, and a flash of gold, and then it was gone, a phantom unheard, barely seen fading from his sight as quickly as he had caught it in his viewer. 'Better them than me', he thought turning up his collar against the rain that lashed against his dripping weatherproofs.

At first light the Saratoga launched the initial flight patrol of the day. A bunch of rookies needed training and the donkey work of flying out into the void far ahead of their home plate was part of the exercise in becoming proficient. Despite closing the gap a little between them and the real position

509

of the Royal Oak, the pilots were going to find something in the water that lay partly submerged many miles in front of the advancing carrier and her escort. The previous eighteen hours had been full of mystery as events unfolded. Certain that something serious had befallen their friends in the comparatively few miles that separated them since their original departure, mid-ocean, the wisdom of her Captain held sway. "I don't see nothing' out there Sir." Called back the wingman after they had completed a couple of low passes. "OK, one more sweep then we'll break for home plate." Turning together in a tight circle the two pilots completed a huge loop within which they should have been able to find the Royal Oak dead in the water. Over the expanse of grey-green sea within their visual ranges they could find no large object resembling a stricken skimmer. The 'kid' saw it first, a twinkling light that caught the corner of his eye as they flashed in and out of a heavy burst of rain. "Wait! I've got something down there on our left." Then it was gone, but not before both pilots had activated the position lock markers on their navigation computers. "Navigation position lock on." The voice activated system initiating an orange marker symbol on each aircraft's sensor display. The flight commander took them on a two-minute leg before turning back towards the marker, dropping down to a thousand feet above the sea. "I've got it," called the lead pilot seeing the flashing beacon on top of the danbuoy's mast for the first time. He took them through a second pass at a very much slower speed than before, the water vapour being squeezed out of the atmosphere by the air passing over their wing roots and by the wingtip vortices, leaving perfectly sculptured curves behind them in the sky. Their existence dissipating into nothingness within seconds of their creation.

"It's a beacon of some kind with a flag, did you see anything Cobra two?"

"Cobra one, not sure, but it looks like a large object floating just below the surface. It doesn't look like an up turned hull though."

"OK Cobra two we'll make a final pass for a photo run."

"Cobra one, roger."

He took them down to a hundred and fifty feet at one hundred and eighty knots before they zeroed in onto their target. "Video on." Said the flight leader watching the miniature display in his cockpit jump into life. The high speed, high definition photo-recon system storing video information of the sea below them. At the completion of their pass over the indeterminate object the flight leader headed back into the sky through the overcast. "Secure video." He paused before issuing the next voice command. "Transmit video data-stream." The computer beeping acceptance of each command as they flashed above the clouds into brilliant sunlight. "Let's go see what's out there, Cobra two."

"Cobra one, roger." Together they climbed to twenty thousand feet heading west towards the Straits of Gibraltar and the Atlantic Ocean. The blue skies blurring at the edges of the horizon where white bedecked cloud tops fused in a fluffy demarcation zone of spectacular winds and reflections.

Sensors picked up the two aircraft barrelling along. Amber indicator lights flashing on and off slowly as first, standard secondary surveillance signals were detected, followed by more sophisticated tactical interrogation pulses. The two pilots continued their patrol just beyond the gates of Hercules, before sweeping the sky in a wide arc on the beginning of their return flight to home plate. Far below them, with all of her sensors running in passive mode, the duty watch on Royal Oak saw them coming and then going with mild interest. William being the most anxious of them all over his responsibility to keep any suspicions at bay over their new-found capability to 'vanish'. The American data stream from the satellite chain high above them giving solid data on their surroundings. A fishing fleet off Santa Maria had spread out during the night making it difficult to plot a course through the area without being spotted. "It's not worth the chance of relying on their hatred of the Spanish to turn a blind eye to a British Naval vessel passing by in the distance." Ruminated Fred as he surveyed the navigation plot. "No, let the computer work it out and if that won't work we'll have to go around them."

They were fifty-five miles off the cape and outside coastal sensor range with the hands finishing off breakfast at 07:45 when a thin blue line across the horizon gave evidence of the weather system moving on. Clear skies meant they had reached the point where the course of their secret dash was about to end. The tactical plot revealing the massive fleet of vessels moving relentlessly towards the English Channel far ahead of them in Biscay. Apart from the two American recon aircraft the only other indications had been the departure of the regular Spanish Maritime patrol from its base in Rota. Following it patiently on the plots as it lumbered in to the sky turning south west towards the narrows far behind them. In the equipment room the duty signal op, monitoring Spanish comms on the harbour networks for signs of abnormal activity, while the duty tech studied the tactical plot and its augmented overlays with absolute conviction. The Chief Tech arrived and locked out the last of the active sensor transmission systems. Then working quietly off to one side he disabled the cloaking device on a foldout panel provided at one of the encoder panels in the equipment racks. With the exception of their forward looking sonar giving a limited range of just over five miles the ship was once more operating as a non-standard deep sea vessel running without the mandatory transponders. Flying the white ensign and with her red crosses uncovered they sped along in the Atlantic swell praying silently for a safe passage home. A phone buzzed off to the side where a seaman picked up the receiver.

"Sir, the equipment room says the ESNF destroyer at Cadiz is preparing to leave harbour."

"Ah, just what we've been waiting for. This is where the brown stuff hits the fan. Thank you." Fred didn't want to disturb Chip who had spent nearly seventeen hours up and about, and had only recently turned in. "It's Fred Sir, sorry to disturb you, but I thought you might like to know the Spanish navy has decided to leave harbour." He paused for effect. "Cadiz."

"Let me know if anything comes our way, I think it most likely." Chip turned over and putting the phone back down looked at his watch, shortly afterwards he sat up looking at his tactical display through bleary eyes.

With the exception of the lookouts, the duty Coxs'n and his co-pilot, the duty watchmen gathered around the tactical plot in a small knot. It was ten minutes to eight o' clock other crewmen came out of nooks and crannies to stare at the main panel like men possessed. "Chief Grey, please patch the tac-plot through to the accommodation lounge, in the meantime." Said Fred inwardly smiling and turning to address the goofers he said to them. "You can watch the fireworks from there, now please, clear the bridge!" People scampered down the flat towards the crew lounge vying to get there first to get a good seat. Sub Pengelly stood back in amazement at the tide of humanity sweeping towards him when he emerged from the Wardroom at almost the same point in time. "What's all this then my lad!" He boomed as a junior seaman rushed towards him. "It's the Spanish ship Sir. It's leaving harbour, they've put the plot up on the viewer in the lounge!"

"Oh, I see. You'd better get there then before you get trampled to death in the stampede!"

"Yes Sir." The lad was gone in a flash as Leyland made his way slowly through an advancing tide of men. "Hello Leyland, is that your morning report you have there?" enquired Fred looking pleased.

"Yes Sir, all ready for the Captain to sign."

"Come and have a look at this?"

"I hear the Spanish navy is about to set sail." Leyland smiled nonchalantly. "It's about time they took some unpleasant medicine." He fitted into the group watching the main display while the dutymen worked away on their smaller consoles. They watched the tugs moving in and around the inner harbour working to pull the heavy destroyer way from the wall, the escorts already waiting for her in the outer harbour. Fred looked briefly over to the navigation plot to see, with some satisfaction, that the fishing fleet was sufficiently spread out to allow them undetected passage. He turned his attention back to the tactical display, watching it intently with all the others. There it was, the moment of truth was almost upon them as the small flotilla assembled in the outer harbour, the ships making way slowly out towards the entrance.

Unnoticed, the thin band of blue sky broadened slightly, heralding the onset of better weather. Accompanied by a steady eight knots of wind outside on their port quarter, veering slowly as the temperature rose under the gathering rays of the sun.

It seemed as though the first escort had made it through the channel when suddenly the target data blinked before settling down to indicate the distress code for a vessel in trouble. The distant observers did not hear the explosions as the intelligent mines sought out their prey with cold precision. Speeding along at eighteen knots in the full knowledge that no other traffic was about, and likely to get in the way, they charged out into the bay line astern, no more than a couple off ship lengths between them. The Cervantez leading the way took the full force of the explosion on her main hull that opened like a cherry blossom in full sun. The gaping hole sucking in huge amounts of water in a gusher completely flooding the forward section, nearly tipping her on her nose. The Rodriguez' Captain barely had time to shout the order that would steer them clear before she ran into the stern of the smaller skimmer, pushing it nose down in a final dive for the bottom. The steeply angled stern scraping all the way down the destroyer's starboard side as she passed by the wreck, with some of the sailors jumping for their lives being sucked into her planes.

"Mama Mia!" exploded the second escort Captain grabbing the wheel turning his more agile craft to the starboard. They successfully avoided dodging the destroyer as she slowed visibly in the water while the up-ended stern of his sister ship hung in the air above water, gently bobbing less and less as the waters cascading into her hull weighed her down. Sweeping around in a wide arc with the intention of circling back to lend assistance to the crippled Cervantez, the Cortez struck two mines vanishing rapidly in the waves until only her port side remained visible, hanging lifeless on the surface. Royal Oak's sensors relaying the signals briefly before they were snuffed out on their tactical display. No one spoke or showed any visible sign of reaction as the plot revealed the outcome of their night's work in stark detachment. The seeds of war having been sown with arrogance now coming home to roost with the enemy in the form of a bitter harvest for those destined to pursue it. While their political leaders slumbered in the sumptuous safety of their ivory towers the subordinates were now paying the full price of it with their lives.

"Mines!" Shouted the young lieutenant on the bridge of the Rodriguez, realising the danger too late. His Captain ringing-down the order himself to go hard astern. A cluster of three mines unleashing their fury on the Rodriguez before she could make way. Her slow moving speed was to save most of her crew when the first mine blew away the forward planes on the port side. The second struck her under the bridge while the third made kiss-and-tell contact with her hull under the long section forward of her main intakes, before opening a huge hole in the bilge. Rodriguez slewed around with her twin power plants going asymmetrically haywire, their drive by wire control systems severely damaged. Revolving about her beam-ends she began settling in the water while a tide of humanity hurled itself over the side hardly waiting for any command decision to abandon ship.

Chip was watching in silence in the privacy of his cabin when the first two targets winked out. Unhurriedly, he walked to the bridge to find all but the lookouts and the 'boat-drivers' staring hard at the unfolding tragedy of warfare. Slowly around and around the stricken ship turned, out of control and going down. They could imagine, but did not hear the Captain's hoarse command to abandon ship as the sea climbed ever closer towards broaching her gun'ls. With wreckage swilling around in the water the proud and angry Captain stepped off his ship into the cold Atlantic Ocean cursing the day he was found by the enemy and had been powerless to fight back. It took forty-five minutes for the Rodriguez to sink. In that time span the majority of the survivors had been drawn along the coast by the swiftly flowing current, placing the mines between them and any rescue boat that might be tempted to find them. A few managed to swim ashore forming human chains to catch others drifting by, while in the main, their

Latin temperament took over as they sat motionless on the rocks watching their shipmates drifting by unaided. The dancing girls of Cadiz would be weeping before noon; their siestas shrouded in black long before the sunset fell upon Hesperia beyond the evening tide.

"That's one in the eye for those Spanish Admirals who think they can attack our country without a fight," said Chip breaking the silence. "Come on everybody, back to work. We've got a long way to go and about an hour or two at the most before they come looking for someone to blame."

"I make that three Spanish vessels sunk at 08:35 by mines laid by Royal Oak. Please enter it into the log William." Ordered Fred, who, without catching his breath continued speaking, "All those who should be abed and ought to be please do so now. By your leave Sir that doesn't include you." Then he added with a smile, the first real smile since he had returned back onboard. "Well done!"

****

The French Admiral shrugging his shoulders at the outcome of his discussion with the war council, turned and passed the day old signal to his Italian counterpart. "Is there an explanation for this Captain Antonio? If so I'd like to hear it." He passed the signal to the Italian who, looking blank, took the electronic pad from the Admiral's fingers. Reading it slowly and still expressionless he read it again. "I have no answer for you at this moment Admiral, but I will find out and let you know."

"We may be at war, but I don't want to see this kind of thing happening to anyone at all. If that hospital ship has been left to sink with no rescue attempt it will not bear well with our political masters in Brussels or Strasbourg."

"Si, it's not good at all Admiral. I will make further enquiries."

"See that you do." The sting of that final remark dug deep into the Italian Captain's heart. At his elevated rank no one expected to be spoken to like that by a senior officer. Apart from the fact that someone somewhere had broken a cardinal seafaring rule, he felt it was a personal reflection upon his own navy and on himself as he handed back the electronic notepad. "Si Admiral he replied the white heat of anger beginning to rise in his throat. 'Someone is going to fall for this.' He thought as the meeting broke up for the morning. 'Nearly two hundred men and women including crew had

515

been lost in his patch of water without anyone responding to their mayday, unthinkable!'

****

In London William Goodfellow sat behind President Warnock who was chairing the Defence Council meeting. His notepad automatically printing on its screen the words of the assembled 'high command' as they were spoken. Various secretaries and aides were doing the same thing, and it went some way to lifting the tedium of the heavy subjects up for discussion. "What I need gentlemen is something more than what we've got now to boost the morale of the people. Bringing his majesty back has been a wonderful piece of good news for everybody, but unless we counter the propaganda campaign in Europe we will find ourselves feeling very depressed before the end of the summer. It's more than just a counter offensive, I know General, but it also goes beyond political necessity. We not only need to give them a victory on which to build more victories, but something that can inspire them against the superior odds we are facing."

"The Bristol invasion has bogged both sides down Sir, they can't move us, but neither can we exactly move them, I can only suggest that we pull the plug out at Bath and Swindon. But I don't think that a small enclave of German sappers and French snipers will constitute a major victory like Carlisle."

"Air Marshall, do you have any suggestions?"

"Give me an aircraft carrier to carry my squadrons to the enemy, so I can bomb the Armada out of the water before it sails around the corner of France, or we might as well sue for peace now."

"That's not helpful, but I see the point. We don't have the time to build you any."

"May I suggest that we close with the Armada now Sir. Our intelligence informs us that while the Spanish took on supplies at St Nazaire, six French submarines slipped out late last night under cover of darkness. We have three in the area now with another three in the North Sea. The First wave of French transport vessels remain damaged or sunk in the Bristol Channel and Port Talbot, and I'm sure the loss of their supplies will hasten their capitulation in Bristol. Then Bath will follow since the enemy is comprised of essentially paratroops with no formal support. They should last a few days at best."

"Well General, what do you think about that?"

"It's sound logic provided we can keep their reinforcements from landing."

"I can continue to provide limited air cover, but bear in mind we are absolutely stretched to the limit." Quibbled the Air Marshall. "Gentlemen, it makes good sense to seed the Western Approaches with submarines. Your attack boats will have to take the brunt of the action. Air Marshall, please arrange to co-ordinate as much air cover you can spare, Liaise with Admiral Watson to integrate both your fighter-bombers with the Naval air squadrons more closely. General, keep up the good work, I'm sure our new recruits will quickly shape up."

"But Admiral, how many of those fast skimmers do you have at present."

"Not many Sir. We have almost forty on active service, and they are being rotated for refit to kit them up with torpedoes and anti-submarine equipment."

"Would they work together with the hunter-killers to harry the enemy before they, as you say Admiral, turn the corner of France?"

"They would prove extremely effective if properly kitted out. Their previous role of coastal and fisheries protection has not suited them for out and out warfare, but they are proving to be very easily adaptable."

There was a pause while the President scanned his notes and at that moment an aide appeared though the doorway heading directly for William, handing him a signal tablet before leaving the conference room. The message contained on the electronic screen reminded him of a subject that he preferred not to think about. The sad loss of the HMS Royal Oak in the Mediterranean was a great dishonour to their enemies and a painful memory. Still here was a spark of good news for the President and also for the Chiefs of Staff. William gently tapped the President's elbow as he laid the electronic tablet on the table next to his hand. The President nodded turning his head slightly towards William in silent thanks. The pause grew a little longer while the other men waited politely. "Gentlemen, it seems as though we have a little good news. USS Saratoga has recovered casualties from the Royal Oak and is making her way through the Mediterranean with a view to bringing them home. President Warnock turned to speak privately with William in muted tones. Returning his attention back to the assembled dignitaries around the table, the president announced the

517

news 'hot off the press', while William was already sending messages to the Foreign Ministry and the Home Office for the respective ministers to meet the President later that day.

The meeting broke up at one o' clock with the signal wires in defence headquarters beginning to heat up with the news arriving from unknown intelligence sources. Admiral Dunham was on his way to his office when an aide caught up with him in a brightly-lit corridor, two floors down. The Admiral looking puzzled folded the handheld taking it with him into the lift. Once upstairs in his office the Admiral phoned around seeking answers to a number of questions, not least of all was the question; 'have you got anyone out there at the moment?' Without fail everyone denied any involvement. The Saratoga had recently passed through the narrows having been buzzed by jittery Spanish air patrols several times, but other than that there was not a whiff of covert operations by anyone, including sympathisers. The Admiral ignored lunch choosing instead to go down the 'hole' to see for himself. When he arrived in the darkened ops room several wall panels told the story of a beleaguered Britain being attacked from all sides.

Concentrating on the Western Approaches panel he asked the operator to zoom in on all targets. He saw three heavy mono-hulled cruisers sailing out of Brest, with their escorts fanning out ahead of them, all heading due south, instead of north. 'There's no denying why they're doing that.' He thought to himself. The operator sat back watching the Admiral pressing buttons and searching in and out with the zoom over an area covering the Atlantic seaboard of Europe from Cherbourg to southern Spain. There was nothing. The subsea data did not support a submarine attack since all of SM10's squadron was split between the eastern seaboard defences and the Western Approaches. "Can you get photo-metric data from this console?" He asked patiently.

"Ordinarily, yes Sir, but we have been relying on non-military systems for that kind of data. The next payload is due in about fifteen minutes." The Admiral waited while watching the operator setting the console up for video download. "Do you have the augmented tactical data facility available?" He asked getting a little impatient. "Yes Sir, we do. Do you want me to punch it up now?"

"Straightaway please." The Admiral leaned in towards the console watching for the augmented overlay to emerge on the screen. Slowly the tactical plot changed as additional satellite sensors came on stream. "There." He said pointing to a tiny object on the very edge of the swirling cloud formation outlined before them. "Put it up on the wall screen if you please." He stood up and walked over to the screen for a closer look. "Speed is fifty knots Sir, heading three six zero. No ident marker or naval transponder code emissions.

"So what is it Lieutenant?"

"I'll increase magnification Sir."

"There's only one type of vessel that steams along at that speed Lieutenant, and that is a skimmer if I'm not mistaken."

"That's the best I can do Sir." There was a pause as both men watched the target move slowly towards the final vestiges of cloud cover. A small knot of interested senior officers watching them from a discreet distance. Admiral Dunham was more than half sure about this target. No other skimmer Captain in the world would be heading north with complete anonymity to prying eyes. "Get me a secure line to the C in C Naval Home Command, quickly now!"

Rapidly and out of earshot, Peter Dunham made known his assumption to his old colleague and partner in crime down in Portsmouth. It was decided that only air cover could be provided once the main target of the Armada sailing up the north west corner of France had been dealt with. Until then, their only hope was good fortune or maybe a submarine if one could be spared. "Look, there's three heavies and their escorts heading south out of Brest right now. That can only mean one thing, they've realised their mistake and are sending a rear guard to patrol their southern extremity. If that vessel is who I think it is they'll run smack into them and with no hope of escape." There was a significant pause on the other end of the line. "Peter, I'll see what I can do and ring you back."

"Thank you."

****

Sub came on watch at noon looking much better for time in the nest. The log showing one hundred and ninety eight miles had passed under the keel between them and the point where they were when the mines had struck. Their current position at seventy miles west abeam Cape Sines. The dash across the Algarve coast and around the corner at Cape St. Vincent had paled to insignificance while they sped towards a position abeam the

519

mouth of the Tagus estuary. The tactical plot exposing several Portuguese men of war powering up in preparation to leave Lisbon naval base. With immediate danger now past Fred had retired to the wardroom where he sat perched between two chairs talking to William who was trying to balance a cup of coffee on his bad elbow. "There you are, reckon I will be able to fly again once we get back in."

"Not on your life. Look at that disastrous wobble you've got there, that makes all the difference between you dropping a bomb on one of theirs or one of ours. Worse in fact than a gun captain with a stutter." They smiled wanly at each other. William put the cup down grinning. Behind the grin he was secretly worried about their chances of getting back home. "As a matter of fact I wanted to ask you something Sir." He said broaching the subject of their survival without actually saying so. Fred shot him a penetrating look. "About as much chance as a snowball in a jet exhaust." replied Fred swiftly. William looked at him taken aback. "Well, I guess that's what you wanted to know isn't it William. Slightly better than the odds you face when your squadron takes to the air - our odds of survival."

"Yes, um, I was going to ask that question."

"Don't think about it, you won't have the time when it happens William. If we can find a way to dodge the oncoming traffic we will but you have to agree that from now on the rest of our journey will be more than a little interesting."

They talked around the houses for a while longer as Chip slept deeply in his cabin. Leyland Pengelly was dhobeying down in the small laundry after having awoken from his morning off, the prospect of filling in endless paperwork in the afternoon weighing on his mind. While his merchant marine counterparts had little to do once their watches had finished, the Grey Funnel Line had, centuries earlier, made it necessary to find work for everyone onboard; from Captains to the lowliest rank of junior lantern wick trimmer. Music emanating from the lounge area gave people a momentary escape from the realities of the past few weeks. By the time lunch was in mid-sway, when Admiral Dunham had spotted the faint smudge on the satellite image, Royal Oak was beginning to wallow in a deepening swell during the crossing of the distant mouth of the Tagus which lay far below the horizon to the east. The Spanish border two hundred and ten miles further north.

Hourly bulletins on the networks only served to make the news gloomier as they moved closer to their destination. Foreign correspondents speaking English laced with continental accents ran opinion polls and summaries of recently produced government statistics provided by eager Mandarins. Despite the negative reporting people onboard remained optimistic on the outcome of what was now being openly admitted as a war. The ship felt deserted with the crew down in their messdecks or cabins or in their respective lounges, talking, playing uckers or card games of one kind or another. A couple of the marines emerged from down below with their one and only prisoner. Walking him down the battered looking cargo deck, empty now of its former passengers, many of whom the enemy pilot had killed in his attack. They took him through the rear doors onto the quarterdeck chaining him onto the railing on a short length of steel chain.

The man was quiet, never speaking to anyone, holding his peace. The object of many individual murder plots hatching in the lower decks, he was allowed out twice a day to get some fresh air and exercise. The pasty faced individual now looking the worse for wear with his clothing and appearance showing that they were well past their sell by dates. The man, allowed a shower once a day when most of the crew were preoccupied with their own pursuits during the evening watch, was kept out of sight and sound during such times the crew were active. The boot-neck guards stood talking among themselves leaving the prisoner on the other side by himself. Meanwhile, the duty watchmen cast anxious eyes over the symbols depicting six vessels heading across Biscay, coming south, and a singleton submarine way out in the Atlantic showing no computed ident derived from signature references.

Sub thought it was a Russian. "They always play dumb." He'd told a mildly interested lookout. The tactical plot alarm blooped a low-level warning indicating that two ships were powering up in the massive lagoon of Lisbon harbour. Although the Portuguese had made no commitment towards joining the hostilities, they were still an unknown factor. The long range plot showed an aircraft leaving Corruna far to the north, heading north west. After an hour it changed course heading due south. The projected track for a box pattern indicating that by mid afternoon the skimmer would be well within range of the maritime reconnaissance patrol. Sub checked their position finding it to be 40° 9'N by 11° 21' W, even by mental arithmetic he could see the reality of an overpass before too long. Two more aircraft clawed their way skywards from Lisbon, one turning west flying directly out to sea overhead Cape Roca. Climbing through the haze on a vector that kept it over a hundred miles distant, while the other headed south along the coast towards the advancing aircraft carrier and her escorts. Fred accompanied by William entered the closed bridge heading for the large plotter. Together they scanned the details looking for a way out. The ident codes proving them to be maritime reconnaissance units while they studied the charts.

Fred found Chip shaving in front of a mirror in his tiny en-suite accommodation. Hitching a seat on the edge of a small table, Fred outlined the situation giving possible courses of action. "Bring it up on the viewer Fred will you. Tell me where we are?"

"About seventy five miles off Cape Mondega." replied Fred lightly. "You know it wouldn't be a bad idea if we closed up with the coast, it's only about eighty miles to Ria de Aveiro, could reach inshore waters in about an hour or so, where we would look more like a native than a fugitive." He added hopefully. Chip came out wiping his face with a towel looking towards the plot. "Mm, let's have a look at the information." He studied the viewer for a few moments rubbing his chin thoughtfully. "Doesn't look very hopeful does it?"

"Dicey to say the least."

"If that Spanish aircraft turns towards us we're as good as sunk, but if that one heading north from Lisbon keeps on its present track, and runs that way to the west... There's a chance here Fred that they'll respect international boundaries and we may have a chance if it turns back towards the north."

"Yes, I agree, let's take her closer in, but keep us well clear of those fishermen."

"Would you say about twenty miles or so off the coast?"

"Twenty miles looks fine."

"Right, I'll take us in," volunteered Fred making for the door. "Oh, I recommend the fish pie, it's the last of the fish until we get home."

"Thanks Fred, what about the lamb and mint sauce?"

"A bit stringy, the lads are taking bets as to whether or not it's goat."

"What does Leyland say it is?"

"He didn't, he went for the oggy, chips and some mushy peas. He said you could trust that anywhere around the world." Fred laughed. "Wise fellow that. Right, I'll join you say, in about forty minutes." Fred nodded leaving him to his ablutions.

The Portuguese aircraft eventually turned north giving a much looked-for break in the tension. Chip checked the radar sensors scowling at the fishing fleet spread out before them en-route. All eyes now turning to the other target echo representing the Spanish 'eye in the sky' which was expected to make a turn any minute. Compensating for the wind speed high above the deep blue ocean, the Spanish pilot kept them waiting until his navigation computer told him that his aircraft had reached the end of his current track. Looking around at the sky on his left he followed-through the turn as the computer banked the aircraft in a perfectly co-ordinated rate one turn. Seeing nothing untoward he watched the DI as the numbers changed rapidly, then finally slowing to a standstill as once again, the computer levelled the wings bringing the nose onto a new heading of 090 degrees magnetic. Sub breathed an audible sigh of relief while noting the change. "I reckon we'll be looking like one of those fishing boats by the time he closes with us," suggested the tactical op standing nearby staring intently at his screen. "I think you may be right," affirmed Chip. "Keep an eye on that and bring the timing forwards in ten minute steps."

"Aye Sir, ten minute steps." Watching the large viewer as the computer updated the target situations in ten minute projections. With thirty six minutes to spare they saw the plotted solution present a promising situation with Royal Oak passing through the fishing fleet at about the same time the Spanish aircraft passed within forty miles on its side of the territorial divide. A compromise was struck where they would reduce speed and direction slightly to conform with the general profile of the fishing fleet, hoping that none of the fishermen would think to look too closely at a naval vessel 'patrolling' their patch of sea. Fraught with problems of this nature, their discovery could only be a matter of time.

The Spanish pilot was flying close to the extended line of the national boundaries between his country and Portugal. Towards the end of their track the plot looked very much the same as projected earlier by the flight navigation computer. He turned his head and grinned on hearing a meaty smack behind him in the fuselage. Lieutenant Esteban was having problems again. He smacked the radar cabinet with the open palm of his hand watching the console display jitter as he did so. "There you are. I told you this sensor system was falling apart." He said triumphantly. "Easy on that!" chided Captain Tomelloso. "We don't want you starting a fire or something."

"Every time I get this aircraft it is the same old problem Sir. Why do they insist on looping the cables around on the floor where one's feet must go? No wonder the damn thing doesn't work properly." The display flickered and jumped as he tapped a little more lightly. "You worry too much Rafael. Look we'll be home soon, another eighty kilometres before we turn north."

"That's not the point Sir. How am I supposed to complete my log if I don't have any data to show for it?"

"Just log it as a defect for now and take what data you can. You're too much the perfectionist Rafael."

"Oh well, I suppose that a fishing fleet or two amounts to something." Said Rafael glancing up at his display from his crouched position in front of the console. The picture still jittered occasionally, but held long enough. He swore. "No range marker! How am I expected to work with this equipment if I can't use it!"

"OK Rafael, go and get a drink and calm down. If you think we can't get any more good data, I can always take us back home."

"Well... there's not much out there." He paused, thinking for a moment looking at his pilot. "Yes, what's the point, let's turn for home, and I'll try to live with what I've got while we track along the coast."

"Si, maybe you can get it working again before we get to Corruna." Captain Tomelloso sank back into his seat and after a short delay, in which he checked his flight plan, he made the required adjustment to the autopilot. The twin engined aircraft responded by banking in a gentle turn to the left where it remained until their new heading approached due north. Levelling off again Tomelloso saw slight discoloration in the sky giving away the presence of a temperature inversion over the mainland just beyond visual range. Lieutenant Esteban stretched in his chair with a deep sigh of dissatisfaction. He logged the fault and the subsequent course change before returning to his screen again. The fishing fleet was slipping off the edge of the picture to the bottom as they drew away from them. Instead he now concentrated on the expanse of water on either side, between their current position and the coast, and out to the west where lay the limitless waters of the open sea.

Far below them the Sub passed a brief message of relief to Chip who was working on the charts for the western approaches in the chart room. Shortly afterwards they resumed their old course and speed drawing abeam Ria de Aver a little after four o' clock. Their revised ETA abeam Oporto had slipped to 17:00 delaying their rendezvous with the Spanish border until twenty four minutes past six, in time for twilight shadows giving way to dusk. Twenty miles off the coast was a little close for comfort, but a necessary evil. The plot showing that Saratoga was turning around the far corner of Southern Portugal, her air patrols fanning in towards home plate for coffee and doughnuts before throwing metal in the air during night flying exercises.

By nightfall the smell of cooking, the soft sounds of music once again, and the empty companionways rattling quietly in tune with the motions of the ship, belying the external realities with an easy atmosphere of warmth and security. The prisoner had been returned to his makeshift cell; fed and watered early. William, Fred and Leyland emerging from their cabins to fill the little wardroom once again with polite conversation, in between watching the news broadcasts from home and around Europe. Amazingly, there were aerial clips of a small number of ships moving down the Tagus towards the sea. With the military summaries over, and with fresh images of a smoking Bristol City centre, the ravages being meted out in Carlisle by the foreign invaders, the tenor of the news from home changed to focus on the forthcoming elections. The commentators moving on from the now 'old hat' news of the king's return home.

At the dawning of the next day golden sunlight tinged high cirrus with brass while nearer the altostratus and bunches of cumulus radiated a deep rose and marzipan high above the shadows along the starboard deck. The strategy seemed to be working. Still flying the union flag they longed for the safety of the night before changing her tactics yet again. So far, all of the Spanish, Portuguese and the French lookouts had missed the small speck upon the ocean, whether by accident or pure oversight, since she was more likely represented as a coastal trader working between the smaller havens and river ports.

The plotters on the Saratoga had their suspicions when they rounded Cape St Vincent to find a long-range target ploughing along at a fair old lick of fifty knots. It fitted the profile of the Royal Oak. Keeping a wide berth from the coast Saratoga's Captain had been happy to oblige the Flight Commander's needs for getting his tyros into the air, and this included fairly innocuous patrols way ahead of the flat top's position. Identified as 'friendlies' long before they came into view, the three aircraft patrol caught up with them as the late afternoon mood of relaxation changed into early evening. Passing high overhead the speeding aircraft peeled off in an informal right echelon heading for home plate. The news that she was up ahead had been received with great relief by those who saw the intelligence data, and especially by the command authorities who had suspected that their discovery of the destruction at Cadiz might have been something to do with their English cousins. The situation had the potential for political embarrassment, as both captains well knew. For having taken the rescued survivors off the sinking Royal Oak, and then to have discovered her after the event barrelling along into the rear of a heavy blockade cum invasion force, might provoke some sticky questions.

For the Royal Oak it would be difficult to explain her position since it was well known by her enemies that she had been sinking, and then to have her appear once again in the Atlantic. It was too difficult to work out. Either they should disembark the Royal Oak's original casualties back onboard the Royal Oak, or they should give her a wide berth pretending that she was not there. The Saratoga's Captain was adamant. They would provide her with as much help as he could give her without incurring the wrath of his superiors and political masters alike. Much later that day as the penumbra of the setting sun revealed the evening star twinkling in her station up above, turning the sea into a grey-black shimmering mass, Royal Oak was about to disappear for a second time. At twelve minutes to eight Royal Oak drew abeam Cape Finisterre in a worsening sea. The hull creaking as each incoming roller lifted her stern in a diagonal skewing motion rolling her in a sickening way. Slowly they passed the corner of northern Spain into the open vestiges of Biscay. A huge anti-cyclone working its way across from the Americas was beginning to make itself felt as the outer fronds of its thickening storm clouds drizzled rain with increasing intensity. The order was given to reduce speed. Deep in the hold, the prisoner was thrown about in his tiny cell as each passing wave crashed and gurgled beneath the hull plates. Cursing his luck and damning his captors to hell with each sickening lurch.

18. DAYS OF TRIBULATION

It could not have been worse. The Armada rendezvous at Brest proceeded up the Channel on the French side with air cover provided by squadrons from Brest, Cherbourg and Le Havre. Consolidation of the fleet with French units from Cherbourg making up the losses inflicted upon them by the British submarine squadrons, who, lying in wait made holes in their ranks. British warplanes were met by French and German resistance, but ran before they could engage the enemy in a cat and mouse game over a broad front of hundreds of miles. The British deploying cruise missiles inflicted much damage on the inshore flotillas assembled at Le Havre, ruining their chances of providing landing craft for the invasion of the southern coast of England. Cherbourg had not been so successful having been adequately defended by the French air force and by anti-aircraft batteries. A low level attack on Wimereaux to the north, just across the narrows knocked out a French communications facility that had been eavesdropping on the British transmissions for sometime, providing electronic intelligence for radio jamming centres further down the coast. A reduced fleet pressed on for Cap de le Hague the following day, giving the reefs and shoals around the captured Channel Islands a wide berth.

The battle of Alderney was a short sharp exchange started by a sneak attack by two British submarines hiding on the bottom. Despite modern technology the non-nuclear boats were almost undetectable with their near-silent plasma powered engines and silent control systems. Two troop carriers went down in the first salvo, trapped in a crossfire emanating from behind undersea ridges. Ridges that none of the escorts could get past for fear of tearing out their bottom plates on the rocks. A large mono-hulled super-destroyer fell apart as a tin fish hit it squarely amidships, tearing a large hole right the way through to a magazine. The aft section split away careering under its own power out of control, leaving the sinking fore-section to disappear beneath the waves. The remaining aft section creating havoc among the fleet as they attempted to avoid collision. Six Zed-6A MkIIs went down hit by missiles from fleet escorts. While the French squadrons handed out another heavy blow to the English flyers with their Rainbow fighters protecting the fleet, supported by German fighter bombers of the Eleventh Jaeger Geschwader. Elsewhere, a wave hopping task force slipped across the Channel outbound towards the coast of France. Unnoticed or unable to scramble an adequate defence the English pilots hammered the airfields at Cherbourg and in the hinterland beyond with no casualties. When news broke of the combined attack on London the two squadrons that had dashed across at wave height, immediately re-routed to English skies making low level zigzag paths over the hill country to cover their tracks back to their secret bases. Swiftly re-fuelling and re-arming they joined the fray over the wastelands and marshes east of London.

The German landing forces had made further successes along the east coast of Britain, without any further interference from their neighbours, the Dutch, the Danes or the Belgians. Despite facing sanctions for their earlier actions in defending the British coast in the first wave of attacks, they now stood on the sidelines wringing their hands to the accompaniment of muted protestations. The attempted raid up the Humber resulted in a withdrawal as the Germans became riddled with small arms fire, missiles and laser cannon, leaving their casualties and their dead to float downstream on the turn of the tide. Middlesborough took a pounding and fell under an immense barrage from capital ships touting heavy guns and laser cannon. South Shields held for a day until there too, heavy bombardments forced the defending native army of Geordies to retire in good order to the city limits. The defending Generals having secretly encircled the city with a wall of steel, with tanks and artillery waiting in readiness to wipe out the consolidating mass of invaders. The infantry drawing them into the trap like those fabled Impis of Zulu fame long ago, who ruled the veldt for many centuries before the Europeans came to their lands. Expecting only a hotch-potch of regulars supported at best by hastily enlisted militiamen, the German advance foundered before it began. Cut to ribbons, begging for release from the winnowing fire of shells and laser cannon. Their counterparts sitting tight in Carlisle unaware of the ferocity of the defence, only picking up the intelligence later in the day.

Marshall Ferrand viewed the same intelligence from the safety of his bunker outside the old city of Orleans shaking his head. "Messieurs, what is wrong with our army today? First we get bogged-down by a piddling little regiment on the south coast, and now they have a complete armoured brigade at their disposal in the north. This is not a police action but an all out war. The generals mewed about the apparent loss of initiatives, not caring to mention the word failure, except one. General Chauvigny was not a mincer of words. "We have been deceived." He said. Deceived by the government as much as by the British."

"What do you mean by that?" Demanded the generals seated at the table with him. "This was never intended to be anything else but a war in which the British were the targets of a well equipped army. Look at the facts mes amis. In the past year we have been slowly building up our forces along the lines of a politically motivated desire to restore order to a troubled region in the union. All the time we have been told the British were just a rabble facing the possibility of an extreme government like the politburo of old Russia. No elections, just a grab for power by carefully orchestrated mob violence against the reasonable voice of the population wanting democracy. Now look what we are facing. Instead of a run down army that can barely defend a barley field we find a well organised fighting force, well equipped with tanks and artillery, with infantry battalions that we didn't know they had. Look at their airforce. They might have had just a dozen or so old Zed6 machines for show, but now they have squadrons of the latest MkIIs, now what do you make of that?"

"At least their navy is struggling, and that is where the key to this operation lies Pierre. If we have control of the air and the sea, then they are as good as lost. Then we can push forward with air cover as we consolidate our beachheads."

"You've missed the point General Auxerre. We will have to commit a lot more resources than we originally planned. Who stands to gain from a politically motivated invasion that will be the end of the Union in this way. And I will add that if the Dutch, Belgian and the Danes make up their minds we will have another bloodbath on the mainland of Europe." The quietly spoken General was shouted down while he sat watching his colleagues a little too passively.

Marshall Ferrand looked sideways at his colleague feeling slightly alarmed. 'True, he said to himself. 'We have not looked at the problem this way.'

"What is the basis of your claim Mon General?"

"Only that history tells us we shall soon see unreasonable demands being made upon ourselves and our neighbours, to expedite this 'police' action."

"Oh, come on, surely you can understand that the federal government has priority over national authority, and this is just a police…"

"Not so." Persisted General Chauvigny. As the political will of those in government step up the pressure, a pressure requiring, shall we say, territorial expediencies resulting in nothing less than forced entry to the coastal ports based on the demand to supply more men and materials to the front. When we reach that point we will be in the grip of a military government across the entire union and no way to back out of it."

"Don't you think that you're being alarmist over this General Chauvigny?" demanded Marshall Agen, in a rich southern accent. Until now he had been carefully watching the interplay between his Chief of Staff and the Generals. "No Sir, I don't. Look at it this way. We see the Turks and the Russians escalating their troop movements at our extremities. The Albanians are ready to cause another war in Macedonia that will split the Balkans down the middle. The rest of Europe waits patiently for the outcome knowing that if we fail and get dragged into a prolonged war here on the western peninsula, this will be sufficient impetus for our neighbours to take a slice out of our cake."

"True, we could not lend any assistance to either the Greeks or to the Macedonians. Since the United Nations moved to Geneva as a whole, leaving the Americans out of world stage events it would be up to us." Ventured Marshall Ferrand, but that is another matter. We must re-evaluate our position and change our strategy now that we can see it is going to take more than mere police action to overcome this problem…"

****

A Spanish alpine regiment pulled off a lightning raid across the rolling countryside towards Bath. Heading north just west of the city they captured the E4 along a deep cutting, effectively severing a supply line to the British regiments pressing their cousins towards the sea in the fight to capture Bristol. For six hours they blockaded the motorway until they were overcome by field troops from the newly formed Gloucester regiment. The French delivering six hammer-blows along the south coast, puncturing Euroroute 27 in six places. The communications centre at Hartland Point was vaporised in a huge explosion delivered by just three German aircraft that had taken off from Rouen earlier in the day. Only one of their aircrews would return whence they came. A three pronged attack being launched upon Hastings, Eastbourne and Brighton coincided with a massive raid on the Thames estuary.

The maritime defences in the west had become reliant on native cunning to harass the enemy's fleet of ships as it passed by. Fast patrol boats lay hidden in the creeks and secret bays and coves on the north Devon coast by day. During the night they came out to hug the coastline until they found their targets, loosing off missiles and torpedoes with devastating effect. Their losses were expected to be high, and in spite of some casualties their guerrilla tactics of hit and run by night served to redress the imbalance of numbers.

The savage attack on the Thames produced high casualties on both sides until the defenders had reached a point of no return. Groups of hidden soldiers waiting for the word released thousands of gallons of oil and gasoline into the mighty river. As the armed transports led by naval units fought their way past Thurrock threatening the river crossing highways. Downstream other units did the same thing, knowing full well such an attack would have to take place at high tide the planners used the oldest tactic of all to repulse an invader -fire. Aircraft and squaddies alike hurled glowing rounds into the growing, spreading film of fuel. Those trapped upstream had no chance, for turning around they had miles of blazing, choking fire to traverse before they could make their escape to the open sea. The kindest thing the defending soldiers could do was to shoot any person moving in the blazing lake. Captains realising the outcome steered their craft to the nearest shore in the hope of getting their troops and themselves off in time before their ships exploded into fireballs. Forming up on land in disarray, these comparatively small groups were mopped up before nightfall, with only a few stragglers getting away in the dark.

The assault on the Scottish capital went unceremoniously into the record books as one of the most infamous events of the war. A delegation of the Scottish Assembly went down the road passing through Haddington to meet the Colonels leading the attack at their bridgehead at Dunbar, taking with them the argument that Scotland and the Scottish people were never involved in any such anti-federalist behaviour. Moreover, unlike their English counterparts had not indulged in anything other than the wrongful imposition of an English political agenda. Obersts Willi Darmstadter and Gunther von Eilenberg waited patiently for the peace mission to finish its rather belated message, delivered in a self-righteous and high-handed manner by one of the lowlander representatives. Darmstadter shaking his head politely brushed aside their aggrieved notions of injustice followed by the curt commands of von Eilenberg to continue the advance. While the whining civilians were wined and entertained by aides in an accommodation tent, the generals moved the front line to Haddington. As the ruse became apparent the aides following orders clapped them in irons placing them under armed guard.

Sappers attached to the Black Watch severed the arterial roads and railways by blowing principal bridges and tunnels, while ships of the Royal Navy launched missiles from the comparative safety of the Firth of Forth, inflicting casualties on the beach head at Dunbar. Heavy artillery and missile batteries were drawn up along the Kilpatrick Hills to the west overlooking the Clyde, while the Lennox and the Pentland hills were similarly manned. It was the Coldstream Guards who led the way in the attack on the main column at Macmerry, turning elements of the advance towards the south. The invading generals hardly believing their luck sent a third of their army down the Dalkeith road to cut them off from the south. To catch the Coldstream Guards would indeed go down in history. Slowly but surely the Coldstreams fell back under a continuing barrage of fire power, while at Wallyford the gallant Cameronians stopped the advance into Auld Reekie with a blistering counter attack that blew away two hundred and fifty men in less than a quarter of an hour. The enemy attempted the coastal route through Musselburgh to be greeted by civilian barricades and other light defences. It was a piric victory when they discovered the town was devoid of humanity. With the advance now slowing to a crawl the two advancing columns of the invading army were literally being drawn further apart. The southern flank, although originally intended to be an encircling manoeuvre had turned into a chase across the fields and down the byways as the routed Coldstreams began to regroup at Dalkeith.

Two enemy submarines lay in wait in the Firth of Forth. They had sunk the Blake and the Windsor Royal as they steamed out of Rosyth, the Blake going down after turning turtle in Inverkeithing Bay. While the Windsor Royal careered out of control, spewing men and machinery into the water until striking Cramond in a gut wrenching collision that saw her turning on her side, where she settled on the bottom ignominiously. Hiding in the shadow of Inchkeith had been an inspirational move by the submarine commanders. They set up a confusing crossfire of torpedoes in a spreading pattern that wreaked havoc among the fleet as much as on the harbour installations. The retreating guards divided themselves into two columns, the first advancing north along the old Dalkeith road into Edinburgh. The second falling back even further to Eskbank cross roads. Two miles down the Loanhead road the German generals realised something was amiss when they found their southern pincer coming under heavy fire from both sides. Trying to make a tactical withdrawal, the Franco-German spearhead found itself 'pinched-off' by heavy fire from the east where hidden Cameronian artillery batteries began knocking holes in their ranks. Finding a weakness in the ranks rallied against them in the south, the German Oberst in the field took his men to Bonnybrigg to wait for reinforcements from Dunbar. By nightfall the artillery opened up from hidden positions in the Pentland and Moorfoot hills. A deadly crossfire from higher ground began to rain down on them with a vengeance. With the tricky Coldstream Guards pinning them down with volleys of sniper fire they stood little chance. Out in the estuary the home fleet floundered in disarray off Edinburgh in the Firth, the defending forces could do no more than a token attack from the north. The smaller skimmers and agile patrol boats led by frustrated captains who could not strike back at their naval enemies; turned their intentions on to the advancing enemy troops instead. Raking the enemy column with their short-range missiles and with laser cannon as it scuttled through Portobello on its way to capture the docks at Leith and thence into the city itself. With their beachhead established at Dunbar, the Franco-German force continued to push troops and EPB units in the other direction along the road towards Berwick where in the latter case, they needed to secure the coast road and protect themselves from attacks in the southern flank.

There was a muted meeting of five ministers within the empty general assembly chamber. The sounds of random shooting going on in the background as the evening wore on. Almost literally foaming at the mouth in rage the leader of the Scottish Unionist party harangued the silent and crushed figure of the Socialist Leader of the house. Where once she had crowed lovingly about their special relationship within the European socialist super state, she had no fire left in her to defend that which she had been warned would turn sour by her wise opponents. Now cognisant of the fact that the federal authorities didn't give a damn about her government's style or political flavour, so much as for the political advantage of controlling everything from their remote fortress-like Parliament building in Brussels or Strasbourg. She was prepared to throw in the towel and declare Edinburgh an open city.

"And what will that achieve for ye!" roared the unionist leader. "Yew don't even understand the proper use of the term, let alone what the realities will be if ye go aboot declaring such a nonsense as that!"

"I'm sorry Robert, ah truly am sorry. Ah couldnae believe it was possible they could dae this to us…"

"Well, Agnes, we tried and tellt ye, but yew wouldnae listen tae anybuddy. There's nae one left for ye to protect by declaring us an open city, so yew might as well get oot like the rest of us before they have us a' surrounded. They'll probably take us oot and shoot uz for all ah know!" There was a long pause before anyone else spoke. "I'm leaving now, "said a lone voice from the back of the assembly chamber. "I hear tell there's a rumour about a resistance group up in the hills over on the west coast. I'd rather try my hand with them, if they'll have me, rather than wait for that lot to arrive and put a bullet in me." The singsong voice of a highland man echoing around the near empty chamber. Ruarie McCloud turned and left thinking of his estate near Plockton. 'What has become of us?' He asked himself sadly as he paced down the semi-darkened corridors of Scottish power for the last time. "Come on Nan, give it up. You're beaten and so are we all. Let's see what we can do to further their hollow victory, rather than give them something or somebody to gloat over." Agnes McGovan stood up to leave sobbing. "Ah, know Robert," was all she could say. Pale-faced and with mascara running over her cheeks she left the assembly for one last time, not as a triumphant politician but as a defeated and scorned woman who had failed to listen to sound political advice. They split up outside in the falling rain, taking different vehicles, promising to meet somewhere over on the west coast as soon as they could form a government in hiding. A gust of wind buffeted the vehicles in an act of defiance as they sped away into the darkened city streets towards the E9.

****

The American Atlantic fleet re-fuelled from bunkers laid down ages before in Reykjavik when the US had cheekily annexed Iceland during the Second World War. The only 'friendly' outpost left in Europe since the days of the Canadian war and the grab for Great Britain had made their presence around the world unpopular. American submarines had been shadowing a Russian fleet heading east in its journey around North Cape. Three Kiev class cruisers, five Yaroslav destroyers, ten frigates and sixteen escorts cum patrol boats in various shapes and sizes.

By dawn, the Marshals in Orleans talked via the tele-video link with the Feld-Marshals in Berlin. There was tacit agreement that more resources were needed if the British were to be overcome quickly. The delays were looking to be a lot longer than anticipated. The Bluff old German general sitting ramrod straight in his chair, sent a hiss of in-drawn breath among his French counterparts as he outlined a suggestion to use the Dutch and Belgian ports as points of embarkation. His argument was sound, based on time and expediency. It was so simple. The Spanish General and his two Colonels nodded in agreement with the Italian military High Command. The French knew it was right from a military point of view, but General Chauvigny had sown the seeds of doubt the day before, and there was a moment of disquiet within the hearts of the assembled brass-hats with an added twist of deja-vous. The media news channels made a shock announcement -it was claimed that it had come from 'leaked' sources high up in federal circles. As part of the deal to alleviate the sanctions against them the federal authorities demanded immediate passage through the low-countries, and immediate availability of their harbour installations. Dallying for time, the three presidents consulted, each other knowing what the other was about to do before they spoke. Each knowing how history had spoken for them twice before.

While Royal Oak pounded her way through the storm-laden seas far to the west, the three presidents released a joint statement. The word was 'No! You will not be given such rights because this is tantamount to a declaration of war against the sovereign states of Holland, Belgium and Denmark.' Shortly afterwards the Russian president, Vassiliev, made a world-net announcement that his White Sea fleet would be sailing into the North Sea to protect Russian interests in the area. Political analysts knew immediately the import of these words. They were going for the oil pipelines on the argument that it was Russian oil and gas that flowed into the EU, even though they themselves did not own the pipelines. The Americans flustered for a few hours before coming out with a brief statement that the Atlantic fleet would be patrolling US interests in the same area. "What interests?" Sneered back the EU foreign Ministry. "One tired old exploration vessel that had to be towed into harbour because its engines could no longer do their job, and a pipe laying barge stranded in Scapa Flow!" In fact the intelligence community had long suspected that the barge was not as it seemed, but an intelligence gathering vessel of some kind. No hard evidence, but too many coincidences to be just plain out of the ordinary. The Federal European Intelligence and Defence Authority, FEIDA, the official face of the intelligence services, had spent a long time trying to get one of their own men onboard as crew to no avail. All crewmen were US nationals rotated on a regular basis with typical TDY regularity. Rumour was rife in the field amongst the hydrographic fraternity that the crew's knowledge of positioning systems and marine pipe laying appeared to be somewhat lacking.

With all the news buzzing around and wallowing in dreadful conditions Royal Oak made slow progress through the storm. It was tough news to bear as they edged ever closer to home. With her cloaking device turned on she pressed homewards beneath a deeply compacted cloud base where she remained impervious to the probing gadgetry of all and sundry. The Admiralty could not prioritise any resources based on a suspicion that one of its lost ships was heading in to the war zone short on fuel and provisions. The Saratoga and her escorts declining to stop at Lisbon due to their 'special mission' status, ploughed on through the waves with her aircraft safely stowed below on her hangar decks. Her flight deck bucking like a highly energetic seesaw in the deep swell.

A second double pronged attack on the east coast at Holderness had secured a tenuous beachhead for the invaders at Bridlington and Aldbrough. While the Bridlington landing was made to relieve the pressure on Middlesborough, the Southern landing at Aldbrough had the hallmarks of an attack from behind upon entrenched positions along the Humber. Even with their centralised resources the British were being hard pressed. Constant air attacks harried their every effort to throw back the invaders where they came ashore or whey they had been dropped from troop carrying aircraft. With the West Country routes smashed, leaving the region effectively cut off from support; the forces west of Taunton had been left in comparative peace.

Presumably, the enemy had considered them to be of insignificant strategic value as a threat to the main thrust of the invasion plan. The dockyards at Devonport and even in Falmouth had been reduced to penury because of canted regulations on defence spending and regional development. The civilian owned yards having gone into receivership without the protection of being government owned, as fanciful policies based on the narrow demands for profitability destroyed the kingdom's ability to maintain a defensive infrastructure around its shores. Fleet maintenance had been reduced to a pitiful plea-bargaining process between two or three major players in the civil engineering markets that actually could afford to retain marine engineering and surveying subsidiaries. In the same fashion grants were only made available for the upkeep of the Euro-routes at the expense of all other roads. Hence the gradual demise of what was once a fully integrated communications system that had been the envy of the world, leaving the western peninsular, and other regions, with little else to survive on except pitiably small local economies in the post-industrial era.

Alarmed at the unanimous response to their demands for free-passage to the coast, the European president called in his committee for internal affairs for a deep and meaningful discussion, prior to meeting with his military advisors. In the first meeting the Commission's attitude was forceful and to the point. Sanctions would be applied and the freedom of passage was not an option that any government could deny the federal authorities. In the second meeting with the brass hats, the Field Marshals and Generals, along with the Admirals and Air Force Chiefs other conclusions were hammered out while the President and his cronies argued for punitive action. With three countries already in defiance of the Commission's directive, and with the distinct possibility of at least another two countries in the form of Norway and Sweden, it was likely that the police action in Britain would take on the proportions of an all out war in western Europe. "We must call on additional resources from the Poles, the Czechs the Hungarian government as well as the Slovenian Republic." Insisted the Presidential advisors. The Defence Chiefs looking serious and sullen in their silent distaste for the hated the academicians who gave policy to the president's office. There was not a man or women amongst them who had ever faced an enemy, even on a one-to-one basis. All were theoreticians with a penchant for the highly inflated salaries and the lifestyles that went with the title of a Presidential Advisor.

General Chauvigny sat back in his chair having recently returned from an intelligence gathering flight over some of the hotspots along the English coast. "Congratulations Messieur Le President, You have not only allowed the Federal authorities to dictate to you a hopeless plan, but without the balance of the experienced opinion of your Generals such a plan spells out that the union is no more…"

"Attention Mon Brave!" Cautioned the French Field Marshall. "Non, it has to be said that this is no simple police matter any more. Just think on this Messieur Le President. The British knew we were coming and had time to build an army, a navy and an airforce that could hold us off. Tell me what happens when this police action becomes a defence of Europe when the war turns against us?" There was a shocked silence as the President struggled to find words. An advisor opened his mouth to be waved down by the General. "You were not spoken to, so do not interrupt the President!" He paused as he watched the German struggle for his composure. "No, that is right, you do not know, because they do not know, your highly paid advisors. So then, I will tell you. They will bring this war onto the European mainland Messieur Le President. Why? Because the Commission in it's blind jealousy for absolute control did not read their history books. Seven hundred years ago we had the same problem when the Holy Roman Empire got too big for its boots and started to give policy to kings on the back of its brow-beating priests who threatened anybody who stood in their way with ex-communication and death. Is there anything different about what the Commission is doing today Messieur? Non, I think not! Unless you find a way of censuring the Commission you will find yourself with a war that will catch us all in its teeth and tear us apart. Already, the British are destroying bases on French soil, and soon it will be your turn. When the Canadians arrive, as they surely will, how do you intend to bring the war to an end? By asking some theoretician who has never worn a uniform? I say again, Non! To bring in any more forces will bring down the European Union as we know it, and who will step into the vacuum? Tell me that Messieur Le President."

Amid the shuffling of feet and the clearing of throats there came no response from anyone else for several minutes. The suave and confident politician, used to deference and weasel words had got the plain truth and it roasted his heart to ashes. An advisor spoke up using the high level gobbledegook of all advisors when faced with a question they can't answer. Someone tugging at his sleeve shut him up forcing the twit back into his chair. An uncomfortable looking EU President spoke briefly confirming his wishes that further troops be brought in to scale up the operation – until further notice. The tele-video screen went blank with a finality that bore down upon the most senior officers in the European Command.

"You'd better take some leave General," advised the Field Marshal flatly, Non, my friend." He held up a censorial hand when the General saw that he was going to reply. "This time you have gone to far. You may have told him the truth, but you hurt his pride and damned yourself into the bargain."

"There is so much to do…"

"It wasn't an observation General, it is an order. For your own safety and for all concerned you must take some leave, now, indefinitely. I will keep in touch and let you know when things have cooled down. Until then keep out of sight." Then the Field Marshal was gone, walking down the corridor and out of sight around a corner.

The General's wife phoned later in the day. The General had warned his family that he would be coming home during the evening. "There are three men waiting outside the house, I think they are watching us." She announced mildly. The SDLF, the uniforms within uniforms, the secret police had already been told to watch him. 'Already!' He thought to himself as he tried to formulate a warning that was not too obvious. Promising his wife that he was alright the General quickly went through a survival plan in his head to get home and get his family out of harm's way.

At midnight on the second day of her Atlantic dash William noted from the electronic log that they were one hundred and seventy miles off Land's End with an expected cloud cover for two to three days more. Crashing along at fifteen knots off-planes in an empty skimmer was not his idea of a good time. He ruminated on the positive effect the cloaking device had had upon their journey, speculated on getting in to harbour before anyone detected they were there. Given their present speed they should make landfall by noon. Everything was damp as the stinging spray lifting from the bows rattled against the wooden hoardings in a constant barrage, finding every small opening to drip constantly into the enclosed bridge. Rivers of salt water ran down the front of the bridge onto the floor where a collection of deck cloths and canvas had been laid down like a miniature coffer damn to prevent the water running down into the flat and into the accommodation areas. Lengths of hosing 'rabbitted' from the engineer's store removing the water to the safety of the network of drains on the cargo deck. The noise was awful, and many times the crew thought about strength of the repairs to their stern. Travelling light made the going rough, but on the other hand the trade-off was such that there were no further loading stresses due to a cargo.

At 05:45 the sky turned slowly grey, thick with scud hurtling along under low cloud as thick as scum floating on top of a brewer's barrel, the coast of England lying some ninety miles over the distant horizon. The cold and wet made for a miserable existence as they lurched closer to home. The early morning news made a meal of the fall of Edinburgh. "It really looks as though the Jocks have had a hard time of it," observed Sub over an early breakfast. "Hardly their fault Sub." Responded Fred trying to cut his ham and eggs with the edge of a fork tine. "If it wasn't for that 'mother-my-dog, earth mother, all peace and let's be pals together' leader of theirs they would have had that skimmer squadron all on the bottom of Bellhaven Bay wishing they'd never been born!"

"That's a bit strong isn't it?" piped up Leyland. "You have an interest in that part of the world?" He asked innocently. "Sort of, they've always been the weakest link one way or another."

"They make very fine soldiers though."

"Yes, they do, provided the politicians don't get in the way."

"The self-appointed intellectuals brigade. You have a point there I'm afraid."

While they chatted over victuals Chip sat up in the cockpit looking around him at the heaving mass of water. Very much relieved to be flying the White Ensign again he was glad to be within striking distance of home. The cloud cover spread itself over most of Western Europe right into Scandinavia. The deepening low skidding to a halt with its centre still somewhere in the Atlantic spun slowly anti-clockwise like a giant Catherine wheel on the weather plot. Rain drummed a continuing tattoo on the deckhead and against the bulkheads. The remaining windows were almost permanently steamed up with condensation making the lookouts' job more difficult. Mr White sat in the right hand seat fervently wishing that he wasn't perched so high. "Right Mr White, I don't think there's any point in taking the helm from up here. Let's transfer it down to the bridge." Unexpectedly relieved he transferred the helm down below and followed Chip down onto the deck of the bridge. Chip looked at the tactical plot sucking his teeth in frustration at the lack of information. The US chain showing many targets at long range, but with the heavy cloud cover preventing adequate filtering there was little hope of obtaining a fully augmented display. The morning passed boringly for all aboard except the men manning the navigation and tactical plotters. Even the big display had nothing on short range to show except a dim outline of Lizard Point beginning to creep onto the upper boundary of the screen. Just Before noon the radio op received instructions from Chip to send a very short message to the Admiralty on a low power transmitter. The message contained one short coded sentence addressed to the Admiral of the Fleet. He went off to the wardroom for lunch as requested by his First Lieutenant; to enjoy the fare rustled up by the galley from their dwindling provisions.

Due to a necessary delay with Admiral Dunham caught up at a meeting of the Security Council, the reply did not come until after lunch. Admiral Dunham had picked up the message mid-conference from a puzzled signals officer who failed to understand the meaning of the message. Only three men alive did, pausing in mid-sentence he looked considerably pre-occupied about something, but had to sit on the message for another fifty minutes. In the constant racket of signal traffic emanating from defence transmitters situated in and around Great Britain, one signal had been received and filtered out by the digital signal processor's algorithm downstream. It was brief and to the point. 'Making Devonport at best speed. Will advise ETA.' It was signed 'Motherwell.' No one in the command chain knew what it was all about. Someone somewhere supposed it to be a coded message for an unknown agent on some mission and left it at that. Other ears picked up news of the message and pondered on its value. Then, discarding the subject as too obscure to penetrate ignored one of the best-kept secrets of the war.

From the south east five enemy aircraft flew in close formation below the cloud base just above the surface. The German fighter-bombers had been repositioned from Sandhausen specifically for the mission. Flying in passive mode and relying on satellite navigation the flight headed straight as a die for their target on the western peninsula. Twenty miles due south of Gerrans Bay the tactical plot 'bloop-blooped' its target alarm shaking the bridge crew from its hopeful reverie on arriving home. "Five incoming aircraft Sir! Speed two five zero knots, zero feet, bearing green zero seven degrees, range ten miles, on the surface!"

"Lock solution sound action stations!" Boomed Mr White loudly. The display rapidly counting down from nine minutes and twenty one seconds.

"They're not ours Sir, the computed back-track places their point of departure somewhere on the French mainland."

"Standby everyone!" Called Chip as men ran to their action stations. "Weapons to auto-fire… ah, William, make each one count please the odds are five to one!"

"Aye, aye Sir, I'll do my best."

"Mr White, the same message to the marines with the hand-held launchers if you please!"

"Aye Sir." With three conventional missiles left in the armoury and only four hand-held missiles they would be rapidly reduced to laser cannon and nothing else. "Keep us running in passive mode for as long as possible!" Chip and Fred went to the plot and punched up the track projection for the fast approaching flight. "Sir, if we're still passive, then they have to be heading for the air station at Helston."

"Or even Goonhilly where the downlink is sited."

"Or both. Do they really need five aircraft for just one target?"

"Signalman, send signal immediate to Naval Air Station Kernow on one two nine, decimal six two five. Voice only. Message is 'five enemy aircraft coming your way through Falmouth Bay, Bravo Zero Whiskey Five.' One time only"

The signal op used the unit's voice command to tune the air comms console and quickly made the transmission while around him additional orders were handed out at lightning speed. "Guns, sector scan only, lock on and fire two missiles on the solution, now, if you please!"

Aye, aye Sir!" William activated the sensor transmitters in a sector scan covering the approaching targets. They could hear the engines now, but could not see anything through the spray and the scud. "Missiles gone Sir!" Fred thought he saw something black and green racing across the surface towards them on the starboard side then it was lost in the murk. "I think I've got them on the starboard side, no, they've gone." There was a rushing sound as the aircraft did indeed pass swiftly by. The sudden presence of their sensor signatures had an almost demolishing effect on the enemy formation as their own sensors picked up the missiles locking onto them. Their flight commander telling them to hold it, increasing speed to three hundred and twenty knots. Looking at his display in disbelief they hurled themselves in formation towards Falmouth with Pendennis castle coming up fast as the principal turning point, fractionally over three minutes away. Racing in a losing battle the five aircraft jinked above the cliffs as the castle flashed by, firing their countermeasures. Two of them peeling off in a tight turn towards the south, still passive, the other three flashing over the hills towards Brill.

One missile lost lock going wide as the aircraft split formation the other remained firmly locked onto the tailpipe of one of the wingmen heading for Kernow air base. "Rudi! Fire your missiles and get out of here!" warned the flight leader with seconds to spare. Nap of the earth flying was one thing, but with a missile locked onto your tail pipe only served to make the adrenaline in one's blood turn a dirty shade of brown. "Jawohl!" Came the immediate reply while he simultaneously launched four missiles from the pylons beneath his wings before pulling up in a sickening vertical turn through the clouds, releasing his bombs in a final attempt to lob them in the direction of the distant target. The missile struck home at five thousand and fifty feet just as young Rudi Kotsen yanked his G-Handle down hard; the second missile had locked onto one of the other aircraft, heading south, by the merest chance, as the change of course brought the couplet back into the frame.

The attack on Kernow airbase was relatively successful. The base had only enough time to throw up a defensive screen with limited effect on the enemy. Asa Schaffenberg's number two caught a burst of laser cannon across his starboard wing that sent him spinning earthwards before he could eject. His number three hit wire aerials on the far side of the hill and was struggling to regain control as his aircraft pitched down, then up with his port wing down, trailing wires. Two aircraft were in flames on the ground and four bombs had impacted either on or close to the runway, a rising crossfire of laser and metal rounds stitched its way through the air towards his tailpipe seeking revenge. Asa executing a tight climbing turn had placed himself on a vector almost perfectly headed down the length of the runway. Without stopping to think and with the missile lock alarm now going off in the cockpit he released his second bomb load, fired countermeasures and jinked around to the starboard in another tight turn. Heading for the deck he flashed behind hangars and the skyline chasing after his number three. "Stegelbahn Drei, go for target two, go for target two!"

"Stegelbahn drei, target two." Came the immediate read-back 'Thank God he's still going' thought Asa as his aircraft shot out across the shoreline. Temporarily out of sensor sight the two aircraft sped along the beaches until they reached Mullion where they turned sharply up and over the rising landscape towards Goonhilly. The targeting systems locking onto to pre-set destinations the 'cruise' computers onboard bounced back lock and each pilot launched weapons. In less than two seconds they had seen the damage already meted out to the satellite tracking station. Large fires were burning from within shattered radomes while laser cannon zapped skywards towards their remaining aircraft. Stegelbahn vier never made it back home, like his fellow pilot at Kernow airbase, he too 'went in' dodging missiles and dropping the intelligent bomb load before yanking on his G-Handle a fraction of a second before one of them slammed home all the way up his tail-pipe.

With his guns jammed and payload gone Stegelbahn drei pulled out in a tight turn after Stegelbahn Führer and Stegelbahn funf, dropping down to six metres above sea level beyond Coverack. Right into the teeth of Royal Oak's hidden position deep among the surface mists. Missiles locked on from nowhere right in their pathway giving Asa no chance but to give the order to break formation and head for home independently. Breaking like a huge trident the three remaining pilots spread outwards and upwards on maximum plasma-burn. Stegelbahn drei would never be able to tell why he survived. Perhaps it was the aerial wires trailing far behind that had saved him from instant death, but one of the short-range missiles fired by a marine exploded close to his aircraft without making direct contact. With a large hole in his tail fin combined with the induced drag from the aerial wires he was having a very hard time of it. With limited control of his elevators and poor command authority over his rudder there was nothing for it but to reduce speed and hope for the best. Stegelbahn funf went down in a ball of flame five miles due east of Royal Oak. Hearing that his colleagues were in trouble Stegelbahn leader cursed his luck as he raced ahead of the third missile, launched by one of the seamen on the foc'sle. Firing countermeasures and dumping a plasma ball he hoped the two would combine to throw off the missile. A loud report went off in the sky nearby as the incandescent countermeasures colliding with the vented plasma cloud ignited in a huge explosion. Everyone on deck looked and cheered as they thought this was the nemesis of yet another hidden attacker. William shook his head. "That wasn't an aircraft."

"No that was a plasma burst. He's damn cunning whoever he is! Standby with laser cannon!" ordered Chip. With the other missile gone, Asa found his ailing companion and spoke into his voice-activated system putting his aircraft onto a converging vector. Together they slunk home as Stegelbahn drei sweated nuggets to control his ailing aircraft. Far behind them Stegelbahn funf's survival beacon jumped into life as the doomed pilot's life jacket brought the unconscious man to the surface.

Royal Oak approached the crumpled heap heaving about in the heavy swell. For although the rain had stopped the winds had not ceased to make their lives any easier. "It's going to be a boat-hook job I can tell," groaned the Bosun's Mate, "a bloody nightmare if you ask me." The tops of the waves almost broaching the side as she slowed to come alongside the domed head bobbing in the water. Tied onto safety lines to stop them from falling into the water, two seamen crouched closely together as the inert body lurched ever closer. First several feet away in a trough, then suddenly inches away at the crest of the next wave. On the third attempt they grabbed the man's collar and heaved him inboard before the water disappeared leaving them to bear the full load of the man's weight. They hustled him through the nearest door on the cargo deck and laid him out carefully with a medic standing over them. "He's still alive, get him to the lounge now, quick as you like!"

There were grumbles of course, but jack always erred on the side of magnanimity when faced with a defeated enemy. Whether it was patching up his wounds or giving him a decent burial with full naval honours. There is a certain dignity beating in the heart of every sailor that would show itself at times like this. If their lounge was being used as an operating theatre, then good luck to him.

By the time Royal Oak slipped past the breakwater she had been running without the cloaking device since Dodman Point. The calmer waters eased their rocking and rolling somewhat as she progressed towards the Homoaze through the sound. Crowds had gathered on the Ho and along the lower road. There were several anxious glances through the intensifiers as the lookouts and others searched for familiar faces. "Bloody hell! They've got dozens of camera crews out there, what's going on?" Someone was heard exclaiming. "Signalman, make signal." Called Chip

"Aye Sir."

"To Admiral of the Fleet, from HMS Royal Oak. Message is as follows. 'I am pleased to inform His Majesty, that Royal Oak is rejoining the fleet at HMD Devonport. Signed C Woodingdean, Officer Commanding, God Save the king!' -Priority is immediate."

Torpoint slipped past as they slowed to come alongside the wall at Devonport dockyard. Crowds on the jetties waving frantically while camera flashes rippled back and forth along the promenades that had once been south yard aeons ago. The small dockyard with its single basin and covered jetties seemed crammed full of people. Sailors were waving their hats while others whistled shrilly with fingers jammed into their mouths. Turning slowly upstream without the aid of tugs Royal Oak prepared to come alongside port side-to. The upper storeys of the Portland stone of the barracks lay in the background with its roofs shrouded in mist. The C-in-C was there with the harbourmaster and other senior officers, but waiting for them, leaning against the railings and shouting at the tops of their voices were the families of the crew. Many of them with tears streaming down their faces, their hair ruffled by the wind. Children either being carried in the crook of their mother's arms or milling around at arms length as they watched the grey hull creep ever closer. Then it was over, the long journey home; the gangway rattled across the concrete jetty and then slid into place with the crowd watching in deep silence. What the crew could not see or appreciate was the image that all those sightseers ashore had to contend with. Her hull and superstructure were pock marked with dents, holes and patches.

The burn marks and slagged runs of melted steel where laser rounds had left their terrible wounding marks of war. The hoardings covering vacant windows on the bridge and the bent cockpit giving silent testimony to the long battle to get home. The sailors on deck having finished their duties disappeared into the cargo deck to fall in with the rest of the assembled crew. Shortly afterwards an armed harbour vessel came alongside and waited for ten minutes while the prisoners were removed beyond the gaze of the assembled crowds. Then it sheared off again heading upstream to drop them off under escort at the barracks jetty.

The C-in-C came aboard to the sounds of two Bosun's pipes twittering in the wind. Chip greeted the Admiral in the usual respectful fashion, inviting him to meet his officers and crew. The Admiral obligingly following him into the side door leading onto the cargo deck. Fred brought the entire ship's company to order as the Admiral stepped onto the deck. With the formalities over the Admiral gave an amazing address to the crew. It began with a message from the king who was delighted to hear of their safe return, and sorrowful to hear of their losses. Wishing them well in whatever they did and wherever they went as the needs of the current situation demanded. Secondly, the Admiral passed on the heartiest congratulations of the Admiral of the Fleet adding that the whole country had been inspired by the exploits of the ship the Royal Oak and her crew over the past few months. "Indeed," said the Admiral proudly, "We were very careful not to let on where you were and what was happening to you. We have given a summary report of your journey and of your actions to the press, and I can tell you that not only are their Lordships pleased with what you have achieved, the whole nation is talking about you. You are all an inspiration to your colleagues in uniform as much as to the public at large. I am pleased to inform you that his majesty has given the order to splice the main-brace!"

Everyone cheered as the news broke. To the people waiting on the jetty it was a welcome sound indeed. It could only mean that the admirals were pleased. With a smile on his face Chip gave the order to dismiss the crew who fell out from the short ceremonial barely concealing their eagerness to get ashore. A tide of uniformed humanity pouring across the gangway to greet families and friends was snapped up by all the media channels and played again and again during the day, and would be referred to in the days to come.

As the families traipsed on board, down into the messes and into the wardroom, the C-in-C and the harbourmaster met with Chip and Fred in Chip's day cabin for drinks and canapés, while waiting for the right moment to broach several things. One of them was the fact that due to the war footing he could only give everyone ten days leave, but arrangements had been made for accommodation at two of the hotels in town. The families had already been billeted in these hotels, and they would be returning to their accommodation where they would find organised parties and babysitters ready to look after the children. For Chip and Fred there was to be a slightly different itinerary. The king wanted to see them both up in London to thank them personally. The Admiral paused briefly and nodding at Fred gave his respects to leave the ships company to their reunion celebrations.

"Your parents are here," said Fred with a slight tremor in his voice. They are waiting in the wardroom. I'll go and fetch them."

"Really, Fred. How long have you known this? I wasn't aware they were coming down."

"They asked me to keep it quiet. You know, a surprise." Fred slipped out through the door sending a steward back to take away some of the debris left on empty plates and to remove the empty wineglasses. Chip's personal reunion with his parents was a tearful moment. His mother relating afterwards how they had never expected to see him again. As the conversation went on Chip had the feeling that they were building up to something, but couldn't find the words. "How's Meg doing? Did she finally sort out that censorship thing? I expect it doesn't apply any more."

"That's why we're here dear said his mother." rubbing his elbow with a free hand. "She died a short while ago, Chip, I'm sorry to say. They came to arrest her just after you left, before President Warnock dissolved Parliament…"

"Oh, no, no, that can't be right. She was so sure they would just put an impossibly high fine on the radio station that she couldn't pay and close her down. She was going to go underground…"

"It never got that far dear," said his mother sadly. "They took her to one of those awful detention centres where they beat her up before letting her go. But she went on the air again and told the world what they had done and they broke down the door and arrested her again." His mother wiped away the tears from her face. "We tried to find her Chip, and when we did they had taken her to their headquarters in Eltham. We tried pulling a few strings, but these people were different."

"Who were they?"

"I don't suppose it matters, government bully boys, some sort of special ESB unit was the rumour. But it was just a rumour."

"What happened?"

"We think they just beat her to death." He looked intently at his son who seemed to be in a far off place. "Somehow the sun has gone out of my life." He said quietly. "I know dear." She paused momentarily before continuing as gently as she could, fighting back the tears for her son. "We went to her funeral at the end of May. It was a beautiful day with a lot of people there to say goodbye. We had a wreath made up for you on your behalf."

Chip turned away to look across the Tamar through the window of his cabin. Drizzling rain had returned to run in tiny rivulets down the glass. From where he stood he suddenly felt as if the future had fallen out of his life and there was a wall in front of him that he could never pass. "Thank you for coming all this way to tell me." He felt his chin shaking just a little, but taking a deep sigh he held his composure. 'After all.' He thought. 'I've seen so much death lately and those of my friends, why can't I hold onto this a little longer?' Shaking his head silently he took another deep breath. He turned to look at the sad faces of his parents. "I don't suppose they know who did it?"

"They arrested about four people a week later so they tell me, but they had next to no proof to pin on them."

"Does Fred know?" He asked lamely. "Yes dear, he does. We met with him while you were showing the Admiral around. You know he's a very nice man and is concerned that you have been hurt this way. Especially, now that everyone else around you has been reunited with their own families." She looked at his father biting the corner of her lip.

An hour later Chip emerged with his parents to find Fred waiting patiently on the other side of the bridge. They had been friends for over five years, ever since they had struck the deal in their business partnership over the Privateer. They regarded one another with mutual concern. Fred had no visitors to welcome him home since his former wife had deserted him years before. Since he was a free agent he spent his time keeping busy and making sure things ran smoothly. Chip could see the sadness lined across his friend's face knowing it was due in part to his loneliness as much to the sad news of Meg's death. "Thank you Fred for your discretion. I appreciate your thoughtfulness."

"Not at all. I know this is a difficult time, and perhaps you will feel more comfortable ashore in a hotel suite. The Admiral has included your parents in the friends and families list at the old Millennium. I'll be there too with the others. I can give the details of the reception this evening later on."

"Reception? I almost forgot. What time and where?"...

The overcast thinned out overhead allowing the setting sun to peep through and gild the black waters of the Tamar. Chip waving goodbye to his parents on the jetty turned to look at their once proud enterprise. He was almost shocked when he saw her battle scars and the extent of the damage. A little later the crew began to trickle ashore for the first time in an age, many accompanied by family and friends. Each one of them felt a tugging at the heart when they came to leaving what had been their home. Many like Chip, had not realised how badly beaten up their floating pride had been until they in their turn had turned around and looked at her under the floodlights. Some silently reflected for a moment on that vision of a near wreck with a kinship that only those who had gone through such things can share, remarking to themselves upon the silence hanging over them without the sounds of her engines or a crew to give her life. Then, the fleeting moment is gone, as they turn once more to walk away with the satisfaction of a job well done and the hope of a long and pleasant parting from the sea. Long after all the fuss had died down, Leyland shuffled over the narrow gangway, "See you tonight Sir," he said quietly and moved off towards a waiting taxi on the dockside.

The Admiral arranged that the Royal Oak be handed over to a team of ship-keepers pending the return of her crew after a well-earned rest ashore. With the keepers in place, both Chip and Fred made their way silently across the brow, turning to look at the only asset that they possessed wondering how they had ever survived. The presence of the armed guards standing at the quayside end of the brow seemed somehow incongruous to them. How could they know? How could anyone know the journey they been through together? They turned to look as the Admiral's car arrived to whisk them away. The guards raised their rifles in full salute, with Chip returning it with a deeper sense of pride. He held his arm up a little longer than most with a grateful thanks to the little ship that had won its battles for him to bring them home against all the odds. As the car drew away the powerful overhead lights were switched off and she was gone.

Glossary of Terms

Caboosh	Small compartment or enclosed space.
Corned dog	Corned beef
CPO	Chief Petty Officer
DTF	Distilled titration fuel
DQs	Detention quarters; military prison
ESA	European space agency
ED	Euro dollar, Eurodollars (EDs)
EIA	European Intelligence Agency
ESA	European standing army
ESNF	European standing naval forces
Europol	European police force
EuroStar	Early European railway linking Britain to the EU mainland
EuroStar	European satellite system with lunar-based signal booster stations
Eurosat	European satellite system
EPB	European police battalion. Much hated quasi-military police force seen as an agency enforcing the political will of the European Commission
FEIDA	Federal European Intelligence Defence Agency
FPB	Fast patrol boat
Genset	Generating set. An engine turning a generator.
GPS	Global positioning system. Satellite Navigation
HE	High Explosive
Hoverbat	Military hybrid all-terrain hover-car using Coanda effect and air steering
Mag-lev	Magnetic levitation -as in the magnetic levitation railway system first developed at the University of Sussex by Professor Eric Laithwaite and his research team in the 1960s/70s
MARIS	Marine information system. General information service for mariners
MCA	Marine computed almanac. Marine database with GPS backup.

MW	Megawatt -laser-gun power classification
MPV	Multi personnel vehicle
Navplan	Navigation plan -for vessels
NIUPA	Non industrialised urban preservation area.
NOTAM	Notice to airmen (notams)
NOTMAR	Notice to mariners (notmars)
OOD	Officer of the day (duty officer)
PO	Petty Officer
Pot mess	A stew beloved of sailors in rough weather, or taken during lulls in action at mealtimes. Variations include corned dog hash.
PU	Pacific Union -of mainland and island nation states
Rattler	US Navy/Marines fighter aircraft (rattlesnake)
Satcomms	Satellite communications
Skimmer	A hybrid, high-speed multi-hulled vessel with aquaplanes. Some might say these are part ekranoplane in their ability to skim over water.
STOL	Short take-off or landing -aircraft.
SSR	Secondary surveillance radar usually referred to as a 'squawk box'
TAC	Diminutive form of the word Tactical; tac/Tac.
Taclink	European military satellite network/link.
Tacsat	Tactical satellite
Tactco	Tactical control console mode
UPA	Urban preservation area
VCTC	Voice controlled tactical console
Villager	US military tactical satellite system
VGS	Vegetable-gasoline substitute
VTOL	Vertical take-off or landing -aircraft
WNA	World news agency
WO	Warrant Officer

About the Author

David de l'Avern was born in Hampstead, and was educated at Streatham Grammar School, London and at Feldon School, Leamington Spa. Sometime later he gained a degree in engineering and business management at the University of Sussex in 1996. He is also a pilot subsequent to 15 years of deep-sea travel in ships of grey where he practised the hidden arts of electronics. Encouraged to read as a child by his well-travelled parents, and having a liking for the English language as well as for all sorts of adventures, he quickly consumed many books all about the sea, flying, and high adventure. Sometimes involved in the production of various 'humorous' articles in various ships' magazines -mercifully lost in the mists of time, he harboured a secret desire to become a serious writer of adventure stories. His interests are aviation, jazz, science fiction, cats, computers and flying model helicopters because the real things scared him half to death during missions. He still works full-time lecturing in mathematics, and occasionally in other things.

Printed in the United Kingdom
by Lightning Source UK Ltd.
132152UK00001B/106/P